"LOOK AT HER, ROI
SHE'S THE MOST BEA
WOMAN I'VE EVER

Marcus held his breath, almost afraid an with the crystalline aura would fade before eyes, like a dragon slipping through the mist. The man with her seemed less substantial, as if he lingered half in the void.

"Didn't you hear her, Marcus?" Robb asked angrily.

Marcus yanked his concentration away from the beauty with the blue eyes. "I wasn't listening. She's so very beautiful she makes my heart ache. What did you say?" Something important was happening, and Marcus couldn't concentrate, couldn't think. He wanted to go drifting in the void forever with this woman.

"She said that we are ghosts, and we will linger as ghosts for a long, long time." Robb's fingers on Marcus' shoulders squeezed painfully tight.

"Ghosts! We can't be ghosts. We're alive. I see you and this room very clearly, I hear the wind and the rain outside, I feel pain where you are bruising my shoulder."

Robb removed his hand, shaking out some of the tension.

"Those two are the ghosts," Marcus continued. "They look like dragons, sort of here, sort of in the void."

"Something strange is going on here, Marcus. . . ."

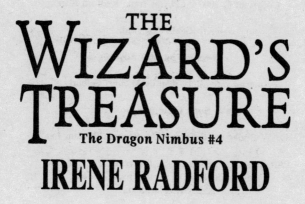

THE WIZARD'S TREASURE

The Dragon Nimbus #4

IRENE RADFORD

DAW BOOKS, INC.

DONALD A. WOLLHEIM, FOUNDER

375 Hudson Street, New York, NY 10014

ELIZABETH R. WOLLHEIM
SHEILA E. GILBERT
PUBLISHERS

First Printing, October 2000

1 2 3 4 5 6 7 8 9

DAW TRADEMARK REGISTERED
U.S. PAT. OFF. AND FOREIGN COUNTRIES
—MARCA REGISTRADA
HECHO EN U.S.A.

PRINTED IN THE U.S.A.

For my Golden Dragon Grandchild,
due to be born the same week
as this book is released.

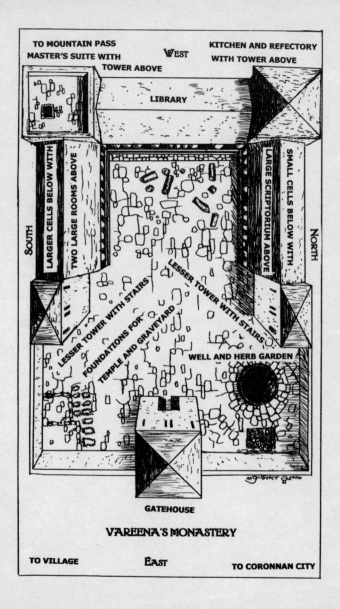

TO MOUNTAIN PASS
MASTER'S SUITE WITH
TOWER ABOVE

KITCHEN AND REFECTORY
WITH TOWER ABOVE

WEST

LIBRARY

LARGER CELLS BELOW WITH
TWO LARGE ROOMS ABOVE

LARGE SCRIPTORIUM ABOVE
SMALL CELLS BELOW WITH

SOUTH

NORTH

LESSER TOWER WITH STAIRS

LESSER TOWER WITH STAIRS

FOUNDATIONS FOR
TEMPLE AND GRAVEYARD

WELL AND HERB GARDEN

GATEHOUSE

VAREENA'S MONASTERY

TO VILLAGE

EAST

TO CORONNAN CITY

PROLOGUE

*T*he cult of the Gnostic Utilitarians bedevils Coronnan. They proclaim the ridiculous notion that hard work is the only medium of value. Magic, to them, is anathema. While they fight for power in the Council of Provinces and among the common people, the coven has gone into hiding in Hanassa where they rebuild very slowly. The rogue magicians of the eight-pointed star have patience. They have waited generations, creating alliances through blackmail, marriage, and coercion.

The numbers within the coven increase slowly. Solitary magicians prefer to remain solitary and secretive rather than join with others of their kind. They distrust everyone.

The University of Magicians still hopes that the dragons will return to Coronnan and restore magic to its honorable place in society—as if the magical energy they emit will automatically force solitary magicians to work together, under the law, with no malice, mistrust, or greed guiding them. They overestimate the honor of men who have tasted power.

And I sit in my lofty fastness, laughing at all of them. Governments rise and governments fall. This scramble for power is merely an exercise to satisfy individual greed.

Even Rovers have succumbed to the power-seeking game. Zolltarn, the current self-styled king of All Rovers, betrays his own kind as well as the coven and the Commune. After centuries of seeking nothing more than their own safety through their separateness, the

Rovers have suddenly found virtue in exploring the disgusting ideas of King Darville of Coronnan. As if peace, law, and justice mean something.

Zolltarn has stolen the child who should inherit the crowns of all three of the kingdoms on this continent. This "king" of the Rovers seeks to raise the child to his own traditions, then place him on the thrones, obligated and obedient to Rover will.

I will remove myself from my protected retreat and intervene if Zolltarn succeeds. Zolltarn and a child with so much political and magical power could rob me of all that I hold dear.

Rejiia, who thinks she leads the coven, has the potential to discover my power. She has thrown herself into her perverted rituals with vigor and stamina, using her sexuality to increase the magic. But I sense her distraction from the stated purpose of the coven. She has other, more personal goals and uses the coven to gain them.

The Commune of Magicians grows stronger. I cannot stop them from this distance, but I can eat away at the trust that binds them together.

I must take pains to see that none of these players finds my power. None of them know the true source of power—magical and political. None of them shall have it. Only I. I will, and can, murder my rivals most horribly if they try to interfere with my power. I have done it before, without conscience. I shall do it again.

Men truly seek only the chaos that rules their hearts.

CHAPTER 1

"So this is the landscape of war," Journeyman Magician Marcus said flatly. "Maybe the dragons should cleanse this battlefield like they did three hundred years ago."

"Dragons cannot cleanse this sinkhole unless they return to Coronnan. We cannot afford to end this war with SeLenicca until the dragons are safely returned from there." Robb, his comrade and also a journeyman magician, argued.

A long moment of silence passed between them as they contemplated the army camp and their possible passage through or around it.

"I think the balladeers need a good dose of reality. I don't see any evidence of glory here," Robb finally broke the silence.

"Just mud and blood, chill and boredom," Marcus confirmed. "Sort of like latrine duty for first-year apprentices." He flashed his friend a smile at shared memories of hardship and mischief.

"Where are we going to find me some new boots in this mess?" He scanned the wide plain at the eastern end of the mountain pass. The once lush river meadows had been churned into a sea of red clay mud.

Marcus shrugged as he wiggled his toes, trying to ease a little of the chill in them from his sopping socks.

The setting sun cast their long shadows against the mud-lashed stubble.

"There are too many idle soldiers lolling about. Too much idle curiosity. Beating you in a game of cartes would be easier than getting through this camp," Robb grumbled.

"But not by much?" Marcus' grin widened. "And once we bring the dragons home from the other side of the pass, we won't have to worry about war or illegal magic for a while."

Robb turned his back on the ugly camp and looked out over the green river plains toward home—if an occasional rest in the dormitory of the new University of Magicians hidden in the Southern Mountains could be called home.

"Cheer up, Robb, we've come this far without trouble."

"For a change."

"In a camp this big, we're just two more soldiers out for a stroll. We'll beg some boots and maybe a bed and a meal from the Battlemages." He pointed to the far side of the camp toward a small group of huts made from stout logs where a blue flag with a dragon emblem snapped smartly in the evening breeze.

"Getting to their enclave could be risky. All magicians, including Battlemages and healers—the only legal magicians left in Coronnan—are feared and spied upon. Let's just find a supply shed and steal some boots." Robb fell into his usual lecture mode.

"This shouldn't be harder than crossing the five miles of no-man's-land between our army and the enemy at the far side of the pass. Pickets and patrols from both sides could cut us down with crossbows without bothering to ask identities first. Here, the pickets and patrols will at least ask for a password or something." Marcus thought out loud.

"But we don't know the password."

"We can find out with a tiny probe of magic." Marcus flashed his friend another grin, unwilling to give in to depression at the first sign of difficulty.

"Illegal," Robb warned.

"So is stealing boots from the supply tent," Marcus retorted.

Robb followed closely in Marcus' footsteps.

Marcus shrugged off the difficulties.

"Good thing you are lucky or my infamous bad luck would have gotten us killed a dozen or more times." Robb turned his face away. On this subject he never fell into lengthy lecture mode. He didn't even ask to play cartes anymore to wile away the long lonely hours around the campfire. Marcus always won.

"I have more lives than a cat, and I bet you my new pair of boots that I'll beat you at cartes tonight," Marcus chortled. He slapped his good friend on the back. For a moment he wished Margit, the apprentice magician assigned to spy for the Commune of Magicians within the royal palace, could join them. The tall, sturdy blonde could liven up any game with outrageous stories of the antics of the nobles and royals she watched so carefully.

Marcus longed for the day he and Margit could settle into a little cottage at the University with a dozen children and apprentices. He'd had his fill of journeying.

"Let's skirt the camp rather than cross it. That's a very wide-open space between the officers' tents and the magicians' huts." Robb ran his fingers through his beard in contemplation. A sure sign that he sensed more trouble than he voiced.

Marcus stumbled on a mud-colored rock that seemed to thrust up at him without warning. He limped for a few paces before the pain in his stubbed toes eased.

"Stop hunching your shoulders," Robb ordered. "Soldiers drill and march endlessly. They should have straight spines and firm steps."

"They also need uniforms." Marcus waved away Robb's objections, replacing them with a delusion of a green-and-gold uniform. His twisted magician's staff became a pike. "Now come along, Robb. We aren't getting any closer to the end of our journey standing here."

"We're gathering information," Robb affirmed, cloaking himself in a similar delusion. "Information is the key to power and . . ."

"Safety," Marcus finished. "I heard the same lecture from Jaylor as many times as you did. And as many times before that from Baamin when he was Senior Magician."

"I miss the old coot," Robb replied sadly. "Old Toad Knees will be honored for a long time by all of his apprentices." They both observed a long moment of silence in memory of their first master.

"Look for anything out of the ordinary or too ordinary—both could be traps." Robb pointed to the first line of pickets near the steed paddock.

"I know, Robb."

"Then why did you step in that pile of steed dung?"

"Camouflage." Marcus paused to scrape the noisome muck from his boot. The worn soles allowed some of the brown liquid to seep through to his socks.

"Some of your luck running out?" Robb quipped.

"Never."

"Let's hope there aren't any Gnostic Utilitarian spies in the area," Robb grumbled. "They'll smell your magic and your boots from half a camp away. Gnuls believe all magic smells like manure—dragon magic or solitary makes no difference to them."

"Another lie that has become accepted as fact." Marcus frowned, no longer willing to keep up the usual banter with his friend. They'd both seen too many atrocities heaped upon innocents because of the unnatural fear of magic spread by the Gnuls. "The sooner we bring the dragons back, the sooner we can help put an end to that all-too-popular cult." Did every mundane in the country truly believe that only hard labor gave work value? That chores accomplished by magic—like transport and communication as well as healing and soil fertility—were evil and deserving of death? Magic was just as hard for a magician as the work was for a mundane.

Robb nodded, his frown quite visible beneath the dark bush of his beard.

They headed boldly through the camp periphery, walking as if they had a purpose. One patrol challenged them. Marcus just shook his head and proceeded. "Orders," he muttered.

The guard shrugged his shoulders and turned his attention back to his patrol.

An invisible line seemed to have been drawn around the magicians' enclave. No one ventured closer than one hundred paces.

"Crossing this barrier could be harder than getting through the pass," Robb muttered.

"Easier," Marcus replied. "The spies watching the magicians never look directly at them. My guess is they don't want to get caught by the evil eye." He grinned at the superstitious nonsense that clung to magicians' reputations.

Despite his bold face, Marcus' neck itched as if one hundred eyes followed every step he made across the untrampled grass that surrounded the ramshackle wooden buildings in a near perfect circle. Each step seemed to make his thin boots heavier and more cumbersome. Was this merely a delusion to keep out uninvited observers?

The blue banner with a dragon outlined in silver seemed to be a beacon, drawing them toward the largest of the buildings. A door beneath the banner stood invitingly open.

Marcus started to step through the doorway without preamble, but Robb held him back.

"For the sake of the Gnul spies all around us, at least look like you are one of the awestruck masses with a message from the generals and knock." He rapped the wooden doorjamb with his fist and waited.

"What!" a querulous voice sounded within.

"Message, sir," Marcus replied.

"Leave it and be gone."

Marcus and Robb exchanged a questioning look.

"The message is private and not written," Marcus improvised. Dared he enter without invitation? Slowly he unreeled a thin tendril of magic, probing the doorway and the darkness just inside. A sharp pain behind his eyes made him wince.

"He's armored," he whispered, quickly withdrawing the probe, hopefully before any witch-sniffers could detect it.

"What?" a middle-aged man appeared out of the darkness. His red-veined and pointed nose was the first feature Marcus noted. Gray streaked his red-blond hair and beard. Worry lines made deep crevasses around his eyes. His shoulders drooped.

"Woodpecker?" Marcus asked. He wanted to rush forward and lend his shoulder to support this frail man. A year ago he'd been tall and robust.

"Who?" the Battlemage peered at the two journeymen, blinking in the fading light as if emerging into bright sunlight.

"Marcus and Robb. Jaylor sent us," Marcus said very quietly. No telling who could be listening.

"Get in here, boys, before someone spots you. Your delusion is very thin. Too thin to fool the witch-sniffers that permeate the army. They'll report you in a heartbeat without regard to the validity of your errand. Lucky to get out of here without being stoned." With surprising strength, Woodpecker grabbed each journeyman by the front of their tunics and yanked them inside the narrow entryway.

A wave of prickly magic set Marcus' skin itching and crawling. Then, as quickly as it had come, it left, leaving him in a bright room filled with comfortable furniture, carpets, and a glowing brazier.

"Where are the others?" Robb asked, peering around.

"In their own huts. My turn to monitor the scrying bowl for activity on the other side of the pass. Now what is so all-fired important that Jaylor could not trust a summons sent through a glass and candle flame?" Woodpecker demanded, wringing his hands and pacing the room. He paused to peer out each of the large unshuttered windows.

"Well . . . actually . . . Jaylor sent us on a quest into SeLenicca, and I need new boots before we cross the pass." Marcus found the shimmer of light across the windows that indicated strong magical armor too distorting to stare at for more than a moment.

"A bed and a meal would be welcome as well," Robb added.

"Is that all? Why didn't you just steal a pair of boots and a bedroll from the pickets that sleep on duty day and night? Why didn't you transport supplies from the University? Either course would prove safer than coming here." Woodpecker ceased his pacing and stared at the two journeymen.

Robb hung his head. Marcus wanted to do the same.

I am no first-year apprentice to cower before authority, he told himself sternly.

"To steal essential supplies from one of our own soldiers would be dishonorable. To transport something as trivial as boots a waste of energy. Surely you have the authority to requisition a pair for me from army stores," Marcus replied.

"What stores? Fewer than half our supplies reach us. The merchants in Sambol wear our boots, eat our food, and hoard our medicines. If SeLenicca attacks tomorrow, most of our men will desert to the other side just to get a good meal," Woodpecker grumbled.

"How could conditions get so bad? Does the king know about this?" Rob asked.

"Of course the king knows. Of course Jaylor knows, too. But what can they do about it with the Gnuls overriding every decision made. You'd think they want us to lose the war and let the sorcerer-king rule us!" Woodpecker threw up his hands at that horrible and contradictory thought.

"We hope our quest will end the war and end the tyranny of the Gnuls," Marcus said.

Woodpecker looked at him curiously. "No, I don't suppose you can tell me your quest. That goes against the rules. Well, I hope you have better luck than the last spy Jaylor sent across the pass. He came back to us in pieces. Many of them missing." Woodpecker's normally pale complexion paled further. He swallowed convulsively.

Marcus tasted bile. Rumors leaking out of SeLenicca for years had hinted that King Simeon—the sorcerer-king—made human sacrifices to his winged demon-god Simurgh.

Ignorant Gnuls considered dragons modern incarnations of Simurgh. If only they could experience the glory of shared dragon magic, they'd know how much good the dragons brought to Coronnan. He and Robb had to bring the near invisible creatures back to Coronnan soon.

"Are the enemy troops massing for an attack?" Robb asked.

Leave it to him to ask the practical questions.

"Curiously, no. They're waiting for something. Something big. Something disastrous for us. Well, come along. I'll take you to the supply hut. I'll try to keep the quartermaster from skinning all three of us alive for daring to ask for something. Anything." Woodpecker strode toward the doorway, still muttering.

Marcus and Robb followed the Battlemage across the camp. They passed dozens of men on the way. All of them moved quickly away to avoid any contact with the magicians.

"Fear is a wonderful thing," Woodpecker continued his litany of complaint. "Fear gives us mages all of the privacy we could want and then some. No one interferes with our work. But they won't help either. *S'murghit!* They won't even feed us. Have to do it all ourselves so they don't taint their precious mundane lives with magic. If I didn't know that King Simeon's rule would be worse than putting up with these lumbird-brained fools, I'd desert to the enemy. Or go outlaw. I'd get more respect in Hanassa!"

Marcus resisted the urge to make the ancient ward against evil by crossing his wrists and flapping his hands. No one went to Hanassa voluntarily. No one except mercenaries, outlaws, and rogue magicians—all determined to make trouble for the rest of civilization. King Simeon hailed from Hanassa before he'd married SeLenicca's very young Queen Miranda. And look at the mess he'd made there!

"Stand aside. I have need of a few things," Woodpecker demanded of the three armed men at the supply hut.

"Orders are no one gets anything until the next boatload of supplies comes upriver," the sergeant sneered. Three gold stripes on the sleeve of his green uniform tunic shone brightly in the freshly ignited rushlights beside the door. His collar and cuffs were threadbare and his left elbow nearly poked through the cloth. But his boots were new and shone with fresh polish.

Marcus nearly salivated with greed at the thought of the warm and dry feet those boots would give him.

"You dare give orders to me, Giiorge?" Woodpecker asked. "Didn't I bind up an ax wound on your left side with barely a scar after you dropped your guard and allowed a wounded enemy to sneak up on you?"

"Um . . ." Sergeant Giiorge shuffled his feet and blushed.

"One pair of boots for my journeyman. He might very well be the one to throw the spell that wins the next battle. You and all of your men owe the Battle-mages more than your lives."

"Two minutes inside. And don't tell anyone I was the one that let you in." Sergeant Giiorge unlocked the door and then gestured to his men to move for-

ward two paces, just enough room for Woodpecker to
get between him and the door. They kept their backs
sternly to the doorway and the activities of the
magicians.

"Not very grateful, if you ask me," Robb muttered.

"The best we can hope for," Woodpecker replied.
He brought a ball of witchlight to his hand and
scanned the shelves inside the hut. A few uniform
tunics, some blankets, and mess kits. Not much left to
supply an army.

"One pair of boots left. Take them and hope they
fit." Woodpecker thrust the solitary pair into Marcus'
hands and sidled out of the hut.

The moment all three of them were clear of the
doorway, Sergeant Giiorge locked it again and resumed his post.

"Follow me back toward the enclave, then leave as
soon as no one is looking," Woodpecker ordered as
they hurried back the way they had come.

At the edge of the empty circle around the Battlemage's hut, Marcus and Robb veered off toward a
clump of trees beside the paddock. Marcus plunked
himself down on the ground beneath the spreading
branches of an oak. Pale green swelled the ends of
the branches with the promise of new life and plenty
of shade come Summer. He pulled off both his boots
and managed to tug on one of the new ones before a
commotion on the other side of the paddock interrupted him.

"Ah-ha!" exclaimed a deep voice. "We have the
boot thieves! Arrest these men." A burly soldier
dressed in a faded green uniform tunic with a single
muddy yellow stripe on his sleeves ran toward them
brandishing a long dagger and an ax. Three more men
with no stripes on their sleeves followed close behind
him armed with clubs.

"Run!" Robb exclaimed. He pulled Marcus to his
feet.

Marcus grabbed the second boot and followed, limping and off-balance.

"Out of the way!" Robb turned to face the enemy, still running backward. He launched a witch bolt that looked like an arrow at the growing number of soldiers in pursuit. Fire fletched and tipped his missile.

"Theft of a comrade's equipment is punishable by hanging," the leader pronounced. His followers screamed more invective.

Marcus couldn't understand a word they said, but their auras displayed intense outrage and bloodlust.

The witch bolt landed directly in front of the leader's feet. He hopped back, careening into his men. They tumbled backward, like so many stacked game cartes.

"Lucky shot, Robb," Marcus panted as they pelted away from camp toward the dubious cover of a shrublined creek.

"Careful aim. I make my own luck."

They had just slid into the chill water of the foaming creek and drawn a deep breath when six men crashed through the shrubs a few paces to their right.

"Keep running!" Robb called, hauling Marcus to his feet.

"How about another witch bolt while I put on my boot?"

"No time."

"We're heading the wrong way." Marcus limped behind Robb as he scrambled up the other side of the shallow ravine. His left sock was soaked and his foot hurt from running across the uneven turf and stones.

"We're heading toward safety."

"But the pass is back that way."

"Later. We'll go after the dragons later."

Marcus dodged a real arrow followed by a knife aimed at his back. "I think my luck just ran out."

CHAPTER 2

"Three wizards and two Rovers beats your two dragons and three turnips!" Vareena laughed loudly. A deep ripple of mirth warmed her heart. She didn't laugh often enough. "That's the first time I have beaten you at cartes, Farrell. Now hand over your treasure." She peered through the misty light of her witchball at her ghostly companion who faded in and out of her vision.

"My concentration slips, Eena," Farrell excused himself. "Since this last fever, I have become quite forgetful."

"Very forgetful, indeed," Vareena said around her smile. "You seem to have forgotten that you bet three acres of land in the Province of Nunio against my two cows and three chickens." She had no hope of ever claiming her winnings. She and the ghost had played this game before. He always bet the same three acres and she always lost the same two cows and three chickens.

Although her ghost required food and medications, blankets and shelter from the weather, he had no need of her dowry. Once trapped inside this ancient building, her ghosts never left.

"Promise me, Vareena, that when I finally pass into the void between the planes of existence, you will take the amulet from around my neck and carry it to my family in Nunio." Farrell paused a long moment, breathing heavily. His hand stole to his throat where he fingered the leather thong that held the silver-encased amethyst. After a moment he shifted his hand from his only treasure to lay it flat upon his chest. He closed his hand in fierce spasm three times, as if clutching the pain of his worn-out heart.

Vareena saw the pulse in his throat beat more rapidly in an irregular rhythm. She wished she could rest her wrist against his forehead to test for fever. A barrier of stinging energy separated her from each of the ghosts who had found refuge here.

"Tell my sister's sons that you are my heir," Farrell resumed when his breathing and pain eased. "Tell them what happened to me, how you and only you have cared for me these past two years. The amulet is the deed to the land. My nephews will care for you and the land."

A moment of hope brightened within Vareena. When this ghost died, her duties here in this abandoned monastery and within the village would ease. She'd be free to do as Farrell asked.

"I would like that very much, Farrell."

"Promise me, Vareena. Promise that you will leave this cursed place and never return."

Vareena shifted uncomfortably upon her stool. She did not want to lie to her ghost.

He reached out to grab her sleeve. As always, the wall of shocking energy repulsed him before he came in contact with any part of her. 'Twas always the same. He was a ghost and she still human. They were destined never to touch until one of them died.

"Women may not own land." A safe answer.

"King Darville changed that law three years ago."

Vareena lifted her head in surprise. She shouldn't be surprised, though. If such a drastic change had taken place, her isolated village near the Western border of Coronnan would be the last to hear of it. The women of the village would hear of it later still. The men here did not like change. They did not like her ghosts. They did not like her. They did not like much of anything.

A measure of hope warmed her heart. She clamped down on it, afraid to allow it to grow and be drowned later.

"I have duties here, Farrell. My family, the village, this monastery. I do not think I will be allowed to leave." She hung her head, refusing to meet his gaze.

"They feed off your generosity, Vareena. They need to fend for themselves. You must leave this place. As you have so often dreamed."

"But . . ." He was right of course.

"For the friendship we have shared these past two years," Farrell pleaded, "promise me that you will leave this place before it curses you, as it has cursed me and countless other men over the centuries. Leave and follow your heart, Vareena."

"My brothers . . . They need me to care for them as my mother did before her untimely death. The villagers . . . I am their only healer."

"They can all tend to themselves if forced to. You do not belong here, Vareena. Your spirit is too bright and loving to be swallowed whole by your family's selfishness. You've given them twenty years since your mama died. Ten of those years ago, you should have married and started a family of your own."

This time she could not avoid his stern gaze. His brown eyes seemed to blaze through the ghostly mist like two dark coals, lit by his fervor. Or his fever.

She sighed a moment in regret. She'd like a family of her own. But none of the men in this village trusted her or honored her because she could see the ghosts and was destined to care for them. None of them had offered for her hand despite her handsome dowry of two cows and three chickens.

"I promise, Farrell. When you pass fully into the void, I will take your amulet and claim the three acres of land in the province of Nunio."

"Good. Now another game, perhaps. With different stakes. I have won your dowry too many times to make it worth anything. Why don't we play for the pile of gold in the library of this place?"

Vareena shuffled the stack of wooden cartes, each one lovingly engraved with a different image and then painted red, black, green, or yellow. "The trick to winning that particular pot is the courage to enter the library to claim the gold. Neither of us will be lucky enough to lose this pot."

"Ah, but what need have I of gold? I am dying, and you will need much money to buy more land in Nunio. Three acres is a fine dowry but not enough to support you."

"Then I will bet a chicken stew, made with the pickled beets that you love so well."

"Not made from your three chickens. Those you must preserve as part of your dowry."

"Those three chickens are sacrosanct. They know it. Even my brothers know it. They refuse to gather eggs lest those haughty ladies peck their eyes out."

"From what I know of your brothers, they deserve whatever fate your chickens hand out."

"Why do you think I always send Yeenos to the coop when his temper is particularly vile." They both laughed at the image of her tall and lanky brother fighting off the aggressive hens, feathers flying in all directions, squawks and squeals setting the entire coop aflurry.

"I hope Yeenos takes the younger three boys with him as well. They deserve some lessons in humility," Farrell finally said, breaking off his weakening laughter.

In the distance a temple bell tolled twice, long and loud.

"That is the priest calling the shepherds in from the hills for supper. I must go now, Farrell. I'll return in the morning with your breakfast."

"Don't bother, Vareena. There is more than enough stew left. Rest yourself and do something that you never allow yourself the time for."

"I could wash my hair." She smiled, anticipating the luxury of a private bath beneath the waterfall half a league below the village. The cold mountain stream was warmed slightly at the base of the fall by hot springs. All the women of the village went there for bathing and laundry, but never first thing in the morning.

"Use the violet-scented soap. I love the smell of violets on you." Farrell lay back on his cot, one arm thrown across his eyes. "I remember the scent of violets in the Spring, how the cows would trample them and the smell would fill the valley." He drifted off into a light doze.

Vareena packed up her mother's precious cartes and tiptoed out of her ghost's cell. He had chosen one in the middle of the southern wing of the old monastery. The rooms were larger here, originally intended for retired magicians and priests rather than novices and journeymen. The south-facing exterior wall warmed the room better than the small rooms of the chill north wing. As she threw her shawl about her shoulders against the Spring chill of early evening, something heavy and awkward tangled in her hair.

She batted at the offending thing and danced about, first on one foot then the other, half panicked. Her heart raced in fear of the giant spiders that hid in the dark recesses of this ancient building.

"S'murghit!" she let loose with an unladylike curse as sharp metal stabbed at her fingers. She examined the offended digit for any trace of a spider bite. Satisfied that one of the critters hadn't landed on her, she sucked the tiny cut until the worst of the sting eased.

Only then did she take the time to comb her fingers through the mass of tight blonde coils that never stayed in place long, no matter how many pins she used or how tightly she braided it.

At last she freed the long piece of leather that supported a curiously fashioned piece of silver. From the center of the amulet, a bright amethyst winked at her in the setting sun.

"You can't get rid of me so easily, Farrell. I won't leave you until you finally break free of the curse that traps you between this plane of existence and the void. Why is it that only the women of my family can see and care for the ghosts who need us. And there is almost always a ghost here who needs us."

*   *   *

An ill wind blows this way. Does it come from our old enemies in SeLenicca? Partly. I sense chill blasts from Hanassa as well as the capital. My easy life of observation and contemplation is in jeopardy. I must stir myself and resurrect powers I have not used in a very long time..

I do not like change. Yet I must change in order to bring my world back to the way it was before. My safety and the preservation of my power depend upon it. Someone will die. Perhaps many someones. I care not. I must ensure my safety. For the heritage I leave my son and daughter and their descendants, I must ensure my safety.

*   *   *

"Who among you miserable excuses for apprentices can tell me which elements must be invoked in order to divert water from a free-flowing creek into an irrigation ditch? And which elements must therefore be excluded from the spell?" Master Magician Withy-Reed intoned to the class.

The short and rotund magician paced in front of his students. He looked the exact opposite of what his working name suggested—as was often the case since most of the nicknames came to magicians while still apprentices.

Of the dozen students gathered on the grassy fore-court of the University, Margit alone raised her hand. She knew the answer. She'd known the answer for weeks. Only if WithyReed offered her the opportunity to answer would she advance through the ranks to journeyman.

Until she passed all of the tests and endured the trial by Tambootie smoke, she was stuck here in the mountain fastness where the University hid from the prying eyes of the rest of Coronnan, and the spies of the Gnuls in particular. Since she had left Queen Rossemikka's employ as a maid, she had no other place to go.

She wondered if WithyReed would pay more attention to her if she and Marcus had announced their betrothal before he disappeared into the wilds of the border country. No one had heard from him or from his partner Robb since . . . since before the dragons came back with Jack.

A stab of fear to the depths of her soul for the man she loved almost shook the answer to WithyReed's question out of her mind. Marcus and Robb often went moons without contacting her. But they always stayed within reach of a summons spell with Senior Magician Jaylor. What kind of trouble had they gotten into this time? She couldn't even hope to chase after them with half-formed plans of rescue until she became a journeyman—journeywoman—magician.

She couldn't became a journeywoman unless she passed the tests set before her by the master magicians. WithyReed refused to so much as let her answer a question let alone take a test.

"Ferrdie?" Master Magician WithyReed called upon a young boy to Margit's right. Ferrdie had been an apprentice for three years now and not passed a single test. But he, too, had nowhere else to go, having been banished from the family homestead by his father because he was left-handed and therefore must be a magician.

"Is . . . is the answer Fire?" Ferrdie stammered. Never once did he lift his eyes to the master.

Margit kept her hand up and tried to capture Withy-Reed's gaze.

"Incorrect." The master magician scanned the rest of the class. "Have any of you studied the treatise written by Master Scarface some three hundred years ago when dragon magic was first discovered and implemented to save Coronnan from three generations of civil war?"

Margit kept her hand up patiently. Learning to read had been difficult for her at the late age of seventeen. But she had mastered the arcane skill and studied all of her assignments thoroughly.

Again WithyReed's challenging stare slid right past Margit and alighted on a moderately talented boy in the back of the group of students seated cross-legged on the grass. "Mikkail?"

"Air!" the boy replied with confidence.

"Such incompetence. I expected better of you. All of you."

"I know the answer, Master WithyReed," Margit said. She thrust out her chin, determined to make the man acknowledge her.

"Since none of you can give me the proper answer. I will give you a hint. Air and Fire are linked as elements. Since the dragons fly through the air and shoot flames to cook their meat and defend themselves—not that anything on Kardia Hodos remains that is big enough to be a danger to a dragon—when a magician gathers dragon magic, he throws spells most closely linked with those two elements."

Margit stood up in the center of the gathering of two dozen students and faced the master. "I know the answer, sir, and the theory behind it."

"When a magician is forced to draw magical energy from the Kardia, as we had to do until recently, then our spells must be rooted in the Kardia. Now what element is left that would be linked to the Kardia?" WithyReed continued to ignore Margit.

Anger boiled in Margit's stomach and heated her face and hands. "Kardia and Water are linked and therefore an irrigation spell must be rooted in the Kardia to draw the water from its natural flow in the creek or river to the unnatural channel dug for irrigation." She clenched her fists until her fingernails drew blood from her palms.

"Ferrdie, have you figured it out yet?" WithyReed acted as if Margit had not spoken at all.

"Why do you ignore me, sir?" she blurted out, thrusting herself directly in front of him. She topped him in height by at least two finger-lengths. He could not ignore her now.

"Sit down, girl. You are here to listen only. Females cannot gather dragon magic, so your presence in the University is temporary. Speak up, Ferrdie, I need you to answer the question."

Margit gritted her teeth and clenched her hands. Oh! to slam one of her fists into the pompous little magician's face. Before she could follow through with her desires, she whipped around and marched out of the forecourt, spine stiff, hands clenched and tears pricking her eyes.

I will not run. I will not give him the satisfaction of running from him.

She met no one between the forecourt and the girl's dormitory on the north side of the quadrangle of timbered buildings. Girls represented over half the apprentices. Females young and old were the most common victims of Gnul persecution. In the last three years, Marcus and Robb had brought more girls here for refuge than boys. WithyReed and the other masters had no right to pretend female magicians would evaporate and never bother them again. She fully intended to achieve journeyman status. Only as a journeyman—or journeywoman—could she even hope to accompany Marcus on his treks from one end of the country to the other. Maybe even—she dared hope—they could travel to exotic locations on other continents.

She stepped into the room she shared with Annyia. The dark-haired child/woman had been savagely beaten and raped by her stepbrothers in an attempt to kill the magical talent they thought she possessed. They probably succeeded. The ignorant fools believed the myth that only virgins could work magic. Withy-Reed and his antique prejudice that demanded male magicians remain celibate until they became masters didn't help the situation.

Jaylor had placed Margit in the same room with Annyia, hoping some of the older girl's confidence and determination would help Annyia break away from her guilt and depression. Margit had little patience with her roommate's tears and frantic starts at every sharp noise.

"WithyReed ignores me because I am female. But if I look like a boy . . . Maybe he'd forget his prejudices for a moment. Just one short moment until he realizes I know what I'm doing."

She marched to the little chest at the foot of her cot where she kept her few personal possessions. The blue tunic and brown trews she had worn on the trek to the University from the capital were on the bottom, cleaned and mended. Beneath them she found her dagger, the one she had used to defend herself in the market square before Jaylor recruited her as his spy.

For a moment her memory put her back in the crowded market square on King Darville's coronation day. She had been selling her mother's baked goods to the hungry throngs waiting for the grand procession after the ceremony. When a foreign spy had threatened her because he did not like the spices in the sausage roll she sold him, Jack had come to her rescue. She'd been more than willing to defend herself with her knife, but Jack had diffused the anger of the crowd and discovered a dangerous plot against the king's life at the same time.

Later that day, as she packed up the last of the unsold food—not much, for the capital citizens and visitors had all been hungry and jovial, quite willing to spend money on such an auspicious occasion—

Jaylor had come to her, wrapped in an enveloping cloak of magic. She'd seen through his delusion and known him for the head of the now exiled Commune of Magicians. He'd asked her to spy for him and offered to begin training her as a magician in return.

Apparently Jack had noticed something important about her when she stood up to the foreign spy.

Margit appreciated the irony of the Council of Provinces trying to outlaw magic in Coronnan when their king's best friend from childhood led the most powerful group of magicians in all of Kardia Hodos.

Margit's mother had threatened to lock Margit in the pantry with a cat when she announced that she would give up selling meat rolls, pasties, and baked sweets in the market in favor of serving as the new queen's personal maid. Her mother didn't know that Margit had learned to open every lock in the city years ago. She had only just learned that magic had enhanced her senses to allow her to do that.

Thank the Stargods her three years as Queen Rossemikka's maid had ended. She couldn't stand being cooped up in the palace any longer. She had trouble breathing indoors, especially in the queen's apartments which always smelled of cat.

"Time to improvise." With three swift slashes of the dagger, she cut her blonde locks level with her shoulders. Then she bound her hair back into a masculine queue with a bit of blue string. She couldn't get her clumsy gown and shift off fast enough.

"Finding and rescuing Marcus will be much easier if I'm disguised as a boy. I certainly won't remain here any longer than I have to. And I certainly won't baby-sit any more apprentices."

CHAPTER 3

A low rumbling ripple along the floor and walls
shattered the veil of forgetfulness that encased
the woman's mind. She braced herself instinctively
against the waving motion and counted to ten. At
four, the quake drifted away to a memory. Her mind
told her that this was not the first kardiaquake that
had rocked Queen's City. Nor would it be the last.
Some instinct she did not have the strength to comprehend told her that the intensity had lessened. But she
could not remember how or why she knew that.

How long had she been wandering the halls of this
damaged palace without being aware of herself?

Her stomach growled. When had she eaten last?

She remembered nothing: not why she wandered
these once-magnificent halls; nor why she haunted this
huge building like a ghost, alone and lost to everything
and everyone she held dear.

Somehow that aloneness seemed almost . . . not
quite, but almost . . . right.

She imagined what the passageways must have been
like when they were filled with courtiers and politicians, ladies and gentlemen who spent their days—and
nights—pretending to agree with the king's demands.
Then she imagined herself, a wispy ghost, drifting behind them, eavesdropping, laughing at the truths they
would never admit to themselves. The king listened to
no one and those who agreed with him, more often
than not, met with disfavor.

They were all small dogs chasing their own tails in

a fruitless race. But she was not part of that and never would be.

How did she know that?

A brilliantly colored tapestry on the wall caught her attention. Women sitting at lace bolsters concentrated deeply on their bobbins and the yards and yards of floating threadwork. The scene seemed familiar. She reached out to caress the woven picture. Her broken fingernails snagged a thread. Immediately she halted her quest to touch some part of her past through the picture and worked the jagged edge of her nail free without pulling the entire thread loose.

Something was wrong. She stared at the dirt encrusted in the cuticle and beneath the nail. Never before had she allowed her hands to become so filthy. No lacemaker did.

Lace.

Her hands curved as if lifting two pairs of bobbins for an intricate stitch. The sensuous feel of carved bone and wood crawled through her. Deep satisfaction at the creation of delicate and airy fabric expanded in her lungs and gave her a sense of rightness.

Lace! Her world revolved around lace.

But not a scrap of it graced her night robe, shift, or the tops of her slippers. If she did not wear lace, she must be a worker rather than a noble designer or teacher. She reached up her hand to her silvery blonde hair. Her fingers drifted through the long tresses without resistance. She wore no cap, nor had she braided her hair properly.

"I must find the workroom," she resolved. "After I find something to eat and wash. Then I must plait my hair." Two gathered braids from temple to nape that broke free until they reached the center of her back then joined into a single thick rope. That was the proper number for a worker.

"Not two plaits. Three at least." Three plaits belonged to the nobility, and four were reserved for the queen. So if she deserved three plaits, why did she not wear any of the precious lace fabric?

"Three plaits," she repeated. That did not settle in her brain as correct, but better than two plaits or . . . shudder . . . must she revert to the single plait of a peasant or lace factory worker until she knew the truth of her identity?

"Three plaits," she insisted. "But first I must wash and eat."

Her feet automatically headed down three flights of stairs to the long, long dining hall. The central table stretched out with places for fifty people. Remnants of food lay scattered about the table and floor where rodents and other scavengers had left it.

Impatiently, she grabbed one of the discarded serviettes and brushed a place clear for herself. She sat down on the tapestried armchair at the head of the table. The large chair was too large. But she knew this to be her place. The view of the room was correct, but the chair did not fit her.

Why? Why didn't it fit? And why had she presided at the head of the table in this magnificent—but crumbling—palace.

While she puzzled out the problem of where to sit, a series of small crashes brought her awareness back to the palace. Brickwork loosened by the kardiaquake fell throughout the building. Perhaps the impromptu remodeling would allow more light to penetrate the workrooms. She smiled again. An act of nature had defied the pompous king and given her the one thing she wanted most—light to work by.

Well, almost the thing she wanted most. Knowing who she was and why she wandered the palace alone might be useful. But knowledge would come, once she returned to her lace.

More richly colored tapestries hung on the high walls of the hall, from just below the narrow windows near the ceiling, to the top of the sideboards. The one depicting the signing of a long-ago wedding agreement sagged, along with the wall and ceiling. A long rent in the fabric separated the politicians from the bride and groom.

A second tear pushed the couples representing the parents even farther away from the two centers of action.

She almost giggled at the subtle irony created by the rips.

Her stomach growled again. She needed to eat. But . . . but the servants had fled the kardiaquakes. No one would bring her soup and bread. No one remained in the palace but herself. Why had she been left behind in the exodus?

Sitting here would not help. She had to find food. A niggle of pride followed her determination to do something for herself. She'd like to see the politicians in the tapestry fetching anything without help.

Servants always entered through that door to her left and food had always been hot. Therefore the kitchen must be nearby.

Cautiously, she traced the route. Footprints in the dust told her that someone else had passed this way, several times in recent days. She placed her right foot delicately into one of them. For a moment the frayed toes of her embroidered slipper fascinated her. She shook off the thrall of following the patterns of the stitches. Her foot fit perfectly into the indentation in the dust.

A quick scan of the array of prints indicated she had passed this way at least four times in recent days.

Scattered prints next to the wall looked tiny. The impression of heavy toes and light heels indicated someone moved furtively along. A small person. Perhaps a child.

She hastened her steps, suddenly afraid of what she might find.

The end of the passage—longer than she thought necessary to ensure hot food in the dining hall— opened into the cavernous kitchen. A hearth opened from each end of the room. Each fireplace could roast an entire beast. A tall man could stand within without getting soot in his hair.

But no fire burned there now, nor had for some time. Cold ashes, mixed with fallen plaster and bricks from the chimneys, littered the floor before both hearths. Scraps of bone and desiccated meat protruded from the layers of debris. A hole in the exterior wall let in a lot of light. Too much light. She examined the jagged hole, not big enough to crawl through and too many loose bricks to be safe. The kitchen had not fared as well as the rest of the palace.

She seemed to remember a number of passages throughout the palace blocked by collapsed ceilings and bulging walls.

How long before the entire building fell on top of her?

"M'ma!" a tiny voice squealed as a grimy form flung itself at her from the depths of one of the hearths.

She looked carefully at the sobbing bundle of mismatched clothing, dirt, and cobwebs.

"M'ma, you found me. They said you died. They said I'd never see you again. They said . . ." the child sobbed into her skirts, clutching her knees so tightly she thought she'd tumble forward and crush her baby.

"M'ma? Am I truly your M'ma?" she asked in wonder. She wasn't alone. Someone remembered her.

Then concern for her child overtook her joy. She stooped down to study her baby at eye level. Bright blue eyes looked back at her from a smudged face, still round with baby fat. Probably about three. That number felt right. Three years. Three plaits. Silvery-blonde hair scraggled out of three plaits that had started out gathered tightly against the child's head. The end of one plait was still held almost in place by a frayed pink ribbon that clashed with her red hair. The second plait had come undone and hopelessly tangled. The center plait wobbled back and forth as if the little girl had tried to fix it herself and failed.

"Are you hurt, baby?" she asked, soothing tangles away from her child's face. The name eluded her. But that didn't matter. They were together.

"I'm hungry." The little girl pouted.

"What have you eaten these past few days?"

"Some of the roast. I found a turnip!" The child's face brightened as she held up half of a withered root vegetable. Tiny teeth marks showed around the edges. She didn't lisp around missing teeth, so she must still be very young. The number three settled in the woman's mind more firmly.

"What a clever girl you are. Where did you find the turnip?" Her own hunger began to plague her insistently.

"Down there." The child pouted as she glanced at a trapdoor and then back to her mother's skirts. A cellar or pantry. More food, assuming the place had not been looted when the kardiaquakes sent everyone in flight from the city.

"You were very brave to climb down there. Will you come with me as we look for more turnips and things."

"A rat scared me." An almost clean thumb crept toward the little girl's mouth.

The woman allowed the child to find what little comfort she could from sucking. Stargods knew when they'd live a normal life, in a normal home, with a normal schedule again.

Schedules.

The concept of following a routine determined by others sounded oddly comforting and right.

She stood and held her hand for the child. "We'll protect each other from the rat, baby. You and I can do anything together."

"I'm Jaranda. Not a baby anymore." The baby rewarded her with a bright smile and clutched her fingers.

"Of course, Jaranda. How could I forget. You are a big girl now. Big enough to hold the door open for me while I climb down. Be sure you stand so you don't block the light."

"Yes, M'ma." Jaranda stood a little straighter and took her finger out of her mouth.

"I don't suppose you remember *my* name, Jaranda?" she asked her daughter.

"M'ma," Jaranda replied importantly.

"Somehow I thought you'd say that."

CHAPTER 4

"Where have you hidden my son, Rejiia?" Lanciar asked the bottom of his ale mug. He didn't really expect an answer. The steed-piss ale of Hanassa didn't even quench his thirst, let alone show him any truths.

Briefly, he longed for a simpler time when King Simeon still lived to rule SeLenicca and Lanciar had only a minor magical talent. He didn't have to think or make decisions. He only had to obey Simeon, and all the wonders of the coven surrounded him with sex and power and influence. He could love Rejiia in secret and experience the thrill of fathering a son on her while Simeon believed the child his own.

But then Simeon had sent him to seek out the man who wielded enough power within the mines to threaten the coven.

Lanciar had discovered Jack. The young magician was just beginning to recover his memory and his talent after some adolescent trauma.

And then the day came when a deep kardiaquake had collapsed the mine. Jack's newly awakened senses had alerted him to the coming disaster. He, with Lanciar's help, had rescued an entire team of slaves. But Simeon's guards and administrators were caught up in the chaos; the entire complex had to be abandoned. All who survived ran for their lives. Lanciar had attached himself to Jack and his friend as ordered.

On the trail out of the mine Jack had drawn Lanciar deep into a questing spell, seeking the dragon that

Simeon had magically wounded and imprisoned. During that long night on a lonely mountain pass, Lanciar's full talent had awakened.

Now he was a master magician having to think and make his own decisions in order to survive, and able to see Rejiia for a selfish, power-hungry bitch who used everyone she came in contact with to augment her own illusion of greatness. Lanciar had to rescue his son from Rejiia's ungentle clutches.

The Kardia rolled beneath his feet. He braced himself against the exterior wall of the tavern, momentarily reliving the terror of being trapped underground in the mine with tons of Kardia pouring down upon him. He owed Jack his life as well as his respect—probably the only truly honest man he had ever met.

But it was a little quake this time and did not deserve his fear. Almost a daily occurrence here in Hanassa, the city of outlaws. None of the ragged denizens of the city seemed to notice the disruption.

Satisfied that the ground beneath his feet was solid once more, he stared into the last few drops of liquid in his cup. Not enough to scry a vision of Rejiia or the child she had stolen from him. The horrible ale served here was too thick to see through anyway.

Should he drink another? Yes. The dry air within this ancient volcanic caldera that housed the dregs of the world left a constant sour taste in the back of his throat.

"Let's try the next tavern," he suggested to the mug. "Maybe someone there has seen Rejiia with a child. Maybe their ale tastes better."

He strolled casually toward the next outcropping of ramshackle buildings. While he wove a slightly drunken path, he kept his eyes moving, taking in every detail of life among the outlaws, mercenaries, rogue magicians, and criminals. No innocents here, and precious few children.

Where would Rejiia have taken her baby if she didn't keep him with her.

That was a sobering thought. What if she had fostered the child elsewhere? How would Lanciar ever find his son if she had?

A party of richly clad magicians strolled past Lanciar. He knew their profession because they all carried long staffs, some topped with intricate carvings or natural crystals, and they all wore flowing robes embroidered or painted with arcane sigils. At the center of the group strode Rejiia, daughter of the late unlamented Lord Krej, and cousin to King Darville of Coronnan. Under other circumstances, she would be the heir to Darville's dragon throne. But her magic, her illicit alliance with Simeon, the murdered sorcerer-king of SeLenicca, and her own murderous proclivities made her an exile from her native country.

Her father's treason against King Darville didn't help her status either. Lord Krej had thrown one too many illegal spells in a desperate attempt to usurp power in Coronnan. His last piece of magic had been intended to turn Darville into a statue of whatever creature reflected his personality—probably a golden wolf. But the new king had worn his enchanted crown that protected him from all magic. Krej's spell had backlashed into his own eyes, transforming him into a tin weasel with flaking gilt paint.

Rejiia had rescued the statue of her father from Darville's dungeon on the king's coronation day. Simeon had had custody of the tin weasel for a time. But when Jack and his companion from the mines— what was his name?—had murdered the King of SeLenicca a few weeks ago, Rejiia had grabbed the statue and taken it with her in a desperate attempt to murder Jack before he could reunite the dragons with the Commune of Magicians.

She'd failed to do more than enhance Jack's status as a master magician in full command of his powers as she fled that battle scene in disgrace. But she'd managed to keep Krej with her during her escape.

No one knew for sure if Krej lived within the tin

casing or not. No one dared probe it lest they be drawn into the statue as well.

As Rejiia toured Hanassa, she levitated the tin weasel behind her in a subservient position, much as Krej had done to her in her youth. Lanciar knew how much humiliation she had suffered under her father. Now she took her revenge.

But she needed Krej animate to fill in the missing ranks of the dispersing coven. Lanciar could stand in only one corner of the eight-pointed ritual star. He was supposed to be anchoring that corner in SeLenicca rather than here, searching for his son.

He no longer trusted Rejiia or any of the other members of the coven. He'd rather work as a solitary magician than ever work magic with Rejiia again.

Lanciar kept his face buried in his mug, pretending to be just another mercenary waiting for a war to break out until Rejiia passed. She shouldn't recognize him with a full beard. He'd added layers of dirt to his hands and clothing to complete his disguise.

The tilt of her head, the sway of her hips, the way her black hair with a single white streak at her left temple fell in enticing waves, curling around her breasts, triggered memories of better times with her. Lanciar felt a stir of his old lust. Pregnancy and childbirth had filled out her breasts and hips without detracting from her long legs and slender waist. She ran long, elegant fingers through the white streak in her flowing name. The eyes of every man in the vicinity followed the path of those fingers.

She didn't need a staff to focus her magic. She had other tools.

Lanciar's heart ached to hold her one more time. He had loved her once. But then she had tried to pass their infant son off as King Simeon's bastard, possible blood heir to all three kingdoms on this continent. When she discovered that Simeon had been half brother to her father, Lord Krej, she had tried to tell the world that the brat died at birth.

Lanciar knew she lied. Lied more easily than she told the truth.

He hardened his heart against her, likening her to the empty mug in his hand.

Rejiia looked his way.

He raised the mug as if taking a long pull on the sour brew to hide his face from her view. He automatically armored his aura and magical signature and buried them deep inside his gut.

Rejiia and her entourage of magicians passed him by without a second glance. He saw no nannies or servants carrying her infant son. Where had she stashed the boy? Certainly not in the bottom of his mug where he looked for answers.

When he lifted his gaze once more, he noticed that Krej had dropped into the dust. The statue remained stubbornly still. Had the spirit of the man revived enough to try to defy Rejiia? Lanciar smiled at the thought of the inevitable battle of wills that would ensue.

A moment later, Rejiia paused and scowled at the statue. She sighed heavily and snapped her fingers. The statue rose a hand's span above the dirt and floated behind her once more.

How long before Rejiia turned her full attention to reversing the spell? Krej's magic would give the coven a seventh magician—if Lanciar decided to remain one of them. They needed nine.

She probably would not attempt to revive Krej until she was ready to depose Darville of Coronnan and claim the Coraurlia—the magnificent dragon crown made of precious glass—for herself.

Then she'd set up Lanciar's son as her heir.

Not as long as Lanciar lived. He planned on keeping his boy safe from the machinations of the coven.

He decided to search Rejiia's quarters in the palace while she paraded around the city causing misery.

Rejiia's not-so-dainty footprints showed clearly when he allowed his eyes to cross slightly. She carelessly left her magical signature of deep black and blood red in each of her footsteps. Easy enough to retrace her path. He placed his own foot atop her prints, allowing her magical signature to mask his own.

One hundred steps, and he faced the gaping cave mouth that served as entrance to the palace of Hanassa. A lazy guard propped up the wall while he cleaned his fingernails with his dagger.

He took one more step toward the cave mouth and halted in mid-stride. A band of Rover men emerged from the palace. Their leader, a middle-aged man with distinguished wings of gray in his thick black hair, followed the same footsteps Lanciar traced—but in reverse. The Rovers trailed Rejiia. Why? Up to mischief certainly.

Their leader grinned widely. Sunlight glinted off his teeth, his eyes twinkled and years of care fled his face. Zolltarn. The self-styled king of the Rovers had beguiled the hardest of hearts and wisest of mages with that smile.

Lanciar closed his eyes and still saw that smile though the image of the man behind it faded from memory.

What plot drove Zolltarn to follow Rejiia?

Lanciar's mouth turned dry, and he wished for another drink.

Lanciar waited until the garishly clad Rovers in purple and red over black—obviously all members of the same clan—passed. Then he followed them.

Sure enough, within a few moments, the Rovers caught up with Rejiia as she toured the city. She kept up the pretense of examining every detail of life trapped within the walls of this ancient volcano as if she intended to govern here—or use the denizens as an army to back her claims to more important crowns.

She paused in front of a silk merchant. All of the goods had been stolen from a trading caravan that dared the pass between the desert kingdom of Rossemeyer and Coronnan.

"I want black! Black with silver embroidery. This entire shipment is useless." Rejiia spat and threw two bolts of costly fabric to the ground. She aimed a crystal-topped wand at the merchandise and set it afire.

The tubby little merchant hastened to retrieve the jewel-toned bolts. He slapped at the flames, threw some of the ever-present dust on them, and eventually backed away from the heat generated by Rejiia's witchfire.

Rejiia drew back her substantial foot and kicked the man in the ribs while he bent down. She laughed heartily while he clutched his middle and moaned in pain. The nearby burning cloth sent tendrils of flame too close to his head and spread to his hair. He yelped and scuttled away.

Lanciar sent a quick spell to negate the witchfire—only magic could douse it.

Rejiia whirled to confront the one who dared to interfere with her games. Blotches of red on her white skin showed her outrage.

Lanciar ducked out of sight.

At that moment of distraction, Zolltarn physically grabbed the statue of Krej and retreated. He and his men seemed to disappear before Lanciar's eyes.

But Lanciar knew Zolltarn of old. The Rover used tricks that mimicked magic, requiring little actual magical energy. Here in Hanassa magicians could not tap the energy of ley lines or of dragons. Both shunned the city of outlaws.

Lanciar allowed his eyes to cross once more and looked for the distortions in light patterns that meant stealthy movement. He had to smile at the trick played upon Rejiia. Her own arrogance had given her a false sense of security. Good. She'd be so outraged at the challenges to her authority she might drop her guard around her son.

Ripples in the light showed all of the Rovers headed for the tunnel exit from the city. The rest of the clan waited just outside the gates with their loaded sledges, and their steeds, ready to flee.

"I expected more subtlety from you, Zolltarn," Lanciar chuckled.

The Rover chieftain flashed his magnificent smile in Lanciar's direction. Zolltarn spoke directly into Lanciar's mind, *The game is not yet finished, young soldier. But time is short. She planned to free Krej this night. The Commune cannot allow that.*

The statue of Krej passed from Rover hand to Rover hand. One wrapped it in silk. Another threw a coarse blanket over it. Then it disappeared inside the round cabinlike structure atop the lead sledge.

Lanciar could find no trace of the statue or the life it contained with either his magic or his mundane senses.

Rejiia whirled and watched the activity.

"After him! I want Zolltarn's head." She stamped her foot, and three magicians ran to do her bidding. "One thousand gold drageen for the return of my father!" she added.

Krej didn't seem nearly as important to her as the blemish to her dignity.

Rejiia's magician entourage wrung their hands in indecision.

Zolltarn turned and saluted Rejiia with his famous smile and a wave of his hand.

"Damn!" Rejiia stamped her foot again.

Was that an aftershock of the previous quake that seemed to drop the Kardia from beneath Lanciar's feet or a measure of her anger?

"When I retrieve my father, I'll have my son back from his Rover wet nurse as well," Rejiia called in the wake of her magicians.

What?

Lanciar burned with anger equal to Rejiia's. Had one of the babies carried by the Rover tribe been his son?

Rejiia drew in a deep breath, held it, and let it out

through her teeth three times in preparation for a trance.

Lanciar mimicked her actions. He'd follow both Rejiia and Zolltarn into the void and back if he had to. Quickly, he sought Zolltarn's mind along the path of his earlier communication. This little bit of magic would drain his energy reserves, but he had to try. He needed to know the Rover's next trick.

He met a blankness deeper than the void. All Rovers had impressive and instinctive magical armor.

Rejiia scrunched her face in an ugly scowl of frustration. She hadn't been able to penetrate Zolltarn's mind either.

A peculiar sparkle appeared in the light surrounding the entire Rover clan and their possessions. All of them disappeared in a flash of crackling lightning.

Wind rushed to fill the vacuum left by their transport to elsewhere. It moved so quickly and violently that bits of wood and cloth, ash, leftover food, and broken tools swirled together in a series of tornadoes.

Lanciar threw up an arm to protect his eyes.

Then all became quiet again.

S'murghit! Zolltarn had mastered the transport spell. Lanciar couldn't follow them. He didn't know the secret of coming out the other side *alive*.

Another flash of sparkling light signaled Rejiia's disappearance.

Double s'murghit! She knew the secret, too.

How was he to find his son now?

He stared at the bottom of his empty mug wishing for inspiration. "I need a drink while I think about it."

CHAPTER 5

Jack inspected long strands of thread dyed in a rainbow of colors. "Katrina said she wanted purple dye," he muttered to the merchant. His neck burned with embarrassment. This arcane feminine errand made him more uncomfortable than the soul-penetrating stare of a dragon.

"This is a lovely shade of lavender," the woman with sparkling eyes said with the slight lisp of a foreign accent. She pulled one long thread free of the bundle and held it against a black cloth for contrast.

"Too pale." Jack suspected his betrothed wanted her threads to match a particular shade. "Amaranth," he said, hoping the plant matched its namesake.

"Ah!" The merchant tossed her dark curls flirtatiously as she retrieved another thread from the bundle. This one had more pink to it and was several shades darker than the lavender.

"That's close. Can I see it against white?"

"White? As in the cream of the queen's new gown or the stark white of SeLenese lace?" Her accent came through thicker with that statement. She must come from Jihab, Jack decided.

Her mouth twitched in laughter.

In another time and place Jack would love to flirt with her.

"Stark white, like lace," he replied.

"Is this for the little lacemaker recently taking refuge as the queen's favorite companion?" The merchant draped the thread on top of a piece of lace.

Jack recognized the pattern as similar to one Katrina was working at the moment.

"Yes, I'm sure that's the color she wants. Enough dye for a gown and three skeins of linen thread." He sighed in relief, grateful this chore was complete. "I just hope I did this right." This decision was harder than passing one of Old Baamin's magical exams.

He searched his scrip for the proper coin without haggling. The coin was real. Three years ago he'd paid for goods with illusory coins. He still felt guilty about it and tended to overpay.

"Anything else I can get for you, soldier?" The woman smiled at him as she wrapped three packets of powder into a clean cloth.

"This will do." He wanted to hurry back to the palace and Katrina. Someone might recognize him and remember the cocky apprentice who had terrorized this market square on the day of the king's coronation over three years ago.

Just then, a man wearing brown robes thrust passersby away from him as he descended from the arched bridge. He wrinkled his nose repeatedly, sniffing the air and holding his right arm out in front of him, fist clenched.

"S'murghin' Gnul," the merchant muttered behind him. She rapidly packed up her skeins of pretty threads and folded her awning.

"The dye?" Jack asked.

She scuttled away without reply.

Before Jack could search her aura for traces of magic, she disappeared around a corner. But if the man who strode purposefully in this direction was a witch-sniffer from the Gnostic Utilitarian cult, Jack dared not use any of his talent. Even reading an aura could alert some of the more sensitive sniffers.

"You there, soldier!" The Gnul pointed at Jack.

Jack's armor snapped into place in instinctive fear. He put on a bland expression and faced the sniffer.

"Me?" He pointed toward his own chest in silent inquiry.

"Yes, you. Apprehend that woman. I must question her. She may be a foreign witch." The sniffer waved obliquely in the direction the dye merchant had disappeared.

"But she didn't do anything but try to sell me some dye," Jack stalled. What made this man think he had the authority to question anyone? Would he go after Katrina next because she was not born in the city and was unmarried?

"Obey me, man! You are obligated to obey the orders of the Council of Provinces."

"I am obligated to obey the orders of my king and no one else, sir," Jack replied. "I do not recognize you as a member of the Council of Provinces. Nor are you one of their retainers." The hair on his spine and nape bristled.

Shoppers and merchants alike began drifting closer, listening avidly.

Jack searched their faces for any sign of an ally. No one looked in the least sympathetic. Their fear of magic gave the witch-sniffers all the authority they wanted. The Gnostic Utilitarian cult had fed that fear with horror stories. Every death within the city—murder, accident, disease, or old age—was caused by a magician's spell. Every financial setback or change in the weather became the revenge of a disgruntled magician. To make matters worse, ritually slaughtered cats, dogs, rats, even goats and sheep were often found laid at the foot of Festival Pylons around the city as if for a magical sacrifice.

Jack knew no magician would leave evidence lying around so openly, even if they needed the blood of the dying animal to fuel a magical talent.

But the Gnuls didn't care about truth, only about instilling fear in the hearts of the innocent so that the cult could take control of their lives.

Nervously, he fingered the short sword at his hip,

wishing the weapon were his staff instead. He knew how to defend himself with a magician's basic tool. He'd worn the blade and guard's uniform barely a full moon.

"Are you protecting the witch, young man?" The Gnul continued to press closer to Jack.

The crowd grumbled disapproval of all witches. Two men threw stones where the dye merchant had had her awning. One of them whistled very close to Jack's ear.

"What witch?" Jack faced the accuser, trying to keep his fear out of his voice and posture.

The witch-sniffer had gone from wanting to question the woman to actively accusing her without benefit of trial or evidence. Every accused had the right to a public trial. He wondered if the Gnuls and their witch-sniffers ever bothered with the legal process.

The crowd went silent and closed ranks in a near perfect circle around Jack and the Gnul.

"The woman who just ran away. The woman you were doing business with. What were you trying to buy from her? A love potion, perhaps, or poison to use on our king?"

Jack allowed a laugh to explode at the nonsense. "All I wanted was some dye for my betrothed to use on her wedding gown."

The crowd didn't think this was funny. Angry mutters began rising. The sound nearly drowned out the sound of Jack's heart pounding too rapidly. One stooped, old woman licked her lips. "Gonna have us a witch-burning," she sniggered.

"Seize this man for aiding a witch!" the Gnul shouted.

"Not again," Jack sighed. The last time he'd come to this market square three years ago he'd fled a man bent on destroying him. Must he do so again?

Two burly men grabbed Jack's arms.

Deftly Jack twisted and shifted his weight. His captors lost their grip. While they stumbled forward, he ducked and slid backward. He'd learned something useful during his three years of slavery in King Simeon's mines.

"Catch that man, he's a witch!"

"Not this time, witch-sniffer." Jack ran. He knew this city from years of scavenging the streets before Baamin and the University of Magicians recognized his potential. He knew places . . .

Before he could change his mind, he dove into the river. Cold water closed over his head. He swam deeper, praying to the Stargods that he had enough breath to take him beyond sight of the witch-sniffer.

Lungs burning and eyes smarting, he broke the surface well downstream from the market island. He heard the tramp of many feet on a nearby bridge as the witch-sniffer raised the hue and cry. Coronnan City was made up of hundreds of little river islands connected by bridges.

Within minutes, the current took Jack past a large residential island. The Gnuls would have to wind their way through twisting alleyways to traverse the island. Then they'd have to cross another bridge to catch up to him.

He recognized the blue-painted rowboat tied to the next dock. "Still using that leaking scow, Aquilla?" he asked the absent Bay Pilot who had befriended him many years ago.

He grabbed the gunwale and heaved himself into the little craft. It rocked, threatening to dump him back into the water. He gasped for air and willed the boat to steady. First one leg and then the other over the side. At last he sprawled facedown in the bottom of the boat.

Then, carefully, he sat up and reached for the oars. A deep growl stopped him. A white-and-brown water dog faced him, teeth bared.

"I think I have a problem."

* * *

Wind howled through the trees like a lost soul moaning over separation from its body.

Robb ducked deeper into his cloak.

Marcus threw his cloak hood back and shook his hair free of restraint, glorying in the power of the storm.

"Typical," Robb muttered to himself. "I'm miserable, and he can't get enough of this storm." He plodded a few more steps in Marcus' wake, searching the path for signs of habitation. With each step he dug his staff into the mud. Maybe grounding his tool of focus in the Kardia would help him see around the rain.

Too quickly, he chilled and lost strength. The little bit of magic drained him.

He caught up to Marcus and shouted into his companion's ear, "We've got to find shelter. Put up your hood. You'll catch your death of cold! This storm is getting worse." He huddled into himself, trying to keep his body warm. Rain dripped from the edge of his hood onto his chest where the cloak gaped.

Marcus shook his head. "The storm will clear. We have time. With luck we'll be through the pass and out of the rain by nightfall."

They had decided to try passing into SeLenicca in a more obscure location, well south of the armies. Their trek had not been easy, plagued with spoiled supplies, poor hunting, foul weather, and general bad luck.

But Marcus hadn't allowed the miserable conditions to dampen his good spirits. That made Robb grumble all the more.

His feet slid out from beneath him, and he landed flat on his face.

Lightning crackled around them, playing bizarre patterns of light across the thick gray clouds. Marcus laughed out loud at the energy singeing the air. "This is almost as good as gathering dragon magic!"

"Look, there's a light." Robb pointed with his staff toward the meager flicker atop a wooded hill off to their right. The flames burned blue and red rather than natural green.

"It's witchlight! We can spend the evening with another magician," Marcus chortled.

"We're mighty close to the border with SeLenicca. I'm not sure I want to meet another magician around here. No telling if he's friendly or not." Robb shivered as he stood up and tried rearranging his cloak. His hood slipped back in the process. Now he was drenched on the inside as well as without. "Never know it's nearly Summer around here. The loss of the dragons combined with the intensive battle magic at the other pass seems to have made a climactic shift."

"Between the two of us, we can take on any magician even without dragons. As long as they don't surprise us. The storm is giving me power."

"Dragons," Robb grumbled. "If we weren't chasing invisible dragons, we'd be home beside a nice warm fire with a mug of spiced wine. Despite the seeming benevolence of dragon magic as opposed to solitary magic, I sometimes think the politics surrounding dragons makes our entire quest worthless."

"If we weren't here, we'd be freezing our bums off as we spy through every corner of Coronnan for Jaylor and the Commune of Magicians. Stop grumbling. Let's see what's up. You said yourself, we need shelter." Marcus marched forward.

"Admit it, Marcus, your infamous good luck has finally run out," Robb grumbled. "I can't remember being colder, wetter, or hungrier on any of our previous quests. Maybe it's time to start planning ahead a little better and making preparations for the next disaster."

"Stop being pessimistic. Of course my luck is holding. There's a light. That means someone with a fire and shelter to keep the fire going. We'll be fine for tonight. Then we can start out new and fresh in the morning, when the storm passes."

"If it passes. Let's just hope that unnatural light

isn't marsh gas or a ghost," Robb said. As they pushed up the hill, he checked his dagger and shifted his grip on his staff for better defense.

"We've traveled the length and breadth of Coronnan for three years now while the Commune has remained in exile, and you always look for the worst to happen," Marcus said lightly. "And it never does."

"I don't have your luck. I have found that preparation and forethought work better than waiting to see what happens. Besides, we're too close to the border with SeLenicca. No guarantees that your luck will continue once we cross the border and run out of ley lines to fuel our magic."

"Ah, but over the border we will find dragons. What better luck than to find a dragon and return with it to Coronnan so that the University of Magicians and the Commune of Magicians can gain credibility once more?"

"This isn't dragon weather. It's foul and unpleasant and *s'murghin'* cold. There aren't any dragons nearby. I'll believe we've found dragons when we actually return to Coronnan with them. I'll believe that magicians will regain honor and integrity from dragon magic when the Council of Provinces reinstates the Commune into the University buildings and Council Chamber and not before."

Robb trudged beside Marcus uphill along an overgrown and narrow game trail.

"Look, Robb, there's a building with nice stout walls. The light is coming from a window niche. We'll have you warm and dry and cheerfully lecturing me with a nice cup of something hot to take the chill out of your innards and your mood." Marcus grabbed Robb's sleeve and pulled him forward at a brisk pace.

Trees crowded their path, sheltering them from the wind if not the rain. Robb looked up to scan the walls that towered above them. "I only sense one life," he said through chattering teeth. "I can't smell any magic, but that is definitely witchlight." He gnawed his lip in puzzlement.

"Witchfire won't throw out much heat. Let's hope there's some dry fuel about to turn it into green flame." Marcus lifted each foot carefully in the slick mud on the upward path. His staff kept him balanced, but he leaned on it heavily.

"How tired are you?" Robb asked, concerned. "Don't try to hide it just because I'm in a foul humor."

"One of us has to keep moving. Otherwise you'd crawl into a badger hole and call it shelter. A hot infusion of Brevelan's special blend of spices will taste very good once we get inside and light a real fire."

They hadn't much left of the tasty treat and had agreed to ration it. Robb agreed they really needed it today.

Soon enough, stone buttresses jutted out from the walls, making their path as crooked as Old Baamin's magical staff. —*S'murghit!* He wished the old Senior Magician hadn't passed on to his next existence. Robb would welcome the old man's cranky wisdom now.

The neatly dressed stones fit together snugly.

"I wonder how old this place is?" Marcus reached out a hand to caress the stones. "I can't sense any residual energy embedded in the stone by the mason who shaped it."

"All I feel is the deep cold of many Winters," Robb added, mimicking his friend in trying to read the wall. The old cold burned through to his bones. "Old enough to harbor ghosts," he said. He touched his head, heart, and both shoulders in the cross of the Stargods. "I'm not sure . . ."

"Oh, come on. We need shelter and a fire. Let's find the gate." Marcus clumped around the perimeter of the wall. Only an occasional window slit broke the smooth surface between buttresses. The rain eased, but the cloud cover lowered.

"Almost a mile around," Robb stated. His breath

made small chill clouds in front of his face. "Wonder if this is an old monastery. There were a number of them during the Great Wars of Disruption. But we only know of one left standing after peace came to Coronnan. Many of them disappeared as people made use of their building stones for other purposes. A few may have been converted into palaces or Summer retreats for the nobility." Talking—lecturing as Marcus claimed—kept him from thinking about the thickness of the haze they nearly swam through. All of his senses were distorted, untrustworthy. He felt . . . inadequate.

"Wonder if anyone has lived here in the last three hundred years." Marcus stared up at the top of the wall, a good twenty feet above their heads.

"We'll know soon enough. Looks like a gatehouse tower jutting out from the main wall on the next corner. Of course we walked the long way around before finding it."

"We walked deasil, as we should. Walking widdershins is bad luck."

"First time I've ever known you to care about your luck. Prepare yourself for anything. An entire band of outlaws could be hiding within these walls."

CHAPTER 6

Robb shifted his grip on his staff and brought it forward, ready to channel magic down its length or flip it and use it as a mundane weapon.

"We'd know if there were hostiles within this building," Marcus said. "I only sense one life. Feels mostly mundane, not a magician at all. Strange. One life with a minimal magical talent I'm guessing; enough power to call a ball of witchlight, but not enough for us to sense."

"Or someone with incredible armor that allows us to sense his presence, but not his magic. Solitary magicians, raised outside the dragon magic tradition, are known to be quite cunning. He could be lulling us into dropping our defenses so as to make us easy prey."

The gatehouse rose out of the walls like a huge malignant growth—nearly a quarter of the wall's width and twice as high. The two young men slowed their steps and crept around the corner.

"This place is defended more like a castle than a monastery," Marcus whispered.

"What do you expect? It was built as a refuge when civil war tore the land apart for three generations."

Marcus shushed Robb with a finger to his lips as he peered around the next corner, staff at the ready.

Robb shrugged and crept forward, peering through the thickening gloom. He kept his larger body in front of his friend. In a fray his brute strength was well teamed with Marcus' agility.

Marcus peeked over Robb's shoulder. The formerly

stout wooden doors hung askew on weary hinges. The wind made them creak with each new gust.

The dense air almost seemed to pour out of that gate. What kind of ghosts and demons hid within it?

Silently, they edged closer. Robb led them through the gap in the doors. Thick oak had shrunk away from dozens of bronze bosses that had reinforced the wood. Green corrosion brushed off on his cloak like soggy mushroom spores. The hinges protested mightily. They both froze in place, waiting, wary.

No one challenged them.

Breathing a sigh of relief, Marcus pushed forward to lead the way across the broad courtyard. They faced a two-story building shaped like a squared-off steed-shoe. Thick columns supported the second story where it hung over the first, creating a sheltered passage. Two of the pillars lay broken in the courtyard.

Robb sighed wistfully. He wished people had more respect for these old buildings.

"That way." He pointed to the glimmer of light creeping under the door of one of the ground-floor cells in the southern wing.

A number of long paces took them across the courtyard. They climbed six steep steps from the courtyard to the colonnaded passage. Marcus rested a hand on the wooden panels, seeking. "One life force, barely stronger than the witchlight," he whispered. "Star-gods! He's dying!" Marcus pushed hard against the door. It flew inward, banging against the wall to their left.

Robb followed closely, alarmed and ready to defend them both with spells and mundane strength. The sight that met his eyes chilled him more than the storm.

An old man, wasted to skin and bones, lay crumpled upon a stark bed that was pushed right up against the narrow cell's wall, barely made comfortable by a thin pallet and blanket. His image flickered in and out of view, like a dragon in sunlight. His long white hair and beard were matted and yellowed with illness and neglect.

A little ball of blue/white/red witchlight nestled in a window niche high above his head. The light did not flicker or cast shadows. So why did the ancient man fade in and out of reality?

Half the time he looked as transparent as a ghost, but his chest continued to rise and fall with great effort. He hadn't passed into the void between existences yet.

"Start a fire. He needs warmth," Robb ordered. He thrust Marcus aside as he raced to the side of the narrow stone bench that served as a bed. "What ails you, elder?" he asked respectfully as he pulled pouches of herbs from his pack.

Marcus busied himself throwing kindling into the rusting brazier beside the bed. The room was small enough that only a little fire would heat the space nicely. He ignited the twigs and leaves with a snap of his fingers and added larger sticks as quickly as he could. At least the old man had prepared for a fire before illness, injury, or just plain old age felled him.

From the fine cut of his stylish robes and trews, Robb guessed that he had come from a noble and wealthy family. Probably a younger son grown beyond usefulness. He and Marcus would have heard of an heir or lord gone missing. After all, they had spent most of the last three years gathering the gossip of Coronnan.

"Save your medicines for yourself, lad," the ancient waved weakly at Robb's packets. His voice faded and grew with his flickering image. "Leave here. Quickly. This place is cursed. Don't get trapped . . ." His breath gushed out of his chest on a dry rattle like leaves stirred in a drying breeze.

At last his form settled into the current reality, a dry husk that no longer held his spirit trapped between worlds. The witchlight died, leaving only the light from the small fire.

Robb gently closed the old man's staring eyes. "I didn't even have time to ask his name," he said sadly. "I'll hate burying him without a name."

"At least he did not die alone." Marcus looked up from the merrily blazing fire. A little heat spread out from the brazier.

Robb and Marcus set about straightening the old man's limbs. When he lay peacefully on the stone bench, looking comfortable and glad that he no longer struggled through life, Robb searched his pockets for some clue to his identity. His fingers brushed against cool metal disks.

He fished one out and stared at the shiny gold. The soft metal glowed in the gentle firelight. It caressed his fingertips and eyes with an almost living color. His jaw dropped as he recognized the one hundred mark on the old-style coin. The face and inscription did not trigger any memory in him.

"Our fortune is made, Robb. He's got dozens of gold coins in his pockets. Dragons only know how many more are stashed around this lonely monastery." Marcus held up a handful of coins. He gulped as he, too, held them up to catch the light.

Robb's vision fractured into a dozen bright rainbows.

The world tilted.

He fought to retain his balance, eyes focused clearly on the gold coin and nothing else. A fine veil of mist seemed to cover everything.

"The Commune can buy a lot of respectability with these. Not to mention books and equipment for the University," Marcus said. His voice came from a great distance. "This gold will liven up our games of cartes."

"We haven't time to daydream about gold and fortunes," Robb replied as he placed two of the coins upon the ancient's closed eyes. A third rested in his pocket. Keeping one coin for himself would hurt no one. And it might give him an edge against survival during his long treks around Coronnan. Unlike Marcus, he had no desire to settle in one place for a long, long time.

He bowed his head a moment in silent prayer. "This man is very dead, Marcus. And he said this place is cursed. We have to get out of here. We need a plan."

"Not until after the storm passes. We can spend the night searching the place for his stash."

"Marcus," Robb began testily. "Marcus! you're fading into the walls. Marcus, don't you dare leave me and take your good luck with you!"

* * *

"Nice doggy," Jack said quietly. He dared not move.

The beast growled again and showed even more of its teeth. Saliva dripped onto the dock above the boat.

"Nice doggy."

"She doesn't like to be called doggy," a man replied roughly.

"Good mopplewogger," Jack said, still not moving. The dog pricked her ears and sat.

"Nice mopplewogger," Jack coaxed. "Don't suppose you remember me, doggy?"

The dog rose up on its long legs growling again.

"Different dog. It's been ten years, wharf rat. You don't have to steal the boat. I'd loan it if you asked," the man said with a chuckle.

"Want to call off your mopplewogger, Aquilla?"

"Ten years and you're still running from bullies. Want to trade that prissy uniform for a real one?"

Jack dared to look away from the dog long enough to take in Aquilla's Guild of Bay Pilots uniform of maroon and gold. His weather-beaten face crinkled in laughter.

"I've made oaths of loyalty elsewhere. Want to call off the mopplewogger?"

"Lilly, come," Aquilla said. The shorthaired dog growled at Jack one last time before returning to her master's side. She sat on Aquilla's foot and leaned her head into him. Absently the pilot scratched her ears.

"So what kind of trouble you running from this time, wharf rat?"

"Witch-sniffers. And I have a name now. Old Baamin decided I wasn't too stupid to have a name after all. I'm Jack." Jack scrambled onto the dock. His clothes sagged and dripped. He must indeed look like the wharf rat he had been as a child. Aquilla had rescued him when bullies had stolen his food and beaten him nearly senseless.

"Your loyalty to the University of Magicians was misplaced ten years ago. It still is. You should have come to work for me. Not many men have an affinity for a mopplewogger."

"I don't seem to have any kind of bond with this one." Jack held out his hand for the dog to sniff. She growled again and he jerked his hand away from her all-too-large teeth.

"That's because she caught you trying to steal my boat. You look like you need a meal and some dry clothes." Aquilla jerked his head toward the cottage above the dock. "Is that a palace guard's uniform underneath all that river muck?"

"Yes." Jack tried to wring some water out of the sodden wool tunic.

"You'll be better off as a Bay Pilot. Every government recognizes the worth of the Guild. Even the Gnuls. Not so the palace guard. Once the Gnuls depose King Darville, you'll be out of a job and quite likely become fuel for their next bonfire. But without the Bay Pilots, no one gets through the mudflats to deep water and the trading ships. We'll always have work." He negotiated the steep path up to his home. Lilly leaped eagerly ahead of him. Jack followed more slowly. His wet boots slipped on the river clay that packed the path.

"The Gnuls had better not find out about your mopplewogger, then," Jack added. "One hint of how these dogs smell the differences in water depth and salinity to show you the way through the channels of the mudflats and they'll burn you all for magicians."

"They wouldn't dare." Aquilla whirled around and faced Jack, eyes wide with horror.

"They'd dare. One of them just accused me of witchcraft because I failed to pursue a woman he chose to question. Her only crime seemed to be that she was single and spoke with a foreign accent." Just like Katrina. "The sniffer had no evidence; no complaints against her; nothing. He just 'smelled' magic in her vicinity."

"Tomorrow there will be another hundred witch-sniffers in the capital. I'm to retrieve them from the port at high tide." Aquilla's face drained of color.

"Make sure your mopplewogger stays hidden belowdecks."

"Always do. But, Jack, what are we going to do? Pretty soon there will be more witch-sniffers than mundanes in the city."

"That is going to present a problem."

CHAPTER 7

Vareena sat before the sparkling fire in the central hearth, contemplating her fate. Not long now. She'd miss Farrell when he passed on. But his death gave her a chance at freedom.

Freedom.

She tasted the word and liked the feel of it in her mouth and her spirit.

Rain spat upon the flames through the smoke hole in the thatched roof. One of the glowing splinters of wood on the edge of the blaze sputtered and died. She didn't bother reigniting it. It had withered to mostly ash now anyway. Like Farrell.

Her spindle lay idle at her feet. She just could not concentrate on keeping her threads smooth and free of slubs while the storm raged and her ghost sat alone up in the abandoned monastery.

He'd pass soon. The fever had returned yesterday, stronger than before. He had no interest in cartes, or tales, or even the chicken stew with pickled beets. A part of her heart sobbed with the coming grief.

But his passing would give her freedom. She fingered the silver amulet through the protective cloth of her shift. Her father and brothers must never find it. They'd confiscate it and sell it for sure. In their eyes women had no rights and could own nothing but the dowry determined at her coming of age.

She'd take her two cows and three chickens with her.

In the outside world, women could own property

and select their own husbands. Farrell had promised her that as well as the three acres in Nunio.

Neither she nor her ghost understood what had brought him here to the sanctuary of the monastery. He had wandered in two years ago, seeking a night's shelter after becoming separated from a trading caravan that was headed for the pass into SeLenicca. After that first night he had not been able to leave. He did not remember dying.

She only knew that he brightened her lonely days, made her feel useful and important. And now he offered her freedom.

At a price. His death.

The wind howled around her father's cottage. Vareena shivered and drew her shawl closer about her. She should have gone to the ancient monastery hours ago. Farrell needed her. He felt the cold so acutely. She would take him her extra blanket though he usually refused the little comforts she offered. She should have gone to him before noon, as she usually did. But the storm had come upon them quickly and she had been hard pressed to get the villagers, sheep, and plow steeds under shelter. Already the creek threatened to flood.

The ghost needed her. She sensed him passing into his next existence, finally. He'd lingered between this world and the void for two years, neither here nor there. Neither alive nor dead. A nameless man—he'd admitted that Farrell was but the name of his boyhood hero, a man he wished to emulate—lost to his loved ones. Only Vareena cared for him. Cared about him.

No one, not even a ghost deserved to die alone. Over the years she'd sat beside five other ghosts as they finally gave up this existence. None of them had lasted more than two years. She'd been only seven when she sat the death watch with her first ghost. Her mother had died suddenly and left Vareena the odd destiny to care for the ghosts who periodically appeared in the abandoned monastery, a calling inher-

ited by the women of her family for nearly three
hundred years. They were the only ones who could
see the ghosts and knew what they needed and how
to provide for them.

Suddenly Vareena stood up. "I'm going back up
there," she announced to her father and five brothers.
Something tugged at her senses. She couldn't sit here
listening to the wind any longer.

"Stay, Vareena. The storm," Ceddell, her father,
objected. He whittled a toy sheepdog for his four-year-
old grandson.

"Let this one go, Eena," Yeenos, the second oldest
brother said, looking her directly in the eye. "Your
ghost is just a drain on our supplies. No work, no
food. That's the rule, for everyone but your *s'murghin'* ghosts!"

"He's lost between here and the void. I can't allow
his soul to depart unguided," Vareena stated.

"Maybe there isn't really a ghost at all. You're the
only one who can see them. Maybe you're feeding a
bunch of outlaws. Why should we take necessary supplies away from our families to feed a bunch of criminals and repair their building. We could use some of
those finely dressed stones ourselves," Yeenos continued, his voice rising with his passion. "I say we tear
down that cursed building." His fist clenched as if he
needed to pound something, or someone.

Vareena backed away from his temper. He'd never
hit her before, but a number of men in the village had
crooked noses and missing teeth from violent connections with his fists.

"I'll go with you, Eena." Uustass, the eldest of the
brood, stood up to join her. "Stargods know, we've
never been able to keep you from your duty. Might
as well do our best to take care of you when you get
a calling."

"Stay, Uustass." She waved him back to his stool
and the leather he braided for new steed harnesses.
"You'll only catch a chill and be miserable for weeks.

Bad enough I'll have to take soup and poultices to half the village in the morning. I don't need to tend you as well. Stay with your children and tell them stories so the storm doesn't frighten them."

Uustass had lost his wife in childbed last winter. He always seemed lost now unless Vareena gave him something specific to do.

"Take him, or you stay," her da commanded. "Lost your mam to a storm. Not lose you." His voice carried the weight of years of experience leading the village, judging misdeeds, and deciding the crop rotation and beast fertility.

No one disobeyed him when he used that tone as if he begrudged each word.

Vareena was tempted.

"Very well. Uustass, take the cloak I oiled yesterday. There's soup in the pot and bread in the hearth oven for supper. Serve yourselves when you get hungry. I don't think this will take long." She fetched her own garment from the row of hooks by the low door. Farrell wouldn't need supper. She knew he would find his way out of his body and into the void this night. Ghosts always passed on during wild storms like this, as if they needed the wind to guide them to their next existence.

As she opened the door, a powerful gust nearly blew her back into the main room of the cottage. "Stargods, I hope I'm not too late."

Uustass took her arm and guided her up the hill to the ancient building on the crest, mostly hidden by trees. His stocky body shielded her from the wind. For her own comfort she blessed him for being so stalwart and ready to aid her when the rest of her people would shun her for her contact with ghosts. Perhaps Uustass hoped to communicate with his recently deceased wife through Vareena's ghosts. Six moons and he still had not accepted the loss of his life mate.

Nothing but ill luck stalked those who communed with ghosts. She'd known that for years.

She fingered the silver amulet again, praying that her luck was about to change. Stargods only knew, her family had suffered their share of grief, with the death of her mother, grandmother, and sister-in-law, with her need to become mother to her family at the age of seven. But they'd been blessed as well. Blessed in ways the villagers rarely recognized. She had five healthy brothers. Two of them were married and helping run their wives' family farms. Her father continued as a wise judge and leader despite his reluctance to utter more than four words at a time. The village prospered most years. Since the war with SeLenicca, trading caravans used the nearby pass more often, bringing trade goods for surplus crops. Even now, when Winter stores grew thin and new crops had yet to ripen, they all had enough to eat and more to share with the ghost.

But he'd be gone after tonight. She choked back a sob. The ghosts were her friends. They listened patiently as she explored the problems of growing up the only girl in a household of brothers, the only sensitive in the village, the only woman in a position to care for all those around her, family and villagers alike. The ghosts understood her.

"Almost there, little sister." Uustass helped her up the last few steps of the broken path to the gatehouse.

The wind ceased to pound at her senses the moment she stepped within the massive walls of the building. But then her ears started ringing in the comparative silence. She clutched her temples, trying to make sense of the noise. A hum, deep in her mind, at her nape announced an eerie portent.

"What ails you, Eena?" Uustass clutched both of her elbows.

She leaned into him, using his solid presence to balance the sudden numbness between her ears.

"The ghost is passing. We must hurry!"

"I wish I understood this strange compulsion of yours to tend these bizarre beings. Yet you can't summon the ghosts of our loved ones. You don't even know if these ghosts were once human."

"Whatever they are when they come to me, they were human once. I must help them . . . him. Something is amiss. Hurry, Uustass." She pushed him out of her way and dashed through the relative comfort of the tunnel beneath the gatehouse into the pelting rain of the courtyard. The day seemed darker and heavier here than out in the teeth of the storm.

Her feet automatically took her toward the cell where she had placed the little ball of cold light so that Farrell did not have to pass his last day in darkness.

Natural green firelight flickered beneath the closed doorway. Vareena stopped short, heedless of the cold sheets of water that poured upon her from the leaking gutter of the colonnade.

"Now what ails you?" Uustass sighed wearily.

"I did not light the fire."

"Then the ghost must have."

"But he was too weak to leave his pallet. I left no firerock and iron to strike a spark."

Uustass drew his belt knife; the one he used to free young sheep from brambles and cut lengths of rope for various chores around the village. Sharp enough to slice through tree limbs the width of his wrist.

A measure of confidence returned. Whoever had invaded the sanctuary of the ancient monastery must respect her brother's strength and purpose.

Cautiously, Uustass pushed the door open. Rusted hinges creaked. He stood back, peering inward, waiting for an attack.

The fine hairs on Vareena's neck stood up. From the safety of the steps she inspected the small visible portion of the narrow cell. She saw only the slack figure of her ghost, fully formed in this reality, his arms neatly crossed on his chest, legs crossed at the ankles and shiny gold coins holding down his eyelids. She doubted he had composed himself so peacefully before experiencing his death throes.

"I only see the body," Uustass said, sheathing his knife. "Just like the other times. Once they've died, they are visible to normal people."

"Wait!" Vareena whispered frantically. "There, to the right. Something moved." Her hand went to her throat as she swallowed back a lump of fear. It lodged in her upper chest, constricting her breathing.

"I don't see anything." Uustass shrugged as he stepped into the room. His hands remained at his sides, not reaching for the tempting gold.

"Watch out!" Vareena rushed to her brother's side. She placed herself defiantly between him and the two figures who stood beside the pallet. Suddenly the narrow cell seemed far too crowded.

Two ghosts stared at her in surprise, one tall and broad, the other slighter. The shorter one stared at her from pale eyes that seemed to burn through to her soul, his mouth agape.

As she watched, he faded in and out of her vision, one moment fully formed in this reality, the next heartbeat a pale outline of a human figure that distorted light.

The taller and darker figure seemed a trifle more solid. He kept his hand on the other's shoulder. They belonged together. Both wore magician-blue tunics and carried long staffs that had become as ghostly as they.

Neither had been a ghost long.

"Two of you?"

"What!" Uustass whirled and faced the door. "Where?"

"Over here." Vareena pointed. "We lost one ghost only to add two more. Both young and healthy. I've never seen two ghosts at the same time before."

"Wonderful." Sarcasm dripped from Uustass' voice as he continued to scan the room. His eyes slid away from the two ghosts as if something blocked his mind from settling on that direction. "Now we've got to dip deeper into our dwindling stores to feed two of them. They'll linger for years before they waste away."

"I'll never be free of this place now," Vareena moaned to herself.

CHAPTER 8

"Look at her, Robb. She's the most beautiful woman I've ever seen!" Marcus held his breath, almost afraid the woman with the crystalline aura would fade before his eyes, like a dragon slipping through the mist. The man with her seemed less substantial, as if he lingered half in the void—sort of like the dead man before he'd gasped his last and emerged from the void.

"Didn't you hear her, Marcus?" Robb asked angrily.

Marcus yanked his concentration away from the slight beauty with blue eyes so vivid they reminded him of Brevelan—Senior Magician Jaylor's witch wife. But this woman had blonde hair that kinked and curled in a bright cloud of silver and gold rather than Brevelan's witch-red.

She was a few years older than he was. Her maturity made her much more beautiful than any woman he could remember.

The ghostly man with her, older by almost a decade he guessed, looked enough like her to be her brother rather than a lover. His protective stance with the knife when he first thrust open the door suggested a family relationship, too.

"I wasn't listening. She's so very beautiful, she makes my heart ache. What did you say?" Something important was happening, and Marcus couldn't concentrate, couldn't think. He wanted to go drifting in the void forever with this woman.

"She said that we are ghosts and we will linger as ghosts for a long, long time." Robb's fingers on Marcus' shoulders squeezed painfully tight.

"Ghosts! We can't be ghosts. We're alive. I see you and this room very clearly, I hear the wind and the rain outside, I feel pain where you are bruising my shoulder."

Robb removed his hand, shaking out some of the tension.

Only then did Marcus realize his friend held one of the gold coins in his left hand, rubbing it absently, just as Marcus did with the coins he'd slipped into his pocket.

"Those two are the ghosts," Marcus continued. "They look like dragons, sort of here, sort of in the void."

"Something strange is going on here, Marcus. Something that will delay us a long time from completing our quest and returning to the Commune with the dragons."

"Maybe these people are kin to dragons. Maybe we can gather dragon magic from them," Marcus suggested, his natural optimism replacing the tiny tingles of fear Robb had planted in his mind.

He took three deep breaths, triggering a light trance. Then he stood with his arms to his sides, palms out, feet braced, eyes closed, and opened himself to the energies swirling through the universe.

Robb did the same.

Nothing filled the empty place above his belly and behind his heart where he stored dragon magic.

Robb shook his head.

"They aren't dragons," Marcus admitted.

"This isn't the end of the quest, Marcus. But I fear it is a long and dangerous side trip away from our true mission."

"Not necessarily. We'll just walk out of here. The rain and wind are letting up. We'll find shelter somewhere else. These folks can bury the old man. They probably know his name at least." Resolutely, he stepped around the beautiful woman and her elusive protector. He marched across the courtyard with Robb in his wake. The ghostly pair followed, the woman directing, her companion darting blank looks in every corner.

They entered the tunnel beneath the gatehouse and pushed open the wooden doors.

Two more steps and they would be free of this eerie old building where darkness seemed to gather. Two more steps to return to their quest.

At the exit through the massive monastery walls, Marcus hit a solid wall of resistance—like running into a magician with incredibly strong armor.

He bounced back into Robb. His friend caught him. Without a word Robb stepped around Marcus and extended his hands to test the blockage.

Marcus jabbed the barrier with his staff. It passed through easily. "I don't sense anything." He tried again to step through the doorway into the outside world. Once more he slammed up against a barrier.

Robb tried and bounced back as well.

"Looks like your luck has finally run out, Marcus. And I don't have a plan. We're trapped."

* * *

Forces are moving against me. I sense the presence of people who will rob me of my power. But I am not the barely talented clerk I was in my youth. I have true power now. I know how to stop my enemies. I am in touch with all four of the elements as none of these modern magicians can hope to be. A little pressure here, a tug against the elements there and we have a kardiaquake. That should delay those who come for me.

* * *

Robb stalked around the perimeter of Hanassa. He knew he'd never been here. Couldn't remember traveling to this remote corner of the world.

It's only a dream, part of him whispered. But the heat of the desert sun, the sour taste of thirst, and the heavy grit that irritated his eyes were too tangible to be merely a dream.

He swallowed heavily, hoping to ease some of the dryness in his throat. Not enough saliva. Not enough strength.

The heavy sand trapped his feet. He couldn't shift them, couldn't think, couldn't plan his next move.

And then the ground rippled beneath him, as if he stood on water like some long-legged bug and the water no longer wanted to support him.

He froze every muscle and gritted his teeth against the waving motion. His stomach tried to turn itself inside out. His eyes refused to focus, and his body wanted to become one with the water.

Arrows rained down upon his head. What could he do? No place to hide. No way to move.

Pain pierced his shoulder. He looked at the source, too stupefied to do anything else. Blood poured down his magician blue tunic, staining his new, brightly polished boots. He stared at them, aggrieved at the spoiling of the pristine leather.

But he didn't have new boots. Marcus did. Why was he wearing Marcus' boots? But these boots fit. He could barely get his foot inside the ones Marcus stole from the army.

He should throw a spell. What spell?

Sweat broke out on his brow and back. The pain in his shoulder doubled, bringing him to his knees.

Hot oil replaced the onslaught of arrows.

It burned his skin and hair. He held his hands and arms over his head, trying desperately to block the continuing deluge of boiling oil. His sweat turned icy. Blisters on his face and arms froze, burst, and peeled.

The new boots couldn't protect his toes from the icy sand of the desert of Hanassa.

Bright light penetrated his eyes with blinding stabs. He looked up to see what new weapon the outlaws of Hanassa brought to bear.

Dark walls surrounded him. Only a single arrow slit window allowed light to escape Hanassa. The world around him turned to darkness. Intensely cold. An ancient cold born of evil.

Wild screams from above and below him blotted out coherency.

He huddled in on himself. All control of himself, his thoughts, his plans vanished. How could he make his own luck if he couldn't think ahead? There had to be a way out of this mess. He couldn't make it right.

A deep sob wrenched upward from his gut.

The sound of his own moan woke him. Only a hint of starlight penetrated his cell in the ancient monastery, keeping it in deep gloom. The storm had abated.

Vareena and her brother must have trudged home hours ago. They had promised to return to bury Farrell the next day. Robb and Marcus had tried an unsuccessful summons spell to Jaylor that left them exhausted and empty. Then they had selected rooms as far away from the scene of death as possible. They'd eaten their dinners in silence and retired.

Robb hadn't traveled to Hanassa and been assaulted from all sides by unknown outlaws. He rotated his stiff shoulders. Chill and an awkward sleeping position plagued his muscles. An insect bite on his shoulder itched. That must have triggered the dream pain of a poisoned arrow wound.

He heaved a sigh of relief that sounded very much like a sob. He sat on the edge of the stone platform that formed his bed in the corner cell, bracing his elbows on his knees.

The dream had been so real. Almost like a dragondream. He shuddered. For years he'd heard stories of how the dragons could impose an illusion so convincing that healthy men wandered in circles for days, not eating or sleeping, ignoring the calls and pleas of friends and family to return, only to die of starvation with a smile on their faces. Always those tales had seemed apocryphal.

Now he wondered what he had done to anger a dragon.

But he wouldn't have awakened from a dragon-dream.

Still shivering with memories of arrows and boiling oil, he called a ball a witchlight to hand and stumbled to the latrine. Best way to banish a nightmare.

Three spiders as large as the largest gold coin crunched under his boots between his cell and the corner latrine. He relished the squishy sound of their deaths. This, he could control.

But when he climbed beneath the blankets again, the dream returned. He forced himself awake and counted the stones in each wall, the floor, and ceiling for the rest of the night.

*   *   *

"I don't love you anymore, Margit," Marcus stated boldly.

The tall blonde stood before him, hands on hips, feet spread, mouth agape. The setting sun backlit her flowing tresses into a wild halo of indignation. And then she started throwing spells, fire, water, wind, dirt clods.

Marcus ducked, holding up his arms to shield his face. He tried to erect a barrier between himself and Margit's fury. Magic dribbled from his fingers like the last dregs of old ale from the bottom of the barrel.

"Let me explain, Margit." When magic deserted him, he always had words. He could charm the surliest of beldames into giving him a night's shelter, a meal, or a tumble in the hay. "We've had some good times together. We've shared the secrets of magicians spying upon politicos and fanatic Gnuls. I was the liaison between you and Jaylor at the Commune of Magicians. But that wasn't true love. You don't truly love me any more than I love you."

"Explain!" Margit hurled rocks with fists and magic. Only one landed at his feet. The others found her targets, his shoulders, his gut, his head. She'd had a lot of practice warding off ravens and jackdaws from her mother's bakery cart in the market square. "Explain! You call that an explanation? What have you found this time? A more beautiful woman, a wealthier woman, a willing woman on the long, lonely nights in the middle of nowhere? I've heard all of your excuses before, Marcus. But this is the last one. I'll kill you before I let another woman have you."

From empty air she conjured metal throwing stars. She aimed their sharp points at his eyes.

His luck had definitely run out. No more could he count on Margit's love and loyalty waiting for him in the capital when he returned.

Fierce, hot pain in his eyes and head jolted Marcus awake. Darkness surrounded him. Had Margit's aim been true and blinded him? Sweat poured down his face and back. He rubbed at the biting pain in his temple and eye. Insect bites.

Gradually, the faint starlight filtered through the high window of his monastery cell. As his eyes adjusted to the dim light, he remembered where he was. He sighed heavily and brought a ball of cold witchlight to his hand.

"Just a nightmare. I still have my magic and my luck." He rolled over and curled into his bedroll, seeking to warm the chill of sweat drying on his skin.

Images of Margit's fury superimposed themselves on his mind every time he closed his eyes.

"I don't love Margit. 'Tis Vareena who has captured my heart." He tried to conjure her image before him, starting with her cloud of fair curls surrounding delicate features, frail frame, and serene demeanor.

Margit's laugh and well-muscled strength kept trying to mask the pictures he held in his mind's eye.

"I love Vareena. Tomorrow I'll find a way out of here so that we can be together. Forever," he repeated over and over again, until exhausted sleep finally claimed him.

CHAPTER 9

"Marcus, we've tried this before." Robb sighed heavily.

"But we haven't tried it this way," Marcus replied. Eagerly he placed his right foot into a crevice in the outer wall. Then he reached for the first secure handhold with a show of confidence he didn't really feel. They'd been trying to escape the old monastery all morning with no luck.

No luck. The words rang ominously around his head. He gritted his teeth and hauled himself up to find the next toehold. The chipped crevice he sought eluded him. As his balance teetered and his arms threatened to give way from the strain of holding his weight so precariously, he pressed his back against the gatehouse tower and wedged his body in the tight corner between it and the main curtain wall.

This would be easier if he'd slept better last night. Even after he'd banished the nightmare of Margit trying to kill him, he had not slept. Every time he'd turned over on the stone bench of a bed, the bed itself had seemed to roll and reshape itself to be more uncomfortable. Good fortune would never return until he escaped this cursed monastery.

From the looks of the deep shadows beneath Robb's eyes, he hadn't slept any better.

They had to get out of here. Today. Now.

"Your theory is flawed, Marcus. Whatever magical barrier holds us here is most thorough. Even the scattered ley lines within the courtyard do not reach the wall. They end abruptly and never do they cross. Our summons spell to Jaylor last night did not leave this complex. I think the thick cloud cover kept it within the walls. The confinement spell must have been constructed to surround the entire wall, not just the obvious exits and easily climbed points. Actually from the way you are bracing yourself there, I believe this to be the most obvious place for a climber to escape." Robb droned on with his logical assessment of their predicament. He held his grounded staff so that the top made little circles at the end of each sentence.

"But Vareena comes and goes with her brother. Why them and not us?" Marcus returned. "She brought us food and blankets this morning. She talks to us. She sees us. But her brother doesn't. Not once could I make eye contact with him while we dug Farrell's grave. Why can Vareena and her brother leave and we can't?" He didn't add that he wanted to follow the lovely blonde. He'd follow her to the ends of the Kardia if he had to, giving up his dreams of a snug cottage and never wandering more than a few leagues from there ever again.

Margit's image reared up before him. She'd never forgive him for deserting her. She'd hunt him down and kill him . . . No that was the nightmare. Margit might make life miserable for him, but she'd never . . . or would she?

He had a nagging feeling that his infamous good luck wouldn't solve this problem for him.

But he had to have Vareena— He caressed the name in his mind as he climbed. Vareena needed his protection. She stood barely as tall as his shoulder. Her willowy figure looked too fragile to withstand a light breeze, let alone stand up to her strapping brother. And yet, from their conversations, Marcus gathered that the entire family of strong brothers and an implacable father listened and obeyed her. She'd remained a spinster to care for them.

"Perhaps Vareena and her brother have the free-

dom to leave because they are mundane," Robb
mused. He stroked his dark beard, eyes crossing in
thought. In another time and place, Marcus might expect a spell to bounce from the end of his staff. But
those ley lines curved and twisted away from each
other as if repelled. Neither he nor Robb had been
able to tap into their energy for more than the most
rudimentary spells.

The summons spell had not exited the walls.

"What does talent or lack of it have to do with
escape?" Marcus wormed his way up the wall a little
higher. His right foot slipped just as he shifted his
balance to move his other foot. Rough stone rasped
his palms and cheek while he scrabbled for a better
position. "*S'murghit!* That stings." His breath whistled
through his clenched teeth.

Time was, he could set his mind to any task, and
luck would carry him through to the end. He always
found a way to come through unscathed no matter
how difficult or dangerous the chore.

Robb bore a number of scars from their adventures.
They enhanced his rugged appeal. Marcus had no
scars to blemish his fair skin and lithe body—yet.

Doggedly he climbed higher, doing his best to ignore the painful scrapes that made him want to curl
his fingers tightly over the wounds.

"This would be a lot easier if the builders had put
in a parapet and walkway for guards or lookouts. This
exterior wall must have been added for protection
after the main building was constructed," Marcus
mused rather than think about his luck and his magic
draining away.

"We must consider the possibility that this monastery was converted to a prison for rogue magicians
at the end of the Great Wars of Disruption." Robb
continued his lecture. "If such were the case, then the
Commune would need a powerful spell to keep the
criminals in. Something in the nature of the magical

border around Coronnan. Until recently it prevented enemies and undesirables from entering the country."

"Flawed logic, Robb. The border broke down when the number of dragons that supplied our magic decreased. When Shayla flew away and took her mates with her, the border dissolved completely. Why didn't this spell?" He didn't want to think what kind of sorcery kept the dragons in SeLenicca. Who could be stronger than a dragon?

Robb made no reply. A quick glance over his shoulder told Marcus that his friend's eyes crossed almost to opposite sockets as he stroked his beard.

"Another puzzle that I must think on," Robb replied after several moments.

"If you don't let your eyes straighten out, Robb, they will remain crossed forever," he chided his friend.

Robb apparently didn't hear him, but remained deep in contemplation.

Marcus reached higher. His shoulders and back ached and his face burned from the previous scrape. If he didn't have an audience, he just might give up and go find a dark corner where he could vent his frustration by stomping a few of the monstrous spiders that thrived in this place. Then he'd nurse his hurts in private.

He edged closer to the top of the wall where it joined the taller gatehouse tower.

At last his left hand clutched the rounded top. Then he pushed high enough to fling his right arm over the top stone and brace his weight. A shout of triumph burst out of his laboring lungs.

It died before it passed his lips. Magical power jolted up his arm to his neck and head. His ears rang and a numbness grew in his head. The blankness spread and he lost his grip. He couldn't find the other wall with his back. His feet went slack.

He knew he fell, but he couldn't feel a thing.

He *did* hear Robb droning on about *his* theory of how one would create such an enduring protective spell that would not disintegrate with the loss of the dragons.

"That *s'murghin'* containment spell is killing my luck," Marcus cursed.

* * *

These men who seek to steal my power are either too stubborn for their own health or too stupid to survive. They have not responded to the dreams of portent I sent them, nor to the subtle persuasion of a kardia-quake. I must think anew. I have time. I am not going anywhere.

* * *

"Your Grace?" Jack hissed to King Darville and Queen Rossemikka from the cover of a flowering shrub in the queen's private garden.

The king stopped quickly, gaze darting for the source the whisper. His hand reached for the ceremonial short sword he always wore on his right hip.

Queen Mikka's fingers arched away from the arm of her husband that she had clung to as they walked. She opened her mouth in a silent hiss, revealing small pointed teeth. Her eyes narrowed, and the pupils showed as definite vertical slits. Jack suspected that her back arched as well and the hairs on her neck stood up. But her richly textured gown fell in wide folds all around her, disguising her posture.

The gown hung too heavily on her thin frame. Since her last miscarriage—a very dangerous one that had required Brevelan and Jaylor to transport to the capital to heal her—Mikka had been listless and pale with little appetite. If Jack did not succeed with his special project soon, she might die of a broken heart.

"Your Grace, it's only me." Jack half rose from his crouched position, then ducked quickly back within the broad leaves and abundant red blossoms. He wanted to sneeze away the heavy perfume of the flowers, but didn't dare. Even here, guards trailed behind the royal couple. Two of them, Jack suspected of being at least spies for the Gnuls, if not actual witch-sniffers. And they closed in upon the royal couple, alerted by Darville's startlement.

After his conversation with Aquilla, he suspected more people than he had this morning. He dared not use even the tiniest of spells as long as any of these men were present.

Darville soothed his wife with a gentle hand to her mane of multicolored hair. She leaned into his caress and kissed his palm.

"I need to speak with you privately, Your Grace."

"My office. You are on duty later today."

"This won't wait, and there are too many curious people hanging around the barracks. I can't get in there yet to change to a clean uniform," Jack insisted. He'd dried his tunic and trews as best he could before Aquilla's fire, but the uniform was crumpled and stained, not fit to be worn in the king's presence.

"Your Grace, what do you fear?" Sergeant Fred asked. He held his functional battle sword at the ready while he scanned the bushes and tree branches for signs of an enemy. Equally alert, his five attending soldiers spread out in a wide circle.

Jack trusted Fred. The slightly older soldier had been with the king for a number of years as personal bodyguard and confidant. Of all the palace guard, only Fred knew Jack's true reason for being in the capital disguised as another trusted soldier.

"Only a bird scuttling in the bushes after a worm, Sergeant," Darville dismissed the six hovering attendants.

Fred gestured to the men to retreat the required ten paces to grant the king and queen an illusion of privacy.

Rossemikka bent to sniff at the red blossoms that concealed Jack from mundane eyes. Her fingers relaxed and when she blinked, her eyes had returned to a normal round pupil.

Darville rubbed the back of his wrist idly. Were the red weals beneath his fingertips cat scratches? The queen must be in a high state of agitation if she allowed the cat persona trapped within her to rise to the surface so readily. She hadn't scratched her husband in weeks.

"Are you any closer to finding a cure for me?" the queen asked in her slightly accented voice. She hailed from the desert kingdom of Rossemeyer where the land was so harsh, the people traded for all of their food and most of their household goods with mercenaries and the fiery liquor called *beta'arack*. "I would be rid of this cat."

"Alas, Your Grace, no. I wish I had found the proper spell. I came today to warn you both of extreme danger. A boatload of witch-sniffers arrived at the port islands this morning." Three islands at the edge of deep water in the Great Bay marked the sailing limit for large vessels. Only shallow draft barges piloted by Guild of Bay Pilot members could negotiate the mudflats of the inner bay. "They await transport into the city. Another one hundred are due to arrive next week. Some of these foreign seekers are extremely sensitive. They may 'smell' the cat within you since it was put there by magic."

Jack checked the position of the soldiers. The two he suspected had inched forward, right arms slightly extended and circling. They kept the signature gesture of a witch-sniffer subtle. But Jack knew they sought him.

Darville must have seen them as well. He shifted his position so that he stood between his beloved queen and the sniffers. Years ago, before he ascended to the throne, Darville had been kidnapped by his cousin, the rogue magician Krej, and ensorcelled into the body of a golden wolf. When Jaylor had rescued him and exposed the plot, Darville had fallen ill from the effects of too many spells being cast upon a mundane within too short a time. The illness had given the

Council of Provinces reason to deny him the crown for many moons.

He could always claim that the sniffers smelled him and not his queen who did have magic in her blood even before the cat had joined her in that body.

"Why don't you just dismiss those men?" Jack mused, not realizing he had spoken until he heard his words.

"Because the Gnuls control my council. Any retaliation against them brings worse reprisals against innocents. I am only the first among equals, not a tyrant. I must defer to the wishes of the lords who help me govern," the king said sadly. "I thought I had pounded some sense into them, but apparently not."

"What will we do, Darville?" Rossemikka turned wide, frightened eyes up to her husband. Her fingers curled again. The cat wanted dominance.

"What we always do. Dissemble, divert, claim they persecute us with unfounded accusations merely to overthrow me and claim the throne for themselves."

"They can't depose you, Your Grace. Your coronation was dragon-blessed. Thousands witnessed B—" he couldn't say the true name of the blue-tipped dragon out loud. The secret of Baamin's origins must remain secret a while longer. "They all saw the same thing I saw. The dragons blessed your crown and your queen."

"But no one has seen a dragon since. Before and after my coronation, the dragon nimbus remained in exile. Baamin returned only long enough to show himself at the coronation." The king grinned widely, letting Jack know that not much remained secret from him.

"Our enemies have grown in strength while the dragons remained in SeLenicca. They now discount the reality of the dragons you returned to Coronnan. The Gnuls will try to kill any dragons who show themselves, claiming them the spawn of Simurgh."

"But what do you want me to do about the influx of witch-sniffers?"

"Can you whip up a storm that will strand them in the port for a time?"

"I don't dare with those two watching everything in the palace so closely."

"Then we must invent a disease that will close the port to all people, but not goods."

"That I can do, Your Grace. I have a friend who will gladly dispense a convincing rumor." Jack eased backward through the clump of bushes until he stood on a path well hidden from the view of the guards. Within moments he was running back to Aquilla, just like when he was nothing more than a scullery lad and wharf rat needing protection from bullies. Gnuls, bullies, what was the difference?

CHAPTER 10

Lanciar tried hard to think in convoluted circles like a Rover. The more he drank, the straighter the path his mind followed. In the end, logic prevailed. Lanciar left Hanassa by the same dizzyingly steep path he had entered the haven for outlaws—on foot.

Zolltarn could not have transported his entire clan and all of their goods far. That much magic was unprecedented, even if the entire Rover clan joined the spell. Logic also told Lanciar that the Rovers must head for Coronnan and the Commune of Magicians. No one else would value the statue of Lord Krej. And no Rover would steal something unless it held value to someone. Besides, Zolltarn had deserted the coven for the Commune three years ago.

Was the entire adventure merely a ploy to lead Rejiia to the Commune? If so, then he had a better chance of claiming his son by following the Rovers into Coronnan than treading in Rejiia's footsteps.

Rumors claimed the dragons had returned to the Commune. Neither Rejiia, nor the entire coven—especially with its depleted numbers—could stand against a Commune united by dragon magic. Dragon magic had its limits when wielded by a single magician. But unlike the coven's blood rituals that enhanced power, or the Rovers' secret ceremonies, dragon magic allowed talented men to join their talents, augmenting the strength of every spell by orders of magnitude. With this united power they could impose laws, ethics, and honor upon their members, and overcome all those who opposed them.

Fortunately for the Rovers, the coven, and solitary magicians, their honor and ethics kept them from going to war against their own people to wrest political power from the Gnostic Utilitarian cult.

Once more he wondered if his old adversary Jack had managed to return the dragons to Coronnan or if he had died beneath the rubble of Queen's City. "We'll have to see if Jack awakened the ability to gather dragon magic as well as my other magical powers," Lanciar mused.

If it would help regain his son, Lanciar would join the Commune and submit to the limitations and laws of dragon magic in order to negate the power of Rejiia and the coven and the Gnuls.

Once outside the volcanic crater of Hanassa, Lanciar found a thin ley line deep within the surface of the Kardia. He drew its meager energies into him. Weak power infiltrated his blood. He needed to get farther away from the mountain fastness before he'd have access to more power.

Three deep breaths triggered his light trance. He used his power to levitate himself down the zigzag path of stairs cut into the steep cliff's side. He kept his eyes firmly on the steps rather than evaluate the deadly drop-off into the ravine below. One false step would send him careening down the mountain. Levitation—exhausting though it was—was less daunting than walking.

A simple thing like looking down this near vertical cliff should not make his stomach queasy and detach his head from his shoulders. He'd spent most of his life training to be a soldier. He should be able to tackle any physical challenge. He'd faced death in battle many times. He'd killed men before, in battle and in magical sacrifice. Still his head reeled if he looked beyond the path.

At the bottom of the cliff, some three hundred feet

below Hanassa's plateau, the land leveled out and showed signs of a little more rainfall than on the desert plateau. Scrawny shrubs and a few fistfuls of grass clung to precious bits of dirt beside the path. Indeed, the path became a road broad enough for men to walk two and three abreast with pack steeds. Two miles farther on, an inn perched precariously atop another cliff beside a thundering waterfall. Caravans and their beasts camped across the river from the inn. A wobbly bridge strung together with odd bits of rope and mismatched planks spanned the rushing stream.

Lanciar's head spun at the thought of crashing through the bridge into the river and then plummeting over the cataract onto the broken rocks one hundred feet below. He gulped and turned his eyes and attention away from such thoughts.

Three pairs of men wrestled in the inn's forecourt, exchanging blows. The pointless brawl spread to several of the spectators. Lanciar spat in the dust in disgust. "Waste of energy and discipline. If you were part of my army, I'd have all of you flogged."

Rejiia might aspire to the title of Kaalipha of Hanassa, but she didn't have the discipline to organize the city, only to terrorize it. Lanciar could do it. If he wanted to. The people of Coronnan, SeLenicca, and Rossemeyer would rise up in rebellion against her tyranny. She'd not last long as queen of any place. Lanciar had to retrieve his son before Rejiia put the boy in the way of vengeful assassins.

Lanciar walked a little way past the inn. He paused, drinking in the colors of the place and the clean smell of the air. Green grass beside the river, red tile roof, bright yellow mud walls, a shrub or two, and bright tents in a variety of colors—red, purple, green, and blue. But mostly the tents were the red and purple with black trim of Zolltarn's clan. A dozen or more dark-haired men and women, dressed in the same colors as the tents, worked hard to rig the tents and start cooking fires.

Indeed, the Rovers had not gone far.

How to approach them undetected? And how to find his son among the numerous babies he'd seen in packs on the backs of the clan women?

He went into the inn and ordered an ale. The first one slid down his throat in welcome relief. He needed to replenish his bodily reserves after the long levitation down the mountain with only a faint and spindly ley line to fuel his talent. Another ale and a meal sent the magic humming through his body once more.

He took his third ale outside while he watched the Rover camp. A pleasant buzz accompanied him. A placid smile spread through him as he sought a place to sit.

"This is too nice a day to do more than watch other people work." He settled onto a bench at the back of the inn beside the corral, beneath a spreading hardwood tree. He didn't know the variety and frankly did not care since it bore plain blue/green leaves rather than the pink-veined, thick and oily foliage of a Tambootie tree.

He could eat a few leaves of the Tambootie to enhance his magic. No. He wasn't that desperate yet. King Simeon's insanity near the end had been caused by addiction to the leaves. He suspected Rejiia's instability stemmed from an overuse of Tambootie as well.

But where the Tambootie grew, dragons flew. Tambootie provided essential nutrients to the huge, winged beasts. Those nutrients allowed them to emit magical energy magicians could gather.

Lanciar opened himself to the air, as if drinking in the power contained within the ley lines that crisscrossed the planet. Nothing.

He'd try again later, deeper into Coronnan where dragons might fly once more.

At first the tents and activity across the rapid stream seemed all a jumble. He might have dozed a bit, lulled by the buzz of insects, the warm air, and the ale. Bright colors flowed behind his closed eyes like the umbilicals of life one saw in the void between the planes of existence.

Travel in the void was dangerous, both physically and mentally. He'd known fledgling magicians who went insane and killed themselves after viewing unspeakable truths about themselves in the void.

He jerked awake and saw anew the arrangement of tents. The black, brown, and dusty green shelters clustered together with their backs to the more garish Rover tents. As in the rest of life, ordinary travelers had turned their backs on the Rovers.

The Rovers gathered their tents and sledges in a large circle around a common cook fire with smaller campfires before each flapping opening. A few of the round huts atop the sledges—bardos, he'd heard them called—had been pressed into service as small dwellings to complete the circle.

Lanciar smiled to himself. Zolltarn must reside in the largest purple tent with red-and-black trim.

Lanciar hunted for some sign of the statue of Krej in the vicinity of that tent. Surely Zolltarn would want to display his trophy.

The tin weasel with flaking gilt paint remained elusive.

A middle-aged woman with streaks of gray in her hair directed a myriad of younger women who scurried about the big tent. She could only be the wife of the chieftain.

Three of the five young women—two still teenagers—bore the signs of pregnancy; one barely showing, one about midway along, the third about to pop. Zolltarn's wives or daughters? The other two girls remained youthfully slim and unburdened with children.

"I doubt I'll find my boy there." He turned his attention to the next tent in line. Three women, three infants. His eyes focused more closely on this campfire. All three infants bore the dark hair common to Rovers—but then so did Rejiia. He dared not hope any child of his union with the witch would result in a blue-eyed blond of the true-blood of SeLenicca. Two of the infants toddled out of their mothers' laps to play in the dirt. The third appeared the size of a child somewhere between three and six moons old. The proper age for Lanciar's son.

He sent a tendril of silvery magic across the bridge and into the Rover encampment.

At that moment Rejiia walked through his magical thread, breaking the connection. She paused before the woman cradling the infant.

Lanciar cursed and tried again to listen to the conversation. He caught only a few words.

"I seek . . . wet nurse . . . Kestra. . . . told to ask . . . claim my son," Rejiia commanded. She stood straight and tall, as regal as the queen she claimed to be.

The Rover woman laughed out loud. Lanciar heard her all the way across the rushing stream without magic. "Kestra, first daughter of Zolltarn, disappeared nearly twenty years ago. Have you not heard the legend of the missing girl and her miracle child? Rovers still seek them."

"Simurgh shit on you! Where is my son?" Rejiia screamed and stamped her foot. Enough magic compulsion accompanied her words to threaten a kardia-quake.

Lanciar braced himself, but the land absorbed Rejiia's frustration.

"If you gave us a child, Lady Sorcerer, then the child is ours. Now go back to your schemes and your politics. As for the child, if he did not die of disease or malnutrition or was not stoned by fearful *gadjé,* then he is lost to you forever." The woman continued to smile, but her eyes narrowed and her muscles tightened in defense.

"Take me to Zolltarn! He cannot steal from me. I'll have the statue of my father from him, now. And my son. The time has come to find a new wet nurse. Zolltarn owes me for his betrayal of the coven. He must not refuse. If he does, he will suffer the wrath of the coven!"

"Zolltarn can refuse anyone. Rovers have no fear of your coven. Zolltarn owes what he chooses to owe. Our debts are not always honored as *gadjé* sluts would. Go away, Lady Sorcerer. Run back to your broken coven."

Bloody Simurgh's hell! thought Lanciar. Rejiia had alerted the Rovers to her pursuit. They'd hide the baby as well as the statue of Krej where no one without Rover blood could find them. Lanciar would never get close enough to separate his son from all of the other children running around the camp.

He'd not take just any child. He wanted his own son, blood of his blood.

Blood.

The boy's blood would shine through his life force when viewed from the void.

Simurgh take them all, I'll have to go into the void by myself, without an anchor to this world. I never thought I'd want to see you again, Jack. But I could use your help right now.

"*S'murghit,* I think I need another drink of this steed-piss ale."

CHAPTER 11

From Aquilla's boat, Jack hastened back to the palace. He trusted the Bay Pilot to pick out one passenger with cool clammy skin and wobbling balance from sea sickness—there was always at least one even in the calmest of seas—and proclaim him ill from some exotic plague. Aquilla had the authority to quarantine all of the passengers. By sunset, the entire load of witch-sniffers would be back aboard their boat and headed out to sea flying a yellow flag of quarantine.

Jack did not trust the witch-sniffers already in the city to cease their torment of innocents. Katrina, his betrothed, was a prime target for Gnul persecution because she hailed from a foreign land and had no legal spouse to protect her.

Once changed into a decent uniform, he sneaked through the palace toward the inner courtyard that caught and held the sunlight. It was there Katrina chose to work at her lace pillow.

He couldn't allow her to delay their marriage any longer.

"Name the day, Katrina." Jack kissed his love on the forehead. He brushed his fingers along the long plaits of silver-gilt hair. She dropped her head onto his chest, hiding her face. He tugged on the plaits where they joined into a single thick rope below her nape, bringing her eyes up to meet his again.

Fear of the witch-sniffers made him jumpy. He had to keep a calm face and manner so Katrina would not panic.

The drone of bees flitting from flower to flower in this private courtyard within the palace sounded loud in his ears, but not as loudly as the pounding of his heart.

"Just tell me when, and I will meet you in any temple in Coronnan City to say my vows to any priest. Just name the day," he pleaded. Once they were married, he might convince King Darville to hasten his promised appointment as ambassador to SeLenicca. Then he could leave the witch-sniffers and their rabid accusations behind before they threatened Katrina.

"I . . . I . . . Jack, I'm afraid," she replied as she turned pale blue eyes up to him.

He wanted nothing more than to wrap his arms around her and protect her from her inner demons as well as from the Gnuls for the rest of their lives.

Since the death of his familiar—a cranky jackdaw with tufts of white feathers over his eyes that looked like Old Baamin's bushy white eyebrows—he'd been empty, emotionally lost. Only Katrina made him feel whole again. With her beside him, he might not need another familiar.

What he needed was to get her out of town.

"You led me across Queen's City during a massive kardiaquake." He brushed a light kiss across her brow. "You bandaged a dragon wing with a special piece of magic lace." He kissed both of her cheeks. She started melting into him, losing the rigidity in her spine. "And you helped me battle the coven with tremendous courage, Katrina. What could you possibly fear after that?"

"I . . . I fear you, Jack." She looked pointedly at his palace guard uniform. The uniform must remind her of the violence inflicted upon one and all by palace guards in Queen's City. The inhabitants of her home tolerated, almost encouraged, that violence. They claimed it kept them safe from contamination by outlanders.

"I fear the intensity of your love for me," Katrina

admitted. "I'm not certain I can return it. After
Brunix . . . You know what he did to me. How can I
love any man after that?"

Jack held her face protectively against his chest
rather than look at the tears in her eyes. Neeles
Brunix, half-Rover, opportunist, and unscrupulous
businessman, had owned Katrina and her lacemaking
talent for three years. The coven had murdered Brunix
and framed Jack for the crime.

"Brunix loved you, too, in his own twisted way,"
Jack cajoled. "He loved his possessions because he
owned them rather than owning them because he
loved them. He did not touch you out of anger, Katrina. In time, the scars he left on your heart will fade.
When you are ready, I will be waiting for you."

"I fear you must wait a very long time. I can't ask
you to do that, Jack. I love you too much to keep you
from finding someone who can return your love." She
broke away from his embrace and turned her back
on him.

Suddenly the little courtyard where she had set up
her lace bolster seemed too small to contain all of
Jack's panic. How could he get permission to take her
away from here unless they were married?

"I'll always love you." He reached out for her but
let his hand drop back to his side before he touched
her. If she did not marry him, how could he protect
her?

"Perhaps by the time you figure out how to separate
the queen from the cat spirit that also inhabits her
body, I will be ready to love you properly." That project had occupied the finest magical minds for over
three years without success.

She fingered the wide piece of lace she had been
working on when he sneaked into the courtyard.

"I'm nearly ready to try the spell, Katrina." He had
a few ideas but not yet enough to try the spell. Right
now, though, he'd try anything to get Katrina out of
the city. "As soon as we know the queen is back to

being one person in one body, King Darville will dispatch me to SeLenicca as ambassador. I need you to come with me as my wife. Only together will we be able to help rebuild your country."

She looked over her shoulder at him, a hopeful smile tugging at her lips. "Home."

"Barely. SeLenicca is changed, torn apart by war and natural catastrophe. Your family is gone. The lacemaking industry is in tatters. Nothing will be as you remember. But it is your home. You belong there. Here you will always be a political refugee, no matter how much the queen favors you." One foray into the marketplace could bring the witch-sniffers down on her as it had on the dye merchant.

"Will you be able to use your magic to revive Queen Miranda from her coma?" Katrina asked. Hope shone from her eyes for the first time since Jack had pressed her to marry him. "With our queen restored, SeLenicca will rebuild, stronger than ever before." She rushed back into his arms. "On the day after you cure Queen Rossemikka of Coronnan, I will marry you. Then we will go home, together."

Jack sealed her promise with a fierce kiss. His first assault on her mouth softened, explored possibilities, deepened to a mutual sharing. They were getting good at this. He kissed her again, pulling her tight against his chest.

She fit snugly against him, as if they were two halves of the same mold. A tremendous ache built within him. He deepened the kiss, needing more of her, all of her, forever.

Home." Katrina repeated when she came up for air. Then she renewed the kiss with vigor and promise.

A playful squeak in the back of Jack's mind alerted him to new observers. He opened one eye and stared into the silvery muzzle of a baby dragon perched on the courtyard wall. Bricks sagged and mortar crumbled beneath his purplish talons. Jack's ungainly tagalong might be only a baby—barely two full years old—but he already exceeded a packsteed in size and weight. He'd grown rapidly in the past months since Jack had first made contact with the dragons.

The stub of his slightly-askew spiral forehead horn also glowed with the identifying color—the rarest of all dragons. That all-important horn might never grow to its full length the way Amaranth kept stumbling and falling on it.

Jack had tried to match the dye to Amaranth's pinky-purple-tipped wingtips, and talons. What had happened to the dye merchant?

He took a long deep breath, anticipating the dragon magic that would soon fill him, augmenting the power he drew from the ley lines that wove a lacy network beneath the Kardia in Coronnan.

"Where did you come from, Amaranth? And where is your mama?" Jack asked aloud, reaching to touch the baby. He could communicate with this dragon mind-to-mind, but Katrina could not. He'd developed a premature rapport with Amaranth when he'd tried gathering dragon magic from him in order to heal the mother dragon's injured wing. The spell had failed, but the bond with Amaranth was sealed long before the baby was mature enough to understand it or cope with the emotions evoked. He barely had the vocabulary to communicate more than his emotions—which he broadcast loudly in a wide band.

At the moment, happiness with a touch of mischief radiated from the baby dragon.

"You must not be seen here, Amaranth. While the Gnostic Utilitarians dominate the Council of Provinces, magic and dragons remain illegal." Jack tried discouraging the dragon. Dragon safety had always come from their elusiveness and near invisibility. Amaranth had trouble understanding the concept of danger.

"Amaranth?" Katrina squealed in delight. She jumped away from Jack and hurried to the wall where she reached up to scratch the baby's muzzle. He opened his mouth and drooled in ecstasy. His meat-ripping fangs bent slightly backward, curved over his lower jaw at a near useless angle—damaged from one too many stumbles while the teeth were forming and vulnerable. Amaranth hadn't made much success as a dragon.

A dozen bricks from the top of Amaranth's perch tumbled to the ground at Katrina's feet. She dodged them neatly.

"Amaranth, where is Shayla, your mama?" Jack asked again, worried about the safety of the wall as well as the baby. More mortar broke away from the courtyard wall as he watched. Six bricks on the top tilted precariously, ready to fly in odd directions.

He placed his hands on the wall just beneath Amaranth. His fingertips touched the dragon's talons; enough contact to allow the dragon energies to flood him. He used the magic to shore up the wall and re-place the discarded bricks.

He hoped the legend that witch-sniffers had more difficulty detecting dragon magic than solitary powers was true.

The dragon nibbled delicately on Jack's hair. At the brief contact more magic dusted him. But it would evaporate the moment Jack ceased touching the dragon.

Amaranth squeaked something in juvenile dragon talk. Jack interpreted his emotions rather than the scattered images. He caught a glimpse of Shayla soar-ing over the bay on a never-ending hunt to feed her twelve voracious babies. Amaranth had seen his moth-er's absence as permission to find Jack for a romp in the bay. And he'd only fallen on his nose twice trying to launch into flight.

"No swimming today, Amaranth." Jack joined Ka-trina in scratching the dragonet. The magic filled his being. As long as he touched a purple-tipped dragon, he could use the power that traditional magicians gathered from the air. His inability to gather dragon magic in the normal way would always isolate him from his fellow magicians, despite his master status and membership in the Commune.

The flood of magic allowed him to find another weak spot in the wall. He used some of the power to strengthen more of the stressed mortar and bricks.

The magic and contact with Amaranth also told him how much the bruised horn hurt. He wanted to reach up and soothe it, find a way to straighten and restore it to normal size. But the dragon had to learn from his mistakes or he would not survive long.

Jack feared that his friend would not survive at all. According to dragon lore, only one purple-tipped dragon could live at any one time, and they were always born twins. Iianthe, Amaranth's twin, exhibited a great deal more grace, caution, and intelligence than this enthusiastic toddler.

But Jack loved this baby and hated the idea of him being sacrificed merely to satisfy dragon tradition. If only there was some way to adopt this baby, to take him to SeLenicca along with Katrina . . .

Amaranth lowered his head for attention to his itchy horn.

"Yes, I see how big the horn grows," Jack cooed. Though it looked more swollen than growing. "But you can't stay here, Amaranth. You need to go home until your mama brings you to the city. You could get hurt if one of the Gnuls sees you."

The Gnuls used the same tactics of fear as the coven to gain followers.

His years of slavery in King Simeon's mines had taught him that violence only begets more violence and the innocent are the ones who are hurt the most. Innocents like the dye merchant and Katrina.

The next squeak from Amaranth sounded like a pout.

"I have work to do for King Darville, Amaranth," Jack apologized to the dragonet for not joining his games in the bay. "Katrina has lace to make. We can't play today. I'll come to the lair soon and we'll spend some time together."

(Lace?) The human word formed decisively in Jack's mind. A picture of the lace shawl that Katrina had used to patch Shayla's wing after Jack's healing spell had failed followed. Though Shayla's magically damaged wing had grown back whole and strong, the lace bandage had left its imprint permanently in the membrane.

(Make lace for my wings?) The dragonet spread and flapped his stubby wings. *(Make my wings pretty with lace?)*

Jack translated for the dragonet.

"Your wings are beautiful as they are, Amaranth," Katrina reassured the baby. "You don't need lace. Though I wish I could find a dye to match you for my newest lace pattern. For now, you just need to grow big and strong like your mama, safely back in your own lair."

Another pout.

"Where's your twin brother, Amaranth? Iianthe must be lonely without you." Jack tried to persuade the dragonet to leave.

(Don't want Iianthe. Want Jack.)

Already the twins must sense the separation soon to come.

An idea hit Jack like one of the dislodged bricks from the wall.

A grin spread across his face and lightened his soul. Some of his problems crumbled like the wall where Amaranth perched.

"Amaranth, there is one way you can stay and play with me forever."

The dragonet and Katrina cocked their heads in curiously similar gestures of acute listening. Jack's heart swelled with possibilities and love for them both.

He smiled fondly at them and the image they presented. Family. His family.

"As a purple dragon, a very rare and special being,

either you or Iianthe must give up your dragon form soon."

The dragon nodded sagely, suddenly more mature and experienced than any two-year-old had a right to be.

"If you transform into a catlike creature, you can help me entice Rosie the cat out of Queen Mikka. Then you can stay with me forever as my familiar. As a dragon, you must make a lair of your own and live alone."

Perhaps, as a cat, Amaranth would lose a little of his awkwardness. Jack had never known a clumsy cat.

"This is a really important task, Amaranth. I really need your help."

As long as Rosie remained joined to Rossemikka, the queen's body would be unbalanced and she could not produce the heir that the country needed so badly for stability. The Gnuls preyed on that instability to spread their litany of fear.

(An elegant solution to our problems, Jack,) Shayla said from a great distance.

Jack sensed her presence, high above the city as she soared on a thermal. He knew she would not be too far away while one of her brood explored the world.

"You agree with the plan?" he asked.

Katrina struck an acute listening pose as well. Ever since she had bandaged Shayla's wing with the unique lace shawl woven of Tambrin thread spun from the Tambootie trees, she had shared a rapport with the dragon.

(How did you know that one of the two forms a redundant purple dragon may take is the flywacket?)

"Flywacket? What's a flywacket?"

(A creature that has not been seen in this land in many generations of humans, but thanks to you, one will once again grace us with its wisdom and life force.)

Somehow grace and wisdom did not fit Amaranth.

"Flywacket, huh? If everyone agrees, we can try it tonight."

"So soon?" Katrina's eyes grew wide with just a touch of panic.

"Tonight! In the central grove on Sacred Isle. There should be enough space there for Shayla and Amaranth and everyone else."

He remembered with joy the day he had found his magician's staff within one of the sacred oaks there. Performing the greatest spell of his life should take place in the same sacred grove. A few weeks ago he thought bringing the dragons home and defeating Rejiia should have been the magical achievement of a lifetime. What awaited him after this?

"Why wait another day? Queen Mikka has been waiting three years to be rid of that cat. Tonight I perform the spell. Tomorrow we will marry. The day after we journey to SeLenicca." He kissed Katrina soundly, wanting to linger. But the logistics of the magic pulled at his concentration. "I have to leave now, love. A spell of this magnitude requires a lot of preparation."

Amaranth squealed in delight. His dragon language rose shrill and piercing. Jack and Katrina both covered their ears rather than linger with another kiss.

"Uh, Shayla, will you call your dragonet? He's making a shambles of this wall and our eardrums."

A dragonlike chuckle sounded in the back of Jack's head. A moment later Amaranth cocked his head and obediently, but clumsily, flapped his ungainly wings for a launch. The dragonet tilted dangerously forward, nearly brushing his nose against a prickly rosebush.

Jack dashed forward to make sure the dragonet didn't bump his muzzle and sensitive horn bud—again—when he crashed into the paving.

At the last minute, Amaranth got enough air under his wings and cleared the courtyard by a talon length. Moments later he disappeared into the air, one more silvery distortion of light on this bright Spring day.

"Tonight, my love. I'll do the spell tonight. Trust

me, everything will be all right. Then we'll go home to SeLenicca." Jack promised.

"I trusted you with my life when all of SeLenicca conspired against me," she replied, looking at her threads rather than him.

"Tomorrow we will wed." He kissed her again, cherishing the warmth of her body in his arms. "Trust me. We will be happy together. I'll never hurt you. Ever."

CHAPTER 12

Vareena opened the sagging gates of the monastery. She must remember to send Yeenos with a work party to repair the hinges.

The villagers grumbled about the extra—and to them unnecessary—work of keeping the old site in good repair. Some, led by Yeenos himself, had refused outright when she'd requested repairs to the broken gutters last moon. She wondered how many more times she could command them.

If the orders had come from Lord Laislac, they would obey without question. But since they came from her, a spinster no man wanted, they questioned their duty constantly.

Did her mother and grandmother have the same trouble with recalcitrant villagers?

What she really needed right now was a bolt of lightning, judiciously aimed at a few reluctant back-sides.

Instead, she had two new ghosts to cater to, just when she thought she'd get a rest from her duties and a chance to escape.

The silver-and-amethyst amulet weighed heavily against her neck. It seemed to taunt her with broken promises of freedom; from her duties, from the scorn of the villagers, from her brothers.

She kept the amulet hidden beneath her shift lest her family steal it from her.

Early sunshine barely penetrated to the monastery courtyard through the ever-present haze. The mist seemed thicker today. "Good morning!" she called cheerfully. In all this haze she'd not see her ghosts easily. They'd have to come to her today. With direct light or within the building, she could see them quite easily as misty outlines with hints of color in their clothing. Hair and eye color tended to bleach out with only vague suggestions of fair or dark. Out here, with the light scattering in all directions and lingering nowhere, even those brief hints of their presence evaporated.

If she couldn't see them, could she pretend they did not exist and make her escape to the promised acres in Nunio?

No. These two new ghosts had only recently passed into their amorphous existence. They needed her.

She took a moment to stand beside the fresh grave among the foundation stones of the original temple in the southeast corner. When the magicians and priests abandoned this place, they had dismantled the house of worship to prevent desecration. "Stargods, watch over your servant Farrell as he passes to his next existence. Guide him with your wisdom. And grant his family peace in accepting his death though they have heard nothing from him in over two years."

Silence hung so heavy in this corner that she wondered if her prayer had escaped any better than any of her ghosts.

Prayers complete, she searched for traces of Marcus' magician-blue tunic, trews, and sash. She suspected the color matched his eyes exactly. Robb on the other hand, with dark, hooded eyes that brooded mysteriously, favored black for all but his identifying tunic and cloak.

She worried about him. He hadn't accepted his transition to ghosthood with Marcus' good humor and optimism.

"Over here, Vareena," Marcus called to her.

Without seeing him, she sensed the smile behind his voice. Her own lips curved upward in response. He told wonderfully funny accounts of their journeys. He made her laugh when her life seemed so hopeless. She searched the curtain wall on the other side of the gatehouse tower for signs of his vague outline.

"No, I'm over here by the well," Marcus called again.

Vareena turned toward the stone circle that enclosed the pool of water. It had once provided for over one hundred men. Now it served only two. She trusted Marcus to direct her correctly. She'd never had a ghost trick her. Or lie to her—unlike the people of her village.

"I brought you breakfast," she said to the air, hoping she directed her words in the proper direction. She'd waited four days to come back. Ghosts never needed to eat more than once or twice a week.

"Thanks, I'm hungry." The trencher of bread and cheese covered by a plain linen cloth floated from her hands. Ghosts could touch inanimate objects in this world, but not a living being. Life energies generated a barrier that repelled ghosts from humans and humans from ghosts.

"Did anyone ever tell you how beautiful you are, Vareena?" Marcus asked. "I would compose poetry to you, but you defy the limitation of words."

She dismissed his admiration. Other ghosts had told her as much. They had no one else to speak to, share their thoughts with, or pass the idle hours. Of course they fell in love with her, or her mother before her, or her grandmother before that.

If she were as beautiful as they claimed, then some normal man would have claimed her as his wife by now.

Nothing could come of Marcus' flirtations. These men were ghosts, after all. And she must cater to them until they died. Quite likely these two could last for the rest of her life rather than a bare two years.

"Step into shadows, so I can see you, please." She

continued to search the area around the well for some trace of distorted light or a wisp of mist.

There! The outline of Robb, the dark and brooding one, materialized on the far side of the well as he slumped to sit on the ground with his back against the stone circle.

"Why bother eating," Robb grumbled. "We're trapped here until we die. Might as well hasten the process and get on into our next existence."

His dark eyes burned through the mist of the gloaming into her soul.

"I wish I could help you," she murmured. Her entire body ached for him, trapped here with no hope.

And then she realized that she ached for herself as well.

"Coronnan is doomed. We'll never find the dragons and return magic to the Commune. Without dragon magic and controls, the lords will tear the country apart. Three hundred years of peace will evaporate like mist in sunshine. I wonder if this gloom ever evaporates. Everything is lost because we sought shelter here during a storm." Robb buried his face in his hands.

"Is he always so gloomy?" Vareena asked, wary of her own sensitivity to his emotions.

"No. I can usually persuade him to look on the bright side." Marcus moved around the well until he crouched beside Robb. "We'll find a way out of this, friend. We always do. My luck will return. It always does."

"And if your good luck has deserted us permanently? As the dragons deserted Coronnan?" Robb thrust Marcus' placating hand off his arm.

"Then you will develop a plan, like you always do."

"I told you yesterday and the day before, and the day before that, your luck has run out and I never had any."

"There has to be a way out of here. I don't know how or why yet, but there has to be," Vareena said.

Did she truly believe that? She must, or she would not have said so.

Her mother had taught her that lies—even those said in comfort—served no purpose. Vareena had never knowingly lied before.

Tentatively, she reached to touch Robb's shoulder, offering what comfort she could—as she would to any living person in the village. Her hand tingled as she neared him. Resolutely she pushed herself closer, resisting the urge to jerk her hand back. The strange sensation in her hand and arm did not really hurt. Felt more like the pinpricks when she lay too long with her weight on a hand or foot.

At last she made contact with him—almost. Her hand did not so much pass through him as curve around a soft mass, not quite liquid, not quite solid. Then the barrier of energy broke through her willpower and thrust her hand aside.

Her hand and arm had not faded when she touched the ghost, however briefly.

Robb looked at her. All of his hurt and despair poured from him into her. Her heart twisted and found a new rhythm.

The world seemed to shift beneath her feet as she sought a new destiny. One that included this sorrowful man.

"I brought a deck of cartes to help pass the time." She proffered the painted sheets of pressed wood.

Robb took them from her. He shuffled them idly. "Maybe I can finally win a game with Marcus now that his luck has deserted him. That's about the only good that's come out of this mess."

"I will help you find a way out of this," Vareena vowed. Her heart ached for the sadness that made Robb's shoulders slump and his mouth frown. "I promise on my sacred duty to serve the ghosts that haunt this place, that I will find a way to help you back into this existence. We will end the curse of this place so that no one becomes a ghost here again."

Perhaps then I will finally be able to claim my acres in Nunio and be free.

* * *

Robb stood in the shadows of the north tower above the kitchen and refectory watching Marcus watch Vareena. After hours playing a complex three-handed game of cartes—which Marcus won quite handily—Vareena had left on errands (she said for the night but only a few hours had passed) and returned again while the sun still rode high in the sky.

Part of his heart rejoiced every time Marcus sighed with longing directed at Vareena. If Marcus did truly love the woman—her maturity might give Marcus the steadying influence Robb thought he needed—then Marcus would forget his longtime passion for Margit. Margit would be hurt, of course. But when she healed, then perhaps, if he courted her very carefully, perhaps Robb could win her heart.

Another part of him coiled in anger against his best friend. How could Marcus be so callous? How could he forget Margit so easily? How could he hurt her thus?

He remembered the first time he'd seen Margit. She had met them in the market square near where her mother sold baked goods.

"Tell Jaylor that the queen swears she will educate any daughters she bears in the ways of Rossemeyer. I presume that means she will bare her breasts and cover her hair. But the Gnuls in the city whisper that magic is not illegal in Rossemeyer and the queen wants her daughters to learn to throw magic." Margit's harsh whisper reached Robb's ears before he realized that Jaylor's spy in the palace had found him before he'd spotted her.

He honed in on the direction of the whisper and spotted several of the queen's maids examining the produce in the cart where Marcus and Robb lounged in seeming idleness. All of the maids were dressed alike in fine green brocade with low bodices and skirts that fell in wide folds to completely cover their shoes. All five of the women had veiled their hair as well. But one of them, the tallest among them, wore her finery awkwardly. She tripped upon the long skirts, had trouble keeping her blonde braids confined beneath the gauzy veil and slouched her shoulders in an attempt to hide the vast expanse of her upper breast exposed by the lack of gown.

Robb nudged Marcus with his elbow. They both stared at the girl with open admiration until she eased away from her companions and sent them a withering glance in reprimand. Robb had lowered his eyes in apology. A brief nod of his head acknowledged her whisper as she reached across them to examine a ripe melon.

Marcus continued to stare at her with mouth slightly open. "I think I'm love," he said quietly when the women had moved on.

"You are always in love," Robb returned. A flare of jealousy burned through him. Marcus attracted any number of women and fell in love with most of them in turn. His rejects found solace in Robb's arms.

He'd never loved anyone. But Margit . . . this new apprentice of Jaylor's intrigued him. Margit. He caressed the name in his mind. Margit.

He could love this girl.

But as their friendship developed, Margit clearly preferred Marcus. Robb's best friend had remained faithful to Margit—as faithful as he was capable of being—for nearly three years, never declaring his love for another until now.

Robb had kept his love for Margit a secret for all that time. He heaved a weary sigh, wondering if something good might come of this disastrous quest after all. If he could return to Margit with comfort and companionship while Marcus chased after Vareena . . .

Vareena emptied her carry basket of firewood and kindling at Marcus' feet. Her brother stood in disapproving silence at the gate. But his stern posture broke frequently as he cast weary glances about the courtyard, seeking what he did not have the talent to see.

Robb allowed his eyes to cross slightly as he sought the aura of the man who escorted his sister so diligently. Spikes of orange fear shot through the multiple layers of fire green. A man of passion without a single hint of magical talent.

Vareena, on the other hand, sparkled around the edges of her aura of bright pink and pale yellow. A minor talent that would go unnoticed anywhere but in this haunted monastery.

Then Vareena lifted her eyes from the firewood to search the courtyard. Her gaze rested on Robb for a long moment. He looked away first. The longing that burned in her gaze embarrassed him. He had no interest in her as a woman, only as a helper in this dilemma. His heart truly belonged to Margit and Margit only.

Reluctantly, Vareena turned to her brother and retreated back to her normal world in the village.

Normal. What was normal anymore?

For years he had trained to work only dragon magic and revile anyone who dared tap rogue powers. As magicians had believed for centuries, Robb had held to the tenet that any use of rogue, or solitary magic, had its roots in evil. That had been normal. Then the dragons had left Coronnan, taking their communal magic with them. Over the last three years Robb had come to accept solitary magic as normal. The wandering life he and Marcus led as journeymen carrying out Jaylor's missions had become normal.

How long would he and his best friend be stuck here before this half existence between reality and the void became normal?

He couldn't allow that to happen. Coronnan needed dragons so that honor and respect could be restored to magic and magicians. Only with dragons could magicians combine their powers, have them amplified by orders of magnitude to overcome any solitary magician. The Commune of Magicians was dedicated to enforcing law, ethics, honor, and justice among themselves and throughout Coronnan. He and Marcus were Jaylor's last hope for bringing the female dragon Shayla and her mates home.

Yaakke had failed, having gone missing some three years ago.

Now he and Marcus must remain missing in this hazy gloaming indefinitely.

Didn't that half-haze ever dissipate from the sky? He kicked the stone wall of the tower in his frustration. All he wanted right now was to see honest sunshine reflecting off Margit's blonde braids.

In the center of the courtyard Marcus arranged the kindling and wood into an efficient campfire. He snapped his fingers and brought a flamelet of witchfire to his fingertip. It leaped from his hand into the kindling, chewing hungrily at the fuel.

They were ready to try a summons spell again, in broad daylight, when they had a better chance of someone being awake at the University to respond. Possibly the containment spell around the monastery weakened the spell to the point a sleeping magician would not notice the faint hum in the recipient's glass.

Robb moved to Marcus' side, staying slightly behind so he could feed the fire without distracting his friend from his spell.

Marcus acknowledged him with a slight nod as he breathed deeply, in three counts, hold three, out three, hold three. His eyes glazed over, and he stared into the flames, seeing something far, far away. Slowly, deliberately, he brought his square of precious glass up to eye level and recited the ritual words that would summon Jaylor, Senior Magician of the Commune.

Robb fought the urge to dive into his own trance and participate in the spell. If dragon magic were available, he could combine his own talent with Marcus' and boost the power of the spell far beyond the sum of their two talents. Without dragons, he could only monitor his friend and keep the fire going for as long as the spell took to reach across Coronnan to the protected Clearing near the University.

"Flame to flame, glass to glass, like seeking like," Marcus chanted over and over again.

Robb grew cramped sitting cross-legged on the hard-packed surface of the courtyard. He shifted uneasily and fed yet another log onto the fire. The sparks leaped high, greedy for more fuel.

His back ached. He reached out with a tiny magical probe and checked Marcus' pulse. He'd been in trance a long time. Surely Jaylor would answer the thrumming vibration of his glass no matter what time of the day or night. If he couldn't, then an apprentice or another magician would intervene with his own glass and flame. He could not imagine a situation that would keep every magician in the Commune and University away from communication at the same time.

The probe lost contact with Marcus' pulse. Robb risked touching his friend. His skin was cool and had taken on the waxy pallor of exhaustion and hunger.

"Wake up, Marcus. Return to your body and your thoughts. Come back slowly, easily." Robb held his friend's hand, infusing warmth and strength into the chill skin.

Marcus slumped and sighed heavily. His eyelids fluttered. He looked up bleakly. "I couldn't get through. I don't think the spell climbed the walls any better than we did."

"My plan didn't work."

CHAPTER 13

"Did you feel that?" Margit asked Ferrdie and Mikkail. She touched the little shard of glass in her scrip. A moment ago it felt as if it vibrated with a summons. Now it lay quiet again.

For years, during her time as Queen Rossemikka's maid and Jaylor's spy in the capital, the summons spell was the only bit of magic she could work. She had mastered all nuances of that spell very well and should know that characteristic thrumming in her glass.

But now the sensation had dissipated like mist in a fog. A summons did not work that way. The glass should continue to vibrate until the one summoned found a flame and a bit of privacy to answer.

She'd known a spell to linger in her glass for the best part of a day.

"Feel what?" Mikkail returned. He looked up from the text he studied at the long library table. Darkness had driven them inside, otherwise Margit would have insisted they continue their reading beneath a tree in the fresh air. She had chosen a table beneath a shuttered window, which she opened to the night air.

Ferrdie looked around anxiously as if expecting to be beaten for doing his homework.

Since she'd adopted masculine clothing and hairstyle, the boys in her class accepted her more readily, asked her to study and practice with them. WithyReed still did not call upon her in class, but the other masters took her more seriously. Almost as if a gown set up a barrier between them.

Or a challenge. Dressed as a boy, she did not threaten their preconceived ideas about females and magic. She wondered briefly how Brevelan, the wife of the Senior Magician, coped with the archaic attitude.

In asking the question, she knew the answer. Brevelan ignored the masters who treated her as subhuman. That irritated the masters immensely because their lofty opinions meant nothing to the wife of their Senior Magician.

Briefly, Margit explained the strange half-sensation that her glass had interrupted a summons to someone else. Both boys touched their glasses within their scrips. Both shook their heads. Mikkail shrugged his shoulders and returned to the treatise written by the ancient magician named Scarface.

"What's this word, Margit?" He turned the scroll so she could see it.

"Complementary," she replied.

"So the elements of Fire and Air are 'com-ple-men-tar-y'." He sounded each syllable carefully as Margit had taught him, so he'd remember the word next time he saw it.

"And Kardia and Water are complementary. I wonder if one could negate a spell by invoking opposing elements?" she mused.

"An interesting theory you may explore as part of your next advancement test, Margit," Jaylor said from the doorway.

All three apprentices jumped to their feet in respect for the Senior Magician.

"Sit, sit, return to your studies." He waved them back to their stools and their books. He carried his younger son under one arm and a cat on his other shoulder. Lately, he was rarely seen without at least one of his two sons and some of the overflow of animals attracted to the shelter of Brevelan's Clearing. The first Senior Magician in many generations to have a family, he took his duties as a father very seriously—especially now that his wife Brevelan was heavily pregnant again. She needed a break from the excessive energy of her two sons and husband.

"Have any of you seen Master Librarian Lyman?" Jaylor asked, looking about the jumbled shelves of the library. They'd lost a number of books in their years of running from refuge to refuge before building a new University in exile. But they'd retrieved many more books from unexpected sources as silent sympathizers found circuitous ways to send the treasures. Not everyone was willing to consign books to Gnul bonfires. Lyman, the ancient librarian, hadn't managed to sort and shelve them all properly. Nor had he appointed an assistant to help him.

Perhaps Ferrdie? Margit thought the job perfect for her meek friend.

"Dozing in the corner," Margit whispered to Jaylor.

"I'll not wake him then. He needs his rest." Jaylor started to back out of the room.

"Master Jaylor?" Margit stopped him. "Did you just sense a summons gone astray?" Her hand automatically went to her scrip, testing the glass again for residual vibrations.

"Did you?" Jaylor's eyebrows rose nearly to his dark auburn hair.

"Aye, sir. But it . . . evaporated. I've never had anything like that come through my glass before."

"Neither have I. Keep alert, Margit. And work on the paper about opposing elements to negate a spell. You'll find some preliminary explorations on the subject over by the last window on the right. Don't wake Master Lyman. He's getting old and needs his rest." Jaylor quietly left the library.

"Master Lyman was born old," Mikkail muttered.

"I heard he doesn't eat. He just inhales the dust from the books," Ferrdie offered.

Margit had to smile. The boy just might break away from the trap of his fears if he could repeat a joke that had followed apprentices for—forever.

"No, I don't breathe book dust, little boy, I eat

apprentices who disturb my nap!" Lyman called from the corner. His wrinkled skin and wispy silver hair almost blended into the shadows as if he were as invisible as a dragon.

Ferrdie cowered behind his book.

"And I was born older than I am now. I don't age, I young," Lyman tugged his beard and winked at Margit. "Now, come along, Margit. Get the study on your topic. Only way you'll make journeyman in time to answer that distress summons you intercepted is to get the paper written and impress the masters that you aren't just a girl."

"Distress summons?" Margit's voice came out on a squeak. The only person she knew who might send a distress summons that would reach her but not Jaylor was Marcus.

Once again she knew a stab of hot fear that her love had been lost and out of communication for many moons.

"Nothing to worry about just yet. He's safe for the moment. But you must push forward to be ready when you need to be."

"How did you know it was a distress summons, Master Lyman?"

"Because I'm older than the oldest dragon, and I've seen it all," the frail old man retorted. "A distress summons that is interrupted is the only summons that hits more than one person like a stab in the side and then evaporates into mist. The sender is lucky someone caught it and is willing to prepare for it. Now, research and write that paper. You don't have enough knowledge and talent to plan ahead as Robb does or to trust in your luck like Marcus does."

"Then I'll have to improvise." She flashed the old man an impish grin.

* * *

These intruders have one hundred days. That is all. One hundred days and they die. They will not figure out how to steal my power in that time.

* * *

"Tell me a story, M'ma," Jaranda demanded. The regal, imperious tone of the three-year-old lost a lot in translation around the thumb she sucked. Her eyelids drooped.

Mother and daughter had consumed every scrap of food they could scrounge from the kitchen and pantry. For the moment they were replete and happy.

What about tomorrow?

All around them, they heard small crashes and groans as weakened walls and ceilings gave way. How much longer could they safely stay here? With atavistic fear, she resisted going forth into the city.

"Come sit in my lap, baby. I'll tell you a story." She opened her arms where they sat on the floor of the workroom. Round bolster pillows spilled yards of soft lace around them. Straight-backed chairs by the pillow stands offered the only seating in the room. So she and Jaranda sat on the floor where they could be together. They had found elegant withdrawing rooms with comfortable furniture, bedrooms with lace curtains, and little private salons all over the palace. All of them had breaches in the walls or ceilings and offered little protection. The workroom remained intact and felt like home. How long? What about food tomorrow?

"Once upon a time, in a country far, far away . . ." she began the story.

"How far away?" Jaranda asked as she snuggled her head into her mother's lap. She sucked her thumb again.

Part of the woman knew she should do her best to discourage the little girl from the baby behavior, but with life so unsettled, their future so uncertain, she allowed Jaranda whatever comfort she could find.

"Many days' travel by barge up the river, farther away than you or I have ever been. Farther away than either of us would want to travel."

"Hmm," Jaranda agreed.

"In this far, far country, there lived a . . . a princess who made lace. And her name was . . . Jaranda."

"That's me," the little girl sighed and shifted deeper into her mother's lap.

"And she lived in a crumbling palace that had been deserted by one and all when an evil sorcerer with dark eyes and hair made the land tremble and the skies shoot flame. Everyone was very afraid. Everyone except the princess. She knew that the only defense against the evil sorcerer was to make enough lace to cover the walls of the palace and heal them. The little princess searched the palace high and low for all of the Tambrin thread she could find. For Tambrin has special magic spun into it . . ."

Jaranda drifted into sleep, a smile on her face.

The woman looked around the workroom with new hope. Tambrin.

If she could find some of the silky thread spun from the fibers of immature Tambootie trees, perhaps she could heal herself, remember her name. Maybe then she would know where to look for family or friends to shelter and feed her and her daughter.

Without disturbing Jaranda, she reached to the nearest strand of lace dangling from a work table. She fingered the fine threads woven into an airy pattern.

Silk. Lovely. But not Tambrin.

She reached a little farther to the table behind her. Linen. The finest spun linen in the world, but still not Tambrin.

She reached again, across her to the left. The lace eluded her. She stretched farther and touched—a hand!

A scream lodged deep in her throat. She wanted to scream, needed to shout her fear to the rooftops.

But that would awaken the baby.

"Nice story, Lady. Tambrin lace is worth six times its weight in gold in Coronnan right now." The man's deep voice flowed around her in soothing tones.

"Show me which of these is Tambrin, and I'll show you a safe place to stay in the city."

Just then the floor rippled beneath them, and the ceiling dropped chunks of plaster on top of her head.

"I think I'd rather take one of these pillows to Coronnan and make my fortune there," she replied.

Only then did she look at the intruder. Tall, black-haired, with eyes as deeply dark as a well, he smiled at her with a mouth full of gleaming teeth. A small pack steed stood patiently behind him. Not a true pack steed. One of those odd little creatures from the mountains of Jehab with exceedingly long ears and shaggy coat. It opened its mouth and brayed long and loud as if it laughed at her, at him, at the world. It displayed an amazing number of oversized square teeth—a lot like its master.

His clothing certainly deserved a smile, black trews and shirt brightened by a garish vest of purple with red trim and silver embroidery. His fringed sash of bright blue hung nearly to his dusty black boots. A dozen or more coins hung from the sash at his waist, from rings in his ears, and dangling from his purple, billed cap set at rakish angle.

Something in the back of her mind whispered "Exotic, interesting." She thought perhaps it should have shouted "Dangerous!" But it didn't.

"I should fear you, but I don't."

"Prejudices have to be learned. Not much to fear from me. I'm just a simple trader trying to make a living. You and a lace pillow filled with Tambrin lace could set us up in a nice palace all our own in Coronnan. No kardiaquakes in Coronnan." A mischievous twinkle in his eyes made his offer nearly as attractive as the man.

"I don't suppose you know my name?"

"Never met you before, Lady." He shrugged, setting the coins to jingling. They formed an almost recognizable melody played on silver bells.

"I suspected you'd say that."

CHAPTER 14

"What was this room used for?" Marcus asked Vareena. They had reached the corner room beneath one of the two large watchtowers. Two smaller towers at the end of the residential wings of the monastery contained latrines and staircases but no observation platforms on their roofs. These corner towers were massive—larger than four of the individual rooms combined. They topped the courtyard walls by at least another story.

Vareena paced the colonnade beside him, thrusting open doors as they passed. He wanted to hold her hand as they explored, but the barrier of energy repulsed him every time.

Robb slunk along behind them, lost in his own grumbling. He'd sat by the well for hours shuffling the deck of cartes. But as soon as Marcus and Vareena neared the tower, he had joined them.

"Looks like an office or study," Vareena said, staring at the slanted writing desk, tall stool, stone visitor's bench, and rank of empty bookshelves along one wall. The desktop and the shelves held only dust.

They explored a bed niche behind a half-wall at the back of the room. In the corner, steps spiraled up into the tower. Indentations in the shallow risers showed the wear of many feet climbing those stairs over the course of centuries of use.

Robb stared at the stairs without mounting them. "Maybe the bathing chamber is up there. Haven't seen any signs of a bath. How did they keep clean?" he muttered.

"At least they have convenient privies in every corner and every level. They're dry. No one has used them for centuries. Maybe we can crawl down one and out of the monastery." Marcus began looking for the private closet that should be behind the stairs.

"What if they drain directly into the river, or into a pit beneath the ground with no exit? Besides the holes are too small for either of us to squeeze through," Robb reminded him.

"We've found nothing. Nothing at all in this place." Marcus slammed one fist into the other. He'd learned not to try putting it through the wall. He had several bruises and raw knuckles to remind him.

"I have a vague recollection of Mam saying that when the numbers of priests and monks declined to only three men, they packed up everything, including the temple stones, and moved elsewhere," Vareena continued. "But that was long, long ago. Before the first ghost came three hundred years ago."

"We need information," Marcus interjected. He wanted to slam his fist into something in his frustration, again. Fear replaced his certainty that all would come out right.

And he could not touch Vareena, the one person he longed to take comfort from.

"Can you bring your mother here for us to talk to?" Robb looked up, hope shining in his eyes rather than his usual pessimism. "Always best to get information as close to the source as possible."

"No." She stared off into the distance, refusing to look at them, all her friendliness and helpfulness faded.

For once, Robb respected her silence and did not press her to comply with his request. Instead, he reached out one of his hands as if to caress her hair in comfort. But he dropped it before he even came close.

Marcus let out a long, uneasy breath. Unwanted

jealousy flared hot. He and Robb had never competed for a woman before—they'd both had a number of liaisons—but always with the other's blessing. They took care to seek out women who did not interest the other. But where Marcus fell in and out of love quite easily, Robb had always kept his heart slightly aloof.

For the past two years Marcus had loved Margit, Jaylor's spy in Palace Reveta Tristile. He thought perhaps this attachment would last forever since it had lasted so long.

Then they'd come here.

He should remain faithful to Margit's memory. He shouldn't begrudge Robb's attraction to Vareena.

But Vareena was so very beautiful, resilient, wise, and mature. And their only hope.

Marcus' heart twisted in silent agony.

"Guess it's natural we'd both want the only woman who can see either of us," he muttered under his breath. He tried to reassert his natural good humor, without much luck.

The endless empty rooms of the monastery depressed him. He and Robb had searched the place, of course, looking for another exit. But he'd hoped Vareena could show them something they'd overlooked. She seemed more ignorant of the layout than they.

"My mam died twenty years ago. She tried to come up here to sit with her last ghost during a wild thunderstorm. Like the one that brought you here. Lightning hit a tree as she was making her way here. It fell on top of her and killed her. I inherited the duty to tend the ghosts that night."

"How old were you, Vareena?" Marcus asked gently.

She held up her hand displaying all five fingers plus two from the other hand while she swallowed repeatedly, working to avoid the strong emotions that gripped her.

"Stargods!" He slammed his right fist into his left palm. Unsatisfied with the explosive gesture, he looked for something else to hit. Robb would do. He caught his breath and closed his eyes in shock. "This place is truly cursed. And all three of us along with it. We've got to get out of here!"

"That is what I have been trying to tell you for two days, Marcus," Robb said quietly. Too quietly. Had he sensed Marcus' earlier anger and jealousy, his need to lash out at his best friend because he was a handy target?

"What's in the other corner room?" Marcus nearly ran the length of the colonnade where he kicked the door open, letting it slam against the stone wall behind it. The bang did nothing to alleviate his frustration.

"The kitchen with storage behind and refectory above." Vareena looked inside. Her posture told him nothing of her thoughts.

He considered probing her mind, letting her memories give him as much information as she possessed—even the deeply buried bits about her mother. Something repelled him. He wasn't even sure his magic would work on her since she seemed partially in the void. The summons spell he'd tried last night had lain dormant within the fire, never passing through his glass. He'd tried three times since coming here to no avail. Maybe all of his magic had died the moment they passed through these walls. He certainly had not had any luck trying to tap the erratic ley lines that passed through the courtyard. They never seemed to rest in the same place two heartbeats in a row.

And the constant haze in the sky distorted his planetary orientation. He had slept only two nights in this place. Well he hadn't really slept all that much what with the nightmares and all.

His latest nightmare involved losing at endless games of cartes, until he finally bet with University money entrusted to him by Jaylor. In a desperate play to salvage his losses he'd bet everything, including Margit.

And lost.

He shuddered and tried to think the problem through—as Jaylor and Baamin before him had taught him.

His connection to the wheel of the stars, the spin of the planet, and the shift of the season told him more time had passed than the two nights he thought he'd spent in the monastery. Much more time. On top of that, his sense of *where* they were in relation to the nearest magnetic pole shifted every few hours.

Perhaps the way the ley lines broke just before meeting the exterior walls had something to do with his reactions. He got a headache every time he tried to puzzle it through. He just wanted out. Now.

He breathed deeply, trying to master his emotions. The failed summons spell had left him frightened and afraid to try again lest he fail and know for certain that all his magic was lost along with his luck.

"Look, Marcus," Robb said in hushed tones. "Look at this!"

Marcus turned his attention away from his fears and looked where Robb had stopped at the center of the central wing of the monastery. He stomped over to his friend and peered inside.

Large and larger. Like the University, this three-story room took up one entire wing of the building, dominating the lesser rooms.

"A library," Robb whispered.

"An empty library." The last of Marcus' optimism slid out of him, into the cold paving stones. "No books, no journals. Not even a cobweb. The rest of this building is filled with spiders and cobwebs, but not here. Only dust and empty shelves."

"Not entirely empty. This bank of shelves in the center is filled with sacks of gold," Robb dribbled a handful of coins out of a rotting canvas sack. He moved around to the back of the shelving unit and reappeared with another sack. "As many back here as in front."

Marcus paced around the massive unit. It could easily hold one hundred or more books on each side. The entire thing was filled with sacks of gold coins and several bullion bars.

"What sunlight penetrates through the gloaming and then through the windows seems to concentrate in this spot." Robb circled the unit in the opposite direction. With each pass the two of them made, the gold seemed to glow more brightly.

"Maybe whoever put the gold here wanted to spend his hours staring at it," Marcus mused.

"Kind of a boring existence," Robb added.

"Who would collect all this gold and just leave it?" Marcus reached out to touch the shiny metal. The coin warmed under his touch. Light reflected off it in warm shades. It almost begged him to pocket it along with the few coins he'd taken from Farrell's corpse.

His heartbeat and breathing slowed. He focused only on the gold. Time seemed to stop . . .

Some moments later he shook himself free of the enthrallment. "Gold doesn't do anyone any good just sitting here in isolation. We need to get it back to Jaylor and the Commune." Hope blossomed again in Marcus' chest. "Think of all that the Commune and University can accomplish with this much gold. New buildings. Books. Tools. Food and clothing for apprentices and journeymen."

"Bribes to nobles to legalize the Commune again." Robb grinned from ear to ear. His previous depression seemed to have eased.

"Stargods save us!" Vareena crossed herself, paused and signed the ward against evil again. "Money is evil. Put it back, Robb."

"Nonsense. The world economy depends upon the free circulation of coins." Robb fell into lecture mode. "Some coins may be cursed by an individual. But the coins themselves are not evil. Evil exists only in the hearts of certain humans. A magician of unusual strength and evil design might place a curse upon coin. But the curse would die with the magician. Since ghosts have been coming here for generations, these coins cannot be cursed."

"Put it back. You have no need for gold. I will provide all that you need while you are here. We do not use gold or silver in our village. We trade for everything we need with the caravans that use the pass, or the Rovers that wander through. The priests have told us that coins are the source of all evil. We grow and make all else that we need ourselves. Put it back! Before you die, put it back."

* * *

These amateurs slept through the kardiaquake I caused. They ignored the nightmares I gave them as if they were of no consequence. What will it take to be rid of them?

They should tremble in their boots at thought of the power I command. I was the first to employ a blending of traditions. Dragon magic is limited in scope for all the strength it employs. Ley line magic cannot be combined with other magicians to enhance the power by orders of magnitude. Blood magic requires a unique personality to endure the pain and to relish the fear and blood sacrifice of others.

But I discovered how to use all three disciplines at once. My offspring continue experimenting with my discoveries. I sired two of the strongest magicians ever. The older is even more innovative than I. The younger is warped by early rejection. She has not the emotional strength to use that trauma to enhance her magic. But the warping in her personality makes her very creative in inflicting pain. She is truly a master of blood magic. She also taps ley lines as a spigot in a cask of wine. But being female she cannot draw upon dragon magic, unless she remains in physical contact with a purple dragon. I think she may have solved that little problem on her own.

I will bring my two children to me. They will know

how to find me with only a little prompting and a few clues.

With their help, I can deal with these matters and be free to enjoy my power.

CHAPTER 15

"Do you have a name, my dark-eyed friend?" the unnamed woman asked.

"Outside my clan, I am called Zebbiah," the Rover merchant replied, nodding his head. "And do you, my new business partner, have a name?"

"If I have one, I have forgotten it." She sighed heavily. "Do you happen to have any idea what I might be called inside or outside my clan?"

"True-bloods of SeLenicca do not have clans," he replied succinctly. "Your blonde hair and blue eyes proclaim you a true-blood."

Jaranda had red hair. Did that make her other than a true-blood of SeLenicca? The woman couldn't remember if that held import in society or not.

"But what am I called?"

He shrugged and set about removing the panniers from his pack beast. He'd neatly evaded her question. She had a feeling he was good at evading issues rather than lying. Good. She trusted him not to lie outright to her even if he did not speak the truth.

"Why did you bring that animal inside the palace?"

Jaranda stirred from her nap. The woman soothed her with a gentle caress through the baby's tangled hair.

"This is not a true palace anymore. More ruins than building. Besides, I didn't dare leave him alone. Beasts are valuable in this city. Someone would steal him."

"Is theft so rampant that the city guards cannot control it?" Something fearful clutched at her heart and throat.

"Aye, Lady. The city guard fled along with all the others. No one rules here now. Law is enforced by the strongest bully who makes his own rules as benefit him and him alone." Panniers off the beast, Zebbiah set about lighting a fire in the nearby brazier. He squatted on his heels, looking comfortable making camp in the workroom of the ruined palace. He looked as if he could make himself comfortable anywhere, any time.

She wished she knew enough about herself to find comfort within her own mind and heart. In this state of not knowing, only Jaranda anchored her.

With a half smile she suddenly realized that her lack of memory offered her a kind of freedom. She and her baby could make a home for themselves anywhere they chose. They could set the rules and style of their home to suit themselves. They need please no one else—except possibly Zebbiah if he stayed with them.

The heat quickly penetrated her bones, and her mind lightened. "I didn't realize I was cold until I touched heat again," she mused.

"Cold can be like that. When it gets really bad, it almost feels like warmth and then you fall asleep and never wake up."

"Will you protect me and my baby from the cold?"

"If I can."

"And from the bandits and bully gangs?" She shuddered.

He paused a moment before answering. "My word as a Rover. I'll do my best to protect you from harm of any kind."

"Even from yourself?"

He grinned, flashing a huge number of teeth, just like his pack beast "My word of honor, Lady. You are as safe from me as you want to be."

A long silent moment passed between them. The woman looked away first.

"You hungry?" Zebbiah asked.

The woman shook her head. "We scavenged in the pantry. But we will need to eat again by nightfall."

"I've food for the three of us. We'll leave at dawn." He fished a pot and some packets wrapped in oiled cloth from one of the panniers. "Is there water?"

"The well behind the kitchen still tastes sweet."

He nodded abruptly and rose from his squat in one graceful motion, without using his hands to brace himself.

"You need anything while I'm out?"

The pack beast shifted his head and began nibbling her tangled hair.

"If you could find a hairbrush or comb?"

He nodded again and left without complaint.

"We'll deal well together, Zebbiah," she whispered. "I'm not sure why I trust you, but I do."

Oversized teeth nipped her ear. She batted the pack beast away. It then began grazing on a piece of lace dangling from a corner pillow. "But you'll have to teach this beast of yours some manners, Zebbiah." She settled Jaranda on the floor and followed the beast to rescue the priceless ornament.

"I don't suppose you know my name?" she asked the beast as she pulled half a yard of lace free of its jaws

"Heeeeeee haaaaaaaw," the beast brayed in answer, or protest.

"Somehow I thought you'd say that."

* * *

Jack waited outside King Darville's private study, impatiently shifting from one foot to the other. He pretended to stand guard while listening with every sense available to him. He needed to speak to the king and queen alone. How much longer before Darville and Rossemikka freed themselves from the increasingly loud political conversation?

Lord Laislac had spent the last hour haranguing his

king. Lord Andrall, the king's uncle by marriage, had spoken a couple of times. Laislac's daughter Ariiell had whimpered occasionally. Jack had seen Andrall's and Laislac's wives enter the room, but so far they had remained silent.

Darville had said little, asking only an occasional question. Queen Mikka probably sat in the window embrasure, basking in the afternoon sunshine, stroking the sensuous texture of her gown with long fingers. She said little during these sessions, but she observed everything and counseled Darville afterward.

Jack did not have to open his magical listening senses to hear the scandal in the making. Long ago, when he'd been a kitchen drudge, considered too stupid to even have a name, he'd learned to listen carefully with all of his senses before entering a room. He'd also eventually learned how to make himself seem invisible in order to avoid the local bullies.

Today invisibility came from his plain guard's uniform and his presence outside the king's study. No one noticed him because he belonged there.

But Jack had to stand still, at attention, hoping his impatience for a moment of privacy with the king and queen did not alert anyone that something unusual was about to happen.

He needed absolute secrecy to summon the Commune for tonight's spell. One whisper of the king and queen involved with magic would bring the wrath of the Gnuls and the lords they controlled down on their heads. None of them would be safe for a moment if the Gnuls found out what Jack planned to do tonight.

He shuddered every time he thought about this morning's adventures in the market square. Fear of magic grew by the day. The dye merchant wasn't the only innocent to be accused and judged upon the spot. Stoning had become a favorite form of execution. It required no preparation and could be carried out before palace guards could interfere. That the Gnuls had grown so bold as to accuse Jack while he wore a guard's uniform told him how strong the Gnuls had grown.

King Darville and Queen Mikka kept bodyguards close to them all the time now. Jack and Sergeant Fred pulled the duty more often than others. Fred was an accepted presence and trusted by king and council alike. Jack was new and unknown to the council, but the king and queen relied upon his magical talent for their safety as well as secret communication with Jaylor and the Commune of Magicians.

"She must marry the boy. He's responsible for this—this outrage!" Lord Laislac screamed within the king's study.

Any mention of marriage piqued Jack's interest.

"The boy is not responsible for his own actions," Lord Andrall replied mildly. "My son was born with only half his wits and never found the rest. For him to marry anyone would be a mockery of the Stargods."

"Well, he certainly managed to become a man long enough to sire a child on my daughter. My daughter who was a virgin when she came to your household for fosterage after her mother died," Laislac sneered this time. But his agitation showed through his wavering voice.

Jack leaned a little closer to the door. He'd been very young and frightened when news hit the capital that Lord Andrall's son, first cousin to then Prince Darville, had been born damaged. The court went into mourning for the beloved lord and his lady, sister to Darville's father, King Darcine.

Jack had rejoiced because at last there was someone more stupid than him. Upon the few occasions the childlike young man came to court, Jack had grown to love and honor him as the Stargods commanded. Few people realized how much love, patience, and truth they could learn from the special people marked by the Stargods.

"But I don't want to marry him, P'pa. He's repulsive! He's ugly. And he smells." That must be Ariiell, she of the whining voice.

Jack had seen her around court a couple of times, frail, pale, and uninteresting. No personality to go with the fair prettiness.

"Well, you certainly found him attractive enough once to take him into your bed," Andrall replied mildly.

"You don't understand! 'Twas but a game. A teasing game, and I . . . he lost control." A long pause followed her slip of the tongue. "He's strong. He overpowered me. I had no choice." She babbled on, trying to make excuses for herself.

Jack doubted that Andrall's son had been much more than a passive participant. He knew the young man too well. But he also knew how often his own patience had been taxed by Katrina, and he had his full wits. Mardall didn't have the reasoning power and emotional control of an adult.

"Gentlemen, ladies. I do not believe a forced marriage is the answer to this dilemma," Darville said in a soothing tone. "Surely a retreat into the country for a year or so, a discreet adoption by a childless couple of good family would serve all of us and no scandal need accompany either party."

" 'Twould serve you, Your Grace. You would not have to acknowledge your cousin's child as your heir," Laislac replied, sarcasm dripping from every word. "Since you can't manage to get the queen pregnant yourself." The insult brought a painful silence.

Jack suddenly turned his full attention to every breath within the room. Lady Ariiell sought to make her child legitimate with a hasty marriage to Darville's only blood heir—discounting the exiled Rejiia and her equally exiled sisters. Should Darville die heirless, then Laislac was the logical choice as regent for his young grandson as monarch. Kings had been killed for less.

This made Jack's errand doubly important. He knew

how to stabilize Queen Mikka's body so she could carry a child to full term and give the country an unquestioned heir.

"I would welcome the stability a legitimate heir would bring to Coronnan," Darville replied. Jack could almost see him pacing back and forth behind his massive desk like a wolf stalking his territory. The king rarely sat still and then only when Queen Mikka held his hand.

"We will discuss this further, when all of us have had time to reflect on all of the options." More likely when Darville had a chance to discuss the alternatives with Mikka. "Remember, Laislac, the plight of Lord Andrall's son is well known. This marriage and his impending paternity would generate more scandal than were Lady Ariiell to give birth to an illegitimate child. Do you really want this?"

"I insist that Lord Andrall and his son honor their obligations to my daughter. They will marry!" Laislac screamed loud enough for the entire court to hear.

A few moments later all of the combatants exited. Lady Lynnetta in tears, comforted by the supporting arm of her husband, Lord Andrall. Their son, Mardall, tripped along in their wake, drooling slightly, smiling happily at Jack's familiar wave. He clutched a stuffed toy—perhaps a well-worn spotted saber cat—and seemed oblivious to the storm that had threatened his quiet, predictable world away from the court. He'd been so quiet, Jack had not realized he'd been in the room.

Lord Laislac looked as if he'd spit thunder and lightning. His wife, Ariiell's stepmother, held her chin up and pursed her mouth in a disgusted pout.

But Lady Ariiell smiled and patted her slightly swollen tummy.

She was up to something.

Jack needed to follow her and find out what.

He also needed to inform the king and queen that he had a possible answer to Mikka's problem. After tonight, Queen Mikka might very well negate Lady Ariiell's ambitions.

Jack slipped into the study and locked the door behind him, both physically and magically.

"Something *else* that requires my attention?" King Darville asked impatiently, lifting one golden eyebrow. He barely looked up from the documents that he read most intently. His leather queue restraint had slipped, and he looked in need of a shave. The last confrontation had taken its toll on him since Jack's witch-sniffer report a few hours ago.

Still the king maintained his gentle smile and politeness while his eyes narrowed in slight disapproval. Better to risk the king's irritation than brave the wolflike smile and bared teeth that betrayed his anger. He glanced at his wife, clearly anxious for a moment alone with her to discuss that touchy situation Laislac had thrown at his feet.

"Your Grace, I believe I have a solution to a recurring problem."

Darville half rose from his chair, his full gaze intent upon Jack's face. "Do we have privacy?" he asked quietly.

Mikka came to his side and clutched his arm. Darville tucked her neatly against his side in a loving and companionable gesture. Her eyes became huge in her too thin face; not daring to hope.

Jack closed his eyes and breathed deeply, listening to all of the small sounds around the palace with extra as well as mundane senses. He heard the shuffle of many feet within the building and out in the courtyards. The murmur of many conversations drifted close to his ear. He sorted through them and dismissed all but one. Just above the subtle shift of stones and Kardia settling into each other, he detected a whisper, two heartbeats, the sputter of a rushlight . . .

He held up two fingers and pointed beneath the floor.

Darville cocked his head and pursed his lips in consternation. "The tunnels," he mouthed the words and pointed to his massive desk.

Jack had heard about the numerous secret passages that riddled the residential wing of the palace. They dated to the earliest construction of the old keep, intended to give the original lord of the islands an escape in time of war. Only one tunnel remained open and well known. It provided a quick trip between the palace and the University complex on an adjacent island. Now that the University served as a barracks, the guards used the tunnel to move quickly between duties, protected from the weather.

But the other tunnels. The older ones were supposed to remain secret from all but the king's closest family and confidants.

Jack drew his sword, actually his staff in mild disguise.

"Fred?" Darville said quietly.

"No time," Jack replied equally quiet.

"Ready?"

Jack nodded.

The king pressed a hidden lever. The desktop slid sideways. He withdrew from the opening quickly, taking Mikka with him.

Unnatural yellow flame tinged with blue lighted the dark hole where the desktop had been. Witchlight!

Mikka gasped and held her hand over her mouth to stifle any further sound. Darville pushed her behind him as he reached for his short sword atop the desk.

A magician eavesdropped on the king. Only a member of the coven would have the audacity to do that.

CHAPTER 16

Jack reached down with his sword/staff, with his free hand, and with his magic to yank a startled scullery maid through the hole.

She squeaked a protest, her eyes wide.

Jack detected no magic in her aura. He'd heard a second heartbeat.

The witchlight torch continued to gleam. The magician who had lighted it could not be far. The coven had grown as bold as the Gnuls if they eavesdropped within the palace.

Jack thrust the maid toward Darville. The king stumbled with his unexpected burden. The two landed in a heap on the floor. Feminine giggles erupted from the froth of flying petticoats.

Mikka grabbed the girl by the back of her bodice and hoisted her away from the grinning king with a ferocious yank. The queen did not return the smile.

Jack reached again into the hole, only slightly distracted by the sight of feminine legs protruding enticingly from the tangle of lacy petticoats—too much expensive lace for a mere scullery maid.

This time his hands came up empty. He peered deeper. The witchlight retreated rapidly.

Should he follow?

"Who was with you?" Jack demanded angrily.

The maid continued to eye the king while patting and shifting her clothing. She giggled as Queen Mikka possessively brushed dust off her husband's tunic. Darville did not look overly distressed at the attention of two attractive women.

"Why, no one, My Lord," the maid replied. She preened and fussed with her mussed gown, making certain Jack saw how low her bodice dipped.

The king kept his eyes discreetly on his wife's face.

"Don't lie, girl. I saw the witchlight within the torch." Jack advanced on the girl until his sword tip touched her throat just below the chin. He hated using violence to intimidate the truth out of her, yet he knew of no other safe way to interrogate her. She'd report magic coercion to the Gnuls and the Council of Provinces.

"Witchlight!" she gasped, crossing herself, then making the older warding gesture of right wrist crossed over left and flapping her hands—a symbolic banning of Simurgh, the ancient winged demon who thrived upon blood. "I never . . . He never . . ." She drifted off into panicky choking noises as she looked pleadingly at Jack and then at the king. "He said we'd just listen . . . gather gossip . . . harmless, he said . . ." the maid stammered her explanation.

"I'll send Sergeant Fred to search the tunnels from both ends," Darville said as he marched toward the door, pointedly keeping his back to the maid. He tried the door.

It resisted.

He turned the key.

It still wouldn't budge.

He looked at Jack, lifting one eyebrow again in a maddening gesture.

Jack blinked hastily, three times and recited the trigger words that would remove the locking spell, hoping the maid was too concerned with her own hysteria and Jack's sword point to notice the delay.

The door flew open at Darville's touch. Three more guards, led by Fred, almost fell into the room, swords and daggers drawn. Three steps, two turns, double over, and balance on one foot. The maid dove into their clumsy dance for balance, further upsetting them. More laughter and delay.

She knew more than she admitted.

"A little late, aren't you, Sergeant?" Jack said, working his cheeks to keep from laughing at their antics.

"Fred, take one man into the tunnels and search for anyone who might have carried a torch of witch-light within the past few moments. And you." Darville thrust the maid into the all too willing arms of the third guard. "Take her to an interrogation room. No one talks to her until I get there. No one. Do you hear me?"

The guard gulped and nodded. His fair skin turned blotchy red in embarrassment.

"I didn't mean no harm . . . only gossip about Lady Ariiell being in the family way. No harm in gossip," the maid protested as the guard dragged her from the room.

"And dispatch some men to search the tunnels from the barracks end and the cove three islands over where His Grace keeps his private boat," Jack added. No doubt the listener had brought the maid along so that she would be caught while he escaped.

The soldiers scrambled to obey Jack's orders as if he were the lieutenant and not merely a new recruit.

Jack smiled to himself. Authority came from within and not from a rank arbitrarily assigned. That had been one of the hardest lessons he'd had to learn.

When the room cleared again and the desk closed, King Darville sat down heavily in the window seat. Mikka curled up against him, like a cat seeking a lap in the waning sunlight. "I am tired of all these plots," Darville said upon a weary sigh. "Let's put your plan into effect as soon as possible. I think we need to summon Jaylor," he said while leaning his head back against the precious glass covering of the window.

"My thoughts exactly," Mikka added, stroking her husband's cheek. The she touched her abdomen, just above her womb, where she had carried five babes and lost all of them before they quickened. "I am willing to share this body only with the children my husband and I conceive out of love. The cat has to go. I have long lost all affection for the pet I once considered the other half of myself."

"I'll need at least three other master magicians, two purple dragons, and you, Your Grace, in the clearing on Sacred Isle tonight as the moon crests the oak trees."

"And is my presence required?" Darville asked. Again that half-ironic gesture of one raised eyebrow.

"Advisable, but not required."

"Is the clearing large enough to accommodate all of those you do require. You must include Shayla in your entourage. I cannot imagine the mother dragon allowing you to play with two of her precious babies without her. And Brevelan, too. She won't want to miss something this big involving her best friend, her husband, and *her* dragons," Mikka added with a smile. She and Darville had shared a number of adventures with Jaylor and Brevelan before duty and responsibility had weighed so heavily upon all their shoulders.

"We may be a bit crowded," Jack admitted. "But I believe Brevelan must stay home tonight. She's expecting again, very soon."

"Yes, she is. Twins this time, I believe." Mikka looked at her hands where she plucked at the satiny texture of her brocade gown. "Even for my best friend, I will not postpone this ceremony. We will have to perform it without Brevelan's supervision."

"Lock the door again and armor the desk against eavesdropping." Darville roused from his seat, leaving his wife there to stare at her own inner thoughts. "Send your summons to Jaylor from here."

"Should be the safest place in the palace for a while. The man with the witchlight speeding away from here should draw the witch-sniffers after him." Jack pulled energy from the nearest ley line to fuel his spells. The magic tingled through his body in welcome waves. He drank it in, relishing the power that fed his talent and energized his mind. The pattern of tingles was different from dragon magic, but more familiar. He knew how to mold this power precisely.

Besides he didn't have a purple-tipped dragon at his fingertips to give him power.

If he'd been able to gather dragon magic from the air, he'd have been accepted by the University and Commune as a child. But if he'd been accepted and nurtured, he'd not have learned the strength and resilience his adventures had taught him. He'd not have met Katrina, or found the lair of the dragons to bring them home.

Katrina wouldn't be planning their wedding for tomorrow if . . .

Breathing deeply in the early stages of a trance, he set a candle upon the desk and sat in the king's chair. He couldn't settle comfortably in the furniture custom-made for the tall and lanky man who paced the room like a caged wolf. Jack moved to the smaller visitor's chair. It wasn't exactly comfortable either, made that way to discourage visitors from lingering unnecessarily. But the size was better suited to Jack's shorter, stockier figure.

Only then did he retrieve a special shard of glass hidden deep within his scrip. Possession of the precious and rare piece marked him as a magician. As a master magician, he was entitled to a much larger, gold-framed piece. Even journeymen used a larger piece than this. But they were harder to hide. And other than an occasional summons to Jaylor, or a bubble of armor to ensure privacy, he wasn't supposed to work any magic while in the capital.

A middling trance settled on his mind. His eyes crossed slightly, and the flame doubled and wavered in his sight. He looked through the glass into the flame.

"Flame to flame, glass to glass, like seeking like, follow my thoughts to the one I seek," he murmured in a singsong. His talent flew along the path of his chant through the glass into the flame. In his mind he watched a tiny flamelet jump from the candle, fly along the desk, drop to the floor and travel along the carpet without igniting the fibers.

King Darville watched the candle, oblivious to the movement of the ghostly flame. It traveled to Mikka's gown, across her lap, and out the closed window in the space of three heartbeats. The queen shifted position restlessly three times during that brief moment. Her own magical talent might make her aware of the spell, but she couldn't participate.

Jack breathed easily again when the flame passed onto the roof of the wing below the study tower. In his mind he followed the tiny spark on its journey far to the South. It gained speed as it traversed the land, uphill, jumping rivers and creeks, through forests, over pastures and plowed fields. At last, it found a nameless little village perched on a cliff above a treacherous cove. It paused a moment as if catching a breath near the triple festival pylon, still decorated with flowers, new foliage, and grasses from the Spring celebrations. Then off again, steeply uphill along a narrow but well-trodden path. At the boulder split by a tree, the path seemed to pass to the left. Jack's mind and the flamelet pressed to the right. He saw the iridescent shimmer of the magical barrier that protected Brevelan's clearing. No human could pass through this barrier without Brevelan's or Jaylor's express wish. But the flame did not live, and Jack's body remained in Coronnan City.

A sudden thrumming in Jack's mind told him the flame had found a piece of glass and sent a signal to the owner that a summons awaited. The vibration of the signal set Jack's teeth on edge. It had set his fingers twitching before a second flame appeared in his glass. Then Jaylor's familiar face emerged, as close and clear as if he sat on the opposite side of the desk.

"What?" Jaylor asked abruptly. His gaze wandered to his left and stayed there. Worry shadowed his eyes and drew his mouth into a deep frown. His beard looked untrimmed, and his hair had pulled loose from his queue restraint.

"Jaylor, I have a solution and need help. Shayla has agreed to meet us with the twin purple-tips on Sacred Isle tonight," Jack replied. Jaylor's distraction worried him. The Senior Magician of the Commune did not allow his students anything but full concentration on any spell and taught by example.

"Not tonight. No time." Jaylor raised his hand in the time-honored signal that he closed the communication.

"But it has to be tonight!" Otherwise Katrina might find another excuse to delay their wedding.

Otherwise Ariiell and Laislac might find a way to grab the position of heir to the throne.

"Not tonight. Brevelan is in labor. It's not going well. I can't leave her, and I won't delegate this chore."

"What's wrong?" Darville asked. "Tell him we can go to the clearing instead of to Sacred Isle. Tell him about the eavesdroppers. Tell him that Mikka . . ."

"Do you want to do this?" Jack looked at his king, slightly exasperated.

"You know I can't. Tell him . . ."

"Jaylor, we can come to the clearing. I can transport Their Graces and Katrina and myself."

"Not tonight!" Jaylor nearly screamed. Then he took a deep breath, composing himself. "Give us three days to recover from the birth. Then we will meet you in Shayla's lair. All of us." He ended the summons abruptly.

"I'd better tell Katrina she has a three-day reprieve," Jack murmured sadly. Three days for her to think up new excuses for delay.

Suddenly, he knew she did not need the three days to find an excuse. She'd make one of her own today.

Without bothering to extinguish the candle or take leave of his king, Jack pelted out of the room, down the stairs, across three corridors, and out into the sunny courtyard where she usually worked. He gasped for breath, seeking a trace of her presence.

Gone. Lace pillow, patterns, and herself. She might never have been here an hour ago when he left her. The ragged wall still showed marks from Amaranth's talons. Jack hadn't dreamed Katrina's agreement to marry. She had promised.

Where would she go?

Back inside, he traced the route to the honored servants' quarters where she slept or sometimes worked by rushlight when rain threatened.

Not a cloud in the sky, he thought to himself. *Why would she retreat indoors on such a fine day? Not too hot, nor too windy. The sun will shine another candle mark at least.*

The other servants nodded to him as he passed, a now-familiar presence in the palace, as was Katrina. He paused outside her door. He knocked quietly. The door swung open at his first touch.

He knew before he looked with his eyes that the room was empty. It looked as if she had never been there.

Gone.

Pillows, lace, patterns, her clothes, and the little trinkets he'd given her to make the stark room a home.

Gone.

He searched the wardrobe, the chest at the foot of the bed, beneath the bed. She had taken the magical lace shawl they'd used to patch Shayla's wing. Katrina had planned to use the airy lace as her wedding veil.

Perhaps she had merely gone to the dressmaker for her wedding gown.

But he knew she had fled.

She'd run away rather than marry him. Run into danger from the Gnuls, and he couldn't protect her.

CHAPTER 17

Vareena picked her way over the muddy paths that wound through the village. Rain had made the packed dirt slick and left puddles in every indentation. The Summer sun had not climbed high enough to remove the shadows and evaporate the water. The haze that shrouded the monastery seemed to be spreading.

What would happen to her village if the gloaming spread here and deprived them all of light, distorted time, and trapped them forever? She'd never break free, trade caravans would cease coming . . . They'd all become ghosts.

She shuddered and wished she were back in bed where she could pull the blankets over her head and pretend none of this was happening.

But the baker's son had burned his hand and arm badly, stoking the fire beneath the huge bread oven. Cold water and lard had not eased the boy's pain, so the family had summoned Vareena out of her warm bed.

She'd have liked to take her time gathering the eggs herself and preparing breakfast for her brothers. Her chickens never pecked her when she reached for their treasures. She sang soothing songs to them, talked to them, treated them as important assets to the farm. They responded in kind.

"What kept you?" snarled the baker's wife. She thrust her hands behind her back, crossing her wrists and flapping her hands. The old ward could not keep Vareena from entering the cottage. The huge mud-

and-brick oven that served the entire village heated the place almost beyond tolerance in this bright Summer weather.

A low moan coming from behind the curtain at the back of the low-ceilinged room grabbed Vareena's attention. Rather than reply to the surly woman, so typical of the villagers, Vareena thrust her way past her. She tore aside the curtain to the dark lean-to that normally contained firewood and food stores for the family.

The baker had set his son Jeeremy on a rough pallet here before returning to his oven. From the grimace of pain that crossed the boy's face, Vareena guessed he had been unable to climb the ladder into the sleeping loft above the cottage's only room.

"What witchcraft you gonna work on my boy?" the baker's wife demanded as she inserted herself between Vareena and her son.

"No witchcraft," Vareena replied, holding herself rigid rather than flinging herself out of the cottage without so much as looking at the boy. The ghosts might trap her in this hated place, but they at least appreciated her, thanked her for the small services she gave them.

"I'll have no witchery, Vareena. Headman's daughter you might be, but I don't have to tolerate your evil ways."

"If you do not want me to heal your son, why did you send for me?"

"Baker made me send for you. He needs the boy up and working, not languishing here screaming his heart out. Had I my way, I'd have treated him myself and let him heal slow. Burns heal better slow."

Jeeremy did not seem to be screaming, merely moaning. His pain reached out and squeezed Vareena's heart. She couldn't abandon him because of his mother's rude intolerance.

"I have a salve made of barks and berries," Vareena said quietly through her clamped teeth. "But first I must cleanse the burn of the lard you slathered on. That might have cooled it a little at first, but such a treatment offers no lasting relief."

"You saying I don't know what is best for my boy?" The woman's voice rose to near hysteria.

"I'll fetch some water." Vareena ducked out of the dark and dusty lean-to rather than issue the angry retort that nearly choked her.

Outside the cottage she breathed deeply, holding each breath within her lungs before letting it out. The cool morning breeze taunted her with hints of other places it had visited before blowing here. It tasted cool and tangy, like salt, everblue trees, and rich loamy dirt. Bits of the mist and haze scattered to reveal patches of blue sky.

A tear stung her eyes. If only she could follow the breeze wherever it led her. She clutched the silver-and-amethyst amulet beneath her shift. If only she could claim the acres Farrell had bequeathed her. If only she and Robb could leave this place together. If only . . .

But none of that would happen. She had to fetch fresh well water and tend to Jeeremy's burns under the hostile stare of his mother. Then she had to take fresh food up to her ghosts. Tomorrow and the next day and the next promised her no difference in her routine. Her freedom fled with the breeze.

*   *   *

They think to keep me in darkness. But I do not need light. I need only my magic to keep safe what is mine. The kardiaquake did not stop them. The nightmares did not stop them. I must try something else. As I send out my senses, seeking another diversion, I see others gathering. They come from many directions. Diverse people with different priorities and warring ideals. An idea planted here. A whisper there.

Soon they will fight among themselves rather than bother with me and mine.

* * *

"Just hold that lace pillow nice and gentle, Lady, while I strap it on tight," Zebbiah said.

The nameless woman did so while she took one last look at the palace where she had wandered aimlessly for . . . at least five days before she awakened and two days since then.

"Zebbiah, do you think I have the right to give myself a name, since neither you nor my daughter remembers my true name?" she asked intently.

Yesterday, while she'd packed the lace, he and Jaranda had scavenged food and other journey supplies. They had tried to leave at dawn as planned. An explosion outside the palace walls had frightened the pack beast. It sat and brayed as if in pain for a long time. It did not understand that the terrible noise was probably only someone clearing rubble. The beast would not rise again, no matter the enticement or provocation, for almost two hours until the city that surrounded them on three sides had quieted.

Now they seemed about to set forth. Into danger? Perhaps only adventure. But she still had no idea who she was or why she and her daughter had been abandoned in the palace. Something about her daughter having red hair rather than the blonde of a trueblood?

"Choose whatever name you like, Lady," Zebbiah said as he secured more straps on his pack beast. The obnoxious creature let out a mournful bray, extending its neck and laying back its ears as the Rover cinched the girth strap tighter. It shifted its rear hooves restlessly. Both the Rover and the woman moved out of range of those dangerous feet.

It kicked back once and arched its back. But since it had not connected with anything, or anyone, it settled again.

"I'll think about a name as we walk to the docks. Are you certain the ferries are still running upriver?"

The traffic on the river she had observed from the palace windows was sporadic at best.

"Sure as sure. My uncle's cousin's nephew has a boat waiting for me. We can pay them with that linen doily you found tucked inside your favorite pillow," he answered, still concentrating on the packing. "Lace still has some value here, mostly to people trading outland, but hard work and sharp weapons have more. We'll save the Tambrin lace for trade in Coronnan."

From the palace windows she had watched the river. Some people left on outland barges, others moved back into the city in small groups. In the city, she had watched a few people trying to clear away rubble and start new buildings, others attempted to rebuild their damaged homes and businesses. No one stopped the looters, or bully gangs that robbed at will. No one traveled alone. Almost everyone, men, women, and children, carried weapons.

She knew that was wrong. Weapons had no place in this peaceful city. She had never carried a weapon, wouldn't know how to use one if she had. What little crime prowled around the edges of civilization should be handled by the city guard—or in extreme cases by . . . She couldn't remember who judged the more serious crimes, only that a feared authority existed.

None of the returning citizens or gangs came near the palace. No one came to check on the unnamed woman and her child who had been abandoned in the palace—except this itinerant trader. She trusted his strong arms and his politeness. Mostly she trusted his greed. He could have stolen the lace and sold it outland at a profit. But that would be the end of that market. By taking her under his wing, he guaranteed a continuing supply of lace. As long as she gave him a valuable product to sell, he would protect her and her daughter.

"Have an eye to everything around you as we walk, Lady. I don't think anyone will accost you on the way. Rovers still have a reputation in this land." He flashed her a smile that bordered on vicious. "I'd like to concentrate on protecting the beast and the lace. So keep one eye on your daughter and the other on everyone and everything around you. Once aboard the ferry, my people will keep you from harm."

As if to emphasize his warning, the sounds of harsh words, blows exchanged, a scream, and running feet came from just outside the walls.

The woman shuddered and closed her eyes a moment. Her people should be working together to rebuild, not fighting and stealing.

"And these relatives of yours will take us all the way to the headwaters of the River Lenicc? All the way to safety."

"He said so. There's a caravan gathering to go over the pass into Coronnan. We'll be safe with them, but we have to get going. The journey is long. As it is, we might have to spend the Winter in an abandoned monastery I know of on the other side of the pass. Find your daughter, Lady, and let us leave."

The ground shook once again as if to emphasize his order. The roof above the lace workroom collapsed, sending bricks and beams spraying over the courtyard. Zebbiah crouched down with his arms over his head and neck until the avalanche of debris ceased.

"Jaranda!" the woman screamed. "Where are you, baby?" Panic filled her heart.

The pack beast brayed again in protest at the disruption. It kicked out and then threatened to park its rear end down on the cobbles.

Zebbiah cursed and kicked the creature to keep it on its feet.

"Jaranda!" she called again. She whirled about, desperately seeking a sign of her child.

"Here I am, M'ma." The little girl skipped over loose cobblestones and fallen bricks from the far side of the courtyard, seemingly unconcerned despite the recent danger. She bounced a ball from the royal nursery.

The woman nearly sagged with relief. She crouched down and hugged her daughter close.

"Lady, you have never questioned traveling so far with me. You, a woman alone and unprotected. Me, a man you don't know, have no reason to trust."

"You have not given me a reason not to trust you. As you said, prejudices must be learned. I have forgotten everything."

They stared at each other for a long silent moment, assessing, weighing, enjoying.

He looked away first.

"Jaranda, my love, I think I would like the name, Trizia. Do you like that name? It means noble lady." She pulled the little girl against her leg in a fierce hug, unwilling to let her stray again, even for a moment.

"You are M'ma," the little girl insisted. She stamped her foot in irritation. "M'ma."

"Trizia doesn't fit," Zebbiah added. He yanked the pack beast's halter to start it moving.

"I thought you'd say that."

* * *

"Twelve, thirteen, fourteen," Marcus counted out loud the number of bags of gold on the first bank of shelves.

He counted because Robb had told him to count. He could not think beyond the straight sequence of numbers, could not plan. If he stopped counting, he'd fall into deep despair.

Yet the more he counted, the heavier he felt. Each movement and thought became an effort. The gloaming pressed against all of his senses. Soon he'd not be able to hold his head up, stand, talk, eat.

"Fifteen, sixteen, seventeen." He gulped back a sob.

The monastery trapped them. His luck and his magic had drained out of him. The future looked hopeless.

"Snap out of it, Marcus," Robb barked. He spoke slowly as if he, too, swam through the thick air.

"It all seems so hopeless." Marcus rubbed two gold coins together in his pocket while he paused. "All this gold stashed away, gathering dust. It could be put to such good use—rebuilding the University, stabilizing the economy, increasing trade."

"Bribing nobles to make magic legal again," Robb added with a grin. But his smile looked false. As false as the hazy light that dominated the entire monastery.

"And the gold just sits here! And we can't get out to put it to use."

"Every bit of information we gather is a step toward finding an exit." Robb placed a comforting hand upon Marcus' shoulder. "We're magicians, trained to think, to plan, and solve problems. We can't always trust in luck. If we plan it right, we'll get out of here."

Warmth and reassurance spread from Robb's touch. Marcus absorbed it, fighting for a small glimmer of hope.

"We've got to make our own luck, Marcus. Maybe there is significance in the number and arrangement of bags. Perhaps these isolated shelves in the center of the room mask an exit we haven't discovered yet. We won't know until we investigate."

"What is happening to us, Robb? I'm supposed to be the one who gives you cheer and encouragement. That's why we work so well together. You think, I plow forward with infinite optimism, making up the plan as we go." Marcus covered his friend's hand on his shoulder with his own and squeezed to show his undying friendship—even in this terrible time.

"We've been in worse scrapes before. Remember that time in Hanic when that farmer caught us hiding in his byre with his daughter. He chased us bare-assed through his fields for almost a quarter league before we got our wits together enough to throw up magical armor?" They both chuckled at the memory. "Think about something pleasant for a while, rather than what we can't do. Think about Margit. Margit always brings a smile to your face."

"Margit." Marcus tried to conjure her image in his mind's eye. Bold and forthright, she had a minor magical talent and had used it in good stead as Jaylor's spy in the royal household. Her dark blonde braids bounced with life as she strode strongly through each task.

But she hated living indoors. And she hated cats; said they robbed her breath. When Marcus had seen her last, she had not known the nature of Queen Rossemikka's problem—that a cat spirit shared her body.

But she had known her own heart and pledged it to Marcus.

A daintier blonde, more mature, milder of temperament and smaller of body superimposed herself upon Marcus' inner vision.

Vareena.

"I bet Vareena likes cats as much as I do," he said to himself.

He shook his head to clear it.

"I wonder if Jaylor has found a solution to the queen's problem?" he mused rather than admit his sense of guilt and betrayal of Margit. He'd loved her and been faithful to her for two years and more. He'd never loved anyone for that long before.

"We won't know what is going on in the capital or the University until we find a way to break the spell trapping us. Now count the bags. Count the pattern of their arrangement. Count the coins themselves."

"And what will you be doing while I count?"

"Counting the graves of the ghosts. Searching the temple foundation stones for another exit. I have this odd feeling that something is missing. Something I should have noticed."

Robb turned to retreat from the bookless library and froze in his tracks.

Alerted to danger, Marcus opened his senses and stared in the direction Robb looked—toward the back of the room into deep shadows from the overhanging gallery and more empty shelves.

And something else. A glittering mist that gathered and coalesced into a vague human shape. Dressed in old-fashioned robes of gold and brown, the figure carried a bloody sacrificial knife and a magician's staff.

"Do you see what I see?" Robb whispered.

"I hope I don't. That . . . that looks like a ghost. A real ghost." His balance and perceptions twisted. He stumbled and clutched the gold-laden shelves for balance.

"That ghost looks very angry indeed!" Robb wasn't standing easy on the rolling floor either.

"Run!"

CHAPTER 18

Marcus skidded to a halt on the slick paving stones at the end of the colonnade. He had to bend over to catch his breath. Still, icy bugs seemed to climb his spine. He imagined the ghost slicing into his back from the base of his spine upward.

Robb careened into him. They looked at each other, eyes wide. Marcus' heart beat loudly in his ears.

Without a word spoken, they took off again, away from the buildings toward the graveyard and the foundations for the old temple.

Vareena stood just inside the gates, holding a covered basket—probably full of food.

"What ails you, Marcus, Robb?" Vareena gasped, clutching her throat in alarm.

"A—g—gho–ghost!" Marcus panted. He leaned heavily against the gatehouse wall as he drew in deep draughts of air.

"But you are the ghosts here. No one else," she protested. She furrowed her brow in puzzlement, tilting her adorable little nose down.

Marcus reached out to smooth tight worry lines from her face. A barrier of burning energy repulsed his hand. He clenched it into a fist instead.

"We. Are. Not. Ghosts," Robb stated breathlessly. "We did not die, leaving our spirits behind."

"You only forget your passing, Robb. You are both truly ghosts," Vareena insisted.

"No, we aren't," Marcus agreed with his friend. "That—thing—haunting the library is a real ghost.

And it is royally pissed . . . um . . . I mean perturbed by our presence."

"If there is truly another ghost in this place, why have I not sensed his presence? Why have I not seen him in all these past twenty years? I assure you, you two are the only ghosts currently residing here." She placed her hands upon her hips and pursed her lips as if reprimanding errant children.

"I beg to differ, my dear." Robb assumed his normal preaching tone, so obviously missing earlier today. "The entity we encountered in the library has most certainly staked a claim there. You admitted that you had not explored any part of the monastery other than the rooms occupied by your guests. The villagers shun the place unless required by you to make repairs, and even then they usually restrict themselves to the residential wing. Why should anyone have disturbed that thing other than your other guests who examined the building out of boredom, or seeking an exit. I can only presume they, too, were frightened away by this true ghost and did not explore further. Therefore, I must conclude that the answer to our quest for escape lies within the library." Robb finally paused to breathe.

"I am not going back to that library!" Marcus trembled. "It wanted to carve out my heart with that sacrificial knife. Didn't you see how much blood it dripped, how it reeked of the grave, and carried the chill of the void between existences?" Had he truly felt all that, or had his imagination filled in the gaps from old stories passed around apprentice dormitories late at night on Saawheen Eve?

"Yes, I did see all that and felt the same unnatural chill," Robb said thoughtfully, tapping his teeth. He began to pace a serpentine path around Marcus and Vareena. "That is how I know it to be a true ghost."

"A ghost is a ghost!" Vareena protested. "I shall prove it to you. You two are the only ghosts here."

She set down her basket, pushed past the two magicians, and marched back along the colonnade toward the library. Her footsteps echoed against the flagstones.

Marcus suddenly realized that he and Robb made no noise as they moved about the old place. Their boots with sturdy leather soles and hard wooden heels should clomp noisily with every step.

The gloaming seemed to absorb the sounds of their passing. He wondered if they stood on the edge of the void between the planes of existence. The sense-robbing blackness of the void when one first entered could also rob a man of his sanity if he did not have a purpose, a question to ask. Only when he held that purpose or question firmly in his mind did the multi-colored umbilicals of life become visible. If one had patience and courage, a man could sort through the life forces that surrounded him in the void that represented all those important to him in reality.

Perhaps . . . If he could summon enough magic for a trip into the void, he could find a way home.

"Robb." He stopped his friend from following Vareena with a hand upon his shoulder. No barrier of energy repulsed his touch as it did with Vareena. "Robb, maybe we are ghosts of a sort. Our boots make no noise, we can touch each other but not her. Perhaps we are at the edge . . ."

"True. Our condition is not normal. But we cannot pass through walls, we require food and drink—we both eliminate bodily wastes regularly. And we have no memory of injury or death. None of that indicates that we have left our bodies behind as we would in death or on a trip through the void. We have bodies. We just aren't truly in one reality or another, but trapped halfway between."

"Isn't that what happens to a ghost? His body is in one reality and his spirit in another."

"Our spirits and bodies remain intact. 'Tis reality around us that wavers."

"You've got a point there. Let's follow and see what Vareena conjurs up in the library."

"An apt description, I believe."

Together they caught up with Vareena as she pushed open the door to the library.

"I don't remember closing the door. Did you close it, Robb?"

Robb shook his head and scrunched his face in a puzzled frown. "I believe the ghost wishes to be left alone."

Marcus tasted the air with his magical senses. Dust, mold, stone older than time, staleness, and . . . and something sour tingling on his tongue that did not belong there.

"It's waiting for us," he whispered.

"Stuff and nonsense. I'd know if another ghost had come here. I'm a sensitive." Vareena resolutely pushed the door open and stepped into the vast room. "Yoohooo! Anybody home?"

Her words echoed around the nearly empty room. Silence followed.

Marcus and Robb poked their heads around the door, Robb above, Marcus slightly stooped. Diffuse sunlight filtered through the dust in broken shafts. "The dust should have settled by now. There isn't a breeze to stir it," Marcus whispered.

"I know," Robb replied.

"Look for the sparkles, for movement."

Vareena walked around the free-standing book-shelves. Her skirts raised clouds of dust in her wake. It swirled and eddied, drifting to new locations. But none of her dust stayed in the air more than a moment or two.

The other dust—the stuff that lingered in the corner far away from her circuitous path—took on a vaguely human shape, the glint of red and metal showed the knife now tucked into his old-fashioned belt sash over yellow tunic and orange sleeveless robe. Brown trews and boots faded into the shadows, making him look almost legless. He made mocking faces at Vareena, waving his arms in a parody of drawing attention to himself.

Eventually, Vareena climbed the spiral staircase to the second-floor gallery. The gloating dust followed her only within touching distance of the cold iron structure. Then it jerked back as if burned.

"Behind you," Marcus hissed at her.

"What?" Vareena turned on the sixth step, looking over her shoulder at them.

"The ghost. In the dust. Behind you." Marcus held his breath, not daring to come closer, yet fearful for her well-being.

"I see nothing." Firmly she marched up the stairs.

"She didn't even look," Robb protested.

"Perhaps she truly cannot see this ghost. Her sensitivities are limited, as is her magic."

"I wonder if all of her other ghosts have been mundane," Robb mused.

"If so, they might not have seen this ghost. If mundanes couldn't find a way out, perhaps the solution lies in magic." Hope brightened Marcus' heart for the first time since coming here.

"But our magic has become quite limited by whatever force holds us here. Without a dragon to combine and enhance our powers, we may not have enough magic to break the spell."

* * *

Ariiell loosened the ties of her gown and shifted the pillows behind her back. She sighed at the relief of pressure on her swelling belly.

Outside her bedchamber her father and stepmother continued to argue over her plight. Her father's second wife wept more than she spoke. "Think of the disgrace of bringing that monster into our family. Everyone will know 'tis not a love match. 'Tis not even a good political move." Lady Laislac choked out the words between sobs. "Better we send her to a convent overseas for a year and foster the baby elsewhere. It's likely to be as hideous as the father."

Ariiell frowned. Her stepmother repeated some of the arguments Ariiell had put forth against the marriage to Mardall. Arguments she expected and hoped to lose.

"My honor is as much at stake as the girl's. She'll never be able to make a more advantageous marriage. Whoever we pawn her off on will know she's not a virgin and will renounce the marriage on the wedding night." Lord Laislac's boots pounded the floor rushes into a distinctive path from his repetitive pacing.

Her father always won family arguments regardless of the wisdom or rightness of his position.

The best way for Ariiell to get what she wanted was to counter her father with the opposite of her goal. In four years of marriage, her stepmother had never learned that little trick. Her father's wife deserved the unhappiness Lord Laislac dealt her every day.

"To bring that . . . that thing into the family!"

"That *thing* is blood heir to the throne," Ariiell's father reminded his wife.

"Precisely," Ariiell whispered to herself. "Mardall will never take the throne. But as long as Queen Rossemikka remains barren, my child is next in line." She smiled hugely, rubbing her tummy.

The baby kicked in response to the slight pressure. A good sign of the child's health and vigor. Her mentor had promised the child would be normal.

"I will be the mother of the next king of Coronnan," she whispered to herself. No sense in losing the battle with her father by stating the truth. "As soon as the marriage takes place and the child is declared legitimate, I must find a way to eliminate Darville. I'll certainly be more successful than those idiots from the coven and the Gnuls who have bungled every attempt these last three years."

She reached beneath the mattress for the book of poisons she had recently acquired. She wasn't supposed to be able to read—no person other than the now outlawed magicians were allowed to learn the arcane art of reading and higher mathematics. But Ariiell had watched the family magician priest as he sounded out the letters and words on letters and reports. The priest was supposed to consign written communications to the fire as soon as he read them to the lord. A little sleight of hand had brought most of those messages into Ariiell's possession.

Careful study had brought the words to life.

So now she plotted out ways to coat the inside of Darville's riding gloves with a fast-acting poison. She'd need time to gather all the necessary ingredients. Time to insert herself into court life. After the wedding.

By this time next year, she intended to be regent for her infant son and the coven.

Earlier today, her guardian from the coven had tried another assassination upon the king. But this one was intended to fail. The coven needed Darville alive until Ariiell's child was born. But they needed him frightened of dying without an heir so that he would name Ariiell's child as next in succession. The man must have failed. He hadn't reported back to her, and the king had not sent word to hasten the marriage.

Time for a change of tactics. In a few hours she'd summon her nameless guardian and give him a new task—the poison ingredients would work just as well on Queen Rossemikka.

* * *

"I think I have a problem, Jaylor. I can't throw the spell. I can't come to the lair in three days or even tonight." Jack schooled his voice and his face to slip through the summons spell on a note of calm. Panic gibbered inside him, demanding he pace, he pound, he seek Katrina in any way possible. He'd even travel into the void by himself, without an anchor, in order to find her.

He sent this summons alone, deep in the night. As he had always been alone. He'd hoped Katrina would be the one to fill the aching void in his life. Now she was gone, too!

He intended to fight to bring her back.

Moonlight filtered through the rare glass window of the king's study tower. Hours of searching had resulted in no new information as to Katrina's direction or means of transportation. The scrying bowl had revealed only that she fled away from him.

The king had had less luck in interrogating the scullery maid from the tunnel. She had disappeared from her locked room before anyone could question her, and no one from the kitchen remembered her ever working there. And yet Jack knew he'd seen her there just the day before . . . a puzzle he did not have time for.

Jack's only hope of finding his beloved lay in Katrina's lack of magical talent. She couldn't transport herself and had to travel on foot or steedback. She'd not get beyond the reach of his transport spell. But he had to have a landmark, something recognizable to home in on.

And every minute he prayed that the Gnuls had not captured her. Their witch-sniffers had ways of shielding their prisoners from searches conducted by mundanes and magicians alike—much as Journeymen Marcus and Robb had disappeared some moons ago.

He wouldn't think about that. He knew he could find Katrina anywhere, any time, once he calmed down. Their souls were linked. His last journey through the void had shown him how the white and gold of her life force had entwined with his silver and purple.

"Calm down, Jack," Jaylor ordered. "What happened?" He looked more relaxed and coherent than the last time Jack had summoned him. The twin girls had made their entrance into the world. One came screaming, kicking, and protesting the transition. The other was much smaller and more placid, almost listless. Not all of Jaylor's worries had ended, just the worst of them. Brevelan and the new babies slept . . . for the moment.

Jack took three deep breaths, almost triggering a deeper trance that would take him into the void then and there. A haunting *Song* drifted through the blackness of the void, tempting him.

(Answers can be found in the void. Are you ready to learn and accept what you find, pleasant or distressful?) Baamin asked. In his current existence Baamin wore magician blue on the tips of his dragon wings. He had befriended Jack more than once.

Jack couldn't see the wise dragon at the moment, but would recognize his voice anywhere.

He held himself tightly to this world.

"Talk to me, Jack. Don't revert to your old habits of silence. In this case, keeping your mouth shut will not solve the problem," Jaylor coaxed. He'd known Jack when he was a nameless kitchen drudge. He'd stood by Jack when he became an arrogant apprentice magician who chose the magnificent name Yaakke out of history. But Jaylor was not there when Jack had to live up to the name he chose. Jack had learned most painfully that the humbler shortening of the name suited him much better. Jaylor could not know how important Katrina had been to his survival through that long and grueling process.

"She's gone," Jack choked out. Slowly, he found the words to explain how and why Katrina had fled rather than face the intimacy of marriage. "I have to bring her back!"

"You need to follow her, certainly," Jaylor replied. "But believe me, you can't force her to come back to you. All you can do is wait patiently by her side and allow her to make the first move." The Senior Magician smiled. His attention drifted as if he remembered something wonderful.

Jack had to remind himself that Jaylor might hold authority over all members of the Commune of Magicians, but he was only a few years older than Jack. And a new father, for the third and fourth time. Balladeers had been singing of his deep and abiding love for Brevelan for four years now.

"Then I'll follow Katrina now."

"No. You will complete your duty to Coronnan, the Commune, and our king! That is our oath as members of the Commune."

Jack's sense of duty to Coronnan, Commune, and king had seen him through years of slavery, terrible dangers, and persecution. It had brought him many rewards, including Katrina's love.

"She's not safe. I can't fulfill my duties to anyone as long as she's in danger."

"I'll send Margit to catch up with her. My apprentice is most anxious to get out in the world. She says that she finds life at the University or at court stifling—she can't breathe properly indoors. But I suspect much of her anxiety centers around the missing Marcus and Robb—Marcus in particular."

"Margit has no training. The only spell she can work is a weak summons. How can she protect Katrina?"

"Margit has learned a lot in the last few moons, and as long as her breathing isn't stifled while indoors, she does have more magic than we thought. She's the best person to be with Katrina right now. They are the same age. They are both in love and having difficulty with the relationship. Margit can talk to her. They can share female secrets, where a man will just frighten your ladylove."

"But . . ."

"No buts. Do your research and planning. Then transport Mikka and Darville to the lair three days hence."

"But . . ."

Jaylor broke off the summons.

Jack slumped against the king's desk. His spine no longer had the stiffness to hold him up.

"Be safe, Katrina. Be safe until I can come to you."

CHAPTER 19

"But I haven't finished writing the paper you re-quested," Margit half-protested Jaylor's excit-ing news. Dawn had barely crested the horizon. She hadn't expected anyone to be out and about so early. The Senior Magician had surprised her in her favorite study perch in an oak tree on the edge of the University compound.

A quest! A chance to journey like a true journeyman . . . er—journeywoman. Could she be con-sidered a journeywoman if she had not undergone the trial by Tambootie smoke?

She both dreaded and welcomed the ritual. Well . . . she welcomed the advancement the ritual offered. But to endure three days in a windowless room, the only door sealed by magic, with only a Tambootie wood fire for light and warmth, strapping huge bands of pressure around her lungs, squeezing the breath from her. Rumor—almost legend—proclaimed that when Jaylor had undergone the trial, the master magicians had had to battle the demons he conjured for three days before sending them back beyond the void.

To be trapped in the room for three days would be bad enough. To be trapped with the monsters of her worst nightmares would kill her. She'd die of suffoca-tion before the monsters could take form.

"Have you finished the research for the paper?" Jaylor asked. He kept looking back toward the clear-ing, eyes clouded, worry making deep creases beside his mouth. Then he finger-combed his beard and turned those deep brown eyes fully on her.

Margit felt as if her skin peeled away, revealing more than just her bones and organs. Her very soul was exposed to this man. He had to know how her heart skipped a beat and pounded relentlessly, how her skin jumped and her toes wiggled, eager to begin the journey this very instant.

Her tree branch became very uncomfortable.

"I think I've read everything others have written about opposing elements and complementary elements. But I need to conduct some experiments before I can know for sure that the theory works."

"You can do that on the road. I suggest simple things like a compulsion on your steed to make it travel faster to appease Katrina's need to flee, then negate it when you find her to delay until Jack can catch up to you."

"Is this quest so very important?" She tucked her book inside her tunic and swung down to face the Senior Magician on his own level. She had to look up at the man who held her career in his hands as easily as he held the reins of the entire Commune and University. Not many men topped her by more than half a hand's span.

"I, the queen, the entire kingdom, have need of Jack's special talents and skills. He is worthless unless he knows for certain that Katrina is safe. Can you do that?" The earnestness of his question lost some of its effect as his attention wandered back to his home in the clearing.

She'd heard that one of the newborn twins was small and sickly, her sister having enough strength and energy for two. Too often, twins were born early—too early for both, or either to survive. She wished she'd paid more attention to how long Brevelan had carried the babies.

"Are Brevelan and the babies all right?" she asked, rather than speculate. The Commune thrived on rumors and gossip, most of it wrong. If the kingdom needed Jack free of concern and fully concentrating on his tasks, likewise the kingdom and the Commune needed Jaylor free of problems in his personal life.

"Nothing you need worry about. Now, have you ever scried in a bowl of water?" Jaylor avoided answering. His eyes remained fixed on the trees in the direction of his home.

"Uh . . . not officially, sir." How much experimentation should she have done on her own?

WithyReed discouraged apprentices from working any spell unless directly supervised by him. Slippy and Lyman, on the other hand, applauded initiative, even competition, among their students.

"Unofficially, then, how much success did you have?"

"None at all." Margit hung her head.

"Come into my study and show me how you worked the spell."

"Uh, can we try this out-of-doors, sir?" She stared at the closed door of his private workroom on the back side of the library. Only one entrance and one window, both facing north, toward the clearing and his beloved wife and children.

Margit didn't care which direction the openings faced. There weren't enough of them.

"Is this unnatural fear you have of being within four walls going to interfere with your ability to work magic?"

"No. I survived three years in the palace as the queen's maid."

"Survived, but did not flourish. Your magical talent has blossomed well beyond our initial test results since we brought you here. What bothers you so about being indoors?"

"There isn't enough air to breathe. Besides, you always have a cat with you. They suck out all the air in confined places."

"Cats." Jaylor stared at her long and hard. "Cats.

Very well. Fetch me the bowl on my desk and draw some fresh water from the well. We'll enjoy the sunshine under this tree. I have to admit, I prefer fresh air myself." He lifted a drooping everblue branch and ducked beneath it to the open place beside the trunk, as private a place as one could have this close to the classrooms, library, dormitories, and workrooms of the University.

"Uh, sir, wouldn't the spell work better with fresh water from a free-flowing creek and a crockery bowl rather than silver?"

"You have been studying! Amazing." He sounded very much like old Lyman. "You are correct, of course. The bowl on my desk is crockery. Take it to the creek and fill it half full. What about a crystal to trigger the spell?"

"Only if it's uncut. Otherwise, an agate works better."

"And you absorbed the entire lesson. Will miracles never cease?" he added on a chuckle. He sounded so much like Old Lyman, Margit wondered if the Commune still needed the ancient librarian now that he slept so much and avoided work even more.

A few moments later, Margit settled on the carpet of everblue needles, the bowl nestled into a little depression before her. She crossed her legs beneath her and began the deep breathing necessary to focus her concentration.

"That's it, breathe deep, one, two, three, hold on three, release on three, hold, one, two, three," Jaylor chanted quietly. "Let the light trance slide over your mind, concentrate on the water. Focus all of your senses on the water. Now think of whom you seek. Picture Katrina firmly in your mind. If you can't remember her features, think of her most dominant characteristic."

"Silver-blonde hair and a lace pillow," Margit mumbled as the picture of Katrina, the last time she had seen her, formed within her mind.

"Yes, the lace pillow. Almost inseparable from her. Now drop the agate into the center of the bowl and watch the ripples, not the agate. See how the ripples reach out from the center, seeking, seeking . . ."

"There!" Margit breathed. In the water she watched the refugee from SeLenicca riding across the river plains away from the capital. Her lace pillow, barely covered with a bright kerchief, and a small pack rested precariously behind her saddle. Her steed plodded, Katrina's shoulders drooped, and her head sagged. Had she ridden all night and fallen asleep while riding?

"Do you recognize any landmarks?"

"Yes, the queen used to like riding across that meadow. I've followed her up that barren hill and around those boulders many times."

"Good, now withdraw from the images slowly."

Margit allowed her eyes to blink rapidly several times while she let loose her breath that had become pent up with excitement. The pictures faded from the water. Sleepiness fogged her mind and made her head too heavy for her neck to support.

"Wake up!" Jaylor clapped his hands sharply right beneath her nose.

Margit shook herself and focused on the tent made by drooping everblue branches. She seemed to return to herself from a great distance. Her stomach growled.

"Now, Margit, think carefully. What did you do differently from the time you tried this on your own?"

"Nothing."

"Something was different. This time it worked very well. Last time you saw nothing. What is different?"

Margit scrunched her eyes closed reviewing the entire procedure. "I've tried several times to find Marcus. Every time, the water ripples and the agate falls and nothing happens."

"Marcus? You've tried to find my missing journeyman?"

"Yes, sir. We—ah—we . . ."

"Are in love. Yes. I recognized the symptoms."

Margit blushed. "I did not think our feelings had become so obvious to others."

"Love is something that cannot hide, Margit. It needs to shine forth and grow. Now go get your breakfast. You'll need to refuel your body while I arrange for riding and pack steeds. You'll need journey food and camping gear for several days, perhaps a week. Master Lyman, Master Slippy, and I will transport you to the place you recognized when all is ready. When Jack catches up with you in a few days, I want you to stay with Katrina, make sure that both of them get safely into SeLenicca and report back to me every night." Jaylor stood up and lifted one of the branches for an exit.

"What about Marcus and Robb?" Margit stayed stubbornly beside the bowl.

"Keep your eyes open for signs of them. I expect they headed for one of the passes to the south of Sambol. Try to steer Jack and Katrina in that direction. I suspect those roads are less well guarded and safer than through two armies at the headwaters of the River Coronnan." He left her alone.

"Oh, and return the water to the creek and the bowl and agate to my desk before you eat."

"Am I a journeywoman yet, Master Jaylor?"

"Probably. But we haven't time for the trial by Tambootie smoke. We'll worry about that later. Find yourself a staff anyway. We'll discuss this further when you get back to me tonight." He hurried back toward the clearing and his family.

"I'm going to find you, Marcus, no matter how much I have to improvise," Margit said to the empty air. "No matter what magical and mundane barriers stand between us, I will find you. Then the two of us will spend the rest of our lives together, traveling the world on missions for the Commune."

*   *   *

"Come, daughter." Lord Laislac grabbed Ariiell's hand and dragged her off the bed. "A priest and the imbecile await us."

"P'pa?" Ariiell sat down on the edge of the high mattress, resisting his efforts to propel her out the door. "What has come over you? Why the sudden hurry?"

She knew the reason well enough. All day the king and queen had withdrawn from court, smiling longingly into each other's eyes. Rossemikka's pale skin had developed a rosy glow, she wore her hair loose about her shoulders, disguising the strange white streaks in the auburn, brown, black, blonde hair. The royal couple laughed and smiled secretly at each other as they held hands.

They acted like newlyweds, in the first flush of love. Disgusting.

They were up to something. Something devious and detrimental to Ariiell.

Rumors flew through the capital. Half the court were certain the queen had conceived again. The other half gleefully named a secret mistress who would produce a child that the royal couple would substitute for the queen's many failed pregnancies.

If Ariiell and her father had any hopes of having her child named heir to the throne, they had to insure its legitimacy as quickly as possible.

"Lord Andrall agrees with me. The kingdom is too unstable to rely on the queen to produce an heir. If she miscarries again, it could well kill her. The brat you carry is the only hope." Laislac yanked hard on Ariiell's arm, nearly dislocating her shoulder before she had a chance to balance on her own two feet. The folds of her gown twisted to outline the huge swell of her baby.

"How far along are you?" Laislac stared at his daughter. "You told your stepmother only four moons."

"Closer to seven," Ariiell dropped her eyes, feigning embarrassment.

"We've no time to waste, then, do we?" her father stated.

She cringed away from him, expecting a hard slap, or a burning bruise on her upper arm. When the hurt did not come, she chanced a glance at him. A wry smile tugged at her father's lips.

"Stargods, I wish your brothers were half as cunning as you. How often did you have to endure the imbecile in your bed before you arranged to be found?"

"Only three times." Mardall, for all of his slow mind and stalled emotional growth, had been a rather considerate lover. More so than some. Mardall wanted to please. Her other lovers—usually within a ritual eight-pointed star of the coven—wanted only their own pleasure and the power of domination. "When I knew for certain that Mardall's seed had found fertile ground, I deliberately made mistakes in arranging the next tryst." Ariiell returned her father's smile. "You'll be the grandfather of the next king, P'pa. 'Twill be easy enough to arrange a joint regency between you and Lord Andrall."

"Tell me, daughter, did you choose to foster with Andrall after your mother died and before I remarried with this in mind?"

Ariiell smiled at her father, letting him draw his own conclusions. If she allowed him to guess part of the truth, he'd not look further for the entire truth.

"Lord Andrall and Lady Lynnetta are very kind and trusting. Too bad they have withdrawn from court so often this last year and more." Ariiell kept her eyes on the floor—she couldn't see her toes anymore for the bulk of the baby. Let her father think what he liked. She'd never tell him that she had anchored the eight-pointed star in Nunio. She'd never tell him how the coven had arranged for her fosterage and her pregnancy.

"Everyone knows Andrall retreats to the quiet of

the country because his heart has weakened. Too much distress over keeping his nephew safe on the throne." This time Laislac laughed heartily. "Rumor claims he has not long to live. Perhaps someone can hasten to give truth to the rumor, eh?" He cocked his head and smiled with half his mouth. His eyes glittered with malice and greed.

Ariiell rearranged her gown to once more draw men's eyes away from her belly to the more enticing swell of her breasts. Then she draped a filmy veil over her hair and shoulders. The belled fringe fluttered in another off-center illusion. Each step created a delicate chiming of the silver ornaments.

"We'll leave for home directly after the ceremony," Lord Laislac pronounced. "You'll deliver safely within the confines of our castle. I shall control the time and place of the announcement of the birth."

"But, P'pa, won't our presence be more advantageous at court, where we can watch Darville and his foreign queen, make certain he does not survive long enough to father a child that the queen might carry full term?"

"We have time. The queen has lost five babes before the fifth month. The last miscarriage nearly killed her. She won't risk another pregnancy so soon. The servants will pack for you. Come. Your groom awaits you."

"Perhaps you are right, P'pa. If Darville witnesses the marriage, he cannot later deny the legitimacy of my child. Best he be born in safety. At court the Gnuls might kill me and the child just to make sure we do not succeed Darville." She clenched her fist in her gown, praying to Simurgh that her father would remain true to form and immediately counter her wishes.

"Precisely. Now come along so the servants can get busy packing."

"But, P'pa!" She couldn't allow servants to dismantle her room. They'd find the book beneath the mat-

tress. She had only had time to acquire half the
ingredients for the poison she wanted to use. She had
not had time to memorize the entire spell and compo-
nents to recreate it without the book.

"Stop acting the fool and come, before Andrall
changes his mind and takes the imbecile back to
Nunio." Laislac grabbed her arm once more. This time
his grip threatened to leave large bruises. "He can do
that after the wedding. We won't need him once he
says the vows. I hope Andrall prompts his son correctly. I don't want any doubts about the legality of
the marriage or the birth."

Ariiell dropped to her knees. If her father dragged
her farther, he'd ruin her gown so that she appeared
at the wedding reluctant and disgraced.

"What now?" he stared down at her, hands on hips.
The lines around his mouth clearly showed his need
to release his temper.

"I . . . I lost my balance. The babe . . ." Ariiell
heaved herself upright, using the bed as a crutch. With
her back to her father, she slipped the precious book
from beneath the mattress into a secret pocket within
an extra fold of her skirt. She redraped the scarf to
further conceal it. The fluttering bells would disguise
and distract anyone from looking too closely at any
misalignment of her gown.

Darville would not long survive the birth of her
child even if she had to steal the transport spell from
Rejiia to return to court.

CHAPTER 20

"You may now kiss the bride," the red-robed priest intoned. His clean-shaven face showed not a trace of emotion.

Ariiell stared equally stone-faced straight ahead at the tapestry icon of the Stargods descending upon a cloud of silver flame. The metallic embroidery had been cunningly worked to take on the outline of a dragon in certain lights. The flickering candles on the altar gave her tantalizing glimpses of the magical creatures.

She wished a dragon would swoop down and whisk away her bridegroom.

"Go ahead, kiss her, Mardall," Lord Andrall prompted his son.

King Darville looked away, his upper lip curled in a feral snarl. He looked as if he'd like to retreat from the dais where he stood beside the priest. Queen Rossemikka was notably missing from the ceremony.

Mardall blushed slightly as he pursed his lips and leaned vaguely in Ariiell's direction. She turned her head so that his damp mouth touched only her cheek. At least he didn't drool. She'd almost cured him of that in the time she was actively trying to get pregnant. One more spell and she thought she'd eliminate the problem.

Ariiell batted her eyes at the king and tried to look hurt at his rebuff. Inside, she nearly shouted in triumph. The marriage ceremony was complete. Her child legitimate and likely to sit on the throne wearing the Coraurlia as soon as Darville died. The coven had achieved their primary aim: one of their own would be heir to the throne of rich and powerful Coronnan.

Power! She did this for power. Political power. Magical power. All she had to do was endure until the baby was born strong and healthy.

The coven would place her at the center of every ritual because of the power and the fulfillment of their dearest and most ancient goal.

"Toast to the royal couple, Your Grace," Lord Laislac suggested. He snapped his fingers to summon his steward.

The servant stepped forward carrying a tray of jewel-encrusted cups and a matching decanter of wine.

"Ohhh," Lady Laislac moaned. She wept loudly into her handkerchief.

"Must we heap hypocrisy upon scandal?" Darville snarled.

Lord Andrall and his lady both gasped. Lady Lynetta clung to her husband's arm, chin quivering.

The bridegroom, Mardall, looked happily around at the marvelous wall paintings and tapestries in the royal chapel.

Ariiell was getting tired of his lighthearted mood already. Nothing seemed to upset him for more than a moment.

"Take the wine away," Darville commanded. "This ceremony may be necessary, but I do not have to like it. There will be no celebration. And there will be no announcements or discussion at court until *I* decide."

"Your Grace, please . . ." Laislac protested.

"We will see how long you can keep this secret," Ariiell told herself silently.

King Darville cocked his head and frowned at her from his position beside the priest. His aunt, Lady Lynnetta, had a similar gesture. With their identical golden-blond hair and golden-brown eyes, they could have been mother and son.

The king's frown deepened.

Had he heard her whisper? She doubted it. He and his line were notoriously mundane, with no trace of magic in their blood at all. He couldn't have learned any listening tricks from Jaylor. They had spent most of their dissolute youth together. But tricks were useless without a magical talent to fuel them.

And Darville's queen, who might or might not have magical power, depending upon which rumor you believed, had not graced the ceremony with her presence. A deliberate snub that Ariiell intended to revenge as soon as she became regent for her baby.

Ariiell smiled at the king, with an expression she hoped beguiled him with innocence. Tradition required him to preside over and bless the marriage since the idiot Mardall was his closest blood relative. Darville needed to appear in accord with the marriage that might produce his heir.

Rossemikka's absence kept Ariiell's hopes and aspirations in a shadowy realm. The marriage was legal, but the royal couple strongly disapproved. She'd have a hard time gaining acceptance at court until she killed Darville.

Never mind. The king would not long survive the birth of the baby.

"You all have leave to depart for Laislac Province," King Darville said. "You still have four or five hours of daylight."

"Leave!" Ariiell choked. "Surely, I cannot travel now." She thrust back her shoulders emphasizing the full extent of her bulging belly.

"By your parent's reckoning you can't be more than four months gone. The best healers in the country tell me you may travel safely," he insisted, daring her to admit the child had resulted from a long-term affair rather than a single incident.

Such an admission would put the blame and disgrace on her shoulders and remove Mardall from all responsibility. She couldn't allow that. She had to appear the victim here to gain the sympathy of the court and the Council of Provinces.

"But . . . but . . ." She couldn't think of a single argument against the king's stern order.

"Surely you wish your cousin to be born at court, Your Grace," Lord Andrall argued. "Surely you want the Council of Provinces to acknowledge the legitimacy of the birth. Our country will gain a great deal of stability with this birth and acknowledgment."

King Darville looked aghast at Lord Andrall, his most loyal supporter and uncle by marriage. Mardall's father nodded sadly.

The king's jaw firmed and his golden-brown eyes narrowed. Wolf eyes. Ariiell suddenly saw herself reflected in those eyes as a small rabbit, easy prey. She shrank away from him, making certain the book of poisons hidden within the folds and pleats of her gown remained out of sight.

"The child will be born away from court. If it survives and displays normal intelligence, I will acknowledge it in the line of succession. Bad enough I have to preside over this mockery of a marriage. I will not endure the constant reminder of events that should not have happened. All of you are dismissed." He turned on his heel and exited through the private door behind the altar.

A dozen guards appeared at the main door, as if summoned by the king's departure. "Your sledges and steeds await you in the postern courtyard, My Lords," the sergeant said. "We will escort you beyond the city limits now." His hand rested easily on his sword.

*   *   *

Lanciar postponed his trip into the void in search of his son. As a military tactician, he knew that intelligence was more important than troop numbers and superior weapons.

So he sat outside the tavern day after day, drinking the sour ale until it began to taste good and watching the Rover encampment. Then he drank some more, relishing the soft haze around his vision. For the first time since he'd left Queen's City in SeLenicca, he did not thirst from his very pores and he did not need to shield his eyes from an overly bright sun.

Day after day he memorized the movements within the Rover encampment. Day after day he learned the faces of the women and the children, which tent or bardo they inhabited, which man they waited for at the end of the day.

Always, he counted more women than men in each dwelling. His heart beat faster at the thrill of two or three women in his bed. Then he clamped down on his emotions and returned to the task at hand.

The dearth of men puzzled Lanciar. Fewer angry and armed men to pursue him when he chose to retrieve his son. But where had they all gone? Only old men and young boys, barely mature enough to mate remained. He saw nothing of men in their prime.

He learned that laundry, cooking, and minding the children were communal chores shared by all of the women. Men and women alike hunted and foraged to feed the entire community.

Visitors from the inn and nearby campground came to the Rover camp to have their fortunes told, their pots mended, or to buy unique silver jewelry and embroidery. Their few coins bought the things the Rovers could not find in the nearby forest or field.

He guessed that the statue of Krej resided with Zolltarn in the largest tent, for it was guarded night and day. Zolltarn rarely emerged from the fabric shelter, and then only when a dispute disturbed the usual quiet of the camp. He did not linger with his clan, did not join in the singing or dancing or storytelling. But once disturbed he would flash his smile and his people settled into their chores without protest. Whatever had caused the noisy disagreement, it dispersed like mist in sunshine.

"Which child are you, son?" Lanciar asked the air

repeatedly. All of the children were treated equally with love and respect. All of the children were tended by at least three adults at all times.

Even if he knew which child to snatch, he'd not travel more than three steps before encountering a vorpal dagger wielded by a very angry Rover. Both men and women carried the nasty rippled blades.

Lanciar trusted his own ability to wield a weapon, but not while carrying a precious baby in one arm.

He knew that Rejiia also watched the Rover enclave, but from the relative comfort of the upper window of the inn. She had commandeered their best and biggest room for herself.

And then the day came when the Rovers broke camp.

Lanciar had seen nothing unusual in their movement. One night they went to bed after singing and dancing around the campfires until nearly midnight—as was their custom—and the next morning they were gone at sunrise.

But this time, they had not used the transport spell. Lanciar found their tracks easily. With an illusory coin, he hired a sturdy steed without much energy and only one speed—slow. But it would walk at that plodding pace all day and half the night without pause.

"Saddle that steed for me, peasant," Rejiia sneered right behind Lanciar. Rejiia gestured to a high-stepping black steed with a blaze of white on its nose and mane that matched her own raven locks streaked at one temple with white.

"I'll see the color of your coin first," the hostler replied calmly.

"You'll see the color of my magic first." Rejiia flung a ball of witchfire into his face.

He screamed and stumbled to a watering trough. Batting at the flames, he plunged his head beneath the water.

The steed pranced and snorted and wheeled, its eyes rolled.

"*S-murghit,* stand still!" Rejiia cursed loudly and let a spell fly. The beast froze in place. Two grooms scurried out of the stable with saddle and tack. They prepared him for riding in record time.

Lanciar sensed the beast straining at the spell. She'd not keep it on a tight rein for long. When it bolted . . .

He hoped Rejiia landed on her lush bottom in the dirt.

For the next three days, Lanciar followed the caravan. The first two nights, the clan camped within shouting distance of villages with inns. He and Rejiia each hired a room. But on the third night, they had passed into Coronnan. The natives here rarely traveled outside their own lands—except for magicians and the occasional trader caravan—and thus had no need for inns. None of their taverns had guest facilities. He made a rough camp beyond the reach of Rover firelight and perimeter guards.

He kept his own fire low, and his noise to a minimum. He'd learned the basic skills of camping behind enemy lines in his first years as a recruit in the Se-Lenese army.

Of Rejiia, he saw no sign. Perhaps she commandeered lodging at the nearest manor. Perhaps she retreated and watched Zolltarn through a scrying bowl. He found no trace of her within a league of the Rovers with his magical or mundane senses and hoped she had given up the chase.

With his back against a tree, Lanciar munched on dry journey rations. He watched the Rovers prepare a rich stew of hedgehog and root vegetables, flavored with a fruity red wine. The enticing aromas wafted on the breeze like a compulsion spell. His mouth watered, and his stomach grumbled.

His bedroll already took on the dampness of dewfall. The fire sputtered from damp wood and threatened to die.

All at the Rover camp seemed warm and dry and friendly.

Lanciar took comfort that his son ate well and slept in a dry cot.

Ah well, he'd endured worse in rough bivouacs while on patrol behind enemy lines.

"Spy," a woman spoke from directly behind his tree.

"*S'murghit!* Where did you come from? I didn't hear you," he cursed to cover his startlement. His magical and military trained senses should have alerted him to her presence the moment she left camp.

"Watch your language, spy. We have children nearby." She glared at him, hands on hips, eyes blazing with outrage.

"Sorry. You surprised me." Good thing the darkness hid his flaming cheeks.

"Spy, you have followed us diligently. You might as well join us. We offer you comfort this rough camp cannot give you."

"Wh–what?"

"You heard me. You've watched us and followed us, learning all you can of our people and our habits. We have nothing to hide. You might as well join us."

"J–join you?" He'd never heard of an enemy openly inviting a spy into their camp. Never heard of Rovers inviting *gadjé* adults into their camp either. Children they welcomed, not strangers over the age of ten.

But the invitation made a twisted kind of sense. They could observe him and control the knowledge he gained under their supervision.

He could get a closer look at each of the children, see which might have fairer skin or lighter eyes than those born to the clan.

"I'll be with you as soon as I put out the fire and gather my bloody bedroll."

"Watch your language or you will never be allowed near your son." She frowned at him sternly.

Lanciar closed his eyes and dipped his head a fraction in acknowledgment of the rules.

She smiled at him and twitched her hips as she returned to the protection of her clan.

"I've heard they have good wine and ale in Rover camps."

"I brew the best ale of all the Rovers," the young woman replied. "Come and join us. If we learn to trust you, perhaps we will introduce you to your son."

"My . . . my son. How did you know I sought my son?"

"Zolltarn knows everything." She flashed a smile as big and enchanting as the Rover chieftain's.

"Lead me to the ale. I think I'm going to need it."

CHAPTER 21

Jack came out of the transport spell inside Shayla's lair. He landed with a jolt to his spine and foot-numbing abruptness. His mind had remained drifting in the void a heartbeat too long. He stumbled and grabbed the closest object to steady his balance.

He hoped Mikka and Darville had arrived in the dragon lair ahead of him and with more grace.

Amaranth let out a squeak of distress and jerked away from Jack's grasp.

"Sorry, Amaranth." He petted the bruised and stunted spiral horn bud on the baby dragon's fore-head. "This will all be over soon."

The dragonet nuzzled Jack's side, keeping his sensitive forehead lowered and out of reach. He radiated bewilderment, excitement, and just a touch of fear. Jack cuddled Amaranth a little closer.

Emotional distraction kept him from adding any other reassurance. He needed to be on the road following Katrina. Jaylor had confidence in Margit's ability to take care of Katrina. Jack didn't trust anyone but himself where Katrina's well-being was concerned.

Amaranth almost purred under his caresses. Magical power flooded Jack's being. The dragonet opened his mind to Jack. Vivid images of the dragonet's daily hunt and swim in the bay with his brothers filled Jack's head.

For a moment he felt like part of the group, a member of the family. He pushed it aside; the only family he wanted now was Katrina.

But the premature bond he had inadvertently awakened in Amaranth did not allow him to shut out the images or the emotions. Nor could he forget his preparation for the spell with Baamin, the blue-tipped dragon who had been his mentor at the old University in a previous life. He'd always have a family with the dragons.

"Amaranth, where is Baamin, the elder blue-tipped dragon?"

(Here, son,) a new voice replied. Soothing, confident, wise.

Jack breathed deeply, more comfortable with himself just hearing the voice of his mentor. His father—though neither of them had known of the relationship while the old man lived in his human body.

For Jack, just knowing that Old Baamin lived on in the dragon body gave him a sense of continuity with the past, something that had been missing most of his life. But at the moment he could not comprehend his life extending forward to new generations, not until he and Katrina found a way to overcome her fears.

"Are you here in the lair, Baamin? Or here in my head?" Jack asked.

(In your head, Jack. There isn't room for me in the lair tonight.)

"Can you check on Katrina for me? Is she safe? Is she lonely?"

(Yes, and yes. You have time to complete your tasks and then catch up with her. She needs this time alone.)

Jack nodded his acceptance of the dragon's words, knowing the old man would read his emotions. Other than himself, he trusted Baamin more than anyone on Kardia Hodos. As long as Baamin watched Katrina, no one would beset her intending harm.

(Stop feeling sorry for yourself and get on with your spell, boy,) the dragon reprimanded him, sounding very much like the master magician in charge of exuberant and inattentive apprentices.

"Is everyone here?" Jack asked the assembly in the

lair. He counted noses: at least ten master magicians and a horde of journeymen and apprentices, Shayla and the two purple dragonets, Jaylor and Brevelan near the slightly raised platform that usually held Shayla's nest. Brevelan sat on a boulder that seemed molded to her slight frame. She held one of her new-born twins, the tiny quiet one that everyone feared might not live, a small scrap of life who held every-one's heart and concern. Queen Mikka sat beside her on another boulder holding the other baby, a squall-ing, squirming bundle of aggressive humanity with an aura big enough for two. King Darville leaned over his queen inspecting the baby. A look of wistful regret passed between the king and queen. They'd lost five babes before Mikka could carry them to full term. The cat spirit within the queen's body caused an imbalance that affected her ability to produce the long hoped-for heir.

"After tonight, maybe you'll have your own brood of sons and daughters," Jack whispered.

Shayla must have banished the other ten dragonets to keep them from interfering with the spell. Ten curi-ous dragon babies could wreak havoc on the simplest of activities. He almost chuckled at the antics that had greeted him the first time he'd encountered the drag-ons in a cave hidden behind a waterfall deep within the mountains of SeLenicca.

Jaylor came out from behind his wife with an out-stretched hand, greeting Jack like an equal. He beamed proudly. Of his two sons, Jack saw no sign. Good. Amaranth's clumsiness created enough chaos in the lair. Two rambunctious and under-cautious young boys would only add to the confusion Jack was about to create.

Jack did not envy the four apprentices assigned to sit with the boys this night. They needed four adults to handle the two boys. Four apprentices or Brevelan.

With one arm draped around Amaranth's neck—to keep him from falling into the campfire ignited for the humans' benefit, Jack nearly stumbled again with an awesome sense of having done this before. And failed.

No. He forced himself to remember that this time he had the backing of the full Commune of Magicians. He had a purple dragon to give him extra magic that he normally could not gather. Never again would he be as alone or lonely as he had been before he met Katrina.

He'd needed Katrina and her Tambrin lace to truly heal Shayla's wing. Tonight he needed Katrina by his side to anchor him, give him reasons for succeeding.

"Your Grace, time to convince your pesky cat to find a new body." Jack bowed to Queen Mikka. "Is everyone ready?"

"Will it hurt?" Mikka asked.

"Perhaps. I don't know, Your Grace." Jack shrugged his shoulders.

"Very well. Let us proceed." Mikka stood up and handed the bawling baby back to Brevelan. As she turned to face Jack, she presented a regal calm. Her multicolored hair, like a brindled brown cat's fur, flowed smoothly about her shoulders. As tall as Brevelan was short, she radiated authority and determination as well as acceptance of tonight's procedures—complete with risks.

Precisely the queen Darville needed to help him govern the fractious lords who sat on the Council of Provinces. The couple ruled by the grace of the dragons. But the lords no longer respected the dragons.

Jack sensed the other magicians arranging themselves around Amaranth in a circle. Shayla nudged Iianthe, the second purple-tipped dragonet to join them. Iianthe held back. He'd always been shy around Jack.

That other time Jack had used a purple dragon to give him extra magic to heal Shayla's wing, Amaranth had willingly joined him. The spell had awakened their unique rapport before the dragonet was mature enough to understand or control it. Iianthe had hidden rather than participate in something new.

"We need symmetry with the original spell that bound the queen and her cat into the same body," Jack announced. He tapped several of the master magicians on the shoulder and indicated they should leave. "That means eight men working around a center point. Your Grace, if you will take the center with Amaranth." He beckoned the queen over. Jaylor followed her.

Four years ago, Jaylor had been the center of the spell. The Rovers had agreed to straighten out his warped magic. Their massive working had involved an eight-pointed star, dance, music, and fire. Mikka and her cat had been on the sidelines then, along with Brevelan and Darville. As the Rovers unraveled Jaylor's talent and then bound it back into his body, the cat had crawled into her mistress' lap and the two had been caught in the spillover of magic.

Jack couldn't let that happen again. Carefully, he positioned two journeymen in front of Brevelan and the babies. Then he beckoned Darville to stand behind them as well. "I want a full bubble of armor around the nonparticipants the entire time," he whispered to the journeymen as he returned to his core of magicians.

Quietly he chalked the important points and junctions of an eight-pointed star on the ground. "We'll need a second fire over there, to balance this one. I don't want the fire in the middle. That will destroy the balance."

Amaranth obliged by igniting the pile of reserve firewood. It blazed merrily and the dragon bounced back to Jack's side.

The spell was taking shape.

"Where's Zolltarn? He needs to be here." Jack looked around, blinking slightly as he roused from his deep concentration and memories.

"He did not respond to our summons." Jaylor shrugged.

The Rover Chieftain obeyed his own rules—rules he made up as he went along.

"He designed the original spell," Jack half protested.

"He's your grandfather, boy," Old Lyman half sneered. "The blood tie is complete." The elder librarian hobbled about the cave with the aid of his staff. Jack was glad he'd kept the old man out of the spell.

Three years ago the Rover spell had put too much strain on Baamin's heart and hastened his death. Jack did not want to be responsible for that happening with Lyman.

Old hurts. He needed to put them aside and make new memories. With Katrina.

"Let's get started." Jack squared his shoulders with new resolve. The sooner he completed this duty, the sooner he'd be on the road, following his love. No matter that departing abruptly, without explicit permission would look like a repeat of his youthful misdeeds that had led him to SeLenicca and Katrina the first time.

Jaylor could not hold him. Only Katrina could do that.

"Amaranth, into the center with Queen Mikka." Jack pushed the dragonet from behind.

Amaranth hung his head and dragged his tail. He knew something strange was about to occur and feared it. Jack was afraid, too. Afraid of failing yet again, afraid of losing Katrina forever. Afraid of hurting his friend, the baby dragon, and the queen.

He couldn't let his fears govern his actions. He had to impart some measure of reassurance and love to Amaranth.

"I need you to help the queen, Amaranth. Only you can do that." The dragonet's head came up, and he emitted a bit of pride. "Remember, when this is over, you get to stay with me forever, as my cat."

(Be your familiar?) The baby dragon looked at him with hope and adoration.

"My familiar?" A peculiar warmth untied itself from his inner knot of loneliness. "Yes, if you like." He half smiled. Something good might come of this night's work after all. He'd have Amaranth's help while he tracked Katrina. He'd have another to share his hopes and fears, to plot and plan, to dream with.

Reluctantly, tail and muzzle drooping, Amaranth trudged to the center of the circle. He paused to look back at Jack three times before he settled on his haunches at the queen's side.

"Touch the dragonet, Your Grace. You need a conduit for the cat to follow out of your body."

She rested her left hand on Amaranth's head, behind the stubby horn, and gently scratched his ears. He began to hum, just like a cat purring.

"Iianthe, here, beside me."

The other purple-tipped dragon slunk behind his mother.

"Shayla." Jack looked toward the mother dragon. Exhaustion seemed to feed upon every little setback in this procedure. He needed to be gone, in search of Katrina. He took a deep breath and continued addressing Shayla. "If Amaranth is to become the flywacket, I won't be able to gather magic from him. I can only gather magic from a purple-tipped dragon, unlike my companions. I need Iianthe to complete this spell. We need the augmented power of dragon magic to make this work. Solitary magic isn't enough."

The other master magicians looked at Jack with small frowns of disapproval.

By the laws of Coronnan and the Commune, he must be able to gather dragon magic or go into exile. But the situation had changed and Jack's solitary magic had saved the Commune more than once.

He frowned back at them. All but elder Librarian Lyman looked away in embarrassment. That old man made his own rules and set his own standards of acceptability. He slammed his staff into the dirt as a prompt to get the spell moving.

Iianthe retreated farther behind his mother. Amaranth began to shift his weight uneasily beside Mikka.

All of the magicians looked at each other blankly.

"I'll get him," Jaylor heaved a sigh. He might be Senior Magician, but except for Jack, he was the youngest and strongest among them.

Shayla nudged Iianthe forward with her muzzle. A touch of her long spiral forehead horn applied judiciously to his rump brought him abruptly to Jack's side.

"Everyone get ready. We may not have a lot of time once I start," Jack warned.

"Perhaps one of us should take over the managing of this spell," Slippy said. He'd taken his name from the eels that nestled near the shore of the Great Bay. Cooked properly, they had a sweet nutritious meat. Handled incorrectly, they poisoned all they touched.

"None of you were there during the original spell. None of you have the *feel* of what happened," Jack asserted.

"Jaylor was there," Slippy corrected him.

"Jaylor was the object of the spell. As such, he was a passive participant."

Silence greeted his assertion.

"Look, nothing would please me more than turning over the entire procedure to one or all of you. I have business elsewhere. Pressing business. But you chose me for this spell. Me. The rogue who was too stupid to have a name, and too irresponsible to follow orders. Me. I developed the transport spell. I saved the entire Commune from Rejiia. I found the dragons and brought them home. You chose me for a reason." Jack clenched his fists in a serious effort to keep from shouting and throwing flashes of fire from his staff.

"What do we do?" Jaylor asked. He ignored the tension that grew almost tangibly among his master magicians.

"Link together, Jaylor to my right with Iianthe between us. Each of you stand on a point of the eight-pointed star." Jack forced his hands to relax as he gently caressed Iianthe's horn bud. Unlike Amaranth's, this one had grown. It had started to spiral into a sharp point.

Shayla crooned in the background. The baby dragon coiled his tail around himself. At least it wasn't sticking straight out and elevated in preparation to bolt.

"Rovers induce a trancelike state through music and dance. They then draw magical energy from all life by reaching out and touching it with their heightened senses," Jack reminded the other magicians. "That's how the original spell began."

There'd be no dancing to recreate a Rover spell tonight. Jack had to remain rooted beside Iianthe in order to gather dragon magic.

But the men of the Commune could sing and move their feet while standing in one place.

Jack gave out his instructions quietly. No sense in spooking Iianthe. He reached for the shoulder of the man to his left. Jaylor placed one hand on Jack's shoulder to complete the circle of eight magicians.

They chanted the poetry of the Rovers, words Jack had dredged up from his memory and sent to the other men to memorize earlier in the day.

And then they marched in place, keeping time with the rhythmic repetition of the song.

Iianthe shifted uneasily beneath Jack's hand. He sped up the chant and the march. His eyes crossed as the power rose within him. It grew, expanded, writhed like a living being in a myriad of colors representing each of the magicians in the circle.

Jack drew a deep breath and grabbed the power, molding it to his will. Between one heartbeat and the next the auras of every being within the circle took on the lavender-and-silver overtones of his magical signature.

Amaranth responded to the compulsion within the

chant, shrinking, collapsing in on himself, absorbing all the light his silvery hide normally reflected. He darkened as he shrank until . . . until . . .

A black cat, so dark its fur reflected purple lights stood beside the queen. It yowled loudly and fluttered black-feathered wings. A flywacket. A creature of legend and prophecy.

In that instant, Jack grabbed at the source of the queen's double aura and yanked.

Amaranth yowled again.

Iianthe reared up, breaking Jack's contact.

The circle of magic dissolved.

Jack doubled over in exhaustion with a curious pain in his gut. Strange afterimages showed around everything he tried to focus his eyes upon.

"I'm free!" Mikka shouted as she sank to her knees. Her head looked too heavy for her neck to support. "I'm free of that blasted cat." Tears of joy streamed down her face. Her husband rushed forward and knelt beside her, scuffing the marks of the eight-pointed star. He cradled her against him, kissing away her tears.

"Are you hurt?" Darville cupped her face in his long-fingered hands.

"A curious emptiness. Tired. A little dizzy—disoriented." Her strength gave out. She collapsed in a faint. Darville caught her.

"Thank you, young man." Darville looked up from his wife's peaceful countenance. "We—all of Coronnan—owe you a debt of gratitude. Hopefully, now we can stabilize the succession without Lord Laislac and his daughter."

"I'd best send you home, Your Grace, before you are missed," Jaylor said. He took a deep breath. His face still looked a little gray.

"No more magic until you all eat!" Brevelan proclaimed.

"Food," Jack murmured, recognizing the cause of some of his disorientation. The afterimages continued to plague his vision like half-formed ghosts. His skin felt clammy, and his knees wobbled. "I need food."

An unknown journeyman stuffed a hunk of bread into Jack's hand, followed by a thick slab of cheese.

Jack ate hungrily, methodically. He had to restore his energies quickly.

"Jack, I'll see you in my study in the morning. We need to discuss security within the palace." Darville swallowed convulsively.

"SeLenicca," Jack croaked. "You promised to send Katrina and me to SeLenicca as ambassadors."

"Later. I need you in Coronnan City more than I need you across the border now that the war is over. We still have an eavesdropping rogue to find." Darville dismissed the suggestion.

"I've got to take Katrina home, Your Grace. Now."

Three deep breaths and the void beckoned him. "Come, Amaranth." The flywacket leaped into his arms. Three more breaths and he sent them both into the void in search of his true love.

CHAPTER 22

Zebbiah hustled Jaranda and the pack beast onto the sailing vessel amidst shouts for haste from the captain and crew—who all looked amazingly like the Rover except they wore blue and green on their black clothing instead of purple and red. The pack beast protested the plank up to the ship's deck vehemently and tried to sit down again in the middle of it.

The woman pushed the animal from behind with a sharp stick, trying her best to keep it from parking its rear anywhere but on the deck. Zebbiah called no orders to her, nor did he look to see if she followed. They had made a bargain; therefore, he must presume she followed.

Eight passengers, all dressed in rough clothing, moved abruptly to the far side of the open-decked vessel giving the Rover and his beast more than enough room to settle for the long voyage upriver.

The woman inspected the other passengers openly. All of the women but one wore a single plait that started at the crown and gathered closely to the head to the nape where it broke free into a thick rope of a braid. Two of them had not bothered with the complex four strand plait but sufficed with the simpler three strand braid. The other woman wore two plaits that started at her temples and stayed close to her head to the nape, then swung free for a short space and joined into a single thick plait halfway down her back. She must come from a merchant family. The others were all peasants.

Not knowing who she was or what her status was, the unnamed woman had gathered her own hair into a thick knot at her own nape. Jaranda's hair, she had tied back with a green ribbon to match her dress. They, like their fellow passengers, wore sturdy dark skirts and vests with white, long-sleeved shifts beneath.

She caught the eye of the woman wearing two plaits. The merchant's wife turned up her nose and spun on her heel to face the water on the other side of the vessel. The peasant women followed suit.

The men talked amongst themselves and paid no attention to the newcomers.

Jaranda did not seem to care about the people. She skipped about looking at everything, watching the crew as they cast off the lines and set the sail.

"Zebbiah, what plagues them?" the woman whispered to her traveling companion.

He looked up from tending to the stubborn beast that carried all their worldly wealth and supplies.

"We made them late. They are displeased." He shrugged and returned to the beast's reins, tethering them to a brass ring embedded into the decking.

" 'Tis more than that, Zebbiah. Displeasure at our tardiness would evoke curses and grumbling, not this silent disdain." Why did she know that? An image, a very old image, flashed across her mind's eye. She stood and watched a parade of noblemen and courtiers as they exited the king's audience chamber. One of them turned and faced her squarely. "This war with Coronnan will benefit no one. No one. We'd be better off governing ourselves than submitting to *his* demands for more money, more war, more slaves, more sacrifices."

She tried to put a name to the man's face. She tried to place herself in the crowd. She tried to remember who *he* was.

The images faded to mists.

"You remembering something?" Zebbiah asked.

"Not quite. Has our country been at war long?"

"Over three years."* No further comment good or bad. No information as to the cause. Just that war had become a part of life.

"And is all this devastation a part of the war?" She swept a hand to include the city behind the docks that drifted farther and farther away.

"Partly."

She raised her eyebrows, waiting for more information. He sat down on a cargo bale and began plaiting a piece of leather he drew from the panniers.

Slightly miffed, she marched over to the women crowding against the far railing. "Good morning, ladies. Are you traveling all the way to the end of the river?" she asked politely.

Two-plaits sniffed as if she smelled something rancid. "Riffraff, tainting true-blood with dark-eyed outlanders," she spat.

"Wouldn't have this problem if the council hadn't made mixed marriages legal so Queen Miranda could marry an outlander," a stout woman added. She wore a clumsy braid that looked as if it had not been washed or combed in a month.

Two-plaits looked pointedly at red-haired Jaranda.

"I don't suppose you know my name, ladies?"

"A name that's too good for you, if you ask me," two-plaits replied and moved as far into the bow as she could, away from them all.

"Somehow, I didn't expect you to say that."

* * *

"Stargods, they make a lot of demands for ghosts!" Yeenos, Vareena's older brother protested. "Bad enough we have to feed two more of them with no respite from the last one. Now they want special herbs and minerals, crystals, and our soap-making cauldrons. I say no. We feed them because the Stargods decree we must. But no more!" He swung his shepherd's

crook in a wide circle before slamming the crook
against a watering trough.

"Yeenos, calm down." Vareena ducked the staff,
well used to her brother's temper. She had seen Marcus do the same thing with his staff. Robb seemed to
have better control of his temper and treated his staff
more gently. "These new ghosts claim that another
ghost, a true ghost of a man who has died, haunts the
monastery and causes live men to become trapped
there, halfway between here and their next existence."

"What else is a ghost?" Yeenos sneered, then he
whistled for his dog to run the sheep farther uphill
from the farmhouse.

"I don't know. But they refuse to believe they are
true ghosts, and they need these things to work a spell
that will lay the other ghost to rest and free them
from the trap." Vareena rubbed her hands together
nervously. She'd have gone to Uustass for help, but
he had led a dozen men to the river this morning with
scythes. The village needed fresh grass and reeds to
repair the thatch on several dwellings and byres.

Jeeremy Baker had gone with them, his burns heavily bandaged but no longer in pain.

"I agree with Yeenos," Vareena's father Ceddell
said, coming over to them from the byre. "We owe
the ghosts food. That was the curse laid on this village
three hundred years ago for refusing hospitality to a
benighted traveler. *S'murghin'* magician." He crossed
his wrists and flapped his hands as he spat onto the
ground. "But we owe them nothing more. I'll not be
spending our resources to find these odd ingredients
for a useless bit of magic." He kicked the water trough
and called his dog to his heels, away from the flock
Yeenos worked with his own dogs.

"But, Papa, if we can end this curse once and for
all . . ."

"We've had priests and magicians alike trying to
end the curse with no luck."

"But these ghosts are magicians trapped by the

curse, not magicians working outside of it. They might have a chance . . ."

"You've gone and fallen in love with one of them, haven't you!" Ceddell raised his voice and his hand in anger.

Vareena stepped back but did not duck. She faced her father, refusing to submit to his violence. She might be as trapped here as the ghosts, but she refused to lessen herself by accepting any man's abuse.

"Your mother did the same thing, before I showed her the wrong of it."

"Showed her with your fists, no doubt." Vareena schooled her voice and features to betray none of her fear or her disgust.

"I'll find you a husband this night. Then you'll give up this nonsense."

"No man in this village wants me. I'll have none you bribe or coerce into the act."

"You'll marry the man I choose for you. The law of the land and the laws of the Stargods decree that you must obey your father." Ceddell raised his clenched fist once more.

Vareena stood her ground. "Touch me, and I move into the monastery permanently. The villagers will have to bring food, clothing, and bedding to me there. They will have to come to me for healing. How far will your authority stretch, Ceddell, once the Ghost Woman removes herself and her witch healing from your household?"

"Enough!" Yeenos nearly screamed at them. His nostrils pinched white and his mouth pursed to a thin lipless line. "This village has borne the burden of this curse too long."

Both Vareena and her father stared at the young man as if he had lost his reason.

"You say these new ghosts are magicians, Vareena?"

"So they claim. I have seen no evidence of their talent other than lighting a fire from a distance. But I can do that."

"Lord Laislac sent around a newscrier three years ago," Yeenos said, almost gloating. "Magic is illegal in all of Coronnan now. I'm going to the capital to talk to the priests, and to the Council of Provinces. I'll get the obligation removed from us. Ghosts or no ghosts, there will be no more food and supplies wasted upon those who haunt the monastery."

"You can't!" Vareena gasped.

"You can't stop me, Eena. It's time."

He whistled one last time to his dog and turned his crook over to his father. Then he stalked into the house and began throwing journey rations into a pack.

Vareena took off running for the hill crested by the abandoned monastery.

"Vareena!" her father roared. "Come back here."

"Never. I have to save my ghosts. I can't let them die of neglect." She had to find a way to bring Robb back to life. Marcus, too. If the Stargods showed any mercy at all, they'd allow her to kiss her love just once in this existence. She'd give up the freedom Farrell promised her for one kiss from Robb.

*   *   *

"How much time do we have?" Robb asked at Vareena's breathless news.

She shrugged her shoulders, inhaled deeply, and spoke. "A week. Perhaps two. Depends if Yeenos changes steeds along the way, or if he talks his way onto a barge."

"We're doomed." Marcus slid to a heap in the corner of the refectory. He wrapped his arms around his knees and began rocking.

Robb wanted to do the same, but refused to give in to the despair that his friend exhibited.

" 'Tis a long way from here to the capital and back." Robb finger-combed his beard. Years ago he had copied the thinking gesture from Jaylor. Now he'd done it for so long that it had become a part of him. "We've walked from the capital to the border often enough in the past three years. Even with magic urging a steed to greater speed and endurance, the trip always took at least a week each direction. Once Yeenos reaches the capital, he'll need to gain an audience, first with the priests at the Royal Temple, then with the Council of Provinces. That could take weeks. Moons. Until he returns with an edict withdrawing village responsibility for us, we have food and supplies. We have time to trap that ghost in the library and get some answers."

"Papa has agreed to village responsibility to feed you two until Yeenos returns. But he refuses you the supplies you need for the spell." Vareena turned her face away from him.

Robb wished he could watch her eyes, know what she hid. But the mist that separated her from the two magicians veiled her eyes and her mind from his probes.

Strange how physical objects retained their crisp outlines, but the people looked as insubstantial as a dragon. He could touch physical objects, lift them, probe them for long-lost memories, but a kind of armor prevented him from touching other people—except Marcus.

Perhaps if they probed the walls rather than trying to climb them, he could discern the nature of the spell that kept them within. Later, when he was alone and could concentrate. Hard to do since the entrapment.

"Can you find these supplies for us?" Robb asked Vareena.

"Some of them. The herbs are common enough. Some of the minerals, but crystals and the cauldron . . ."

"We've got little crystals in our supplies. We've got a little cooking pot. They will have to serve for now. A smaller spell. Less chance of success, but perhaps enough to show us what *can* be done."

"I'll bring you what I can." She rose up on tiptoe as if to kiss his cheek, then reared back, repulsed by the energy barrier. "I'll go now." A tear formed in the corner of her eye, like a perfect dew drop glinting in the sun. Then she ran off on her errand.

"Stargods! She's in love with you," Marcus choked on a sob. "I might as well curl up and die. I've lost everything."

"What are you talking about?"

Marcus moaned and buried his head in his knees. "I can't do anything right, can't even love the right woman!"

"Marcus, stop wallowing in misery and help me. We have a ghost to trap."

His friend only moaned again.

"Marcus." Robb stalked over and shook him by the shoulder. "What are you talking about. Until we got here, you were madly in love with Margit—and she with you. Before Margit, you loved that little dairy-maid in Hanic. You are always in love with someone. Now you *think* you love Vareena, and you *think* she loves me. You aren't thinking straight."

"I can't think of anything else but Vareena. This place twists everything back to her." Marcus clutched Robb's hand in a painful grip that bordered on desperation.

"Perhaps this place does cloud our thinking." Robb had kept visions of Margit in his heart and his dreams for a long, long time. He focused hard on her each night before sleeping to stave off the recurring nightmares of attack and fruitless defense. But she obviously had strong feelings for Marcus. He did not want to come between his two best friends if their affection was genuine.

Now?

"What a tangled mess." He slumped down beside Marcus and draped an arm around his friend's shoulders.

Marcus rested his head on Robb's shoulders and sobbed.

"Vareena loves me," Robb mused. "I love Margit, Margit loves you, you love Vareena . . ."

"I love you, too, Robb," Marcus sobbed. "You are right. My feelings for women are temporary. Illusions. My love for you will last forever."

Horror shuddered through Robb. He stood up jerkily, putting as much physical distance as he could between them.

"Snap out of your adolescent hero worship, Marcus. I'm going to climb the tower, see if a summons spell works from there—above the level of the walls."

CHAPTER 23

Unlike my son, those who seek to capture me are bumbling beginners. My son would have known how to break my spells and leave this cursed place. My daughter, too. They did not need this paltry dragon magic to bring them anything they wished. Nor did they need the convoluted and time-consuming rituals of the Rovers.

And yet these amateurs do not panic easily. They have been trained to think a problem through—as Nimbulan did. I could have trained them better.

Let us see how they handle my next little trick. Their own fear will force them to leave me alone long before I finish with them. They shall die in another ninety-seven days if they remain here. Soon I will be alone again with my power.

* * *

The nameless woman surveyed the long line of pack steeds, sledges, merchants, and other travelers who had banded together to cross the pass safely into Coronnan. Every traveler had to be wary of bandits, out-of-work mercenaries, and rogue magicians. They were too close to the border of Hanassa for comfort.

A flash of memory lanced her mind right between her eyes. Images of battles, war, displaced families, hungry people, noble and peasant alike, fire, flood, kardiaquakes without end.

She clutched the mane of Zebbiah's beast for balance as the world spun around and around, taking her with it.

"M'ma!" Jaranda screamed.

She fought her way through the maze of images to find the coarse, mottled brown-and-gray hide of the pack beast. It brayed loudly, threatening to sit again in protest of her fierce clutch on its mane.

Her memory flashed again to another steed, one she rode, a docile little mare that was greatly intimidated by the mighty war stallion beside her. Her husband sat atop that horse, surveying the battle below. She had eyes only for the red-haired man who commanded the troops. "I was too young to see beyond the glamour of being in love with the notion of love," she whispered. "I worshiped him." He was a powerful general with tangled political connections, a strong and handsome man: what more could an idealistic young girl ask for in a man? He took care of her, protected her from . . . she couldn't remember from what, only that she cherished his domineering presence.

And she thanked him daily for the child he had given her.

"Jaranda," she whispered.

"M'ma!" Jaranda tugged on her gown. "Wake up, M'ma. I'm scared," the little girl implored.

"Jaranda," she said again, louder, firmly. "Jaranda, my love. Do you remember your father?"

Strange, she felt no sense of loss at the man's absence. No regret. She focused entirely on her daughter, stooping to put herself on the same level as the child.

Jaranda shook her head. Her thumb crept toward her mouth.

The woman gently restrained her from the baby habit of insecurity. "This is important, Jaranda. If I know your P'pa's name, I might remember my own."

"You're M'ma. You don't need 'nother name." Jaranda thrust out her lower lip. A tear trembled in the corner of her eye.

"I am your M'ma, little one. But these other people need to call my by another name. I 'm not their M'ma, after all." She touched the edge of her hem to her daughter's eyes, blotting the half-formed tears.

"I don't remember P'pa. 'Cept he was big. He filled the doorway when he came to watch me at night. He thought I was asleep. He wouldn't have come if he knew I was awake." Jaranda flung her arms around her mother's neck and hugged her tightly, nearly strangling her.

"We don't want P'pa. He scared me. I like Zebbie better."

"Yes, I like Zebbiah, too, Jaranda," she choked out, fighting the pressure on her throat from the little girl's enthusiasm. She stood up and gently held her daughter's hands.

She turned to find the dark-eyed man watching her.

"You remember something." His usually expressive eyes took on a hooded look, and he refused to meet her gaze.

"Where is my husband, Zebbiah? Why did he not come for us in the palace when everyone deserted me?"

"Many men died in the war." He bent to fuss with the harness on his pack beast.

"Dead?" A huge weight seemed to lift from her chest. "I'm a widow." She had to restrain herself from jumping in glee. "I guess the marriage was not happy," she whispered to herself. Jaranda renewed her stranglehold, on her knees this time.

"Serves you right." A bulky man, managing the sledge behind her spat into the dirt. "Can't trust outlanders. Especially those with dark eyes. Brown or blue as dark as midnight, don't matter, they's all signs of outlanders," he sneered. "Best you don't remember the man what give you a child with outland hair. Best you take her and your dark-eyed lover out of SeLenicca. We don't need no outlanders tainting our blood or telling us what to do."

"And yet you travel outland. By the looks of the goods on your sledge, you intend to stay there a long time." She raised an eyebrow at him in irony at his hypocrisy.

"Prejudice has to be learned, Lady," Zebbiah said quietly.

"And I have forgotten my prejudices along with my name."

"Common enough name," the bulky man snarled again.

"Do you know my name, traveler?"

He turned his back on her, refusing to answer.

"Somehow I thought he'd say that. But I'll remember eventually. I've started to remember. The rest will come." She brushed Jaranda's dress free of dust. "Let's get started. The day is too beautiful to waste on the past and regrets and prejudices." She whistled to the pack beast. It brayed in an obnoxious imitation of an agreement and plodded along behind her. The other steed riders and sledge drivers followed her lead.

"Your M . . . Your Ladyship, get back in line," the caravan leader snarled, pushing ahead of her. But he kept marching, no longer finding excuses to delay.

"Excuse me, do you happen to know my name?" she asked the leader, assuming a place just behind his left shoulder.

"That ain't your place in line, Lady. Get back with your outland lover."

"Why did I know you'd be as evasive as the others?"

* * *

Jack stood on a promontory overlooking the vale where Margit and Katrina made camp. Even after three days, he struggled to reconcile the double nature of his vision. The massive spell to separate the queen from her cat had sapped his energies to a dangerously low point.

Amaranth balanced easily on his shoulder. Corby used to perch in much the same spot. Amaranth was heavier, but more willing to please and become an extension of Jack's magic and personality. A friend. His rich fur brushed Jack's face and they both leaned into the caress, needing each other.

Jack had cried the morning he could not wake Corby, but he'd accepted the loss. Corby had been his only—if somewhat reluctant—friend for a long time; much longer than jackdaws normally lived. Corby deserved his rest. Hopefully, he'd pass peacefully into his next existence, into a life without the wild adventures reserved for a magician's familiar.

Amaranth chattered his teeth in anxious anticipation of the coming adventures.

"They've come a long way in so short a time," Jack mused as he stroked Amaranth's fur. He'd stalked the two women for three days, not daring to approach closer lest Katrina reject him. He'd also husbanded his strength. That last spell had drained him of more energy than usual. More often than not, he was so tired he saw double.

"We're very near the border with SeLenicca. I don't like them camping without a bubble of armor."

But if Katrina would *Sing* as she had *Sung* in SeLenicca, she might create her own spell of invisibility that Margit couldn't duplicate. Jack had to chuckle at how many villages and homesteads had eluded him on his quest, all because the women unconsciously *Sang* spells of protection for their loved ones as they went about their daily chores.

The flywacket ruffled his feathered wings, getting used to their size and the skin flap that hid them when at rest. He rubbed his cat's muzzle against Jack's chin, eager for more caresses.

(Steeds.) Not so much a word as an image of two fleet and one pack steed picketed beyond Margit's fire,

but sheltered by an outcropping of rock. Jack could not have seen the animals without Amaranth's help.

"They've stopped early. Still hours of daylight left," he mused. As he watched, Katrina and Margit both rubbed the insides of their thighs through their journey trews. Riding had taken its toll on unfamiliar riders.

"Is it time to let the girls know we've followed them?" Jack asked Amaranth, not really expecting an answer.

Amaranth purred, devoid of opinion. Jack supposed the true cat spirit he'd liberated from Queen Mikka vied with the dragon intelligence for dominance inside the flywacket. They'd compromise soon enough. Then Amaranth would reawaken his true telepathic communication with Jack.

Something alien churned inside Jack, and the base of his spine itched as if it needed to twitch. The smell of Margit's roasting hedgehog filtered up to his nose in hundreds of component odors. He grew dizzy trying to sort them.

"I guess you are channeling your heightened senses into me without knowing it, Amaranth," he commented.

The flywacket perked his ears and continued purring.

"Maybe I'll stay up here one more night. I'll join them tomorrow," Jack mused.

"Mew," Amaranth agreed.

The wind shifted to the East, behind Jack. It smelled of rain with a slight tang of salt. Another storm approached from the sea.

Margit sneezed three times in quick succession.

Katrina draped a blanket over the apprentice magician's shoulders.

Jack crouched down to observe closer. Margit getting sick was not in his plans. She'd delay them. He hoped that once in her own land, Katrina would learn to trust him again, learn that he'd never hurt her, even

if they must remain celibate the rest of their lives—a
fate he certainly hoped to avoid.

(Not sick,) Amaranth insisted.

"Well, nice to hear you speak again, friend," Jack
murmured, stroking the flywacket's neck and back.
His fingers lingered on the slight bump of the extra
skin that had rolled back to release the wings.

(Lonely for Katrina. She lonely, too.) Amaranth
launched into a long glide down the rock face. He
landed beside Katrina, tucked his wings neatly away
and began an obligatory bath.

Both women squealed, Margit half-frightened, Katrina half-delighted, at their visitor. Margit shifted her
bottom to a rock on the opposite side of the fire from
the flywacket.

"I hate cats!" Her words came distinctly to Jack's
ears, despite the wind that blew in the opposite
direction.

True to the perverse nature of all cats, Amaranth
followed Margit. He rubbed up against her arm and
attempted to crawl into her lap. Margit jumped up
with a yelp and began walking circles around the
camp. The flywacket followed her lazily.

Katrina tried luring the black cat into her lap. Amaranth crouched on the other side of the fire, shifting
his front paws in hunter mode, ready to leap.

But Jack saw the cat's trajectory in his mind and
Amaranth's. He'd land directly on Margit's shoulder,
not Katrina's lap.

"Thanks for making my decision for me, Amaranth." Jack climbed down to retrieve his familiar and
restore order in the camp. "I just hope you haven't
created more problems than you solved."

CHAPTER 24

Lanciar threaded his way along the line of march toward Zolltarn's sledge. The stern and wily clan chieftain popped a whip just above the left ear of the lead pack steed. The animal quickened its pace a bit. The other steeds followed suit.

The tin weasel, perched on the raised front of the sledge, seemed to wink and drool at the evidence of Zolltarn's control of the dumb beasts. Its tail lost some of its rigidity and bristled.

Lanciar quickly crossed his wrists behind his back and wiggled his fingers in an abbreviated ward against evil. The statue was inanimate. It couldn't move. Could it?

Zolltarn smiled and so did everyone else in the caravan, including Lanciar, the tin weasel forgotten. That happened a lot. Whatever mood sat on Zolltarn's shoulders infected the entire clan. Was this part of their connected magic; all of them subtly linked so that what one experienced the others shared? Lanciar hoped not. If that were the case, he was falling under their spell. He needed independence and privacy to steal his son. If he ever found the boy.

"You have something to ask me?" Zolltarn spoke before Lanciar could open his mouth or even frame his question.

"You lead us in a strange direction," Lanciar said.

"The road leads us. We follow it," Zolltarn replied in typically cryptic Rover fashion.

"The road branched three ways less than an hour

ago. You could have chosen any one of those directions."

"This road seemed more enticing."

"This road leads to the mountains. The pass into SeLenicca is haunted by demons and ghosts as well as bandits."

"Ghosts have no reason to trouble Rovers. Bandits have learned to leave us alone. And as for demons? Demons can be our friends." The Rover leader smiled and squinted his eyes in an expression that looked like mischief personified.

Lanciar refused to repeat the ward behind his back. He'd have to learn to deal with Zolltarn and his smile sooner or later, hopefully later, after he left the clan with his son.

"Rovers are not welcome in SeLenicca," Lanciar argued. "The land has been stripped of resources. Why borrow trouble, when you can roam Coronnan and live off its lush bounty?"

"My grandson travels this way. I sense that he needs me." Zolltarn lifted his head and sniffed the air. His eyes took on a glazed expression.

"Who calls you, Zolltarn?" Lanciar asked.

"As I said, my grandson."

"You have so few men in the clan. I'm surprised you allowed the man to leave."

"In the way of the People, the man goes to his wife's clan. For my grandson to marry within the clan would violate our laws against incest. He will rule his wife's clan one day, as I rule my wife's."

"You have not brought in new husbands for the many women here. Instead you indulge in polygamy."

'You have been brought into the clan. As have many orphaned children."

"I travel with you. There is a difference." But his senses became suddenly alert to the nuances in Zolltarn's tone. There was only one child that interested him.

"Is there a difference? We take in the son, so must we take in the father."

"I will leave when I have accomplished my mission."

"Will you?"

"*S'murghit,* I will."

Watch your language! He distinctly heard Maija's reprimand in his mind.

Lanciar looked around for Zolltarn's youngest daughter. She frowned at him from three sledges behind him. For once he did not look away and feel ashamed, but boldly held her gaze until she smiled and nodded.

Only then did Lanciar turn his attention back to the Rover Chieftain's challenge. Inwardly he shuddered against standing in such close proximity to a dark-eyed outlander; having his son raised by outlanders. Prejudices pounded into him as a child remained firmly rooted in his gut and the back of his mind.

At one time he'd loved Rejiia. By that time, he'd spent enough time in the company of foreign soldiers and diplomats to overlook many things about outlanders. But still he resented them, felt dirty having to touch one. He'd overlooked Rejiia's black hair because she had an incredibly lush body and an insatiable sexual appetite. True-blood women were notorious prudes. She also had piercing and beautiful blue eyes—the blue of an endless night sky in deep Winter. True-bloods of SeLenicca always had blue eyes (though several shades lighter than Rejiia's) and blond hair.

But she and her lover King Simeon, Queen Miranda's red-haired consort, had stolen the crown from Simeon's meek little wife. Rejiia had claimed that her son was fathered by Simeon, hoping to put the child on the throne of SeLenicca as well as Coronnan with claims to Rossemeyer and Hanassa. But Simeon had turned out to be her father's half brother. Then she claimed the boy died at birth to avoid the taint of incest.

But Lanciar knew the child to be his, sired during a particularly passionate coven ritual when The Simeon had occupied himself exclusively with Ariiell. She'd been a simpering virgin at the time and screamed loudly enough to satisfy even The Simeon. Rejiia had never screamed during sex and always participated with all of her strength and emotions—even during her first ritual when Simeon claimed her virginity.

Lanciar wondered if she'd indeed been a virgin or merely used her magic to create that illusion.

You can't trust a dark-eyed outlander. The oft repeated phrase burned into Lanciar's mind.

"I'll leave when I accomplish my mission," he reiterated.

"You have met my daughter Maija," Zolltarn continued as if Lanciar had not spoken. "A comely girl."

"She's a good cook." Lanciar wasn't about to admit how beautiful he found the girl with her flashing eyes, bright smile, long legs, and lush bosom. He didn't really mind her reprimands about his soldier-bred language. From that first night when she'd asked him to abandon his campsite and join the clan, he'd admired her.

But the promise of a romp in her bed had remained an elusive taunt between them. All he wanted from her was a romp. A commitment for more would tie him to the clan and he did not want to stay with them any longer than necessary. He wanted his son free of Rover ideas and morals—or lack of morals.

He sensed a trap in Zolltarn's words and the girl's seduction. And he'd witnessed almost no immoral conduct or indiscretions.

"Maija has no husband. She has courted a number of suitable men from other clans but found none of them to her liking. Not all of the men are willing to follow me because I am a powerful magician and have ties to the Commune of Magicians. They know that once they mate with one of mine there is no escape. They remain part of my clan even if their bride dies."

"I presume, then, that the choice of mate belongs to the women in your clan." Lanciar found himself edging away from Zolltarn, off the road, away from these people and their alien customs.

" 'Tis the way of the Rovers. Once she chooses, she must be faithful. Before she chooses, she must remain untouched. Upon occasion we have relaxed that rule and met with disaster. My eldest daughter Kestra died and her child was stolen from us because we sought a different solution to our needs. Never again."

"I'm surprised you have not pushed Maija to choose sooner, bring new blood, another man into the clan."

"Ah, but now she has chosen. And she will take your son into her household as soon as he is weaned." Zolltarn stared directly at Lanciar.

"I think I need a drink."

"Maija brews the best ale of all the Rover clans."

* * *

Eight black articulated limbs quested outward from the slime-coated, bulbous body of the spider. Vareena stared at the malevolent creature, frozen by fear.

Poison dripped from the clacking pincers on the forward limbs. Its eyes, positioned near the joint of each leg, flashed demon red. The thing could easily enclose her fist within its eight arms.

Her heart pounded as loud as festival drums. Cold sweat trickled down her back.

The spider inched forward, tasting the air with each legtip, glowing as redly as its eyes.

"Stargods protect me," she whispered, trying to edge away from her stalker. The stone walls on three sides of her hard bed within the monastery stopped her retreat.

The spider moved forward faster than she could edge away from it.

Could she run for the doorway before it swung out on its web and latched onto her vulnerable neck?

Surely Robb must sense her fear, hear her thudding heartbeat, and come to her rescue.

The door remained stubbornly closed. The entire monastery was wrapped in the preternatural silence of the gloaming.

The spider came closer.

Panic propelled Vareena out of bed and across the room. She tugged at the door. It remained firmly closed and latched. She kicked it and bruised her toes. She pulled with both hands. It did not even rattle.

Something heavy and hard landed on her hair.

She screamed . . .

And awoke in bed drenched in sweat.

Cautiously, afraid to move lest she bring the spider upon her, she brought a wisp of witchlight to her fingertip.

Search as she might, she could not find the spider. An empty and torn cobweb hung from the far corner of her cell. She'd thrown witchfire at it before claiming the room as her own.

The sweat beneath her shift chilled rapidly. She needed to move or wrap the covers more tightly about her. But if she did that, she might disturb the spider.

The door burst open. Marcus and Robb, both bleary-eyed with sleep-tousled hair stood side by side. Each carried a large ball of witchlight. The directionless light illuminated every corner of the room.

"Spider!" she hissed at them, almost daring them to search her blankets.

Marcus strode forward with confidence and whipped the bedcovers away from her. He shook them vigorously.

Nothing scuttled away from his search.

"You must have had a nightmare," Robb said behind a yawn. "We've both had them since coming here. Go back to sleep. The dream will fade with the dawn."

"I can't go back to sleep." She wished one of them, either of them, both of them, would hold her tight and banish the fear with their strength. Their ghostly energies kept them from touching her.

"Then get up and do something. Best way to banish a dream is to use the privy and let it drain away. Bake some bread, clean something, count the bricks in the wall. You'll be sleep again in moments." Robb backed out of the room.

"He's right, Vareena. You need to do something to shake yourself free of the dream." Marcus shrugged and exited as well.

"He's right." Vareena stood up and took stock of her cell. No shadows hid from her witchlight. "Childish fears. I won't let them rule me." With determination, she dressed and went to find flour and yeast. Time to start baking bread for breakfast.

* * *

My powers are weakening! My enemies have weathered every disaster I throw at them. Yet still they gather. Still they plot against me.

Once, long ago, when I was just beginning, all others thought me weak and of little consequence. But I showed them. I gathered secrets as a miser gathers gold. I gathered power and I learned to use it subtly, so that they never knew from whence the attack came. I taught my children to do the same. They became almost as powerful as me.

To protect myself and the source of my power, I must delve deep into my memories for a spell that will drain away all that these thieves hold dear. Then, when they are weak and vulnerable, I will scatter them, make them wander lost and alone, powerless. If that fails, I must murder them all.

CHAPTER 25

The unnamed woman sat staring into the crackling fire. Zebbiah and Jaranda had left her alone while they made a game of fetching water and washing the roots he had gathered earlier today. Her heart warmed whenever she saw the two of them together. Zebbiah would make an admirable father for the little girl.

Would he make as fine a husband?

She nudged the notion aside while she concentrated on the flames. Images from her past flitted in and out of her view.

She tasted a name on her tongue. *Miranda*. A common enough name since a former king and queen of SeLenicca had given the name to their only child nineteen years ago.

Miranda. The name tasted smoky, like the air on this crisp and clear night in the middle of a remote mountain pass.

Miranda.

Could that truly be her name?

She stared into the green-and-yellow flames, seeking answers, wondering if she'd asked the right questions.

Images danced with the flames, teasing her mind. The strong, red-haired man with deep blue eyes, older than she by many years, dominated every scene she managed to mine from the deep recesses of her fragmented memory.

Jaranda's eyes. Her daughter had inherited those midnight blue eyes. True-bloods tended to have eyes as pale as their hair and skin. Washed out. As depleted of color as the land was depleted of vitality and resources.

She heaved a sigh and tasted the name again. She heard it whispered behind her back by the other travelers. It resonated within her as if it belonged.

Queen Miranda had married a red-haired outlander: Simeon the sorcerer-king. In her youth and naïveté, Queen Miranda had granted him joint ruling powers. Then she had turned over the government to him so that she could spend all of her time making lace—the proper place for a woman in her culture.

But Simeon had imposed crushing taxes on her people. He had forced a war with Coronnan. He had enacted stringent laws. For even the tiniest infraction of the new laws he had exacted the extreme punishment, slavery or execution. The executions had been carried out as sacrifices to his blood-thirsty demon god Simurgh.

And yet Simeon himself had broken every law he enacted. He'd taken several mistresses—one of them, Rejiia, his own niece. He'd consorted with foreigners. He'd paid no tithes to the temple as required, yet he stole temple funds for his own bizarre religion.

And then he had outlawed the ancient and beautiful worship of the three Stargod brothers.

SeLenicca had crumbled under his crushing rule.

Change had come to SeLenicca. Dramatic, catastrophic, and none too soon.

The SeLenese had long believed that they were the Chosen of the Stargods. The land was theirs to exploit. Nurturing the land, growing crops, and raising livestock had been delegated to lesser peoples in other countries. By the time Miranda came to the throne, the Chosen of the Stargods had bled SeLenicca of all her natural resources. They had nothing left except their arrogance, their prejudices, and their lace.

Dared she believe that she and the meek woman who had allowed all that to happen while she closeted herself with her lace were one and the same. Did she want to be that woman?

What other reason for one and all to desert her and her young daughter in the palace when they fled the kardiaquakes and the fires and the flooding? What other reason than to condemn her for their troubles?

Miranda.

"I'll do better when I return. But first I have to find the strength to be the kind of queen my people need. I need to remember everything, not just bits and pieces glued together with supposition."

A noise alerted her to the presence of another. She wasn't ready to face Zebbiah and Jaranda yet, so she continued staring blankly into the fire. Part of her senses remained focused on the shuffling steps and wheezing breath of the intruder.

Not Zebbiah.

She listened more closely and shifted her eyes, but not her head, to catch a glimpse of whoever hovered behind her, near the pack beast and the panniers; the panniers filled with her lace pillow and countless yards of priceless lace.

"You there!" She stood abruptly and whirled to face the caravan leader.

He held a long strand of lace, as wide as two joints of her pointing finger.

"Thief!" she screamed as loud as she could.

The leader took off running, trailing the lace behind him.

"Stop, thief!" she screamed again.

Loud footsteps ran closer. Men crowded close to her. Off to the side she caught a glimpse of Zebbiah running in pursuit.

"The leader stealing?" someone whispered behind her.

"What have we let ourselves in for."

"We can't continue with a thief for our leader."

"Is it truly theft to steal from a Rover and his mistress?"

The thief stumbled, tripping over the long strand of lace he tried desperately to gather as he ran. Zebbiah tackled him. They both landed facedown in the dirt.

"Leader, I accuse you of theft from the queen!" Miranda announced. She fought the hole in her gut that felt like he'd stolen her soul as well as her identity when he stole the lace. "The presence of Tambrin lace in your hand is all the evidence we need to convict you."

Stunned silence rang around the campfires at her pronouncement.

'You are sentenced to exile. Escort him from the camp," she ordered.

"But who will lead us? Who will guide us?"

"You caused this!" the stout merchant woman with two plaits from the boat shouldered her way to Miranda's side. "You and your slutty ways. If you'd married a true-blood we'd not have had your outland husband bring the wrath of the Stargods down on our heads. If you'd acted the queen and ruled rather than surrendering to your sorcerer husband, he'd not have ruined our beautiful land. Now you consort with another outlander. Aren't true-bloods good enough for you? We should exile you!" She raised a fist as if to hit Miranda.

The former queen stood straight, facing her accuser.

Excited whispers broke out among the men and the few women in the caravan. They retreated a step or two, leaving Miranda alone in the circle with her accuser.

Jaranda broke into wild cries.

Zebbiah wrestled the purloined lace from the thief.

"It seems to me, I am headed into exile, as are you and the rest of these people. What more can you do to me?" Miranda finally spoke. "But thievery from me is only a symptom of this man's dishonesty. Do you truly wish to risk traveling so far with him? Do you truly wish to be led by a man who will steal from each of you as easily as he does from me? I am no longer your queen. Decide for yourselves how you will treat a thief. I am going to eat my dinner." She sat down on her rock beside the fire once more.

"Somehow, I thought you'd find a rod of iron in your backbone once you started to remember," Zebbiah said quietly. He cuddled Jaranda close to his side.

Miranda took the lace from him and began rolling it into a neat coil, brushing dust from it as best she could. "How long have you known who I am?"

"Since the beginning. Who else would haunt the palace like the most beautiful ghost this world ever saw?"

"Why did I know you'd say something lovely like that?" She smiled up at him, welcoming his open admiration of her.

*   *   *

Marcus waited until the faint sounds of Robb settling back into his bed filtered through the wall separating their rooms. Barefoot, he crept across to the doorway and waited again. Vareena had quieted, too. The chill of the ages seeped from the stones into his feet. But he dared not put on his boots. He needed quiet and privacy. Not even the ghost must hear him.

He was convinced the ghost had given or augmented Vareena's nightmare. He had to be stopped. And Marcus had to be the one to stop him.

He'd oiled the leather hinges of his door this afternoon with a bit of fat from his breakfast bacon. The door opened silently. He closed it again behind him, leaving it just slightly ajar so that even the click of the latch would not alert another to his movements.

A tiny bit of light showed around the edges of Robb's door, as it did most nights. For some reason the absolute darkness within the monastery bothered him. He set a ball of witchlight in his window each night and let it fade as he fell asleep.

Vareena's room was dark, but a little light glowed from the refectory.

Marcus welcomed the dark tonight. He needed stealth.

Thirty paces down the colonnade brought him to the doorway of the corner master's suite. No one else seemed to have noticed that this room remained unused by those seeking sanctuary here. The previous prisoners should have sought the relative luxury of the larger room with its own privy. Even he and Robb had instinctively chosen rooms at the end of the wing of the building rather than bunk in here.

Why?

In asking the question, he knew the room must contain answers to the entrapment puzzle. But the answers were hidden and not easily ferreted out.

The door opened easily and silently at his touch. He'd greased these hinges as well as his own. Once inside, with the door closed, he brought a ball of cold light to his palm and held it aloft.

Nothing seemed changed, or out of place. An ordinary room reserved for the most senior magician who would administer the place from the office portion of the room. The bed niche behind the half wall would allow him to rest in relative privacy. From here he had easy access to the tower observation platform where he would monitor the movements of the stars and moon in the endless wheel of time.

Marcus had seen many towers and many observation platforms in his career. Answers might lie in the stars, but those patterns were subject to interpretation. What he needed was communion with the ancient spirits who had lived here long ago, when the first ghosts came here to die.

Inanimate objects could absorb strong emotions. Stone walls might reveal things that people forgot.

He placed the ball of witchlight in a niche beside the tower stairs. It nestled in there as if born to the place. The builders must have placed the small opening there as a night light for weary magicians moving up and down the staircase when they watched the stars for omens and portents of the future as well as answers to the present.

Breathing deeply, Marcus stared at the wall that adjoined the library, seeking a vulnerable place; some stone that might have been struck in anger or frustration, a place where a weary man had leaned for a moment of rest.

A trance settled on his shoulders, and the light in the room seemed to magnify. The tiny chinks and crevices blazed forth. The stones and the mortar took on a luminescence. He could see every fleck of minerals on the surface.

There! The stone a little below shoulder height, five blocks away from the doorway, seemed to have a handprint outlined in tiny glowing dots of white marble within the granite. Marcus placed his own left hand over the handprint. His longer and narrower fingers spread beyond the print, but his palm seemed an almost perfect match.

Already, he got a sense of the man, shorter than himself, probably stouter. And there, a darker splotch, about his nose level, where he had rested his head. He mimicked the posture.

Beneath his ear, the stones seemed to pulse. He let his trance fall deeper, penetrate the wall taking him . . .

Betrayed! The one who has claimed to be my friend our entire lives, has betrayed me. He knows nothing of the reality of politics or economics, nothing of the agreed of men. He knows only magic, the theories and techniques. Now he expects me to step aside and allow him to govern all magic and magicians in Coronnan. He'll botch the job for certain. Without me working beside him to keep lords and merchants honest in their dealings, he'll be bankrupt and disgraced before a moon has transpired.

But I will not be there to drag him out of the muck of politics and economics. This time his insults and disdain go too far. I shall take myself and my meager savings to another. Another man will pay me well to be his Battlemage. My so-called friend will have to face me in battle. He shall come alone and unprepared, because I am not there to do the work for him beforehand.

But first I must secure what is mine! No one shall find it in three hundred years.

Marcus jerked away from the wall as if burned. The anger of the man scorched the very walls of this monastery. His palm continued to tingle and radiate heat. He'd learn nothing more tonight.

"Ackerly. I think his name was Ackerly," he whispered as he made his way back to bed.

CHAPTER 26

Robb sat atop the open northwest watchtower above the kitchen and refectory, watching the stars. The haze thinned up here, giving him a clearer view. Many hundreds of years ago, hundreds of magician priests, and retired magicians, healers and Battlemages had taken turns sitting up here watching the same stars. He found the familiar constellations, noting their position in the sky automatically. His planetary orientation told him that his observations were correct—something he couldn't discern down in the courtyard. The great wheel of stars around the moon had moved seventeen days since he and Marcus had arrived.

And yet they had only slept three nights. Time as well as magic became distorted within the monastery.

Another storm massed clouds to the west. But it would not arrive until tomorrow or the next day in real time, depending on the winds that pushed it. He didn't think it would hit with as much severity as the last one, if it reached them at all. The time distortion might very well push the weather elsewhere. Only one storm in a thousand hit the forgotten enclave, and then only those storms of unusual fierceness.

The scent of yeast bread rising wafted up to him from the refectory. What was he to do with Vareena and her obvious infatuation with him? "She loves the idea that I might take her away from here more than she loves me," he decided.

Idly, he tossed pebbles off the roof thinking of noth-

ing and everything. Mostly he avoided thinking of
Marcus and his declaration of love.

How could he ever feel close to his comrade again?

They had traveled the length and breadth of Coronnan several times these last three years. Many times
they had faced danger together. Many more times they
had fled from it. Never had they questioned their
friendship or their dependence upon each other. But
that need had never crossed over the unspoken sexual
boundaries Marcus now teetered on.

They both enjoyed women, looked forward to the
day they could commit to just one. That they both
wanted Margit hadn't seemed to matter. Margit loved
Marcus. Robb had convinced himself he'd learn to
love another someday.

But now? He'd rather watch the pebbles he threw,
feel the rhythm of his shoulders and arms as he got the
knack of aiming them to different parts of the monastery.

The stones landed in the packed dirt of the courtyard with tiny "plunk" sounds. He cast the next pebbles farther, aiming for a peculiar twist in the silvery-
blue ley line. It landed on the slate paving stones
around the well with a satisfying "thwack." The next
six pebbles also landed anywhere but on top of a ley
line. Curious. The lines might be illusory, part of the
confinement spell. He put more energy into the next
pebble, a slightly larger piece of rubble from this roof-
top observation post. It soared over the walls of the
monastery to land silent and unseen.

"So, things can get out of here. People with magical
talent can't." But could a spell?

Shrugging his shoulders, he lit a candle and dug out
his shard of glass. He went through the motions of
setting up the summons spell without thinking. Just
before he sent his mind through the glass into the
candle, he sat back and looked up at the stars once
more. They twinkled at him invitingly.

"It's worth a try." He moved the candle to the parapet and sat below it, aiming his spell upward. Three

deep breaths sent him halfway to the void. Another three breaths and the stars sang in his blood. All of his senses hummed in harmony with the world. He drew power from the stars, from the stones, from the ancient trees.

"If this doesn't work, I'll try probing the walls."

He took another three breaths for courage. "Like seeking like, flame to flame, glass to glass, my mind to a receptive mind. Heed my call of distress. Hear my plea for release." The rhythmic words poured from his mouth and his mind through the glass into the flame.

Reluctantly the flame pried itself loose from the candle and soared upward, much diminished in size and intensity. It flew beyond the walls, beyond the spell that bound it to Robb. It arced high and wide, flying on and on until Robb lost all trace of it in his glass and in his mind.

The candle guttered. The glass fell from his nerveless hands. He collapsed in a heap upon the stones, utterly exhausted.

The chill of morning dew awoke him. Automatically, he reached for the precious piece of glass. Pain slashed across his fingers. He yelped and jerked his hand away from the glass, sucking on the bloody cut. His glass had shattered when he dropped it.

His glass. The very symbol of his magical talent. His most precious tool along with his staff. A part of him. Broken. Shattered into six fragments too small to use for even the simplest of spells.

"S'murghit!" he yelled at the top of his lungs. *"Bloody, tartarian Simurgh!"* He threw the largest piece as far and high as he could, then the next shard and the next. When he still needed to release more energy, he grabbed the piece of gold in his pocket and threw it.

The world shattered. Light blazed. The stones at his feet tilted and whirled. Two heartbeats later his senses righted and he looked out at the world with a new clarity.

The gloaming retreated downward, leaving him above the haze.

"What the . . ." He retreated cautiously back down the staircase to the ground level. The coin glinted at him from the vicinity of the gate, enticing him to return it to his pocket where it belonged.

Robb raced down the stairs to retrieve the coin before he lost it. He paused in the arched entryway of the stairs. No one yet stirred in the monastery. He could retrieve the coin without observation.

He took fifty silent paces across the courtyard. Then stooped, about to place the little bit of treasure in his pocket—protected, out of sight. Hoarded.

The rising sun glinting through the crack in the sagging gate caught his attention.

"Just once more. I'll try the gate just once more." Holding his breath he pushed against the heavy panels. They creaked open.

Hastily, he looked over his shoulder to check if Marcus or Vareena came to investigate. The courtyard remained empty.

One more deep breath for courage and he—

Stepped through the gateway into the outside world.

Astonishment kept him pressed against the gate, afraid to step away lest his knees give out.

"I'm free?" he whispered to the winds. Two steps away from the stout walls confirmed it. He could walk away from here. Send help back for Marcus and Vareena. He could tap the formerly crazy ley lines that now ran straight and thick. He could . . .

He had to go back.

Marcus would disintegrate, physically and emotionally without him. He owed it to Marcus to go back.

The coin greeted him upon his return.

"So you are the culprit." He gritted his teeth and picked up the shiny piece of gold. "And my guess is your original owner was a miser. A miser who refused his next existence rather than give you up."

Once more the world tilted and light flashed, momentarily blinding him. When he opened his eyes again, a misty veil lay over everything.

"Coronnan has waited years for the return of the dragons. A few more weeks will not make so much difference."

"Robb, is everything all right?" Marcus appeared at the doorway to his cell, running his fingers through his tangled hair and blinking sleepily.

"Yeah, Marcus, everything's going to be fine." *If I can figure this out, so can you. You need the success to bolster your luck more than I do. I'll wait until things get really desperate to show you the truth—if you haven't figured it out by then.*

* * *

"Get that cat away from me!" Margit screamed as she jumped away from Amaranth for the fifth time.

"What a sweet creature," Katrina gathered Amaranth into her lap. "Such a *big* cat. Did you truly fly here or did you just jump from the rocks above us?" She petted him with enthusiasm.

"He's with me," Jack said quietly as he scrambled down the last of the rocks. He had to work hard to retain his balance, never quite certain which image was real and which a ghost.

Margit jumped again, startled. "You're supposed to let your armor down when approaching the camp of a magician. I could have blasted you with . . . with . . ."

"With what, Margit? What spell could you devise that would catch me off guard?" Jack smiled, trying hard to keep any sense of triumph out of his voice. From what he'd seen, Margit would make a competent journeywoman someday. Master status would elude her talents.

"I—I'd have thought of some—something." Margit worked her nose and mouth in peculiar gyrations.

"Jack," Katrina said quietly, still stroking Amaranth.

"Ahhhchooo!" Margit sneezed strongly enough to nearly extinguish the fire. "Get that cat away from me."

"Katrina," Jack acknowledged the woman he loved, ignoring Margit completely.

"I suppose you've come to take me back," Katrina said quietly, burying her face in Amaranth's blacker than black fur.

Did she sound accepting or defiant? Jack couldn't tell while Margit continued to sneeze her head off right next to him.

"No, Katrina, I've come to join you, keep you safe on this journey you've chosen."

"I thought that was Margit's job."

The apprentice magician sneezed again, three times in quick succession.

Katrina shifted to a rock on the far side of the fire, taking Amaranth with her. She looked up at Jack with hopeful eyes.

Margit continued to sneeze.

"I hope you will welcome my company," Jack said tersely.

Katrina looked up at him without answering, eyes huge in the firelight.

"Something is different about you, Jack. You are . . . almost vulnerable. Like you were when I first met you."

"Lonely. Missing you as I would miss my breath or the beat of my heart."

Her chin quivered slightly. She bit her lip.

Jack waited a moment, hoping she'd say something, anything to reassure him. "I'll not press you to marry me, Katrina. I know you fear it. But I need to know you are safe. I need to be close to you, look at you, touch you." He stroked her long, silky plaits.

Margit might not have been there except for her sneezes. Which tapered off as Jack moved away from her.

The funny feeling churned in his gut again, and his tailbone needed to twitch. He knew a sudden compulsion to wash his hands and face—especially behind his ears—in the nearby creek.

"And who is this new companion of yours, Jack? I know you miss Corby, but I never thought I'd see you with a cat," Katrina continued, as if their future together did not lay between them like an open wound.

"That is Amaranth." Silently, Jack sent the flywacket an image of rubbing his black fur against Margit's trews.

"Amaranth?" Katrina looked up at him, love and trust shining in her eyes. Could this be just another ordinary conversation catching up on the news?

"The redundant purple dragon has taken a new form. He's truly my familiar now." Jack perched on a rock next to Katrina; close enough to reach out and hold her hand, but not so close as to threaten her.

"It's as if he now absorbs all of the light he used to reflect." She tried to stop the black cat from hopping off her lap, but he wriggled free of her grasp and slunk over to Margit. She had her back to the fire and for a moment her sneezes had abated.

"Amaranth," Katrina called him back.

Under Jack's prodding the flywacket circled Margit three times, each circuit bringing him closer to her until he rubbed his face against her boots and then her knees.

"Get away, you awful creature." Margit hopped and jumped farther away from the fire. But she did not sneeze.

Jack sent Amaranth another mental command to return to Katrina and stay with her. Amaranth arched his back and stretched, leaning first backward, tail up, front legs extended. Then he leaned forward, stretching his back legs one at a time. At last he shook himself and leaped over the fire, extending only the tips of his wings for balance. He landed next to Katrina and sat. He accepted a few ear scratches, then began to lave his front paws.

Jack wanted to fish the soap out of his pack and join his familiar in the cleansing ritual.

Margit whirled to face him, eyes huge, hands fishing within her scrip. "Did you feel that? You must have. It was stronger this time, more urgent."

Then Jack put aside his own horrible fears and opened his awareness. His glass thrummed, very lightly; almost as if he had already answered the summons that had brought it to life.

"What?"

"A distress call. From that direction." She pointed. "West by southwest."

"I barely felt it before it was gone."

"That's the nature of a distress call, sent out to any magician who might intercept it."

Jack looked at her quizzically.

"That's what Lyman says. And I'm betting it's Marcus. I'm following it. Now." She stooped to pick up her pack at her feet. "You two don't need me anymore."

"Wait, Margit. You can't go now. It's dark. The road is uncertain, and we're very near the border. Who knows what kinds of bandits lurk in the foothills." Jack gritted his teeth and grabbed Margit's arm to detain her. His insides coiled in mistrust and an urge to flee.

The moment he touched her shoulder, Margit sneezed three more times in rapid succession.

He whirled quickly and sought Amaranth's aura, clearly outlined in the firelight. Only the pale purple signature color outlined his black body with energy. Jack sought Katrina's single aura of crystal and white, like her lace. Margit shone three shades of yellow between sneezes that shifted all her energy to orange while she purged himself of some foreign humor in the air.

Then Jack took a deep breath and sought the first

stages of a trance. He stared at the silvery umbilical of life that trailed from his body.

Very few master magicians could see their umbilical anywhere but in the void. Fewer still ever had a glimpse of their true signature colors in the umbilical.

Along with Jack's signature silver and purple—darker than Amaranth's—he saw a strange coil of life entwined with his own. Red, black, yellow, brown, and a touch of white.

The same colors he'd sensed around Queen Mikka. The same colors as the cat she had lost when she absorbed her pet's spirit.

"Ladies, I think I have a problem."

CHAPTER 27

Lanciar shifted the bundle of kindling under his arm for better balance. Satisfied that he'd not drop the load of small sticks and dried grasses, he swung his free arm jauntily and whistled a gay tune as he strolled through the line of trees bordering a chuckling creek. This simple life of trekking across the countryside with the Rovers appealed to him. Almost like being back in the army without the worry and responsibility of seeing to the discipline and well-being of a thousand men under his command.

Indeed, discipline never seemed to be a problem with the Rovers. Their mind-to-mind links with Zoll-tarn gave them a sense of unity and purpose he'd never achieved in the army.

For a moment he felt very alone and left out of the clan. The whistling tune died in his throat. Alone. As he had always been alone except for those few brief hours when he and Jack had sat on a cold mountain trail while they traversed the void together seeking a way to center and awaken Lanciar's magical talent. Linked to Jack by mind and magic, he had known a short time of belonging with the universe at large and with one other person.

The next morning he and Jack had parted with hostility. And then, because of his misguided loyalty to the coven, Lanciar had betrayed Jack. Lanciar had never heard if the young magician had survived. He hoped so, even though they belonged to opposing forces on both the magic and mundane planes. Jack's honesty and unwavering loyalty deserved better than Rejiia had given him.

Guilt made him long for a tall mug of Maija's ale.

"What troubles you, spy?" Maija asked from directly behind him.

Lanciar gasped and whirled, ready to defend himself with his staff and magic. He'd never get used to the Rover's ability to creep up on him unannounced. Inanely, he was still clutching the kindling, recognizing its importance to the camp as a whole.

"What do you want?" he asked rather curtly. His irritation at his own failings suddenly became her fault.

"I thought you might like to meet your son, spy."

"I am not a spy. I have a *s'murghin'* name." He couldn't allow hope to overshadow his caution.

"Watch your language," she replied curtly. "Until you are one of us, we do not acknowledge your name. When you join us, we will give you a name worthy of our clan."

"When will I join you—if I decide to join your clan?"

"When you and I are married. When you and I soar through the heavens on a cloud of bliss on our wedding night. Then you will know the ecstasy of belonging to a clan." She moved closer. Her scent—soap, berries, and feminine allure—filled Lanciar's senses with longing.

Lanciar swallowed against a suddenly dry mouth.

"Come with me now, spy, and I will introduce you to your son. For the sake of your son, you will marry me. For the sake of your son, you will moderate your language, you will join with us, strengthen our clan with your strength, with your weapons, with your magic." She drifted closer yet. Her sweet breath fanned his cheek.

Slowly he shifted his mouth closer to hers. Closer until his lips brushed hers ever so lightly. Fire lit his veins and blanked his mind to all but Maija.

"Come," she whispered, taking his hand and leading him back to the encampment.

Men and women alike erected the circle of tents and bardos with swift efficiency. Trained soldiers didn't set up camp any better.

Still holding his hand, Maija led him to the small red tent with black trim beside Zolltarn's huge purple one. Together they ducked inside the long strands of wooden beads that served as a curtain. The aromatic incense of Tambootie wood greeted him from the beads as well as the fire. His senses reeled under the onslaught of hypnotic humors.

Lanciar blinked rapidly for several heartbeats, waiting for his eyes to adjust to the gloom of the tent interior and for his senses to balance. Maija continued to hold his hand. A fine layer of sweat moistened his palms. His mouth continued to dry. He swallowed convulsively several times, wishing he had a mug of Maija's very fine ale.

At last he spotted the curtained cradle swinging between two upright stands set beside the narrow pallet where Maija slept alone each night. A series of gurgles and coos came from the depths of the gauzy linen drapes over the peaked half roof of the cradle.

Lanciar dropped the bundle of kindling in his haste to reach his son. The Tambootie smoke had heightened his magical senses. One glimpse of the child's aura told him that he had sired this fragile scrap of humanity. He slid to his knees beside the cradle, fumbling with the coverings. Desperate to see the boy, afraid that Maija would hide the baby again if Lanciar took too long, he ripped away the fine linen.

His son stopped wiggling and cooing for one long breathless moment while father and son studied each other. Then at last the boy smiled, revealing toothless gums. He drooled and waved his hands about, happy with his life, with his full tummy, and his clean diaper.

"He is the most beautiful baby in the world," Lanciar gasped.

"Because he is your son." Maija beamed at him.

"Have you given him a name?" Lanciar spoke in hushed tones lest he startle the babe and set him crying. He offered the boy a finger to grasp.

A tiny fist wrapped around the digit with amazing strength and pulled it toward his mouth. Instantly, the baby began gnawing on it.

"Is he hungry?" Lanciar kept his finger where his son wanted it.

"No. He just needs to taste you in order to fix you in his tiny mind," Maija replied. She continued smiling hugely. "He's also beginning to grow teeth. His gums itch."

Lanciar finally gathered enough of his wits to look the boy over. Fine black hair with just a hint of a curl in it. Pink skin, much fairer than the olive tones of the Rovers. And incredibly deep blue eyes, the color of midnight at the full moon.

Rejiia's eyes.

Lanciar allowed his eyes to cross so he could study his son's aura. Undistinguished layers of purple, blue, red, green, and yellow frothed about him. He hadn't yet developed enough personality to push one color through to dominance.

"Marry me, and we will raise the boy together. You need never be separated from him again," Maija said. She lifted the babe into her arms, one hand beneath his bottom, the other supporting his head as she held him close against her shoulder.

"And if I choose to take my son back to my own land?"

"You will never see him again," she replied sternly.

"Then I will marry you." He swallowed, trying to get rid of his increasingly dry throat.

And then he noticed, eyes still crossed, how Maija's aura completely engulfed his son's, replacing it with her own dark purple-and-red coloring, extensions of Zolltarn's colors. The boy would never have an identity or personality of his own as long as he remained with the clan.

Lanciar had to get him away from here and soon.

"But first I need a drink. A very long and cold drink. Let me hold the boy while you fetch the ale."

"I will take him with me to the wet nurse. He will be hungry again soon."

"But . . ."

"When we marry, you may hold him all you wish. Until then, he belongs to the wet nurse."

"I'll get my own ale. And lots of it."

* * *

Jaranda fretted and cried. Her face flushed with fever. Her mother held her on her shoulder, gently rubbing the child's back.

"Hush, baby. Hush," she murmured over and over.

Jaranda pouted and stuck her thumb into her mouth.

"Zebbiah, she's feverish," Miranda called to her traveling companion. "We have to find someplace warm and dry. My baby needs rest and nourishing broths. We have to stop!"

Zebbiah frowned, looking up and down the line of march. "We need to stay with the caravan. These parts aren't safe," he said quietly. "Look, she's fallen asleep. I'll carry her for a while. She's just not used to traveling."

"It's more than that, Zebbiah. I remember a time of great sickness the Winter she was born. I remember the funeral pyres—the terrible smell. Most of all I remember the fear every time someone spiked a fever in a matter of moments. I will not let my baby die because you refuse to leave the dubious safety of these thieves and vagabonds."

"Lady, if I take you to a place where you can rest, will you make lace for me to sell?" Zebbiah asked in a whisper.

"Travel dust kept me from working the pillow by

the campfire. These thieves and vagabonds have already tried to steal the lace. They'd steal the glass beads, silk threads, and bag of lace for the price of a meal. If you find me a quiet place with a roof and a fire pit and proper food, I'll gladly sit and make lace every day as long as the light allows." Until she remembered everything.

She'd gladly separate from this caravan to get away from their fellow travelers. None of them had spoken civilly to her since they'd ousted the leader. And they kept their distance, making sure each evening to light their fires well away from Miranda, Zebbiah, and Jaranda.

She had pieces of her memory, her name and that of her husband, flashes of faces from the past, but little else.

"Lady, where I plan to take you, I'll have access to witchlight come Winter. You'll be able to make lace in the darkest corner in quiet privacy."

"Witchlight?" she gasped, frightened and exhilarated by the danger of sorcery. Often enough on this long trek through the mountains she'd seen the other travelers make the ward against witchcraft and evil whenever Zebbiah passed. She knew the motion of crossed wrists, right over left, and then flapping hands from a deep memory that seemed a part of her from her very beginnings. She wished she knew the origin of the gesture. Then perhaps she could understand the nature of the magic it warded against.

Something flapping, like a bird's wings . . .

She yanked her mind back to the immediate problem. Letting herself drift with minor remembrance often led to a true memory. But she didn't have time for that now.

"Yes, take me to this place, and I will make lace for you to sell while my baby recovers. Turn the place into a home, and I might stay there forever, content to make lace and raise my child in peace." Easier than returning to SeLenicca to take up the reins of government.

"Peace I cannot guarantee for long. But not many people know of this abandoned monastery. Most who know of it shun it because it is haunted. I have yet to meet a ghost there. It is not far from here, a day at most. We will break away from the caravan at the first bird chirp."

Jaranda stirred in Zebbiah's arms, snuggling close to him. She slept peacefully, thumb slipping free of her mouth. Something solid and honest about the man soothed her more than her mother's presence.

"We leave before dawn," the woman agreed.

"Take your baby now. I will make sure we camp close to the hidden path within the hour. I don't want to have to backtrack. Not on the open road. These vagabonds and thieves might well follow and attack us as soon as we are out of sight. I need to make plans to divert them."

CHAPTER 28

"We've only the one room above, the rest of you must take pallets in the great room—or the stable. Take your pick," the innkeeper announced. "Caravan came through from the pass yesterday and ain't left yet." She stood with fists atop her broad hips and a frown making deep creases in her heavy jowls. A thick wooden rolling pin with numerous dents sprouted from one of his fists. She looked as if she'd used it often to keep order in her tavern.

"I will have the private room to myself!" Ariiell stated firmly.

"I am the lord of this province, daughter. I shall have the room, with my wife, of course." Laislac glared at her with equal stubbornness. His face darkened. He'd explode with flying fists in a moment.

"I am a new bride and I carry the heir to the throne of all Coronnan. I believe I take precedence here."

Mardall giggled beside her. A bit of drool escaped his lips. His mother gently wiped it away with a lace-edged handkerchief.

"Protocol is useless in a situation like this." Andrall shouldered his way between Laislac and Ariiell. "If truth be told, Lady Lynnetta is senior in nobility to all of us. She is the daughter of one king, sister to another, and aunt to the current one. The only sensible thing to do is for all six of us to share the room above. Our retainers will bed down here and in the stable."

"Oh, why couldn't we have waited to leave Coronnan City. Then we could have traveled by our usual route, taking hospitality from minor lords who treat us as we deserve. Instead we have stayed with ungrateful merchants. Now we must spend tonight in this foul inn that breeds disease and crime," Lady Laislac wailed and sobbed into her own handkerchief—not nearly as fine as Lady Lynnetta's.

The innkeeper frowned more deeply. She looked as if she'd gladly throw them all out to fend for themselves in the nightly drizzle.

"We left in midafternoon because the king commanded it," Andrall reminded them all. "If we had gone to my own castle at Nunio, we'd be there by now. 'Twould be more seemly for the child to be born in his father's ancestral home."

"I want my daughter comfortable, in familiar surroundings, where *I* can protect her and the babe." Laislac faced his new great-brother, his face darkening further. "You know the threats by the Gnuls. They want Darville to die heirless so the kingdom will fall into chaos. My daughter and her child will be safe in Laislac. Nunio is too close to the capital and the Gnuls."

"The Gnuls are everywhere, even in Laislac. Ariiell and the child would be safer in Nunio where *I* can protect them," Andrall returned. "I, at least, have some battle experience."

Ariiell motioned her maid to take her bag up the rickety staircase to the attic room. She slipped away, leaving her elders to their arguments.

Once inside the drafty space between the main floor and the roof, she dismissed her servant—a spy for her stepmother and probably the king as well—and locked the door. She shoved a table and chair in front of it for good measure.

"Alone at last!" She dug a small candle and piece of glass out of her personal bag of toiletries. The wick burst into flame with a thought. Then she settled down to summon her mentor. Rejiia would find a way to force Darville into recalling her to court. The mission of the coven was at stake.

"Flame to flame, like seeking like," she intoned the ritual phrases as she breathed deeply. The flickering green bit of fire drew her focus deep within the many layers of color, so like an aura, but more primitive and pure. She was content to sit there staring at the light magnified by her bit of glass.

A hazy yellow/green/blue glow rippled across the clear surface, vibrating slightly with the thrumming magic she had channeled through it.

Her spell must be weak and diffuse because she did not know where Rejiia hid. An answer might take a long time in coming . . .

"What!" Rejiia's explosive reply burst through the glass before her image solidified. Anger and impatience blazed in her midnight-blue eyes. Her black hair crackled about her puffy face in wild disarray. Dark shadows ringed her eyes.

Ariiell had never seen her in such disorder. She could almost smell the Tambootie leaves on Rejiia's breath. The drugs within the tree sap might enhance magical power, but it led to certain insanity.

"Rejiia, I need your help . . ." she began.

"Of course you do, you inept little . . ." Rejiia clamped her mouth shut and closed her eyes for a brief moment. When she returned her attention to Ariiell, she appeared calm, gentle, patient, and wise. Her eyes were clear and the familiar lean planes had returned to her cheeks and chin. A demeanor befitting the Center of the coven, a position Rejiia guarded jealously. Even though pregnancy should allow Ariiell to anchor the eight-pointed star rituals, Rejiia had not relinquished her place since her own pregnancy had ousted the late King Simeon from the center.

"What troubles you, child?" Rejiia asked. An aura of love and forgiveness flowed through the glass. But her hair still needed a good brushing.

Ariiell didn't trust that projected image any more

than she trusted Rejiia to do anything except advance herself and the cause of the coven.

"Darville has exiled my entire family from court, Lord Andrall and Lady Lynnetta as well."

"Did the marriage take place?" Rejiia asked anxiously.

"Of course. Darville presided beside the priest. The entire ceremony was duly witnessed and recorded. The child is legitimate. But Rossemikka did not attend. 'Twas not a state event. I doubt anyone outside the family knows of it." Ariiell allowed herself a small smile.

"And the idiot?"

"With us."

"Good. Keep him, close. Sleep with him if you must. We need him alive and well until the child is born."

"I must return to court, Rejiia. That is the plan. I must be there to poison Darville and his foreign queen as soon as my child is acknowledged the legitimate heir."

"Plans change. I leave the poisoning to your guardian who is still in the capital." Rejiia lifted her hand in the gesture to end the summons.

But Ariiell had the book of poisons. Her guardian— whatever his name and status in the coven might be— had asked for it several times. She smiled to herself.

"The plan will not change. My son will rule Coronnan and I shall be regent. The coven will rule Coronnan through me," Ariiell replied sternly.

"Plans change," Rejiia stated firmly. Her eyes narrowed with secrets.

Suddenly Ariiell did not trust Rejiia to work in the coven's best interests. She worked only for herself.

"There may be another heir. I must investigate," Rejiia continued. "I am needed elsewhere."

"The coven has decreed that I must remain at court. Now help me return there. Shall I summon the full coven in council?" Ariiell asserted her rights.

"Very well, where are you?" Rejiia sighed and rolled her eyes upward. Dark shadows made her brilliantly blue eyes look as deep and fathomless as the Great Bay at midnight.

Ariiell shuddered with a sudden chill. Rejiia's anger could be formidable. She wasn't certain her own magic was strong enough yet to challenge the black-haired, black-hearted woman for the Center of the coven.

Quickly, Ariiell gave Rejiia a brief accounting of her location, still about five hours' hard steed ride east and south of Castle Laislac, not too far from the small pass through the mountains into SeLenicca.

"Really?" Rejiia's smile brightened. She laughed loud and long. The echoes of her mirth rippled through the glass to bounce off the walls of the attic room. Rejiia might have been next door. "How interesting. At dawn, you must proceed south on the main road for approximately one league, then turn north by northwest on a drover's track until you reach the small village perched on a rolling meadow by the river. Above the village at the top of a wooded hill is an abandoned monastery. Go there and wait for further instructions."

"But that is out of the way! What excuse can I use to separate myself from all these people. They guard me closely." As they should, since she carried the heir.

"You'll think of something. Just get there before noon. The entire fate of the coven depends upon you arriving in time . . . Never mind what for. Just do it. You'll know why when you arrive." Rejiia ended the summons with a snap of her fingers.

The glass turned cloudy with soot from the candle flame. It ceased vibrating with rippling colors and became once more inert.

The sounds of Rejiia's misplaced laughter still vibrated in Ariiell's ears.

Deflated by hunger and exhaustion from the spell, Ariiell fell back upon the single bed. Sleep wanted to claim her, but her mind spun with possibilities and plans.

* * *

"I don't like the smell of this," Zebbiah said quietly.

Miranda started out of a drifting sleep at the pressure of his hand over her mouth. She nodded briefly to acknowledge her understanding of the need to say nothing. He removed his hand slowly. Reluctantly? Did his fingertips truly caress her cheek and mouth?

"Our former caravan leader is scouting the perimeter of the camp. I don't want him to see which way we travel."

"The pack beast?" Miranda mouthed the words.

"Tethered away from the other animals."

"Will he protest?" They both grinned at the thought of the trouble the stubborn beast could cause them if he chose.

"I know a few tricks."

Miranda rose from her bedroll, careful not disturb her still sleeping daughter. Gently, she wrapped the baby in the covers and carried her to where Zebbiah indicated the pack beast waited.

At first she couldn't see the animal, only smell his dusty hide. Then, in the predawn stillness, she heard the click of teeth snapping at a tuft of grass just ahead of her, on the other side of the scraggly bush of d'vil's weed. The thorny vines had a tendency to reach out and grab unwary passersby and cling, and twine, and choke, and infect. The stuff grew everywhere that men had not burned it out and poisoned the roots.

How to get through the bush to the pack beast? Serve the obnoxious creature right for getting caught in the mass. It might starve before they could untwine all the branches and drop them in the campfire.

A flash of eldritch blue fire brightened the entire sky to the south. Miranda ducked, putting her back between the fire and her baby. She tried to cover her head from the unholy beings that might swoop down

on them out of that fire. She tried to make the cross
of the Stargods, but found her movements hampered
by her burden.

Jaranda whimpered from being clutched so tightly.

Miranda settled for flapping her crossed wrists, hoping the antique ward against evil was sufficient protection.

The camp erupted in screams and flailing limbs.
Men ran in opposing directions. Women crashed into
each other as they tried to escape the eldritch light.

The former leader stumbled into their midst thrashing his arms about, his back aglow with blue flames
that did not consume his shirt or skin.

Miranda wanted to run, too. Where? Masses of
d'vil's weed blocked her path. She could escape only
into that terrible blueness.

The Zebbiah was beside her. "Good girl. You
didn't panic."

Swallowing the lump in her throat, she glared at
him. "Why didn't you warn me this was but a Rover
trick?"

"Didn't want to spoil the surprise." He grinned,
flashing his magnificent white teeth. "This way." He
waved toward the pernicious vines that grew thick between them and the pack steed.

"How?"

He grinned again and swept the vines aside with
one arm. Strangely, they did not cling to his shirt or
dig sharp spines into his flesh.

"Another Rover trick?" She eyed the vines suspi-
ciously.

"Rover magic."

This time she did cross herself, no longer sure she
could trust him. Or wanted to.

CHAPTER 29

"Do you think we should go back to the library and investigate?" Marcus asked Robb and Vareena. They were lounging around the well, listening to the bees feast on the blossoms of hundreds of overgrown herbs and flowers. No other sound penetrated the high walls. Marcus' fingers itched to get in there and start pulling weeds, pruning, and thinning.

He decided that when he had a place to call his own, he'd spend lots of time in an herb garden, meditating as he worked.

Maybe his restlessness pushed him to work among the growing things. Maybe this half-death made him long for contact with living things.

He needed to confront the ghost, throw the name of Ackerly at it, give it a chance to tell its story. But he also wanted Robb to be the one to find the answers. He deserved that. He'd been right. They had to make their own luck and opportunities.

The villagers, led by Uustaas, had left them enough food for a week. They didn't need extra blankets in the warmer weather, and the villagers had no reason to leave their work just to amuse two ghosts and their keeper. Vareena had turned her back to her brother and refused to speak to any who tried to break down her wall of silence.

When the outsiders had left—most of them with unseemly haste—Marcus had seen tears in her eyes. He wanted to hold her in his arms and chase the tears away with kisses. But the barrier of energy had repulsed him quite effectively.

Confronting the ghost seemed the only way to end this half-existence.

"Promise me, Robb and Marcus, promise me, that when you find a way to break the spell that holds you here, you will take me with you." Vareena seemed to be looking far beyond the restrictions of the monastery walls.

Both magicians nodded mutely.

"Have you noticed that the big spiders crawl everywhere but inside the library," Marcus added as a challenge to his partner.

Robb's head came up abruptly. He stared at Marcus a moment, then grinned with half his mouth. He knew something.

"Poking around the library has to be better than sitting out here doing nothing." Robb heaved himself to his feet.

Marcus followed suit, curious as to what Robb hid.

"Have you figured out how to avoid the true ghost?" Vareena asked.

"We need information," Marcus stated firmly. How many times had Jaylor, and before him Baamin, pounded that idea into his thick head. Information was the key to power. Information was the key to problem solving. Depending upon luck only worked when backed by information to point him in the right direction. He squared his shoulders, swallowed his instinctive fear of the ghost and marched in Robb's wake. He knew something, too.

Vareena shuffled along behind him, still shredding the petals from a daisy. She hummed a tune with a catchy repetitive rhythm under her breath. He'd heard that song before. It played itself over and over in his mind without end, like an obsession. Even the bees in the herb garden around the well seemed to buzz in time with it.

"You know what I miss most in this place?" Marcus remarked.

Robb kept walking. Vareena caught up with him and rewarded him with a smile. The haze seemed suddenly thinner, and the bees hummed louder.

"I miss music. We have no instruments. We don't sing or dance to pass the too many idle hours. Even the birds are silent here." He continued staring at Vareena, hoping to lock her gaze with his own. If only he could look deeply into her eyes, he could convey all of his feelings.

"I thought I heard music on the wind, last night," Vareena said. "I thought it was the villagers."

"The wind was from the wrong quarter," Robb announced as he grasped the latch on the library doors. "This place plays tricks on your mind and distorts truths." He paused a moment for a breath and then thrust both sides of the double portal open.

"Hey, you, Ghost of this library. I'm not afraid of you. What are you going to do about it!" he called into the echoing emptiness.

"Who are you, Ghost? Does the name Ackerly mean anything to you?" Marcus grinned at Robb's look of surprise.

"Where'd you come up with that name?

Marcus shrugged. "I probed a wall last night."

"Do you know who Ackerly was?" Rob's eyes remained wide and fixed on Marcus rather than on the gathering of mist under the gallery.

"I read it somewhere in a history book."

"You read it in Nimbulan's journals. The founder of the Commune of Magicians had an assistant named Ackerly who betrayed him. They fought with magic, and Ackerly died. No magician since has been named Ackerly."

"Ah, that explains some things." Marcus started backing out of the library as if afraid. He needed Robb to find the next clue. He needed his friend to succeed.

"First time I've ever known you to be the timid one, Marcus."

"That was before my luck ran out."

"Then make your own luck." Robb marched into the library and stood in the precise center of the room, legs spread sturdily, hands on hips, head thrown back in defiance.

The gold lay temptingly to his right and left.

"Stargods, Robb, you don't even have your armor up." Quickly, Marcus brought forward his own magical shields and extended them to his friend.

No sooner had his protection snapped into place than the misty form drifted forward. It glowed with a dark yellow, almost goldenrod color, around the edges. The dripping sacrificial knife pulsed with preternatural colors, seemingly growing sharper and hungrier by the moment.

Marcus gulped but stood his ground. Robb still stubbornly refused to armor himself.

"Come and get us, Ghost of Ackerly the traitor," Robb taunted. "Kill us so you won't be alone. Kill us and you will share this monastery and all its secrets with us as we become true ghosts as well."

The ghost reared back, stopping three arm's lengths from the two magicians.

"What are you afraid of, Ackerly?" Marcus asked, trying very hard to make his voice strong and assertive. "Afraid that if we join you as ghosts, you'll have to share something?"

The ghost moved his head back and forth, looking first at the knife, then at Robb and Marcus.

"Well, I guess he won't interfere if we take some of this gold to the villagers to pay for our keep," Robb said.

"Gold!" a new voice exclaimed from the doorway.

Marcus looked over his shoulder, keeping the ghost and Robb still within his perceptions.

Vareena tugged on the hand of a tall, dark-haired man with wings of silver at his temple. He wore black garments trimmed with garish purple and red. He smiled, and all the light in the room seemed to sparkle off his teeth.

"Please, sir. You must leave here at once before you are trapped by the ghost," she protested, trying desperately to keep him out of the library. "The gold is but an illusion. Gold is the source of all evil," she added another argument.

"Gold by itself is the source of much pleasure and joy. Only a curse can make the gold evil. Only a curse cast by a Rover can harm a Rover, child," the man gently disengaged Vareena's hands from his arms. "Gold!" He turned his attention back to the bags dripping coins of many nations and denominations. "Gold to ensure our freedom, and our welcome wherever we might wander. Now I will truly be king of all the Rovers in Kardia Hodos. We must have a celebration and a coronation!"

Almost quicker than thought he dashed to the shelves and grabbed a handful of coins. A dozen or more people trooped into the room behind him and each also grabbed as many coins as they could hold in both hands. All of them hummed that obnoxious little tune that still repeated endlessly in Marcus's head.

Lightning flashed. The world tilted. The veil of mist flew from the chieftain and the rest of the Rovers, bringing them all sharply into Marcus' view and dimension. Even the ones who had not yet touched the gold shifted.

"Oh, no," Marcus groaned. The gold was indeed cursed. And he and Robb had fallen into its alluring trap. He fingered the gold in his pocket, longing to cast it aside and be free again.

Then he remembered what he had read about Ackerly, confirmed by the emotions trapped within the wall: a miser who loved his gold more than his life, his magic, or his honor.

Marcus looked to see if Robb had been watching.

But his friend's attention remained entirely on Ackerly.

The ghost, in turn, stared at the intruders, eyes wide in shock and horror.

"You have to make your own luck, Robb," Marcus whispered. "I can keep the secret a little longer until you figure out the answer. You deserve this triumph, if for nothing else than to prove yourself right and me wrong."

CHAPTER 30

"Stop staring at the dumb steed and mount it!" Margit ordered Jack from atop her own mount. "We go through this every morning and every morning, for the last three, you stare at the beast an hour before you get up the courage to mount. I'm tired of waiting for you. We've a long way to travel yet."

Margit's steed pranced closer to Jack. He shied away from the animal as well as from the placid pack steed he had ridden yesterday. At least he'd learned to cope with the double vision and now knew which image of the steed might step on his foot and which was only an illusion.

Morning had passed halfway to noon. Jack had tried mounting the beast four times and had not yet come close to touching the animal.

He eyed the steed warily. "I never used to be afraid of these critters. I've ridden wilder beasts over the years. Why now?"

The cat inside him squirmed uncomfortably. Amaranth swooped low upon Margit, laughing at her discomfort as well as Jack's.

"Surely you can master the spirit of a cat, Jack. You have the strongest soul of any man I have ever met." Katrina sidled her steed close enough to Jack to ruffle his head.

He inclined his neck to lean into her caress. A deep thrumming sound began in his chest and climbed to his nose.

Why didn't he retreat from this beast? Because Katrina rode it. He trusted Katrina more than himself at the moment.

The thrumming deep inside him matched the tingle in his fingers and behind his eyes, almost like the summons spell gone astray. He'd tried for three nights running to anchor the distress call that both he and Margit had intercepted and failed. He sincerely hoped the alien presence in his body hadn't interfered with his magic.

The cat—Rosie, as it thought of itself—purred in accompaniment to Katrina's caress.

At least Rosie liked Katrina. He remembered a time when Rosie was still within Queen Mikka that the cat took a sudden and unexplained dislike to her husband. Darville had worn scratch marks repeatedly.

The pack steed sidled and shifted closer to Jack. He jumped back hastily.

Margit laughed again.

"You didn't sneeze when Amaranth touched you because he isn't a true cat," he grumbled at the apprentice magician. "But you sneeze every time I think about coming near you."

"My instincts are true, Jack. I have the purrrrfect defense against you." With another chuckle she dug her heels into her steed. "Now, let's go find Marcus. We can't delay any longer." Her beast lunged forward at a rapid clip.

"I'll walk." Jack decided, handling the reins of the extra steed to Katrina.

"She's right, Jack. We have a long way to go to Queen's City."

"A long time for me to figure out what to do with this troublesome cat. At least the queen is free of it. My spell didn't completely fail." He smiled up at her as he trudged up onto the road from their campsite. He'd spent quite a bit of time obscuring all traces of their presence. Most of that time he'd been merely stalling.

"Why didn't the cat go to Amaranth as you directed? I would think it would want to return to a cat's body after all this time." Katrina kept her mount walking at Jack's pace. Margit trotted ahead of them.

"I'm guessing that Rosie has gotten used to the superior intelligence of humans. She—it—recognizes the difference between being a pet and controlling a human." Jack stuffed his hands in his pockets to keep from licking them and laving his ears.

"I'm sorry, Katrina, but I think we'll have to postpone our wedding again until I solve this problem."

Katrina half-frowned but didn't say anything.

"I do still want to marry you, when you are ready," he reassured her.

"I know, Jack. Strange, now that you want to postpone the wedding, I want it more than anything."

They both chuckled.

"We'll work it out, love. By the time we get to SeLenicca, we'll work it out."

Amaranth flew past them, nearly brushing Jack's head with his extended talons. He dropped onto the pack saddle of the steed Jack should be riding and set about preening his wings.

"I take it you like the body you inherited," Jack said to his familiar. He wanted to caress the soft black fur of his friend, but Rosie prevented him from coming any closer to the steed. How had the queen managed to ride so fearlessly these last three years?

Amaranth purred his contentment while continuing his bath. As he lifted his hind leg to wash the fur along that quarter, his talonlike claws embedded into the pack saddle for better balance. But he missed the saddle and clutched the steed's mane. The steed spooked and reared, rolling its eyes and screaming its outrage.

Amaranth shrieked and flopped around, trying desperately to disengage his claws.

With a long and frightened neigh the steed bolted. Katrina tried to hang onto the leading rein. It whipped through her fingers, cutting deeply as it burned free of her grasp. Her steed pranced wild-eyed and nervous at the strange noises and the smell of blood. It gathered its legs under it, ready to bolt after its companion.

* * *

Lanciar watched as one by one the Rovers winked out of sight, including the children—including *his* son. His jaw dropped. A fly buzzed around him. He knew he should close his mouth and yet. . . .

"I wish I hadn't drunk so much." He had trouble thinking clearly. His head buzzed and his eyes ached.

Beside him, the unknown blonde woman sobbed as she dropped his arm and buried her face in her hands.

"Oh, no," she moaned, rocking from foot to foot. "Not more ghosts. More ghosts for my people to feed. They'll surely forsake the Stargods now and let us all starve."

The air smelled strange, slightly acidic, slightly rancid sweet, like a spell gone wrong. The wind rushed into this bizarre building, filling the vacuum left by the disappearing people. But not enough wind to account for the loss of all these people.

He remembered the fierce gusts that rushed through Hanassa when the Rovers had transported out. Then the Rovers had disappeared all at once from one heartbeat to the next. Now, they vanished one at a time like links in an anchor chain disappearing beneath the water.

They'd stumbled onto something strange—to say the least.

He wished Rejiia had accompanied them so that she could explain the phenomenon. His former love had an instinctive grasp of otherworldly puzzles.

Jack, too, would be a great help.

He had to find his son and flee. Now. Before things got worse.

Feeling almost blind with numb senses and numb magic, he grasped the doorjamb for balance. A burning energy repulsed his hand. He peered more closely at the spot. His magic kicked in, opening all of his senses.

"What?" The dim outline of another hand—almost invisible, like a dragon sliding in and out of view—shone with a silvery energy. He traced with trembling fingers the almost-visible hand up a black-clad arm to a shoulder and a black vest trimmed in bright purple and red. An abundance of silvery embroidery shone through the misty veil that seemed to separate him from the man.

"Zolltarn?" Lanciar gasped.

"Of course. Who else would I be?" the Rover leader sneered, then flashed his amazing smile. Lanciar immediately felt more comfortable, ready to listen to the older man's wisdom. But his voice sounded as if it came from a great distance.

"What happened to you? You—you're as transparent as a ghost," Lanciar said.

"Nonsense, boy. You are the one fading in and out of view. Come in, come fully into the room. Then you will be one of us. You must be one of us if you hope to marry my daughter." Zolltarn opened his arms as if to embrace Lanciar, an all too familiar and disarming gesture. The curious burning energy kept them apart.

Lanciar breathed a little easier. He knew Zolltarn's charm all too well, knew how he lulled suspicions with the little deceptions of friendship.

"One of the clan," Lanciar stated flatly. He'd resisted all attempts by the Rovers to draw him into their direct mind-to-mind connections by ritual or coercion. He'd postponed his marriage to Maija for days, keeping his individuality for as long as possible by sheer force of will.

He wanted a drink. Desperately.

"Can you help me?" He turned to the sobbing blonde.

"Stay out of the library. Stay away from the other ghosts, the true ghost as well as all these new ones.

Just turn around and walk out the gate before you, too, are cursed and trapped here forever." She gulped back her tears and faced him resolutely. "Get out now! And take me with you. I forsake my destiny though I'll be cursed through all my future existences. I cannot be responsible for all of these ghosts." She gulped back a new round of sobs and stiffened her spine. "I'm sorry, Robb. I must also forsake my love for you."

"I'm not leaving without my son," Lanciar told her. He looked for a trace of the smallest children among the Rovers. They should be too young to be linked with the Rover magic. But each one had been in the arms of a Rover woman. If touch or proximity to the library turned one into a ghost, then he'd lost his son, too. Forever?

"What do you know of this curse, woman?" He grabbed her arm, shaking her gently. "I've got to find my son among them. Help me find my son. Then I will leave and take you with me. Not before."

" 'Tis my destiny to serve the ghosts, not to understand them. They cannot leave here and must be fed. Your son is lost. Leave now before you too are cursed." Her eyes widened in horror. "I've never had more than one ghost before Marcus and Robb came. Now there are dozens. Dozens! Where will I find enough food for them all? Now I will never be allowed to leave this cursed place."

The statue of Krej sat in the place of honor at the front of the lead sledge—Zolltarn's conveyance. The hideous visage seemed to wink and grin at Lanciar in silent laughter as yet more gilt paint flaked off its tin hide. One front paw seemed to shed its metal coating and become true fur.

"I'll think of something. I need some ale in order to think." Lanciar wove through the scattered sledges seeking Maija's bardo. She did indeed brew the best ale he'd ever tasted.

But maybe he'd had too much already.

* * *

What strange being is this who stares at me from his perch atop the Rover conveyance? I can see the true nature of a man as a ghostly aura around the tin statue with the flaking gilt paint that renews itself only to flake off once more. Another ghost, as I am. Another with a mission. Shall I release him from his tin prison so that his gold will become real and cease to flake? I could possess the gold then. But that would deprive him of his life.

I sense that soon this ghostly man will separate from the tin statue that traps him. If he is not released before then, both the inert beast and animated spirit will drift forever in time, unanchored in any reality. He will cause havoc in all realities if that occurs. He has not much time.

But this place is a strange meeting of vortexes. Anything can happen, and time moves differently here. That is how I know my children live though three hundred years have passed. They must survive. Otherwise all I did for them is worthless.

I will know this man's true heart so that he can not betray me as others have.

As long as I have the gold, I can accomplish anything. Gold is power.

CHAPTER 31

"Katrina!" Jack sent a magical probe into the steed's mind, forcing it to remain in place. He gulped down his fear and grabbed the reins, yanking them down hard to keep the steed under control. His stomach heaved in fear of the steed and for Katrina's safety. His magical bond with Amaranth stretched thin to the breaking point.

"I am stronger than this!" he muttered through gritted teeth. "First things first." He lifted Katrina free of her skittish mount. He cradled her in his arms, soothing her shock and pain. A cursory examination of her bleeding hand showed him deep cuts from the leather.

"I don't have the healing touch, love, but I'll do what I can," he apologized. "It's going to hurt terribly, but I have to wash it."

She nodded, white-faced. "I trust you," she whispered so softly he wasn't certain he heard her as she clung to him with her free hand, resting her head upon his shoulder.

He kissed her temple and carried her to the creek beside the road.

Margit wheeled her horse and galloped back to them. "I'll take care of her. You go after that demented cat of yours," she said. "We can't afford to lose the supplies on the steed." She swung her leg over the saddle horn and dropped to the ground in one swift movement.

Jack released Katrina reluctantly. He took off running after the steed that was rapidly disappearing in the distance. "Stop, *s'murghit*," he panted. He couldn't call up his FarSight or enter the beast's mind while he put all of his energy into running. He didn't dare stop running lest the steed and Amaranth got too far away.

The steed would not cease its blind flight until Amaranth stopped shrieking and flopping about in panic. He could still hear his familiar protesting in the distance.

Quiet, my friend. Quiet, he whispered directly into the flywacket's receptive mind. The bonds between them guided his words. *Hush, little one.* He repeated the lulling words over and over, all the magic he could muster while maintaining his ground-eating lope.

At last, winded and nearly doubled over, gulping in huge draughts of air, he sensed that Amaranth worked his talons free of the tangled mane and the padded leather of the pack saddle. But the steed plunged on and on.

Jack repeated his quiet litany, seeking the equine brain. Steeds usually responded to humans, being nearly as physically compatible as cats. This one's panic blocked all of the normal channels of communication and control.

He sensed Amaranth launching into flight, having had enough of the steed's wild thrashing through the thickening woods.

Track it Amaranth. We can't afford to lose it! he called to his friend.

Amaranth swooped onto Jack's shoulder instead, barely digging in his claws at all. He kept his feathered wings half engaged, flustered, frightened, and bewildered. His voice reverted to baby shrieks. No telepathy at all.

"Go after the blasted steed, Jack!" Margit ordered him with mind and voice.

"Go, Amaranth. You can do this. The steed did not hurt you. Hunt it and show it to me as you fly."

Amaranth rubbed his face along Jack's cheek, heaved a sigh, and pushed himself into the air.

The absence of his weight on Jack's shoulder left him feeling terribly alone, almost empty. He stared after his familiar for several long moments, then returned to the women.

Katrina sat on the creek bank with her head between her knees, and her left hand held out for Margit's ministrations. Margit knelt beside the water rinsing a bloody rag. Mud and everblue needles stained the knees of her leather trews.

"I can't make it stop bleeding, Jack," Margit said. A touch of panic edged her voice. "It's stiffening up, like there's a tendon damaged."

Katrina gasped, then bit her trembling lip.

Jack knew her thoughts without reading her. She feared she'd never hold her lace bobbins again.

Margit closed her eyes, then spoke without looking at either of them. "Jaylor's going to kill me if I fail in this mission. He told me specifically to take care of her." She worked her cheeks in an effort to control her own panic. "Even last night when I reported that I was an unnecessary extra on this mission, he ordered me to stay with her."

"Let me see," Jack took her place beside Katrina. He concentrated on sending out an aura of calm authority to both of them.

When Margit's eyes quit darting about, he took Katrina's hand gently, probing the wicked cut across the palm, just below the finger joints. His eyes saw torn flesh and new puddles of blood. His magic found the severed blood vessels and gashed tendon. He took three deep breaths to trigger a trance.

"Are you going to cauterize it?" Margit rested her hand on his shoulder as she watched.

"Sort of." Jack narrowed his focus. "A healer would do this without effort and without pain to the patient. Just bear with me, Katrina." A nearby ley line winked at him with silvery-blue energy. He tapped it to fuel his work.

A little magic bound him to his love. A little more opened his TrueSight to the layers of tissue and energy in her hand. Flesh became translucent. Beneath it, he saw the pulsing vessels, the twitching joints, the binding tendons and cartilage.

"Sing something, Katrina. Sing your magic to match my own," he breathed, still within the throes of his trance. "You knew how to heal burned-out ley lines with your *Songs*. *Sing* to heal yourself now."

"I—I can't." She grimaced. Her pain became a visible layer of blackened red infiltrating all the layers of her aura. She kept trying to tug her hand out of his grasp.

"Trust me?"

"With my life."

He caught her frightened eyes with his own gaze. In a moment she quieted. Her breathing slowed to match his own.

A small *Song* of magic worked its way out of his heart into his voice. Their song. The little lullaby she'd sung in their prison cell. The one that had spawned tiny, spidery ley lines of energy where no ley lines had existed for many centuries. Together they had discovered the magic all women invoked when singing over mundane tasks. Unconsciously, they set up layer upon layer of protection for those they loved.

He'd tapped the ley lines Katrina had brought to life to release their shackles and aid their escape while Queen's City shook and crumbled in the aftermath of multiple kardiaquakes.

Slowly, gently, with the *Song* still lighting his mind and his magic, he sent a needle-fine probe of magic to the first small blood vessel. He encouraged it to mend. Then the next, a larger one this time. He needed a second, hotter touch to make it seal off.

Katrina gasped and tried to wrench her hand away. He held her tighter, seeing precisely how much pressure he exerted with his solid hand against her seemingly transparent flesh.

A moment more and the last vessel closed. He encouraged the tendon tissue to knit and expel foreign matter so tiny only Jack's magic could see it. Then he brought the muscle and skin together, binding them loosely with magic. Best if they finished healing on their own.

At last he sat back on his heels and withdrew from the intimate contact. Sweat poured from his brow and his heart pounded erratically. Too tired to eat, he just wanted to curl up and sleep. He closed his eyes and still saw the pulses of energy and layers of color in the hand he kept within his own.

"You did it, Jack," Katrina said quietly. "I knew all along you had the healing touch. It only hurt a little."

Judging by the quieting layers of energy in her aura, that was a lie she almost believed.

She brushed a stray lock of hair off his forehead. Her fingers lingered and traced his cheek. He turned his face just enough to kiss her palm.

"It will be stiff for a few days, while it finishes healing. But you'll be handling bobbins with ease after that," he reassured her.

"Time to get moving," Margit said brusquely. She stood up and brushed her trews clean of the creekside debris. "Has your cat found the pack steed yet?"

"He's working on it." Flashes of images began to penetrate Jack's mind. Tall trees, rising terrain as they neared the mountain barrier between SeLenicca and Coronnan. A scatter of small buildings at the base of a hill. More trees and then—atop the hill a jumble of stones with many pack steeds and sledges milling among the stones. A great deal of black with purple-and-red trim adorned the saddles, packs and rounded huts atop the sledges. He knew who owned them.

He sat up straighter, pushing Amaranth to focus more closely on the stones.

Not jumbled haphazardly. Worked stone stacked

carefully and mortared into thick walls. A steedshoe-shaped building—squared off at the corners—with an exterior wall connecting the two outthrusting wings and forming a wide courtyard.

And there, quietly nickering to one of the smaller beasts harnessed to a sledge, stood Margit's white pack steed.

"Found him!" Jack stood up, dragging Katrina with him. "Only a mile or two off, that way." He pointed west and slightly south where they could see the beginning of the rising ground and the dense forest around the hill. The line of everblues blocked their view of the building.

Margit threw dried meat and journey bread at Jack from her pack as she leaped astride her mount. "Eat as we ride. You need to replenish energies lost while working magic. We need that steed and its supplies. If we delay, it may wander farther."

More slowly, Katrina stuck her foot into a stirrup. Jack pushed her into the saddle. Then, closing his eyes and forcing Rosie to the back of his consciousness, he clambered up behind her.

The cat within him roiled and wanted to spit. He fought it. His need to remain close to Katrina overcame the cat's hissing fear. More like a need to have its own way than a real fear.

Jack almost laughed out loud at this insight. "I'll match you stubborn for stubborn, cat," he said to himself.

Katrina looked over her shoulder at him in question.

"I think I found a solution to my problem," he whispered into Katrina's ear as he wound his arms around her waist. "Our steed found a bunch of Rover steeds. I believe they belong to my grandfather. The original spell that bound the queen to her cat was danced by Rovers. We'll have my grandfather's people reverse it for me and put the cat into Amaranth's body where it belongs."

"Rovers." Katrina gulped and stiffened in his arms. She did not urge her mount forward.

Neeles Brunix, the man who had owned her for three years; used and abused her for his own gain, had flaunted his half-Rover connections, the same blood mix as Jack.

CHAPTER 32

"There's a village," Margit whooped. "We'll purchase supplies and a new pack steed here. No sense going off on a wild lumbird chase after the other one." She set her heels into the sides of her mount.

Katrina did likewise.

Jack bounced uncomfortably on the spine of the animal, clinging to Katrina for dear life. The cat spirit rose sharply to the front of his senses. His back arched, the hair on his nape and along his backbone stood up. A curious itch in his bottom felt as if a tail twitched in agitation. He swallowed the angry hiss that climbed from his gut to his throat like a too-long-suppressed cough. Rosie *really* did not like this steed.

"I am stronger than you," he hissed at the cat.

"What?" Katrina spared him a look over her shoulder while she gripped the reins firmly with her right hand, fully in control of her mount. She rested her bandaged left hand in her lap.

"Nothing, love. Take this path angling off to the south." He relived the course Amaranth had flown in pursuit of the errant steed. Even now the flywacket perched atop a high stone tower, trying to make sense of the images that wandered in and out of his vision. Jack couldn't make sense of them either. He hoped the confusion came from Amaranth's youth and lack of experience and not what he feared.

"But Margit . . ."

"Margit will follow. Her mission is to take care of you. She won't let us stray too far without her."

"Her true mission is to find Marcus. She can do that a lot easier without me. And now that you have come to see me safely into SeLenicca she will go off on her own, no matter what Jaylor orders."

"And leave you without a chaperone? Not likely. She knows her best chance of finding Marcus and Robb is to stick with me. Just guide this monstrous beast up that path to the top of the hill. I have a feeling we'll all find answers up there."

He blinked rapidly trying to sort the curious double vision. Amaranth's continuous feed of bizarre images, much clearer now that he perched atop a tower than when he flew, overlaid his own sensory view. He had to fight for balance the entire time. Then Rosie had to add her own confused perceptions, relying more on scent and sound than sight. Jack nearly lost his meager breakfast.

Amaranth sensed Rosie's need to understand through her other senses, and he began to relay scent impressions more than visual. Too many bodies confined together. Too many bewildered steeds. Strange cooking smells that relied heavily upon timboor, the fruit of the Tambootie tree, and something very old on the verge of decay.

And then Amaranth focused sharply on a curious statue perched atop the largest and gaudiest of the Rover bardos. A tin weasel. At one time the statue had been dipped in gold and the outermost layer had begun to flake off. The flywacket knew the weasel form, but could not understand why the statue did not smell of weasel.

Krej. Jack's heart fell. Another problem for him to deal with before he could take Katrina to SeLenicca.

(Gold!) the flywacket proclaimed.

At one time the dragons had told Jack that they valued gold and jewels almost as much as humans. Gold represented the power of the Kardia, a symbol of the beauty of life.

Rosie recognized the value humans placed upon gold and reared up, ready to make Jack pounce.

Hold back, Amaranth. Do not announce your presence or betray your wings. I will be there, in a few moments. We can investigate together, he ordered his familiar.

Ruthlessly, he forced Rosie away from the front of his consciousness. It fought him every finger-length of the way.

Amaranth reluctantly folded his wings but continued to peer avariciously at the statue.

Jack closed his eyes again, reducing the onslaught of sensations. His stomach slid back down from his throat to about the middle of his chest. Manageable.

Silently he called Amaranth to him. Maybe if he could reduce the number of perspectives, he could conquer the queasiness.

Amaranth remained stubbornly in place. *(Must keep the gold from disappearing like funny men,)* the fly-wacket returned.

"What funny men?" Jack muttered.

Katrina pulled on the reins and looked back at him questioningly. He motioned her forward.

Then another view of the monastery with a thick haze over all. The vague outlines, as if viewing them through a thick fog, of mingling steeds and Rover bardos superimposed onto his already distorted visions. This one came from high above them. Briefly he caught a glimpse of himself and Katrina atop the lumbering steed. He watched them climbing the long trail that circled the hill half a dozen times before ending abruptly at the tree line a few yards from the gatehouse tower.

His stomach lurched again. "Don't fly, Amaranth," he pleaded with his familiar. Then he realized that the new view came from yet another source. A dragon flew above.

"Shayla?" he asked the unseen observer.

"Shayla?" Katrina looked up in delight.

(Baamin,) the blue-tipped male dragon replied with a chuckle. *(Shayla's son fares better than you do, young Jack.)* Another laugh rippled across Jack's consciousness. *(You can sever the link between your minds upon occasion.)*

"I don't want him to feel lost. We need this time of constant contact to solidify our bond." Jack looked up trying to catch a glimpse of the magician turned dragon who had been his mentor and father figure as well as father in another life. "You taught me that with Corby, my first familiar."

Katrina patted his hand. "How sweet, Jack. I hope you are as considerate of our children." She must have heard the dragon. Unusual. Normally, only Shayla communicated with her.

"I'm glad you are still thinking of our future." Jack nuzzled her neck, drinking in her unique smell and the silkiness of her hair.

(There will be many times when you do not wish a third participant in your life, Jack. Amaranth will wait for you.) Baamin broke off his verbal and visual contact. Abruptly, Amaranth's contribution ceased as well.

Jack sensed a tiny squeak of protest from his familiar just before his vision centered upon what his eyes could see alone.

Relief came to his stomach with a sense of emptiness. The cat settled into a contented purr within him. The vibrations centered at the base of his spine. Since his attention was no longer divided between the cat and the flywacket, Rosie had nothing further to contribute.

Jack almost panicked at the loss of Amaranth's familiar presence in his mind. They'd been linked constantly since before the purple dragonet's transformation. He took a deep breath and accepted the temporary separation. Temporary, he reminded himself and the cat.

You know, if you had gone into Amaranth's body

as planned, you wouldn't have anything to be jealous of, he reminded Rosie.

The cat continued to purr without further comment, setting up an almost sexual satisfaction within Jack as the vibrations radiated out from his spine. His bottom stopped itching, as if his invisible tail curled around his hips in contentment.

"What was that all about?" Katrina asked.

"Did Baamin show you the view from above?"

"I only caught bits and pieces through a thick fog. My contact with him is not as—as complete as it is with Shayla. But I sense his approval of me. He wants to deepen our contact. What is that strange building atop the hill that he seemed so concerned about?"

"I'm guessing from the shape it's an abandoned monastery from long ago. People who aren't supposed to be there have recently taken up residence."

"What people?"

"Rovers." The bardos atop the sledges were distinctly Rover in construction and painted design. But why had the owners neglected the sledges and pack beasts? Rovers always attended to their animals very carefully before seeing to their own needs. Always. Steeds carried nearly as much value to them as the gold coins they wore on their sashes and caps. Only children represented more wealth than gold and steeds.

The distinctive purple and red that dominated the colors of those bardos proclaimed them the possessions of Zolltarn, self-styled king of all Rovers, member of the Commune of Magicians, and Jack's grandfather. That clan had an abundance of babies born in the last four years—to replace the men who had died quite suddenly the year before Zolltarn changed his loyalties from coven to Commune. The dragons had a hand in the loss of those men, and the Rovers had never quite trusted them as a source of magic or as a benign presence since.

Zolltarn used dragon magic and his membership in

the Commune to serve his own ends. Only he of all master magicians dared ignore a summons from Senior Magician Jaylor.

"I might have known that Zolltarn would end up with the statue of Krej," he muttered.

"Amaranth. I need you to look again. Where are the children, where are the Rovers for that matter? They wouldn't abandon their steeds and bardos." He relinquished the moments of quiet single vision in favor of information.

He saw again the bardos still harnessed to the steeds; the riding steeds wandering about the large courtyard, grazing on the overgrown herb garden; a woman he did not know sitting on the step beside the well, face buried in her hands, her shoulders heaving with sobs. Beside her stood a familiar and unwelcome figure. He sensed more than recognized the aura of his old enemy Lanciar from SeLenicca. What was *he* doing in Coronnan? And if Lanciar was about, Rejiia could not be far behind.

Then the Rovers and several other figures emerged from inside the building. They looked nearly transparent, outlined in silver like a dragon. All of them had become ghosts!

At that moment Katrina stopped their steed abruptly at the gate tower. Jack slid from its back, half planning to dismount, half falling from distorted balance and perception.

"We've got some real problems here. Stay outside the walls, Katrina. Whatever happens, you and Margit stay outside the walls." He walked quietly through the gate, keeping to the shadows.

"Your problems are my problems, Jack." Behind him, Katrina dismounted and followed closely on his heels.

* * *

Vareena rose from her seat by the well and marched out into the courtyard. Steeds milled about, placing their burdensome sledges at odd angles. She stumbled over an abandoned pack, slipped in a fresh pile of dung and landed heavily against the sledge cabin. A tin weasel with flaking gilt paint grinned down at her as it teetered on its porch.

"S'murghit!" she cursed in very unladylike tones. "I refuse to be responsible anymore. I'm leaving." She righted herself and aimed for the gate.

"Wait, you can't abandon us. You're the only one who knows what's going on," the blond man who remained human grabbed her sleeve and kept her from retreating out the gate.

Another steed—taller and stockier than the beasts that had come with the Rovers—blocked the exit. Its sides heaved as if it had run a long distance. She'd not shove it aside without help, not for a while yet anyway.

"You can leave this cursed place with me," she said flatly, shoving her way through the crowded courtyard. Ghosts began appearing among the steeds. She bounced away from them into more animals, dogs and chickens as well as the pack beasts.

"No, I can't leave. They have my son. I can't find him without your help, and I won't leave him with these people."

"A child?" Vareena stopped short, heart aching for the lost souls condemned to this place. Why had this man been spared but not his son?

"My son is still a baby, a tiny baby with black hair and brilliant blue eyes. Please help me find him. Please help me to hold him one more time before this terrible curse takes him from me forever." The man who had appeared so confident when he walked through the gate looked helpless now. A great deal of pain and longing poured out of his eyes.

"Vareena!" Marcus pelted out of the library into the courtyard. "Vareena, don't leave me, please. I need you. I love you," he panted as he skidded to a halt scant inches from her.

"Marcus?" Vareena peered at his insubstantial form, not certain she had heard him correctly.

"Yes, Vareena. I love you. I have from the moment I first saw you. Please stay. I can find an answer to this problem. I know I can." He rammed his right fist into the pocket of is trews while his left hand reached out tentatively as if to brush a stray lock of hair from her brow. A sharp tingle of energy repulsed him before he made contact with her.

"No, Marcus, you do not love me. You can't." *Not Marcus*, her heart wailed. *Why couldn't it be Robb. 'Tis Robb I love. Will always love.*

Having acknowledged her attraction to the dark-haired magician, she knew she could not abandon Robb or his friend now. She needed to see this through to the end, even if she remained here the rest of her life, like her mother, and her mother's mother before her.

Once cursed by the monastery and the hoard of gold, the women of her family were cursed forever.

Her last hope of freedom slid away.

CHAPTER 33

"Making your own luck doesn't always work," Marcus said as he trudged back to the library from Vareena's side. She'd stay to help. Now he needed to stay by Robb until his friend also figured out the source of the curse.

He watched the Rovers step through the constant veil of mist into his reality. His heart lodged in his throat. How could he push Robb to discover the secret with all of these Rovers complicating things?

"This is bad luck for all of us," Robb agreed.

The hair on the back of Marcus' neck stood on end. An unnatural chill climbed his spine. He whipped around to face the ghost of Ackerly. The misty form coalesced into a nearly solid being. His aura pulsed brighter as he sped across the massive library, sacrificial knife raised over his head.

"He's a Bloodmage," Robb hissed. "He gains power from inflicting pain and drawing blood!"

'Zolltarn, look out!" Marcus called. He dove for the Rover, knocking him to the ground. Ackerly's knife sliced through the air where Zolltarn's neck had been. In the same movement, Marcus drew Zolltarn's long dagger and turned on the ghost.

"Eat iron!" he yelled, stabbing at the air around him.

A wail of pain and frustration pierced his ears. He wanted to clutch his ears and curl into a fetal ball but dared not shift his attention away from the knife. The ghostly sound faded.

An eerie silence fell upon the library. No one moved. No one breathed.

"M–my thanks, young magician," Zolltarn said. He remained on the flagstone floor staring about him, eyes wide, showing more white than black. He tried working his mouth into one of his engaging smiles and failed. "I owe you my life and my soul."

Marcus nodded but kept searching for the ghost.

"Best we all retreat," Robb said, ushering the Rovers away from the gold.

One young man sneered at Robb, still clutching an awkward double handful of coins.

"Go!" Zolltarn said, resuming his natural authority over his people. "The gold will still be here tomorrow."

"And many tomorrows after that," Marcus muttered. "Unless my luck changes."

"Make your own luck," Robb reminded him, patting him on the back.

Together they retreated, blades at the ready.

But the ghost remained quiet and out of sight.

"I think saving the life and soul of a Rover chieftain is a bit of luck," Robb continued when the haze separated them from the darkness in the library. "Rovers have power, and Zolltarn is more powerful than most. He's indebted to you."

"What did he mean that I saved his soul?" Marcus asked quietly.

"I meant that for a Rover to lose his life to a Bloodmage binds his soul to the murderer. When that Bloodmage is a ghost . . ." Zolltarn shuddered rather than complete the sentence. "My debt to you is immeasurable, young magician. I offer you any of my daughters as your wife."

"Uh . . . no thanks. I may have spent the last three years wandering, but the Rover life is not for me. I want a nice little cottage with a wife and a dozen children and a dozen more apprentices." He felt immeasurably lighter for having voiced his longtime dream. The possibilities seemed firmer.

Robb raised his eyebrows at him. A big grin tugged at his mouth. "By any chance did you ever tell Margit this is what you want out of life?"

Marcus shrugged. Had he? No matter. He loved Vareena now. He'd likely never see Margit again.

"We will be on our way, young magicians," Zolltarn dismissed them. "We had planned to spend some time here and celebrate the marriage of my daughter Maija to soldier Lanciar. But we do not willingly share space with the ghost of a Bloodmage." He bowed deeply, all the while edging toward the gatehouse.

"Good luck getting out of here," Marcus snorted, keeping his attention on the library.

"What?" Zolltarn stared at him with eyes narrowed in speculation.

"Explain the situation to Zolltarn, Robb. I'm going to see if we can persuade the ghost to drop his knife." Marcus took a deep breath and stepped back in the direction of the library.

An unholy screech from atop the walls interrupted Robb before he could speak. Lumbird bumps raced up Marcus' arms and spine. Both he and Robb turned toward this new menace, blades at the ready for the ghost.

"Stargods, save us all!" Zolltarn crossed himself three times, flapped his wrists in the ward against Simurgh and crossed himself again. "An evil creature out of myths! What strange place is this?"

A black cat swooped down on black-feathered wings. Its blacker than black fur seemed to absorb all the sunlight. The beast let loose with another of its eerie cries, half yowl, half the screech of an enraged eagle.

Everyone ducked as it passed.

Marcus heard many strange invocations against the ancient winged demon Simurgh. As soon as he felt the passage of air on his hair from the cat's flight, he glanced up to follow its trajectory. Surprisingly it landed neatly on the outstretched arm of a Rover-dark man standing in the archway to the gatehouse. He might have the coloring of a Rover, but he dressed like a Commune magician in blue tunic and trews. Behind him stood a blonde woman. The misty veil of unreality separated them from the rest of the milling crowd of Rovers. Marcus was certain neither of them had been in the courtyard a few moments before. Neither of them was dressed in the garish purple and red on black. But the man's eyes bore the same shape and intensity as Zolltarn's.

He'd seen those eyes before.

"Stay out of this cursed place," Vareena ordered, marching quickly up to the newcomers.

"We seek only a night's shelter," the stranger said.

"With the spawn of Simurgh on your shoulder you seek more than that," Zolltarn challenged. But his smile returned full force, driving away the sense of foreboding that hovered among his people.

"Perhaps I seek my grandfather," the stranger returned the smile. He clutched the hand of the young woman behind him and strode forward.

"Jack, have you returned to the clan at last?" Zolltarn asked, striding to meet him. The Rover spread his arms wide intending a fierce embrace. Jack remained in place, arms firmly at his side. Zolltarn bounced off him before Jack could rebuff him. Zolltarn frowned deeply. Jack merely nodded with a grimace.

"You look like a ghost, Grandfather," Jack said, peering at all of the Rovers with curiosity.

"I know that man," Robb whispered to Marcus.

"He does seem familiar, but I've never met Zolltarn's grandson. I know a lot of men named Jack, none of them magicians. A magician would change his name to something more lofty to command respect," Marcus replied. "Jack doesn't seem like a Rover name either."

"Perhaps you knew me under another name, before I learned of my heritage. Before I earned Master status in the Commune," Jack said.

Marcus searched his memory for any apprentice or journeyman with Rover heritage.

"Um . . . Yaakke had very dark hair and eyes," Robb reminded him.

"Yaakke? The lost journeyman?"

"One and the same. And this is my betrothed, Katrina of SeLenicca."

"You escaped SeLenicca?" Lanciar pushed his way toward them—of all the Rover party, he alone remained fully human. "Thank the Stargods you survived."

Vareena followed Lanciar, shaking her head.

Marcus moved to Vareena's side. "It will be all right. We'll get this fixed soon," he whispered to his love.

She had eyes only for Robb.

"Aye, Lanciar, no thanks to you, I survived," Jack said, ignoring the others. His voice and face remained calm, almost devoid of emotion. But his eyes took on a haunted look. "I survived. With Katrina's help, I escaped Rejiia's foul prison, and the kardiaquakes and the destruction of Queen's City. The last I saw of you, you were meekly obeying her orders and boasting of your membership in the coven." Both men's auras flared with wild and violent emotions.

"But did you find the dragons?" Marcus moved to stand between the men before they engaged in a physical, or worse, a magical duel. The barrier of energy around him repulsed them in opposite directions.

Vareena tugged on Katrina's hand, urging her toward the gate. But Katrina held firmly to Jack, or Yaakke, or whoever he was now. Older, more mature and sure of himself with only a trace of the cockiness of his youth.

"Yes, I found the dragons and returned them to the lair, again with Katrina's help."

"Then magic is legal again in Coronnan?" Marcus asked. His dream of a home and family at the University shifted slightly from a cottage in the woods to a suite of rooms in the massive stone building in the capital.

"Not exactly," Jack and Zolltarn replied at the same time.

"Marcus!" a new voice announced herself from the gateway. Margit raced across the crowded courtyard, bouncing off of one ghostly Rover after another, heedless of the angry voices and offended travelers. "So this is where you've been hiding. This is where you came just to get away from me!" She raised her fist and slammed it into his jaw.

The anger behind her blow pushed her through the energy barrier and knocked Marcus flat on his bum.

* * *

Iron! They fight me with iron. I have no defense against that base metal. So cold. And yet it burns. Not like my gold that warms to the touch and invites me to caress it. The young whelps must have watched when I could not follow our keeper up the iron staircase.

The iron cannot push me into my next existence. I want no other than what I have. I have the gold and that is all I need. I do not even need my children—proud of them as I am—as long as I have the gold. But iron will give me terrible pain that will not go away. Ever.

I must make them flee. None of the others who have visited me have given me so much trouble. The others were company of sorts. I was content to let them fondle a piece or two of gold. They could not leave with it. And so I retrieved it upon their deaths. Quiet deaths mostly, with a peaceful passage into their next existence. They can only last one hundred days or less living under my curse. And I still had the gold.

But these magicians tax me greatly. They have the

gift to undo three hundred years of protecting my gold. I shall whisper the secret into their dreams. 'Tis their greed that keeps them here. Tonight, I shall whisper into their dreams. All of them. By morning they will either flee or kill each other. One way or another, I shall be free of them all.

* * *

Ariiell eyed the side trail with suspicion. Why would Rejiia send her up there? This must be the wrong road.

But they'd passed no others. She had watched diligently for signs of the place Rejiia needed her to go. With just a touch of TrueSight she discerned the signs of many steeds passing this way recently. Steeds and sledges.

No respectable trading caravan would travel up this narrow and nearly overgrown path. They would seek the village up ahead.

She sniffed the trail with her mundane nose, made more sensitive by magic and pregnancy. This was a talent Rejiia and the coven did not know about. She could identify individuals by smell from one hundred paces, she could tell what Cook prepared for dinner before the dishes began cooking. And she knew that the passing steeds pulling the sledges had left a great deal of dung on the path.

She would not traverse this trail. No matter what Rejiia ordered. She would not go there!

"I'll not follow orders blindly anymore. I carry the heir. I shall make all my own decisions." She kicked her placid mare into a sprightly trot, leaving the noisome trail behind.

"Why did you tarry there, daughter?" Lord Laislac asked as she rode alongside him.

"I thought it might lead someplace interesting." She dismissed the topic.

Lord Andrall immediately looked back over his

shoulder at the trail and up the hill. As his gaze came to the crest, his eyes widened. "I do not like well-traversed trails branching off to old ruins. They speak of outlaw hideouts."

"An abandoned monastery." Laislac kept his voice light, but his eyes remained fixed on the same spot as Lord Andrall's. "The locals proclaim it haunted and do not go near. Outlaws heed them."

Ariiell squinted and called up her FarSight. Nothing but a pile of old stones shrouded in mist.

"Tales of haunting are often spread by outlaws and bandits to keep the locals away. I'm going to investigate." Andrall yanked his reins so his steed would make the tight turn onto the trail. Mardall steered his own mount to follow his father.

"Milord, you cannot go there alone!" Lady Lynnetta protested, hand to her throat.

"Half of the men with me, weapons at the ready. The rest stay close to the ladies," he called to the troop of retainers behind them.

"Not without me," Laislac muttered.

"No, P'pa," Ariiell protested. Amazing, just when she decided not to obey Rejiia's orders, her father proceeded to force her to follow them. "You cannot leave us with such meager protection." She waved to indicate her stepmother and Lady Lynnetta. Then she placed her hand on the bulge of her belly in silent reminder of the importance of the child she carried.

"No one will disturb you on the main road. Go up to the village if you are frightened." Laislac pushed his steed onto the side trail.

Lord Andrall looked as if he would protest the safety of the road and village. Then he firmed his jaw and turned in the wake of his great-brother. The men at arms followed. The retainers and servants milled about, uncertain of which way to go.

Ariiell rolled her eyes up in exasperation. "I'm not

going to be left behind." She joined the trek up the hillside. Behind her the others followed her lead.

"This had better be good, Rejiia."

In the back of her head she heard a malicious chuckle.

CHAPTER 34

"Where'd he go?" Margit stared at the space where Marcus had just been. She shook her hand to free it of the curious burn on top of the bruising from connecting so firmly with his jaw. "The bastard must have used the transport spell to disappear on me again. *S'murghin'* coward couldn't tell me to my face he expects me to sit quietly at home bearing his brats and babysitting his apprentices! What makes him think I want that kind of life? What makes him think . . ."

"I'm right here, Margit, right where you dumped me on the ground." Marcus' voice came to her from a great distance.

"Where?" She looked around for the source of his voice. Only Jack and Katrina with the blasted fly-wacket and another man and woman and a lot of steeds and sledges stood in the courtyard. "Where?" she repeated.

"Right here!" the once-beloved voice sounded angry now. "You could have told me your dreams. Instead you let me ramble on about my hopes for the future and you never said a word. You could have told me you don't really love me. You only wanted to use me as a means to wander the world."

The thickening fog distorted the air into a vague manlike shape, like looking at a dragon, but . . . but dragons had more solidity.

"You never said anything to me about settling down. All you did was retell your adventures on the road. I thought you wanted to keep traveling, take me with you on your journeys." Margit gulped back a sob, trying to rekindle the anger that had propelled her. "Jack, what's going on?" She looked to the one magician who might figure out this puzzle.

"Your anger must have heightened your senses for you to see him in the first place," Jack sighed. "Engage your TrueSight, Margit. Then look slightly to the side of the distortion. Do you see him?"

"I'm not sure. He looks sort of like a scrying image gone awry, almost there but not quite."

"I'm here, Margit. And our betrothal is off. I've found another. Vareena." His voice caressed the name. The figure that might be Marcus reached out as if to embrace the short woman standing off to the side. But he didn't touch her.

Vareena heaved a weary sigh and stepped away from him. She'd be pretty if she weren't so old. Nearly thirty. Past being a spinster. Margit classified her as a maiden aunt, destined to care for her brother's families, if she had any.

'Robb, tell him that I do not love him," Vareena said wearily. "I cannot love him." She sounded more exasperated than aggrieved.

"I can't tell him anything, Vareena." Another ghostly voice that sounded like Robb but not quite, from somewhere near the largest of the sledges.

Margit looked closely. Definitely another man shape within the light distortion. And beside him another and another. The flutters and fluctuations in her perceptions made her dizzy.

She closed her eyes to regain her balance. When she opened them again, the wavering light remained.

"What's going on, Jack?" She looked at his solid body rather than at all of the almost-people who milled around the courtyard. Katrina looked as bewildered as she. Only Vareena and the other man who did not seem a part of the entire proceedings acted as if all was normal.

"I was just about to find out when you interjected with your rather—um—forceful opinion," Jack replied. The corners of his mouth twitched even though he kept them in a stern frown.

Just then a caterwauling rose all around them, like a thousand cat fights all at once. Chills ran through Margit, but she didn't sneeze.

"Now what?"

"They're all fighting over the gold," Marcus said. He sounded as if a great weight pressed against him.

Margit's heart almost moved in empathy with him.

But the hurt was too great.

How could he have just presumed she wanted a home and children? Kardia Hodos was a big planet, and she intended to see all of it.

No, he hadn't heard. He hadn't listened. He never listened to anything but what he wanted to hear because he presumed his luck would make everyone agree with him.

"Your luck just ran out, Marcus," she muttered as Jack and two blobs of watery light moved toward the loudest of the disagreements.

And then she heard something that chilled her even more than the screeching fights and arguments by unseen ghosts: the distinctive hiss of long metal blades sliding out of wooden scabbards.

She whirled around to find a new party of a dozen steeds ridden by nobles and men at arms.

* * *

"Whatever happens, do not touch the gold," Robb whispered to Jack. He slammed his weight into two Rover men who grabbed each other by their shirts, clutching fingers far too close to the vulnerable throats of their opponent.

"Zolltarn!" he yelled at the top of his lungs. "Zolltarn, control your people!"

Jack bounced off two women, one heavily pregnant. They separated, mouths agape, panting for breath as they stared at the man who had the audacity to interfere. The burning energy that must separate the women from the normal world kept Jack from touching them directly, but his impact against the barrier should have been unpleasant enough to force them apart.

Someone grabbed the back of Robb's shirt and spun him around. Then a fist connected with his jaw and stars spun before his eyes.

"Robb!" Vareena screamed. And then she was kneeling beside him, hands reaching out to examine the huge ache in his teeth that spread from his chin to his eye. This time she forced her hand through the burning energy. Her fingers caressed his jaw, featherlight. The sharp pain eased to a dull ache.

For a moment his gaze caught hers. Suddenly his heart raced in his chest, opening him to new emotions, new truths about himself. A kind of serenity filled him. All because she touched him.

"We'll discuss this later. Right now, I have a brawl to break up." He heaved himself to his feet, wishing he could return her caress, perhaps kiss her cheek in tentative promise. "Later," he affirmed to them both.

The world seemed suddenly brighter and all of their problems surmountable.

And then the world tilted, light flashed, and the misty veil around the world expanded.

A gaggle of newcomers at the gate flashed swords. "Where'd she go?" Lord Andrall shouted.

Robb felt his skin grow cold as he recognized the king's adviser and his lady and their simple son astride the magnificent steeds clustered around the gatehouse. The other lord and lady could only be Lord Laislac and his second wife—his first wife had died quite mysteriously, and with a scandal Robb couldn't remember, some years ago. Their attention all focused on a very pregnant young woman—now in the ghostly reality—wrestling with a Rover woman over a scarf heavy with gold coins.

"Give it to me, you ignorant slut. I need that gold. In the name of the coven, give me that gold!" she shouted.

"Get out of here now, Vareena," Robb implored. "Run as far and as fast as you can. Save yourself from the coven."

*   *   *

Everyone and everything in the courtyard stilled. The name of the coven had that effect on people.

Marcus looked around to see who had invoked them. The band of magicians was dedicated to the overthrow of every peaceful government in all of Kardia Hodos. His gaze lighted on the young woman in elegant velvet riding clothes. Hints of red glistened within her blonde hair. Her aura almost shouted magical power within the orange-and-yellow layers.

He blinked and looked again, more closely. She had touched the gold a Rover woman had fastened to a sash. In touching the gold-laden sash she joined the growing crowd of those trapped in this other reality. She broadcast greed to any receptive magician within a league's distance. So did the Rovers.

"Did I hear someone say gold?" One of the lords at the gatehouse dismounted hurriedly. If he wasn't careful, he'd trip over one of the Rovers and become a ghost himself.

"Lord Laislac." Vareena dipped a hasty curtsy to him.

He ignored her.

Marcus already knew Lord Andrall and his lady. He'd heard tales of their simple son. The other woman in the party must be Laislac's wife. The one he'd married in haste after his first wife quite conveniently fell from the castle ramparts. Or was pushed. The scandal had circulated in the capital for a few weeks and then disappeared in the wake of newer gossip. Laislac had married a much younger woman the day the official mourning period ended.

Marcus peered around Zolltarn's sledge to see if any of the Rovers acknowledged the presence of nobility. They didn't seem to care. But the statue on top of the sledge, the tin weasel with flaking gilt paint, began to rock and shift. Both front paws and about half of the tail seemed to have shed its tin coating. A spot of drool dripped from the exposed teeth—real teeth, not metal castings.

"Robb, Jack, look at Krej!" he called, fascinated by the partial animation. At one time Krej had been the most powerful lord of the land—first cousin to Darville's father and regent during Darville's magically induced illness at the beginning of his reign.

"Krej and Lanciar in the same area?" Jack held his staff out, prepared to use it as a defensive weapon, physical and magical. "Rejiia can't be far away."

Katrina touched Jack's shoulder and pointed to the top of the southwest tower. Marcus followed her pointing finger with half his attention, keeping one eye on Krej.

Atop the tower the light sparkled with new magic. The wind blasted outward and down into the courtyard whipping dust into everyone's eyes. Marcus forced himself to keep his gaze trained on the area. He didn't know the secret of the transport spell, but he'd witnessed it often enough to know when someone used it.

Black and red dominated the spot. The light coalesced into the figure of a black-haired woman with a silver streak running from one temple down the length of her waist-length tresses. Her black gown molded to her tall figure, outlining all of her curves and emphasizing the length of her legs.

"Rejiia," Jack confirmed.

Marcus' armor snapped into place. Beautiful, deadly, vicious. Krej's daughter. She'd learned a lot from her father before the lord had thrown one spell too many and had it backlash off King Darville's sword and crown. He'd been captive in the weasel

statue ever since. Without Krej's disdainful supervision, Rejiia had learned a lot more about magic and
about evil than her father had ever dreamed of.

She would continue to menace Coronnan until she
sat on the throne with the Coraurlia—the magically
charmed glass crown in the shape of a dragon—on her
head; or until someone managed to kill her.

"Release my father!" she called in an imperious
tone. But there was a tightness in her neck muscles
and the way her hand clenched around a small wand
set with a black crystal on the end. She must use the
wand as most magicians used a staff. A pretty and
feminine affectation. And undoubtedly just as deadly
as the woman who used it. She pointed the crystal
directly at the statue of her father.

The tin weasel rocked again, but it remained firmly
anchored atop the sledge.

Then Marcus noted that Zolltarn rested his hand on
Krej. He flashed his brilliant smile at Rejiia. She
flinched ever so slightly.

As long as Zolltarn had some of the enchanted gold
in his possession and touched the tin statue, the statue
traversed both realities and was subject to the magic
of neither. A dark aura surrounded the statue, as
black as the void.

Something was terribly wrong with Krej.

Rejiia must have sensed it, too. She disappeared in
another flash of light and swirl of wind. Just as suddenly, she reappeared directly in front of Zolltarn and
the statue.

The black aura moved higher. The statue rocked
harder, puffing up to almost twice its normal size.

Marcus jumped to stand between Margit and Vareena and the magic about to go awry.

CHAPTER 35

"Give him back to me!" Rejiia said through clenched teeth. Her body seemed as tightly controlled as her jaw.

"And what of our son, Rejiia?" Lanciar asked. "Don't you care anything at all about the child the Rovers hide from you?" The mass of Rovers and newcomers separated for him as he marched over to her side. Outrage poured from him like a leaking bucket. Magic power raced from his fingertips up his arms to his shoulders. He wanted nothing more than to backhand the woman and knock her clear out of his life into her next existence.

"The child is just one more crime for which Zolltarn and his Rovers must answer to the coven. My father is in greater danger. Release him!" Rejiia reached out with her hand and her magic to encircle the tin weasel.

Light flashed, and the world tilted. Rejiia joined the Rovers and the others trapped in some reality different from Lanciar's.

Part of Lanciar wanted to laugh. Disgust invaded a bigger part of him.

"Is this place truly safe?" A new voice asked from the gateway. A feminine voice speaking Lanciar's native language.

Only Katrina turned to look at this newest additions to the mob. Rejiia continued to struggle with Zolltarn for possession of Krej.

"Your Majesty," Katrina gasped as she bent her

knees into a full curtsy. In the same motion, she tugged on Jack's sleeve to bring his head respectfully lower than the trail-weary woman.

Miranda cradled a small child in her arms. Yet another Rover held her arm at the elbow.

This new Rover wore the same red-and-purple trim on his black clothes as Zolltarn's clan. Lanciar did not recognize him from his weeks on the road with the Rovers.

Lace spilled from the panniers on the back of their pack steed. But it wasn't quite a steed. Then the beast opened his mouth and extended his neck, bellowing an obnoxious braying sound around a mouthful of big, square teeth. A team of trumpeters could not have attracted more attention.

Everyone in the compound turned to face this new greeting.

"Who?" Zolltarn asked.

Lord Andrall and Lord Laislac immediately bent a single knee to her presence. Their wives followed suit—sometime during the fray they, too, had dismounted.

"Your Majesty, may I present your new ambassador from Coronnan," Katrina said, daring to raise her head a little. She pushed Jack forward. He stumbled to one knee. The flywacket remained firmly on his shoulder, flaring his wings just enough for them both to catch their balance.

"Your Majesty, my position as ambassador to Se-Lenicca has not been confirmed by the Council of Provinces, only promised by His Grace King Darville."

"Miranda," Lanciar breathed. "When did she come back to life?" In asking the question, he knew the answer. The moment Simeon died, his spells would have dissipated. The sorcerer-king had kept his wife—the hereditary ruler of SeLenicca—comatose for weeks to keep her from revoking the edict of joint monarchy. She had planned to strip him of power and divorce him. His blatant affair with Rejiia had pushed her beyond forgiveness.

"Queen Miranda," Marcus gasped. "What in the name of the Stargods is *she* doing here, dressed as a peasant and in the company of a Rover? I thought the SeLenese did not acknowledge outlanders as human."

"They don't," Lanciar confirmed. "It seems some changes are happening in SeLenicca."

"Rise up, all of you," Queen Miranda said. She blushed and looked to her escort. "I am queen no longer. SeLenicca is in ruins. I have no government. Today I am no more than this trader's partner. I make lace for a living."

Katrina smiled brightly. "So do I, Your Majesty."

"You will have a government again," Jack affirmed. "King Darville is committed to helping you rebuild your country."

"With what? The land is bankrupt. My people are scattered and disillusioned."

Rejiia seemed to have been forgotten in this new development. Lanciar spared her a probing glance. She raised her wand as if to strike Zolltarn on the head with it. Did she have any magic to accompany the blow? Her emotions were out of control and so must her magic be. She reeked of Tambootie.

Lanciar guessed the dragon weed was pushing her into insanity, just as it had Krej and Simeon before their downfalls.

"We have a vast hoard of gold here, Milady Queen," Zolltarn announced with all the enthusiasm of a minstrel at an Equinox Festival. "You have only to claim it."

"No!" a dozen or more voices protested. "The gold is mine."

And then the ghost of Ackerly erupted from the library. His misty white form flew broad circles around the courtyard, slashing with his sacrificial knife at all who held his gold.

Rovers and armed guards alike in both realities beat at the wraith with daggers and cook pots and anything else made of cold iron that came easily to hand. One Rover slashed the sleeve of another open with a dagger. He received a fist in his jaw in return. Another dozen brawls erupted, spilling over to the newcomers who had not yet had a chance to claim any of the hoard.

Still the ghost circled the compound, screaming and slashing with his dripping ritual blade. Two men fell to the ground screaming, dripping blood from scalp and back wounds.

Lanciar waved his hands at the being. Just as it flew past him, knife aimed at the great vein of his neck, Lanciar dove beneath a sledge. The wraith howled his disappointment but kept circling, seeking a new victim.

"Maija, if you love me even a little, you will help me make sure Rejiia does not escape justice this time," Lanciar pleaded with whoever might hear him. A second later the weight of a gold coin rested firmly within his palm.

Black stars clouded his vision and his head felt as if it floated somewhere around the tower roofs. The ground beneath him seemed to slant sideways.

He braced himself to keep from sliding out from beneath the sledge and into the extended brawl. Quickly everything settled and Maija lay beside him, eyes wide and moist.

He kissed her lips lightly. "Thank you, Maija. Now help me make certain none of these people leave until we sort this all out. We have to stop Rejiia from stealing my son or reanimating her father. Stop her forever."

"I knew you loved me," Maija cried, throwing her arms around his neck and returning his kiss most soundly

"Later, Maija. I promise that once this is over we

will marry and I will stay with you. We will raise my
son together with any other children we happen to
have." He held up the coin she had given him and
smiled. "What happens if we drop a coin deep in the
undergarment pockets of all these people?"

Maija returned his grin. "I have listened to all these
people argue. The gold is what traps them here in a
ghostly existence."

"Then we must keep them all here for a time. Especially Rejiia. She must not leave, and she must not
liberate her father from the statue."

"With your promise to marry me, with my clan as
witness, we are already married and bound to each
other for all time." Another kiss with her body
pressed tightly against his distracted him a moment.

"Then we must work together for the safety of the
clan. Help me keep all these *s'murghin'* people here."

"Watch your language around the children!" Maija's eyes, sparkling with mischief, belied her stern
frown.

"Will you please help me keep everyone here?"

"Even the *gadjé* nobles and their retainers?"

"Especially the *s'mur*—um—*gadjé* nobles and their
pregnant daughter. If she escapes before we sort this
all out, she will alert the coven and bring them here
from the far corners of Kardia Hodos." He kissed
Maija's cheek—her mouth was too dangerous with its
open invitation to linger with her. Then he extricated
himself from her arms.

Maija crawled over to the nearest Rovers who
rolled on the ground punching each other. She lightly
removed a coin from the discarded cap of one of
the men.

"Is it one of the ghostly coins?" he asked as she
handed it to him.

"Aye. See how old it is?"

He nodded as he picked out the outline of a long
dead monarch. The date on the inscription connected

it to the province of Faciar before the unification of
Coronnan and the foundation of the Commune of
Magicians.

"Only the ghost's hoard is that old."

Rejiia had both hands upon the tin weasel. Zolltarn
worked to keep her from wrenching it away from his
grasp. Sweat dripped from both of their brows. The
statue retained all of Krej's mass as a full-grown man.
Neither of them could lift the thing easily. Both of
their magical talents seemed depressed by the ghostly
reality of the gold.

Lanciar crawled out of his cover, careful to avoid
the swooping ghost. He walked right up to Rejiia and
Zolltarn. Neither took any notice of him. The weasel
was more tin than gilt these days and the front legs
and all of the tail seemed to have lost most of the
metal, taking on a decidedly furry texture. The backlashed spell was wearing off.

Would Krej survive? Would he emerge as a man?
Or did the spell have to be reversed instead of wearing
out in order for him to become other than a weasel?

Lanciar didn't care. He was about to irrevocably
sever all of his connections to the coven. Perhaps
break it apart once and for all.

"This is for deserting our son, Rejiia, and for not
giving me the right to raise him as I choose." He
dropped the antique coin down the front of her bodice. It lodged neatly between her ample breasts.

Rejiia screeched in her most annoying voice. She
clutched her temples and reeled. Zolltarn tumbled
backward in full possession of the heavy statue. He
landed flat on his back with Krej sitting on his chest.

Then Rejiia's already ghostly form dissipated more.
Lanciar could barely make out an outline of her or her
aura. Both had been clearly visible while she merely
clutched Krej on the other side of Zolltarn's ghostly
grasp.

"Neatly done, my boy. You'll make an admirable
Rover!" Zolltarn proclaimed around heavy gasps

for air. He remained a silvery outline. The Blood-mage ghost and his wicked knife were more substantial.

"Zolltarn's had the wind knocked out of him," Lanciar said. "Marcus, Robb, somebody help him up."

Lanciar had difficulty seeing the men he called to for help. But Jack and Katrina remained clearly visible, along with Vareena and Queen Miranda and her party. He must have slipped back into reality when he let loose the coin into Rejiia's bodice. Rejiia's violent transition had kept him from noticing the sense-shattering shift.

One by one the nobles became opaque ghosts. Strange that the mundanes were more visible than those with magic. Rejiia and Zolltarn were the hardest of all to see.

Then Maija popped back into full view. She smiled at him. The sun seemed to burst through the clouds and brighten his day. She had definitely inherited that smile from her father.

"Let's hope you have a few more scruples than your father," he muttered as he moved to join her.

"Changing sides again, Lanciar?" Jack confronted him, keeping him from Maija. He leveled his staff, aiming the tip directly at him.

"Trust me, Jack. Please, trust me just this once. I know which side offers me the best hope of regaining my son and raising him in a loving family, learning to use magic responsibly."

"I don't believe you any more than I did back in King Simeon's mines. You were a spy for him and the coven then. I know you still spy for them."

"Traitor!" Rejiia aimed her wand directly at Lanciar.

Lanciar saw two brief blasts of fire, one purple and silver, the other red and black, then there was nothing.

* * *

"Enough," Marcus said. "I've had enough." He took a deep breath and fingered the three gold coins in his pocket.

Robb, Jack, Vareena, and Margit looked at him strangely. He smiled at them. Only half his mouth turned up.

"I'm sorry, Robb, you really deserved to figure this out first, but I can't take any more of this. I'm getting out." Deliberately, he sank his hand into his pocket and retrieved the three coins.

He held them up to the sunlight. They glinted enticingly, begging him to hold them, caress them, keep them forever.

He closed his eyes and gathered his strength. With a mighty effort he threw them at Ackerly. "Take these back, you cursed ghost. I have no more use for your hoard. I want to live poor rather than remain trapped here with your riches."

Ackerly snatched the gold out of the air as he circled the compound once more. He juggled his bloody knife while he fumbled to hold onto this returned wealth. For a moment he looked as if he might drop them both. Then he sighed and disappeared into his library.

Light flashed blue and white and red. The world tilted. Up and down exchanged places three or four times. And then Marcus found his feet firmly planted on the ground. The misty haze that had covered his vision for so long lifted and he could see Vareena and Margit quite clearly along with Queen Miranda and her party. Robb, the Rovers, Rejiia, and the pregnant woman and her party remained insubstantial forms.

But the heavy fog remained across the top of the courtyard.

A moment later Robb emerged from his haze to stand before him with a big silly grin on his face. "I was waiting for you to figure it out."

Marcus hugged him tight and slapped his back.

Robb returned the comradely embrace.

"Now what do we do?" Marcus asked them all.

CHAPTER 36

"It seems to me that part of completing a quest is cleaning up the messes along the way," Jack said quietly. Guilt immediately heated his face. He'd left a terrible mess in SeLenicca.

But he was going back there, with Katrina, to do what he could. And the gold seemed to be one of the answers to that country's many problems. If they could convince Ackerly to give it up and remove the curse.

At least he'd temporarily stunned Lanciar enough to keep him from interfering.

"Our quest is a bit redundant," Robb replied. "We were sent to bring the dragons home and possibly find you. You seem to have completed both of those tasks quite handily. Our duty to the Commune is to return to the University for a new assignment." His face fell, as if that were the last thing he wanted to do. His eyes strayed to Margit and Vareena.

"Marcus and Robb, do you intend to leave this situation unsettled?" Jack asked. "These Rovers and the others trapped between the void and reality, with a ghost to haunt them, need a solution. So does the village that will impoverish itself trying to feed them." Jack needed to prod them into making their own decisions. He couldn't do it for them. They'd never become master magicians if they relied on others to make their decisions.

That had been a hard lesson to learn and one the cat within him truly resented. Rosie was more interested in watching than leading. He had to get rid of this cat and soon. He had enough problems without Rosie complicating things.

"I've never known a Rover to willingly give up anything they possessed. Why did Zolltarn offer a fortune in gold to a foreign queen?" Marcus interjected.

"Why give away the gold, Zolltarn?" Jack raised his voice over the sounds of many people arguing. Even the lords and their ladies fought over who could bow the lowest to the improbable queen in their midst even though the queen remained substantial and the nobles had become ghosts.

The Rover chieftain opened his mouth in a toothy grin. Jack continued to look at him questioningly rather than succumb to the seduction within that smile. He knew his grandfather too well.

"With a Rover sitting beside the queen of SeLenicca." He nodded to their kinsman holding Miranda's hand and guarding the pack beast and its treasure trove of expensive lace from the light fingers of a number of the combatants. "And Rover gold to rebuild the country, my clan will have a homeland. We will have the freedom to roam there forever."

"You won't end a thousand years and more of prejudice against dark-eyed outlanders with a little bit of gold," Jack reminded him.

"And the people of SeLenicca may not allow their queen to marry another outlander. Look what the last one did to us," Katrina added. "With the help of that black-haired bitch." She almost snarled as she jerked her head toward Rejiia.

The coven witch had returned her attention to Zolltarn and the tin statue.

"Katrina?" Jack had never seen her so aggressive, or so angry. But then, Rejiia had made her watch Jack's torture. Afterward, she had left Katrina to share his dank and miserable cell and die chained apart as the city collapsed around them.

Memories of that awful night pushed Jack closer to Katrina. Silently he reached for her hand. United, they had defeated Rejiia and her lover, King Simeon. Together they could conquer the world.

"I need to return to the University to find a way to lay Ackerly to rest and lift the curse from the gold," Marcus said.

Jack almost didn't hear him.

"What about us?" Margit asked belligerently. Her fist clenched as if she intended to knock him flat once more.

"I don't know, Margit. We need to talk. We need to find out if our dreams for the future can ever find a common ground. But first, I need to solve this problem." He captured her gaze for a long moment. Margit looked away first.

If a breaking heart could make a sound, Jack heard it in her sigh. But no tear touched her eyes.

"Come on, Robb. Let's pack and get out of here. We have a long walk back to the University."

"I think I'd best stay here, Marcus," Robb replied. "Vareena and I have much to discuss. And someone needs to try to restore order to this mess."

"Yeah, maybe the time has come for us to work alone. We've always relied on each other and that is a good thing. But some things can only be done alone."

"I can't give you the secret of the transport spell until you are confirmed a master magician, Marcus, but I can send you on your way in a matter of heartbeats rather than weeks. We don't have time to wait for you to walk there and back," Jack offered.

"And my brother Yeenos may return at any time with an edict from the priests and Council of Provinces removing our responsibility to these ghosts," Vareena reminded them. "We have to free all of these people before then."

"And free yourself as well," Robb added. "As long as there is a chance someone will wander in here and become a ghost, you will feel honor-bound to remain here. I can't allow you to do that, Vareena."

Jack took a moment to assess the status of the cap-

tured people. Marcus and Robb had returned from
the gloaming. Katrina, Margit, Zebbiah, and Queen
Miranda had never transferred into a ghostly state.
All of the Rovers seemed to be gone, as well as Rejiia.
Rejiia and Zolltarn continued to tussle over possession
of Krej. The Rovers and the nobles continued to argue
and brawl.

The noise began to make his head spin.

Amaranth screeched and flapped his wings, not liking the loud chaos much either.

"I'll take the offer of the transport spell." Marcus
firmed his chin. "Though the way my luck has been
running lately, I'll probably get lost in the void."

"I did that once, Marcus." Jack could smile now at
the devastating mistake that had begun his adventures.
But he'd been young and too arrogant of his talent
then. "Have you undergone a trial by Tambootie
smoke?"

"Of course. We all do upon advancement to journeyman from apprentice. It centers the talent and
opens true life paths," Marcus replied.

"And protects young magicians from the inconsis-
tency of raging growth and change when we reach
puberty," Jack confirmed. He hadn't undergone the
important magical trial when he'd become lost in the
void. His body and talent had rebelled against each
other. "I'll make sure you don't get lost. But just to
be sure, I'll send Amaranth along with you to guide
you home."

And that way, he'd also have some privacy with
Katrina. If this mob would ever settle down.

"One problem at a time," he told himself.

* * *

Vareena joined the Rover girl kneeling beside the
blond man Jack and Rejiia had reduced to immobility.

Rejiia, who seemed to be everyone's enemy, had
time and attention only for the hideous statue. But
the Rover chieftain had secreted it once more inside

one of the funny looking hovels atop the sledges. Vareena had watched him hand it over to a subordinate who in turn passed it to another and another until she'd lost track of who had it.

"Where have you hidden my father?" Rejiia screeched, much like the flywacket. With magic, she blasted open the door of the closest bardo. While the wooden panels smoldered, she began pawing through the possessions inside. She discarded clothing and boxes, cooking pots and camp furniture in her desperate search.

"Get away from my things!" a Rover woman howled at Rejiia in protest, louder than the ghost of Ackerly had. She launched herself at Rejiia's back, fingers arched to claws and teeth exposed to bite.

Rejiia flicked her wrist and her assailant landed on her back in the middle of the compound. Rejiia continued her disorderly search.

"Murderer!" Maija screamed. She dove after Rejiia. "You murdered Lanciar for no reason." The two women rolled out of the bardo, the Rover clinging to Rejiia's back, fingernails raking the fine, white skin of Rejiia's neck and face.

"But he's not dead," Vareena said quietly. Beneath her fingertips, the pulse on Lanciar's neck pounded in a regular rhythm. Surely Maija had felt the same life sign.

Lanciar opened his eyes a crack. "Wha . . . what?" he croaked.

"Hush. I'm trying to sort this out," Vareena whispered.

Then Jack, Marcus, and Robb joined the attack on Rejiia. First one, then the other aimed their staffs at the woman.

"Get off me!" Rejiia fought Maija with one hand while her other plucked at something invisible that seemed to be encircling her.

If only the brawling Rovers would be quiet, she

could figure out more of the complex relationships in this strange group. For a moment she understood Marcus' disgust with the entire situation. She wanted little more than to leave the mess and let these people sort it out themselves as best they could.

"You cannot bind me," Rejiia proclaimed. "I lead the coven. My magic is stronger than yours." She bucked backward, much as a plow steed rejects a rider. Maija sprang free of her victim, a sly smile on her face.

Jack directed Marcus and Robb with his staff. The three men circled Rejiia three times, each chanting something slightly different in a language Vareena did not understand. She was only aware of the fact that they did not speak in unison.

"Three different spells to break, each with a different solution," Maija told her. "Even Rejiia will have a hard time getting out of their bindings.

With each circle, Rejiia's movements became more restrained. Her hands and arms pressed tightly against her sides, immobile. Only her mouth remained free and she spewed invective on every head.

"Oh, shut up," Vareena finally exclaimed. "I'm sick and tired of all this noise and chaos in *my* monastery."

"*Your* monastery? My dear young woman, this entire province belongs to me and only me!" Lord Laislac said. He puffed out his chest and attempted to look down his nose.

"At the moment, milord, you, your lady, and your daughter are all ghosts trapped within these walls. I have inherited the responsibility for this place and the ghosts it holds. Therefore, you belong to me at the moment, and I said, 'Shut up!' "

Stunned silence followed her words. One by one the Rover brawls stilled. The combatants dusted themselves off and offered a hand up to the people they had been fighting only moments before. Only the pregnant girl continued to tussle for possession of a coin-laden scarf.

"That goes for you, too." Vareena shoved herself between the two women. The energy barrier that separated her from the ghosts forced the last combatants apart. The scarf tore and both women moved to attack Vareena. They bounced off her into the arms of their families, waiting to receive them.

"Now, Robb, see that Rejiia is locked in one of the towers," Vareena ordered. "Please."

"One of the lesser towers, I think." Robb grinned back at her, still anchoring Rejiia with magic from his staff.

"Jack, you and Marcus go to his room and do whatever it is you have to do. Zolltarn, see that your people find places to settle. Lord Laislac, I suggest you do the same for your party. And as for you, Ackerly, you'd better stay in the library where you belong."

Surprisingly, everyone obeyed her.

Satisfaction nestled comfortably on her shoulders.

"You can't have the big room," the pregnant girl said imperiously to Zolltarn. "I carry the heir to all of Coronnan. Therefore I am entitled to the biggest room with the private facilities."

Zolltarn snarled at her. The expression carried almost as much weight as his smile.

The girl backed away from him, but she did not bow her head or lower her eyes.

"You, Lady whoever you are, can have the scriptorium above the south wing all to yourself. I'll stand guard at the foot of the stairs if necessary to keep you there and out of mischief." Vareena glared at her.

"That will not be necessary, miss," the other lord said. "The six of us will settle into that same scriptorium. My daughter-in-law will not disturb you." He bowed slightly and offered his arm to his lady. They retreated in silent dignity.

Lord Laislac and his lady followed suit. The moonfaced young man with a little drool at the corner of his mouth copied the men in offering his arm to the

pregnant girl. She batted it away and huffed in the
wake of her elders. The simple boy shrugged and
flashed a smile to one and all.

"Good luck," Vareena called to him, utterly
charmed. "I wish I could do something for him," she
said to herself.

"Perhaps we can do something for him," Jack said.
"But that is a plan I cannot implement without some
serious consultation with the Commune. Marcus is
ready. Do you want to see him off?"

"I . . . uh . . ." What did she want? Marcus had
earned her respect as a clear thinker and leader in
this adventure, but he wasn't Robb. "I think I'll remain out here and keep order. My eldest brother has
just arrived at the gate looking very puzzled. I'd best
inform him of this newest crisis and arrange for food
for all of these people. You and I may have to go
hunting later."

She picked up her skirts and rushed to the gate to
confer with Uustass. She hoped he had some better
ideas for provisioning two dozen Rovers, two lords
and their retinues, an exiled queen, and a host of
magicians.

"Hurry back, Marcus. We need whatever answers
you can find quickly."

She'd never wanted to leave this place more. Freedom beckoned to her just beyond the room where
Jack and Marcus had firmly closed the door against
intruders. She fingered the silver-and-amethyst amulet.
Boldly, she pulled it from beneath her shift. She
needed to see it in the sunlight as a symbol of the
future freedom she only dared dream of.

* * *

*These invaders with their iron and their greed do not
frighten me. But the wounds I suffer from their iron
will plague me forever. For that they must pay.*

They have betrayed me, as Nimbulan did. As my son

*and daughter did when they rejected me as their father,
preferring Nimbulan to raise them.*

*They will all die before another night passes, or they
will wish themselves dead. In this place, such wishes
come true.*

CHAPTER 37

Marcus stuffed his few possessions into his pack. Excitement fluttered in his belly, making his movements jerky and imprecise.

"Be sure to check on Old Lyman," Margit said, throwing open the door to his room with a bang.

Marcus jumped a little at her abrupt entrance. Then he settled into his packing once more.

"He was ailing when I left. Sleeping more than waking and acting a little confused when he did bother to open his eyes."

"Lyman is older than dirt and always acts confused. Untangling his cryptic statements is one of the best learning tools at the University," Marcus countered.

"Ask about Jaylor's newborn twins as well," Jack added right on Margit's heels. He caressed his ever-present flywacket, murmuring to it. "Gossip among the Masters said that one of the twins was too small and weak to survive long. Such a loss will devastate Jaylor and Brevelan. We need them both hale and thinking clearly as long as the Gnuls have power in Coronnan."

"Yeah, I noticed Jaylor was acting distracted, always wanting to be back at the clearing rather than in the University. I thought he was just acting the new father," Margit confirmed. "But there wasn't the triumphant shout announcing the births either."

"I'll check on both of them—not that I can be of any help. Now can we get on with this? Is there anything special I should know or do to survive the transport spell?"

"Marcus, good, I caught you before you left," Robb burst into the little room, Vareena right behind him. It was getting crowded in here.

Presumably Katrina was helping Queen Miranda settle in with her daughter and Rover escort. Otherwise, she'd be pressed as close to Jack as Vareena was to Robb.

"I'll be back as soon as I can, Robb." Marcus indulged in one last back-slapping hug with his friend and partner. "Thanks for showing me how to take responsibility and not trust in my luck so much."

"I think today is my lucky day," Robb looked into Vareena's eyes for one long adoring moment before turning back to Marcus. "Check out Nimbulan's diaries for any reference to Ackerly. There has to be a clue there as to how we can separate him from the gold."

"Look in the library for early references to exorcism of ghosts and blood magic," Jack added. He began his deep breathing in preparation for a trance. "Just think about the courtyard of the University. There's a big everblue tree with a bank of calubra ferns at the base on the north end."

"I know the place." Marcus breathed deeply on his own, fixing the memory of the University firmly in his mind as he'd seen it only a moon or so ago. "I always pictured Margit nestled in among the lower branches for a shady study place."

"How did you know?" Margit asked.

The sense-robbing blackness of the void closed around him before he could answer.

Before he could register the mind-numbing cold and the tangle of colored umbilicals that entwined with his own life force, a sharp jolt through his feet brought him into the exact spot he had visualized.

"Merawk!" Amaranth protested in the branch above with a flutter of wings and scraping of talons

on bark. Then the creature flapped his wings and flew up the cliff face behind the library toward Shayla's lair. He had his own errands to run.

Marcus took a deep breath that smelled of home.

"Marcus, you are the last person I expected to invade our meditation session," Master Slippy exclaimed. The lanky magician gestured to the silent students sitting cross-legged all around the compound. The leaves on the trees around them had faded and begun to change color and the sun angled quite low.

"How—how long have I been gone?" He had meticulously counted the days in the monastery—difficult because of the perpetual twilight the gloaming had imposed upon him. High Summer should still brighten the courtyard.

"Many moons. Since early last Spring." Slippy looked puzzled.

"The ghost was right. Time does move differently in his domain."

"Time cannot be distorted, boy," Slippy reprimanded him. "I thought I taught you better than that."

"Maybe time isn't distorted, but our perceptions are. I need to report to Jaylor, right away."

"Not today, young man. Our Senior Magician is sorely troubled at home. I could have told him that families interfere with magic. But he wouldn't listen. No one listens to me anymore."

Marcus noted the increased amount of white hair in Slippy's faded strawberry-blond queue. The hairline on his forehead had receded another finger-length since Marcus had last seen him as well.

"This will not wait, Master Slippy." Marcus kept his voice down in deference to the apprentices hard at work within their own minds. "There is great trouble brewing in Laislac near one of the minor passes."

"Another invasion? I thought SeLenicca broken and beyond organizing anything."

"That is probably true since their queen has taken

herself into exile at an abandoned monastery. No, the trouble involves the coven, and the Rovers, and a ghost, and . . . it's too complex to relate all at once."

"Then come into the library. These pesky students can survive without supervision for a while. In the absence of Jaylor and Lyman—he's truly ill—I guess I am the most senior of the masters and the one you should report to."

"Is . . . is Master Lyman truly so ill?" Marcus had difficulty imagining the University without the elderly librarian. But then everyone grew old and died eventually, even Old Baamin, Jaylor's predecessor as Senior Magician.

Everyone died eventually and passed on to the next existence. So why hadn't Ackerly passed on? What chained him other than his lust for gold?

A sense of urgency drove him to ask one last question before diving into his research.

"Master Slippy, have you heard any rumors from the capital about the priests or Gnuls breaking the sanctuary of that abandoned monastery?"

Slippy stopped his slow steps toward the library abruptly. "How did you know that Hanic's successor is mounting an armed force to guard a party of engineers that are supposed to tear the place apart stone by stone and kill anything that lives within?"

Marcus had to stop and breathe deeply.

"What ails you, boy. You are as pale as a ghost." Slippy clutched his arm.

"An apt description," Marcus mumbled. He welcomed the extra support while he fought for balance. "When are the engineers leaving the capital?"

"Two days ago, riding with all haste, guided by a local. A young man petitioned to destroy the place, the village too, if they encounter resistance."

* * *

Lanciar woke abruptly. He opened his eyes to dim stone walls and a fierce stabbing pain pounding in his temple. The ache in his lower back competed with the burning sensation on his wrists and ankles for dominance.

"Am I alive?" His words came out in a dry whisper. He grimaced at the increase in the knife stabs behind his eyes.

"You'd probably hurt less if you had drunk a whole barrel of ale," Jack said. His tone offered no sympathy and certainly no mercy. "From what Maija tells me, that is not usual for you."

Lanciar tried to lift his hand to rub his eyes, his temples, his aching hair. The burning sensation on his wrists increased.

"You are restrained by magic as well as mundane manacles," Jack informed him. Still no easing in his tone.

Lanciar risked lifting his head to look and wished he hadn't.

"Where's Maija?" he asked, knowing she'd soothe his hurts with cool towels, kind words, and ale.

"Waiting outside, wringing her hands and wailing to her father. Hard to believe that beautiful girl is my maternal aunt." This last piece of news came out in a confused mutter.

'Then you are the legendary child of the missing Kestra," Lanciar repeated the gossip he'd heard while traveling with the clan. Zolltarn's oldest daughter had been ordered to conceive a child with the most powerful magician in all of Coronnan. The resulting child should have prodigious magical talents to open the dragon magic barrier that had surrounded Coronnan at the time. But Kestra and her escort had disappeared before she could rejoin the clan. All of the Rover clans had searched for her and the child ever since.

"My father tells me that Kestra was my mother, and therefore Zolltarn is my grandfather." Jack added no details to satisfy Lanciar's curiosity.

"Then we will shortly be family, Jack. I intend to marry Maija and raise my son with the Rovers—honorable rogues that they are." A sense of satisfaction settled upon Lanciar. He wasn't certain he loved Maija, not like he had loved Rejiia. But his affection for the sprightly Rover girl would endure a lot longer. He'd work had to be sure of that.

He'd even watch his language around Maija. And he'd drink a lot less ale. Maija wouldn't have to brew so much and would have more time for him . . . and dared he hope? . . . for their children.

"Your son?" Jack asked.

"Rejiia rejected him at birth. I won't allow her to kidnap him away from me again."

"I thought Simeon fathered her child and that it died at birth. Not unusual, considering Simeon was her uncle. The close blood tie could damage the child."

"Lies. Rejiia lies as naturally as she breathes. She wanted the child to be a secret. When she brought to fruit all her convoluted plans to conquer all of Kardia Hodos through magic, she'd produce the child as heir to the three kingdoms. But she didn't want the responsibility of raising him. She can't love anyone but herself."

"And possibly her father."

"Not much longer if the spell keeping him within the statue isn't reversed soon. I think Krej is dying. Let me up, Jack. I'm no longer a threat to you."

"You've lied to me before. You were the coven's spy in King Simeon's mines where I was enslaved for three years. You betrayed me to Rejiia and Simeon. You gloated over me while she tortured me."

"I have renounced my membership in the coven. And I truly regret my misguided loyalty to Rejiia. She and Simeon coerced me into betraying the only truly honest man I have ever known." He caught Jack's gaze with his own, imploring him to understand.

Jack remained stone-faced and unforgiving.

"My son needs me, needs the family the Rovers have offered us. You, Jack, are a part of that family whether you want to be or not."

Jack blanched a moment. Then he firmed his jaw. "What makes you think you can be a father to the child? From what I hear, you look for too many answers in the bottom of your ale mug and never find them, so you have to refill the mug until you pass out."

Lanciar had no answer for that. Even now his mouth watered for the taste of Maija's ale. He knew he drank too much, had drunk too much ever since he'd discovered the depth of Rejiia's betrayal of him and the coven. "I need the clan as much as my son does. Their petty thefts and chicanery are minor irritations. I would like to reform them, but doubt anyone could. Throw a truth spell on me if you must to determine my intentions."

"You know as well as I do that if you lie while under a truth spell, you will die—quite horribly." Jack breathed deeply. For the first time since this terrible interview had begun, his eyes relaxed.

"Yes, I know that. I also know that you awakened my magical talent, so you have delved into the depths of my soul. You can ferret out my secrets easier than I can. Throw the spell and know that I have renounced the coven once and for all."

"I wish I could take your word for it. But I've dealt with the coven too many times. I know from experience how they gain power from pain, their own or what they can inflict upon others." Jack flinched as he spoke.

Lanciar understood how deep his scars must run.

"I speak the truth, I have no need to fear your spell, Jack."

"Just be glad Katrina is not here to take fright and thus weaken my resolve." With a simple gesture blue sparkles shot from Jack's fingers.

Lanciar just had time for a single breath before numbing cold settled over his entire body. A veil of blue haze covered everything—not unlike the few moments when he'd held the gold in his hands. And then all of his aches and pains disappeared, replaced by that terrible cold. His mind drifted free of his body and he looked down upon himself and Jack from somewhere near the narrow window at the top of the room.

His perceptions expanded. He wanted to drift into the haze, free of hurt, free of tangled emotions, free of . . .

Off in the distance he sensed things that he thought he'd left behind in SeLenicca: Many steeds pounding the Kardia as they raced forward, men cursing and sweating as they drew weapons, fear, excitement, determination. All the things that accompanied men as they rode to battle. They rode here to the monastery. When would they arrive? Where did they come from?

"To whom do you owe allegiance, Lanciar, soldier of SeLenicca, member of the coven?" Jack asked.

Lanciar's attention returned to the little room in the monastery. He had to answer every question correctly and end this interview quickly. He had to make preparations to protect the ones he loved. "I owe allegiance to my son, to myself, and to Maija, daughter of Zolltarn, chieftain of his clan of Rovers." His voice came from a great distance. And then he realized that his body had spoken what was in his heart.

"And what will you do when the coven commands you?"

"I will fight them with every tool at my command. I will fight anyone who seeks to harm Maija and my son," he answered rather fiercely. How long did he have to prepare for the coming attack?

"Why have you turned upon the coven?"

"Because they threaten my son." But the coven did not employ armies. Who commanded the troops coming here?

"Do you still love Rejiia?"

"No." The answer came more readily than he expected. He'd loved Rejiia passionately, devotedly.

He'd schemed with her to cheat Simeon of the son he craved. He'd lied and stolen for the coven. He had betrayed Jack, possibly the only true friend he'd ever had. But no more. His son and Maija claimed him now. And the rest of the Rovers, and the motley band trapped here.

"And if Rejiia kidnaps her son from you?"

"I will follow her to the ends of the Kardia Hodos and do all I can to protect my boy from her manipulations."

"How will you revive Lord Krej?"

"I won't unless asked to by you and Zolltarn, backed by whomever you take orders from."

Suddenly Lanciar was sucked back into his body. Before he could register what was happening, he blinked and the blue haze disappeared. His extremities took longer to warm up, but the burning pain around his wrists and ankles ceased.

Jack looked depleted, almost as badly as he had on that lonely mountain pass where the two of them had traveled the stars and awakened Lanciar's latent talent. Jack ran a shaking hand across his eyes and then dropped onto the stool in the corner of the room.

"There's an army on its way here," Lanciar blurted out.

"How far?"

"I don't know. But I sensed them during the spell. They ride hard, have ridden hard for a time."

"We'd best make plans."

"I'm best qualified to do that."

Jack nodded. "We still have to settle the matter of the gold. We have to have a plan before we go into battle.

Lanciar nodded. His mind quickly reviewed the layout of the monastery and their limited weapons.

"Marcus and Robb found it. They should determine who deserves it, if anyone. But only after they remove the curse. If they are able to do so."

"I'd like it to go to Queen Miranda. SeLenicca does

not deserve what we did to it." And if the approaching army came from SeLenicca the gold might appease their anger. They needed Miranda's cooperation. "The people of SeLenicca are arrogant, determined to remain superior and separate from the rest of the world. But most of them are innocent of the evil the coven brought there. We need to help them rebuild."

"Somehow, I didn't expect that from you, Lanciar," Jack said after a long moment of silence. "I have to admit I half-hoped you'd try to lie and I could watch you die. For both our sakes, I'm glad you told the truth. Now I know why Katrina is so frightened of me. I scare myself sometimes. You can get up whenever you feel strong enough."

Lanciar wiggled his toes and rotated his hands. A bit of chafing remained. "Where'd you get the manacles, Jack?"

"Left over from my days as King Darville's bodyguard."

"We might need them on Rejiia." She could complicate the battle plan taking shape in his head.

"I doubt they'd hold long. She has one formidable talent."

"What are we going to do with her? Now that she knows the transport spell, she can't be kept out of Coronnan."

"I have some ideas. But they are dangerous. Thanks to her, we all have a very big problem."

"On top of many other problems. Perhaps the combined might of the Rovers will hold her until Marcus returns with some answers—if he gets back in time. Your Rover blood will allow you to join with them. Maija assures me that once she and I are married, I will be able to join her clan in their mind-to-mind link."

"I've resisted that link," Jack replied, staring blankly at the floor. "I worked too hard to find out who I was and what was important to me to risk losing myself in the clan. I'll work with Andrall and Laislac as we plan a defense. You can work with Zolltarn."

"I look forward to losing myself in the clan rather than in the bottom of a mug of ale. I'll need a clear head to get through the next battle."

CHAPTER 38

"Where are you going, Lord Andrall?" Ariiell asked in panic.

How could she have been so stupid as to reveal her connections to the coven? Something about the sight of all that gold in the hands of filthy Rovers. Something compelling. The gold was enchanted. That was the answer. She had to possess it, learn its secrets. Then she could use it to buy influence, bribe and coerce the rest of the coven to give her the center position of power.

For now, she sat huddled before a small fire burning in the hearth against the outside wall of the scriptorium of this ancient and chill monastery. She didn't believe for a moment that some enchantment trapped her here. She could overcome any curse laid upon her. Her magic was strong and growing stronger because the baby anchored her more firmly to Kardia.

She shivered despite the heat thrown out by the fire she augmented with magic. These old stone walls held the chill of the ages, a chill that burned all the way to her soul. She had to get out of here, quickly, before the ancient cold hurt the baby.

But everyone—her parents, Mardall, his parents, and all of their retainers—watched her with suspicion and fear.

"I am going to consult with the resident magicians. King Darville must be informed of these latest developments," Andrall stated coldly. "He may have exiled me because of your behavior, Ariiell, but I still support him as my king, my wife's nephew, and . . . and my friend." He rose from his camp stool and walked resolutely to the door.

"You intend to rob me and my child of our rightful place in the succession," she accused bitterly.

"If necessary." He stalked out of the large room without bothering to bow to anyone.

'You owe me respect. I carry the heir to the throne. I carry your grandchild!" Rage propelled her off her own uncomfortable camp stool—all their luggage could provide. She kicked the offensive piece of furniture into the fire. This Simurgh-cursed place did not have so much as a chair to ease the pain in her back.

"My husband owes you nothing, slut," Lady Lynnetta sneered. "You seduced my boy. You brought this exile upon us. And now you profess loyalty to the coven. You will never hold power within Coronnan. I hope the Stargods punish you appropriately."

Lady Lynnetta's reputation for sweetness might have won her the respect of the court, but Ariiell suspected no one had ever heard her speak with so much malice.

The idiot continued to smile and laugh and drool, taking pleasure from helping the servants unpack.

Ariiell marched to the door in Andrall's wake. She refused to remain in this room any longer.

She'd keep Andrall from contacting King Darville. She had the magic at her fingertips. And when all was in place, she would release Rejiia from her prison in the small tower across the compound. Rejiia would be so grateful she'd give up her position in the center of the coven rituals.

"Are you forgetting, Lord Andrall, that magic and magicians are still illegal in Coronnan? If you deliberately use magic to contact our king, you violate numerous laws and put King Darville in jeopardy of losing his crown," she whispered to him in a malicious hiss at the foot of the tower stairs. She knew her words would carry up the stairwell to any of the avid listeners in their party.

"By your own admission of ties to the coven, you make yourself and your child illegal as well." Lord Andrall looked down his long patrician nose at her.

"Have you ever seen me throw a spell, Lord Andrall? Do you have any evidence that I *belong* to the coven? Perhaps I merely used their name to invoke fear and obedience in a woman of an inferior race," Ariiell replied sweetly. She hated following on his heels, pressing her arguments. He should stand respectfully still and hear her out.

"The chaos your accusations cause cannot help anyone but the Gnostic Utilitarian cult. And they will hunt you down and torture you without mercy. You and any other followers of the coven they find." Andrall turned his back on her again and proceeded into the courtyard.

Ariiell refused to admit defeat. She stamped her foot angrily and followed closely.

The magician named Robb and the older woman who seemed to be in charge stood by the wall conversing. Their rapidly waving hands and slightly hunched posture broadcast their anxiety.

A veil of mist made them look like ghosts. Who was alive and who dead in this place? Another reason to leave as soon as possible.

Ariiell studied them closely as she and Andrall came closer to them. She'd be able to think more clearly if this *s'murghin'* mist didn't cover everything.

How could she use their upset to her own advantage? Robb was certainly ripe for loss of concentration if he tried a summons. And just who would receive the summons? Who in the king's court had enough magic to be in constant communication with the Commune of Magicians?

She intended to eavesdrop and find out. The Gnuls would pay handsomely for that information. The coven would also receive the news with delight. She

must escape this horrible place—alone—before Andrall's overblown sense of morality revealed her untimely admission. News of a magician in close contact
with the king would set the Council of Provinces to
depose Darville and put her child on the throne. Possibly before the birth!

Lord Andrall stopped short, staring at the older
woman beside Robb. She was handsome in an aging
sort of way, but not worth this mouth-agape stare.
Ariiell alone in this hodgepodge of captives should
have invited such open admiration.

Ariiell stamped her foot in frustration. Lord Andrall
continued to utter incomprehensible choking sounds
rather than come to the point of his mission. Ariiell
needed Lord Andrall and Robb to discuss a summons
to Darville so she could learn the name of the king's
magical confidant.

"Wh . . . where . . . who . . . that amulet . . ." At
last Andrall pointed to the rather clumsy and ugly
jumble of silver and amethyst hanging around the
woman's neck.

"This is mine." Vareena immediately clasped the
jewelry defensively.

Robb put an arm around her shoulders in a touching display of affection. Disgusting!

"Then . . . then that amulet can only be yours because you stole it," Andrall spluttered. "What have
you done to my brother? He would not have parted
with that symbol of inheritance while he lived!" He
reached to tear the amulet from her neck.

Magical power tingled through Ariiell. *Yes!* This is
what the coven had tried in vain to teach her. She
could feed off strong emotions, drain people of power
by absorbing all of their energy. She longed to let a
spell, any spell, fly from her fingertips before it dissipated. But what? What could she do that would not
get her into more trouble.

She wiggled her fingers and the knot in the leather

thong that held Vareena's amulet loosened. The thing dropped into Andrall's outstretched hand.

"Farrell gave that to me on his deathbed. I nursed him for two years while he resided here in this monastery. With the amulet comes a bequest of acres in the Province of Nunio," Vareena replied proudly. Her spine looked like it was lashed to a broom handle or her magician lover's staff.

"Farrell? So that's the name he gave you," Andrall mused, tracing the silverwork on the amulet lovingly with his fingertip. "Farrell. He always wanted to be a hero. But poor Iiann never had the courage to do anything but run away." The lord closed his eyes and grimaced as if in great pain.

Ariiell had heard that he had suffered from a weak heart recently, that he'd kept to his home more frequently because of it. What would happen to her plans if she encouraged his heart to fail?

Without his accusations, she had a better chance of gaining the crown for her child. Without his testimony, no one else would have the courage to remember her untimely confession to membership in the coven.

"She murdered your brother for the land," Ariiell whispered into his ear. She used the last of the magic from his anger to fuel her words with compulsion. He had to believe her. He had to condemn this spinster on the spot. And then she'd feed off his pain and give him more.

"Your bother died of the effects of age and loneliness and grief that he could not return home one last time." Vareena reached a placating hand toward Andrall and the amulet.

"Where is he buried? I'd like to pay my respects."

"No!" Ariiel bit her tongue to keep from saying more out loud. She raised her hand to push some of her own outrage into Andrall, to keep his anger at a fever pitch.

Red trails of magic compulsion dribbled from her fingers, dissipating uselessly in the dust.

Robb finger-combed his beard. Laughter sparkled in his eyes.

"How dare you laugh at me!" she hissed at him.

He merely raised his eyebrows and pointed to his chest in mock surprise.

Ariiel suppressed a snarl.

"Over there," Vareena pointed to the far corner of the herb garden, ignoring Ariiel. *How dare she!* "He's with the other ghosts who have perished in this cursed place. The foundations of the old temple seemed appropriate for their last resting place."

"Don't believe her!" Ariiell had no more magic to push Andrall into drastic action. If only the coven had taught her to tap a ley line. But her fellows did not believe the ley lines worth bothering with. They relied on rituals filled with music, dance, nudity, and sexual perversion to enhance their powers. Ariiell had no power to tap unless she could push these strangely placid people into violent emotions again.

"My lord," Robb interrupted, "I was with your brother in his last moments. He died peacefully, anxious for his next existence. Will you honor his bequest to Vareena?"

"Of course."

"No, you can't! You have to condemn her for murder right here and now!"

"Oh, shut up, Ariiell. Go back to the room and behave like the lady you want to be." Andrall dismissed her with a bored wave of his hand.

The trio ignored her as they approached the graves in the corner by the wall.

"You can't do this to me," she murmured quietly. "I still have the book of poisons. I can still take control." A nice little demon let loose within these walls ought to liven things up. Rejiia would know how to conjure one.

*   *   *

"Stay with me, Zebbiah," Miranda called anxiously to her friend. His face faded into mist and then re-formed in this reality followed by his body. Twice now, he'd drifted off into the strange haze with the rest of his clan. Both times she'd been able to call him back. But this time he seemed to have difficulty get-ting all of him to step free of the engulfing mist.

Her lace pillow lay forgotten beside her. She dared not lose herself in the lace she loved. The entire pur-pose of their long journey had been for her to sit and make their fortune with her work. Zebbiah's anchor to this reality was still too tenuous for her to concen-trate on anything but him and her daughter.

She rocked Jaranda gently in front of the little fire Zebbiah had built in one of the large second-story rooms. Possibly this had been a smaller scriptorium, possibly a classroom. It covered nearly half of one wing with an identical room adjoining it.

The pack beast brayed obnoxiously and Zebbiah freed himself from the gloaming. He'd had a time coaxing the pack beast up the circular stairs, but he refused to be separated from it or the packs loaded on its back.

"I never thought I wanted to sever my link to my clan before," Zebbiah said, dropping his head into his hands. "Their blood calls to my blood. It is a comfort and an asset most of the time."

"Except when danger to them threatens you as well." Miranda reached out and touched his hand.

His expression brightened and the last little bit of mist around him seemed to evaporate.

"In times of danger, the mind-to-mind link and ac-cess to magic helps the entire clan. Each of us has all the others to draw upon for help, for strength, for courage. This time, they draw upon me as an anchor to life outside this fog. They drain me."

"This . . . this link, does it allow all of you to partici-pate in the . . . the activities of one of your numbers?" Katrina asked. She'd been pacing the room while she examined the lace and the pillows that Miranda had liberated from the palace. Her fingers constantly tangled the lengths of edgings and she nearly shredded one particularly fine cap while moving about the room. Curiously, she kept to the edges, looking out of the row of windows at every pass.

"Sometimes. Why do you ask?" Zebbiah watched her carefully, as if he saw something more than a normal eye could discern. The strange mist started to gather around him again.

Miranda grabbed his hand, and the mist went away. For a time. Fatigue clutched her heart. How long could she keep him here before he fully joined the others? She wished she could see them as easily as the magicians seemed to. If even a dim outline appeared to her, she'd feel more comfortable with their looming presence. As it was, she constantly looked to see if an unseen eavesdropper hovered nearby.

Her back itched as if a thousand eyes watched her every breath, waiting, ready to attack her.

"Was Neeles Brunix, the owner of a lace factory in Queen's City, one your clan?" Katrina ceased her pacing for a moment at the cost of the linen lace doily that unraveled beneath her anxious fingers.

"Brunix, *bah*!" Zebbiah spat the name. "His mother was of our clan. Technically that makes him one of ours. But his father's people raised him to despise us. He took what he wanted of our rituals and customs and perverted them to suit his needs. We never admitted him to our special link."

"Yet you did business with him." Katrina held up the remnants of the doily.

"Rovers trade where the trade is best. Brunix provided us with the best lace. Brunix gave us many unique designs. The palace lacemakers had not enough imagination to try new things." He grinned at Miranda in a sort of apology.

"I designed this piece and several others in your pack. He stole the patterns from me during the three years he owned me. My lace." Katrina nearly shook with the emotions that racked her.

Miranda sympathized with her. Designing and working a pattern required a great deal of diligence, dedication, and devotion to the art. To have it stolen represented almost a sacrilege to a true lacemaker.

Except that the women who designed lace for the palace workers had been locked into specific forms and techniques, never taking a chance on something new and different.

Miranda wanted nothing more than to let the world pass her by while she made lace now. She wouldn't even mind the invisible watching eyes as long as she had the bobbins in her hands and the rhythm of the pattern in her body and mind.

"Whatever happened to you, the clan did not participate in, or sanction the actions of Brunix," Zebbiah comforted Katrina. "Too often have our people been enslaved over the centuries by those who do not understand our ways, who fear anything they do not understand. We deny anyone the right to own another. All should be free to rove as they choose. As we choose."

"But your people steal. You hide behind half truths and you take children from their rightful parents!" Katrina resumed her pacing. Her words sounded more a recitation of oft told tales than an accusation.

"When people refuse to sell us things we need to survive, we often take those things, but we leave something of value behind in payment—just not always what the original owner thinks has value. Half a truth is better than a lie. Parents often give us unwanted children—those who are deformed or simple or sometimes just one too many mouths to feed. The only children we steal are those who are beaten and treated as less than dirt by their parents." Zebbiah answered each of her accusations in turn with resignation.

Katrina nodded. "Jack says much the same thing."

She resumed her pacing. This time she alternately touched the walls and ran her fingers through her already disheveled hair.

"I never thought about slavery before," Miranda mused. She brushed damp hair off Jaranda's brow. She seemed cooler, sleeping easier than before. Perhaps the fever had broken. "I never thought about my people before. All I cared about was my lace. I was happy to allow Simeon to take the burden of rule from my shoulders. I was happy not to have to think about the hardship of others. I can't let that happen again. Slavery in SeLenicca must end."

A hole opened in her heart. If she took over the responsibilities of the crown—responsibilities she had inherited but never been allowed to exercise by her parents or husband—then she'd never have the time to work the lace as she had before. She'd never have the concentration to design new patterns or lovingly recreate old ones.

But then, SeLenicca must never again become dependent upon lace, only one export, to support the entire economy. Her people must be trained to other tasks. The land must be nurtured rather than exploited. Her people must become self-sufficient, as the Rovers were self-sufficient. Only she could change the entire culture of SeLenicca. She had to go back.

Jaranda whimpered in her sleep. She thrashed in her mother's arms. Her movements mimicked the rhythm of Katrina's pacing.

"Katrina, what ails you?" Zebbiah asked before Miranda could.

"This place." Katrina hugged herself. "The cold follows me. My arms are all lumbird bumps. If I were trapped here, as your clan and nobles are, then I do not think I would want to live."

"Come sit by the fire. Let it warm you," Miranda urged, trying to ignore the chill that climbed her spine and set the hairs on her neck standing straight up. " 'Tis your fatigue talking, nothing more."

The invisible eyes seemed to increase and move closer, sensing her unease, ready to pounce at the first sign of weakness.

"No!" Katrina protested too violently for the nature of the suggestion. Then she breathed deeply, forcing calm. "Fire. The ghost of Ackerly fears fire." Slowly she walked closer to the cheery blaze, as if she forced one foot in front of the other.

"No, P'pa, no," Jaranda whispered in her sleep. "Don't kill me, P'pa. I'm too little to sacrifice."

"Wake up, Jaranda." Miranda shook her baby. Memories of Simeon and the tortures he delighted in crowded around her vision, forcing out the present. "Wake up, baby. It's only a dream. Wake up."

"M'ma, don't let P'pa take me to the fires."

"We must leave this place, *cherbein* Miranda." Zebbiah stood up, grabbing the packs in one graceful movement. "The ghost will poison all of us if we do not leave. Now."

Jaranda's eyes opened and she stared over her mother's shoulders. "Go away, P'pa. Go away. You are dead," she sobbed.

"Don't leave me alone here!" Katrina protested. Her eyes darted frantically all around. "Do not leave me with Simeon's ghost. If he haunts this place, then Brunix will, too."

"I would say let us all leave immediately, but we have nowhere else to go," Miranda reminded them.

CHAPTER 39

"Found it!" Marcus whispered excitedly. He looked around the library for someone to share the good news with. The place was deserted. All the apprentices seemed to prefer taking their books outdoors to study. Had Margit started that tradition? He had had more than enough of the out of doors to last a lifetime.

At least now he knew how to lay the ghost to rest. He even had an idea of how to remove the curse from the gold. But he needed help.

This information should go to Jaylor first. Marcus gathered the texts he had studied repeatedly for days. Too many days. How long before the army reached the monastery?

Moments later he knocked upon the door to Jaylor's office. The wooden panels echoed emptily within. He rapped again, a little louder and longer.

Jaylor always spent the midafternoon in his office while the children napped and he could guarantee at least a little time without familial interference. Puzzled, Marcus sent an inquisitive probe into the room. It circled aimlessly, encountering only empty air and dust.

"You won't find our Senior Magician anywhere near the University, Marcus," Slippy said coming toward him from the direction of the courtyard. "One of the twins is dying. He's with his family."

"Where he belongs," Marcus replied. "But I need to talk to him. Now. It's important."

"I doubt he wants anyone near except his wife and his sons." Slippy shook his head. "I sent a message to our representative in the king's court to inform His Grace. Jaylor and Brevelan may want to share their grief with their oldest friends, but no one else."

"I wondered why everyone was so quiet today." Actually he hadn't noticed the lack of activity or the conversations in unusually hushed tones until now. His concentration had all been on his research. He looked at his books, weighing them in his hands. Now what? He had to get back to the monastery soon. He'd wasted too much time already.

"May I be of assistance?" Slippy looked pointedly at the books Marcus carried.

"Do you know anything about time travel?" Marcus asked.

"Never! Impossible." Slippy sniffed with disdain.

"I didn't think I'd be lucky enough to find the help I need right off." Marcus excused himself and went in search of Old Lyman. If anyone had ever traveled through time and lived, Layman was the most likely candidate.

Marcus hadn't seen the ancient librarian in any of his usual haunts about the library. He turned his steps toward the master's quarters on the opposite wing of the sprawling University. But that didn't feel right. Lyman loved his library and his books. Even if he were dying, he'd want to be there, not in some sterile bedroom.

Marcus found him in a deep recess at the back of the second gallery, near an open window that looked at the cliff face, between his books and the dragons. The best place for the old man.

Lyman turned rheumy eyes on Marcus as he tiptoed closer. "Who?" His question came out of tired lungs almost like a whistle, or the call of a baby dragon.

"It's Marcus, sir. I have a question that only you can answer." He knelt beside the old man's pallet.

"Marcus? You can't be here. You are lost between here and there, now and then."

"I found my way back home, sir."

"That is hard to do, boy."

"Easy enough once you have the scent in your mind. In spirit I've never left." In that moment he knew that the one hearth to light his days and cook his meals and the one bed at the end of the day that he craved was here, at the University. But the one smiling face to greet him at the door, cook his meals, warm his bed? He'd loved Margit. He'd loved Vareena. Did either woman belong to his heart and his life forever?

The image of a smiling woman with a cloud of blonde curls and a twinkle of mischief in her eyes while she dealt cartes came to mind.

Expelling a huge, pent-up breath, he shed a lot of the weight of indecision.

Lyman closed his eyes and turned his face toward the window. "My time is nearly come, boy. I must leave this body behind very soon. Ask your question and let me get on with this."

"Master Librarian, I need to lay a ghost to rest and remove the curse he placed upon a hoard of gold."

"Ghosts are easy to get rid of. Curses are not."

"How do I trick Ackerly into telling me how he laid the curse so that I may reverse it?"

"Ackerly, eh? Always knew that man would not give up his gold even in death. He'll not tell you, boy. He invented the tricks you plan to turn on him. The gold must remain cursed even after you lay him to rest."

"Won't the curse dissipate once his presence no longer nourishes it?"

"If the curse has lasted three hundred years beyond his death then it will not fade in time to save those now cursed by the cursed gold."

"Then how do I . . . ?"

"You must go back in time and watch him throw

the spell. Ackerly was tricky. He probably used a mixture of solitary, blood, and dragon magic. You'll have to use an exact reversal of his ritual. One slip and you fail. One slip and you and the gold become one."

"Trapped in the gloaming forever," Marcus finished for him. "How do I travel back in time?"

"Jack will have to guide you. He's done it before. I'm too tired." Yet he heaved himself to his knees.

Marcus offered him an arm for support. Surprisingly the old man leaned heavily upon him. Lyman had always asserted his ability to get around in fierce defiance of his age. "Brevelan's child is nearly ready to give up the fight. I must be there when she does. Take me to the clearing, boy."

"Shouldn't you rest, sir? Here, where you are at home, between your books and the dragons?"

"Ah, to be a dragon again," Lyman sighed. For a moment his face took on a vacant expression as he looked far into his past. "I had hoped to tell my story to Jack. He's the one who deserves to know this, but there isn't time. Be sure to repeat this to him word for word."

"Save your words, Master Lyman. You are too weak to walk and talk." Marcus didn't know how to handle the stubborn old man. Surely, if he were indeed dying, he'd want to conserve his strength and remain in this existence as long as possible.

Unless he looked forward to his next existence.

"Let me call for some help. We'll carry you, Master."

"Nonsense. I'll not have my story repeated among the apprentices like some ancient legend that grows with each telling. This is for you and for Jack. Jack earned the right to hear the truth. You, my boy, are merely the messenger." Lyman fixed him with a fierce gaze. For an instant, his watery old eyes blazed forth in silver-and-purple lights, whirling in a hypnotic stare.

The world faded from Marcus' perceptions. All that existed was the elderly librarian's voice.

"Listen and learn, young Marcus. Learn that many aeons ago, before weak and insignificant humans learned to harness the power of dragons, or cared to, when the Stargods were but pups dreaming of their first outrageous adventures, I was born Iianthe, twin purple-tipped dragon to Hanassa."

"But only one purple-tip can live at any one time," Marcus heard himself protest the old man's litany. Somehow, in the process of speaking, they had descended three staircases to the ground level.

" 'Twas the destiny of my twin Hanassa to choose another life-form or to die. In choosing, he must find a new life path that would benefit all of Kardia Hodos. He chose to become human. But he was weak and envied the power of the Stargods. He wanted to control all that he touched. And so he sought to mimic the gods and awakened many dark powers. Plagues followed in his wake and eventually the humans, with the power of the Stargods to back them, exiled my twin to the land we now know as Hanassa. There he ruled for many generations, choosing to inhabit the body of one of his descendants as each body wore out."

"Hanassa, the home of outlaws and rebels and rogue magicians." Marcus nearly whistled on his exhalation. "How did he take new bodies?"

Lyman waved away the question. "Hanassa became the home of the outcasts and misfits of society. That city of outlaws was, and is, a bloodthirsty place and saw many terrible tortures before Hanassa finally died. But seven hundred years passed before he gave up his last body. That is a tale you will find in the journals of a magician named Powwell. It is hidden in my room, beneath a loose board in the flooring. Only Jack should read it, but you will have to take it to him. I know you will read it. You were always a curious one. If you or Jack chooses to share the tale, think long and hard about who can safely carry the knowledge." The old man's voice cracked with dryness and he ceased walking while his knees sagged. "Powwell was Ackerly's son. His journal may help you lay the ghost to rest."

They had made it as far as the path to the clearing.

"Rest, Master. I'll take the journal to Jack."

"No time to rest. Jaylor's daughter is eager for her next existence. She is tired of fighting to retain possession of her body." Lyman took a deep breath and continued his tale and his final journey.

"When Shayla birthed a new pair of purple-tipped dragons, my existence as Iianthe had to come to an end. I should have passed into the void and gone on without memory of my past. But Hanassa had not completed his destiny. I had to live out the life he had forsaken. So I chose the body of an old man and joined Nimbulan in his search for a way to control magic and make it ethical."

"But that was three hundred years ago!"

"Haven't you been listening, boy? I already said I had lived over seven hundred years as the purple-tipped dragon Iianthe. I have worn out dozens of aging bodies in the past three hundred years. Always, there was one more task to complete, one more life to save, one more apprentice to guide forward. Now this body is giving out and I still have work to do."

"Jaylor's daughter! You plan to take the baby's body the moment she gives it up." Inspiration dawned in Marcus at the moment Lyman's knees gave up the fight to walk all the way to the clearing.

"The little girl has not the determination to fight for her life. If she would hang on only a while longer, her body would heal. But she will not. So I must."

"Climb onto my back, Master. I'll carry you the rest of the way."

Marcus draped the old man's arms over his shoulders and hoisted his legs near his hips. Old Lyman weighed next to nothing.

"Be sure to tell the tale to Jack word for word,

except for the last. No one else must know where I send my spirit next."

"I'll tell Jack to look for you in the most unlikely place, right under his nose."

"He'll think I've given Amaranth a little sense and grace." The old man wheezed heavily in something approximating a chuckle.

"Only a little way to go, Master." Marcus could see the eldritch shimmer of the protective barrier that surrounded the clearing. They'd not get through it without Jaylor's or Brevelan's permission. And they were undoubtedly distracted at the moment.

"Close enough. The spirit knows no boundaries imposed upon frail bodies. Remember Powwell's journal." Lyman grew limp, slipped down, and breathed his last in Marcus' arms.

CHAPTER 40

Jack awoke in a cold sweat. His heart beat in his chest. He lay on cold stone, without so much as a few rushes to ease his sleep. He dreamed of the time Rejiia had sent a magical probe through his eye in that noisome dungeon cell. Memory relived the shafts of pain. Only by massive willpower had he kept the probe from stripping his mind and leaving him a brainless hulk. But he had babbled endlessly about the transport spell. Thanks to him, Coronnan's greatest enemy could now travel anywhere she chose without restraint.

The ancient stone walls of his cell too closely resembled the prison beneath King Simeon's palace. Disoriented, he lay on his pallet for many long moments, desperately afraid he had not broken free of that dank and miserable deathtrap.

Then sanity returned. He knew he rested in the old monastery near a small mountain pass between Coronnan and SeLenicca. He knew that Katrina rested just the other side of this wall in her own cell. They had survived Rejiia's tortures once. He'd not let the witch capture him again.

He sent out a probe automatically, seeking Rejiia's location. Surprisingly, she remained in the tower prison he and Robb had made for her yesterday. Why hadn't she used the transport spell to free herself from this prison?

Because one of Ackerly's coins remained on her

person and the curse on the gold kept her here. She hadn't been able to remove her magical restraints either.

Why?

Because the gloaming—that frightful place that traversed two realities while retaining part of the void that lay between them—limited the amount of magic that could leave a magician. Jack, Robb, and Marcus had not fully entered the haze at the time of the spell since they had none of the cursed gold on them, so their magic might be stronger than Rejiia's. She was still in her ghostly form.

He hoped. He feared she might use hidden talents to overcome any of the obstacles in her way. She'd done it before, popping up in odd places without warning at moments when she could inflict the most damage.

Resolutely, Jack threw off the bedroll and placed his feet on the stone floor. The midnight chill banished the last fog of his nightmare.

While he slept, the approaching army had days to travel closer. If he hadn't sent Amaranth back to Shayla, he could send the flywacket in search of them.

"Best check on Rejiia. Make sure those magical chains still hold her." Though the chains that held Rejiia had been woven by three separate magicians, none of them would be as strong as he liked.

He ran a hand through his sweat-damp hair and heaved himself upright. This old building never seemed to warm up. He threw on his clothes and boots, pulling on extra thick stockings to ward against the chill, and made his way into the colonnade. A faint glow of green firelight flickered beneath the doorways all along the outdoor passageway. The others must feel the chill as badly as he did.

Out in the courtyard he could almost see the stars in their slow dance across the universe. He drank in the crisp night air, grateful that his nightmare had been merely a memory dream and not reality. His planetary awareness centered and he knew precisely where and when he was despite a slight time distortion caused by the gloaming.

He opened his senses, seeking a similar awareness of Rejiia. His magic shied away from contact with her. Ever since her mind probe had debilitated him, he'd fought coming in contact with her again. Surely she must sense his presence and draw power from his discomfort.

His mind touched hers. She dreamed restlessly, thrashing within her bonds and the fears that plagued her. Jack shied away from intruding on her privacy.

But this is Rejiia, he reminded himself. The safety of many people relied on knowing what she planned and what she feared.

From across the courtyard he slid into her thoughts. Seeking. Endless seeking. Her quarry always just beyond her reach. She ran. She stumbled and fell. The gray weasel with gold tipping the ends of its fur slipped easily through her hands. And behind her, danger loomed. Every time she failed to capture the weasel, the unnamed danger came closer. Her life depended upon capturing the weasel.

And then she woke on a cry, sweating as badly a Jack had.

He pulled back from her dreams before her waking thoughts sensed his presence.

And then the dreams of all the others descended upon him with equal clarity. Everyone in this cursed building dreamed their greatest fears. They saw their closest friends as deadly enemies. More than dreamed, relived their most vivid horrors. Almost like a dragon-dream.

Despair haunted them all. Many considered death a relief from their misery.

Anxiously he searched the skies for the presence of a dragon. Who among the nimbus would visit this kind of terror upon innocents?

None. He knew that.

Baamin! he called. *Baamin, what transpires here?*

He knew the answer before the blue-tipped dragon had a chance to reply. The ghost tried to drive them to kill each other or to suicide before Marcus returned with a spell to remove the curse from the gold.

"Jack!" Katrina cried in panic. He dashed the few steps to her doorway. She threw open the door as he skidded to a halt before her.

Clad only in her shift, she trembled with more than cold. He wrapped his arms around her. "Wake up, Katrina. It was only a nightmare."

"Jack, he was here. Brunix was here and he grabbed hold of me. He still owns me. I'm still his slave! I'll kill myself before I live as his slave again."

"Hush, Katrina. Brunix is dead. I watched him die. His last words commanded me to take care of you. He loved you in his own perverted way. He'd never truly hurt you alive or dead. It was only a nightmare, preying on your worst fear."

I'll have my revenge on you, Ackerly, he swore silently. *I'll make sure you rest silently in a deep, deep grave. You will never haunt my Katrina again.*

Others have tried and failed. You will fail as well. You will always fail, the ghost taunted him.

Jack shut out the ghost's voice.

"Just hold me, Jack." Katrina clung to him until her trembling ceased.

"Go back to sleep now, Katrina. 'Twas only a dream and can't truly hurt you." Gently he kissed her brow and eased away from her. He'd gladly go on holding her all night. Now was not the time to discuss her reluctance to marry him.

"Stay with me, Jack. I don't want to be alone." She pulled him close again, burying her face in his shoulder. Her fingers clutched his tunic with fierce strength.

"Katrina, is that a good idea?" He tried to hold her away, allow them both to gain some perspective, and keep his desire under control.

"Yes, Jack, this is a very good idea. Together we

can keep the dreams at bay. Besides, tomorrow may never come and I want to die with you beside me." She kissed him soundly and pulled him down onto her bed.

* * *

Robb approached the baker's hut cautiously. Vareena kept close to his heels. Her hand constantly touched the silver-and-amethyst amulet she wore on a thong around her neck.

"That thing won't protect you from mundane dangers," Robb said testily. He had not slept well, the old nightmare coming time and time again no matter what he did to banish it. Vareena's eyes looked hollow with dark circles beneath them. She had probably spent the night searching for spiders in her bed.

From the wary jumpiness of all of the Rovers and extra guests around campfires in the courtyard before dawn, he presumed they, too, had had nightmares of their greatest fears. Except Jack and Katrina. Those two had emerged from their room holding hands and smiling at each other as if they'd just discovered the greatest secret in the world.

Maybe they had.

"I think the baker and his son are more likely to give us extra bread than his wife." Vareena directed him around to the oven and away from the nearby hut.

"Unusual. In my years on the road, I've always found the women more interested in charity than the men."

"Charity to handsome young men is different from charity to the ghost woman no one fully trusts even when they depend upon her for healing." The stony blankness that came over her face betrayed more of her hurt than any amount of anger or tears.

Robb pulled her close against him. "She's just jealous of how beautiful you are."

"I'm a spinster, available, and therefore I must be a whore as well as a witch."

"No one will say those thing about you once I take you away from here. Besides, you'll be too busy marveling at the wonders of our world. I'll show you bemouths swimming in the great bay. They are as big around as the baker's oven and longer than two of them put together. And their hide is so tough spears bounce off it. But they are the most beautiful iridescent blue. You can see every color of the ocean in their hides. And then there are the dragons flying above. You have to look very close to see them at all. I saw one at King Darville's coronation three years ago. It was a blue-tip. Light slides around them, challenging the eye to look anywhere but at them, but they are so magnificent, elegant, graceful, and perfectly proportioned that you can't look anywhere else. There are gold mines deep in the kardia, black holes where no light shines at all and towers in the capital that look like they are climbing to the sky—or to the dragons. If you want, I'll even take you to the jewel markets in Jihab where you can find the finest loose gems as well as stones set in gold and silver. Or maybe you fancy the spice traders in Varnicia?"

Robb painted the pictures in his mind of all the places he wanted to see for himself and show her. Let Marcus settle in his little cottage with a wife and a dozen children. Robb still needed to see more of the world. He liked the idea of sharing his adventures with someone.

His breath caught for a moment. Vareena would make a comfortable traveling companion. But then, so would Margit, or Jack, or even some of the Rovers. He wondered if his attraction to Vareena was merely part of her talent to soothe and calm those in need.

"Robb." Vareena looked up at him with puzzled eyes. "Robb, I thought you would take me to my land in Lord Andrall's province."

"We'll go there to make your claim. But you've been trapped in this village all your life. Now you have the opportunity to view the world." Why were people so fond of one hearth, one bed, one life mate when the entire world awaited them?

"I want to live on my land, work it, nurture it, know where my place is in this world. Can you understand that?"

"Yeah." But he didn't really. He withdrew his arm from her shoulder. "I think I understand. Marcus has the same dream."

"I'm sorry, Robb, but I think I love the idea of owning something permanent more than I love you."

"And I was just so grateful for all you've done for us, that I mistook it for love." He had to look away from her.

After a moment he had the courage to face her again. "We'd best get the extra bread and head back. We're still needed back at the monastery before we can pursue our dreams." Separately.

Somehow removing Vareena from his view of the future didn't hurt as much as he thought. Jaylor and the Commune still needed him in the field. *He* still needed to be in the field.

"I knew we should have talked last night," he mumbled.

"If we had, we would still have ended up going our separate ways, but I would not have had the hope of you beside me in the morning to get me through that night of terrible dreams. Twice I considered killing myself—or someone else—just to end the dreams." She wrapped her arms around herself and shivered.

"Me, too. Thank you for that little bit of hope." He kissed her temple and stepped up to the baker's oven.

A wiry man turned from the opening where he shifted several loaves around with a wet wooden paddle. A young boy held out his arms, covered with thick padded cloths, to receive any finished loaves the baker retrieved.

"Master Baker, we appeal to your charity and your sense of responsibility to those in need," Robb said quietly by way of introduction.

"Be off with you, filthy Rover!" Baker turned on him, waving the massive paddle at his head.

Robb leaned away from the blow but held his ground. "I am no Rover," he said quietly.

"Thieves all of you!" Baker advanced with the paddle once more. His bellows had attracted the attention of others in the village. Some of them handled shepherd crooks and belt knives as if they intended to use them.

"Stop this all of you! Stop and think what you are doing. We need bread for the monastery. Nobles and warriors have come there as well as Rovers." Vareena tried to step between Robb and the baker.

Robb held her back. He hadn't her confidence that the locals would not attack.

"Mercenaries from SeLenicca," a man with a crook shouted. He swung it like he knew how to use it for defense.

Robb brought his own staff to the ready. He didn't want to blast these people with magic. Magic had a bad enough reputation in Coronnan without him adding more distrust and fear. But he'd bash a few heads if he had to.

"Why should we feed the enemy?" An older man with an air of authority stepped forward. He carried no weapon. He didn't need to.

"Who told you Rovers and mercenaries from SeLenicca came to the monastery yesterday?" Robb asked.

"Didn't need to be told. We saw them all arrive. Thieving Rovers can feed themselves." The village elder stepped forward, fist raised. His people followed.

All of them had red-rimmed eyes and their gazes darted about warily. Some jumped in alarm as they brushed against their neighbors.

Could the ghost have sent his terrible nightmares this far?

If so, there would be no reasoning with these people until they'd had a good night's sleep.

"Get away from here, Vareena," Robb whispered as he pushed her behind him.

"I will not run from my own people. From my own father." She stood her ground.

"Then you die with your Rover lover, for you are no daughter of mine." The village elder advanced. He grabbed a knife and crook from his neighbor.

"You would kill me, P'pa?" Vareena still did not move out of range of the rocks some of the children picked up. Robb knew from experience that children often had the best throwing aim.

Sure enough a rock flew through the air directly at his head. He ducked, but it grazed his temple. Fire followed its path across his skull. Warm moisture oozed down his cheek.

"Robb!" Vareena screamed.

"Run, Vareena." Robb threw up his magical armor around himself. But he couldn't extend it to Vareena and fend off the press of bodies that followed the rocks.

He lashed out with his staff, tripping the closest man. He fell forward into Robb's armor and bounced backward into his comrades. They clutched and scrambled for balance.

Robb used the diversion to put several arm's lengths between himself and the irate villagers.

Stupidly, Vareena stood rooted in place. She held up her hands, begging her people to listen to reason. Her eyes showed her bewilderment at their actions.

"Just because you would never hurt a soul, doesn't mean they won't," Robb muttered. His armor snapped into a wider circle to include her. He grabbed her around the waist and threw her over his shoulder.

He took off running, back to the haunted monastery. Back to all of the problems and anxious demands that had sent him out in search of bread.

"Time for a new plan," he muttered.

CHAPTER 41

Margit sat in the shadowed ell between the lesser tower at the south end of the west wing and the exterior wall. She braced her feet against one of the few remaining foundation stones of the little temple that used to serve the monastic community. She needed the tension in her thighs and calves to maintain control of the emotions roiling in her gut.

Marcus didn't love her.

She pushed harder against the stone before a tear could shatter her control.

One of the shadowy rovers—she could almost see these "ghosts" if she crossed her eyes and drew on every bit of magic she possessed—stood guard at the only ground floor entrance to the round structure at her back. More Rovers guarded the second-story and roof-top entrances. This lesser tower topped the exterior wall by only a few handspans and did not rise above the gloaming—the great towers on the western corners rose a full story above the defensive walls and pierced the constant haze. Inside the circular room at the base of the tower, Rejiia paced around and around her prison. Her footsteps and heavy sighs filtered through the stone to Margit's extended senses. Sometimes she heard Rejiia climb the turret stairs and pound on the doors. Mostly she just paced.

She'd done this all night long after waking screaming from some pain or nightmare. Margit had listened from the observation platform atop the northwest tower where she had attempted to sleep. Never one to remain indoors if the weather were anything but the most hostile, Margit had rejected the tiny cells available. Better to fall asleep under the stars than trapped by four walls.

But sleep had eluded her. When she wasn't crying over the loss of Marcus, a sense of airless dread had pursued her even to the open air. So she had listened with her magic to all of the inhabitants, looking for the source of her unease.

Everyone within the compound seemed to have awakened screaming, in a cold sweat at one time or another. And yet, even with her senses wide open, Margit couldn't isolate the cause.

A loud thud within the lesser tower where Margit sat now sounded as if Rejiia had thrown her entire body as well as her magic at the door of her prison. The woman had a fierce temper if she still beat aimlessly at anything and everything that defied her.

Margit withdrew any lingering magic from her mundane sense to avoid touching the witch or being touched by her.

Yet she sympathized with Rejiia. Many times during her three years as Queen Rossemikka's maid she had railed at the confinement of the palace. The only thing that kept her there for so long was the dream of advancing to journeywoman magician so she could wander the world at Marcus' side.

But Marcus had had his fill of wandering. He also, it seemed, had had his fill of Margit.

She refused to be bound by his dream of hearth and home and dozens of children and apprentices. She had her own dreams.

She'd accept whatever quest Jaylor chose to give her, alone or in the company of another, as long as she did not have walls confining her or cats fouling the scant air within a building.

The ache in her heart spread to her head. Marcus had never considered her wishes in his plans. He'd never even asked what she wanted out of life. That betrayal hurt as much as the idea of spending the rest of her life indoors, cooking and cleaning for him and his brats. And he loved cats, frequently trying to arouse her sympathy for some stray whenever he visited the capital.

Some subtle variation in the light caught her attention. She sensed more than saw the Rover at the doorway shifting restlessly from foot to foot. He'd been there since before dawn. Margit would be restless and tired by now, too. Something about the changes in light around his ghostly outline made her open her magical senses again, straining to see his posture and possibly an aura.

At the same moment, she became aware of a subtle difference in the way Rejiia and her magic moved. The witch focused her beating against the magical and mundane chains that bound her. The wall at Margit's back no longer vibrated from her assault. And yet a great deal of magic beat at her senses.

A subtle voice in the back of her mind suggested that the lock was open. She needed to shift it. She needed . . .

"Compulsions are illegal, Rejiia," Margit chortled as she recognized the nature of the magic drifting around her. "The lock is in place. Shifting it will merely open it for you. Commune magicians are trained to be immune to magical coercion. But that Rover isn't."

She stood up, alert to any other changes in the compound. No more time to feel sorry for herself or worry about sleep loss. The best cure for a broken heart was action. She smiled, anticipating a fight. She twirled her staff, seeking the best defensive grip.

But if Rejiia relied on magic, Margit needed help. Marcus had not returned—probably wouldn't for days. Robb had gone to the village with Vareena. That left Jack and the Rovers. By his own admission, Jack was half Rover, Zolltarn's grandson. Her prejudices told her not to trust either man. But both had sworn oaths of loyalty to the Commune.

The Rover at the doorway drifted closer. His hands reached behind him. Margit couldn't tell more because of the blasted haze that made the man nearly invisible. But she knew that no lock could resist a Rover for long.

She placed two fingers against her teeth and blew. A sharp whistle reverberated through the courtyard. Several shadowy outlines lifted their heads to look in her direction. Jack and Katrina among them.

At least Margit could see those two along with Miranda, her Rover lover, and Lanciar, the soldier from SeLenicca. None of them had passed into the gloaming.

With her magical senses extended, Jack and Katrina's auras became fully visible to her. They complemented each other in shades of purple, silver, and white. Except . . .

Jack's aura had a strange double layer; a reversed reflection of the purple and silver that could also be bronze and black depending upon how the light hit him. Queen Rossemikka's aura also had a bizarre reflection that doubled the layers of energy about her. Jack did indeed have a problem.

He only took about three heartbeats to assess the position of the Rover. He turned his head toward the Rover guard. One of the indistinct outlines raised a hand and pointed at the figure outside Rejiia's prison door.

Instantly the guard jerked as if coming awake from a doze.

Rejiia's magic recoiled, too, as if she'd been stung by a bee.

That strange mind-to-mind link all Rovers seemed to share at work again. So why wasn't Miranda's lover a ghost, too?

And then Margit felt the faintest brush of tingling

air against her arm. Instinctively, she swatted at the butterfly-light touch. Her hand encountered a barrier of energy extremely close. One of the ghosts stood next to her. She peered closer, letting her eyes cross, looking for distortions of light, a remnant of an aura, anything that might tell her who stood so close, so quiet she couldn't even hear him/her breathe.

Jack and the ghost who was probably Zolltarn approached the guard. They stood for several moments talking to him in heated whispers in a language Margit did not understand. The ghost who stood next to her must be someone different. An unwanted eavesdropper.

One of the nobles or their servants? Jack and Lanciar had made certain they had all passed into the gloaming to keep them here until the situation was resolved.

"Why didn't Rejiia try this earlier, while we slept?" Jack's words came to Margit quite clearly.

"Time is distorted here," Zolltarn said. His worried voice sounded as if it traversed a great distance, but was more distinct than his body. "If I have lost my planetary orientation, then so must Rejiia. She might not know what time it is. She might not have been able to control her temper until now."

"I know what it's like when the loss of one's sense of where and when goes askew." Jack shuddered visibly. "But Rejiia has always been able channel her temper into ruthless cunning. Why not now."

"Because Ackerly has invaded all of our dreams and made us react without thinking," Zolltarn replied.

"Who needs to think?" the invisible one next to Margit said on a breath. "Don't think. Just turn your backs for one long moment."

Margit almost didn't hear her, but as soon as the words penetrated her consciousness she recognized the petulant tones of Ariiell, the pregnant one who thought the world owed her adulation.

Ariiell almost floated between the Rover guard and the door. She must have cloaked herself in some kind of invisibility spell for Jack and Zolltarn not to notice her. But the spell probably kept her from noticing anyone not in the gloaming.

Ariiell hunched over the lock and proceeded to fiddle with it.

"Oh, no, you don't, you conniving bitch." Margit launched herself at Ariiell in a full body tackle. She bounced against the barrier to the gloaming. Her entire front burned. But Ariiell stumbled away from the lock. A tiny bit of the mist that surrounded her faded along with her invisibility spell.

"Get away from me, you filthy peasant!" Ariiell screeched. She arched her fingers as if to claw at anyone who stood in her way.

"You won't get that door open, Lady." Zolltarn hauled her to her feet without regard to her delicate condition or sensibilities.

"Do not touch me, Rover." Ariiell spat at Zolltarn's feet. "And I am more than a lady. I carry the heir to the throne of Coronnan. I'll have your head when I am regent."

"You'll have to wait for King Darville to die first. And now that we've been warned, we'll protect him." Margit inserted herself between the door and the guard, making sure Ariiell could get no closer.

"But . . . but you can't. I have the coven backing me," Ariiell spluttered. Her haughty demeanor drained out of her, leaving a greatly diminished and confused young woman.

"Oh, shut up, you ignorant twit!" Rejiia's harsh voice came from behind the sealed door.

Just then Robb pushed his way through the crowd. "If you want your child to inherit the crown, then you have to stop using magic now, Ariiell." He leaned close to her, speaking each word distinctly. "Do you know what happens when a child's magic is awakened prematurely because the mother thoughtlessly throws spells—if the child survives the ordeal of birth? Usually a premature birth." Anger suffused his face with bright color.

Margit had never seen him display such passion. Usually he fell into a long pedantic lecture. Interest pricked, she noted that Vareena hung back from the confrontation. The air of possessiveness she'd displayed when they left this morning seemed to have blown away.

"Well, I'll tell you what happens—what happened to Brevelan's first child," Robb continued with barely a pause for breath. "The child never speaks. He doesn't need to because he has direct mind-to-mind communication with anyone who has a bit of magical talent. But he is totally incapable of communicating with mundanes. How can a king rule if he can't communicate with his Council or the vast majority of his subjects. Those of us with magical talent grow up surrounded by other magicians, we seek out others of our kind when we are away from our comrades. So we expect everyone to be able to do what we do. But only one in one thousand is born with any magical talent at all. Only one in one thousand of those have enough talent to qualify for admission into the University. Only one in one hundred of those will ever reach master status."

"Mundanes mean nothing." Ariiell dismissed his tirade with a disdainful wave of her delicate hand.

"You've been working magic your entire pregnancy. I can smell it on you." Rob did not let up. His eyes almost glowed with intensity.

Margit gritted her teeth. She knew there was a reason she shouldn't settle down with Marcus to produce baby after baby—as Brevelan had. She wasn't ready to give up her magic yet. She had too much more to learn. Too many more places to go and sights to see.

"Any one of the Rover midwives will be able to tell you the child's awareness is awakened very early in the womb. It grows eager to be out in the world, to see what all of the magic is about." Robb finally breathed. He stood straight again and relaxed his shoulders. But Margit suspected his words were intended to reach more ears than just Ariiell's. "The child will come early, before you are ready. He'll tear up your insides in his eagerness to be out in the world before he is ready to breathe air and eat food. If you survive, you'll never bear another child."

"Is that the fate of my son? Will he ever learn to speak? Will he be able to lead a normal life?" Lanciar, the soldier from SeLenicca asked. His slender cheeks took on new hollows and shadows. "Stargods, Rejiia ate the Tambootie while pregnant. What did that do to her?"

"Your son is too young to know the extent of Rejiia's folly while carrying him," Zolltarn said. He reached out a hand as if to pat the man's shoulder in reassurance. But of course he couldn't bridge the energy barrier that separated him from the real world where Lanciar remained. "Rejiia has always been indiscriminate with her spells and her concerns for others. That is why her Rover wet nurse spirited him away from the witch. With our special links, we hope to give him a home and family that will protect him from the violent prejudice of the outside world."

"I knew I had decided to join you for a good reason." A half smile lighted the soldier's face.

"King Darville has already been alerted that the child you carry is no longer qualified to succeed him," Marcus said, strolling into the group.

Margit's heart skipped a beat in joy at sight of him, but then slowed to its normal dull thud. She would always love this man, but her destiny lay elsewhere. A deep sigh heaved its way up through her chest. When it was gone, she felt lighter, more confident. She was in charge of her destiny for the first time in a very long time.

"When did you get back?" she asked, keeping her tone neutral and polite.

"Just now. I heard most of what Robb said so eloquently." He looked at her longingly, then shook himself free of any lingering ties.

"No! You can't do this to me." Ariiell's eyes went wide. Her pupils contracted to mere dots. Her mouth pinched. White showed around her nostrils. "I am to be queen. The coven promised. I will have all of your heads."

No one answered her.

"You will obey me this instant. I am to be queen. My son will be king. Darville will be put to death. The coven promised." Her voice grew louder, more shrill.

The crowd drifted away, tired of her tantrum.

"Come back here," she screeched, tearing at her red-blonde hair. Crimson splotches showed on her neck and cheeks. The whites of her eyes dominated her face. "I am queen!" She lifted her hands in a classic gesture to throw a spell. Blue-and-yellow witchfire streamed from her fingertips toward Zolltarn's retreating back. The flames fizzled and lost energy a mere arm's length from her hands. Dull sparks flowed to the ground and winked out. "Where is my magic?" Ariiell fell to her knees moaning. "I have to have my magic. Oh, baby, lend me some magic." She clutched her belly and rocked back and forth continuing her self-absorbed litany.

"Come, Ariiell. I'll take care of you." Lord Laislac knelt beside her, lifting her gently to her feet. "I feared this might come to pass." He looked around at the others in apology, especially Lord Andrall and Lady Lynnetta. "Her mother succumbed to insanity. She threw herself from the top of the tower of Castle Laislac, convinced she could fly. My daughter seems to have inherited the same weakness in her mind. Her use of the Tambootie in coven ritual may have hastened her infirmity."

Sadly, he led Ariiell back toward their second-story room in the opposite wing.

"She is welcome to shelter in our home until the child comes. We will raise it, love it, as our only grandchild." Lady Lynnetta reached an imploring hand toward them.

"We are used to caring for . . . well, for our son." Lord Andrall gestured toward Mardall who led the Rover children in a quiet game that involved drawing complex patterns in the dirt.

"I have an idea that might help you with that, Lord Andrall." Jack grinned from ear to ear. "I have a rather pesky, but intelligent cat who needs a good home."

"Before we do anything, I have to let you know that some very angry villagers are on their way here. They plan to dismantle this place stone by stone to end the tyranny of the ghost once and for all," Robb said.

"They will be aided by a troop of soldiers with a commission from the priests in the capital," Marcus added. "They are led by Gnuls and employ three witch-sniffers. With or without permission, they intend to capture and burn any magicians they find here."

Jack and Lanciar nodded to each other in confirmation of that statement.

Why hadn't they told her? Margit fumed for a bit, wishing these men had more confidence in her. She could help. She knew she could, if they'd just let her.

"We have work to do, folks," Marcus continued. "That ghost has to be laid to rest and the curse removed from the gold before the others arrive."

"What can I do to help?" Margit leaped at the chance to finally *do* something. They wouldn't think to ask her unless she volunteered.

"That depends upon how friendly you are with dragons." Marcus cocked his head and raised his eyebrows in an endearing gesture.

Margit needed to run to him, hold him tight, kiss him one more time. Maybe they could work things out.

But he turned his gaze elsewhere. No longer interested in her love.

The joy at her sense of freedom battled with the heavy ache in her gut. "I'll just have to improvise to get through this."

CHAPTER 42

"The good news is that Jaylor's daughter is gaining strength and vitality by the hour," Marcus told his companions from the Commune as they closeted themselves in the large suite Zolltarn had appropriated for himself. "The bad news is that Master Lyman has gone to his next existence."

That statement felt quite strange. Marcus knew where Lyman had gone. He'd chosen a new existence but not necessarily in the way one expected.

Jack sank down on the floor in the corner. "I wanted to be there with him. He . . . he and I had a kind of kinship."

The blank mask that descended over Jack's features told Marcus how close the young master magician and the elder Librarian had become.

"He wanted you there, Jack," Marcus consoled. "He said to look for him where you least expect."

'Probably right under my nose." Jack's laugh became choked. He swallowed deeply and then remained silent.

There is more to his story. I'll tell all, later, in private. Marcus sent his telepathic message on a tight line. With all of these other magicians in the room anything more might be intercepted. Lyman had been most emphatic that his story was for Jack alone.

"This feels almost as bad as when Old Baamin died." Robb sank to the floor beside Jack as if his legs would no longer support his weight.

"About time the old coot gave up and let someone

younger and more vital govern his beloved collection
of books." Zolltarn stretched within his comfortably
padded chair—the only piece of furniture in the room
besides the built-in bed platform and slanted writing
desk that was either too heavy to move or anchored
to the floor. The chair and the bedding had come with
the Rover.

"I really liked Old Lyman," Margit said. "He understood why I preferred to study outdoors rather
than in his stuffy library. He even showed me a little
spell that would keep the rain off the books so I
wouldn't have to come inside."

Marcus touched the book tucked into his tunic that
Lyman had directed him to in his last moments. One
of these days, when life had settled into a pattern
again, he'd have to ask Jaylor if any of his ancestors
had been named Bessell. That young companion of
Powwell—the author of the book—had developed an
attitude of benign defiance very similar to Jaylor's before he'd become Senior Magician. He also had an
almost identical magical signature to Jaylor.

Old Lyman had known every word in every book,
the name of the author, and where he'd shelved it. He
probably suspected the family connection. He would
indeed be missed.

'Speaking of Old Baamin." Marcus jumped back to
the subject he needed to follow. He took a moment
to survey all of their faces and to make sure he had
all of their attention. "The old blue-tipped dragon who
brought me here is named Baamin." He closed his
eyes a moment as he relived the exhilarating, stomach-
dropping moments of flight. The sight of the thick gray
fog that surrounded the monastery had troubled him
at first. But the view from above had also given him
a bit of understanding. The building existed halfway
into a different dimension from the rest of the planet.
That explained the time distortion and the weakening
of magic within its walls.

He waited a moment for the others to absorb the

hint he'd given them about Baamin's new existence. Robb looked up from his fascinated gaze at his hands in his lap. He cocked his head and winked one eye. Margit didn't seem interested at all—but then she had never known the rotund little magician who had governed the Commune and the University for decades.

Zolltarn chortled aloud. "I knew the bas . . . the master would find a way to come back to haunt me!"

Jack merely looked blank again. He was very good at that. He'd learned early and well to hide his true emotions in silence.

"You knew that one of the dragons is named Baamin, Jack," Marcus said, almost accusingly.

"He rescued me from SeLenicca," Jack said quietly. "He was also my father in his previous existence." His last words sounded so softly Marcus wasn't quite sure he'd heard him correctly.

"Your father?" Robb asked. He rolled to his knees and peered at their comrade. He used his standard pin-you-in-place-with-my-eyes look. A lecture usually followed that ploy. But this time Robb waited for an answer.

"A long story of a Rover girl seducing a very powerful magician the night before his installation as Senior Magician of the Commune. Her clan wanted a child who could break down the magical border that kept them out of Coronnan." Jack recited the tale as if it had happened to someone else. "The woman died protecting her baby as she escaped from Hanassa. The baby disappeared. It took the dragons to find him again."

Marcus wondered briefly if Master Baamin had known of his son. He was the only one who believed Jack as a child had any intelligence at all when the rest of the world considered him too stupid to even have a name.

"Kestra," Margit supplied. "I've heard legends for years about the missing Kestra and her miracle child.

We all believed them to be Rover myths with no basis in reality."

"Kestra was my oldest daughter," Zolltarn admitted proudly. "Jack is my grandson. And a mighty magician he is. Who else but my grandson could have brought SeLenicca to its knees, killed The Simeon, defeated Rejiia in open battle, and returned the dragons to Coronnan!" More a statement than a question.

"I had a lot of help from the Commune and from the dragons. Katrina's love saw me through the worst of it. Simeon's and Rejiia's arrogance didn't help them any either," Jack retorted. "Don't forget we still have to battle Rejiia and do something about her father in the tin statue."

"With a heritage like that, no wonder you made master magician before you turned twenty." Marcus slapped his forehead with his hand. No one knew for sure exactly how old Jack was. Well, maybe Zolltarn knew.

Robb shook his head and ran his hands across his eyes. "What does a dragon named Baamin have to do with laying the ghost to rest before the villagers and soldiers arrive to tear this place—and us—apart, stone by stone?"

"Old Lyman told me just before he died that in order to remove the curse from the gold we have to travel back in time to watch Ackerly lay the spell upon the gold. He said Jack knew how to do it."

"The only time I did it, I had the help of a dragon." Jack grinned. "We'll have to solicit his help again."

"A blue-tipped dragon named Baamin, by any chance?" Robb asked.

When had Robb become so succinct of speech?

"A dragon named Baamin helped me go back in time to view my beginnings." Jack eased himself up, keeping his back in the corner, using the walls as a brace. "There are dangers. We may not have time to do this."

Marcus touched the book beneath his tunic superstitiously. "It's the only way, Jack. We have to know his ritual down to the last detail in order to reverse it. And we have to reverse it. We can't afford to leave the gold tempting people into the gloaming. I surveyed this place meticulously before Baamin landed. There is a thick fog around it. Even without touching the gold, a person enters the edges of the gloaming whenever they walk through the gatehouse. And it is spreading, reaching down to the village."

He let them think about that for several long moments. "Besides, if Robb and I succeed in this and in laying the ghost to rest, Jaylor will promote us to Master Magicians," he ended on a more optimistic note.

"Going back in time is worse than being trapped in the gloaming, Marcus." Jack looked him directly in the eye.

"Nothing is worse than that half-existence," Robb insisted.

"Nothing is worse than having the rest of the world pass you by, where an entire week of real time feels like only a day in the spell fog. We will end the curse or die trying," Marcus insisted.

"You may very well die. Your time in the past is very limited. The longer you stay, the harder it is to return. You fade and fade into mist until there is nothing left of you to return. You have to pick the exact time on the exact day. Lingering is not an option. Nor is repeating the process."

"And the cost of the spell?" Robb asked.

"You become part dragon in order to go back in time. You are never fully content afterward to remain merely human. The longer you stay in the past, the more the dragon in you takes of your soul."

"Well, then, let's hope that Ackerly's son recorded accurately the time and day Ackerly fought with his superiors and disappeared from the first University." Marcus held up the little book in triumph.

A heavy vibration traveled through the floor slates.

Jack blanched and braced himself as if anticipating a kardiaquake.

"We haven't much time," Zolltarn warned. "Do you hear that banging? That is a very angry mob trying to break down the gates to our refuge."

* * *

"This won't hold them long," Lanciar said as he helped Lord Andrall shove one of the bardos in front of the outer gate. The angry shouts from the villagers on the other side of the meager barrier echoed menacingly around the gatehouse tunnel.

The noise made his head ache worse than the nightmare sounds made by the ghost last night. He'd dreamed repeatedly that Rejiia had stolen his son and was using the baby as a focus for her tortuous rituals to raise power. Rather than have the dream—vision almost—repeat endlessly he had walked the colonnade until the others roused at dawn. They, too, had wandered about heavy-eyed and listless.

"Do you have a better suggestion?" Lord Andrall sat on the sloped edge of the sledge, adding his weight on the barricade. He had discarded his single piece of gold to free himself of the gloaming. But he hadn't told Lord Laislac or any of the others in his party how to emerge from the perpetual mist.

Lanciar found the man much easier to work with when he could see him and a barrier of energy did not separate them.

The sound of men and tools ramming into the gate pounded in his ears. The wooden planks of the outer door buckled under the pressure.

"We don't have much besides these bardos to block the outer gate. This one is all that will fit in the gatehouse. We'll have to close the inner portal—if it will still close—and push the rest of the sledges in front of it." His military training quickly assessed the situation and made his decisions almost before he thought them through.

"Weapons?" Lord Andrall tilted his head.

"A few of your retainers have swords. Most of us have daggers and eating knives. We also have five magicians." He shrugged his shoulders.

"You . . . you will kill my people?" Vareena looked ghostly pale. She swayed slightly as she wrung her hands.

"Please sit somewhere, Vareena, before you fall down," Lord Andrall suggested. "We will do our best to spare these frightened villagers while defending ourselves."

"Let's just hope our magicians find a solution to the problem of the curse before they break through," Lanciar added. Then he began directing the closing of the inner gate.

The assault on the gate came again, stronger this time. More of the wooden planks screeched and buckled. Lanciar dragged Lord Andrall off the sledge and into the courtyard. "Get that inner gate closed now. Use magic if you have to. Two more bardos ready to move in front of it!"

Just then, the flying black cat—had he heard Jack call it a flywacket?—swooped into the courtyard. It landed neatly on the stonework around the well. Before it could begin to preen its wings, it caught Lanciar's gaze.

A blurred and confused image of mounted soldiers racing through the foothills to this lonely spot on nearly blown steeds flashed before his mind's eye. The scene repeated itself twice more, becoming clearer each time.

Just then the four other magicians emerged from Zolltarn's lair.

Jack stretched his arm for the flywacket to perch on. The bird/cat (or was it dragon/cat) pushed down with his wings once and glided over to his companion. They stared deeply into each other's eyes for a moment. "I think I need a drink," Jack said as if cursing.

"Somehow I thought you'd say that," Marcus replied. His eyes had the same half-glaze as Jack's. He'd probably shared the information.

"*S'murghit!* I think we have a problem," Lanciar muttered.

"Watch your language around the children," Vareena hissed at him.

"We haven't time to do all that we need to," Marcus protested.

"Then we'll have to improvise," Robb replied.

"Time to make our own luck, people," Queen Miranda insisted upon hearing the news. "Magicians, get to work on whatever spells you have to cast to lay the ghost to rest and remove the curse of the gloaming. Lanciar, you and Lord Andrall devise and direct a battle plan. I shall keep you informed of the attack from the top of the tower."

Lanciar didn't wait for Andrall to finish bowing to the queen. "Rovers," he shouted, "on the ramparts with any loose rubble you can find. Start tearing the walls down yourselves if you have to. Throw it at the attackers, but watch your aim. We want to scare them off—not kill them. Ladies, boil water to pour down on the villagers. That should hurt and discourage without seriously maiming and killing."

Everyone hopped to obey as if he were truly a general and not just a middle-rank officer.

Lanciar nodded his head to his queen. She didn't know how run a battle, but she knew how to delegate to someone with experience. She might have been a flighty, self-absorbed teenager when she turned over the rule of her country to Simeon, but now she showed the makings of a true leader. He looked forward to negotiating with her for the free passage of Rovers through her country.

The pounding on the gate increased, followed by a shriek of shattering wood.

CHAPTER 43

Marcus pulled the book out of his tunic and stared at the plain leather cover for a moment. He bit his lip while he prayed for the strength to complete the next task.

He called to mind the passages Powwell had written about his father, Ackerly.

A memory of the night he had read Ackerly's emotions in the stone wall of the master's suite flashed through him. Emotions he had dismissed because he did not understand them became clear. Ackerly was proud of his son.

His son, Powwell, had not been proud of the man who sired him but had never acted the father.

"Maybe, if we do this right, we won't have to take a dangerous trip through time," he said. "Maybe . . ."

"Your guess is as good as mine," Jack replied after communing with his flywacket for a moment.

"We can't allow the greed the gold inspires to go beyond these walls. I believe it possible that once the stones are torn down the gloaming, and the spell, will spread as far as the stones are scattered." Robb had returned to his normal lecture mode.

Marcus felt better with this one return to normal. "Then let's do it. All of you, Zolltarn and Lanciar, Margit, Robb, anyone with a bit of magical talent, come with me."

"My Lord Andrall, will you direct the defenses according to our plan?" Lanciar called to the lord.

Andrall saluted him and began tossing orders right and left.

Satisfied, Marcus took two firm steps toward the library.

Vareena blocked his path resolutely.

"Vareena, this could be dangerous. You'd be more help trying to soothe the villagers," Robb said gently.

"All the ghosts within this monastery are my responsibility. All of them," she insisted. "That includes Ackerly. I will be there to guide him into his next existence. I must."

Marcus shrugged his shoulders and smiled. "When this is all over, may I escort you to your lands in Nunio, and perhaps call upon you upon occasion?" Stargods! He loved her strength and determination.

Vareena bit her lip, then jerked her head up and down once in assent.

Marcus suddenly felt much more confident of the outcome of this day's work. "Come along, then, all of you. Just be prepared to duck on command and avoid that ritual knife of his. He may be a ghost, but his weapon isn't."

In single-file, they moved into the shadowed coolness of the library. Diffused sunlight streamed through the high windows around the gallery, highlighting the centuries of accumulated dust. Instantly, the dust motes beneath the gallery began to swirl and concentrate. Ackerly formed more quickly than usual. Marcus saw the knife first, just before the ghost sped toward him, aiming the blade for his eyes.

"Scatter," Marcus called as he dived beneath Ackerly. A preternatural chill ran down his spine. Childhood fears of monsters beneath the bed made his teeth chatter.

He clamped his jaw shut as he read one of the final passages in the journal he carried. Still lying prone, he turned the book so that it caught some of the light from the gallery windows.

"Listen to what happened to your son, Ackerly,"

he said with what little control he had left. "Listen to how you tainted everything you touched, especially the lives of your only two children—bastard children at that. 'I shall not accept a new existence when this one passes. Life hurts too much. Love hurts more. When my sister Kalen died in the pit beneath Hanassa, a large hole ripped open in my gut and it has never healed. Her death was as filled with torment as her life. Her ghost has haunted me since. When I die, her spirit will be free, not before. I have never wanted to inflict that kind of curse upon anyone. My years of seeking the best forms of healing—even though they dipped into rogue magic—have not been enough to remove the curse laid upon us by our father. I have not truly loved anyone since Kalen died. I have not fathered any children. Ackerly's line and his curses die with me. There will be no reincarnation for any of us.' "

Marcus sensed stillness throughout the library.

"By the Fire of my body, the Water of my blood, the Air that I breathe, and the Kardia of my bones, I call forth the restless one who dwells only in sadness and refuses to live!" Zolltarn shouted to each of the four corners of the room, the four cardinal directions.

Vareena repeated his chant four times facing each of the four walls.

Margit followed suit. As did Jack.

"That sounds like a coven ritual," Robb whispered.

"Who cares, as long as it accomplishes something positive," Marcus replied.

LIES! Ackerly's voice boomed through Marcus' mind.

He clamped his hands over his ears in a futile effort to block out the reverberations and the need to crawl out of the monastery in abject defeat.

"It's just the ghost. There is nothing to fear. We can handle him," Marcus muttered to himself over and over.

"Lies! You wish to steal my gold. All lies. Everything is lies." Ackerly flew around the room so rapidly Marcus couldn't separate the trail of dust from his ethereal robes from the cloud of dust around his hair. His voice had become audible to mundane senses. His emotions must be roiling and totally beyond control.

Lanciar kept the ghost from fleeing to the courtyard with wild slashes of his iron sword at the doorway.

"Your life and your death have all been lies," Marcus announced. He noted that Ackerly stayed away from Zolltarn, Lanciar, Margit, and Vareena. The haze seemed to thicken around them, a misty veil deeper than the half existence Ackerly had created for himself and his gold.

"What good is the gold, Ackerly? What good did you accomplish by hoarding it all these centuries?" Marcus had to keep the ghost occupied until Zolltarn finished his conjure.

Gold is power. I have power as long as I have the gold.

"You have nothing. Power exists only when it involves other people. Hidden away here you have power over nothing. Not even yourself."

I have the gold.

"Hoarding the gold makes you a failure. You won't use it to buy land or trade with foreign countries. You can't buy influence in politics. You can't help the poor. You are a failure, Ackerly. A failure in your life and in your death. You can't even get to your next existence properly. And your greed kept your son and daughter from seeking their next existence. You denied them their due. You FAILED!" Marcus taunted the ghost.

You know nothing. Without the gold I am nothing. Ackerly's wails became shriller, more desperate.

"With the gold, you are less than nothing," a new voice said softly.

Everyone in the room turned to look at the figure that stood at the top of the spiral iron stair. More fully formed than Ackerly, the light still shone through the man. His curly dark hair stood out around his head in a kind of halo. Old-fashioned blue robes, similar to what master magicians still wore for formal occasions, fluttered as if in a breeze. He anchored his staff against the first stair.

Vareena took a step closer, staring at the man's tired gray eyes. Compassion, as well as inner pain, radiated from those eyes. Those eyes had seen more pain and destruction than a man three times his age. Marcus doubted he'd seen more than thirty summers. And yet he seemed ageless, timeless. He held his twisted staff in his right hand, a miniature hedgehog in his left. A familiar that had followed him into death.

The hedgehog bristled and wiggled in response to Powwell's emotions.

A curious shadow stood behind his left shoulder, a darker, shorter, duplicate of himself.

Not too different from Jack's double aura, or the one that Queen Rossemikka possessed.

What strange entity haunted him?

"We could not have conjured your son if his soul resided anywhere but drifting aimlessly in the void," Marcus said quietly. He knew Ackerly heard him.

"I am Powwell, of the Commune of Magicians. You called me across time for a purpose," the new entity announced.

"We called you to confront your father." Marcus found the courage to speak first.

"My father is not worth the time and trouble. Your true need and purpose must be great indeed to risk calling me forth from the void."

"Your father has also refused his next existence. He and his gold have cursed this place for nigh on three hundred years. We have called you to heal him," Zolltarn answered the man's plea. He had, after all initiated the spell.

"You were the greatest healer of your time," Jack added. "And you could not heal yourself because you never had the opportunity to confront your father. I thank the Stargods that the dragons gave my father the opportunity to continue his destiny as a dragon so that I could confront him and find myself in my heritage. We give you the same chance."

"For all of our sakes, acknowledge Ackerly and guide him to his next existence," Vareena concluded.

"I hate to interrupt this sentimental reunion, folks, but the door around Rejiia's tower is smoking," Lanciar hissed from the doorway. "She'll be drawn to the magic swirling around us all like iron to lodestone."

"I repeat, the man who sired me is not worth the trouble and danger you face when drawing me across time and distance." Powwell turned away.

I refute your accusation! Ackerly screamed. The cloud of dust approached the iron stairway. *I dedicated my life to making Nimbulan's life easier, more organized. I fed him when he was too exhausted to think. I made sure all of his equipment was at hand while he waged battle on the enemies of Coronnan. I supported him all our lives and he betrayed me. As you, Powwell, and your sister Kalen betrayed me.* He stopped short at the bottom step.

Once before the iron in the stairway had repulsed him. He could approach no closer to his son.

Could Powwell cross the barrier iron placed between them? There were higher and thicker barriers to contend with first.

"You betrayed Nimbulan, the greatest magician of his age, perhaps of any age. You tried to kill him with an overdose of Tambootie, and then you usurped his position in the University. You sold the services of half-trained apprentices for gold. You manipulated and coerced the lords of the land for gold. You did nothing for others, only for your own selfish greed," Powwell accused. He kept his back to his father.

The gold was to be your inheritance. I did not want either you or Kalen to be left destitute and dependent because of the wars. Ackerly held out a hand to his son in entreaty.

"Then why did you secrete the gold here where no one could find it? Why didn't you acknowledge your two bastards and at least give them names? You did nothing for us. Kalen died barely two years after you did. She was still a *child*. The victim of yet another who sought to use her talent for their own gain and without regard for her soul."

I left clues. If only you had sought them. You were both children when I departed Coronnan. If I had left the gold in an obvious place, it would have been stolen from you. You might have been murdered for it.

Powwell turned back to face his father. He took two steps forward only to stop, or be stopped by the iron stairs.

Marcus sensed something important was going on. He needed to listen and learn, perhaps heal his own hurts by their example.

The scent of woodsmoke drew his attention to the doorway. Flames shot upward across the courtyard. The door to the lesser tower exploded outward.

Rejiia stalked through the fire, free of her bonds.

CHAPTER 44

Jack watched as Rejiia, with a deceptively subtle gesture, knocked flat three determined Rover women armed with rolling pins. Black-and-red spikes of magic radiated from her aura. Everything that came in contact with those layers of energy was in danger.

How had she overcome the magical dissipation of the gloaming? Then he realized he could see her quite clearly. She had discarded the coin that trapped her between dimensions as soon as she broke the bonds he, Marcus, and Robb had wrapped around her.

And she reeked of Tambootie. The leaves of the tree of magic, which she probably kept about her person at all times, could temporarily enhance her powers. But once the effects of the drug wore off . . .

Three more women, Zolltarn's head wife in the lead, jumped to attack the renegade witch with pots full of boiling water. Everything they threw at the determined woman bounced off her armor and back in the faces of her attackers.

The women cowered away from her, covering their eyes.

Around them, Rovers, nobles, and the others confronted the villagers with whatever weapons came to hand. Miranda stood on the observation platform of the northwest tower calling to Lord Andrall the activities of each attacker still outside the walls. The noise of that battle distracted Jack from the impending magical duel with his old enemy.

Rejiia's eyes burned with her need for revenge.

Flames nearly shot from her gaze. But her hands shook. With pent-up emotion or a side effect of the Tambootie?

Jack wanted to cower away from Rejiia and the memory of what she had done to him in the prison cell in Queen's City. The last time he'd battled her, she'd been calm and controlled, almost mocking in her superiority.

But she'd fled in defeat when confronted by a united Commune.

The weasel statue of her father, Lord Krej, rocked on top of the bardo as she passed. The muzzle and ears had joined both front legs and the tail in becoming realistically furry. His mouth opened, and he drooled. More of the tin casing dropped away from his head. Not a trace of humanity touched his features.

Before Jack could think of a ploy to stop or delay Rejiia, the inner gate split and tumbled forward on top of the jumble of bardos. Hopefully, the maze of sledges and cabins, of milling steeds, squawking flusterhens, and bawling children would slow them down until Ackerly's angry influence had been negated.

Where were the soldiers and Gnuls from the capital? How much time did they have? Amaranth didn't know and didn't care. He only wanted to hide his head under a wing and pretend all this chaos and noise would go away.

Jack sent him safely into the air to search.

He had no idea how the breach in the defenses of the monastery would affect the curse on the gold. Would it spread or dissipate? Maybe nothing at all would affect it but a true reversal of the curse. Whatever, they had to finish before the army with the Gnuls and witch-sniffers arrived.

His fellow magicians looked anxiously back and forth between the melee at the gate and Rejiia's advancing menace.

Jack waved them over to the gate. "Take care of

Katrina for me. I'll be with you shortly," he said. "Rejiia is mine."

"And mine," Lanciar added. He took up his position shoulder to shoulder with Jack. "We may have been enemies once, but in this we are allies."

"We forged some interesting bonds on that frigid mountain pass . . . comrade," Jack replied.

"Friend. And kin."

Jack needed more time to forgive Lanciar. He nodded his acceptance that one day they might walk side by side as friends. One day. Not yet.

Together they faced their foe.

"Jack, Rejiia's element seems to be fire," Margit said, almost breathless.

Jack raised an eyebrow at her.

"I did some research on opposing elements for Jaylor. Air and Fire are linked. Water and Kardia oppose them. Use Water and Kardia. You can negate her magic without harming the others around her. Trust me."

Across the courtyard the other magicians joined the Rovers and nobles in shoving obstacles in front of the invading villagers. Queen Miranda moved atop Zolltarn's large bardo with Lord Andrall for more immediate observation and direction of the defenses.

Amaranth showed Jack images of the soldiers led by Vareena's brother on the far side of the river. They were still almost a league from the ford. Without the professionals backing the locals and urging them to battle, Jack and his companions had a chance to end this without giving or receiving serious injury.

With the transport spell, he could then evacuate all of the magicians from the place and keep them safe from Gnul persecution. Zolltarn could tend to his own people quite nicely.

Rejiia raised her hands, fingers arched, fire at her command, murder in her eyes.

"Let's see if your research works, Margit, because I don't have any other ideas," Jack muttered. He took a deep breath and began his spell. "Gather together, drop by drop, seek your like, find the path," he chanted calling upon the element of Water to oppose Fire. "Gather to a trickle, spread to a stream, climb to a wave."

All the water in the courtyard that had been flung at friend and enemy alike responded to his plea, willingly bonding with its own kind. It gathered in puddles that traveled quickly to join with other rivulets streaming from the well. Then the puddles piled on top of each other, fed by the deep underground spring, forming a wall of water traveling forward toward Jack.

"Air rush to fill the emptiness," Lanciar chanted beside him. "Join with Water, swell the wave. Oppose each other in battle, aid the brave."

The wave grew and spread wide. A strong wind pushed it higher yet. The two elements raged where they met, churning each other, adding pressure to the path they followed.

At the moment the wall of water reached Rejiia's back, Jack and Lanciar both dropped their hands. "Water seek your complement. Ground in the Kardia taking Fire and Air with you," they chanted together.

The wave crested over the witch. For a moment Rejiia was lost within the roaring water, pushed forward, off-balance. She thrashed about, spluttering for air.

Water retreated. Fire sought its opposite, ready to do battle, and fled her fingers to ground itself harmlessly in the Kardia.

"Aid me, Air, reignite my Fire," Rejiia called, still spitting water from her mouth. She emerged sputtering from the rapidly dissipating Water, hair drenched and scraggling in thin and tangled tendrils. Her once elegant black-and-silver gown hung upon her body in ugly, misplaced lumps. Her skin looked pasty. The boost to her magic given by the Tambootie was wearing off.

Air ignored her, rushing onward.

"From North, South, East, and West and the lesser points between, I call upon the coven to come forth. Aide me, brethren. Defeat our enemies now and forever," she called, turning a full but wobbling circle with her arms outstretched.

Again the magic fizzled as soon as it left her body.

"They aren't coming, Rejiia," Lanciar taunted her. "Your summons never left the compound."

She raised a fist and shook it at him in anger. Some of her lumpy padding dislodged and settled near her waist.

Lanciar giggled slightly. "All those tempting curves were nothing more than cotton padding," he said. A touch of magic projected his words to the farthest corners of the embattled courtyard.

More giggles rippled around the crowd, many of them from the throats of villagers. Much of the anger that had propelled them dissipated, much like the water retreating toward the well.

"You can't do this to me!" Rejiia screamed. Frantically she pushed at the lumps in her clothing, only misplacing them more. Her hands trembled. A convulsive shudder vibrated her entire body. She looked as if her knees would no longer support her.

At that moment Jack realized that humiliation was the one weapon Rejiia could not fight—especially not with her magic drained and an exhausted body. She'd not restore herself soon without more Tambootie. He detected no more leaves in her possession.

"She couldn't even bother enhancing her appearance with a magical glamour. She just used the common artifice available to any *mundane* woman," Jack chortled.

"I'll show you magic!" Rejiia raised her hands again. This time she held half a dozen metal stars in each palm. When accurately thrown, the wickedly sharp points could take out an eye, or penetrate to the heart.

Jack sobered immediately. He needed to be in the

courtyard, standing atop one of the ley lines to command enough magic to wrap Rejiia in a bubble of armor strong enough to contain those stars. He edged forward, Lanciar in his wake.

"Merawk!" Amaranth screeched from atop the tallest tower. He spread his wings and swooped down, talons extended. Sunlight hit his feathered wings, making them glisten purple. He seemed to grow, to shed the light his black body absorbed. He skimmed over Rejiia's head, grabbing several tufts of her dripping hair.

"Yieeeeee!" Rejiia's screech echoed and amplified as it bounced off the stone walls that confined them all. She dropped the throwing stars to clutch her scalp.

Amaranth shrank back to normal size as he swooped about, displaying his trophy.

The weasel rose up on its hind legs and nipped at the flywacket's tail feathers.

Amaranth screeched, compounding the noise. He flew higher, scattering tufts of Rejiia's hair.

A bald spot showed clearly just off center of her head.

"Krej is nearly free of the spell," Zolltarn gasped. "We must stop him from running."

"Or transforming back to a man," Jack added.

"I don't want to go back to the days when he was regent," Robb said as he ran up from the gate area. The fray at the entrance had given way to astonished gasps and stares.

"I don't think he can become a man again," Lancier said, pointing to the now animate animal. "His humanity is so deeply buried within the tin, it will take magic to bring it forth again. He's been a weasel for three years. A weasel he will stay."

Jack had the impression of dozens of people frozen in mid-scramble across the barricade of bardos. Their anger dispersed, much as Rejiia's magic had.

Some of the villagers scuttled away, crossing themselves repeatedly, making the flapping wrist ward against Simurgh in between each invocation of the Stargods.

Then he realized that the Rovers were much easier to see. The haze had thinned. Sunlight began to penetrate to the courtyard.

"The gloaming is fading. We have to finish this now, before Rejiia manages to escape again," he said to Lanciar and anyone else who cared to help. He raised his hands once more to find a spell, any spell that would trap the witch.

Just then the weasel broke free of the last of its tin casing and leaped from its perch on the bardo.

Lancier flung his arm forward as if launching a spell or an invisible spear.

"Come back here," Rejiia screamed and dove for the slippery animal. It eluded her grasp. "Don't you dare leave before I'm ready. I am your master as long as you are enthralled. I will be your master when you live." She crawled after the elusive animal into the midst of the sledges.

A pain ripped across Jack's gut, leaving him dizzy and disoriented. What was he about to do? He touched his temples, trying desperately to ground himself. His eyes crossed and lost focus.

Then his vision cleared of the afterimages he'd seen ever since Rosie took up residence in his body. His bottom no longer itched as if to twitch a tail.

"Rejiia and Krej, Krej and Rejiia, father and daughter, daughter and father, bound together by blood and by magic, cling to each other in the chase," Lanciar said quietly as he traced a sigil in the dirt with his toe. He followed with more words, spoken too rapidly in a language similar to Rover, but . . . Jack didn't have the concentration to think through a translation.

More pain attacked every joint in Jack's body. He needed to fall to his knees. He didn't dare.

And then Katrina was there, holding him, giving him the strength he needed to continue, as she had done in that dank and miserable dungeon cell beneath Queen's City.

But this time the weakness that assailed him felt like a kind of freedom.

Rejiia continued to crawl after her father, coaxing now rather than screaming. She stopped to groom her wet and straggling hair. Then she returned to her determined chase.

"Did I see her lick her hand and wash her ears?" Jack asked. Feeling suddenly lighter, he patted his gut, his backside, all of his joints in turn. Rosie did not respond. He risked a minor trance to search his inner being.

"Katrina, I think I've just lost one of our problems." He couldn't help grinning.

Then Rejiia did pause in her mad scramble beneath the sledges to rub dust off her hands and lick them.

"What?" Jack eyed Lanciar carefully.

"I just put a compulsion upon her."

"Compulsions are illegal," Marcus reminded him.

"I'm not a member of the Commune and not bound by their conventions. Yet."

"What did you do to her?" Jack asked again.

"She'll follow the weasel until one or both of them dies. And until she catches it—alive—she can't throw any magic."

"She'll be tracking that thing for years before she realizes she's under a compulsion!" Marcus chortled.

"All Lanciar did was enhance her own inner demons," Jack added. "She's been obsessed with her father since before his spell against Darville backlashed and turned him into a weasel. I think that was why she embraced Simeon as a lover. He looked so much like her father, and Rejiia controlled that relationship from the beginning." He didn't add that with the cat persona embedded with her own, the compulsion would compound. No one could outstubborn a cat.

"Even when Simeon thought he commanded the

world, Rejiia gave him the commands," Lanciar mused. "She controlled him as she never could her father."

"How long does a weasel live?" Marcus asked. "What happens when Krej dies? Are we back to battling Rejiia?"

"I don't think so." Lanciar whistled a jaunty Rover tune. "That compulsion won't go away unless she captures the weasel *alive*! She'll search for him even after he dies."

"I think we need to get back into the library," Robb reminded them. "The gloaming is lifting, but not gone. Vareena needs our help."

CHAPTER 5

Vareena watched and listened as Powwell and Ackerly continued their bitter litanies against each other. Over and over, she tried to project love and peace into their hearts. She'd done this for every ghost who came under her care. She had to show these two lost souls the lighted path through the void to their next existence.

'Twas her destiny, her purpose in staying so long in this cursed and unforgiving place. If she could not help these two, she would never have freedom, even if she left.

Ackerly and Powwell rejected every offer.

"Stop it, both of you!" she finally insisted. "Stop and listen to yourselves. You just repeat the same arguments over and over, phrased a little differently, but accomplishing nothing." She stomped her foot in frustration.

Both ghosts paused and looked at her, acknowledging something outside their own bitterness for the first time.

"You have both been trapped in this half-life, this nothingness, for three hundred years. You've accomplished nothing in that time, a true reflection of the nothing you accomplished in life."

Both opened insubstantial mouths to protest.

"What did you achieve?" she asked Powwell.

"I was the greatest healer of my time. I researched the healing arts and brought new techniques to ease the pain and suffering of many," Powwell intoned.

The little hedgehog perched on his palm bristled as if protesting the statement.

"According to this journal, written in your own hand, Powwell, many of those techniques were borrowed from rogue and blood magic. All of them have been rejected by the Commune since then. Your legacy is forgotten." She held up the little book.

I taught many new magicians in the University while Nimbulan wandered aimlessly in search of something that eluded him all his life, Ackerly returned.

"Our histories tell us that Nimbulan found dragon magic and brought an end to the Great Wars of Disruption. You died opposing him in the final battle of the war." Vareena allowed the silence to stretch for another endless moment. "We remember Nimbulan with love and adulation. No one remembered either of you until Nimbulan's journals were found."

Nimbulan found peace with his wife and family. He died at the age of ninety, content with his life and his death. I was there. I guided him to the void that final time. Powwell almost choked on this thought/words. His words and form faded to a mere echo inside Vareena's mind. If he faded much more, she'd lose contact with him altogether. *He was the greatest man of his time. More a father to me than you, Ackerly. He loved me, nurtured me, wept with me when Kalen died.*

"Then accept him as your father and seek a new existence. Continue his greatness by passing beyond your misery and seeking happiness and good in a new life." Vareena sensed Powwell's hesitation. His form wavered, strengthening and fading in his indecision.

"And you, Ackerly. Give up your gold, give up this illusion of power. True power is in the kind of love Nimbulan gave his family, his apprentices, and his country. You are reviled as a traitor by those who do know of you. You can have the kind of power Nimbulan had in your next life if you only try. You can have a family to nurture and love next time. But you have to give up the gold."

Powwell reached out a hand to Ackerly. *Join me, Father, in this new quest. Begin your healing alongside me.*

Ackerly lifted his hand as well.

The solid iron of the staircase blocked them.

Tears in her eyes, Vareena ran to the first step. She had to brush Ackerly's ghostly robes. Chills racked her body at the unnatural touch. Just a small taste of what was to come, if she succeeded.

She couldn't turn back now. She had to succeed. She had to end this here and now.

One at a time she mounted the steps until she stood halfway between the two ghosts. "Let me guide you both forward." She held out a hand to each. Bare finger-lengths separated her hands from theirs. "You have to try harder. You have to reach beyond your fears, beyond the limitations of this existence."

Both ghosts leaned forward, bending around the iron barrier.

Still they could not reach her.

Then Powwell shifted his staff. He grasped the butt end and pushed the crystal-studded head down. It dropped on the second step.

Ackerly couldn't reach it without touching the deadly iron. Vareena grasped the crystal at the end of the staff. Ackerly held out the hilt of his knife for her questing hands. She clutched them both tightly.

Light, power, love pulsed through the staff and the knife. They washed over Vareena in endless, daunting waves. The onslaught of emotions drained the strength from her knees. The intricate pattern of the iron stair pressed through her gown, bruising her mortal flesh. She fought to remain conscious, to keep the tunnel of light open for the two souls who must take the first steps toward their next existence.

The magical tools burned her palms. The iron stairs seared her knees. Light pierced her eyes, until she knew she must close them or be blinded for life. Her aching need for freedom intensified. How could she leave if she couldn't see? How could she work her meager acres without her sight? Who would love her, a blind spinster with burn scars hampering her grasp and her walk?

Still she clung to the tools, binding father and son together.

"Vareena!" Marcus and Robb cried.

She couldn't see them. The staff and the knife continued to vibrate, continued to bind her to her ghosts. She sensed Ackerly and Powwell lifting free of the confines of their half-existence. Sensed their spirits joining, melding, leaving her behind.

Their joy flooded her. "Take me with you," she whispered. "Take me away from the hurts of this life, from the weight of my duty and responsibility."

"Not yet, Vareena. You have too much life to live and love to give." Marcus eased the staff from her hands. "I'll help you heal. I'll take care of you, if you let me."

She heard the wooden staff land on the stone floor with a clatter. The knife followed, its blade shattering.

Robb lifted her free of the staircase. Both magicians held her close, crooning soothing words. Each loving her in his own way.

"You're safe now. The Rover women are coming to heal you." Marcus kissed her temple, smoothing tangled hair out of her eyes.

"Lord Andrall has pledged his protection of you and your acres."

"You are safe now."

She couldn't tell which man spoke, only that they both took care of her as she had taken care of them and all the ghosts of this place. She leaned into Marcus, cherishing the strength of his arms supporting her.

Thank you, Vareena. Thank you for your gift of love and healing, Powwell and Ackerly both whispered across her mind.

She opened her eyes. Too much light still blazed around the edges of her vision. The gloaming lifted.

She could see only a few dark figures at the center of the brightness. But she could see.

She saw a tiny hedgehog scuttle away from the staff under her skirts, seeking protection and love. She stooped to cradle it in her burned hands.

Thorny, the creature announced his name to her.

"I guess that makes you a magician after all," Marcus said around a huge smile. "Powwell left you his staff and his familiar."

A gift of love and healing for a gift of love and healing." Powwell's voice echoed around the library, spreading to the courtyard.

The mist of Ackerly's spell lifted from all around. The gold lay inert and uncharmed upon its shelves, ready and waiting to be put to use.

IRENE RADFORD

THE DRAGON NIMBUS HISTORY

☐ **THE DRAGON'S TOUCHSTONE (Book One)**
0-88677-744-5—$6.99

☐ **THE LAST BATTLEMAGE (Book Two)** 0-88677-774-7—$6.99

☐ **THE RENEGADE DRAGON (Book Three)** 0-88677-855-7—$6.99
The great magical wars have come to an end. But in bringing peace, Nimbulan, the last Battlemage, has lost his powers. Dragon magic is the only magic legal to practice. And the kingdom's only hope against dangerous technology lies in the one place to which no dragon will fly . . .

THE DRAGON NIMBUS TRILOGY

☐ **THE GLASS DRAGON (Book One)**
0-88677-634-1—$6.99

☐ **THE PERFECT PRINCESS (Book Two)**
0-88677-678-3—$6.99

☐ **THE LONELIEST MAGICIAN (Book Three)**
0-88677-709-7—$6.99

Prices slightly higher in Canada   **DAW: 188**

KATE ELLIOT

CROWN OF STARS

"An entirely captivating affair"—*Publishers Weekly*

☐ **KING'S DRAGON**   UE2771—$6.99
In a world where bloody conflicts rage and sorcery holds sway both human
and other-than-human forces vie for supremacy. In this land, Alain, a
young man seeking the destiny promised him by the Lady of Battles, and
Liath, a young woman gifted with a power that can alter history, are about
to be swept up in a world-shaking conflict for the survival of humanity.

☐ **PRINCE OF DOGS**   UE2816—$6.99
Return to the intertwined destinies of: Alain, raised in humble surroundings
but now a Count's Heir; Liath, who struggles with the secrets of her past
while evading those who seek the treasure she conceals; Sanglant, believed dead, but only held captive in the cathedral of Gent, and Fifth Son,
who now builds an army to do his father's—or his own—bidding in a world
at war!

☐ **THE BURNING STONE**   UE2813—$24.95
Liath and Sanglant, made outcasts by their love, are forced to choose
their own path—lured by the equally strong claims of politics, forbidden
knowledge, and family, even as Alain is torn apart by the demands of
love, honor, and duty.

Tanya Huff

Praise for #1 *New York Times* bestselling author Linda Lael Miller

"Miller delights readers… The coming together of the two families was very well written and the characters are fraught with humor and sexual tension, which leads to a lovely HEA [happily ever after]."
—*RT Book Reviews* on *The Marriage Season*

"*The Marriage Season* is a wonderfully candid example of a contemporary western with the requisite ranch, horses, kids and dogs—wouldn't be a Linda Lael Miller story without pets… The Brides of Bliss County novels do not have to be read in order but it would be a shame to miss some of the most endearing love stories that feature rugged, handsome cowboys."
—*Fresh Fiction*

"Fans of Linda Lael Miller will fall in love with *The Marriage Pact* and without a doubt be waiting for the next installments… Her ranch-based westerns have always entertained and stayed with me long after reading them."
—*Idaho Statesman*

"Miller has found a perfect niche with charming western romances and cowboys who will set readers' hearts aflutter. Funny and heartwarming, *The Marriage Pact* will intrigue readers by the first few pages. Unforgettable characters with endless spunk and desire make this a must-read."
—*RT Book Reviews*

"All three titles should appeal to readers who like their contemporary romances Western, slightly dangerous and graced with enlightened (more or less) bad-boy heroes."
—*Library Journal* on the Montana Creeds series

"An engrossing, contemporary western romance… Miller's masterful ability to create living, breathing characters never flags, even in the case of Echo's dog, Avalon; combined with a taut story line and vivid prose, Miller's romance won't disappoint."
—*Publishers Weekly* on *McKettrick's Pride* (starred review)

LINDA LAEL
MILLER

Always a Cowboy

HQN™

ISBN-13: 978-0-373-78969-6

Recycling programs
for this product may
not exist in your area.

Always a Cowboy

This edition published by arrangement with Harlequin Books S.A.

For questions and comments about the quality of this book,
please contact us at CustomerService@Harlequin.com.

® and TM are trademarks of Harlequin Enterprises Limited or its
corporate affiliates. Trademarks indicated with ® are registered in the
United States Patent and Trademark Office, the Canadian Intellectual
Property Office and in other countries.

www.HQNBooks.com

Printed in U.S.A.

Dear Reader,

Welcome back to Mustang Creek, Wyoming, home of hot cowboys and the smart, beautiful women who love them.

Always a Cowboy is the story of Drake Carson, the second of the three Carson brothers, and Lucinda "Luce" Hale. Drake is a true cowboy with a ranch to run, plus stallion trouble and a mountain lion trying to wipe out his whole herd of cattle. He certainly has no time, or so he thinks, for the likes of Luce, a stranger and a trespasser to boot.

Luce is doing a postgraduate study, and her subject is wild mustangs and their interactions with livestock. She is one determined city woman, willing to climb over fences and hike for miles, rain or shine. Luce wants to know all about ranching, and ranchers—one in particular.

If you read the first book in this new trilogy, *Once a Rancher*, you'll recognize a lot of the characters, and I hope you'll feel right at home in their midst.

The third book in the series, *Forever a Hero*, features the youngest Carson brother, Mace, a combination cowboy/winemaker, and the woman whose life he once saved.

Ranch life runs deep with me; I live on my own modest little spread, called the Triple L, and we've got critters aplenty: five horses, two dogs and two cats. And those are just the official ones—we share the land with wild turkeys, deer and the occasional moose, and I wouldn't live any other way.

My love of animals shows in my stories, and I never miss a chance to speak for the silent, furry ones who have no voices and no choices. So please support your local animal shelters, have your pets spayed and neutered and, if you're feeling a mite lonely, why not rescue a four-legged somebody waiting to love you with the purest of devotion.

Thank you for bending an ear my way, and enjoy the story.

With all best,

Linda Lael Miller

For Doug and Teresa, with love

CHAPTER ONE

THE WEATHER JUST plain sucked, but that was okay with Drake Carson. In his opinion, rain was better than snow any day of the week, and as for sleet…well, that was wicked, especially in the wide-open spaces, coming at a person in stinging blasts like a barrage of buckshot. Yep, give him a slow, gentle rainfall every time, the kind that generally meant spring was in the works. Anyhow, he could stand to get a little wet.

Here in Wyoming, this close to the mountains, the month of May might bring sunshine and pastures blanketed with wildflowers—or a freak blizzard, wild enough to bury cattle and people alike.

Raising his coat collar around his ears, he nudged his horse into motion with his heels. Starburst obeyed, although he seemed hesitant about it, unusually jumpy, in fact, and when that happened, Drake paid attention. Horses were prey animals and, as such, their instincts and senses were fine-tuned to their surroundings in ways a human being couldn't equal.

Something was going on, that was for sure.

For nearly a year now, they'd been coming up short, Drake and his crew, when they tallied the livestock. Some losses were inevitable, of course, but too many calves, along with the occasional steer or heifer, had gone missing over the past twelve months.

Sometimes, they found a carcass. Other times, not.

Like all ranchers, Drake took every decrease in the herd seriously, and he wanted reasons.

The Carson spread was big, and while Drake couldn't keep an eye on the whole place at once, he sure as hell tried.

"Stay with me," he told his dogs, Harold and Violet, a pair of German shepherds from the same litter and two of the best friends he'd ever had.

Then, tightening the reins slightly, in case Starburst took a notion to bolt instead of skittering and sidestepping like he was doing now, Drake looked around, squinting against the downpour. Whatever he'd expected to see—a grizzly or a wildcat or even a band of modern-day rustlers—he *hadn't* expected to lay eyes on a lone female. She was just up ahead, crouched behind a small tree and clearly drenched, despite the dark rain slicker covering her slender form.

She was peering through a pair of binoculars, having taken no apparent notice of Drake, his dogs or his horse. Even with the rain pounding down, they should have been hard to miss, being only fifty yards away.

Whoever the lady turned out to be, he wasn't giving her points for alertness.

He studied her as he approached, but there was nothing familiar about her. Drake would have recognized a local woman. Mustang Creek was a small community, and strangers stood out.

Anyway, the whole ranch was posted against trespassers, mainly to keep tourists on the far side of the fences. A lot of visiting sightseers had seen a few too many G-rated animal movies and thought they could cozy up to a bear, a bison or a wolf and snap a selfie to post on social media.

Some greenhorns were simply naive or heedless, but others were entitled know-it-alls, disregarding the warnings of park rangers, professional wilderness guides and concerned locals. It galled Drake, the risks people took, camping and hiking in areas that were off-limits, walking right up to the wildlife, as if the place were a petting zoo. The lucky ones got away alive, but they were often missing the family pet or a few body parts when it was over.

Drake had been on more than one search-and-rescue mission, organized by the Bliss County Sheriff's Department, and he'd seen things that kept him awake nights, if he thought about them too much.

He shook off the gruesome images and concentrated on the problem at hand—the woman in the rain slicker. Wondered which category—naive, thoughtless or arrogant—she fell into.

She didn't appear to be in any danger at the moment but, then again, she seemed oblivious to everything around her, with the exception of whatever it was she was looking at through those binoculars of hers.

Presently, it dawned on Drake that whatever else

she might be, she *wasn't* the reason his big Appa-
loosa gelding was so worked up.

The woman seemed fixated on the wide meadow,
actually a shallow valley, just beyond the copse of
cottonwood. Starburst pranced and tossed his head,
and Drake tightened the reins slightly, gave a gruff
command.

The horse calmed down a little.

Once Drake cleared the stand of cottonwoods,
he stood in the stirrups, adjusted his hat and followed the woman's gaze. Briefly, he couldn't believe
what he was seeing, after days, weeks and months
of searching, with only a rare and always distant
sighting.

But there they were, big as life; the stallion, his
band of wild mustangs—and half a dozen mares
lured from his own pastures.

Forgetting the rain-slicked trespasser for a few
moments, his breath trapped in his throat, Drake
stared, taking a quick count in his head, temporarily immobilized by the sheer grandeur of the sight.

The stallion was magnificence on the hoof, lean
but with every muscle as clearly defined as if he'd
been sculpted by a master. His coat was a ghostly
gray, darkened by the rain, and his mane and tail
were blacker than black.

The animal, well aware that he had an audience
and plainly unconcerned, lifted his head slowly from
the creek where he'd been drinking and made no
move to run. With no more than a hundred yards

between them, he regarded Drake for what seemed like a long while, as though sizing him up.

The rest of the band, mares included, went still, heads high, ears pricked forward, hindquarters tensed as they awaited some signal from the stallion.

Drake couldn't help admiring that four-footed devil, even as he silently cursed the critter, consigning him to seven kinds of hell. The instant he pressed his boot heels to Starburst's quivering sides, a motion so subtle that Drake himself was barely aware of it, the stallion went into action.

Nostrils flared, eyes rolling, the cocky son of a bitch snorted, then threw back his head and whinnied, the sound piercing the moisture-thickened air.

The band whirled toward the hillside and scattered.

The stallion stood watching as Drake, rope in hand and ready to throw, drove Starburst from a dead stop to a full run.

Before Starburst reached the creek, though, the big gray spun on his hind legs and damn near took wing as he raced across the clearing and up the slope.

Drake and his gelding splashed through the narrow stream, and up the opposite bank, the dogs loping alongside.

But hard as he rode, the whole experience felt like a slow-motion sequence from one of his brother Slater's documentaries. He and Starburst might as well have been standing still for all the progress they made closing the gap.

The stallion paused at the top of the ridge, he

and his band sketched against the stormy sky. Time seemed to stop, just for an instant, before the spell was broken and the whole bunch of them vanished as swiftly as if they'd melted into the clouds.

Drake knew he'd lost this round.

He reined Starburst to a halt, grabbed his hat by the brim and slapped it hard against his left thigh before jamming it back on his head. Then, still breathing hard, his jaw clamped down so hard that his ears ached from the strain, he recoiled his rope and fastened it to his saddle.

Harold and Violet were at the foot of the ridge by then, panting visibly and looking back at Drake in confusion.

He summoned them back with a shrill whistle, and they trotted toward him, tongues lolling, sides heaving.

Only when he'd ridden across the creek again did Drake remember the woman. Coupled with the fact that he'd just been outwitted by that damn stallion— again—her presence stuck in his hide like a burr.

She stood watching him as he rode toward her, her face a pale oval within the hood of her slicker.

With bitter amusement, he noticed that her feet were set a little apart, as in a fighter's stance, and her elbows jutted out at her sides. Her hands, no doubt bunched into fists, were pressing hard into her hips.

As he drew nearer, he noted the spark of fury in her eyes and the tight line of her mouth.

Under other circumstances, he might have thrown back his head and laughed out loud at her sheer audacity, but at the moment his pride was giving him too much grief for that.

He hadn't managed to get this close to the stallion—or his prize mares—for longer than he cared to remember. While he hated letting them get away so easily, he knew the dogs would be run ragged if he gave chase, and might even end up getting their heads kicked in. They'd been bred for herding cattle, not wild horses.

They were disappointed just the same and whimpered in baleful protest at being called off, which only made Drake feel like more of a loser than he already did.

Harold and Violet, named for two of his favorite elementary school teachers, ambled over to him, tails wagging. They were drenched to the skin and getting wetter by the minute, but they were quick to forgive, unlike their human counterparts, himself included.

Just then, Drake's chestnut quarter horse, a two-year-old mare with impeccable bloodlines, caught his eye, appearing on the crest of the ridge. Hope stirred briefly, and he drew in his breath to whistle for her, but before he could make a sound, the stallion came back, crowding the mare, nipping at her flanks and butting her with his head.

And then she was gone again.

Damn it all to hell.

"Thanks for nothing, mister!"

It was the intruder, the trespasser. The woman stormed toward Drake through the rain-bent grass, waving the binoculars like a maestro raising a baton at the symphony. He'd forgotten about her until that moment, and the reminder did nothing for his mood.

He was overreacting, he knew that, but he couldn't seem to change course.

She was a sight, he'd say that, plowing through the grass the way she was, all fuss and fury and wet through and through.

Drake waited a few moments before he spoke, just watching her advance on him like a one-woman army.

Miraculously, he felt his equanimity returning. In fact, he was mildly curious about her, now that the rush of adrenaline from his lame-ass confrontation with the stallion was starting to subside.

Drake waited with what was, for him, uncommon patience. He hoped the approaching tornado, pint-size but definitely category five, wouldn't step in a gopher hole and break a leg, or get bitten by a snake before she completed the charge.

Born and raised on this land, where there were perils aplenty, Drake understood the importance of practical caution. Out here, experience wasn't just the best teacher, it was often a harsh one, too.

As the lady got closer, he made out her face, still framed by the hood of her coat, and a pair of amber eyes that flashed as she demanded, "Do you have any idea how long it took me to get that close to those horses? Days!" She paused to suck in a furious breath. "And what happens when I finally catch up to them? *You* come along and scare them off!"

Drake resettled his hat, tugging hard at the brim, and waited.

The woman all but stamped her feet. "Days!" she repeated wildly.

Drake felt his mouth stretch in the direction of a grin, but he suppressed it. "Excuse me, ma'am, but the fact is, I'm a bit confused. You're here because...?"

"Because of the horses!" The tone and pitch of her voice said he was an idiot for even asking such a question. Apparently, she thought he ought to be able to read her mind—ahead of time, and from a convenient distance. Just like a woman.

Silently, he congratulated himself on his restraint—and for managing a reasonable tone. "I see," he said, although of course he didn't see at all. This was his land, and she was on it, and he still didn't have any idea why.

"The least you could do is apologize," she informed him, glaring. Her hands were resting on her slim hips, like before, causing her breasts to rise in a very attractive way.

Still mounted, Drake adjusted his hat again. The dogs sat on either side of him, looking on with calm and bedraggled interest. Starburst, on the other hand, nickered and sidestepped and tossed his head, as startled as if the woman had sprung up from the ground like a magic bean stalk.

When Drake replied, he sounded downright amiable, his tone designed to piss her off even more, if that was possible. If there was one thing an angry

woman hated, he figured, it was exaggerated politeness. "Now, why would I apologize? Given that I *live*
here, I mean. This is private property, Ms.——"

She wasn't at all fazed by this information. Nor
did she offer her name.

"It took me hours to track those horses down," she
ranted on, flinging her arms out wide for emphasis.
"In this weather, no less! I finally get close enough
to observe them in their natural habitat, and you...
you..." She paused, but only to take in a breath so
she could go right on strafing him with words. "*You*
try hiding behind a tree for hours without moving a
muscle, with water dripping down your neck!"

Drake might have pointed out that he was no
stranger to inclement weather, since he rode fence
lines and worked under any and all conditions, white-
hot heat and blinding snowstorms and everything in
between, but he felt no need to explain that to this
woman or anyone else on the planet.

Zeke Carson, his late father, had lived by a creed,
and he'd drilled it into his sons early on: never complain, never explain. Let your actions tell the story.

"What were you doing there, anyhow, lurking behind my tree?" he asked moderately.

She bristled. "*Your* tree? No one owns a tree. And
I wasn't *lurking*!"

"You were," he contradicted cheerfully. "And
maybe you're right about the tree. But people can
sure as hell own the ground it grows out of, and that's
the case here, I'm afraid."

She rolled her eyes.

Great, he thought, half amused and half annoyed, a tree hugger, of the holier-than-thou variety, it seemed.

The woman probably drove one of those little hybrid cars, not that there was anything wrong with them, but he'd bet she was self-righteous about it, cruising along at the speed of a lawn mower in the fast lane.

Impatient with the trail his thoughts were taking, Drake made an effort to draw in his horns a bit. He was assuming a lot here.

Still, he made every effort to protect and honor the environment, trees included, and if she was implying otherwise, he meant to set her straight. Nobody loved the natural world more than he did and, furthermore, he had a right to ask questions. The Carsons had held the deed to this ranch since homestead days, and in case she hadn't noticed, he wasn't running a public campground. Nor was this a state or national park.

He leaned forward in the saddle. "Do the words *no trespassing* mean anything to you?" he asked mildly.

Although he didn't want it to show, he was still enjoying this encounter, and way more than he should have at that.

She merely glowered up at him, arms folded now, chin set at an obstinate angle.

Suddenly, Drake was tired to the bone. "All right. Let's see if we can clarify matters. That tree—" he gestured to the one she'd taken refuge behind earlier and spoke very slowly so she could follow "—is on my ranch." He paused. "I'm Drake Carson. And you are?"

The look of surprise on her face was gratifying. "*You're* Drake Carson?"

"I was when I woke up this morning," he drawled. "I don't imagine that's changed since then." He let a moment pass. "Now, how about answering my original question? What are you doing here?"

She seemed to wilt, and Drake supposed that was a victory, however small, but he wasn't inclined to celebrate. Her attitude got on his last nerve, but there was something delicate about her. A kind of fragility that made him want to protect her. "I'm studying the horses."

The brim of Drake's hat spilled water down his front as he nodded. "Well, yeah, I kind of figured that. It's really not the point, though, is it? Like I said before, and more than once, this is private property. And if you'd asked permission to be here, I'd know it."

She blushed, but no explanation was forthcoming. Her mouth opened, then closed again, and her eyes went wide. "You're *him*."

"And you would be…?"

The next moment, she was blustering again. Ignoring his question, too. "Tall man on a tall horse," she remarked, her tone scathing. "Very intimidating."

A few seconds earlier, he'd been in charge here. Now he felt defensive, which was ridiculous on all counts.

He drew a deep breath, released it slowly and

spoke with quiet authority. He hoped. "Believe me, I'm not trying to intimidate you," he said. "My point—once again—is that you don't have the right to be here, much less yell at me."

"Yes, I do." Her tone was testy. "Well, the being here part, anyway. And I don't think I was yelling."

Of all the freaking gall. Drake glowered at the young woman, who was standing next to his horse by then, unafraid, giving as good as she got.

"Say what?" he asked.

"I *do* have the right to be on this ranch," she insisted. "I asked your mother's permission to come out and study the wild horses, and she said yes, fine, no problem at all. She was very supportive, as it happens."

Well, shit.

Why hadn't she said that in the first place?

Moreover, why hadn't his mother bothered to mention any of this to him?

For some reason, even in light of this development, he couldn't back off, or not completely, anyway. Maybe it was his stubborn pride. "Okay," he said evenly. "*Why* do you want to study wild horses? Considering that they're...*wild* and everything."

She was undaunted. No real surprise there, although it was frustrating as hell. "I'm getting my PhD, and my dissertation is about the way wildlife, particularly horses, co-exist with the animals on working ranches." She added, "And how ranchers deal with them. Ranchers like you."

Ranchers like him. Right.

"Let's get something straight, here and now," he said, feeling cornered for some reason, and wondering why he liked it. "My mother might have given you the go-ahead to bedevil all the horses you can rustle up on this spread, but that's as far as it goes. You aren't going to study *me*."

"Are you saying you don't obey your mother?" she asked sweetly.

"That's it," he answered, without a trace of good-will. By then, Drake's mood was back on a downhill slide. What was he doing out here in the damn rain, bantering with some self-proclaimed intellectual? He wasn't just cold, tired and wet, he was hungry, since all he'd had before leaving the house this morning was a slice of toast and a cup of coffee. He'd been in a hurry to get started, and now his blood sugar had dropped to the soles of his boots, and the effect on his disposition was not pretty.

The saddle leather creaked as he bent toward her. "Listen, Ms. Whoever-you-are, I don't give a rat's ass about your thesis, or your theories about ranchers and wild horses, either. Do whatever it is you do, stay out of my way and try not to get yourself killed while you're at it."

She didn't bat an eye. "Hale," she announced brightly, as though he hadn't spoken. "My name is Lucinda Hale, but everybody calls me Luce."

He inhaled a long, deep breath. If he'd ever had that much trouble learning a woman's name before, he didn't recall the occasion. "Ms. Hale, then," he began, tugging at the brim of his hat in a gesture that was more automatic than cordial. "I'll leave you to it. While I'm sure your work is absolutely fascinating, not to mention vital to the future of the planet, I have plenty of my own to do. In short, while I've enjoyed shadowboxing with you, I'm fresh out of leisure time."

He might've been talking to the barn wall. "Oh, don't worry," she said cheerfully. "I wouldn't *dream* of interfering. I'll be an observer, that's all. Watching, figuring out how things work, making a few notes. You won't even know I'm around."

Drake bit back a terse reply and reined his horse away, although he didn't use his heels. The dogs, still fascinated by the whole scenario, sat tight. "You're right, Ms. Hale. I won't know you're around, because you won't be. Not around *me*, that is."

"You really are a very difficult man," she observed almost sadly. "Surely you can see the value of my project. Interactions between wild animals, domesticated ones and human beings?"

LUCE WAS COLD, wet, a little amused and *very* intrigued.

Drake Carson was gawking at her as though she'd just popped in from a neighboring dimension, wearing a tutu and waving a wand. His two beautiful dogs, waiting obediently for some word or gesture from their master, seemed equally curious.

The consternation on the man's face was absolutely priceless.

And a very handsome face it was, at least what

she could see of it, shadowed by the brim of his hat
the way it was. If he resembled his younger brother,
Mace, whom she'd met earlier that day, he was one
very impressive man.

She decided to push him a bit, just to see what
happened. "You run this ranch, don't you?"

"I do my best."

She liked his voice, which was a deep, slow drawl
now, not mocking like before. "Then you're the one
I want."

Open mouth, she thought, insert foot.

"For my project, I mean," she added hastily.

His strong jawline tightened visibly. "I don't have
time to babysit you," he said. "This is a working
ranch, not a resort."

"As I've said repeatedly, Mr. Carson, you won't
have to do any such thing. I can take care of myself,
and I promise you, I won't be underfoot."

He seemed unconvinced. And still irritated in the
extreme.

But he didn't ride away.

Luce had already been warned that Drake wouldn't
take to her project, but somehow she hadn't expected
this much resistance. She was normally a persuasive
person, and reasonable, too.

Of course, it helped if the other person was somewhat agreeable.

Mentally, she cataloged the things she'd learned
about Drake Carson.

He was in charge of the ranch, which spanned
thousands of acres and was home to lots of cattle

and horses, as well as wildlife. The Carsons had very deep roots in Bliss County, Wyoming, going back several generations. He loved the outdoors, and he was good with animals, particularly horses.

He was, in fact, a true cowboy.

He was also on the quiet side, solitary by nature, slow to anger—but when he did get mad, he could be formidable. At thirty-two, Drake had never been married; he was college-educated, and once he'd gotten his degree—land management and animal husbandry—he'd come straight back to the ranch, having no desire to live anywhere else. He worked from sunrise to sunset and often longer.

Harry, the Carsons' housekeeper, whose real name was Harriet Armstrong, had dished up some sort of heavenly pie when Luce had arrived at the main ranch house fairly early in the day. As soon as Harry understood who Luce was and why she was there, she'd proceeded to spill information about Drake at a steady clip.

Luce had encountered Mace Carson, Drake's younger brother, very briefly, when he'd come in from the family vineyard expressly for a piece of pie. Harry had introduced them and explained Luce's mission— i.e., to gather material for her dissertation and interview Drake in depth, thus getting the rancher's perspective.

Mace had smiled slightly and shaken his head in response to Harry's briefing. "I'm glad you're here, Ms. Hale, but I'm afraid my brother isn't going to be a whole lot of use as a research subject. He's into his work and not much else, and he doesn't like to be distracted from whatever he's got scheduled for the day. Makes him testy."

A quick glance in Harry's direction had confirmed the sinking sensation Mace's words produced. The older woman had given a small, reluctant nod of agreement.

Well, Luce thought now, standing face-to-horse with Drake, they'd certainly known what they were talking about, Mace and Harry both.

Drake was *definitely* testy.

He stared grimly into the rainy distance for a long moment, then muttered, "As if that damn stallion wasn't enough to get under my hide like a nasty itch."

"Cheer up," Luce said. She loved a challenge. "I'm here to help."

Drake gave her a long, level look. "Why didn't you say so in the first place?" he asked very slowly, and without a hint of humor. He flung out his free hand, making his point, the reins resting easily in the other one. "My problems are over."

"Didn't you say you were leaving?" Luce asked.

He opened his mouth, closed it again, evidently reconsidering whatever he'd been about to say. Finally, with a hoarse note in his voice, he went on. "I planned to," he said. "But if I did, you'd be out here alone." He looked around. "Where's your horse? You won't be getting close to those critters again today. The stallion will see to that."

Luce's interest was genuine. "You sound as if you know him pretty well."

"We understand each other, all right," Drake said. "We should. We've been playing this game for a while now."

That was going in her notes.

She shook her head in belated answer to his question about her means of transportation. "I don't have a horse," she explained. "I parked my car at your place and hiked out here."

The day had been breathtakingly beautiful, before the clouds lowered and thickened and began dumping rain. She'd hiked in all the western states and in Europe, and this was some gorgeous country. The Grand Tetons were just that. Grand.

"The house is a long way from here. You came all this way *on foot*?" Drake frowned at her. "Did my mother know you were crazy when she agreed to let you do your study here?"

"I actually enjoy hiking. A little rain doesn't bother me. I'll take a hot shower when I get back to the house, change clothes and—"

"When you get back to the house?" he repeated warily. "You're staying there?"

This was where she could tell him that Blythe Carson was an old friend of her mother's, and she'd already been installed in one of the guest rooms, but she decided not to mention that just yet, in case he thought she was taking advantage. She was determined not to inconvenience the family, and if she felt she was imposing, she would move to a hotel. She'd planned to do just that, actually, but Blythe, hospitable woman that she was, wouldn't hear of it. Lord knew there was plenty of room, she'd said, and it wouldn't make any sense to drive back and forth from town when Luce's work was right here on the ranch.

"You live in a beautiful house, by the way," she said, trying to smooth things over a little. "Not what I expected to find out here in the wide-open spaces. All those chandeliers and oil paintings and gorgeous antiques." Was she jabbering? Yes. She definitely was, and she couldn't seem to stop. "I mean, it's hardly the Ponderosa." She beamed a smile at Drake. "I was planning to check into a hotel, or pitch a tent at one of the campgrounds, but your mother wanted no part of that idea, so...well, here I am." Why couldn't she just shut up? "My room has a fabulous view. It'll be incredible, waking up to those mountains every morning."

Drake, understandably, was still a few beats behind, and little wonder, the way she'd been prattling. "You're *staying* with us?"

Hadn't she just said that?

She smiled her most ingenuous smile. "How else can I observe you in your native habitat?" The truth was, she intended to camp at least part of the time, provided the weather improved, simply because she wanted to enjoy the outdoors.

Drake himself was one of the reasons she'd chosen

the area for her research work, but he didn't know that. He was well respected, a rancher's rancher, with a reputation for hard work, integrity and intelligence.

She'd known, even before Harry filled her in on the more personal aspects of Drake's life, that he was an animal advocate, as well as a prominent rancher, that he'd minored in ecology. She'd first seen his name in print when she was still an undergrad, just a quote in an article, expressing his belief that running a large cattle operation could and should be done without endangering wildlife or the environment. Knowing that her mother and Blythe Carson were close had been a deciding factor, too, of course—a way of gaining access.

She allowed herself a few minutes to study the man. He sat his horse confidently, relaxed and comfortable in the saddle, the reins loosely held. The well-trained animal stood there calmly, clipping grass but not moving otherwise during their discussion.

Drake broke into her reverie by saying, "Guess I'd better take you back before something happens to you." He leaned toward her, reaching down. "Climb on."

She looked at the proffered hand and bit her lip, hesitant to explain that, despite her consuming interest in horses, she wasn't an experienced rider—the last time she'd been in the saddle, at summer camp when she was twelve, something had spooked her mount. She'd been thrown, breaking her collarbone and her right arm, and nearly trampled in the process.

Passion for horses or not, she was anything but confident.

She couldn't tell him that, not after the exchange they'd just had. He would no doubt laugh or make some cutting remark, or both, and her pride smarted at the very idea.

Besides, she wouldn't be holding the reins, handling the huge gelding; Drake would. And there was no denying the difficulties the weather presented, in terms of trailing the stallion and his mares from place to place.

She'd gotten some great footage during the afternoon, though, and made some useful notes, which meant the day wasn't a total loss.

"My backpack's heavy," she pointed out, her drummed-up courage already faltering a little. The top of that horse was pretty far off the ground. She could climb mountains, for Pete's sake, but that was small consolation; she'd been standing on her own two feet the whole time.

At last, Drake smiled, and the impact of that smile was palpable. He was still leaning toward her, still holding out his hand. "Starburst's knees won't buckle under the weight of a backpack," he told her. "Or yours, either."

The logic was sound, if not particularly comforting.

Drake slipped his booted foot out from the stirrup to make room for hers. "Come on. I'll haul you up behind me."

She handed up the backpack, sighed heavily. "Okay," she said. Then, gamely, she took Drake's hand. His grip was strong, and he swung her up behind him with no apparent effort.

It was easy to imagine this man working with horses, delivering breach calves and digging postholes for fences.

Settled on the animal's broad back, Luce had no choice but to put her arms around Drake's cowboy-lean waist and grip him like the jaws of life.

The rain was coming down harder, and conversation was impossible.

Gradually, Luce relaxed enough to loosen her hold on Drake's middle.

A little, anyway.

Now that she was fairly sure she wasn't facing certain death, Luce allowed herself to enjoy the ride. Intrepid hiker though she was, the thought of trudging back in the driving rain made her wince.

She hadn't missed the irony of the situation, either. She wanted to study wild horses, but she was a rank greenhorn with a slew of sweaty-palmed phobias. Drake had surely noticed, skilled as he was, and he would have been well within his rights to comment.

He didn't, though.

When they finally reached the ranch house, he was considerate enough not to grin when she slid clumsily off the horse and almost landed on her rear in a giant puddle. No, he simply tugged at the brim of his hat, suppressing a smile, and rode away without looking back.

CHAPTER TWO

WHEN DRAKE CAME in for supper that night, he was half-starved, chilled to the bone and feeling as though he'd worked like an old cow pony and still achieved next to nothing.

He'd seen the mare he'd bought for a small fortune and personally trained, out there on the range that day, but he sure hadn't won her back. Which only added insult to injury. That whistle had always brought her right to the pasture fence at a full run for an apple or a carrot and a nose rub. It had almost worked today, but not quite, not with that young stallion keeping watch.

Drake hadn't found the latest missing calf, either. He'd repaired one of the gates on the north pasture—and discovered he had exactly the same problem with the one just east of it. Then he had to call the vet to come out because he had a cow dropping a calf and she was in obvious trouble...

Every single minute of the day had brought new problems.

Add to that the young graduate student who, for some reason he couldn't understand, was now living in the same house. *His* house. He'd deposited her near the porch when they got back, and he'd ridden away. Surely that was polite enough. Especially since he wasn't interested in being part of her "study."

He remembered to take off his boots in the nick of time, leaving them on the porch. Harry would lynch him if he mucked up her floors, after delivering a loud lecture of the how-many-times-do-I-have-to-tell-you variety. In his sock feet, he hung up his coat and headed for his room. A long shower and a hot meal would solve *some* of his problems.

But not all of them.

He met Luce Hale as soon as he'd rounded the corner and stepped into the hallway. Actually, he practically body-slammed the woman and would have sent her sprawling if he hadn't been so quick to grab her by the shoulders.

Getting another look at her, he realized she was a hell of a lot prettier than he'd thought at first, now that she'd shed her rain gear. In fact, she was *very* pretty, with her long chestnut hair and incredible tawny eyes, and that tall, toned and athletic body of hers. Seeing her in the formfitting jeans and pink shirt she'd changed into, he could believe she'd done plenty of hiking.

He, on the other hand, probably looked as if he'd been hog-tied and dragged through a mudhole. He might've had to do some hiking himself earlier, come to think of it, when a bolt of lightning spooked his horse while he was checking out a broken gate. On foot, he'd managed to catch hold of the reins just before Starburst lit out for the barn and left him behind—no matter how loudly he whistled.

"S-sorry," she stammered as she hastily stepped back. "This place is the size of a hotel—I keep getting turned around."

This part of the house did involve quite a few hallways and bedrooms. The plantation-style setup was hardly a cozy bungalow. The size of the place meant it was easy for Drake and both his brothers— and now Slater's wife, Grace, plus her stepson—to continue living there without colliding at every turn. Each brother had his separate space.

Slater was out of town half the time, anyway, filming on location. Mace sometimes slept at the winery in his comfortable office, and Drake was out all day. So while they lived in the same house, they often didn't see one another except at dinner. The situation was a little different now, since Slater and Grace had a baby on the way, but Grace and his mother got along well and spent a lot of time together.

"Dining room is that way." He pointed.

Luce, evidently, was in no hurry to get to the table, and her project was very much on her mind. "Do you normally get home this time of day? Will you be going back out?"

Oh, great. So it begins. The "study" of his movements and the inquisition that would undoubtedly follow.

"Yes."

She nodded, obviously making a note of his answer.

Drake had an urge to sigh, but didn't. This was *not* what he needed right now.

Or ever.

He was going to have a word with his mother about this situation and her failure to discuss it with him.

Still, he made an effort to be civil, if not cordial, grumpy mood notwithstanding. "I sometimes eat with the ranch hands—they have their own kitchen, off the bunkhouse—and I have to go out and see to the livestock after supper, close the gate to the main drive, check the stables." That was enough information for one evening, as far as he was concerned. Under normal circumstances, he didn't say that many words in a whole day. "Please excuse me, I really need a shower. Sorry. I didn't do your formerly clean shirt any favors when I, ah, ran into you."

It didn't help when Ms. Hale grinned as she surveyed his disheveled appearance. "Can't disagree with that."

"It's been a long day and it's far from over," he said as he walked away. Drake wasn't usually self-conscious, but he was aware that he wasn't at his charming best, either. If he ever *was* charming.

Slater could be charming. Mace was smooth, when he wanted to be. But Drake was no talker, smooth or otherwise. He tended to be distracted and was always either busy or tired, or both.

Meeting a beautiful woman in the hall while covered in dirt didn't exactly boost his confidence.

And judging by Luce's teasing smile, she thought the situation was funny.

Well, that was just great. On top of everything else, he was stuck with a city girl who planned on following him around day and night, asking dumb questions and making notes.

The uncivilized cowboy in his natural habitat.

He flat out wasn't interested. Not in the role of lab rat. The woman, unfortunately, was another story.

And that just made things worse.

Once he'd reached his room, he shut the door hard, kicked off his boots, peeled off his shirt, which stuck to his skin.

At least he didn't have a farmer's tan going, he observed, after a glance in the mirror; what he had was a *rancher's* tan. He was brown from elbow to wrist, since he had a habit of rolling up his sleeves when the weather was decent, and the brim of his hat saved him from the famous red neck.

Tanned or not, he felt about as sexy as a tractor— and why the hell he was thinking along such lines in the first place was beyond him. Luce made for some mighty fine scenery all on her own, but that wasn't reason enough to put up with her, or have her stuck to his heels 24/7.

Besides, she was a know-it-all.

He moved to a window, looked out, drank in what he saw. Even in the rain, the scenery was beautiful.

Drake's bedroom was on the eastern side of the house, which was convenient for someone who got up at sunrise, his favorite time of day. He never got tired of watching the first dawn light brightening the peaks of the mountains, of anticipating the smell of damp grass and the fresh breeze. He liked to absorb the vast quietness, draw it into his very cells, where it sustained him in ways that were almost spiritual.

He loved the sights and sounds of twilight, too. The lowering indigo of the sky, the stars popping out, clear and bright—unsullied by the false glow of crowded communities—the lonely howl of a wolf, the yipping cries of coyotes.

Drake had little use for cities.

Sure, he traveled now and then, for meetings and a few social functions his mother dragged him to, but Mustang Creek suited him just fine. It was small, an unpretentious place, full of decent, hardworking people who voted and went to church and were always ready with a howdy or a helping hand.

Crowds were rare in those parts, except during tourist seasons—summer, when vacationers came to marvel at Yellowstone or the Grand Tetons, and winter, when the skiers and snowboarders converged. But a person got used to things like that.

Drake left the window, went into his bathroom, finished undressing and took a steaming shower, letting the hard spray pound the soreness out of his muscles and thaw the chill in his bones.

Afterward, he chose a white shirt and a pair of jeans, got dressed, combed his hair. He considered shaving, but he was blond, so his light stubble didn't show too much, and anyway, there was a limit to how much fuss he was willing to undergo. He was starting to feel like a high school kid getting ready for a hot date, not a tired man fixing to have supper in his own house.

Shaking his head at his own musings, he looked at the clock—Harry served supper right on schedule, devil take the hindmost—and then he made for the dining room, which was downstairs and on the other side of the house.

As far as Harry was concerned, showing up late for a meal was the eighth deadly sin. If he was delayed by an unexpected problem, she understood and saved him a plate—as long as he let her know ahead of time.

If he didn't, he was out of luck.

And he was so ravenous, he felt hollow.

He had one minute to spare when he slid into his seat. The dogs, Harold and Violet, immediately headed for the kitchen, since it was suppertime for them, too. They had it cushy for ranch dogs, sleeping in the house and all, but they weren't allowed to beg at the table and they knew it. Plus, they both adored Harry, who probably slipped them a scrap or two, on the sly, just to add a little zip to their kibble.

Tonight, the beef stew smelled better than good. Harry knew how to hit that particular culinary note. Stew was one of her specialties—great on a rainy day—and he was starved, so when she brought in the crockery tureen and set it in the middle of the table, he favored her with a winning smile.

Harry didn't respond, except to wave off his grin with a motion of one hand.

So far, Drake thought, he had the whole table to himself—not a bad thing, when you considered the extent of his brothers' appetites.

Harry left the room, returned momentarily with a platter of fresh-baked biscuits and the familiar butter dish.

Things were looking up, until Mace ambled in and took his place across from Drake. Slater soon appeared, along with Grace, smiling and sitting down in their customary chairs, side by side. Drake and Mace, having risen to their feet when their sister-in-law entered, sat again.

If their mother, Blythe, was around, she was occupied elsewhere.

Once settled, everybody eyed the soup tureen, but nobody reached for the spoon. In the Carson house, you waited until all expected diners were present and accounted for, or you suffered the consequences.

"Where's Ryder?" Mace asked. They all liked Grace's teenage stepson and considered him part of the family.

"Basketball practice," Grace replied, arranging her cloth napkin on her lap. Drake and his brothers would have been all right with the throwaway kind, or even a sheet of paper towel, but Blythe and Harry took a dim view of both, except at barbecues and picnics.

Luce trailed in then, looking a little shy.

Slater, Mace and Drake stood up again, and she blushed slightly and glanced down at her jeans and shirt—blue this time—as though she thought there might be a dress code.

Drake drew back the chair next to his, since there was a place setting there and his mother always sat at the head of the table.

Luce hesitated, then seated herself.

Harry bustled in, carrying a salad bowl brimming with greens.

"Go ahead and eat," she ordered good-naturedly. "Your mother's having supper in her office again. She'll see all of you later, she said."

Having delivered the salad, the housekeeper deftly cleared away the dishes and silverware at Blythe's place and vanished into the kitchen.

For a while, nobody said anything, which was fine with Drake. He was hungry, fresh out of conversation and so aware of the woman sitting beside him that his ears felt hot.

He helped himself to stew and salad and three biscuits when his turn came and hoped Luce wouldn't whip out a notebook and a pen and make a record of what he ate and the way he ate it.

There was some chitchat, Grace and Slater and Mace all trying to put Luce at ease and make her feel welcome.

Relieved, Drake ate his supper and kept his thoughts to himself.

Then, from across the table, his younger brother dragged him into the discussion.

"So," Mace began, "have you warned Luce here that she ought to be careful because you like to swim naked in the creek some mornings?" He paused, ignoring Drake's scowl. "I'm just saying, if she's going to follow you around and all, certain precautions ought to be taken."

Drake narrowed his eyes and glared at his brother, before stealing a sidelong look at Luce to gauge her reaction.

There wasn't one, nothing visible, anyway. Luce seemed intent on enjoying Harry's beef stew, but something in the way she held herself told Drake she was listening, all right. She'd have had to be deaf not to hear, of course.

Drake summoned up a smile, strictly for Luce's benefit, and said, "Don't pay any attention to my brother. He's challenged when it comes to table manners, and he's been known to dip into his own wine vats a little too often. Must have pickled his brain."

"Now, boys," Grace said with a pleasant sigh. "Let's give Luce a little time to get used to your warped senses of humor, shall we?"

Slater met Drake's gaze, saying nothing, but there was a twinkle in his eyes.

Mace pretended to be aggrieved, not by Grace's attempt to change the course of the conversation, but by Drake's earlier remark. "My wine," he said, "is the finest available. It won't pickle anything."

"That so?" Drake asked. In the Carson household, bickering was a tradition, like touch football was with the Kennedys. He was beginning to enjoy himself, and not be so worried about the impression all this might make on Luce. "I seem to remember a science project—the one that almost got Ryder kicked out of school last term? Something about dissolving a tenpenny nail in a jar of your best Cabernet."

"Stop," Grace said, closing her eyes for a moment.

Luce giggled, although the sound was nearly inaudible.

"Why?" Mace asked reasonably. Like Drake, he loved Grace.

"Because it wasn't a tenpenny nail," Grace replied, looking to Slater for help, which wasn't forthcoming. Her husband was buttering his second biscuit and grinning to himself.

"Your problem," Mace told Drake, "is that you are totally unsophisticated. To you, warm generic beer from a can is the height of elegance."

Let the games begin.

"*I'm* unsophisticated?" Drake raised his brows. "This from a man who wore different colored socks just the other day? That was sophisticated, all right."

Mace looked and sounded pained. "Hey, it was dark when I got dressed, and I was in a hurry."

"I bet you were," Drake shot back. "Come to think of it, little brother, those might not have been your socks in the first place. Guess it all depends on whose bedroom floor you found them on."

"Oh, for heaven's sake," Grace said, tossing a sympathetic glance Luce's way.

"Are they always like this?" Luce asked.

"Unfortunately," Grace answered, "yes."

Just then, Blythe Carson breezed in, carrying a place setting and closely followed by Ryder.

"We've decided to join you," Blythe announced cheerfully.

"Thank God," Grace murmured.

Ryder, holding a bowl and silverware of his own, sat down next to his mother. "Basketball practice got out early," he said. He nodded a greeting to Luce and reached for the stew.

Blythe Carson, more commonly known as "Mom," sat down with a flourish and beamed a smile at Luce. "How nice to see you again," she said. "I hope my sons have been behaving themselves."

"Not so much," Grace said.

"Hey," Slater objected, elbowing his wife lightly. "I have been a complete gentleman."

"You've been a spectator," Grace countered, hiding a smile.

"All I did," Mace said, "was warn Luce about Drake's tendency to skinny-dip at every opportunity. Seemed like the least I could do, considering that she's a stranger here, and a guest."

"Hush," said Blythe.

Harry reappeared with a coffeepot in one hand and a freshly baked pie in the other.

Once she'd set them down, she started whisking

stew bowls out from under spoons. When she decided a course was over, and that folks had had enough, she took it away and served the next one.

Blythe sparkled.

The coffee was poured and the pie was served.

Ryder excused himself, saying he had homework to do, and left, taking his slice of apple pie with him.

The others lingered.

Grace, yawning, said she thought she'd make it an early night and promptly left the table, carrying her cup and saucer and her barely touched pie to the kitchen before heading upstairs.

Blythe remained, watching her sons thoughtfully, each in turn, before focusing on Mace. "Seriously?" she said. "You brought up skinny-dipping?"

Luce, who had been soaking up the conversation all evening, and probably taking mental notes, finally spoke up.

She smiled brightly at Slater, then Mace, and then Drake. "I enjoy skinny-dipping myself, once in a while." She paused, obviously for effect. "Who knows, maybe I'll join you sometime."

Blythe laughed, delighted.

Mace and Slater picked up their dishes, murmured politely and fled.

"I'd better help Harry with the dishes," Blythe said, and in another moment, she was gone, too.

LUCE TURNED TO DRAKE, all business. "Now, then," she said, "the wild herd has almost doubled in size since you first reported their presence to the Bureau of Land Management several years ago. What accounts for the increase, in your opinion?"

The change of subject, from skinny-dipping to the BLM, had thrown Drake a little, and Luce took a certain satisfaction in the victory, however small and unimportant.

The room was empty, except for them, and Luce was of two minds about that. On the one hand, she liked having Drake Carson all to herself. On the other, she was nervous to the point of discomfort.

Drake, she noticed, had recovered quickly, and with no discernible brain split. He'd probably never been "of two minds" about anything in his life, Luce thought, with some ruefulness. Unless she missed her guess, he was a one-track kind of guy.

Now he leaned back in his chair, his expression giving nothing away. And, after due deliberation, he finally replied to her question.

"What accounts for the increase? Well, Ms. Hale, that's simple. Good grazing land and plenty of water— the two main reasons my family settled here in the first place, over a hundred years ago."

She wondered if he might be holding back a sarcastic comment, something in the category of any-idiot-ought-to-be-able-to-figure-that-out.

She had, in fact, taken note of the obvious; she'd put in long hours mapping out the details of her dissertation. She wanted his take on the subject, since that was the whole point of this or any other conversational exchange between them.

Okay, so she wasn't an expert, but she was eager to learn. Wasn't that what education was all about, from kindergarten right on up through postgraduate work?

She decided to shut down the little voice in her head, the one that presumed to speak for both her and Drake, before it got her into trouble.

"What makes it so good?" she asked with genuine interest. "The type of grass?"

His gaze was level. "There's a wide variety, actually, but quantity matters almost as much as quality in this case." A pause. "By the way, there are a lot more wild horses in Utah than here in Wyoming."

Zap.

"Yes, I know that," Luce replied coolly, determined to stay the course. She hadn't gotten this far by running for shelter every time she encountered a challenge. "And I realize you would prefer I went there to do my research," she countered, keeping her tone even and, she hoped, professional. "Bottom line, Mr. Carson, I'm not going anywhere."

"Why here? Why me?" For the first time, he sounded plaintive, rather than irritated.

"Fair questions," Luce conceded. "I chose the Carson ranch because it meets all the qualifications and, I admit, because my mother knows your mother. I guess that sort of answers your second inquiry, too—you're here, and you run the place. One thing, as they say, led to another." She let her answer sink in for a moment, before the windup. "And, I will admit, your commitment to animal rights intrigues me."

That was all Drake needed to know, for the time being. If she had a weakness for tall, blond cowboys with world-class bodies and eyes so blue it almost hurt to look into them, well, that was her business.

He surprised her with a slanted grin. "I know when I'm licked," he drawled.

The remark was anything but innocent, Luce knew that, but she also knew that if she called him on it, she'd be the one who looked foolish, not Drake.

Bad enough that she blushed, hot and pink, betrayed by her own biology.

He watched the whole process, clearly pleased by her involuntary reaction.

She had to look away, just briefly, to recover her composure. Such as it was.

"This can be easy," she said when she thought she could trust her voice, "or it can be har—difficult."

Wicked mischief danced in his eyes. "The harder—more difficult—things are," he said, "the better I like it."

Luce wanted to yell at him to stop with the double entendres, just stop, but she wasn't quite that rattled. Yet.

Instead, she breathed a sigh. "Okay," she said. "Fine. We understand each other, it would seem."

"So it would seem," he agreed placidly, and with a smile in his eyes.

Luce would've liked to call it a day and return to her well-appointed guest room, which was really more of a suite, with its spacious private bathroom, sitting area and gorgeous antique furnishings, but she didn't. Not only would Drake have the last word if she bailed now, she'd feel like a coward—and leave herself open to more teasing.

"We have one thing in common," she said.

"And what would that be, Ms. Hale?"

Damn him. Would it kill the man to cut her a break?

"Animals," she answered. Surely he wouldn't—couldn't—disagree with that.

He looked wary, although Luce took no satisfaction in that. "If I didn't like them," he said, his tone guarded now, and a little gruff, "I wouldn't do what I do."

Like all ranchers, he'd probably taken his share of flack over the apparent dichotomy between loving animals and raising them for food, but Luce had no intention of taking that approach. Would have considered it dishonorable.

She enjoyed a good steak now and then herself, after all, and she understood the reality—everything on the planet survives by eating something else.

"I'm sure you wouldn't," she said.

Drake relaxed noticeably, and it seemed to Luce that something had changed between them, something basic and powerful. They weren't going to be BFFs or anything like that—the gibes would surely continue—but they'd set some important boundaries.

They were not enemies.

In time, they might even become friends.

While Luce was still weighing this insight in her

head, Drake stood, rested his strong, rancher's hands on the back of her chair.

"It's been a long day, Ms. Hale," he said. "I reckon you're ready to turn in."

At her nod, Drake waited to draw back her chair. As she rose, she watched his face.

"Thank you," she said. Then she smiled. "And please, call me Luce."

Drake inclined his head. "All right, then," he replied, very quietly. "Shall I walk you to your room, or can you find your way back there on your own?"

Luce laughed. "I memorized the route," she answered. Then, pulling her smartphone from the pocket of her jeans, she held it up. "And if that fails, there's always GPS."

Drake smiled. "You'll get used to the layout," he told her.

"Here's hoping," Luce said, wondering why she was hesitating, making small talk, of all things, when most of her exchanges with this man had felt more like swordplay than conversation.

"Good night—Luce." Drake looked thoughtful now, and his gaze seemed to rest on her mouth.

Was he deciding whether or not to kiss her?

And if he was, how did she feel about it?

She didn't want to know.

"Good night," she said.

She left the dining room, left Drake Carson and was almost at the door of her suite before the realization struck her.

She'd gotten the last word after all.

CHAPTER THREE

DRAKE ROLLED OUT of bed at his usual time, ignored the clock—since his inner one was the real guide—and pulled on his jeans.

Harold and Violet both got up, tails wagging.

Boots next, hat planted on his head and, seconds later, he was out the door. He'd grab coffee at the bunkhouse. Red, the foreman, was always up and ready, and that seasoned old cowboy could herd cattle with the best of them. Drake drove his truck over just as dawn hit the edge of sunrise and, sure enough, he could smell coffee.

Red, who did a mean scrambled egg dish and some terrific hash browns, was already done eating, elbows on the farmhouse-style table, something he never did when he ate up at the house. He nodded good morning and went back to his book, which happened to be *Shogun* by James Clavell. Drake wasn't surprised at his choice. Red looked like a classic, weathered Wyoming ranch hand, which he was, but he also fancied himself a gourmet cook—he could give Harry a run for her money now and then—and he listened more often than not to classical music.

The package wasn't all that sophisticated, but there was a keen intellect inside.

Drake fed the dogs, helped himself to a plate of eggs and potatoes, ate with his usual lightning speed and got up to wash the dishes. That was the arrangement and it was fine with him. He'd had to cook for himself in college and discovered he didn't have the patience for it. He'd survived on hamburgers fried in a pan, sandwiches and spaghetti prepared with jarred sauce. Coming back to Harry's or Red's cooking made all those winter morning rides to feed the stock, with the wind tossing snow in his face and biting through his gloves, worth it. If Red cooked breakfast, he would wash up, no problem.

"How's the horse lady?" Red put a bookmark between the pages and shut the novel, setting it aside.

Drake braced himself for a sip of coffee—Red was a great cook, but his coffee could strip the hide off a steer—before he answered. "Enthusiastic college girl. Bright, but has no idea what she's getting into. I have the impression that she likes to be outdoors, since she hiked all the way to the north ridge, can you believe that? But I don't think she really knows anything about horses, wild *or* domesticated."

"The north ridge?" It wasn't easy to surprise Red, but he just had.

"Yup. I gave her a lift home on Starburst, but she was planning to walk it. Go figure."

"Can't."

"Me, neither." Drake spent nearly all his time

outdoors, and if he had the right weather, he sometimes canoed and did some fishing in the Bliss
River, but he wasn't a hiker.

"The outdoorsy type. That's good. You need a
dainty debutante like you need a big hole in your
John B. Stetson."

Such a Red thing to say. Drake didn't need another female in his life right now, period. He had his
mother, Harry, his niece, Daisy—Slater's daughter
by an earlier relationship—and, now that Slater had
finally settled down, his sister-in-law, Grace. The
men were getting outnumbered even before the arrival of Ms. Hale.

Drake shrugged. "She's pretty, I'll give her that."

"That so?" Red grinned. "Easy on the eyes, huh?
And you've noticed."

"I'm not blind, but that doesn't mean I want her
here." That was the truth. "I just plain don't want
the complication."

"Women complicate just about everything, son."

That he agreed with, at least based on his own
observations—and experience. So he changed the
subject. "Move the bull to the high pasture for a few
days? I think he needs new grazing. After that, we'll
get feed out and tackle the faulty gate."

"You're the boss."

Technically, he thought, but Red was the one who
really ran the show. Drake was born and raised on this
land, but Red had more ranching experience. Drake

always asked for his advice and ended up regretting the few times he hadn't followed it. "He's getting old."

"Sherman? That he is."

"So…what do you suggest?"

"We need a new bull." Red got up and refilled his cup. "Been meaning to say it, but I know you don't want to part with that critter. Don't move him. He's getting touchy in his old age. Just retire him. Sherman has more gray on his snout than I do in my hair. Out to pasture will work fine. We have the land to keep him in comfort."

"My father raised that bull." Drake's throat tightened.

"I know. I was there. I'm hurting, too. Think of it this way—he's done his job. If I thought a recliner and a remote would make him happy, I'd give him both. Sherman is a tired old man."

He'd asked, after all. Drake ran his fingers through his hair. It wasn't as if he hadn't thought about it. He exhaled. "I don't disagree. Not from a practical point of view, anyway. Auctions, then? Or do you have another bull in mind?"

Red scratched his chin. "I might go into town and ask Jim Galloway. Been meaning to stop by and see him and Pauline, anyway. He knows most of the livestock breeders in the state."

Jim was the father of one of Slater's best friends, Tripp Galloway, a pilot who'd returned to his roots and, like Drake, had taken over the family ranch near Mustang Creek after Jim remarried and retired.

"Good call." Drake managed to down the last of his coffee—not easy, since it was particularly make-your-hair-stand-on-end this morning—and set down his cup. "I'm going to help you with the horses and then ride out."

"Sorry I'm late."

The breathless interruption made him swivel toward the plain wooden doorway. He saw with dismay that Luce Hale stood there, hair pulled back in a no-nonsense ponytail, wearing a baggy sweatshirt with well-worn jeans, backpack in hand. She added, "That is one very comfortable bed, so I slept longer than I intended. Your mother should run a hotel. Where are we headed?"

We? First of all, *he* hadn't invited her to the party. Second, the woman couldn't even ride a horse.

And damned if Red wasn't snickering. Not openly, he'd never be that rude, but there was laughter in his eyes and he'd had to clear his throat—several times.

He should be at least as polite. Grudgingly, he said, "Red, meet Ms. Lucinda Hale. Ms. Hale, Red here runs the operation but likes to pretend I do."

Red naturally shuffled over to take her hand, playing it up. "Pleased to meet you, ma'am. So you're here to study that worthless cowpoke?" He leveled a finger in Drake's direction. "Hmm, prepare to be disappointed. Kinda boring would be my take on him. I've tried to take the boy in hand, but it hasn't worked. Nary a shoot-out, no saloons and he has yet to rescue a damsel in distress, unless you count the time Harry had a flat tire and he had to run into town to change it, but I swear that's just 'cause he's more afraid of her than he is of an angry hornet. Would you like a cup of coffee, darlin'?"

Red was ever hopeful that someone might like his coffee—he called it Wyoming coffee, which was quite a stretch, since he seemed to be the only one in the entire state who liked it.

Okay, she was an annoyance in his already busy life, but Drake was about to rescue a damsel who'd be in true distress if she agreed to that coffee.

He said coolly, "I'm off to the glamorous world of feeding the horses and then fixing a gate. I also need to look for a missing calf and am fairly sure it's a goner. Please don't let the excitement of my day overwhelm you, but come along if you want. You'll have to skip the coffee."

She tilted her head to one side, considering him, obviously undeterred. "I need to see if the wild horses affect how you run your business. Therefore, I need to know how you run it in the first place. I want to find what you do day-to-day."

Why hadn't she picked a topic she actually knew something about before deciding on this venture? Like buying shoes, for instance.

Not fair, he corrected himself. She *had* trekked all the way to that ridge—in hiking boots, no less, nothing fashionable about those—and she'd found the horses. Maybe he was underestimating Ms. Hale. She was certainly determined, no doubt about that.

"Follow along. Be my guest. If you enjoy the smell of manure and hay, I'm more than happy to escort you to the stables."

For that condescending statement he received a derisive look. "I can find the stables on my own. I promise I won't get in your way. This project is important to me, and as far as I can tell, it's important to you."

He failed to see the logic there. "How so?"

"What if I can help you figure out what to do?"

Drake was honest, but he was also diplomatic—or so he hoped. He fought back a response that included *How the heck could you help me?* and substituted, "I look forward to your suggestions."

LUCE COULDN'T DECIDE if he was just being sarcastic, but at least he was courteous.

She'd meant it.

"You don't think I can help?"

He walked next to her, toward a weathered structure bordered by a fenced enclosure. Several sleek horses were grazing and lifted their heads to watch as they approached, curious but unafraid. Some of them nickered, wanting his attention. "You don't know horses."

"Wrong."

She was above average height for a woman and still reached only his shoulder. He was one tall man. She'd mostly seen him on horseback or sitting at the dinner table with his brothers, who were also tall, so she hadn't realized.

He looked skeptical. "How am I wrong?"

"I don't know them the same way you do. I've worked on a lot of studies, read the literature, done my homework, so to speak, but that doesn't mean I completely understand their behavior. I do, however, understand the situation."

She'd describe his expression as unconvinced.

"That's fine," he said. "You go about your business and I'll go about mine."

"Suit yourself."

You are *my business.* She didn't say it out loud, but it was true. She found it disconcerting to recognize that he might be more interesting than those beautiful horses. When her thesis topic had first come to her, she'd wondered abstractly how wild horses impacted the environment.

Here she was now, and she had a Zen-like feeling that maybe fate was toying with her. At first he'd caught her attention because, from what she'd read, they shared similar views on ecological issues, but there was more to it.

Drake opened the stable door. "After you."

The place smelled earthy, lined with rows of neat stalls, and Drake was greeted with soft whinnies as the animals poked their heads over the stall doors. He was gently companionable with each one, unhurried in his attentions. Luce was moved by this, but not really surprised; the way the dogs followed him

around, quiet and devoted, had told her a lot about
the man. In her experience animals had more insight
than people normally did, so that said something
very positive about Drake Carson.

"Anything I can do?"

"I doubt it." He carried a bucket of water into a
stall and softened that by adding, "By the time I
told you what to do, I could probably have done it
myself."

"Probably," she conceded, "but keep in mind, I'm
a fast learner."

He turned, empty bucket in hand, and gave her a
measured look. "Good to know."

She caught on quickly that they were no longer
talking about feeding a barn full of horses. Her response was tart. "Isn't it a little early in the morning
for sexual innuendos, Mr. Carson?"

"I figure all twenty-four hours of the day are good
for those." He led out his big horse and she scooted
aside. "I'm going to saddle up and ride out now. You
do whatever you want to, but I have a gate to fix and
that has nothing to do with wild horses and everything to do with keeping the cattle in that pasture."

"I can't ride along?"

He went into a small room and emerged with a
well-worn saddle. "Grace's horse, Molly, is in that
stall." He pointed. "Saddle her and follow me if you
like. For now, I need to move along. Have a nice
morning."

It took him about three minutes to saddle his

horse, slip on the bridle and mount up. Then he was heading out, the beautiful dogs trotting alongside. She'd yet to even hear them bark.

Learn to saddle a horse—that was item number one on her to-do list. But first she hurried to the doorway to see which direction Drake had gone. Maybe she couldn't ride or fling saddles around with any confidence, but she was wearing her hiking boots, had a bottle of water in her pack and a sack lunch Harry had handed her as she'd hurried out the door. If dinner the night before was any indication, there could be something magical in there.

Perfect day for a walk.

That obnoxious cowboy wasn't getting rid of her as easily as he thought.

Besides, she was hoping to take more pictures of the horses. She'd gotten some good shots, but she hoped to do that each and every time she was close enough to manage it. She'd already caught an excellent image of the stallion; she knew more about horses than Drake gave her credit for. It was obvious to her that the magnificent animal was the one in charge of the herd—even before she'd listened to the conversation at dinner. He was beautiful, too, with clean lines and fluid grace.

If she could find Drake, she'd photograph him at work, whether he liked it or not. Better to ask forgiveness, as the saying went, than permission. Besides, it wasn't as if she was going to publish them or anything. They were purely for research purposes.

Having a physical record would help her organize her notes when she began the process of writing the actual paper. As she hefted her pack and left the barn, the sun-gilded Tetons felt like familiar friends, the glory of the setting an undeniable perk. There was still snow on the peaks, and the air was crisp and fresh.

Lovely, lovely day.

CHAPTER FOUR

IT HAD ALREADY been one hell of a day, and there was still a long trail ahead.

Drake tried to concentrate on fixing yet another gate hinge so rusted it was next to impossible to remove the screws without help. Red had sacrificed some of his considerable pride by turning the job over to a younger man. Luckily, the old bull in the pasture beyond hadn't figured out how easy it would've been to bust the thing and make a run for it.

Slater was lending him a hand by holding the gate steady.

As he worked, Drake mulled over a more complex problem.

He felt guilty for ditching Lucinda Hale on a daily basis this past week. It wasn't as if he didn't understand her zeal for the animals. It was just that at the beginning, middle and end of the day, or *any time* he really didn't need a shadow, she seemed to appear. And what made it worse was the fact that he couldn't stop himself from worrying about her.

Drake totally understood her objectives, but this was his land, so every creature on it was his to take care of, with the exception of his brothers, who could handle themselves. He even worried about Red, since he was showing his age but refused to slow down. In his entire life Drake had never known the man to go to a doctor. Once, Red had fractured his arm breaking a colt and the vet had been handy, since he was taking care of one of the horses. So Red had asked him to set it and wrap it in an Ace bandage, then used a makeshift sling made from an old halter and lead. They'd all shaken their heads over that one, especially the vet.

With a motion of his hand, Drake indicated the bull grazing nearby. "Red's going to ask Jim Galloway to recommend the best stock breeder he knows, not just in Bliss County, but in the state. We could use some new blood." He dropped a crowbar into his tool kit and wiped his brow. "Damn hot out here. Shades of summer, I guess."

"Not much of a breeze, either," Slater observed, using a cordless drill to put the first screw into the new hinge. "That sure isn't usual in Wyoming."

Drake grimaced. "I swear it only happens if you're repairing a fence. That'll make the breeze die down every single time. I'll do the dirty work and hold it in place."

The gate was heavy, but his older brother knew his stuff and the hinge was done in a matter of minutes. Slater leaned against the fence and crossed his arms. "So, still no missing calf?"

"Nope." Drake had searched as far as anyone

could in country this size and hadn't found anything; that was predictable. "Not a trace."

"Too bad—but here comes trouble of a different kind." Slater's grin was wide. "I think your campaign of avoidance is about to go south, brother. I have to give you credit. Up until now, you've been fairly successful."

Damned if his brother wasn't right. Drake saw the unmistakable outline of the female figure walking toward them, the sun catching the chestnut glints in her hair. Any trace of guilt was wiped clean by his irritation. He muttered, "I know you find this just hilarious, but how would *you* like it if some eager film student wanted to follow your every movement?"

"Hmm." Slater nodded with exaggerated introspection. "Grace might not approve of this answer, but between you and me, if the nonexistent film student looked like Ms. Hale and I wasn't happily married, I would have no objections at all."

"She knows nothing about running a ranch."

Slater burst out laughing. "So maybe you should teach her? I think that's why she's here."

Starburst had the gall to lift his head and whinny in greeting as she walked up. Her cheeks held a slight flush, but otherwise the hike apparently hadn't been that much of a challenge. Slater was watching in obvious amusement, so Drake tried to respond with equanimity. "You found us, I see."

"And I did it without a horse," she shot back defiantly.

He let the gibe pass. "Red will teach you to saddle one if you give him a sweet smile. Grace's mare is gentle enough." *For a greenhorn.*

"Why do I feel I'm being patronized?" So much for his attempt at subtlety. "Plus, you've been avoiding me."

That was true. Slater was clearly enjoying the exchange. From the corner of his eye, Drake could see his brother grinning like a damn fool. "I'd say you *are* being patronized," Slater said.

Luce seemed to be as annoyed by that as Drake was, so at least they had one thing in common.

"The wild horses are back on that ridge," she said curtly.

Drake's attention sharpened. "The entire herd?"

Luce nodded. "I spotted them as I walked up here. The stallion was standing at the top, watching me. A hundred feet away is my estimate."

Drake felt a prickle of alarm. That was *way* too close. "A hundred feet?"

"Yes. That's what I said." In the next moment, she turned breezy. "I go looking for them every day, and when I'm lucky enough to be in the right place at the right time, I sit there as quietly as I can and try not to spook them. The big guy's starting to get curious about what I might be up to." A pause. "Should we go over and take a look if you're done here?"

They could. Why not? Slater was still smiling to himself as he gathered up the tools, not even bothering to pretend he wasn't taking in every word.

Drake considered Luce's invitation. He had plenty of other things to do, but he wouldn't mind an opportunity to recover at least some of those mares. There were other considerations, of course. Starburst was not a small horse, and he might spook the herd. Size-wise, he and the stallion could stand shoulder to shoulder; they were both males, but Star was gelded.

If the stallion got aggressive, Starburst would come out the loser.

More likely, though, the wild horse would turn his mares and head for the hills, as he'd done all the other times.

Another part of Drake's brain was caught upstream in the conversation. A hundred feet? She *had* gotten awfully close to those horses, and she didn't seem to have the first clue how dangerous they could be.

"I'll walk up there with you," he said reluctantly. He asked his brother, "Mind unsaddling Starburst for me and letting him graze with the cattle?"

"Nope." There was still a wicked glint in Slate's eyes. "Have fun hiking in those boots."

"I *live* in these boots," Drake retorted. "I'll be fine, big brother."

"Just sayin'."

"Thanks for your concern," Drake responded drily. "You can put salve on my blisters and rub my feet when we get back."

"I think you'll have to find someone else for that." Slater raised his brows and turned to Luce.

"No way." She smiled. "If anyone's entitled to a foot massage, it's me. I'll have walked up there *twice* today."

"I learn something new about you every day." Drake took his rope from Starburst's saddle, in case it came in handy. He doubted he'd get close enough to use it, but stranger things had happened.

"You don't know as much about me as you think you do. We only met eight days ago."

He couldn't possibly ignore that one. "Maybe it just seems longer. Let's go."

He received a well-deserved lethal look for that comment. "If you're ready, cowboy."

She led the way, sticking to the open areas, which told him she really wasn't a greenhorn when it came to this sort of country.

She provided him with a very nice back view. Following her was no hardship.

He knew the trail to the ridge as well as anyone and better than most. Certainly better than she did. But she walked with a sense of purpose and he climbed behind her. Slater had a point about his cowboy boots, but he could cope. Those mares had cost the ranch a small fortune.

Sure enough, Luce was right. The group of horses was at the top, quietly cropping the grass, half-hidden by a line of aspen. Ever vigilant, the stallion noticed their approach, lifted his head and allowed them to get decently close, with little more than a warning snort. They stopped obediently behind a small group of bushes, fairly well hidden, but the stallion made clear that he knew they were there.

Luce whispered, crouching next to him, "Smoke's in a good mood today."

She'd named the horse. *That figures.*

Those mares were valuable, he reminded himself again, and losing them permanently would have an effect on the bottom line. "Smoke? That's original," he said sarcastically.

"Hey, he's gray and black. Pet names are not my forte."

Drake sighed. "That's no pet, that's more than half a ton of testosterone and muscle. I couldn't take him, even in a fair fight. Think teeth and hooves."

He might have come across as peevish; he was used to riding, not walking, and he'd broken a light sweat on their impromptu stroll. His companion, on the other hand, looked as if they'd been cruising some city park, throwing bread at ducks in ponds or whatever people did in places like that.

She gave him an assessing stare. "Yet I feel you *are* about to beat him—but not on a physical level."

That was absolutely correct. "Yup. I'm going to win this one. I want my horses back, and he needs to go somewhere else."

Easier said than done, of course. That horse had no respect for fences at all. He'd kicked his way through more than one to get at the mares. Drake had thought about building an enclosure like the ones they used for bull riding at rodeos. But getting him into it was quite the challenge. Although he and Luce had barely met, he sensed that she wasn't going to agree with what he had to say next. "A tranquilizer dart is probably my best bet at this point. I'm going to hire someone to do it because that horse knows me. He's smart. He knows exactly who runs this ranch. I'm a good shot, but this is about as close as I've ever gotten to him and I doubt I could do it from here."

As predicted, she turned to scowl at him and said firmly, as if she had some authority over the situation, "No. You aren't shooting him with anything."

SHE'D GOTTEN SOME pretty good snaps of Drake Carson, shirtless, as he fixed that gate. He had impressive muscles and a six-pack stomach. Cowboy poster-boy material. Maybe someone needed to do a calendar with ranchers, like they did with firemen and athletes. She'd be happy to put him in it and leave it turned to that month forever. She had his grudging permission to shoot a few pictures of him if she wanted, but he hadn't been very enthusiastic.

That was nothing compared to what was about to happen, though. They were about to get in a really big argument. She could feel it coming. Whenever she had a strong opinion, she couldn't help expressing it, as her entire family would point out.

She stood up. "Smoke isn't going to understand. He'll hate it. Suddenly going to sleep and waking up somewhere else? How would you like that? Come up with some other idea."

All the horses lifted their heads at the raised voice. Drake straightened, too. "You have a better one?"

"Not yet." She shook her head. "I just don't want that."

"Hell, neither do I. *You* come up with something else and I'll listen."

"I'm thinking on it." She wasn't thinking about anything else. Well, except him.

Here, among the horses, the mountains, the blue sky, he looked like the real deal, a cowboy all the way. Of course, that was probably because he *was* the real deal—and his authenticity wasn't compromised by the exasperated expression on his face. She liked how he habitually tipped back his hat and then drew it forward.

"As I told you, I'll ponder it," she couldn't resist saying.

"*Ponder?* Really? Is that how you think we talk out here?"

"It's a perfectly good word." She stood her ground. "People from California say it all the time."

"Yeah, maybe a hundred years ago." He gestured at the horses. "Smoke—if that's what we're going to call him—would be fine after the trank. But the point is, he has to go. He's wreaking havoc with the ranch's working horses. Get it? Put that in your thesis."

"What if I could coax him into coming close enough so you could just catch him?"

"What?" He looked incredulous. "You can't. He's a wild stallion."

"I think I could."

He let out a long, slow breath. "You can't even *saddle* a horse."

"That's a skill I intend to learn. Can I give it a try? By the way, I'm well aware that we aren't talking about a domesticated animal. If we were, I wouldn't be here."

Drake threw up his hands. "This is the most ridiculous conversation I've ever had. He isn't going to do it."

"Let me try before you shoot him."

That riled him. "I'm not going to shoot that horse or any other horse, for heaven's sake! I'll sedate him and have him moved to federal land set aside for wild horses. *Not* the same thing."

It wasn't as if she didn't know that, but still…it was fun to tease him. She couldn't believe she was about to ask this, but she'd been pretty brazen already. "Can you wait two more weeks? I need that much time for my study, and you've had this herd around for a while, anyway. Then I promise I'll get out of your hair. I was planning on staying a month."

A bribe of sorts, and a shameless one.

His cooperation in exchange for getting rid of her. She figured he might go for it.

"A month!" He seemed properly horrified.

"You'd have one less week with me—if you'll just hold off a bit."

He took the deal. He smiled grimly and jerked

off his glove, then thrust out his hand. "Let's shake on it."

Solid grip. He didn't try to break her fingers or anything, which she appreciated, since she could tell he'd reached the end of his patience.

He had the bluest eyes she'd ever seen.

Was there any chance he'd actually pose for a formal photograph? Maybe next to that giant horse of his... Uh-uh, she thought wisely. This would *not* be the right moment to ask more of Mr. Drake Carson.

Instead, she said simply, "Thanks."

"Don't mention it," he muttered as he stalked away. "All I ask is that you be a man of your word."

"I'm not a man," she called out to his retreating back.

"I've noticed that," he said.

He didn't turn around.

CHAPTER FIVE

THE WEEKLY POKER GAME was set up at Bad Billy's Biker Bar and Burger Palace. Drake could use a cold one, so he approved of the choice. He spotted two of his friends already at the table, then sauntered up to the bar and nodded at Billy in greeting. "Who's waiting tonight? Thelma?"

"Sure is. Full of piss and vinegar, too. Got into a fender bender on her way to work. You know how she loves that old car. You boys be on your best behavior."

"Thanks for the warning." Thelma was a crusty older lady who, like Harry, tolerated no nonsense. Billy didn't need a bouncer; if anybody dared misbehave, Thelma effectively booted him out, although how she managed it when she was only about five feet high—and that was on a tall day—was a mystery. She never had a problem getting her point across, either. "Tell her I'll have my usual, and be polite about it, okay? Especially if she's in a no-bullshit mood." The place seemed busier than ever that night.

Billy laughed, a low rumble in his wide chest. "You are a wise man, my friend. Our Thelma has a soft spot for you, but she's about reached her cowboy quotient for the day, so I'll go ahead and draw your beer myself."

Tripp Galloway and Tate Calder were halfway through their first mugs of beer, elbows resting comfortably on the nicked wooden table. Tripp hooked a foot around a chair and tugged it out so Drake could sit. "You're late, but Spence texted and said he was tied up, so you don't get the slow prize this time. He figures maybe twenty minutes."

Drake took the chair. In the background a jukebox was playing Willie Nelson and the place was loud, but never so loud that you couldn't talk to the people at your table. One of the many reasons he disliked big cities was the noise—restaurants where you couldn't hear yourself think, much less converse with the person next to you. Traffic snarls, horns honking, sirens blaring. The skyscrapers and office buildings made him feel hemmed in, and the smell of exhaust fumes followed you everywhere. Give him the sweet scent of long grass in a clean breeze.

Tate said, "I need to warn you that Thelma's on the warpath and she's headed this way."

"Billy mentioned that she was in some kind of snit," Drake muttered under his breath, just before she plonked down his beer.

"Carson, you're always running late. And where's that worthless Spence Hogan, anyway? I spent some quality time with him earlier."

Spence was the chief of police, and whatever else

she might be, Thelma was no criminal. Drake wondered what she meant, although he wasn't stupid enough to ask.

Thelma had ringlets of gray hair, pale blue eyes, and wore her glasses on the end of her nose. As far as Drake could tell, she didn't actually need them; they seemed to be mainly for effect, probably so she could glare at people over the top.

Then he abruptly remembered and said, "Oh, the accident. Yeah, I heard. Sorry about Frankie."

She'd named her 1966 bright yellow Impala Frankie, and since this was Mustang Creek, he knew that car well. "That out-of-town asshole had no insurance. It's going to cost me seven hundred bucks to fix the car. I can take that idiot to small claims court, and Spence is going to make sure his license is suspended, but that won't do Frankie any good, will it?" She blew out a loud breath. "I'm *really* pissed off."

Now, there was breaking news.

"As soon as Spence gets here, your food will be out."

Tripp made the mistake of saying, "We haven't ordered yet."

Thelma sent him a look that would've scared the average grizzly bear. "All of you will have the special."

Every one of them wanted to ask what the special might be, but none had the guts to do so.

"Get it?" she demanded, just in case they didn't

know what was good for them, which was whatever Thelma *thought* was good for them.

They sure did. Not one of them said a thing as Thelma walked away, ignoring a table full of customers madly waving to get her attention.

"I was kind of hoping for the bacon cheeseburger, but I'll take whatever she sets in front of me," Tate said. "Whew. I wouldn't want to be the guy who made that grave error in judgment and hit her car. That had to be one hell of a conversation."

"If I was Spence, I'd throw him in jail for his own protection." Tripp drained what was left of his beer.

Drake didn't disagree. "Now, back to the menu... I'm praying for chicken-fried steak, but I'll roll with whatever happens to come my way. Did Red have a chance to talk to your dad?"

"About the bull, Sherman? Yeah, Jim will handle it—does him good to get involved. He misses that sort of thing."

Jim, Tripp's stepfather, had run the ranch for a long time before Tripp took over. Drake nodded. "I feel regretful about it. Sherman was great in his prime, but he's not doing real well right now. Slowing down, you might say."

Tripp got that faint grin on his face. "So, tell us about the student. The one who's cuter than a pup in a little red wagon. That's Red talking as you might've guessed, via Jim."

"I already figured that out." Drake took a long cool drink. It tasted great. "She's fine. She's *trying*—

in more ways than one." Tripp rolled his eyes at the pun, but Drake ignored him. "She's a pretty graduate student who has no idea what she's doing."

"How pretty?" That was Tate, also grinning.

"Very," he admitted, remembering the gold highlights in her hair.

"That's what we heard." Tripp was clearly teasing, but before Drake could respond, he lifted a hand. "I actually think that what she's doing is important. I'll bet most of America isn't even aware we have wild horses, much less that they can be a problem. My two cents' worth."

Spence's arrival stopped the discussion. He slid into the fourth chair at their table. Tall, with a natural air of command that wasn't overstated, he was both confident and good at his job. "Thelma's still mad, I take it."

"She's steaming," Drake informed him. "Don't try to order off the menu, my friend. She's decided we're all having the special, whatever that might be."

"Gotcha." Spence grimaced. "You should've been there when Junie got the call. She's a seasoned dispatcher and even she was shaking her head. When Thelma asked that I personally respond, Junie threw me under the bus and said I would. Both of my deputies were laughing their asses off."

They were all laughing, too, but instantly sobered when Thelma showed up with Spence's beer, glowered at him and asked, "That noninsured yahoo in prison yet?"

"Took him there myself. Straight to the dungeon section. He's chained to the wall." Spence said it with a straight face.

Thelma did have a sense of humor and it finally surfaced. "See that he gets no food or water."

"Yes, ma'am."

"Your food will be right up. I'll bring another round when you start your game. But then I'm cutting you off. Y'all have to drive home." She stalked back toward the kitchen.

Spence said mildly, "I could point out that I walked from the station and Melody's having dinner with Hadleigh and Bex, so she's picking me up. But I think I'm just going to keep my mouth shut."

"Good idea." Tripp nodded. Since Hadleigh was his wife and Bex was married to Tate, they were undoubtedly doing the same thing. Drake had planned on having only two beers, anyway, so the decree didn't bother him at all.

Their weekly poker game usually took a couple of hours. He'd be completely sober when he drove back to the ranch.

The special ended up being chicken-fried steak, mashed potatoes and garden-fresh green beans, which meant it was his lucky night. Until he saw who was walking through the front door...

Ms. Lucinda Hale.

Drake couldn't believe it. She spotted him and waved. She looked different with all that long hair in loose curls and a denim skirt that reached only midthigh, with some sort of frothy pink top that left her slender arms bare. Didn't matter how she looked, though. She was still his nemesis. Or, if that was too fancy, he could just call her a pain in the butt. *Focus.* Poker night.

He waved back. What could he do but be polite? Tate narrowed his eyes. "That's her? The graduate student? *Pretty*'s an understatement, I'd say."

"Whatever." He finished his first beer in a gulp and grumbled, "What she's doing here, I don't have a clue."

"Maybe she heard that Billy serves the best burgers in town and decided to try one." Tripp looked amused at Drake's discomfort, especially when Luce started to walk toward them. "Here she comes. No offense, but I've never thought you were all that irresistible myself."

That was *not* worth responding to.

They all stood when she walked in their direction.

"Hello." Luce smiled at them, leaving Drake no choice but to introduce everyone. Once that was done, she said, "Please sit down and eat. I didn't mean to interrupt. Mace is parking the car. Nice to meet all of you."

About two seconds later, his brother strolled through the door, the slightest hint of a smirk on his face, as if he knew their arrival would annoy the hell out of him. Mace waved a casual hello and Luce went off to join him at a table in the corner, near the antique jukebox.

As if they were on a date or something. It definitely got to him, which he'd have to think about later.

"I guess you're not the irresistible one, after all." Tripp was joking, but his gaze was speculative. "You might want to adjust your expression, Carson, because Mace knows you even better than we do and he'll be able to read it loud and clear."

"What expression?" He caught the hint of defensiveness in his voice. Damn.

Spence said to Tate, "Two brothers after the same girl. Not a good scenario, is it?"

Tate took a bite and chewed for a minute as though he was thinking it over. "Especially if they live in the same house. Nope, not good at all."

"I'm not 'after' her," Drake snapped. He knew they were ribbing him, but he was afraid his current level of annoyance wasn't solely because Mace had deliberately brought her to Billy's to irritate him. They were best friends, yet they had fought like two male bighorn sheep their entire lives, arguing so much that even Slater had given up trying to tone them down. Unless it got physical, which it had once or twice when they were teens.

"Why aren't you?" Tripp asked that as if it were a legitimate question. "Attractive and obviously smart. Gorgeous eyes. Does she snore or something?"

"You've known Hadleigh since she was six. I just met Luce. She's only been around for about a week. Our arrangement, if you can call it that, is strictly business." He paused. "So I couldn't tell you if she snores. I haven't slept with her."

"He's always been the bashful type." Spence was doing a lousy job of hiding his glee. "Tripp has a point, though. A woman like that, following you around, living in the same house—seems like an opportunity not to be missed."

Tate had to throw in his opinion, too, of course. "Bex told me she's going to be here all summer. That's plenty of time to win her over. Unless Mace beats you to it."

"You three are worse than my mother. All I want to win at the moment is our poker game. Can we change the subject?" The chicken-fried steak was delicious, he was hungry and he rarely took a night off except for their poker game, so he wanted to enjoy it. If Luce felt like having dinner with his brother, that was her choice.

It didn't upset him.

Not at all.

Well…not much.

A reasonable voice inside him said he resented the intrusion she'd brought into his life, but another nagged that maybe he wasn't as indifferent as he wanted to be.

Thelma used the same tray to deliver their second round and stack up their empty plates. She cocked a brow in challenge. "Food's good?"

"Great," they answered in unison.

"I'll tell Billy. Deal the cards. Hard to believe,

but the four of you are the only customers I've seen tonight who didn't make me say to myself, *Damn, it's them.* Hey, Carson, what's your girlfriend doing here with your brother, anyway?"

He would've explained that Luce wasn't his girlfriend, but Thelma sashayed away before he could comment, moving toward another table, muttering, "Keep your panties on, dammit. I've only got two hands."

They probably all looked shell-shocked. "Did we just get a compliment? From *Thelma*?" Spence whispered when she was far enough away to be out of earshot.

Tate said, "Can't be."

Tripp sat immobile. "I think we did."

Drake said, "Maybe she likes us. Let's not ruin it. You heard the lady. Hurry up and deal the cards."

MACE CARSON WAS entirely too pleased with himself. "Told you so," he said smugly.

Luce was torn between tossing her glass of wine at him—Mountain Vineyards, of course—and just laughing. She decided the waitress was too scary and she didn't dare make a mess, so he won the lottery. "I don't know what you think you're going to accomplish," she said. "Drake and his buddies are playing cards, and you and I are only here because Harry's cousin came to town unexpectedly and she took the night off."

"My mom is friends with Cindy, too, so coming

here seemed like a good plan. The three of them will sit and gossip on the veranda all evening. Did you notice that Slater and Grace went off with Raine and Daisy? And Ryder's hanging out with Red."

She wasn't fooled. "But *you* chose when and where we'd go—just to be sure I'd intrude on your brother's evening with his friends."

His mouth twitched. "Not a ton of restaurant choices in Mustang Creek."

"Whatever lucky woman's out there waiting for you, she should be warned that you're a smooth liar."

He didn't even pretend to dissemble. "You think she's lucky, huh? I'm honored."

Luce watched him over the rim of her wineglass. Of the three Carson men, he was perhaps the most complicated. Slater was brilliant and driven. Drake was the pragmatic, down-to-earth type who dealt with life head-on. Mace was harder to figure out. All she knew with certainty was that he liked to needle his older brothers and would've been disappointed if they hadn't returned the favor.

Luce liked him. There wasn't the same pull she felt with Drake, but chemistry was an unpredictable thing. "Hmm. She'd need to be sassy. Sophisticated. Smart. And she has to be able to handle you."

"You fit the bill." His smile was flirtatious.

"I'm not sophisticated." She wasn't particularly; she'd always been more of an academic than the polished type she pictured at his side. He was equally aware that they weren't well suited in a romantic sense. And he obviously had some intuition about her and Drake—or at least her attraction to Drake—since he was pressuring his brother. She liked him all the better for his matchmaking because she found it both funny and touching. "I'm all about hiking boots and skinny-dipping in the river. You want someone who can pick up a wine list and recognize every single label."

"I don't like snooty women."

"That's not what I said, is it?"

"No." Mace was drinking one of his own red wines, and apparently enjoying the conversation. "I'll wait for her to come along. In the meantime, you and my brother?"

She had no idea what to say. She raised her shoulders in a helpless shrug. "I don't think he even likes me."

"Think again. I recognized that scowl on his face when I walked through the door. It wasn't because you were here. It was because you were here with *me*."

She regarded him dubiously.

With a cheeky grin, he added, "Trust me on this one, Ms. Hale. He just doesn't know what to do with you. Whoops, badly put. He knows what he'd *like* to do with you, but the thought of being part of a research project affronts his desire for solitude. You could put Drake in a time machine and take him back about a hundred and fifty years, drop him anywhere in the American West, and he'd fit right in. Even when we were younger, he hardly ever watched TV or played any video games. When we got home from school, he did his homework as fast as possible so he could saddle his horse and ride out. Harry used to get on him because he missed supper so often."

As Luce took another sip of wine, she was tucking this information away for reasons that weren't really connected to her graduate thesis. The hum of the restaurant had faded into the background. "Yet he went to college, even played a collegiate sport."

Mace leaned his forearms on the edge of the old wooden table, which had seen years of use. "Not going to college wasn't an option. Our father made that clear very early in our lives. What we did after college was our decision, but we were going to college, all three of us. And yeah, Drake is one hell of a tennis player. Think about it, though. Unless you play doubles, that's not a team sport. Slater played football and I ran track, but you should see Drake rope a calf. He's got incredible aim, so that's why he chose tennis. If I was drowning and needed someone to toss me a flotation device, I'd sure hope he was around."

Fascinating. And not what she needed. She was a bit too fascinated already.

"Do you suppose he'd ever let me film him doing that? The calf roping, I mean?"

"Doubtful." Mace shook his head. "Slater might be Mr. Showbiz, but Drake is camera shy. I remember that he had to be bribed with this vintage pickup truck he wanted before he agreed to have his senior pictures taken. He just wanted to skip the whole thing. Some sort of compromise was reached because he said yes to the pictures and he got the truck. He and Red restored it. They're kindred souls."

She'd met Red and could agree with that. "Hard to reach. Softhearted, but they hide it well."

"See, you're observant. What else have you picked up on? Have you decided he's worth the effort?"

Luce kept her cool. "I've decided you're jumping to a few conclusions here."

"I doubt it."

The reappearance of the grouchy waitress ended that conversation. Luce couldn't recall ordering, but she got a plate of fried walleye with homemade coleslaw and thick-cut fries, and Mace got a burger loaded with all the extras. Mystified, she asked, "How did she know what I was going to order? That's impossible."

"There are some questions better left unasked." He gestured at his plate. "Usually, I arrive, she brings me a drink, then she delivers the food. Maybe she's a witch or something, but like my brother, she tends to hit the mark."

The fish was delicious, crispy and paired with tartar sauce made from scratch. She'd barely finished the last bite when the poker party broke up and the players headed for the door, probably eager to get home to their wives and kids. Drake, the only bachelor in the bunch, didn't keep late hours, either, since he got up before dawn.

Speak of the devil... He stopped by their table. "How was your dinner?" he asked.

"Delicious." She waited; he seemed to have something to say.

"Good." He planted a hand, palm down, on the table, looking at her intently. "Finish your wine. You're coming with me. Mace can find his own way home."

When the ultimate cowboy gave you an ultimatum, it was kind of hard to ignore.

Mace was grinning behind his wineglass and his eyes twinkled. "Sure. Home. The place where we grew up. Sure, I can find it on my own."

"Don't even try to be funny. It's never worked for you before. I just want to show Luce something—not that it's any of your business."

"Wonder what that might be," Mace speculated, his tone easy and unhurried.

A muscle tensed in Drake's jaw. "Your tactless comments are getting on my nerves, little brother."

Time to run interference.

Luce finished her wine in an inelegant gulp and smiled apologetically at Mace. If she hadn't known what Mace was up to, she would never have agreed to leave one brother, who'd treated her to dinner, for the other. But he was the one who'd set everything in motion, so she interrupted whatever he was going to say next. "Thanks for dinner. So…what's your advice?"

He gave Drake a once-over. "He's harmless enough."

Drake didn't look flattered. "Don't be so sure."

Luce stood up hastily, aware that Mace could be right and Drake hadn't liked her coming to Bad Billy's with him. Even though it was none of his business. Her reaction to this was both positive and negative. So far, all her interactions with the Carson family had run that way. Three very different brothers who got along well, but there was some head-butting now and then. And she just happened to be the reason for this latest bout.

Drake steered her toward the bar. "I'll be a second. I need to talk to Billy."

Billy—a former biker, or so she'd heard—was busy pouring drinks. Smiling, he paused when Drake walked up. "You boys seemed to like the food okay. I see you stole Mace's woman. That didn't take long. Ain't you slick, cowboy."

"She isn't Mace's woman." Drake sounded emphatic. "Anyway, here's Thelma's tip. I didn't want to leave it on the table. Tell her it's from all of us."

Billy's eyebrows rose as he took the thick wad of bills. "Let me guess. Seven hundred dollars—enough to take care of the car repairs. That's real thoughtful of you."

Drake shrugged. "She brought us chicken-fried steak and beer. The least we could do is help her fix Frankie."

"Dammit, son, don't make me tear up in front of a pretty girl. It'd ruin my reputation. I'll see that Thelma gets this."

Luce would give a lot to see Bad Billy all misty-eyed, but Drake was already leading her toward the door, his fingers firmly around her wrist. Outside, the night was clear and, according to the weather report she'd heard earlier, unseasonably warm. "Do you mind telling me what I need to see so badly that I rudely abandoned your brother?"

He opened the passenger's-side door of his truck for her. "Explaining would defeat the purpose. *See* is the operative word here. Hop in."

CHAPTER SIX

THE MOON ROSE slowly above the mountains, right on cue, spreading its silvery light, and while he certainly knew she'd seen a full moon before, he was convinced she'd never seen one quite like this. Drake thought it was spectacular and he never tired of it.

Since he was going to watch it, anyway, she might as well come along.

Okay, the truth was he *needed* her to see it. If she wanted to have a true Wyoming experience, this was one of the best. He pointed. "This way."

He'd driven his truck as far as possible, but it was still a considerable walk, although he knew she wouldn't mind that part. Luce gave him an inquiring look and he just shook his head. "Worth it. Trust me."

"I am, obviously," she said drily.

He led her over the rustic pass, since he was the one who knew where they were going, and because there might be snakes. Rattlers usually left the vicinity as fast as possible when human beings showed up, but if they were startled, it was a different story. He'd been raised to pay attention, and he did.

The sound of rushing water told him they were

getting close. When they got to the stream, he eyed her impractical open-toed shoes and without a word picked her up, ignoring her sudden gasp of protest, then waded across. Once he'd set her down on the other side, she straightened her skirt and glared at him. "I could've carried my shoes."

She did have the world's prettiest eyes, even when they were staring at him indignantly.

"That was easier, wasn't it? Look around. I think this might be the most beautiful place on earth."

In the twilight, a small waterfall that fed into the stream from a rocky outcrop glimmered. There was a natural bench in the form of a flat stone about six feet wide. He gestured toward it. They were in a small theater of aspens and ponderosa pine, and the air smelled like fresh water and meadow grass. "Have a seat and let the show begin. We're right on time."

"On time for what?"

"Wait for it. Watch the tree line."

The sunset was even *more* spectacular than usual—or at least he felt as if it was. The rows of trees were illuminated in a glow that intensified as the moon came up. With the mountains behind, and a starry sky above, the veil of the waterfall reflected the light.

Luce's eyes widened, and Drake heard her catch her breath as she took it all in.

Oh, hell, he *was* falling for her. He'd always wondered how it would feel if that ever happened—he was thirty-two now and it hadn't yet—but he knew this *was* happening.

He'd once told Slater that when the woman of his dreams walked into his line of vision, he'd know it.

That might be true, but he wasn't sure he wanted it to be Lucinda Hale. They lived in different states, an obstacle in itself, and he sensed that her interest in him was based on her intellectual pursuits— but it might have evolved into something more. He couldn't pick up the ranch and move it somewhere else, so unless she was willing to completely change *her* life, it wasn't going to work.

How had he gotten himself into this situation?

Wait, *he* hadn't done it. She had.

Was he really that serious? He'd met her only a short time ago.

Maybe he was...

"That's so beautiful," she whispered. "Drag me out of a bar and carry me across a river anytime."

"Count on me."

The hell of it was he wanted to reach over, haul her into his arms and prove he meant it, but he wasn't comfortable with this kind of emotional impulse. He led a simple life and liked it that way. He got up early, saddled his horse, went to work and came home. Yup, simple.

Luce was throwing a hitch in his stride. She was a complication, and that was the truth.

It didn't help matters when she turned and smiled

almost tremulously. "I could very easily fall in love." She amended quickly, "With Wyoming, I mean."

Damn, he was going to kiss her, and the worst part was that she knew it, too. There was an expectant look on her face, and when he leaned in and slid his arm around her waist to pull her close, she accepted it willingly, one hand coming up to rest on his chest.

It was quite the kiss, starting tentatively, but then it deepened with alarming speed. Still, he didn't care to analyze it. Luce was warm and pliant against him, her hair smelled like flowers and was tangled around his fingers. His heart was pounding and—

A familiar sound broke them apart, and to his complete shock, he saw the stallion, probably less than a hundred feet away. He'd come up here to drink from the stream and snorted again in displeasure at their presence. Then he lowered his head and drank, anyway, always vigilant but apparently thirsty.

If he could've had a conversation with that mare-thieving bastard, Drake would have pointed out that *he* was the one who should be ticked off.

To make it worse, Luce seemed to forget the kiss entirely. "I can't believe it," she said in a hushed voice. "Look how close he is!"

"Yeah, he sure is." Drake spoke in his normal tone, because while he had affection for all creatures on the planet, he was greatly irritated by this one at the moment.

"Shh. You'll scare him away."

"That would be fine with me. I don't have a tranquilizer gun, and if I did, there's no way I could transport him from this spot, anyway. So I guess if I spook him, it doesn't bother me too much."

"We agreed you weren't going to do that. Use a tranquilizer gun, I mean."

Oh, good. Great kiss followed by an argument. "We didn't *agree* on anything. *You* made the declaration that you'd become his new best friend, and I told you flat out that you were delusional."

"I do remember you being extremely closed-minded now that you mention it." She stood up and Drake gave an inner sigh.

Smoke, the coward, turned and melted into the shadows. Smart horse.

"*Practical.* That's a better word." He stood, too. He might as well ride fences tonight, even though Red had it handled. Never hurt to check twice.

"Whatever," she muttered and started to walk toward the stream, stopping to yank off her shoes, holding them in one hand. "No need to carry me, by the way. I can take care of myself."

"Look, the herd's growing. If I wait too long, it'll be impossible. So I'm not going to wait. I can't afford to."

"The government will auction them off!"

"But not to a slaughterhouse or the glue factory, if that's what you're worried about. I wouldn't condone that, either. The real problem is that you're getting unreasonably attached."

Those gorgeous eyes sent him a death glare to rival Thelma's. "*I'm* unreasonable?"

REALLY?

In just one evening, Drake Carson had ordered her to leave a restaurant with him, picked her up without warning, kissed her senseless and then infuriated her. It was becoming pretty clear that he did things his way, and if she didn't like his approach, he wouldn't lose sleep over it.

Oh, the moon rising up over the mountains was gorgeous, no question about that. Not to mention romantic, which might've been why she was so drawn into that passionate kiss. She could tell that her research project meant little or nothing to him, and *his* agenda was what mattered. It was his ranch, true, but he hadn't done anything about the horses yet. Maybe they could figure something out…

Maybe *she'd* figure out what that something could be.

She splashed through the cold stream, finding the bottom rockier than she'd expected. She gritted her teeth and went on, the current swirling around her thighs. She understood he was running a business; that part was fine. But the fact that he seemed to think she was pursuing a frivolous degree set her teeth on edge. No, he'd never *said* that. He really didn't need to.

Drake Carson was bullheaded, and that was all there was to it.

To make matters worse, he knew she was mad and didn't try to talk about it. He just walked behind her and didn't stop her when she rushed forward to open her own door. He closed it, climbed in the driver's side—both of them wet—and started the truck.

Clearly, if it was up to him, they weren't going to have a conversation.

Well, she had a news bulletin—it *wasn't* up to him, not entirely.

Luce began by asking, "Why did you kiss me?"

"I wanted to." He put the truck in gear and drove down the rutted track.

"I could swear you don't even like me. I told Mace that earlier."

"Mace is nothing but a pain in the ass."

"*And* he's your brother, and a really nice man."

"Nice? When did *that* happen?"

"You're joking and you know it."

"Luce, what do you want from me?" He kept his tone even. "I assume you realize I'm attracted to you. Not sure I want to be, but there it is. I don't do casual, so that means it has to be serious, and in the end, you're going back to California. It might be better if we stayed away from each other, but you're there every time I turn around. This is a hard rock or a deep pool situation for me."

He had a point. She murmured, "I don't think that's quite the right saying. Devil or the deep blue sea? Between a rock and a hard place?"

"Close enough. That's Red talking. He always

says that you could be stuck on a hard rock or drowning in a deep pool."

She laughed. "I can imagine him saying that. So what now?"

"If you want to fall in love, Wyoming is your only choice."

That was honest. A play on her words, but honest.

Still, this was moving far too fast. "I don't know if I want to fall in love—with you *or* Wyoming—at all. Anyway, I can't fall in love—in just a couple of weeks."

"It does seem to defy logic, but my impression is that logic doesn't enter into falling in love."

Time to give him some perspective. "I was kissed by a sexy cowboy near a waterfall during a full moon while a wild stallion intruded on the moment. Let's not confuse romantic with deeper feelings."

Drake only grinned. "I'm sexy?"

"Oh, yes." She wished he wasn't.

"Nice to know you're inclined to think of me that way." His smile flashed again.

"Like you didn't already know that."

"I'm not sure I did."

"Just do me a favor and don't play that card, okay? You're totally aware of what's going on between us. And by the way, I don't do casual, either."

"So—what, are we making a pact not to get involved?" He did that thing with his hat, tipping it and then adjusting it back down. "I'm not positive it works that way. That choice isn't yours—it's made *for* you."

"Voice of experience?" She looked at him curiously, hanging on to the car door, since they were bumping along on something that only resembled a road. "Have you ever been in love?"

"No details available. This isn't a sorority gossip session."

Fine. Whatever Drake's opinion of her, she actually did respect his privacy. So, no questions.

No reason *she* couldn't be honest. "I thought I was in love once, but the man I fell for slept with my roommate. She blamed him, and he blamed her. I blamed them both. End of story. I lost a friend and a fiancé in one fell swoop. I did thank her, though, for saving me from making a big mistake. I got the flat-screen TV when I moved out. That gave me some satisfaction. She could watch the empty space on the wall."

"Ouch, but she did do you a favor. Faithful is not negotiable in my book."

"*The Cowboy Guide to a Successful Relationship*? I assume that's the title." She didn't conceal her amusement. "Let me guess. Chapter One is 'Never Discuss Previous Relationships.' What's Chapter Two?"

"Chapter Two is 'Avoid Beautiful Graduate Students Because They're a Passel of Trouble.'"

"What trouble have I caused you?"

He didn't budge an inch, but his mouth twitched with laughter. "I sense it coming."

"Do you now?" She was laughing, too. "So you think I'm beautiful, or were you just trying to be polite, since I said you were sexy?"

"You'll discover that I don't say anything I don't

mean. Then again, I didn't mention you by name, did I?" He spoke in that low deliberate drawl she found so charming. "But yes, I think beautiful applies."

Maybe changing the subject would be a good idea. He was right; she was going to gather all the information for her thesis this summer and then return to California. Involvement with Drake was the last thing she needed. Her whole life was in California, including every member of her family. "So tell me, why did you give a seven-hundred-dollar tip to a waitress who was so grumpy I hesitated to ask her for a glass of water?"

"Someone hit Frankie."

Luce wrinkled her brow. "Frankie is...who? Husband? Dog? Cat?"

"Car. She doesn't really have the money to fix it. We all pitched in. This is Mustang Creek. She lives frugally, takes care of her elderly mother, and everyone knows she loves Frankie." He shrugged in a nonchalant way. "We all brought money for the poker game, so we pooled it together and gave it to her."

"That's generous of you."

"I've known her my whole life."

Softly, Luce said, "I'm guessing Chapter Three is titled 'Loyalty,' right?"

"If it isn't," he responded as they reached the paved road, "it should be."

CHAPTER SEVEN

SOMETHING WAS UP.

When he came in for lunch the next day, after that moonlit kiss he and Luce had shared, Drake saw Harry's knowing smile, and before he could ask any questions, she presented him with one of his all-time favorites—a corned beef sandwich. He devoured it and would've counted himself a lucky man, but Mace came into the kitchen before he was finished. The smug grin on his brother's face would have made it hard for a saint to resist punching him out on the spot.

Drake was no saint.

"What?" He set aside his plate and forgot all about having seconds of the potato salad. Harold and Violet, waiting patiently at his feet, were obviously hoping for leftovers.

Mace tried to look innocent but didn't quite pull it off as he plucked a sandwich from the board and spooned up enough potato salad to satisfy a bull moose. "What? You and Slater cross paths today?"

"Not yet."

Come to think of it, when he'd passed Grace in

the hall, she'd also had an amused expression on her face.

What now?

For starters, he wasn't going to pass up the extra potato salad, and he never gave the dogs any table scraps, so he ignored them. He took his own sweet time eating, even rinsed his plate. Only then did he take the bait. "You going to elaborate? Just tell me. You're obviously dying to."

Mace had his mouth full, so he finished chewing and swallowed before he answered. "He's in his office. Maybe before you head out again, you should see him."

The fact that Mace found this funny was not a good sign, whatever was going on. Drake maneuvered the hallways to the back of the house, the dogs following. Slater was at his desk, talking on his cell phone, but he waved him into a seat. Drake chose to stand and gaze out the window, because that was one damn fine view. His father had known what he was doing when he'd selected this room for his office. Plus, he wasn't going to stay long, anyway.

Slater ended the call. "Sorry about that."

He turned. "No problem. We're even if you'll tell me why everyone's acting like there's something I don't know that they all find hilarious."

Oh, great, another big grin. His older brother said, "Can't thank you enough."

"What the hell does that mean? Thank me for

what?" Drake was getting exasperated and he didn't
care who knew it.

Slater touched a key on his computer. "I've been
struggling with how to start the new documentary.
We've begun some of the filming, but I needed an
opening. It's all about Wyoming, specifically this
area—and you handed my opening scene to me on
a platter. Sterling-silver platter, in fact. Look at this."

The minute the image came up, Drake understood
the snickers. It was certainly a familiar one. Moon
rising, mountains, waterfall glistening, a wild stallion in the background…

Man and woman kissing.

"You had cameras there last night? At that very
spot?" Drake took off his hat and wanted to throw it
across the room, but he ran his fingers through his
hair instead. "Damn, Slate, that was kind of a private moment!"

His brother leaned back in his chair. "Now, think
about it. How in the hell would I know you'd conveniently show up—cowboy hat, boots and all—and
kiss the girl? I just wanted to catch the waterfall and
the moon rising, so we set up remote cameras. We
handle things that way all the time. The stallion's an
extra perk. I can't *not* use this shot. The chances of
getting something like this are out of the ballpark.
This *is* Wyoming. I'm opening with it."

Oh, *that* was good news.

His brother went on, going all Showbiz. "It's great
footage. I showed it to my assistant, and he about

flipped out. Sent it to the director, and he couldn't believe it, either. Done, and on the first take, too. No actors involved, and the staging and lighting are perfect."

This *was* his brother. He would've told anybody else what they could do with their perfect staging. Slater was Slater, though, and he was telling the truth—he hadn't planned on filming that kiss. It had just happened. No one's fault, but Drake's level of enthusiasm for sharing his love life—if that term applied—with the world was hovering around minus twenty.

So he looked for a way out. "Don't you need our permission?"

"Yeah, I do. I'm counting on you to sign, and to persuade Luce to do the same. You ought to be able to convince her—the two of you seem to like each other well enough, if that kiss is any indication."

This was a headache he didn't need. At least he and Luce weren't really recognizable, he thought as he studied the screen. They were practically silhouettes. "Well, I'm guessing since those were remote cameras, they kept on rolling, so you also caught us having an argument and her stomping off. I wouldn't count on me influencing her."

Slater didn't look fazed at all. "And yet I *am* counting on it. Grace said it might be the most romantic moment she's ever seen—which made me question whether or not I've been handling things right."

"She's pregnant with your child, so you've obviously done things just fine." Drake rubbed his forehead. "Did you *have* to show it to other people?"

"Mom walked in when I was reviewing the film to ask me a question. Most people wouldn't recognize you from your profile, but she would. Of course, she told Harry and Grace. They both asked to see it. Grace is kind of dangerous right now that she's in her last trimester, so I couldn't refuse. And I learned a long time ago that if Harry asks me to do something, I should simply do it. You can't disagree with me on that."

"Someone told Mace."

"Drake, if the way you dragged Luce out of Bad Billy's didn't start everyone talking, then I don't know what would. I heard about it from Raine, and she'd heard it from someone else because she and Daisy were out to dinner with us during that little scene." He paused, looking closely at Drake. "Oh, and I'll need Luce's permission in writing. My lawyers will be in touch."

"Lawyers?" This was getting worse by the minute.

"They handle situations like this. Don't act as if you don't know that."

He did, but still...

"I don't want to be part of your movie."

"You didn't intend to be part of it, but it's going to be perfect. You didn't have to act or anything. You just behaved naturally, and it was exactly what I needed. So you and I both won. Look at the picture again. Classic."

Hell, double hell and triple hell.

"It's that damn horse." Slater could easily get another couple to kiss in the moonlight by the waterfall, but that horse was so beautiful—when he wasn't kicking down fences and creating other chaos. "Fine with me, but *you* get to ask Luce about the footage. I've got a full afternoon and she's being fairly testy with me right now. You stand a better chance."

He stalked out the door and ran into her in the hallway. Figured. She was in full-on outdoor gear, ponytail and all. "Slater needs to talk to you," he said, trying to sound as normal as possible. "He's in his office, and just so you know, this isn't my fault."

"What does that mean?" Luce wasn't letting him off the hook. She caught his arm as he tried to leave. "What isn't your fault?"

"This." He grabbed her, kissed her the way he had the night before, then let her go. At least she didn't smack him, but he did see her bewildered look when he spun on his heel and walked away.

Chapter Four of his book should be titled "Romantic Moonlit Kisses Are a Bad Idea."

BLYTHE WAS ON the porch, watering her flowers. Luce went out there and sat down, sighing deeply. "Your sons are giving me fits."

"Welcome to my world." Blythe glanced over with a smile hovering on her lips. "Specifically?"

"I know you saw that picture of me and Drake." She felt a flush hit her cheeks.

"I could lie," Blythe told her, "but I'm not good at lying, and besides, why should I? I saw it. Slater is elated and I don't blame him one bit. That shot couldn't be orchestrated in a thousand years. Drake would never do that in front of a camera on purpose and that horse is definitely an…interesting addition."

Luce gave a small hiccup of a laugh. "Drake's going to view him as more of a nuisance than ever."

"I assume you mean the horse. Well, Drake viewed *you* as a nuisance when you first got here, but he seems to have decided otherwise in a very short period of time. I was going to have a cup of tea. Care to join me?"

"I'd love to."

"I'll be right back. We'll sit at the table in the corner."

It was a pleasant afternoon, pots of pansies vibrant in the slanting sunlight on the veranda-style porch. When Blythe returned with a tray holding an old-fashioned teapot and two delicate floral china cups with saucers, Luce hurried to take it from her, letting her hostess choose a chair first.

"Of course, Harry insisted on the oatmeal chocolate chip cookies, since she was just taking them out of the oven." Blythe sat down and reached for the teapot, pouring them each a cup. "She makes those for Drake, lemon bars for Slater, and Mace's favorite is her blue-ribbon-winning pie. If asked, I'm fairly sure the boys would describe her as the most thoughtful tyrant in Bliss County. Now, then, what are you going to do about Drake?"

That was certainly direct.

But so was the picture, and he'd just kissed her *again*. Drat the man. Not that she'd pushed him away or anything...

The raspberry-lemon tea was wonderful. "I have no idea," she said with a rueful smile. "I don't know if I *can* do anything about him. He lives here and I live in California."

"His father lived here and I lived in California." Blythe took a dainty sip. "I really fell for that hard-working, honest-as-the-day-is-long cowboy. Slater looks like my late husband, but Drake *reminds* me of him more. Stubborn as all get-out. He's also a very good, kind man. Intelligent and yet compassionate enough that children and animals are instinctively drawn to him."

Luce nibbled at a cookie. She could level with Blythe, and she did. "You don't have to sell me on Drake. You saw that film."

Blythe's smile deepened. "I did indeed. A lot of people will see it. You're fine with that?"

"No one will know who I am. I told Slater I was okay with it."

"There are worse things than a woman being kissed by a handsome young man."

She couldn't agree more. "Everything in life is about timing. Did you catch that bus on schedule? Or if you missed it, did you also miss being in an accident? Did you walk across the street at the wrong time? Did your parents divorce when you were in high school? Did you catch your fiancé with your best friend? All kinds of scenarios like that. I just don't know if this is the right timing for us."

Blythe laughed, the sound light and musical. "Honey, you can't wait for 'right.' There's no such thing when it comes to love. I'd never tell you what to do, but to me, effort is the key to any relationship and I'm living proof that you have to do your share and maybe a little more if you want a man like Drake."

Luce shrugged. "I'm not convinced it's an option."

"Sure it is! Keep in mind that Drake's never going to be forthcoming, especially regarding anything emotional. That's just who he is. Mace expresses himself effectively, Drake not enough and Slater's in the middle."

That didn't bother her too much. He was a loner and she understood that, but he was also an intelligent, articulate man who *could* talk about his feelings; he wasn't inclined to do it.

Talk about being between a hard rock and a deep pool… Red needed to write his own book of quaint sayings and shelve it right next to *The Cowboy Guide to a Successful Relationship*.

"So I chose the difficult one, didn't I?"

"Maybe." Blythe didn't evade her question. "In a lot of ways he's the easiest. He does what he's going to do and that's it. He's never going to pull you in fifteen different directions, and he won't lie to you.

If you want it straight from the hip, that's exactly what you're going to get, like it or not."

Chose was a dangerous word. It implied that she'd made a decision. Perhaps she even had...

Blythe took difficult and made it simple. "He's worth it."

It would be different if Luce disagreed. But Mace had said the same thing.

"I wasn't looking for this."

Blythe took that in stride. "Sometimes it just finds you."

"Now you sound like Drake."

"Or maybe he sounds like me?" She smiled. "We *have* spent some time together in our lives."

That did bring a laugh. "Okay, I concede that he might sound like you. Pragmatic and down-to-earth."

Grace pulled up just then, got out of her car and slammed the door. Hard. She stalked up the steps— as much as a very pregnant woman could stalk— and dropped her purse on the wooden floor of the veranda. "If I could drink, I would, but I can't. Is it wrong to say I had a bad day at the resort? That doesn't seem right. Who could have a bad day at a beautiful resort? Me, that's who. Some of those cookies have my name on them. Don't risk both your lives by eating them all while I go to the bathroom for about the four hundredth time today."

Blythe was unfazed. "Harry made an extra batch."

"She has a good sense of how the universe works. I'll be right back."

Blythe was laughing out loud, but she had a sympathetic look on her face as her daughter-in-law disappeared into the house. She settled comfortably back in her chair. "Near the end it gets rough. Childbirth right in front of you and either you don't know what to expect or you *do* know what to expect. Between a—"

"Hard rock and a deep pool?" Luce supplied helpfully. "According to Drake, it's one of Red's favorite sayings. It's become my new favorite, too."

"Red is quite the character, no doubt about that." Blythe poured another cup of tea. "Speaking of babies, this is a personal question, but I do hope you want children."

Wow, talk about moving too fast.

Luce didn't have a facile response to that one. She was rescued by Grace, who returned to the porch and lowered herself into a chair with a sigh of relief. She'd discarded her shoes in the meantime and come out barefoot, her red hair loose, and accepted a cup of tea and a cookie. "I've been waiting for this all day."

Through a mouthful, she added directly to Luce, "Slate loves the footage of you and Drake. Thank you. He's been struggling with how to open the film. No pun intended, but that's picture-perfect."

He might be happy about the picture, but Drake wasn't. Faintly, Luce said, "My pleasure."

CHAPTER EIGHT

IT HAD BEEN a long week.

Drake had come to the conclusion that those shots of him and Luce might be the death of him.

Mostly because everyone knew about their unwitting role in the film, and the ranch hands had plenty to say. His current infamy—because he'd kissed a young woman under a moonlit sky—was drawing laughs from everyone, and not just on the ranch.

"Hey there, Romeo, what can I do for you?" Jack Dunlap, who ran the hardware store, grinned unapologetically. He was a tall, lean man with iron-gray hair who always wore suspenders and, if there weren't any customers, wasn't averse to stepping outside to smoke a cigar. The place was a labyrinth of packed aisles, but he knew where to find every nut, bolt and screw, and tell a customer exactly how to use every item he sold.

Romeo. Drake was pretty sure he could thank Mace for the new nickname, although he couldn't prove it. In a very short time, it seemed that everyone in Mustang Creek had heard the story. It didn't help that the entire population of Bliss County was fascinated by the idea that Slater was filming a documentary right there. His out-of-town crew was staying at the resort, eating at the local restaurants, shopping at the stores, so it could've been one of those blabbermouths. He'd decided to ignore it all.

When he could, anyway.

"I have a list." He handed it over to Jack. "Most of it's for Mace. He's planning to build a newfangled contraption for fermenting a certain kind of wine, I guess. I just need the usual to do repairs in the stables."

Jack slipped on a pair of spectacles and surveyed the list. "Can do. Take me about fifteen minutes. Heard what you did for Thelma. She's hopping mad at you."

That was Thelma, but it probably meant she was hopping mad because he'd found out she'd cried over the gesture in front of people. They were in real trouble now.

"Did it for Frankie," Drake said blandly. "And it was all of us. Point me in the right direction and I'll help you with this list."

"Back of the store, last aisle, for those hinges. I'll get the rest."

As Drake headed toward the right section, he rounded a corner and came face-to-face with one of the few people he truly detested. Reed Keller straightened, a box of roofing nails in his hand. "Carson. Or I guess I should call you Romeo?"

He tolerated it from Jack, but he had his limits.

"Keller." Drake nodded curtly, trying to ignore the man's smirk. He walked past as swiftly as possible. They'd clashed since grade school when he'd caught Keller pushing Mace around, and their relationship hadn't improved in high school, when Keller deliberately went after Drake's girlfriend.

The ploy had worked for him, too. She and Drake broke up, Keller had gotten her pregnant—there went Danielle's dreams of college—and married her. They had a couple of kids now, but he'd heard they'd recently separated.

Not his business.

Still, seeing the guy at all added a sour note to his day.

Exactly fifteen minutes later, just as Jack had promised, Drake was in his truck, on the way home. He thought the day was improving—until he saw Red outside the barn with Luce, leaning on a shovel and definitely chatting her up. He had the distinct feeling there was another Romeo reference in his future.

He parked the truck, texted Mace that he'd bought his supplies so his brother could come and unload them.

Unfortunately for him, Luce looked *very* cute in a pair of jeans and a T-shirt, with her hair whipped back into a no-nonsense ponytail as usual. She was wearing her hiking boots and held a lightweight backpack slung over her arm.

"Hey, Romeo." Yup, just as he'd predicted. Red obviously thought he was being funny.

Luce blushed. Drake took it in stride. "First time I've heard that today? Uh, not really. Word of warning, I'm starting to lose my sense of humor over this."

Red adjusted his position. He might be older, and was certainly wiser, but he understood boundaries. He raised his hands. "Just joshing, son. Usually, you let it roll off your back. What has you as grouchy as a grizzly crawling out of his cave on a spring day?"

"Yeah, well, word about that film is all over town." He took out the bag with the new latches for two of the stalls and slammed the door of his truck.

Red winked at Luce. "Who cares if the world knows you kissed a pretty girl?"

Exasperated, he avoided looking directly at the woman in question. "I don't particularly care, but surely people have something more important to talk about. Slater kisses Grace about fifty times a day— I'm always walking in on them by accident. No one hangs around talking about it. I'm going to replace those two latches and then ride out to the north pasture. Mind helping Mace with his stuff?"

"Don't mind at all." Red ambled toward the truck.

"I feel I should apologize for something, but I don't know what." Luce smiled tightly.

Drake wasn't taciturn by nature, or didn't think he was, anyway, and he relented, meeting her eyes. "It isn't you. I ran into someone who called me that, and while I don't mind being razzed a little, I didn't appreciate it from this person. We have some history. You have absolutely nothing to apologize for."

He was the one who'd kissed *her*, after all, not just once but twice, and he really wouldn't mind doing it again, but next time he'd check for hidden cameras.

"I'm hiking up to the ridge to see if the horses are there again this afternoon," she said.

"If you want to wait a few minutes, I can take you most of the way." That was the least he could do. He hadn't been very cordial since he'd run into Keller, but he shouldn't take it out on anyone else, particularly not Luce.

She didn't look too enthusiastic. "On your horse?"

"Yeah, on my horse. If I tried to walk everywhere on a ranch this size, I wouldn't get anything done. I do use the ATV sometimes, but it spooks the cattle. Horses work best. Always have and still do. Luce, you're the one who thinks you can tame a wild stallion! Maybe you need to get used to horses. I'm talking about real horses. Not just horses as an abstract idea or an academic interest."

Defensively, she shot back, "All I want is for Smoke to trust me so I can get close enough to observe them better. I never said I'd tame him, nor did I say I want to ride."

"Riding him would be a neat trick."

"You know full well I didn't mean him."

He was just teasing her, but also serious. "Your choice. It's quite a distance on foot as *you* know full well. Starburst and I can take you about halfway. I just have to change out these latches on a couple of stalls. Won't take me long."

She was still thinking it over when he walked away, but he did have things to do, and as much as she might promise she wasn't going to interfere with his daily life, she already had. He found it entertaining that she was so eager to be around the wild horses, and yet Starburst, who was perfectly well behaved, intimidated her.

He used his handheld drill to remove the old latches on the stalls, attached the new ones quickly and then put his tools away.

As it turned out, Luce had decided to wait.

Judging by the tilt of her chin, she'd done it because he'd practically dared her, but he knew one thing.

He was looking forward to that ride.

DRAKE FELT WARM and solid as Luce sat behind him on the saddle. She was determined to put on a brave front, so when he urged the big horse into a gallop, she did her best not to panic.

As promised, he took her about five miles in easily half the time it would've taken her to walk, reined in near a field of grazing cows and dismounted to lift her off.

She appreciated the courtesy and was getting used to the fact that Drake Carson was a man of old-fashioned manners. A man who took care of other living creatures and was used to physical work, he thought nothing of picking up another person—

literally!—and transferring her from point A to point B.

"It isn't smart to hike out here alone, especially if you're not used to rugged country. I hope that's come to your attention," he told her in his low drawl. "Don't be fooled by all the scenic wonders—the place came to be called the Wild West for a reason. Lots of bad-tempered critters around, besides wild horses. We have venomous snakes, bears, big cats. And of course people can be the most dangerous predators of all. I can't stop you, but I can tell you I don't like it."

Fair enough. He was giving her practical advice without being dictatorial, and she appreciated it. "I carry pepper spray."

"Not a bad precaution. But all I'm saying is be alert. An animal, human or otherwise, can catch you unawares."

Smiling, she said, "So you want me to survive to annoy you another day? I'm surprised."

"No, you aren't."

Okay, she wasn't. Not really. He wasn't just another good-looking cowboy; he was a kind man, a decent one. Whether he liked her or not, he wouldn't want any harm to befall her. "Drake, I—"

He raised a hand. "Look, be careful, okay? There's no cell service as you go higher up. I sure hope you put on sunblock if you won't wear a hat."

"You aren't my big brother. Stop with the lecture."

"Lecture's over." He swung onto his horse in a

single smooth movement and touched the brim of his hat. "And just so we're clear, I'm happy I'm not your brother. Have a nice walk. Wave hi to Smoke for me."

With that, he rode off and left her standing there, watching him go. She squared her shoulders. The ridge where she knew the horses frequently grazed was still some distance away. She headed off in that direction, and thanks to his advice, she was more aware of her surroundings rather than simply preoccupied with her destination. It was a lovely sunny day so, yes, she'd put on a combination of insect repellent and sunscreen. The wildflowers were entrancing, and since she wasn't a botanical expert, she didn't know specifically what kind they were. But every variety was beautiful. Yellow, blue, red, violet...

She heard the familiar snort and immediately halted. The horses were much closer than she'd realized, having moved down toward the ranch. She was starting to grasp the dynamic of how the horses interacted with the ranch, which was exactly what she wanted.

They did intrude periodically, but then they made themselves scarce.

Smoke was there, on the fringes of his herd, watching her. He had an elegant head, reminiscent of Spanish horses in historical pictures she'd seen, and although he was cautious, she got the impression that maybe, just maybe, he knew she wasn't a threat. Such as when he'd drunk from the stream even though she was there.

He turned away and went back to grazing, cropping the long grass.

To her mind, that was progress.

Some of the mares in the herd were used to people, so she didn't worry too much about them. She eased closer very cautiously so they didn't all run. Unfortunately, Drake was right; she didn't know enough about horses. Still, she was learning more every day.

The mares with foals watched her, as did Smoke. When he lifted his head, she stood her ground and waited. Evidently, he'd confirmed that she wasn't a threat, because he didn't come any closer, but let her stay perched behind some sort of conifer, probably a Douglas fir. She got some good snapshots and started on her notes, sitting cross-legged behind the tree. The mustangs tolerated her presence. Smoke was paying attention, but he obviously wasn't worried, and that was her goal.

Trust.

It couldn't be bought, and it couldn't be sold, and in her view, it was the most important commodity in the world. Smoke trusted that she wasn't there to threaten anyone, so he wasn't worried about her.

Step one.

She did observe some of the horses taking an interest in her, but the stallion quickly shut that down. She assumed they were some of the mares Drake had griped about losing. Smoke shooed them back into the group, and he got no argument.

She wrote: *It's interesting. He's a dictator and yet protects them all. From what I understand, when the younger males start to challenge him, they'll either win or be driven out. Not a democracy. His private fiefdom is under guard at all times.*

When she looked up again, she suddenly noticed that one of the foals was missing.

She checked her notebook twice. The little black one with the white star on his forehead was gone. She'd carefully noted them all over the past few weeks, describing them, and she was horrified. She even tried to call Drake, but he was right; her cell didn't work up this far.

Darn it, there were tears in her eyes.

As if Drake could fix it. As if he could rush in and save the day, find the colt or filly and solve the problem.

Luce sat down on a fallen log. Okay, she told herself, maybe she didn't know how to ride horses, but she did love them. Where did that little one go?

The sound of a horse nickering made her look up. Smoke stood about twenty feet away. She felt that an unspoken understanding had passed between them and that he recognized her concern.

"I hate to lose any of them," she said quietly, at the risk of sending the horse flying away because she'd spoken. "I can't even imagine how you feel."

The stallion took a tentative step toward her, then another one, until he stood less than a yard away. She couldn't believe it.

Under other circumstances, she might've taken his picture, but this wasn't that kind of moment.

This was…private.

Not that she was an expert, but she estimated that he got close enough to take in her scent. His breath ruffled her hair. She stayed perfectly still. Then he whirled around in a graceful movement and galloped off.

CHAPTER NINE

DRAKE WASN'T SITTING on the porch because he was waiting for a certain hiker to show up, safe and sound.

Nope. Absolutely not.

A man had every right to sit on his own porch and enjoy a cold beer.

No reason to worry about Luce because she happened to be a tenderfoot.

No reason at all.

He wasn't fooling his older brother. Next to him—in one of those rocking chairs their mother insisted on that were actually quite comfortable—Slater said, "Relax. She isn't an idiot. Far from it. Grace tells me Luce is a very experienced hiker."

Was he that transparent? He sure as hell hoped not. Drake summoned up his most indifferent expression. "I'm just sitting here having a beer. How'd the filming go today?"

"Nice try, Ace. Sometimes deflection works, but not tonight. Don't worry, I'm not going to initiate a deep, soulful discussion about your tender feelings. I'm saying the woman intended to camp up near that ridge during this whole study deal, so just because she's staying with us doesn't mean you get to monitor when she comes home—like she's a teenager out on a date or something. She knows better than to miss dinner. If she isn't smart enough to keep on Harry's good side, then I've severely misjudged the woman."

Drake nodded. Being late for dinner...no way you'd want to do that.

He could deny his concern, but he doubted that would work. "I should have ridden up there."

His brother mimicked their mother's skeptical expression. "You have time for that?"

"I'm sitting here having a beer with you, aren't I?"

"A rare occasion."

It was true. He didn't knock off this early very often.

"I was basically done for the day."

His brother wasn't buying it. "No, you're sitting on this porch worrying about her."

Maybe. He couldn't disagree. "Big mountains out there."

"Yes, big mountains. Drake, it isn't a bad thing to admit you're concerned about Luce."

He thought it over, boot heels on the railing. This was going to be a beautiful sunset. "I don't think that the words *concern* or *worry* really apply. I just wish she'd show up so I could forget about her and not have to wonder if she's been eaten by a bear—or attacked by a wild horse. That would sure make my life easier."

Slater choked on his beer, laughing and wiping at his shirt. "A woman shows up and makes your life easier? Oh, yeah, happens all the time." Then he sobered. "She might make your life better, but not *easier.*"

"So speaks a married man."

"So speaks a happily married man. Grace is the love of my life, but is it easier? Nope."

"Wait until that baby arrives." Drake chortled as he imagined his older brother changing diapers. That mental image made the beer taste even better.

"Well, laugh it up all you want, but I think you've caught the same disease I have, and there isn't a cure."

"You're talking about love. Lust isn't the same thing."

"I agree. Completely."

That shook him more than a little. "She's smart and she's pretty. With the full moon and all, it was… just a kiss."

"I kinda thought the same thing with Grace. Just a kiss. Wrong. But at least you can relax. Here she comes."

Drake knew his relief was telling. He had to force himself not to get to his feet; he managed to stay camped in his chair until Luce reached the porch. Then he *had* to stand or his mother would have his head. Slater got up, too. His faint smile was irritating, but Drake could live with it better than with Keller's.

Luce sent him a direct look. Her shirt had wet spots

on it from perspiration and she seemed distressed and out of breath. Yet she still managed to look damn beautiful, even after hiking about a million miles. "We've got a missing foal."

Her expression asked what he was going to do about it. That signal came through loud and clear.

"Okay," he said tentatively, waiting for her to explain.

"It isn't okay at all! I mean *missing*. I was there all afternoon. He's gone."

There could be any number of explanations. Horses got sick, just like any other creature. The foal could have wandered off and gotten lost. Mares were vigilant, but mistakes did happen in the natural order of things. Or there could be a predator stalking the horses, like the one taking his calves now and then. He said in what he thought was a patient tone, "I get it, Luce, but you can't expect me to ride herd—so to speak—on a bunch of wild horses. I've lost calves, too."

He and Slater exchanged a glance. "You thinking what I'm thinking?"

"Sure am." This wasn't news, more like an unwelcome update. "It's a big cat." Drake threw it out there as he grew more certain. "I thought it was wolves, but no, a mountain lion's staked out territory around here. He's got to be big, too. Remember that mauled deer I found last year?"

His brother nodded. "Could be a she. And if she's got little ones, she'd be more dangerous than a male."

That was a valid point. He turned toward Luce. "You're not going up there alone, not anymore."

She obviously resented his authoritative tone. Leaning against the porch railing, she snapped, "Excuse me? *What* did you just say?"

Perhaps he should've put it differently, but he stuck to his guns. "How much clearer do I need to be?"

"There's this part where you get yourself declared my legal guardian. Otherwise, you don't have jurisdiction over what I do and don't do. I believe you mentioned earlier today that you can't stop me."

"I've changed my mind. Carson ranch, Carson rules."

"How am I supposed to study the horses, then?"

"Figure it out, but you aren't going up there alone."

She pulled the high card, taunting him. "I bet Harry would back me up. I know your mother and my mother would."

"Maybe." But in this case, maybe not. Harry was no stranger to how things operated in these parts, and if there was danger, he didn't think either of their mothers would be on board. "I doubt it, though. You aren't a regular part of a mountain lion's diet, but on the other hand, they aren't picky. They've attacked people before. You don't weigh more than the last calf I lost."

"Oh, that's comforting. Are you comparing me to a cow?"

Drake groaned. He'd stepped into that one. He'd said *calf*, but maybe he should just abandon this particular tack. Instead, he turned to his brother. "What do you think?" he asked. "She shouldn't go up there on her own, right?"

"If I want to be part of an argument, I'll hang out with my very pregnant wife. I'd advise you to take Grace with you, Luce, but I doubt she's up for the long walk—and she insists on working until the day she goes into labor. However, I maintain that at this time she could kill a mountain lion with her bare hands." Slater rose, saying over his shoulder, "See you two at dinner. Have fun resolving this."

He beat it, and Drake envied him that option. He sighed. "Luce, I worried about you all afternoon."

Finally, he'd apparently said the right thing. She leaned back against the railing, arms tightly crossed. But she softened. "Oh," she said in a quiet voice.

"I had work to finish, but I was too distracted because I was anxious about you."

"That's sweet."

Probably the last thing he'd ever wanted to be called was *sweet*. It was better than her being mad at him, but sweet? "I don't want you eaten by a rogue cougar. I hardly think that qualifies as sweet. Don't feel special, okay? I don't want *anyone* eaten by a big cat."

"I was referring to how you worried about me all day."

"Afternoon," he corrected.

She waved a hand loftily. "I'm going with *all day*."

The breeze stirred her ponytail; he wished he hadn't noticed that.

And the flirtatious smile she gave him did something interesting to his composure. He made an effort to lean casually against the railing, too. "Look, Luce, Slater can put up remote cameras near the ridge. Then you can skip going off by yourself and still watch the horses."

"That's like sitting on the couch watching television! No, thanks. I came all the way here for the full experience."

And his mother referred to *him* as stubborn? "You can't stay up there by yourself for weeks. Are we really going to continue this conversation?"

"Nope. I'm off to have a shower before dinner. Harry told me she's making French chicken. Not sure what that means, but I trust it'll be fantastic."

It was, and *he* trusted that this discussion wasn't over.

Dinner was divine.

The chicken, simmered in white wine with garlic and then served with crispy potatoes, and a salad tossed with homemade green goddess dressing would have shamed the most elite foodie place in California.

"So, Moonshine, how's the still coming along?" Drake asked between helpings. Luce was fairly sure he was going for his third.

Mace responded, "It's not a still. I'm trying out

what I think will be a better fermentation process for a small line of liquors."

Drake looked at Luce and said in a loud whisper, "It's a still. No wonder he wanted me to buy the stuff for it, so *I'll* look like the guilty party if he gets caught making his illicit potions."

"What you know about making wine—or any kind of potable—could fit in the stomach of a tree frog." Mace plucked a roll from the basket on the table. That quaint expression had Red written all over it. She choked, laughing, on a sip of wine.

"How big is the frog?" Slater asked helpfully with a grin.

Mace grinned, too. "Real small. One of those little green ones about the size of your fingertip."

"It isn't useful knowledge in my chosen profession." Drake said it in a superior tone. "By the way, that last lemon bar has my name on it."

"Like hell it does," Grace piped up. "You all sit there swilling your wine and I can't have any, so that last lemon bar is for me and Junior."

"I'd listen to her, guys. She's in as good a mood as a rattlesnake branded with a red-hot poker." That was Ryder, Grace's teenage stepson, and his grin echoed Slater's. He was fifteen, Blythe had confided. His father was in the military, and even though he and Grace were divorced, she'd taken on her ex-husband's child, because his birth mother had no interest due to a second marriage and other children. Luce was under the impression that his father was gone most of the time, so when Slater and Grace got married, Ryder had been part of the deal.

The Carsons were an interesting family, to say the least.

Drake immediately passed the plate to his sister-in-law. "You win hands-down, Grace."

"You've always been my favorite. Thank you." She grabbed the last cookie.

"Hey!" Both Mace and Slater said it.

After dinner, the ritual seemed to be that the men cleared the table while the women, including Harry, sat and had a cup of tea or decaf coffee. The dining room suited the overall grand style of the house, and the table was obviously an heirloom that could comfortably seat the whole crowd. There was a stunning quilt hanging above an old sideboard, and Luce couldn't help commenting on it. "I love that as a wall decoration."

"It's by Hadleigh Galloway," Blythe told her. "She owns the quilt shop in town. She does beautiful work. You can commission one if she doesn't have what you want. I promise you won't be disappointed."

The image of wild horses immediately danced through her head. "Really? I might stop by there."

"She's super nice, too." Grace yawned. "Is it too early for bed? Maybe I ate too much."

"Or maybe there isn't a lot of room in there for food. He's growing like a weed," Harry suggested with a kindly twinkle in her eye, although her expression was stern. "I just ordered a book online about making homemade baby food. No jarred stuff for the new addition."

They'd learned that it was a boy, but Grace and Slater had refused to reveal the name they'd chosen, to the amusement of the whole family, Luce gathered.

Grace certainly didn't argue. "If you make it, I bet he'll eat it when the time comes for solid food. Anyway, I'm off to bed. I have a romance novel waiting for me and hopefully about ten hours of sleep."

Blythe was laughing as her daughter-in-law departed. "I enjoy this experience a lot more when someone else is going through it. But I can't wait to hold this one in my arms, even though the last thing we need around here is another male."

Harry got up, too. "Ain't that the truth. I have to go to the kitchen to see what's happening. Those boys could be doing anything. I hear a lot of banging of dishes and pans."

"Who knows?" Blythe shrugged, still smiling. "They need to be managed. I'll go with you."

That left Luce to wander out onto the veranda by herself, tea in hand, until Drake suddenly joined her. "I was banished," he informed her. "I wash, they're supposed to dry and put away. But Harry took over my job, probably because of you. My mother not so subtly suggested we go for an evening stroll. That's how she put it—stroll."

He sounded disgruntled enough that Luce sent him a mischievous smile. "I take it there's a country song out there called 'Real Cowboys Don't Stroll'?"

"I couldn't tell you. Now, I'm going to *stroll* to the stables to check on the horses like I do every night, so if you'd care to join me, feel free. It's another pretty night, but Red says tomorrow's going to be as blustery as an old hag on a rant."

"Oh, come on, he didn't say that. You're making it up. I think you're all teasing me by inventing Red-speak."

Drake looked boyishly unrepentant. "Okay, yeah, I did make that up. But doesn't it sound like something he'd say? What he did say is that the weather's going to turn. That man should've been a meteorologist. He's right. You can count on it." He gestured toward the porch steps. "I know you've walked your share today, but shall we?"

It really was another lovely evening, and for once the incessant wind wasn't blowing. Maybe it was the calm before the storm. "Thank you. I need to walk off dinner, anyway. If you think Red should've been a meteorologist, I think Harry should be a chef somewhere in Paris, basking in her four-star rating. The chicken was superb."

"Not gonna argue with that one." He followed her down the steps and walked beside her, slowing his pace to match hers. "How's the research paper coming?"

Nice of him to ask, especially since he hadn't wanted anything to do with it in the first place. "I'm still making notes," she told him. "I have pictures and videos of the horses, and I know this is a sore subject, but thanks to your descriptions, I've identified the mares that were yours and belong to the herd now. So to sum up, it's coming along nicely."

"Glad to be of help," he said sarcastically.

"I'm not trying to rub salt in a wound, I swear it."

"I believe you." He had his hands in his pockets and his expression was reflective. "I also believe that life involves weighing decisions, and figuring out if they're good or bad. I realize some people don't bother with that—they see only one approach, which is usually whatever they've already decided. I have to consider every situation from as many angles as possible." He shrugged. "All I can do is my best. The reality is that these wild horses are a problem for someone in my position."

"I know. I owe you an apology, or perhaps a couple of them. I'm too focused at times. I admit that."

"Darlin', if you think I haven't noticed that you're too focused at *all* times, you're mistaken. In my defense, this is my life and this is who I am. I can't change that."

Truer words were never spoken. He was *him*. Drake Carson.

"Why would you want to?" She meant it. "We don't understand each other all that well, but I wouldn't want you to change. And I wouldn't try to change you."

His response was unexpected—a low groan. "Don't do that."

"Don't do what? Give you a compliment?"

"No. But my mother always told me never to get involved with a woman who wanted to change me. It's a life lecture she gives all her sons. She likes you already, so I'll keep that information to myself."

She liked Blythe, as well. "*Are* we involved?"

Maybe she'd just said the wrong thing.

"You tell me."

She winged it. "Yeah, it might be leaning that way. Like a knotty pine on a windy slope."

"Not bad, but my try at Red-speak was better."

This time she really did give him a playful punch in the gut. It was flat and well muscled, which didn't surprise her because she'd seen him stripped to the waist. "Quit that, or I'll beat you up," she said.

"Think you can take me?"

Maybe she was falling in love with him because of his smile. He didn't show it often, but when he did, it was memorable.

"Oh, come on. My saying was a good effort, right?"

"It was too poetic. It should be more like 'Does manure fall in a horse stall?'"

"Well, I'll take that advice."

Then he kissed her for the third time. Best one yet. They were in each other's arms, and Luce knew this was exactly what Blythe had intended, and yet it was hard to resent when it turned out so well. There was a lowering dusk and privacy, and Drake's body against hers...

He lifted his head. "I forgot to check."

Luce had to admit she was dazed from that kiss. "Check?"

"For cameras." He scouted theatrically around. "I don't see any, but that means nothing. I'm not Showbiz with his diabolical staff, planting surveillance equipment everywhere, so I don't get how they think. Who knows where they might've put one? Under a bale of hay? Strapped to the belly of a horse? It's possible."

One of the things she liked most about him—aside from that smile—was that he had a dry sense of humor. Grace had told her he was one of the funniest people she'd ever met, and Luce could see why. "You're being paranoid," she told him, hiding her own smile.

"Damn straight I am. After what happened last time, shouldn't I be?"

"No one will know who we are."

"Really? Is that why everyone around here is calling me Romeo? But that's not even my point. It was supposed to be just you and me. First kiss. Alone."

He certainly didn't have to take Romance 101. He got an A—due to his natural talent, she supposed. "A kiss is more than just a kiss?"

"Wasn't it? To you?"

"It was." Luce took a breath. "Do you even have to ask me that?"

"No." He let her go and walked about five feet away. "I didn't see this particular storm on the horizon, that's all."

"I'm a storm? Isn't *that* too poetic?"

"Kind of." He swung around. "I'm afraid if I kiss you again, we're going to end up on some horizontal surface, comfortable or not."

"And since neither of us do casual—"

"And you live in California," he interrupted, but he reached for her again and pulled her against him, their mouths no more than an inch apart.

Who knew what might have happened next if Ryder hadn't come down the path to the stables just then, carrying a small sack of apples. He stopped dead in his tracks when he saw them in an embrace. "Oh, uh, s-sorry," he stammered, looking embarrassed. "I was going to give these to the horses…"

Drake didn't miss a beat. As he released her, he said in an easy tone, "I was about to check on them, so that works. Let's go do it. Luce?"

"I'll wait here and admire the view." Luce chose to not join them, but she stood on the path, gazing up at the starlit sky.

"Sure. I'll see you in a few minutes."

After they'd walked away, she whispered out loud, "Well, *now* what do I do?"

The stars didn't answer but twinkled cheerfully back. Even Venus, hanging low on the horizon, just smiled serenely.

CHAPTER TEN

THE STARS WERE not on his side.

Not that he was a big believer in the zodiac or in horoscopes, but he could tell he wasn't going to win anytime soon. Unless you counted one very intent graduate student and a slew of horses he'd never wanted in the first place, he was on his own. So Drake was resigned to navigating this love business without any other guidance.

Oh, his mother and Harry would be glad to chime in, but he had a feeling he knew what their advice would be.

Get together with the pretty girl and settle down. Have babies.

Ryder wasn't helpful. "She's really cool."

"Luce?" He fed Trader—an aging gray gelding who was extremely picky about letting anyone come close to him—an apple. "I think so," he said slowly.

"Kinda noticed that." The kid was too grown-up for his age, but at the same time, refreshingly honest. His expression was sheepish. "Sorry I showed up right then."

"Don't worry about it." That had probably been

for the best, anyway. Although privacy seemed to be in short supply these days… Still, despite that, he wouldn't have traded where he lived for anywhere else in the world.

"What she's doing is pretty interesting." Ryder handed an apple to one of the mares. He was a natural with the horses, which had surprised everyone, since he was a city kid who'd been transplanted from Seattle to Mustang Creek.

"*She's* interesting, for sure."

"What's going to happen with the wild horses?"

Oh, great. All he needed was another bleeding heart on Luce's side. "I have to run a ranch. They can't stay here."

"You aren't going to shoot them!"

"Jeez, Ryder, you know me better than that. Do I seem like someone who'd shoot them?"

"Okay, no. Sorry. But we already have horses. Can't we keep those other ones, too? The wild horses?"

He checked the water in one of the stalls. "The size of that herd has doubled since they decided to take up residence. A few of them isn't a problem, but a lot of them really is. Where would you suggest we keep them? We need the grazing land for the cattle. Our horses are useful. The wild ones aren't, and they impact the ecological balance. And let's not even talk about our missing mares. I've lost stock and I've spent time and money repairing fences. They're an expensive nuisance—especially that damned stallion."

Ryder frowned. "Guess I hadn't looked at it that way."

"I have." Luce was standing in the stable doorway of the stable, her arms crossed. He couldn't help noticing that the light caught her hair.

He handed over the last apple, patted the neck of the horse munching away and turned to face her. "But your whole purpose is to study them—and protect them, right? Not to interfere with the herd."

"At the beginning. Now I see the whole situation with…more complexity." Her voice was soft and her eyes looked like shimmering gold.

Had he really just thought "shimmering gold"? He was an idiot.

He weighed every response he could make that might reverse the idiot progression, but he couldn't find one.

Fortunately, Ryder spoke up. "This place kind of grows on you. I didn't want to come here at all when Grace told me where we were going, but now I like it." *Way to go. Good sell.*

The only question was how she'd respond. "I like it, too."

Nothing definitive there, but he'd take it. Drake muttered, "Then stick around."

Why'd he say that? He had no idea. When she'd arrived, he'd wanted nothing more than for her to leave pronto.

She quickly caught on. "Is that an open invitation?"

Ryder started to get the gist of their conversation.

He hurried toward the stable door. "Uh, I've got some homework to do."

They both watched him scoot outside.

"He just ditched us for homework. That's a powerful rejection of our company right there." Drake put the bucket away and washed his hands in the big metal utility sink.

"He's a nice young man."

"Thanks to Grace. And Slate, too. I sometimes forget he isn't actually their kid. Ryder might've gotten into real trouble if both of them hadn't stepped in. When Showbiz first asked me if the kid could work here, I was skeptical. However, I will say, if you work with Red, you *work*. He doesn't tolerate anything but the best you can give. Ryder stepped up."

"Good for him. And good for you."

"I didn't do anything."

"Drake, yes, you did. Grace told me you helped out so much with Ryder she can't thank you enough."

Sure, he had empathy for kids trying to find their way. Who didn't? "It isn't easy being a teenage boy," he said. "Your body changes, more and more people expect you to take care of yourself, to act responsible. You start to look at girls in a whole new light. I believe I was looking at you like that when he walked in on us." He needed to clarify something. "Feel free to weigh in, but I don't think our agreement to stay detached is working out."

"Not so much," Luce agreed. Then she added in

an offhand tone, "Oh, I'm camping up on the ridge tomorrow night."

Like hell.

He stared at her. "Didn't we recently have this conversation? No, you aren't."

"I'm not doing this project on a sort-of basis. I have to observe the horses at night."

"You do know you're trying my patience."

"No, I'm objecting to your assumption that you have the right to tell me what to do. Not the same thing."

"Luce."

"I have it on excellent authority that I'm not the mainstay of a mountain lion's diet. Wait, that would be yours. The authority, I mean."

"I'll join you."

"On the ridge? Oh, *that's* a good idea."

"You aren't staying up there alone." He paused, then said recklessly, "We can share a tent, tell campfire stories, roast marshmallows, stuff like that."

At least he'd made her smile. "Yeah, I'm sure that's precisely what we'd be doing."

"Remember, the weather's supposed to get nasty. We might have to stay in the tent."

She tilted her head, all that fabulous hair brushing her shoulders. "That's what you're going for, isn't it, cowboy? Same tent?"

"Same sleeping bag, something like that."

"I'm not going to be able to stop you, am I?"

She had that right. He offered her another option.

"You could abandon the whole idea and sleep alone in a nice, safe, dry house. Or you can share a tent with me."

"I've camped alone before, and a little rain won't hurt me, and—"

Drake cut her off. "I think we have a date. Now, let me walk you back to the house, and then I need to close the front gate. After that, I'm going straight to bed. It's been a long day."

LUCE SET ASIDE her almost-empty cup of hot chocolate, hoping that the splash of peppermint liqueur Harry had dashed in with a sly wink would help her sleep. Her secret recipe, the older woman had confided, guaranteed to cure whatever ailed you.

Somehow, Luce thought a cup of heavenly chocolate might not do the trick for her particular affliction.

What she needed was good old-fashioned therapy in the form of girl talk.

There was only one thing to do—call Beth Madison, her older sister and best friend.

After only one ring, she got an answer. "*Mi chica!* What, you psychic? I was just thinking about you. How's life out there in the Wild West? Please tell me they have indoor plumbing."

Considering that she was sitting at a polished mahogany desk in a guest room that could vie with a suite in the most elegant hotel... She glanced around at the silk bedspread and pillows, reading lamp and chair, wall-mounted television with about a million channels, plus a private bathroom. "Yes," she said drily. "They do, believe it or not."

"That's good news. I'm relieved. Men can pee in the woods and all, but for us it's a dicier proposition."

Luce was already laughing, which wasn't unusual after about two seconds on the phone with her older sister. "I often spend all day outside. You get used to the lack of facilities. What are you doing? It's not too late to call, is it?"

"I'm doing yoga. I need some form of relaxation after the diaper I just changed. Who knew a six-month-old could wipe out a whole outfit and his crib sheet in one fell swoop? Or do I mean poop? I won't go into the dreadful details, but a bath was involved. Is it too early for potty training?"

"Six months is probably pushing it, but I'm not an expert. My impression is that they have to be able to walk and maybe even talk." Luce laughed again, knowing that Beth adored her son, born after years of trying. "Have you decided whether you're going back to work?"

"Greg and I talked it over, and after several different versions of what added up to basically the same conversation, I'm going to work part-time from home. I'm on the computer all day, anyway. Who cares if I'm sitting in my sweatpants—I still need to lose about ten pounds—at home, or in an office. I think it'll work for all of us if I cut back a little, since it means I can stay home with Ian."

"Makes sense to me. Day care is good, but Mom is better, right?"

"That's our take on it. Baby sister, why'd you call? There's a reason. I can hear it in your voice."

Beth knew her. Luce fiddled with the handle on her cup for a second and then sighed. "I need some advice. You love Greg."

"I must. I live with him, endure his sometimes annoying habits, and we just had a baby together. And let's not forget I married him. You stood beside me at the wedding, remember? Oh, no way! Who'd you meet out there in the wilderness?"

That was her sister. Quirky at times, but always smart as a whip.

"Picture a tall, blond cowboy. Pure Wyoming, from his Stetson down to his dusty boots. He keeps his conversation sparse but really knows how to kiss."

"Woo-hoo! You found *your* cowboy."

"*My* cowboy?"

"Those sound like your requirements. Tall, good-looking and knows how to kiss. You were about fifteen when you spelled that out."

"I'd read a few too many Western romance novels."

"That you pilfered from Mom. I did the same thing. I still read them, by the way. For that matter, so does she. Tell me more about him."

"He doesn't discuss his feelings. He's close to his family, cares about animals and works long hours, but that's not enough of a description. I think, with him, any kind of relationship is an all-or-nothing deal."

"Oh, decision time, is it?"

It felt that way... "Beth, you're jumping to conclusions. I have the job of my dreams lined up in California. Plus, you and Mom and Dad are there."

"You can come and visit us."

"It isn't that simple. I don't even know what I'd do if I stayed here, and worrying about that is presumptuous, anyway. There's no guarantee he'd even *want* me to stay. He told me he isn't interested in casual relationships. I believe that, because if you look like him and *are* like him, you'd certainly have plenty of opportunities..."

"Did you listen at all to what you just said?"

She had. Part of the reason she'd called was to work it out in her own mind. Beth was always a good sounding board. "I'm in trouble, right? I've known the man for less than a month."

"I want to meet this slow-talking, fast-moving dreamboat. Invite him to California."

Only Beth would use the word *dreamboat*. "We aren't serious. We hardly have a relationship! I'm not sure if he'd go, anyway."

"Aren't you? Sounds to me like he would."

Luce tapped her fingers on the desk. "How do you *know*?"

"Good question. I wish I had a better answer, but I guess it's a sense I'm getting. An intuition, if you prefer. Despite what you say, you're responding to this guy and he's responding to you. So…invite him."

"That's not helpful."

"You hate it when I give you advice."

"I listen, but I don't always follow your advice. I just needed to talk to someone about Drake."

Oops. She hadn't intended to mention his name.

Beth pounced. "As in Drake Carson? *That's* who we're having this deep sisterly discussion about? Does Mom know? She'd be thrilled."

"Don't tell her."

"All right." Beth meant it, but her answer was accompanied by a disappointed sigh. She was a person who could keep her mouth shut if she had to. She had flaws—who didn't?—but that wasn't one of them. "If you don't want me to, I won't say a word, but I'm positive she'd be thrilled."

"Thrilled about what? I can't promise anything. He might know how *he* feels, but I'm…uncertain about myself. Am I in love with him? I'm starting to think so. But all the changes to my life plans have to weigh in, too, right? I've been told more than once that he's worth it."

Beth sighed. "You've worked this all out. I'm so glad, because I need to get to sleep soon. My son still wakes up about six times a night. I hate people who tell me their newborns slept through the night on the second day they took them home. Congratulations on figuring everything out and making me do nothing. I knew I adored you."

When they ended the call, Luce stared at her phone and laughed softly. Okay, perhaps she *had* figured it out—to a certain extent. Did she want Drake? She did. He represented an ideal she'd held close her whole life.

However… Kind, compassionate and all those other qualities were important, but there was also the fact that he couldn't and wouldn't change his life. She'd have to do everything on that end. What was more, he was going to relocate those horses. She saw his point, but damn, she hated it. If it was up to her, the entire Carson ranch would be wild-horse heaven.

Her dissertation was getting more and more difficult to write. She powered up her computer and went back to work, anyway. Tomorrow was another day, as Scarlett O'Hara had declared, and she'd analyze it then.

CHAPTER ELEVEN

WHAT DRAKE WAS doing felt like taking out a billboard ad on Times Square, but he didn't have much choice, did he?

He needed shaving cream and toothpaste, but that wasn't the main reason he'd made this trip to town. He eyed the display on the drugstore shelf and reminded himself that he wasn't sixteen, so he shouldn't be embarrassed. But this *was* Mustang Creek, and all the Romeo jokes were about to get worse. If he'd had the time, he would've driven out of Bliss County and shopped someplace else, where everyone didn't know him. But he didn't have the time; he was already going to use part of his morning to ride up with Luce, help her find a decent campsite. He had one in mind, since he and his brothers used to camp out in that area as kids.

He picked up a box of condoms and resigned himself to the fact that the cashier had greeted him by name when he entered the drugstore. He tried to look impassive as he walked to the counter to check out. Maxine was a sweet lady, but she played bridge with his mother in some women's church club, and there was something about buying condoms from a grand-mother of six that made him feel like an adolescent.

With luck he'd need them. Maybe he should look at it that way. Maybe Maxine would just scan it and not notice.

She noticed, of course, with raised eyebrows. At least she didn't address it. Well, not directly, anyway. "How's Grace doing?"

He swiped his credit card. "Good. As far as I know. Slate jokes about her being touchy right now, but she's fine. I think she looks beautiful. He does, too."

Maxine handed him the bag. "You are a very dip-lomatic young man."

"I'm a cautious man," he said and then winced at the unintended reference to his purchase. "Grace re-ally *is* beautiful. I'm not just saying that."

"I've seen her." Maxine was now laughing at him as he tried to scramble around what he'd said. "That she is. Tell your mother and Harry I said hello."

"Sure will." He hotfooted it out of there. With Maxine's tendency to share information, it was a lost hope that everyone would think all he wanted was a clean shave. They'd almost certainly guess he wanted something else—and they'd know what that something else was.

Worrying about it gained him nothing, though, and he preferred not to waste his energy, so he drove home. He hadn't caught the weather report that morn-ing, but he usually didn't bother with it anymore.

Red was invariably correct. And this morning, as he'd predicted, there was a hint of rain in the air—a higher proportion of humidity, which signaled a change from sunshine and blue skies. Unlike Red, Drake wasn't a human barometer, but he'd lived out-doors pretty much his whole life. He could feel a front coming in.

Maybe he could talk Luce out of plans to camp up on the ridge.

Maybe he couldn't.

He already knew he'd lose the argument.

Maybe he didn't want to talk her out of it.

THE MORNING WAS GORGEOUS, but there'd been a red-dish glow on the horizon at daybreak, and Red had warned her as he saddled Starburst that the weather might turn ugly at any time. He eyed her backpack and shook his head.

She assured him she'd be fine.

Drake had suggested they ride up together so he'd know where her campsite was, if she was hell-bent on doing this—his term, not hers. She was more than capable of pitching a tent on her own, but what he'd said made sense; if he really was going to join her later, he should know where to find her.

As she thought about spending the night with him, her stomach did an unfamiliar flip-flop.

"Wait for Drake," Red advised, slapping the side of the horse. "This fella does whatever that boy says, but he doesn't listen to anyone else."

Oh, yeah. Like she'd jump on and ride off. "No worries. Starburst and I are on good terms."

"He does seem to like you. Here you go." He handed her the reins and left her there, holding the horse. Her entire life, she'd heard that if you were nervous around horses or dogs or any other critter with four legs, they knew it and they reacted. So she stood very still and let Starburst take a gander. He was...huge. He sniffed her hair and nuzzled her shirt and apparently decided she wasn't all that interesting. To her relief, Drake walked in just as she was starting to feel she'd fallen short of the horse's expectations.

Drake looked startled, coming in wearing the usual ensemble of faded jeans, boots and, since the air was cool this morning, a red flannel shirt over his white T-shirt. Naturally, his two sidekicks trotted in right on his heels. "*You* saddled him?"

"No. Of course not! I couldn't saddle a turtle."

"That's what I thought. Ryder did it?"

She could swear the dogs had that same inquiring expression.

"No, Red."

Drake did laugh about the turtle comment, although that wasn't flattering.

She needed to learn the art of saddling a horse before she left Wyoming. A whole summer on a ranch and no saddling skills? Yup, she needed to learn.

"Red wouldn't leave you here alone with this big guy. No way."

She took exception to that. "He says Starburst likes me."

Drake nodded. "Starburst's kind of picky about people. I think he knows *I* like you, so he behaved himself. He's a decent guy." Drake affectionately patted the animal's neck.

Luce was relieved to hand over the reins. "I assume that's what Red thought, too, or he's just so used to horses he figures everyone is as comfortable with them."

"Hard to tell with Red. He seems like a down-to-earth soul, but he's a sight more complicated than that. He might've thought that you needed a nudge and counted on Starburst to realize it, too."

"Do I need to apologize for not growing up on a ranch?"

He shook his head. "Now, don't try to make me feel sorry for you."

"Sorry for me?"

"Everyone should grow up on a ranch."

It wasn't as if she didn't realize she was being teased. "My parents have a beach house in Malibu, besides the place in Napa."

"Little rich girl, huh?" He regarded her in that singular way he had. "You very carefully avoid the subject of your family. You want to study wild horses, but you're obviously not used to being around the domestic variety. Your camping equipment is top-of-the-line, and even though you dress down, I think you seem like a Napa girl. I'm guessing you got the invitation from my mother because she knows your family."

It didn't surprise her that Blythe hadn't completely explained the situation to her son, considering the shameless matchmaking going on.

Okay, maybe it was time to come clean. Luce looked into those very blue eyes. "My mother and yours were best friends all through school in California. They took vacations together and were bridesmaids in each other's weddings—real best friends. *I* wrote to your mother, but I suspect there was a private conversation between the two of them. Trust me, I would never have agreed to stay at the house if I didn't know something about the person who invited me."

"I wondered."

"Yes." She put her hands on her hips. "Why didn't you ask before?"

"That information should be offered, not gained by prying into your life."

A valid argument—and perhaps an example of why animals liked him so much. He was laid-back and considerate and didn't invade a person's space. Usually...

He shrugged. "I just *did*."

"Right," she conceded. "And I answered. Now I'm headed up there." She pointed in the direction of the mountains. "If we're going together, let's get moving."

He checked the cinch, probably out of habit. "We can. Let me saddle your horse first."

Her *what*?

"Drake, listen, I—"

"You'll take Grace's mare, Molly, since she's gentle. It'll be faster for both of us."

He was already opening a stall and leading out a very beautiful horse and slipping a halter on her. "Wait while I get the tack. Give her a carrot. Hold your hand out flat like this." He demonstrated. "That way she won't accidentally bite you, because she does love her carrots. I'll be back in a minute."

Luce tentatively held out the carrot he'd given her, following his instructions. It worked out—hand intact, horse docile and happy as she crunched away.

Drake returned with the tack and made short work of it, expertly handling the straps and stirrups, then turned to help her into the saddle. "Ready? I'll take your pack."

As she handed it over, he looked at her skeptically. "There's a tent in here?"

"Seven pounds or so. All-weather, plus a thermal blanket. I've camped before. Oh, and a lunch, courtesy of Harry."

"Then you're ready."

No, she really wasn't. "I didn't count on this when I got up."

"On what? Riding a horse? Things aren't always what we expect them to be. Happens to all of us. I'll give you a leg up. Just relax, and she'll do the rest."

He caught her around the waist and balanced her as she tentatively put one foot in the stirrup. "It'll be fine," he reassured her.

Easy for him to say. However, she did manage to land in the saddle. As he adjusted the stirrup length, he said, "Hold the reins loosely and only use them to communicate with the horse, let her know what you want her to do. This little lady is well trained or Slate would never let Grace ride her. She'll probably just do whatever my horse does. The worst thing that can happen is you fall off, and even the most experienced rider takes a tumble now and then. You get up, dust yourself off and climb back on—just like that old cliché says."

Two seconds later, he was in the saddle, too, and Molly was docilely following Starburst out of the stable.

Once she'd begun to relax, and the horses were walking at a sedate pace, the experience wasn't as intimidating as she'd feared. In fact, with Drake right next to her, the ride was a surprisingly soothing and pleasant experience. Beautiful mountains, handsome man, cool breeze… What more could a girl want?

He pointed to a huge animal grazing by itself in an enclosed pasture. "That's Sherman. Jim Galloway's lined up some good leads on new bulls for me. Sherman's done his time. My father picked him out and I'm pretty fond of that cranky critter. I'm hoping to get one a lot like him. He's dangerous—all bulls can be dangerous—but he's cooperative unless he's riled up. He hates change, so if we keep his routine the same, he's fine. By the way, did you know Slate wasn't always Mr. Showbiz? He competed on the rodeo circuit for a couple of years during college. He was decent at it, too. Those trophies in his office aren't just for his documentaries."

"I noticed them when I was in there." She stopped, not wanting to mention the image of a moonlit kiss. "Come to think of it, I haven't seen *your* office.

His smile was wry. "Don't have one. I keep a ledger and receipts on an old table in the tack room and I bring them to the accountant once a month. Can you picture me sitting in an office? No, thanks. My mother handles everything to do with the house and, of course, Mace takes care of the winery."

"I see what you mean. But I can't picture you in tennis whites, either, although I know you played in college."

"I needed something physical to do if I couldn't have all this for four years." He gestured at the vista around them. "Sending that ball over the net at a hundred miles an hour releases the frustration."

"I heard you could've gone pro." She was pushing it, getting so personal, but that wasn't any more personal than what he'd done—yanking her into his arms and kissing the heck out of her.

"I hate crowds."

That was the Drake Carson she was coming to know. Explanation over in three words. *A possible Grand Slam title and cheers from the stands? No, thank you. I'd rather saddle up, ride out at dawn and get back after dusk, dirty and tired.*

The man wasn't interested in glamour, but she wasn't, either. All those fancy wine-tasting parties with appetizers and swirly dresses were fine once in a while, but they weren't anything special. Not to her—no doubt because she'd grown up with people who talked about the stock market at dinner and drove cars that cost more than some people's houses. Drake was right; she was a rich kid, and her parents would've been happier if she'd decided to become a doctor or a lawyer. Ecology was just more interesting. She loved nature and that was why she enjoyed hiking so much. Looking at film and photographs of the great outdoors was fine, but experiencing it was very different. When her father had suggested a trip to Europe, he'd meant Rome and Paris and London; she'd accepted his offer and hiked the Alps instead.

"I prefer being outside myself." Luce drew a deep breath. "This is a breathtaking place, but so is Napa."

"Are we making comparisons here? Or choices?"

What a question! She floundered for an answer. "Should I be? The only choice I made this morning was to let you force me up on this horse."

"You chose to *let* me *force* you? Hmm. Sounds like a bit of a contradiction."

"Give me a break," she said tartly. "I'm concentrating on not falling off."

"Or into my arms?"

Now she truly had no idea what to say. Drake

Carson was teasing her. Again. She came up with a
retort, although it took her a moment. "At least you
don't seem to have any lack of confidence, despite
your flaws." A little weak, perhaps, but it was the
best she could do under the circumstances.

They were in a meadow of wildflowers that
smelled heavenly. He swept off his hat and scratched
his head, pretending to consider that, but his mouth
was twitching with laughter. "Flaws, huh? Care to be
more specific? I'm always up for self-improvement."

"No, you aren't. You do what you think you
should do, and that's that."

"I hate to be the one to tell you this, but that's not
a flaw. You'd better pick another one."

"You...you argue with your younger brother a lot."

"Nope, that doesn't work, either. *He* argues with
me. Go on." He replaced his hat and adjusted it. "If
you continue at this rate, I'll start to feel damn near
perfect."

"You're...too tall," she said with a laugh.

"Too tall for what?"

She didn't respond but rushed into her next bogus
complaint. "You talk to your dogs more than you
talk to people."

"Hey, Harold and Violet are smarter than most
people. So if I want intelligent conversation, I usually do pick them. They're also very good listeners.
Besides, aren't I talking to you now? That was a compliment, by the way. I said *most* people."

"So, you're saying I'm smarter than your dogs?"

"Oh, heck, no. I was talking about people, re-member."

If she could throw something at him, she would, but then she'd probably fall off and there was nothing available to chuck in his direction, anyway. She agreed with Grace; he was very funny.

And far too attractive.

He pointed at a spot she recognized. "I'm thinking we should pitch the tent there, by that spring. I'd leave Molly with you, but I can't, not with the other horses nearby." He studied the location, a small, protected valley. "Good cover for when it starts to blow."

She looked at the cloudless blue sky. "Are you sure—"

"I'm sure."

CHAPTER TWELVE

THE CLOUDS WERE THICKENING.

"You aren't going to leave that pretty little girl up on that mountain by herself."

Drake glanced up. Red wasn't asking, he was *telling*. Right behind him stood Ryder, and the kid looked as bent out of shape as the old man.

Well, they could back off, both of them. He'd been busting his ass to get everything done so he could take off and he didn't need them crowding him. "Uh, no, I'm not. I'm waiting for Jax Locke to get here so I can talk to him about those two sick cows."

"Wind's picking up."

"You told me it would." Drake straightened. "I checked my phone and the Doppler confirms you have it right, as usual."

"Get going. I'll talk to the doc." For the second time that day, Red had Starburst saddled and ready to go. He handed over a large insulated bag. "This here's a present from Harry. Supper. Don't know what's in there, but I bet it's good."

He'd bet on that, too. He accepted the cooler. "Any instructions?"

"Didn't think you needed any. Just do what *comes* naturally, son." Red guffawed at that remark. Luckily, Ryder had gone back to mucking out stalls.

Oh, news about the condoms had gotten around for sure, but by now Drake was resigned to that. "I meant for the food, Red."

"Sorry, couldn't resist that one." He was still chuckling. "Nah, Harry knows a campfire meal might be kind of difficult tonight, so she kept it simple. No instructions. All she said was *enjoy*."

Drake sensed another bad joke on the way and staved it off by mounting his horse with lightning speed. "I trust you to deal with the situation if those cows need to be quarantined. I don't want the entire herd getting sick."

"I was handling cattle before you were born. Good call to bring in the vet, but I'm guessing he'll agree with me that those two just ate some plant they shouldn't have. I've seen it before." Red waved him off. Drake pointed at the dogs. "Stay."

Both obediently sat down. At least *someone* listened to him.

It was one thing to spend a stormy night in a tent with a beautiful woman, and another to share the experience with two wet dogs.

He went before Red could repeat *enjoy*. He wouldn't have put it past the old coot.

The air smelled like rain, and that rising breeze sounded faintly like a wail. Part of him said he shouldn't have left Luce alone for most of the day, but another part reminded him that she was an intelligent and determined woman, smart enough to take care of herself. Besides, he'd had plenty to do. The first time they met, he'd explained that he wouldn't babysit her, hadn't he?

And yet... If he could, he'd keep an eye on her all day—and night.

He was looking forward to the nighttime shift, in particular.

The darkening sky told him the storm was bound to roll in before sunset. He squinted up at the slate-gray clouds roiling overhead and gave Starburst a gentle nudge to pick up the pace. The horse didn't like the distant sound of thunder, his ears going back.

"You'll have shelter soon," he said reassuringly, patting the horse's neck. "I chose a good spot."

He had. It was a place where he and Slate and Mace had fashioned a lean-to for their horses, back when they were teenagers and still camped out fairly often. It was hardly master construction, but he'd left it because it reminded him of those outings, and no one saw the place, anyway. Truth be told, he'd replaced part of the roof last fall, just in case he ever had the urge to spend a night.

Good decision. The trees sighed as he got closer to the ridge, and flashes of lightning illuminated the silhouette of the mountains.

When he pulled up and slid off the horse, the drizzle had already started, and his boots made a soggy noise as he hit the ground.

Although the tent had been pitched, it was empty. Oh, hell.

He stood there, holding the reins, trying to make a decision. He figured that was the moment he first knew he was in love with Luce Hale, because he was ready to jump back on his horse and go looking for her.

Good luck with that. There was a lot of country out there, and she could walk places he couldn't get to on horseback. He wasn't even sure what direction she'd gone.

She'd done some camping; she wasn't inexperienced.

She'd know enough to come back to the site—wouldn't she?

Drake hated waiting around, but right now, it was the most sensible thing to do.

Another hour passed before Luce finally turned up, and by then, the weather was really going to hell. The wind was practically tearing the tent off its pegs.

He was inside, fretting, thinking he couldn't recall the last time he'd been so on edge.

When someone unzipped the flap of the tent, he actually ran a shaking hand over his face.

She was back. Thank God.

He was instantly furious. "It's about time! Where've you been?"

Luce stumbled through the opening, lost her balance and landed squarely on top of him. There was no room to stand—and he had no objections at all.

It took him two seconds flat to realize she was soaking wet and shivering. Her teeth were chattering. "I jumped in the stream. Not like I had a lot of choice. Oh, thank heaven, you're warm. Take off your shirt."

She certainly wasn't warm. Wet, cold and delightfully female. But she was shaking so much he could hardly understand her.

He stripped off his T-shirt and dropped it. "Jumped in? Why?"

She wrapped her arms around his neck. "I'll get to that. For now, just help me off with my clothes. I'm so cold my fingers don't work."

Well, he wasn't about to refuse that request. He did have questions about her fall in the river, but…

"Hold still." He unfastened the buttons on her blouse. Underneath she wore a camisole thing with a built-in bra; he helped strip that off, too, and she settled against him, bare breasts to his bare chest.

It felt as wonderful as he'd predicted. This had been coming all along and he'd known it, but he hadn't expected it to happen quite this way. Outside, the wind was shrieking.

He asked," You aren't hurt?"

She buried her face in his neck. "No…no. Frozen, but not hurt. What do you do up here, pour ice into your rivers?"

"Mountain runoff." He kissed her underneath her ear. They were very close to altogether naked. He'd had fantasies about this. Her hair was damp and he smoothed it back, combing it with his fingers. "Any warmer?"

"Yes, thanks."

"Get as close as you want."

"I want closer. Take off my jeans."

That would be his pleasure, as long as she was okay with it. His voice was huskier than he'd intended. "Luce, if I do…"

"Take them off. While you're at it, take yours off, too."

"You sure?"

"I am. But I'm so seriously cold I know I couldn't work the zipper."

It was really going to happen. He helped her out of her wet jeans and some very sexy panties he hoped she'd selected just for him. He'd probably set a world record at getting out of his own clothes.

He held her until she stopped shivering. In their intimate position, there was no doubt that she could feel he was interested in a lot more. Her arms were tight around his neck, but they relaxed bit by bit until she sighed against his chest. "Much better."

"Is it okay for me to let go of you for a minute to get something from my pack?"

She artlessly kissed his jaw and ran a hand over his bare chest. "Hmm. What would you need at this particular moment?"

"I assume you'd prefer that we use protection. I'm old-fashioned enough to like things done in the right order."

"Oh! Yes. Glad you're thinking straight. Maybe my brain is still frozen." She shifted onto her side so he could reach over. He'd brought a battery-powered lantern, and the light revealed every supple curve and hollow of her perfect—in his opinion, anyway—body. Nicely rounded breasts, feminine hips that emphasized her long athletic toned legs…

His hands weren't quite steady as he found what he needed and rolled it on.

"Red was right about the storm."

"He always is," Drake agreed as the tent shuddered under another blast from Mother Nature.

"Harry said you need the rain."

"We do."

"I started back here when the sky was getting so dark, but—"

"Luce, stop talking about the weather." He brushed his thumb across her lower lip in a slow caress, pulling her close again.

"Um, sounds like a good idea. Kiss me?"

"That's an offer I won't turn down."

He thought he did a thorough job of it and then moved lower to her breasts. He took a taut nipple in his mouth. There wasn't a single mention of the rain now pelting the tent. There might've been a gasp of enjoyment he missed because of the storm's noise, but he certainly got the message from the arching of her body and the way her fingers ran through his hair.

His own message to Luce was loud and clear.

He wanted her. He'd always believed that meant for his entire lifetime, and that desire and passion were naturally linked to commitment. But now, with the wild storm rushing through, he wasn't going to do anything except make love to her.

The big questions were left for later. The growing love affair, the proposal, the response...

He wasn't ready to propose. Not because he didn't want to head in that direction, but they hadn't really talked about her return to California. Right now, they didn't need to have that conversation.

He slid his hand over the smooth curve of her hip, down her thigh and upward to touch her intimately. She quivered against him, not at all shy about how much she enjoyed it, her thighs parting in unspoken invitation, her hands tightening urgently on his shoulders.

He'd been trying to go slow, take his time, make sure she was ready, and that he wasn't rushing things because his body was sending him signals like the sudden flashes of lightning outside. But apparently she was impatient, too.

"I'm in love with you," he whispered.

He stopped whatever response might have been with a searing kiss. He'd just needed to say it.

HERE SHE WAS, making love with a very sexy cowboy. As usual he didn't want to talk; all he wanted was to get to the business at hand.

She might ask later how he'd learned what he was

doing so well, but she doubted he'd answer. Every touch had been reverent and gentle, and he certainly knew his way around a woman's body. And that brief declaration—good timing. But she wasn't interested in talking. Not yet. Maybe one day they'd have that discussion, but not now. She didn't own his past and he didn't own hers, either.

But…he was in *love* with her?

If anyone other than Drake had said that, she might've thought it was nothing more than an opportunistic line. Drake wasn't like that.

He truly did mean everything he said. Down to the last word.

She wasn't prepared for any life-changing discussion, but she decided she had to say *something*, meet him halfway. "I think about you from when I wake up in the morning until I go to sleep," she admitted. "Is that love? Help me out."

The way he responded was so Drake. "Can't right now. I'm kinda busy."

Busy translated into driving her crazy with his mouth and hands. When he finally did slide deep inside her, she was already on the edge, so that didn't take long at all.

They moved together naturally and were so lacking in awkwardness that she might've marveled at it, but at the moment she couldn't think anything remotely profound.

Sexy cowboy, score one. She wasn't sure she was still breathing after her first orgasm. After the second, she didn't recall her own name. Then, with a fine sheen of sweat on his skin and his face buried in her still-damp hair, he went rigid and groaned in pleasure. They lay there in the breathless aftermath, intertwined, sated, silent. He finally lifted his head. "The storm's passing. Tent stood firm."

Luce traced the arch of his brow with a fingertip. "So far, so good. It could've blown away and I probably wouldn't have noticed."

"Could be a rocky night. Who knows what might happen next." His grin held pure male satisfaction.

He didn't seem inclined to let her go, which was okay with her. Despite the events of the afternoon and the volatile weather, she felt safe nestled there against him. "Could we just live right here?"

It must have been the afterglow talking. He'd never once mentioned marriage and she'd avoided the subject, as well. She was instantly appalled that she'd spoken out loud.

Luckily, he didn't seem fazed. "Too far from the day-to-day on the ranch. Getaway for the weekend, maybe? A nice little log cabin. I bet Slate and Mace would pitch in to build it because they'll want to use it, too. That's a great idea."

"I wasn't suggesting—"

"Suggest away. You could convince me of anything right now." He raked back her hair, feathering the strands with his fingers. "Unfair advantage."

The lantern light and the fading sound of thunder did lend a romantic ambience, and the rain had let up, too.

She looked into his eyes. "I think the advantage is all yours."

"Hope that's true, but we can debate it later. In the meantime, Harry sent us a present. If you aren't starved, I am. Let's see, I spent all afternoon worrying about you and working like a fiend so I could get up here, you fell into an ice-cold river and I still don't know why, and we finally acknowledged something I think we both figured out a long time ago. Oh, I have a dry shirt in my pack. Why don't you wear it so we can have dinner?"

She was hungry, too, she realized now that everything was ramping down.

Or…ramping up.

"I'll borrow the shirt, thanks. And anything Harry sends me is welcome."

"We'll eat first, but after that maybe you could tell me why you fell in the river."

"Deal."

A few minutes later, she was sitting across from him, eating a fabulous Greek sandwich that involved feta, olives and marinated meat she assumed was lamb. The cucumber salad was tangy, and Drake had brought a bottle of Mountain Vineyards wine she'd never tasted before; it was a mellow red she really liked.

Life was good, even sitting in a tent in stormy Wyoming.

It could be good all the time. He'd made the first move. Luce weighed her words carefully. "I have to finish my degree. I can't fall in love right now."

"I have to finish my sandwich. Keep going. Why?"

He looked incredibly sexy in jeans and nothing else, and yes, he did seem hungry. He kept eating.

She gave up. Why fight it. "Okay, fine. I'm in the same untenable position. But there's a difference. You have ties here and I have ties somewhere else."

"*Untenable?* How many people use that in a sentence?"

She would've tossed the rest of her sandwich at him, but it was too good to waste. "You do realize that the reason you aren't married is because you may be the most exasperating person on earth?"

"I'm not married because I hadn't met you yet."

She had to fall for the most forthright, no-nonsense man on earth—and that was exasperating in its own way. She hadn't wanted to discuss it yet, but he'd brought it up.

Love. And marriage?

She chose to deflect the topic. "I can confirm that you do have a mountain lion problem."

The tactic worked. He choked on his last bite. "Excuse me. You can confirm this *how*?"

"I was hiking back here when I noticed something following me. He wasn't shy, either. I turned around and he was standing right behind me."

"Are you okay?"

The single most ridiculous question ever asked. She had to smile. "I think you inspected every inch of me, so you should know I'm fine." Then she shrugged. "He—the lion—was beautiful. He just watched me, but since I thought running would be a bad idea, I chose the stream. I guess he doesn't like that cold water any more than I do. I stayed in until I was positive he'd gone."

Drake helped himself to another sandwich. "This is where I get to remind you that I didn't want you up here alone in the first place."

Luce ate a large bite of salad and washed it down with wine. "Excuse *me* for making the argument that I'd probably be in more danger getting into my car and having some idiot on his cell phone run a red light. The mountain lion was there stalking the horses, not me. Remember the missing foal?"

"I remember. Those big cats have large territories." Drake rubbed his forehead.

"In any case, Smoke scared him away. I'm not going to get all melodramatic and say he saved my life, but maybe he did."

"The stallion scared him away?"

"Yes." She took more salad, spooning it out of the plastic bowl. "That's exactly what happened. I was watching the horses all day, and when they bolted, I thought it was because of the storm. I decided I should come back, and that was when I realized I was being followed. I turned around and saw the cat, but Smoke came out of nowhere at full speed, and I jumped in the stream."

"The horse saved you?" He still seemed incredulous.

She nodded.

Drake seemed to be striving for patience. "Give me a minute to put this together. So you're out all afternoon watching the horses, taking pictures and making notes. A wicked storm blows up, so you decide to head back to the tent. Then a mountain lion follows you and a rogue stallion chases him away. Do I have this right? Quite the eventful afternoon, Ms. Hale."

"Oh, and don't forget when you and I made love."

"Not likely I'll ever forget that." His voice dropped in timbre and he held her gaze. "I did just say 'ever,' didn't I?"

She hadn't planned to say this yet, but... "My sister thinks I should invite you to California for a brief visit." She hesitated. "I know you're really busy, but if you could find the time, maybe we could go for a couple of days? My parents have a house very close to your grandfather's vineyard. That's how my mother met yours, remember? They both grew up there. You could see him, too."

He didn't respond to that, but his brows rose. "Your family has a country house?"

"Look, the Carson ranch isn't exactly a slum, so I don't want any rich-girl comments. My parents don't support me. They haven't for quite some time.

I want to inform you, though, that I'll have student loans to pay off."

He seemed amused at her defiant statement. "Good information. You do realize it doesn't reflect badly on you that your parents are successful people."

She was probably too sensitive about the subject. "It always makes me feel as though my accomplishments are due to them, not me."

Drake just shook his head. "You do very well all on your own. Mind if I eat the rest of that salad, or do you want more?"

Therapy, Drake Carson–style. *You're okay and pass the salad.*

She passed it. "I *can't* be in love with you," she said again.

"But you are?"

The least she could do was be as honest as he was. "Yes."

He handled it with his usual composure. "I'll take a weekend and we'll go to California. Red can manage the ranch for a few days."

CHAPTER THIRTEEN

LUCE WAS ASLEEP next to Drake, one arm curved over her head. He could see one enticing bare shoulder, and her lips were slightly parted.

He'd kiss her awake, but he had a feeling she could use the sleep. He, on the other hand, rarely slept past dawn. Drake eased out of the sleeping bag, doing his best not to disturb Luce and succeeding except for a small sleepy murmur. Yanking on his jeans, he pulled a clean shirt from his pack. Then, dressed and barefoot, he made his way over to check on Starburst, giving him a handful of the oats he'd brought along. Then he sat on a fallen pine, stretched out his legs and watched the sunrise, inhaling the crisp air that still smelled of rain in the wake of the storm.

He didn't have enough moments like this. Oh, lots of solitude, but he was usually on a ranch mission of some sort. Rarely did he just sit and breathe and indulge in the luxury of reflection.

So Luce wanted him to meet her parents. That was as good as a *yes* to a question he hadn't yet asked. The stumbling block was that they were facing a long-distance relationship, at least for a while.

He was torn over whether or not that kind of marriage could work, but the decision seemed to have been made for him.

And now, in addition to relocating the wild horses *and* trying to recover some of his mares, he'd have to do something about the mountain lion. It had been poaching on Carson property since last fall. Ironically, *without* the horses here, the problem was likely to get worse. The foal Luce had noticed was missing probably wasn't the first. Animals, like people, fell into certain behavioral patterns, and not only that, the young ones were an easy food source for a large predator. A friend who was a park ranger had told him once that he never failed to advise families hiking in the mountains not to let their children or dogs run ahead on the trails. Kids should walk between the adults, he'd said.

Wyoming was a wonderful place to live but, like anywhere else, it had its dangers. No hurricanes or tidal waves, but there were plenty of other things to be cautious about—blizzards, forest fires and tornadoes among them.

"You seem deep in thought."

He glanced up to see Luce emerging from the tent, dressed in a set of clean clothes, her hair in a ponytail. She could pull off a face free of makeup unlike any other woman he'd ever met. She was naturally beautiful, fresh-faced and vital.

"Just mulling over the dynamics of the universe," he said, summoning a smile. "Sleep well?"

"You know exactly how I slept because you were beside me."

"Uh, that's right, I sure was. Wouldn't mind doing that again."

Drily, she said, "How come I think you aren't referring to sleep?"

"You have a suspicious mind?" The smile came more easily this time.

"I hate to be the one to tell you, but you don't do innocent very well. Now, if you'll excuse me—"

"I'm going with you." He'd stood when he heard her voice and he reached out to touch her cheek. "No argument. I'll turn my back to give you privacy, how's that?"

Of course, she argued, anyway. "I was out here by myself all of yesterday. I've been up here alone plenty of times before. I don't need a bodyguard."

"I'm really fond of your body. I'm guarding it for me. Purely selfish reasons." He picked up his rifle, which he'd brought out with him and hoped he wouldn't have to use. But he knew the cat was close, so better safe than sorry. No way was she hiking anywhere alone.

Luce didn't look very happy, but obviously understood that he wasn't going to budge. He thought it was possible that she muttered the words *stubborn ass* as she walked into a copse of small pines.

When she emerged safely and bent to wash her hands in the small spring, he admired the graceful curve of her spine and said, "I could use a good cup of coffee. What about you? Should we pack up and ride back to the house?"

She shook the drops off her fingers and he could swear he saw a tinge of color in her cheeks. "Everyone there is going to know we spent the night together."

"Yeah, that's true." He almost made a comment about his trip to the drugstore but stopped himself in time. All of Mustang Creek knew by now, but she didn't have to realize that. "Last I heard, you and I are both adults and unattached. If we want to sleep together, that's our business."

"I don't care so much about everyone else, but I do care about your mother, mine and Harry."

"The three most conniving matchmakers in history?" He didn't put the brakes on fast enough to stop that one. "You have to be kidding, Luce. Two of them lured you here to Wyoming, and one of them made dinner for us last night. What about those heart-shaped cookies… Oh, *that* wasn't a hint? Do you think Mace included the wine and the glasses? Don't overrate him. He isn't that sensitive. No, it was Harry. She and my mother are probably doing fist bumps over their morning tea."

"That would be flattering," Luce said with a laugh.

"They both like you."

"They both love *you*. That's different."

"I know. I'm not saying they aren't both great. I'm saying you don't have to worry that they'll be anything but happy about it. The two of us getting together, I mean." He was the one likely to endure a talk on how he should go about choosing a ring. Yeah, he was looking forward to that. No doubt someone of the female persuasion would want to go along so he didn't mess it up. He could rope a bull, but there were clearly misgivings in some quarters about his ability to select a suitable ring.

"Any chance Slater caught it on camera? I'm talking about the fist bump."

"Hell, no. He'd never risk his life. Between the two of them, they could certainly take him. Grace would help. He'd be toast."

"You do realize you have an eclectic family, right?"

She'd lightened up, if her laugh was any indication.

"They're an interesting bunch. Let me help you with the tent, and then I'll saddle Starburst."

He thought she'd put up a fight, insist she wanted to camp out again, but maybe despite her comfort with the outdoors, her experience the night before had made an impression. Sure, he and his brothers had camped out many, many times, but they'd brought their rifles, knew how to store food to avoid attracting unwanted guests, and they'd grown up knowing you had to keep your eyes open. Practice and familiarity counted for a lot.

She said without equivocation, "I can handle the tent. Go get your horse."

If he forced the tent issue, he had a feeling he'd be in trouble.

IT WAS NICE to slip into the house unnoticed and bolt straight to her bathroom for a shower. As she stripped off her clothes, she registered soreness, partly from horseback riding and partly from...well, uninhibited sex. On the positive side, the shampoo and conditioner might make her hair manageable again. And she needed a chance to think about the night before.

She already had an offer from a private college for a teaching position once she completed her graduate degree, assistant professor, not associate or full, but she was still in her twenties; there was plenty of time to advance in the academic ranks. She'd gotten a teaching certificate as part of her undergrad program.

As she'd pointed out to Beth, what would she *do* in Mustang Creek?

She'd put a lot of time into figuring out her future. Drake was totally mucking that up.

She did hope this wasn't a problem with trust on her part. Previous men in her life, notably her erstwhile fiancé, had proven to be jerks, but Drake wasn't, and intellectually she understood that. In her heart...she just wanted to make sure she was independent, confident, solid on her own.

It was her problem to solve.

The hair was indeed a challenge, but she won the battle, wielding conditioner and a hairbrush. Because she was self-conscious, she decided mascara was in order. It was closer to lunch than to breakfast, and she found the entire family in the dining room, chatting and having Sunday brunch.

She walked in, and all conversation paused but slowly resumed as she took her seat That was followed by cheerful hellos from everyone present.

"I'm a little late," she said apologetically.

"Yep, you are." Drake, the king of the three-word sentence, rose with his empty plate in hand. "Listen, I'm running behind. Gotta go."

But he didn't leave the dining room right away. Instead, he leaned over and kissed her in front of his entire family, just a light brush of his lips on hers. "See you later."

Luce was speechless. Everyone else was grinning. He used his elbow to open the door and disappeared into the kitchen. Grace jabbed Slater in the ribs. "Admit I called that one."

Blythe interjected, "I think *I* called it."

"Saw it coming from the start," Harry said serenely. "Luce, can I pass you some biscuits and gravy?"

CHAPTER FOURTEEN

"WANT TO FLY-FISH the Bliss?" Slater propped himself against the doorway. "Where's Ryder, anyway? Isn't this his job?"

Drake wiped his forehead. "Believe it or not, he went to the movies with Red. Some sort of John Wayne marathon at the theater downtown. Red's been talking them up to the kid. They were both so excited I told them just to go. Ryder called Grace to ask if it was okay, and then they lit out of here."

"So you're voluntarily mucking out stalls?"

"I am, but fishing sounds better. Feel free to pitch in and, after that, yes to the Bliss. You're done filming for this afternoon?"

Slater picked up a shovel from the wall rack. "I'm not a slave driver. It's Sunday, after all. I'm going to bet half my crew is watching John Wayne, along with Ryder and Red, and the other half is at Bad Billy's. I gave everyone the day off."

It was true that there wasn't a lot to do in Mustang Creek, and that had always been okay with Drake. Plenty to do on the ranch and there were mountains practically in his backyard. He did go skiing now and then, but fly-fishing was more his kind of thing. They'd all gone with their father as boys and those afternoons were among his fondest memories. Being with his dad. The quiet, the sunshine, the gleaming water. The thrill of getting a hit on your line…

"We going or what?"

He turned to see Mace carrying their fly rods and a tackle box, hip waders draped over his arm.

Drake gestured around him. "Get busy mucking. Two more stalls and we can go. Showbiz is on board with helping, as you can see. How about you?"

His younger brother muttered a word he'd never say in front of his mother or Harry, but he obligingly set everything down. "I'll do the straw and feed. I'm not touching Heck, though. Slater can brush his own damn horse."

They'd worked together so many times the work was done in minutes, and then they all piled into Slater's truck. Mace was in the back, and he patted a cooler on the seat next to him. "I told Harry we'd be bringing back trout. Don't make me do all the work because you both suck at fishing."

"Yeah, right," Slater said sarcastically.

"After the storm last night, a successful haul might be a neat trick," Drake observed. "River's going to be high and muddy. I thought I'd end up somewhere around the south pole the wind was blowing so hard."

He shouldn't have said it, because—predictably—

Mace jumped on it. "I'm sure you clung to Luce for comfort, Romeo."

There were two ways to react to that sort of comment, and he chose the high road. "I did, as a matter of fact."

Both of his brothers laughed. As they turned onto the county highway, Slater asked, "So, is it pretty serious or just a fling?"

"I agreed to go to California with her." He really hadn't meant to let the proverbial cat out of the bag. Luckily, his brothers wouldn't tell if he asked them not to, and he did. "That happens to be top secret information, by the way. Mom and Harry are running the show too much as it is. If they get wind of this, I'll know it was one of you two."

Slater shook his head. "Not necessarily. You'd better hope Luce doesn't tell Grace. They seem to like each other and they aren't too far apart in age. I get the impression they talk."

Mace was his usual cheery self. "They probably complain about the two of you. I know I would."

"We could just drown him in the river," Drake suggested caustically.

"That's a plan," Slater agreed. "Think we'd get caught?"

"Hmm. Spence is a smart lawman. He might catch on."

"Yeah. We'd have to be clever about it."

"Thanks to Spence I'm saved? Good to know." Mace took it in stride. He might be a wiseass, but he did have a sense of humor. "I'll thank him later. Why do I get the feeling I'm going to be the last holdout Carson bachelor?"

"Because no one would ever want to marry you?" Drake muttered. Apparently, he viewed that as a logical observation.

"I'm choosing not to take offense at that."

"If you two start arguing again, I'm going to park the truck and walk the rest of the way, and you can follow," Slater said. "Then you guys get stuck with bringing the gear." He was probably only half-kidding. He'd been the peacemaker for a long time.

"Don't worry about it. I'm not going to waste an afternoon off. The river looks high, but there's not too much runoff." Drake, looking out the window, was happy to see the water running clear. The Bliss had to be one of the most beautiful rivers in the world. Crystal-bright and rippling gently, it had a variety of trout and also grayling. "We did need that rain. No significant runoff."

Slater parked in a flat grassy area they'd used before, then it was waders on and flies tied. As he waded into the water, Drake felt a twinge of nostalgia and sorrow that the fourth of their party was long absent and would never join them again.

Mace echoed his thoughts. "This always reminds me of Dad."

"I know." Drake flicked his pole. "For me, that's good *and* bad. I like to remember him, but missing him is still painful."

Slater, a few feet away, water swirling around his thighs, murmured, "Try having your wife expecting his grandchild. I grieve for him, and for the fact that my children won't know their grandfather."

At this stage of his life, Drake could only imagine that feeling. He was distracted from his melancholy mood a moment later, when he got a clean strike and the battle was on. Fly-fishing was truly a sport. It wasn't just hauling them in once they took the hook; it was wearing them out enough so you could net the fish.

He won in the end, a nice rainbow trout. He turned to his brothers. "The score is currently me one, you two zero. I don't know what Harry's backup plan is, and I'm sure she has one, but I'm having trout for dinner."

"Whoa, don't get too smug, brother of mine." Mace's pole had suddenly bowed.

"Try landing that fish," Drake told him. "Let it run."

His brother *was* playing it expertly, giving line and taking it back. "The day I need fishing advice from you is the day hell freezes over."

"Seems to me I'm the only one who's actually caught a fish so far." Drake cast again, working the line with what he considered his lucky fly.

At the end of it all, everyone was having trout for dinner and Slater had caught the most fish. Go figure.

"I'm just lucky," he said when they got back in

the truck. "Beautiful wife, wonderful daughter, and let's not forget I'm a better fisherman."

Mace rubbed his jaw. "If he's better at anything, it's at being conceited. I've always thought that. How about you, Drake?"

"Yeah, he's full of himself, all right." He stowed away the poles.

"You two are poor losers."

"You get to clean them, remember that."

"Yeah, Harry's Law." Slater rolled his eyes. "She'll bake a double-layer chocolate cake and make coconut frosting from scratch, but she won't clean a fish."

"So clean it and remember she cooked the fish."

"Thanks." Slater slanted him a derisive look. "It seems to me we'll *all* be cleaning fish, correct?"

Mace gestured expansively. "Hey, I'm starting to feel blessed 'cause I caught the least, so I won't—"

"No, no," Drake interjected. "You don't get a free pass for that."

Slater backed him up. "We'll make it a family affair. One for all and all for one. We're the Three Carsoneers, aren't we?"

Drake and Mace booed. "Jeez, that's feeble," Mace said.

"The fish are all in the same cooler," Slater added. "You can't tell which measly few are yours."

Mace grumbled, "Fine. But if you're going to brag the whole time, Slate, you might want to keep in mind that I know stories about you in college that

I doubt Grace has heard. Like the one when your buddies bet—"

"Okay, no more bragging," Slater interrupted in mock terror.

"Thought you might feel that way." Mace grinned and so did Drake, listening to the lighthearted banter. All three of them worked so much they rarely had a chance to spend time together. As kids, they'd often gone riding, fishing and camping as a trio. There were a lot of arguments, but those usually blew over as fast as that storm the night before.

The storm.

Luce, soaking wet and clinging to him, and the very different kind of storm that followed. He hadn't asked and he wasn't going to, but he wondered if her betraying jerk of a former fiancé had been her only lover. She wasn't shy by any means; however, he had the feeling that she'd been shocked by the intensity of her sexual response.

He shouldn't have kissed her in front of everyone, but their evolving relationship was hardly a secret. Hell, their first kiss was going to be in a movie!

Time to broach an important subject. "I want to surprise Luce. I'm thinking we should build a cabin up on the ridge. Do you two agree? Nothing fancy. A bedroom or maybe two, small kitchen, but we'd have to bring in coolers for food. We'll need a camp shower, and we could set up a wood-burning stove for heat. If we wanted to, we could put in a generator for electricity. We could run that off a small propane tank. Glorified camping."

His brothers jumped in with both feet. Slater said with conviction, "River-stone fireplace that burns wood. Grace would love that. Two bedrooms—I have children, remember?—and a nice deck."

"An outdoor grill for cooking." Mace was part of the project. "A good one with a burner on the side. Put it on the covered deck, so if the weather's bad, you can still cook. We'll need to improve the horse enclosure, too."

Slater said, "I agree with that. Plus a fire pit for sitting around. When we're ready to build, we should get the logs from the property and have the mill strip them for us instead of buying lumber. For the floors, we could use some of the siding from the bunkhouse we remodeled for the winery."

"That old barn door would make a fantastic dining room table." Mace looked thoughtful. "I could refinish it."

"And we could use the chairs up in the attic," Slater suggested. "Those are antiques from our grandmother, and I've always felt bad that they've just gathered dust for years. Hadleigh Galloway could reupholster them."

This was quickly spiraling out of control. "I was thinking simple," Drake said in protest. "Did I even mention a dining area? What kind of home-improvement TV shows do you have time to watch?

All I want is a small rustic cabin, not something that could be featured in a magazine."

"Be quiet." Slater frowned at him. "We need a place to eat. So we're doing a dining room. It would be great to have a place to go for weekends. Yup, it's a brilliant idea. Can't believe *I* didn't come up with it."

Mace said, "He's full of himself again. I'm so telling Grace that story."

Drake shrugged. "Go for it, I say."

THE WILD HORSES had moved.

Luce had made a diagram of where they usually grazed, and they weren't there. Interesting. Smoke had decided on different territory.

They were closer to the ranch again, which she suspected would not make Drake happy. For her purposes, it was easier, since she wouldn't have to walk for hours.

There was a beautiful new foal.

Pure Smoke. He was gray, with that same black mane, and she was riveted. The mother was one of Drake's stolen mares, and Luce snapped pictures on her phone and took more with the high-tech camera her father had given her for Christmas.

Wonderstruck, she allowed herself to dream that by the time the colt had matured, she might be skilled enough to train and ride him.

Of course, the little one *could* be a filly, but she had a feeling she'd guessed correctly.

Would she even be here when the foal was grown?

Not wanting to pursue the prospect of either going *or* staying, she shifted her attention back to the magic of the moment.

She felt a sudden thrill. She'd come to Wyoming in the hope of having experiences like this. She was learning so much and her ambitious approach to this project made more and more sense—to her and, she thought, to Drake Carson, too. Whether he was ready to admit it or not.

Drake. Before her arrival here, before that first meeting, she'd never imagined what he might come to mean to her.

She texted him the picture. He might be annoyed—this was the stallion's handiwork, after all—but she suspected otherwise.

When she got back to the house, she went straight to her room, fired up her computer and downloaded the pictures. She emailed one to Beth and one to her mother. She was in the middle of putting her notes into a more logical order when Blythe knocked on her open door and stuck her head in. "I know you're working, but care to run into town with me? I want to order a special gift for your parents' anniversary and your opinion would be invaluable."

Her gift would be showing up for the surprise dinner party Beth was hosting for them. She hadn't told Drake about it, although he was her designated date—designated by her, anyway. He'd agreed to California for a weekend; might as well meet her whole family at once, like ripping off a bandage. If she knew Beth, the party would be casual and fun, cocktails by the pool, and her mother's favorite caterer would do the food. Lots of children everywhere, since most of Luce's cousins were older than she was and had growing families.

"I'd love to go." She saved the file. "Let me change. It'll only take a minute."

"Sweetie, you're fine in jeans. Where we're going, the business owner will be dressed the same as you are. You'll like her, too. I know you met her husband, Spence Hogan. Melody makes the most artistic pieces in this entire state. When she got married, she moved to Spence's ranch and turned her own house into a studio. No specific hours—you have to call ahead or drop in and hope she's there. You aren't allergic to cats, are you? Ralph, Waldo and Emerson are usually there, too. I have no idea how she wrangles them back and forth with a little one to boot, but she manages it."

"Her cats are named that?" Luce went to grab her purse. "That's clever!"

"She's an artist, what can I say?" Blythe laughed. "I love her free spirit. She's beautiful, too, but I don't think she realizes it, just like you. She's a jeans kind of girl. What you have on right now is perfectly okay."

That was a nice compliment—the one about being beautiful—but she didn't think Blythe was exactly unbiased.

If Drake loved her, the entire Carson family was going to love her, too. Hands down, no questions asked. They were that sort of family. Look at how they treated Raine, the mother of Slater's child, even though she and Slater were never married. Regardless, she was part of the family.

The drive into Mustang Creek wasn't too long. They pulled into the driveway of a small well-kept house with a neat yellow car. Blythe parked her sleek Mercedes next to it and twirled her hand. "We're here. Get in tune with your creative side. She has a display of her work, but mostly she does commissioned pieces. That's excluding what she sells to the shops in town."

Melody Hogan answered the door in jeans and an old T-shirt that announced she'd graduated from Mustang High School. As Blythe had said, she was strikingly beautiful, a vibrant, energetic blonde. A baby wailed somewhere in the background.

With a smile, Melody said, "Welcome to the land of chaos. We're having green beans today and, as you've no doubt guessed, *somebody* around here hates anything green." The child's cries escalated, and Melody winced. "Sorry about the noise."

"If you think I haven't heard a baby cry before, think again," Blythe said, obviously right at home. "Melody, this is Lucinda Hale—aka Luce. Her mother's a dear friend of mine, and I need a special anniversary gift for her." She waved one hand. "Go handle the green bean crisis. We'll check out some of the pieces on display in your studio."

Melody Logan nodded gratefully. "Look around all you want. I'll be back." She sighed, heading for a nearby door. "Bananas?" she muttered to herself. "Or mashed carrots?"

Smiling, Blythe led the way to Melody's studio-gallery. The space was cozy and colorfully cluttered and, somehow, elegant, too. There were cases of jewelry, bracelets and earrings, and unique custom-made clocks on the walls, along with a few paintings, mostly landscapes.

A couch stood near the fireplace, currently occupied by three napping cats so similar that they might have been cloned. A worktable scattered with sketches and a baby monitor sat next to a computer.

Luce was immediately drawn to the charm bracelets, one of which would be a perfect gift for her sister's upcoming birthday. She was particularly interested in a charm that featured a mother's hand clasping a baby's.

"Do you suppose Melody would do a horse charm?" Suddenly inspired, she pulled up the picture on her phone. "Look at this little guy. He and I just met today."

"Melody would do it." Blythe's mouth held the hint of a smile and there was a twinkle in her eye. "You should give it to Drake."

That made her laugh as she pictured one of these delicate pieces on his brawny wrist. "I was thinking of me, but he won't approve of that, either. He and Smoke have a love/hate relationship."

"He told me you named the stallion. I hadn't seen him up close until that image Slater's film crew took. He really is a beauty. I like the name Smoke. It suits him." Blythe turned back to the display. "Look at these gorgeous rings. Get Melody to show you her engagement ring. My friend Lettie Arbuckle tricked her into making it, and Melody didn't know it was intended for her. It's truly a work of art."

As far as Luce could tell, everything was.

When Melody came back, there was a suspicious yellow stain on her shirt, and she was shaking her head and laughing. "Nap time. Even the bananas were rejected. But give him the right stuffed animal and he's out like a light. It's nice to have a nursery here where I work. Now, what did you have in mind?"

"Like I said, I need an anniversary gift, but it actually has to be for both of them." Blythe gestured at one of the pieces in a display case. "I remember you made Lettie a set of rings that would fit on the neck of a wine bottle. They each had a charm. My friends live in Napa, so a wine-related gift works well. They entertain a lot, so I'd need six of them. Would it be possible for you to do this in two weeks?"

Melody nodded. "Of course. The ring and the chain aren't the issue. I need an idea about the charms. Want them all the same or six different?"

"I was thinking the letter *H*, done in pewter." Blythe turned to Luce. "Sound good?"

It did; it sounded like a very tasteful gift and perfect for her parents. But Luce had already cottoned on to the fact that this wasn't why she'd been invited on Blythe's shopping expedition. She waited for it—and she didn't have to wait long. Very casually, Blythe said, "Oh, Melody, please show Luce your ring. I was telling her how lovely it is."

Drake was going to die laughing when he heard that one of the "conniving matchmakers" had invited her on an excursion to look at engagement rings. Melody extended her hand. The ring, a sapphire surrounded by small diamonds, was exquisite. "I wasn't aware I was making it for myself," Melody explained, "but maybe you've heard that story."

Might as well play along. "Gorgeous," she said with a smile, "and yes, I've heard it."

"Blythe is about to ask you if that would be the kind of ring you'd like and what center stone you'd choose. She'll do it wearing her most innocent face. I have informants in the Carson household."

"That Grace!" Blythe threw up her hands. "What a traitor. If I didn't adore her and she wasn't about to give me a grandchild, I'd be offended. I'm just trying to help my son, who's a wonderful person but who's likely to walk into a jewelry store somewhere, squint at the case for five seconds and then say, 'That one looks fine to me.' Now, if he was buying her a saddle, he'd really take his time and know what he was doing."

Luce was touched *and* amused. One of the cats rose and yawned and then stretched and the other two did the same thing. They settled back down, facing the opposite direction, once again in the same pose.

"We haven't even discussed marriage. He hasn't asked me yet."

"He will," Blythe said with conviction.

Melody echoed that. "From what I hear, he will."

Luce's phone beeped, signaling an incoming text—from Drake. Dinner out? Just us?

Was that timing or what?

She responded, Yes. Then she told Melody, "Should the subject ever come up, I've always loved rubies."

"Good choice."

CHAPTER FIFTEEN

DRAKE WAS ABSURDLY nervous and couldn't understand why.

The evening ahead was no big deal, just dinner at the resort his sister-in-law managed.

Calmly, Drake changed into a white button-down shirt and tan slacks, thought about wearing a tie, but he'd have to borrow it from Slater, since he didn't own one. Hated the things actually.

Finally, when he figured he was as presentable as he was going to get, he texted Luce.

Meet me downstairs in five minutes?

Hey, Cowboy, she texted back. I'm already down here, ready and waiting. If you're primping, stop it. I've seen you covered in dirt and you've seen me sopping wet.

He couldn't stop himself. Not to mention, naked. That was the best part. Be right there.

Taking Luce—or anybody else—out for a formal dinner was a little out of character for Drake, but he ᵢ more one-on-one time with her.

When he got downstairs and saw Luce, he had to catch his breath.

Hot damn, she looked good. She wore a skinny black dress, shoes with heels and some sort of long sweater in a silvery gray. All that luxurious hair was loose and she'd gone a little Hollywood with the makeup, compared to her usual outdoorsy style. It wasn't excessive or anything and he definitely approved.

Drake wasn't a hermit. He dated, but not very often, since he was always working. Occasionally, he'd meet someone through friends or at community events, and he'd even gotten semiserious a time or two, especially back in college. So far, though, he'd never met anyone like Luce.

Maybe because there *was* no one like her.

He gave her a deliberate once-over. "Damn."

That was eloquent. He wanted to groan at his own awkwardness, but she laughed, so maybe it wasn't too bad. "I was going to say that about you," she said.

He opened the front door and, for the second time in two nights, ordered Violet and Harold to stay. They both looked disappointed—those two had expressive canine faces—but they immediately sat down.

As they went down the steps toward his truck, Luce asked him, "How did you train them so well? My mother's Yorkies are the cutest dogs, but it took obedience school to get them to listen. I can't picture you doing that."

"I got them as puppies and I just talked to them. They caught on fast. Animals are so much smarter than most people give them credit for. It's just a question of whether they choose to go with what you tell them to do. They both learned right away that if they didn't do what I asked, I wouldn't take them with me the next time. So they do it. These two have to be some of the best herding dogs anywhere."

"I believe it." Somehow she managed, even in that skimpy dress, to get gracefully into the passenger seat of his truck. In retrospect, he should've borrowed his mother's expensive classy car. His truck was expensive, too, but probably not what a lady wanted to ride in to a nice dinner.

She didn't seem to mind.

"What a beautiful evening. Very different from last night." She gazed out the window as they went down the drive. "Wyoming has such beautiful sunsets. I love the mountains."

He did, too. "California doesn't do too poorly in that department, either. I've visited my grandparents fairly often, especially when I was younger."

Luce gave him a sidelong look. "I'm surprised we never met. My mother's always throwing some sort of party and your grandparents always come."

He shrugged. "For all I know, we did. Remember, I'm a lofty six years older than you. Until I turned twenty-four, you were beneath my notice." His grin held a tinge of humor. "Not to mention underage, and I don't do that any more than I do casual. By the time

I graduated from college, the ranch was waiting for me. It's far easier for my grandparents to visit here than the reverse."

He didn't add that elaborate social events bored the hell out of him, and they had his entire life. Even as a kid he'd preferred taking a long afternoon ride or reading a good book in a secluded place, preferably outdoors.

"Speaking of which, I'm hoping a specific weekend will be convenient for us to fly out there."

Uh-oh. "Why?" he asked cautiously.

"An anniversary party for my parents."

He almost groaned at that announcement. He managed to stifle it, but only just.

She added lightly, "I believe your mother's also invited."

"My mother? That should be a relaxing, romantic trip."

"You were looking for romantic? That's reassuring."

"After last night, do you doubt it? But the idea of meeting your whole family, with my mother right there, sounds worse than a root canal."

"You'll like them. Anyway, I'm going to change the subject. I really want that new colt—Smoke's baby. I sent you his picture."

He stopped dead in the very act of pulling out of the drive onto the county highway, hitting the brakes and looking over at her incredulously. "What exactly would you do with it?"

"Eventually ride him." Her mouth was set in a firm line and she stared straight ahead.

"I see." He didn't discount the possibility that she could do anything she set her mind to because she'd succeeded quite often in his opinion. Her plan to study wild horses in unfamiliar territory didn't seem as illogical as he'd originally thought. She could handle herself well outdoors, and quite frankly, she'd managed to get a lot closer to the herd than he had. In his defense, he didn't have all day to sit around taking pictures and writing notes, but still… Luce had shown dedication and resolve.

He knew he'd have to tell her he was rounding up help to move the horses. She'd asked for time, and the two weeks they'd agreed to were up.

"He'll need his mother for a while," he said calmly. "Red can train a horse like nobody else, but he's getting a little old to hit the ground that often. Slate, Mace or I can do that part."

"I can have him, then? The foal?"

"I sure as hell want that mare back, so yes, if we can work it out." *Here comes the hard part.* "If you want that horse, you'll have to move to Wyoming, Luce."

"Mind clarifying that?"

He gave an exasperated sigh. "You know what I'm saying."

"I'm not sure I do." She'd finally turned to look at him. "Drake, if there's a question dangling in there, just ask me."

So he did. "Marry me?"

"We've known each other less than a month and slept together once."

"The amount of time that's elapsed since you started annoying the hell out of me doesn't really matter, and thank you very much, but it was more than once last night, remember? I'll feel vaguely insulted if you don't."

Her laugh was encouraging. "Oh, yeah, I remember. You do know how to charm a girl, by the way. *Annoying the hell out of you?*"

"Maybe that wasn't well put. How about—annoying the ever-lovin' hell out of me. Better? I could elaborate and tell you that I think about you all day instead of concentrating on what I should be doing, I've had more sappy thoughts since I met you than in my whole life and I've even wondered if our children would have my eyes or yours. That's it. I'm done."

She was quiet, her face averted. Then she said, "That could be the best proposal in history. Yes."

"Yes?" He swerved a little, then straightened the truck.

"Yes."

Well, that was settled. He muttered, "So, I think I should meet your parents. I mean, before we tell the world."

Now she was truly smiling. "That is so sweet—and so old-fashioned."

He smiled at her. "I like to do things right."

She let that one pass. There were plenty of things

Drake Carson "did right"—in and out of bed. "We'll figure something out."

"Hungry?"

She nodded.

"Me, too," he answered. "Let's go to dinner, have a glass of Mountain Vineyards wine and see what Stefano has on the menu for tonight. I had the lobster ravioli last time I was there, and while Harry is a wizard, that's not in her repertoire."

"It sounds like I'm going to have a remarkable evening." She looked him right in the eyes and hers were luminous. "You have no idea how happy I am."

Wrong. He was just as happy. Maybe happier.

SHE TEXTED BETH, just two words, as Drake went to park the car after dropping her off at the entrance to the resort.

He asked.

The reply was immediate. I knew it!

You can't say a word to anyone. Drake wants Mom and Dad to know before we make any announcements.

I won't say a word. If I wasn't breast-feeding I'd drink a glass of champagne to celebrate. See you soon. Can't wait to meet him.

Well, she'd had to tell *someone* and her sister was a logical choice. She was tempted to tell Grace, too, since they were becoming friends. But Grace was married to Drake's brother and part of sharing a life was, after all, sharing everything. When Drake chose to tell his family they were engaged was up to him.

The resort was perfect for the area, rustic but classy. Luce could tell that while it catered to affluent clients, there was no sense of exclusivity. Western-style hospitality was the attitude, and the theme of the decor, too.

Drake steered her toward the restaurant entrance with a hand on her elbow. The place was high-end but low-key, she thought with admiration. The art was impressive—spectacular landscapes, exquisite horses, portraits of Native Americans in ceremonial dress. Several pieces were obviously Melody Hogan's work, such as the clever mobile fashioned from old spurs and stirrups.

Soft instrumental music played, and the tables were beautifully set, with white cloths, candles and gleaming china and silverware. A distinct change from Bad Billy's.

"Lovely," Luce said as they were shown to their table and Drake pulled out her chair. "But I would expect that with Grace in charge."

"She's a perfectionist. So is Slater. No wonder they get along so well." Drake sat down and smiled in a way that suddenly made her feel vulnerable. "I'd love it if you told me what makes *us* get along so well—despite our differences. Quite frankly, I can't quite put a finger on it."

"A love of adventure?" she suggested. "Or that I annoy the hell out of you."

"Could be," he agreed. "I—"

When he stopped in midspeech, Luce first thought it was because the waitress had arrived with their menus, but it took her about two seconds to realize that wasn't it.

The nervous waitress passed them the leather-bound menus with a tremulous smile. "Hi, Drake. It's good to see you. Can I get you all a drink?"

"Danielle. I didn't know you were working here." His voice was even, but the impassive look on his face spoke volumes. "How are you?"

"Getting a divorce. Which you've probably heard."

He nodded.

"Otherwise, I'm managing. I just got this job. Your sister-in-law really helped me out. Grace persuaded the restaurant manager to take a chance on someone who's been a stay-at-home mom for fourteen years. You know Reed. He's determined to make this as nasty as possible. The kids and I are living with my parents right now. But you don't need to hear my sad story. How's your mom?"

"She's fine. And I *asked* how you were. Which means I wanted to know."

"I guess. Well, thanks. Um, I'd better get to work. Drinks?" She flipped back the pad she was holding, pen poised, but her hand wasn't steady and her smile was forced.

Luce homed in on it. She just *knew*. He'd been in love before—he'd said so—and it was with the woman standing in front of her.

She couldn't blame him. The woman was one of those delicate blondes with a flawless complexion. She wasn't heavy, but not thin, with nice curves. She could still pass for a high school cheerleader.

Drake ordered a bottle of chardonnay, Mace's label, of course.

Luce knew she shouldn't ask, but she couldn't help it. "What's the story?"

He did his usual thing. "Long time ago."

"But you were serious."

"We were young."

"Quit with the three-word sentences and *tell* me. It seems to me that we're committed to a permanent relationship now. And I have to say, I don't understand why any woman would give you up."

His smile resurfaced. "I appreciate that, Ms. Hale."

She raised her eyebrows in question.

"High school romance. It might've gone further, but she got involved with someone else. Never liked the guy, but it was her life and her decision. Not a big deal."

Luce sensed that it *had* been a big deal for him. A healed wound still left a scar. He wasn't the kind of person to take betrayal lightly and she knew exactly what that felt like. A different waitress showed up then with their wine, which confirmed that the old romance—the broken romance—was significant for them both. Luce had the feeling that they weren't going to see Danielle for the rest of the evening.

After the tasting ritual, the new waitress poured them each a glass. Drake didn't comment on the change in waitress. This would be life with him; if he didn't want to talk about it, he wouldn't bring it up. On the other hand, if *she* brought it up, he wouldn't argue but would respond directly.

"Shall we toast?" She admired the golden liquid in her glass. "This looks like that wine Mace served at dinner recently. I loved it."

"Could be. He's an alchemist. All I saw was a label I recognized. I usually drink beer."

"Like I haven't noticed." She noticed everything about him. He looked fantastic dressed up, but she still thought he was sexy as hell in jeans and dusty boots, wearing his favorite hat.

He raised his glass. "To us. To our future."

"Our *bright* future."

Their glasses touched and she knew she'd remember that light, delicate sound for the rest of her life.

The menu was an eclectic mixture of Italian, classic Spanish and, of course, things like elk steak and buffalo chili. She chose linguini with a delicate crab sauce; Drake opted for paella and, of course, ate every bite. Their plates had just been cleared when Danielle came rushing up to the table. She'd disappeared from the dining room at least half an hour before.

"I'm so sorry to interrupt, but I'm so glad you're still here." There were tears in her eyes and her mouth was trembling. "Can you help me? I've been waiting for my dad to pick me up because my car's in the shop. My mother just called. They think he had a heart attack and they're doing tests, but I need to go to the hospital right now. Can you give me a lift? I can't call Reed, and even if I could count on him, it would take him a while to get here. I know we've had our differences, but…please? My dad's in intensive care. My mother was hysterical. I could barely understand her on the phone."

Drake didn't hesitate. "Take a deep breath." He stood and pulled out his wallet to extract a credit card. "We haven't gotten the bill yet. Luce, can you take care of it with this, please? I'll run and get the truck."

"Thank you." There were tears running down Danielle's face and Drake handed over his napkin so she could wipe her face before leaving the table.

Was it possible to fall even more in love?

Luce wasn't sure, but he was convincing her otherwise. As he swiftly walked out the door, she put her arm around the shoulders of a complete stranger. "He'll get you there. Let me go take care of the bill."

"Catherine probably has it ready," she said through a small sob.

She did, and the young waitress processed it quickly, obviously aware something was wrong. "Is Danny okay?"

"She's pretty upset because of her dad. We're running her over to the hospital."

"Tell her if she needs me to pick up some of her shifts, I will."

That news brought on a fresh spate of tears when Luce got to the doorway where Danielle was waiting. "After all those years with Reed, I swear I'm not used to people being nice to me. I *knew* Drake would help."

Luce had the feeling there was something else she was saying. *Even after I treated him badly...* But this wasn't the time to worry about that. She stood in the doorway, and when the truck pulled up, she helped Danielle inside, settling her in the backseat of the extended cab.

As it turned out, the regional hospital was about twenty minutes away. Drake drove with his usual calm, but maybe a bit faster, while Danielle talked to her kids on her cell. Evidently, they were home alone, and worrying about their grandfather.

Luce felt double-sorry for those children. Their parents were in the middle of what sounded like a messy divorce, and now this.

It was a memorable way to spend the evening of her engagement, no doubt about that.

CHAPTER SIXTEEN

HE COULD'VE IMAGINED a better end to the evening, but maybe some things were simply meant to be.

Drake was happy that Luce seemed okay with doing this for someone she'd just met, and he was still flying high from her saying yes to his proposal.

A lifetime ago, he and Danielle had lost their virginity to each other, spent warm summer nights by the river talking about their future and been practically inseparable. Was he glad she regretted marrying Reed? No, definitely not. He'd like to think he wasn't that mean-spirited. Besides, then he wouldn't have been free to find the right woman, all these years later.

He parked as close as possible to the main entrance. "We'll go in with you."

Danielle had been sobbing quietly for most of the drive. With the combined stress of the pending divorce, having to move out of her own home, starting a new job and now this, Drake wondered if she could even locate the intensive care unit on her own. She looked almost dazed. He was uneasy about just dropping her off.

Luce met his eyes and nodded. From the ridiculously small stylish purse that matched her outfit, she'd extracted a packet of tissues for Danielle. She'd also turned to cast worried glances at their passenger more than once.

Luce murmured, "We'll come with you, make sure you and your mother don't need anything. What about the kids? Will they have had dinner? We can stop and pick up a pizza or something for them."

"Nathan is fourteen. He can heat up some leftovers, but it's kind of you to offer."

He wouldn't have thought of that, but he certainly wasn't opposed to doing it. "They could probably use a pizza. I know I would've preferred it at their age. We can also give them an update on their granddad once you've seen your mom."

"That would be wonderful." She looked miserable but sounded grateful.

He went to the desk to be directed to the intensive care unit. Coming here brought back memories of his father's death that he didn't want to revisit, but it wasn't as if he hadn't been back a couple of times since then. Once for a broken wrist when he'd been handling an unruly cow. On a later occasion it was because he'd had to admit his stomach pain was getting worse; they ended up removing his appendix.

All in all, though, he'd just as soon skip hospitals.

The friendly woman at the reception desk pointed him in the right direction and they hurried over to find Danielle's mother, Louise, in the waiting area, white-faced and exhausted. The community was small, so Drake saw her now and then at different events, and she looked as if she'd aged about ten years since they'd last run into each other. That was at the fall farmers' market, where he'd obligingly stopped to buy some pumpkins for the front porch. Picking out pumpkins wasn't really one of his skills, but his mother had asked him to do it. Louise had been there, and she'd helped him. She'd been his first-grade teacher, and at one time, he'd envisioned a future with her daughter. So they did have some history.

After she and Danielle had hugged, he asked gently, "How's Walter doing?"

"He's going through bypass surgery. He's in serious condition, but stable." Louise wiped her eyes. "He's always been so healthy. He's never even had a cold that I can recall."

"I know," Drake said. Danielle's father was a cattleman through and through. "He's tough. Remember that." He paused. "This is Luce Hale. We can stop by the house and check on the grandkids, if you want. We're glad to help in any way we can."

Louise smiled weakly and acknowledged Luce with a nod, then said, "I'd appreciate your looking in on the children. Please remind them to feed my cat. He's getting old. He needs medication for his joints and it has to be sprinkled on his food. So if you could—"

"Done."

He wanted to help, as he'd said, but he also wanted to get the heck out of this shell-shocked environment. Luce didn't say anything at all until they got back to the truck. When she'd clicked her seat belt in place, she finally spoke. "I hope you understand that I'm both confused and impressed by your sense of self. Or maybe more to the point, your sense of selflessness. Your kindness and generosity."

There was no real response to that in his estimation. He chose "Ah."

She reached over, gave his arm a squeeze. Her tone was light, but her expression was serious. "Listen to me, Carson. You can handle anything without blinking an eye. This has been one crazy evening and you just seem to take it in stride."

"What else are you supposed to do? Could you order that pizza? Let's say half sausage and half pepperoni. Leave the vegetables off, since some kids like 'em and others don't... Have I mentioned I hate lima beans? Don't ever serve them to me, please."

"Have I mentioned that I don't cook? You aren't in any danger of lima beans and I've never heard of them on pizza."

She *hadn't* mentioned that she didn't cook, but then, this could only be described as a whirlwind romance. They hadn't had time to talk about details—important ones—like that.

"I think lima bean pizza might be a big hit in certain circles," he said, realizing his life had dramatically changed this evening, "but I'm not destined to be a fan, and I can pretty much guarantee those kids won't be, either. So let's stick to the pepperoni and sausage variety. The number's in my phone."

"With Harry there, you still buy pizza?"

Legitimate question. "I sure do. Lunch for the hands once in a while. She deserves some time off."

"And when she fixes you lima beans?" Luce was laughing as she took his phone.

"I eat them," he admitted, "but not happily. She makes this thing called lima bean stew that both of my brothers love, so she serves it fairly often. To-matoes, onions, whatever else is in there I like, but not the lima beans."

"The things we do not know about each other." She pressed a button and a moment later ordered a thick-crust pizza from the only decent place nearby.

When they'd picked it up, he drove to Louise and Walter's house. To his dismay, he saw a car parked outside—a car he recognized. He somehow doubted Reed was welcome at the house where Danielle had grown up, but at least he was paying attention to his children.

He told Luce, "I wish we hadn't offered to deliver the pizza because that's Reed's car. Danielle's soon-to-be ex. He and I don't like each other. Not exactly a state secret. I should warn you. Reed probably won't be very cordial."

"I'm getting the impression he's not what you'd call a prince."

"You have no idea."

"I have some idea. Danielle's very…what's the word? *Downtrodden* might work."

He hated that, too. The Danielle he remembered was bright and beautiful, with high hopes and a buoyant disposition. The woman he'd seen tonight bore almost no resemblance to that memory, and he disliked seeing the unhappiness in her eyes.

Reed, of course, met them at the door.

LUCE WAS A good judge of people, or in any case, she thought she was, and the man staring them down didn't impress her. He was nice-looking with dark brown hair and regular features, wearing what she was starting to think of as the typical Mustang Creek uniform of jeans, boots and a button-up shirt. But he wasn't friendly, as Drake predicted. He leaned against the doorjamb with one shoulder and crossed his arms in a classic gesture of defiance. "Oh, look, it's Romeo. My wife called our son and said you were coming. May I ask why?"

Luce instantly understood why Drake resented hearing the Romeo nickname from certain people.

To his credit, Drake ignored the open animosity. "Just dropping this off. Ran into Danielle at the restaurant when she got the news about her dad. She wasn't sure what the kids would eat. I figured one less worry would be good."

"Knight in shining armor, huh? I always wondered if she'd leave me for you. When Danielle said she wanted a divorce, you were the first reason that came to mind. We split up and a few weeks later she runs straight to you. How long have you two been seeing each other?"

Luce was conscious of two things. One, that the man had been drinking, and two, that fists could easily come into this conversation. They were about the same height and weight. Reed Keller might be impaired, but he was also very angry. A risky combination.

"We haven't," Drake said flatly. "At all."

"I don't believe you. She's been seeing someone."

"I don't care if you believe me or not. Your marriage failed, but I had nothing to do with it." Calm as ever, Drake held out the cardboard box. "Before you get belligerent, have I mentioned this is my fiancée? Give your kids the pizza. Tell them their grandfather's in stable condition."

Danielle's husband seemed to notice Luce for the first time. He said sardonically, "You going to get married to him, Ms. Whoever-you-are? Save yourself and don't. That's my advice. I don't care who it is, Carson or not. Just…don't."

Drake didn't exactly drag Luce down the sidewalk, but almost. She was surprised he didn't pick her up and carry her; maybe he wanted to keep his hands free for a fight.

When they were back in the truck, he started the engine and muttered, "That actually went better than I expected."

"You've got to be kidding me! I was ready to call

911. That guy is a real jerk," Luce said. "How did she live with him for so long?"

They pulled away from the curb. Drake took a moment to answer, the streetlights outlining his profile. "He isn't always a jerk. I don't like him, but that's a problem between him and me. In case you couldn't tell, he doesn't like me, either. He got her pregnant, but he did marry her. Yes, he wanted her to stay home, not go back to school and not work. I guess he was pretty controlling. But…she made her own choice, too. She's smart, so she knew—to some extent, anyway—what she was buying into when she married Reed. As far as I know, her family didn't pressure her to do it, even though she was pregnant. And I don't think he's ever lifted a hand to her or his kids, because around here I would've heard about it. I'm not a fan, but what you saw tonight was a guy whose wife is determined to divorce him and he's apparently hurting because of it."

Luce still felt rattled by the acrimonious exchange. After a moment, she asked, "You always so fair-minded?"

"I was just assessing the situation. Being rational. Looking at both sides."

He meant it, she knew he did. "She made a poor decision. Choosing between you and him? I should've said a *very* poor decision."

"I hope so. Since *you* agreed to marry me."

She had. It still felt surreal.

He went on. "Yet I think you were just advised

that might be a poor decision. Let's not talk about how I dragged you off to take an ex-girlfriend to the hospital. The night is young. Who knows what might happen next?"

It'd been an eventful evening. He'd had only one glass of wine, while she'd had two, and she was feeling uninhibited. "My bedroom or yours?"

"I like that plan. The evening's looking up again. Either one. You pick."

"Whichever isn't going to draw attention to the fact that we're spending the night together."

"It doesn't matter. We've discussed this before. We're both consenting adults." His sidelong glance was brief but held a world of meaning.

"Your mother talks to my mother and I want them both to approve of me." She confessed what was hardly a secret. "I know, I'm a grown woman and all, but I'm not promiscuous and I'd rather not be viewed that way."

Drake broke out laughing. "No one, sweetheart, would *ever* view you that way. Luce, you're the quintessential nice girl. Why else would I fall so hard?"

It was probably his way of explaining that she'd betrayed the fact that she wasn't very experienced in bed. She couldn't decide if she was chagrined by his comment or not. "I suppose that's a compliment."

"I'm in love with you. I asked you to marry me. What do you think? I like everything about you."

That made it better. Sort of. Should she protest the "nice girl" label or live with it? "Talking about nice… You're just as guilty. You were even decent to Danielle's husband when he accused you of having an affair with her."

"I told him the truth. Married women are off-limits in my book."

"Cowboy code, huh?"

He shrugged. "My code, anyway. Straight from the chapter titled 'Things to Do and Not to Do So You Can Still Look at Yourself in the Mirror.' You don't steal a man's horse and you don't steal a man's wife."

Luce laughed. "I'm going to guess the horse is more important."

He grinned in response. "Damn straight. You can live without a wife, but you need a horse."

"Hmm, I'll keep that in mind. Starburst first, me second. I'm trying to come up with a name for the new man in *my* life."

He took his eyes off the road for a second to glance at her. "The foal? He's not yours quite yet, but I'll work on it. Why are you so convinced it's a colt and not a filly?"

"I just am. What do you think of Tinkerbell?"

He turned onto the county road toward the ranch. "That's cruel. Poor horse couldn't hold up his head. Try again."

"Precious?" She couldn't keep a straight face.

"Oh, yeah. Now we're headed in the right direction. Better than Tinkerbell, anyway. Try again."

"What about Moonflower?"

"I'll knit him a skirt to go with that one."

"*You* know how to knit?"

"Hey, I have a lot of hidden talents. Actually, no to the knitting. But if you name that horse Moonflower, I'll learn."

This was one of the reasons she'd fallen in love with him. Grace was right; he was so funny in a droll way. Luce got serious. "I was kind of thinking Fire."

"As in, where there's smoke there's fire? Not a bad choice. And if it's a filly, that should still work. I like it."

They drove into the lane. The front porch light glowed as the house came into view in the distance. Her pulse had already started to accelerate, and she sincerely hoped no one was sitting there, reading a book and sipping tea. It really wasn't all that late.

Luckily, the porch was deserted when Drake parked the truck. As always, he hurried to open her door, but when she got out, he kissed her with a passionate hunger—a preview of what was about to happen. "We never settled this. My room," he murmured against her mouth. "I get up early. It's at the opposite end of the house so I won't disturb anyone."

She didn't care where they went. "Fine with me. Just don't pick me up and carry me in, please. I can tell you're thinking about that, and if we passed anyone in the hall, I'd be mortified for the rest of my life."

He admitted with a wicked smile, "You know me. I *was* thinking that might be faster, but okay."

CHAPTER SEVENTEEN

LUCE DISCARDED HER SWEATER, an action he found sexy as hell. Anticipating the rest of the outfit's removal had him on edge—and he was more than willing to help her get naked.

"Let me unzip your dress." He didn't wait for an answer, taking her shoulders and turning her around, sliding down the zipper.

He pressed his mouth to the nape of her neck, lifting all that silky hair out of the way. Her back was beautiful, smooth and feminine, and as he traced her spine with his fingertips, she gave a sexy little shiver.

She didn't comment on the minimal decor in his room. Bed, dresser, lamp and one comfortable armchair—that was it for him. It wasn't as though he hung out there much. The quilt with its mountain theme he'd bought from Hadleigh, and there was a pegged rack for his hat and coat, as well as a hand-woven brown rug, but otherwise he'd kept it pretty simple. She turned around to face him. "Kiss me."

No way could he resist *that* invitation, especially when she was so irresistible in a slinky bra and barely there panties. He really kissed her. A "this is the night we got engaged" kiss. In about a minute they were on the bed and she was busy unbuttoning his shirt. To his mind this was how it was supposed to be. Both so attracted it was inevitable, like the sun coming up on the horizon.

They made love in a breathless rush of desire and newfound emotion and ended up damp and twined together. Pleasure had taken on a whole new dimension. He wasn't possessive, but he sure as hell wanted to keep her in his life.

She touched him. "I could get used to this."

"Sex?" He relaxed with her in his arms. "Oh, count me in."

"I meant just being with you."

He tried for lighthearted, but he couldn't quite manage it. "That works." Then he cleared his throat. "Luce, after we go to California, I want you to come back to Wyoming with me. How can we figure this out?"

He shouldn't have pushed. She drew back, and her body tensed. "I have to finish this degree. I'm doing it for myself and I don't know if you understand this, but I've spent a lifetime trying to please my parents and friends. This is for *me*. You love what you do. I want that. I'm happy about being a wife, but I want to be more than that, too. I don't want to wind up—I don't know—like Danielle, working at some job because I need it, not because I love the work." She paused, shook her head. "Not that there's anything wrong with waiting tables—that isn't what

I meant—and I'm not implying that you'd ever…" Finally, in a despairing gesture, she threw up her hands. "I want to teach students about ecology, inspire the kind of awareness that might save a species, or even the planet… You of all people know how I feel."

He absorbed her words, let her settle down a little.

"I hear what you're saying," he said after several minutes. Then he raked a hand through his hair, his other arm tightening around her. "How long will it take to finish your degree?" he asked.

"Until December."

He winced. "Ouch," he said. "I'm not sure I can be away from you that long."

"Mr. Carson, that might be the best thing you've said to me since the day we met." She playfully ran a finger along his stomach. "Maybe the university will let me do most of the remaining course work online. But I need to do this, one way or another."

Luce's tenacity was one of the qualities he loved most about her. He moved back onto her warm body. "It can't be December," he said, only half teasing. "We'll have to figure out something else."

She gave him a twinkly smile. "Think about a Christmas wedding."

"I'm thinking about a Christmas wedding night."

"I can tell that you are." She stretched suggestively beneath him.

He kissed her throat. "Will your parents like me?"

She laughed. "My mother will, for sure. She's one

of the scheme team, remember? And my father will be okay with my choice of husband, since you've never been in prison and you're gainfully employed. Dad's priorities are simple." She touched an index finger to his mouth when he raised his head. "And my sister will adore you—I think she already does. Beth is a free spirit, so be prepared."

He cupped her breast, stroking her nipple. "I'm adaptable. My father told me once that ranch life forces you to change the game plan in no time flat. One minute you've got sunny skies, the next pouring rain. A dust storm could follow. You just never know."

She gazed up at him. "You still miss him a lot, don't you?"

"Yeah." He exchanged his caressing thumb for a flick of his tongue, not sure this was the moment to talk about his dad—although he'd brought the subject up. Luckily, she sensed his feelings and left it alone.

"I like your room. It's very…serene."

If she was willing, he was in the mood for a repeat performance of what they'd just done. "Feel free to stop by anytime. This is a room with a beautiful view."

"It doesn't face the mountains."

"I was talking about right now and I'm not looking out the window but at you."

She did that cute thing and blushed. "Nicely done. And I'm looking back at you, by the way."

"I think I noticed that."

"I thought you might have." She arched into his caress. "Maybe we should stop staring at each other and get down to business. Again."

"Yes, ma'am. You're insatiable. I like that."

"Only when it comes to you."

Only you. This wasn't the time to talk about her romantic history. Or his. They'd had enough of the past tonight with Danielle. It was an interesting experience to fall in love again, older and wiser. As a teenager, his psyche had processed information very differently. Lust colliding with immature emotion wasn't a good combination. This time, at least, he was aware of what he wanted and needed—as a man and not a boy.

"I love you." He wasn't really telling her; he was telling himself with a sense of wonder. "I can't believe it."

"Thanks." She urged him closer. "If I didn't know what you meant, I might've taken offense."

He kissed her again. "I just never thought I'd feel this way."

"This *is* going awfully fast," she whispered.

"I hope you aren't insulting my stamina."

She laughed. "So far, no complaints in that department."

"And I'll do my best to keep it that way." He shoved back the tangled sheets so he could see her better. "Can we have our wedding soon? Location doesn't matter to me."

"Um, just keep doing that and you won't hear any argument from me."

He did as he was told. She wasn't voluptuous, but those graceful curves were so feminine, so perfect… He stroked her intimately. "This?"

"Exactly. Don't stop what you're doing."

As if he would. "You have my word."

"I THINK I NEED to write a chapter in *The Cowboy Guide to a Successful Relationship*." Luce was limp in his arms after another earth-shattering climax, resting against Drake's chest. "Can I coauthor it with you?"

"Oh, I'm dying to know what your chapter would be titled."

"'Cowboys Are Not as Simple as They Seem.'"

"Oh, thanks. I'm not happy we seem simple in the first place."

"What I mean is that you're so straightforward, but you're also sensitive. For that matter, Red is, too, along with Slater and Mace. You love animals, you'd do anything for your family, you rescue damsels in distress—"

He interrupted her. "I think you've been reading too many fairy tales."

"Okay, I loved them when I was a kid, but that's beside the point."

Although the moon was no longer full, light spilled in through the window, which had no drapes. He might not have a view of the mountains, but stars were visible in a vast sky and it was utterly quiet except for the far-off lowing of cattle.

Whatever she might have said next was interrupted by someone knocking on the door with alarming urgency.

"Drake." Male voice and it didn't sound happy.

Quickly Drake jumped up to grab his jeans. "Be right there!" he called.

Luce dived under the sheets. It was one thing if people knew she and Drake had been sleeping together, but quite another to be caught bare-ass naked in his bed.

Red opened the door. "Let's go. Right now. We've got trouble."

Drake didn't hesitate but picked up his shirt and thrust his arms into the sleeves. "Bad?"

"I'm hardly going to roust you out of bed otherwise, son." Red sounded grim. "Sorry to bust in like this, Luce."

Luce nodded. "Anything I can do to help?" she asked tentatively.

"Maybe. An extra pair of hands never hurts. Don't wear your favorite dress or anything. We'll be out front. Grab a towel and his cell phone, will you?"

Actually, one of her favorite dresses was the only thing available. She waited until the door shut behind Drake and then slipped into it. She didn't bother with her perfect matching shoes because something in Red's voice told her this was not a perfect situation at all.

She found Drake's cell on the nightstand, ran into the bathroom for a towel and dashed out the door. She wondered if she needed a jacket, since it had started to cool off, and then didn't care when she opened the front door and saw the blood.

All over the front porch.

Harold was on his side. He was licking Drake's hand, but he wasn't moving in any other way. The big German shepherd's fur was matted with blood. Drake said tersely, "Luce, call Jax Locke. It's in my contacts. Tell him to get here right away. I mean *right* away. Throw the towel over to Red, please. This dog's been mauled pretty bad."

Luce's hands were shaking, although Drake appeared calm.

She found the number, got referred to a service and left a message, but about thirty seconds later, the phone rang back. Dr. Locke said, "Drake? What's going on?"

"I—I'm...Luce Hale...his fiancée." She was stammering. "Something...it must've been big, maybe a mountain lion, got hold of Drake's dog. There's a lot of blood."

"Harold? On my way. You guys tell the dog to hang in there. I mean it. Animals understand."

Drake was already doing that, talking softly to the dog, crooning words of encouragement. She was almost more worried about him than Harold—not to mention Red. Both of them were on their knees next to the dog, who was wrapped in the towel. Blythe came out, tying her robe. "I was still up reading and heard voices." Then she caught sight of Harold and gasped. "What's going on... Oh, no! Have you called—"

"He's on his way." Drake's voice cracked. "Let's hope he can do something. I just asked Red and there's no trace of Violet. I'm thinking that big cat got a little too close to the house. Dogs spook them. But mountain lions don't usually act this way. Something is off here."

Red shook his head. "I was asleep. I heard a commotion that woke me out of a sound sleep, like when a Canadian clipper starts wailing through the trees. I ran out of the stable and found Harold like this about five feet from the porch. Brave guy."

"No Violet?" Blythe looked as if she might cry but was struggling against it. Luce was having the same problem.

"Perhaps she's hiding," Luce suggested.

Blythe hugged her. "Yes, let's hope so."

There was an unspoken message between them. *Or else Drake will be devastated and neither of us can take it, and...*

"No Violet." Red looked tired but confirmed it. "I've called and called that dog. She's feisty and maybe the fight stirred her up. She's smaller than Harold, but she might've chased that lion right up the mountain."

"It's possible." Drake glanced over at them. Luce recognized that remote expression. There was blood on his forearms and his T-shirt, even smeared on his face. He was doing his best to hide his response and act calm, but he wasn't. Luce could tell he was shaken. She was, too.

It seemed to take forever as they waited, but she suspected maybe a new record was being set for traveling the distance between Mustang Creek and the ranch.

Headlights shone up the drive, and within a minute of skidding to a halt, a young man was out of the car and dashing up the porch steps. He stopped for a second, looking at the dog and all the blood. "Oh… damn it. You weren't exaggerating."

Drake was petting Harold's head, soothing him. "I know. Just do your best, Jax. Thanks for coming out right away. We didn't want to move him too much."

Locke snapped on disposable gloves and went to kneel by Harold. The dog whined as he was examined, but it was a weak sound at best. "Good call on not moving him more than necessary. I have to stitch him up and give him a couple shots, but he's a big dog, and in my opinion, he'll survive this. We'll have to wait and see. Bad news is it'll take a little time. Where's his sidekick?"

"Violet is missing."

Locke paused, frowning at them. "That's bad."

Blythe offered a timorous suggestion, repeating what Luce had said earlier. "Maybe she's hiding?"

"Shepherds don't usually hide, Mrs. Carson. Anyway, I don't think she'd leave Harold."

It was true. Luce had never seen one of those dogs without the other.

Drake got up and walked away for a minute, his expression once again remote. Both Luce and Blythe let him go. Red said forcefully, "I'm going to grab my rifle and go look for her. I'm useless right now and I don't like the feeling. The doc's already here, so if she's hurt and we can find her, we can do something about it."

Luce said instantly and ridiculously, "I'll go with you."

"Like hell you will." Drake had apparently needed a minute to collect himself; he stalked back up onto the porch. "Luce, you're barefoot and wearing a dress, and even if you were wearing a suit of armor, I don't want to risk you getting hurt. Stay here and help Jax. Red and I will go out. Mom, can you get the big flashlights, please? I'm going to get my rifle as well and wake up Slate and Mace."

Blythe went inside with alacrity and Luce might have resented his commanding tone, but she didn't know what to do and Drake was probably right. She'd be more of a hindrance than anything. She did say, "I want to help."

"Then do it like I said, by staying put. I have enough problems at the moment. I'm worried about how this animal is acting. Harold and Violet wouldn't have tangled with it if they hadn't felt there was a threat. If Red found Harold a few feet from the porch, the animal came right up to the house. Not normal mountain lion behavior. And listen to me, if you think you're going anywhere out there alone after what happened tonight, you're dead wrong. My mother isn't setting foot outside, either, not by herself, until we get this situation taken care of."

Normally, she would've argued, but she was starting to think he was right. He disappeared inside and came back a couple of minutes later with his brothers. He'd thrown on a clean shirt and washed his face. All three of them had rifles.

Slater and Mace swore out loud when they saw Harold, their faces grim.

Luce was an animal lover through and through, and she didn't want them to kill the lion, but she also knew they needed to stay safe. She knew Drake well enough now to know he didn't want to kill it, either, but his mother was a slender woman who was also an avid gardener. She was often outside, alone, tending to the flowers and the herbs she planted every spring for Harry, and Luce was truly getting an education about the realities of ranch life.

Jax Locke was still working on the dog and, without looking up, said, "Priority one is finding Violet, but be careful. That cat did not get off uninjured. Not all this blood is Harold's. I'd usually trust this dog not to bite me, but I sedated him, anyway. I don't have to tell you that injured animals are hard to handle. And that also means your already dangerous friend out there isn't going to be happy."

"I'm pretty unhappy myself." Drake jerked his head toward the stables. "Let's go."

At that moment Luce jumped up and caught his arm, just before his foot hit the top step. "Hold on. Did you hear that? Listen! I swear I heard a dog bark."

They all went still, and just when she thought she'd delayed them for nothing, it came again, faint in the distance. Not a coyote or a wolf, but a dog. Even after her short time in Wyoming, she knew the difference.

"That's her bark. I'd know it anywhere. Thanks." Drake gave Luce's hand a grateful squeeze before all three Carson brothers ran down the steps, hell-bent for leather, as Red would say.

CHAPTER EIGHTEEN

"NORTH."

Drake agreed with Slater and had already turned Starburst in that direction. "Yep."

He wished there was still that romantic full moon, but it was waning and the night was pretty damned dark. At least they could follow the sound, which meant they didn't need to search every inch of terrain. If she could bark, Violet was alive. He was damned fond of that dog, so he wanted to keep her that way. Harold was bigger, so he probably went after the cat first, but Violet was as quick as lightning.

He felt for her. If the mountain lion had hurt Harold, she'd go after it. That was the only reason she'd ever leave him.

They rode by the west pasture, then slowed to see if they could hear her She wasn't much of a barker unless it was necessary, so when it came again, he figured it *was* necessary.

"She's got it cornered somewhere," Red said with conviction. "There's nothing like hunting a big cat in the dark to let a man know if he's got fire or just smoke in his britches."

Drake might have laughed if he wasn't so worried. He'd have to use that one on Luce someday. She'd probably accuse him of freestyling again.

"I know that dog," Drake muttered. "She's fighting mad. Tomorrow I'm calling Ed Gunnerson. He's handled relocating lions before. Man, between this critter and the wild horses, you'd think we'd issued some sort of open invitation to ruin my peace of mind."

"But those horses also brought you a gift, son," Red said in a dry tone. "Unless I'm mistaken, you weren't exactly alone when I knocked on your bedroom door."

Slater murmured, "Why does that not surprise me?"

"We're getting married." Drake was spared having to say anything else, since Violet barked again and this time it was close enough that Mace unsheathed his rifle.

His younger brother said pragmatically, "I'm the best shot. You all manage the situation and I'll be ready if it goes south. Not anxious to do it, but I will."

He was right. Mace was the most accurate marksman Drake had ever seen. It just came naturally, like brewing up those concoctions of his. He had a very focused mind.

"Deal," Drake said. Violet always obeyed him, but on the other hand, this was a different scenario. Normally, he'd just whistle for her. But he was worried that if she turned around to come to him, the injured lion might attack her. At least Mace was likely to hit the target effectively—if it had to happen, which none of them wanted. At one time Mace had contemplated the military to become a sniper or law enforcement for a SWAT team position. He was really that good.

When they finally found the dog, she had, as they'd predicted, treed the big cat. Listening to Violet's ominous growling, Drake wasn't surprised that the mountain lion stayed put on a large branch about twenty feet up, although it was snarling right back.

"Violet, come." He could tell she didn't want to, but she trotted toward him with no apparent injuries except a long bloody scratch on the top of her head. His heart twisted at the sight of her, and at the same time, relief washed over him like a flood tide.

"What do you want me to do?" Mace asked. All three of Drake's companions looked at him expectantly. His ranch to run, so his problem to solve. Just like the wild horses. His brother added, "I don't have a clear shot."

"I'm reluctant to kill it," Drake replied.

Even with the powerful flashlights, the animal was difficult to see because of the foliage, but they knew where it was.

"He's going to continue to be a pain in your backside," Red pointed out, sitting his horse with the ease of an old cowboy. "I understand your position—that critter up there is just doing what comes naturally—but now's your chance."

He was right. However, it *felt* wrong. The animal needed to go, but relocation seemed a much better option.

"Let me talk to Ed," he said finally. "He's handled this kind of thing before. After what this cat did to Harold, you'd think I'd be inclined to tell Mace to give it a try. But if we can handle it another way, I'd prefer that."

"Your call." Slater sounded as calm as usual. "I don't want to have to kill it, either. Although I'm going to walk my pregnant wife out to her car every morning until we fix this. After that run-in with the dogs, I doubt the cat will come near the house again, but who knows. I wouldn't have expected it to in the first place."

"Yeah, who knows what it'll do." Red thoughtfully rubbed his chin. "Had a friend with a cabin on Big Pine Lake and he said he woke one morning and there was the biggest bear he'd ever seen looking in the window, eyeing him up. About gave that die-hard ole cowboy a heart attack, and I can tell you, he doesn't scare easy."

Red had a story for every occasion, including, of course, this one. Drake said wryly, "I hope he's still alive and well." When Red grinned, giving him a thumbs-up, Drake added, "Good to know. I plan to emerge from all of this in the same condition. Let's just take Violet home. I'm not sure if Jax needs to stitch that wound on her head or not."

Red nodded. "Looks like she could maybe heal

on her own, but if we aren't going to end the battle right now, we might as well go home, boss. Hey, girl, let's go see Harold."

Violet followed, wagging her tail, and the rest of them fell into line.

Red always called him *boss*, but Drake had to acknowledge that they had a careful balance of wisdom and authority between them, and he rarely ignored what Red had to say. Part of it was that he knew Red was as worried about both dogs as he was. Red was also a lot more sentimental than he let on.

When they got to the house, every single woman in residence was hovering over the injured dog. Harry wore an impossibly old bathrobe, while his mother, Grace and Luce were all fully dressed. Harold rested in a corner of the veranda, and Jax Locke immediately abandoned a cup of coffee, got to his feet and crossed the room to examine Violet. "Thank God you found her," he said. "Come here, girl—let's have a look at you."

The dog moved slowly as she approached Jax, but she seemed sound. In the end, all Violet needed was first aid, a shot of antibiotics and some loving attention.

Drake took Luce's elbow as everyone else went back into the house. As she looked at him questioningly, he pulled her close and said, "Get some rest. I'm going to grab a sleeping bag and stay out here on the porch with Harold and Violet. In his condition,

Harold can't make it to my room and I don't want to move him. You can go back to my bed or use yours."

"I'm sleeping out here with you."

How did he know she'd say that? He had a feeling he was going to suffer from acute exasperation—and crazy, grateful love—for the rest of his life. "Why would you want to do that, Luce? Isn't a comfortable bed more appealing than a hard floor?"

She ran her fingers lightly through his hair. "I'd just lie awake and worry about you and the dogs, but if you were right next to me, I might be able to get some shut-eye, buckaroo."

For a moment, Drake hesitated, torn between wanting Luce beside him and wanting her to be safe inside the house. He didn't think the cat would be back tonight—or ever, for that matter—and if it did show up again, Violet would let him know. His rifle was within easy reach, too.

He could protect Luce—and the dogs—if he had to.

Anyway, it was a given that the determined Ms. Hale would do as she damned well pleased, regardless of what he said.

He was sure of one thing—come hell or high water, he wasn't leaving Harold.

So he shrugged. "Suit yourself."

I'm camping out on the porch of a Western mansion with a handsome cowboy and a dog who was mauled by a mountain lion.

LUCE SENT THE TEXT to Beth's phone, then grabbed a pillow from her bed. That message would have her sister calling her back first thing in the morning, if not before. Beth was the queen of tantalizing texts such as: At mall and hoping I don't get arrested for murder.

The explanation for that one turned out to be about a purse she'd ordered, a hard-to-find item in a "positively delicious" color. When Beth went to pick up her bag, she discovered that a clerk at the expensive boutique had accidentally sold it to someone else. In the end, she bought the same purse—in black—at a discount store. Beth might have loved the original purse, but she was nothing if not practical.

Introducing Drake to her family was going to be interesting. His down-to-earth, sensible approach to life was not how she'd grown up, that was for sure. However... Blythe and her mother were lifelong friends, and Blythe had certainly married, by all accounts, a true Wyoming cowboy. She'd left California, where her wealthy family was as close to royalty as anybody could get, and settled into her new life. Luce had met Drake's sophisticated grandfather a couple of times. She highly doubted he could—or would—saddle up a horse and go after a mountain lion to save a dog.

Drake had laid out two sleeping bags on the porch floor. He was already half-asleep and she was tired, too, so she crawled into hers. The events of the evening piled up in her mind.

"Hmm," he said, draping one arm over her. "We aren't likely to forget *this* night."

Violet, lying next to Harold in his makeshift bed, lifted her head at the sound of Drake's voice. Luce replied, "I agree with that."

"We could have killed it." His face was shadowed and he looked weary. "I opted not to do it. I think we have a young rogue cougar that's just discovered a convenient food source. A lot of ranchers have had this problem."

"Some take the low road."

"Who could blame them? All of us considered bringing down the cat. One shot and it would be over, problem solved. Fact is, there are *some people* I wouldn't mind wiping off the face of the earth, but I'm more tolerant of animals. Most people know when they're committing a crime."

That pro-animal attitude of his was part of the reason she'd fallen for him. "I support that decision."

He spoke quietly enough not to disturb Harold, who was still sleeping off the sedative. "We're not going to be that couple with twelve dogs and fourteen cats, are we?"

"No." She shook her head. "It's too heartbreaking to lose one. How's he doing, anyway?"

"Harold? Violet will tell me if there's something wrong. He's a ranch dog. He's been hurt before. Not like this, of course, but he's had his share of injuries. Jax is a very good vet, and he wouldn't have left if he was worried. We got lucky when he moved to Mustang Creek. I trust him."

She did, too. Dr. Locke was obviously competent and empathetic, but forthright. It was heart-wrenching to see Violet standing guard over her injured sibling, but also heartwarming. Luce understood why Drake had decided to sleep outside, because Violet would be torn between her loyalty to him and her need to protect Harold. This way was much easier. It made sense for his dogs—and that was important to Drake.

Luce was surprisingly comfortable in her sleeping bag. The night sounds were soothing, the stars twinkled and the air smelled fresh and clean. While Drake might get a few hours of rest, she doubted he'd actually sleep.

On the other hand, she was exhausted. "Hmm, tell me a bedtime story."

His laugh was muffled. "What?"

He looked all cowboy, with his mussed-up blond hair and his arms now linked behind his head. Getting a pillow obviously hadn't even occurred to him.

"You know," she murmured, "the kind of story that helps kids doze off. I'm so tired I'm not sure I can sleep. I need a story."

"If you're looking for *The Princess and the Pea*, I'm afraid I don't really remember that one."

At least she'd coaxed a smile out of him. "Just make something up."

"You do realize you're pretty high maintenance."

"Not compared to my sister. Have a beer with my

brother-in-law and see if he doesn't agree. Come on now, you can invent some yarn. You know Red, for heaven's sake. Has he taught you nothing?"

"I believe he told me when I was about fourteen to steer clear of women because they're a pain in the ass."

Luce jabbed his shoulder. "I didn't notice you feeling that way earlier this evening."

He clasped her hand and kissed each finger in turn. "I don't feel that way now, either. Nice of you to keep me company. Story? Okay, I'll give it a try. Let's see. Once upon a time—"

"You'll have to do better than that, Carson. Not very original." She liked being close to him, even though they were in separate sleeping bags. He grinned. "Hey, give me a chance. I've had an eventful evening. Okay, I'll start over, since you have such exacting standards. How about... Once, out on the range, there was this innocent, unsuspecting cowboy, minding his own damn business."

She couldn't help commenting, although she really was dozing off. "A good start," she mumbled, "but if you're referring to yourself, I don't think *innocent* applies."

"Do you want to hear the story or not?" His thumb stroked her wrist.

"I'm on the edge of my sleeping bag." And snuggled in with her comfy pillow and Drake right next to her. He wasn't the only one who'd had an eventful evening.

"I'm going to ignore that comment. Anyway, this extraordinarily good-looking and talented cowpoke ran afoul of a willful woman—and all hell broke loose."

Luce made a sound that could be described as a snort. "I think *extraordinarily* is a bit over the top. However, I might buy *noticeably*."

He went blithely on. "She seduced him with her hair. Sort of like that Rapunzel girl who lived in the tower. You know the one I'm talking about?"

He loved her hair? She really was drifting off. "Uh-huh."

"But a wise old bowlegged wizard warned him she might put a hitch in his normally peaceful existence and the darned fool didn't listen to what was plain common sense. He got involved with her, anyway."

"Maybe the cowpoke was stubborn and hard-headed."

"Hey, who's telling this story?" Drake ran his finger over the curve of her right brow.

"You are."

"That's what I thought. So, anyway, he wants to ignore her, but he can't. He *wants* to, mind you, but he just…can't."

"Noble of him."

"I think so. He was trying not to take advantage of her."

"What made him think he could?"

"She looked at him a certain way."

"Oh, I see, a love at first sight story."

"Ha-ha. Could be, I guess. Want me to keep going? You seem to be down for the count."

"No, no, I'm still awake."

Drake laughed softly. "Yeah, I can tell."

It was the last thing she remembered.

CHAPTER NINETEEN

HE HAD MYRIAD problems to solve.

Luce slept next to him with her face turned away and, between her and Harold, he doubted he'd close his eyes. So he'd resigned himself to a sleepless night.

Fine with him. He needed to figure things out.

He might've made a mistake by not telling Mace to end the issue with the big cat, but a man had to live with himself. Luce's entire thesis centered on how people and wild animals interacted and, in principle, anyway, he thought they could usually respect each other and achieve a balance.

But…not always. Animals were as individual as human beings. They had their routines and habits, and the lion had to go. He'd decided that last night. It wasn't about vengeance; he knew the critter was operating on instinct, but he couldn't risk letting it roam free. He had to think about the livestock.

Hell, he had to think about *people*.

Harold stirred and Violet was immediately on alert, as was Drake. Part of the reason he was sleeping outside was to make sure the dog didn't hurt himself by getting up too soon. Harold truly was a ranch dog, used to working. The possibility that he'd struggle to his feet once the sedative wore off was very real.

Drake said quietly, "I'm here."

The dog settled back down. Maybe it was sentimental, but he wanted to be there when Harold woke up in the morning.

He wasn't the only one, as it happened.

Slater wandered out with a blanket and feigned a yawn. There was a reason he was a producer and not an actor—he couldn't fake a damn thing. "Can't sleep, and I didn't want to keep Grace awake, tossing and turning. Thought I might camp out here for a while."

Luce stirred but didn't wake. Drake stifled a laugh. "You were checking on Harold, weren't you? Make yourself comfortable, if that's possible. How long do you think before Mace shows up?"

"Two minutes, tops. I met him in the hall." Slater slapped down his blanket and sank on top of it. "He was trying to pretend he wasn't coming this way. Hmph."

"Slate," Drake said, "if you're going for casual, it isn't working."

"We're brothers. Therefore, I'm worried about you *and* the dog. Hell, Drake, all of us love Harold—even if his name is a mite on the stupid side."

Drake ignored the name comment. He had his

reasons for calling his dogs what he did. "He just came to. Tried to get up, then changed his mind."

His older brother relaxed. "You know," he said, "it's kind of nice out here. I haven't done this in a while." He sighed companionably. "I remember sleeping out here a lot when we were kids. I'll never forget the night you and Mace got into it over a candy bar we'd snitched from Harry's stash in the pantry. While the two of you were brawling, I ate it myself—for the sake of peace and goodwill."

"Mace was just as annoying back then as he is now," Drake said. "We probably would've duked it out over something else, if not that chocolate bar."

"Who's annoying?" Sure enough, it was Mace, dropping his bedroll to the floor of the veranda.

"You are."

He shook his head in mock disgust. "Talking about me behind my back," he muttered. "I thought better of you." He executed a yawn only slightly more convincing than Slater's had been. "How's Harold? I came to keep him company."

"He's holding on," Drake said.

A moment later, their mother came out, too, toting a blanket and a pillow. She surveyed the now-crowded porch with a resigned look on her face. "Nobody mentioned a family campout," she said. "I'd think *one* of you might have invited me."

"This seems to be a drop-in kind of deal," Mace told her. "Come as you are, and all that."

Everyone was keeping it down, but Luce was so

exhausted, even the extra voices didn't wake her. At least, Drake thought, they hadn't all wandered out here and found him and Luce sharing a sleeping bag.

Blythe wasn't naive, but she *was* his mother, and Drake would have been embarrassed as hell.

"Remember when we used to do this with Dad?" Mace asked. "I was considered one of the coolest kids at school when I told them we had a 'sleeping porch.'" He leaned forward a little, peering at the dog. "I see Harold's awake. That's good. Means he'll be okay."

"Quiet," Drake cautioned, watching Luce sleep through all the arrivals, wondering if she was going to be chagrined in the morning at waking up to a crowd scene. He shifted closer to her. "She's really tired."

"Of you?" Mace said. "Sure, who wouldn't be?"

"Don't be a wiseass."

Slater intervened, as usual. "I agree with Drake. If the two of you start to bicker and somehow wake up my pregnant wife, I can't answer for what might happen next. I might just end the argument myself, or I might let her loose on you two. Watch it. She's a force to be reckoned with at all times. That red hair does not lie."

Drake loved Grace. A former police officer, she knew how to put her foot down.

So did his mother. "They aren't going to argue. Go to sleep. You especially, Drake. There are more than enough of us to look out for Harold and Violet, not that Violet can't take care of herself."

The Blythe Carson method. Clear and succinct. It had worked when they were kids, and that tone was still mighty effective. Drake closed his eyes. He'd doubted that he'd catch even a wink, but it did help to know that there were other eyes and ears tuned in.

Five seconds later, he'd zonked out.

LUCE WOKE TO the smell of coffee, the scent of fresh bread and voices. She didn't even know where she was until Violet trotted over and licked her hand. She sat up on the hard floor of the porch and pushed her hair away from her face.

Daylight. She'd rarely slept that long. Or that deeply.

It seemed that breakfast alfresco was taking place on the veranda.

The round table at one end held a makeshift buffet, with muffins, a carafe of coffee and a pitcher of juice. There were also plates of sausages, along with a big glass bowl full of mixed fruit. People were sitting in various chairs or on the steps, talking and eating.

As she blinked in confusion at the blankets everywhere around her, Harry breezed through the door carrying a platter. "Scrambled eggs. And if anyone asks for ketchup or hot sauce, I'll have their hide."

Blythe, wearing some sort of lacy robe over silk pajamas, gave Luce a sunny smile. "Good morning, honey. If you're hungry, there's plenty."

Drake was, of course, nowhere in sight. Just her

luck. Luce had on pajama pants patterned with tiny cows—a pair her sister had given her and christened "the moo pants"—and a faded old T-shirt. Crawling out of her sleeping bag was embarrassing; on the other hand, she'd apparently been snoozing away in front of Drake's entire family for who knows how long.

"I, er, might run inside for a few minutes." She made a beeline for the door, since a swift exit seemed prudent. When she got to the bathroom, she saw that her Rapunzel hair was out of control. She rarely wore makeup, so she'd done nothing to remove it, and there were definite dark smudges under her eyes. She scrubbed those away, tamed the hair and put on a pair of jeans, a better shirt and a pair of slip-on shoes. She was late for breakfast yet again.

The Carson household was generally unpredictable. It wasn't every day a girl woke up to discover that she'd slept on a porch, watched by half a dozen people. What *was* predictable was their softhearted attachment to the dogs.

She still found it hard to believe that she was going to become one of these people, a member of their family. She hadn't known Drake very long, but the doubts she'd experienced during her first engagement just weren't there.

How odd to realize it.

This was perfect for her. Okay, sort of perfect. She had the handsome cowboy, and the ranch life she was settling into so easily. But…her family was still in California and she'd have to give up her teaching dream…

Nothing worth having came without sacrifice, she reminded herself. Once she had her master's, maybe she could look for something with the park service. She wasn't cut out to bake cookies and pack school lunches—at least not as a full-time vocation. Centering your life on family appealed to her, but she wanted a professional life, too. In a word, she wanted it *all*.

She hoped to teach at the college or university level. The closest college in this area was quite a drive, even if she managed to land a position there. And completing her PhD, which was another lifetime goal, seemed unlikely if she lived on a remote ranch.

She also guessed babies would be involved at some point. After all, Blythe had already brought up the subject.

There were certainly some things she and Drake needed to discuss—sooner rather than later. Maybe when he was her captive on the plane to California, strapped into the next seat, she could bring up subjects like the actual wedding. She had the distinct feeling that the kind of elaborate wedding her mother was going to want would not be welcome news; Drake was bound to prefer something simple. Beth's wedding had involved a string quartet, hothouse orchids and waiters in tuxedos. Their mother was adamant when it came to entertaining. Beth had confided that she'd just thrown up her hands and bowed out of the decision-making process, except for choosing the dress.

"Have a seat." Blythe offered her a plate. They were alone on the porch now. "Drake is off moving cattle, Mace left for the vineyard a few minutes ago and Slater has a meeting with some of his investors, so he's flying to Cheyenne. Grace went to the resort. She's cutting back her hours but isn't quite ready to stay home and wait it out. I'm going to relax here with the dogs, keep an eye on them. I spend most of my time out here, anyway. I have this new book I'm itching to read, and poor Harold gives me an excuse to indulge myself. What are your plans?"

That was a transparent question. Luce was sure everyone in the household knew Drake had forbidden her to go out on her own, and they were waiting to see how she'd handle it. "I'm going to work on my paper. Don't worry. After last night, I won't go out by myself. But truthfully, that mountain lion's been out there the whole time. Maybe it followed me, and maybe it didn't. Life is full of risks."

"I'm not going to disagree with that. Risk is everywhere. Falling in love is a risk." Blythe sent her a matronly, knowing look. "Have some fruit salad. Bex Calder's recipe. I had to practically bribe it out of her. It's so good."

Not sure what to say, Luce helped herself to a bowl of fruit salad and a muffin. She felt her future was spinning out of control. Unexpected things, positive things, were happening, but *she* wasn't controlling them any longer. She said faintly, "Thank you."

"Your mother's looking forward to meeting Drake. Well, she *has* met him before, when he was much younger. And my father's thrilled we're all coming."

Luce couldn't picture the austere man being thrilled about anything, so she took a bite of her muffin instead of commenting. It was delicious, made with bananas and white chocolate, among the more notable ingredients. Finally, she said, "I mentioned the dates to Drake. I got the impression that when we go doesn't really matter. I assume he'll want to spend some time with his grandfather."

"He and his grandfather don't get along all that well." Blythe looked resigned. "You've met my father."

Luce nodded. She certainly didn't know him well but had a clear memory of the distinguished elderly man, owner of a renowned winery.

"Well…" Bythe sighed. "My father and my husband didn't see eye to eye, either. To Dad, ranching is something people should pay to have someone else do for them. It's fine to own the property and stock, but choosing to be a true rancher baffles him. He couldn't rope a calf or break a horse to save his life. He was raised in wine country and, to his mind, being a vintner is a cultured thing to do. Getting dust on your boots is not. I won't use the word *snob*, and he loves Drake, but they don't understand each other. My father can taste a glass of wine while wearing a thousand-dollar suit and tell you exactly what grapes were used. My son can move a thousand cattle to a different pasture. Both of them are capable and stubborn as all get-out, and just different enough to strike sparks off each other. Yet I love them both. Have you set a date for the wedding?"

The...what?

"He *told* you he proposed?" She was going to strangle the man. They'd agreed to break the news together.

"Drake?" Blythe smiled and poured her a cup of coffee. "Of course not. Sons don't tell their mothers anything that personal, but he didn't have to tell me. Remember when you and I went ring shopping? Cream in your coffee and no sugar, right?"

"I remember the ring shopping," she said, slightly startled by the abrupt shift from jewelry to coffee. "And yes, right. Cream and no sugar, please."

"And here I thought I was being subtle about the wedding."

Yeah, as subtle as a sledgehammer. Luce had to ask, "Um, how often do you talk with my mother?"

"Now and then."

The coffee was wonderful and she needed some caffeine. She took a long sip. "Why do I suspect that means almost daily?"

"Now that you're here, we chat a little more often than before."

"Drake wanted to talk to my father before we announced our plans."

"That doesn't surprise me. I won't say a word, but your mother's already emailed me several pictures of wedding gowns she thinks would suit you. I'm afraid I did mention the film footage Slater's crew caught of my son kissing her daughter. Forgive me, but having been friends all these years, how could I *not* tell her about that?"

That dratted picture. Still, Luce couldn't really blame *his* mother for telling *her* mother. After all, she herself had blabbed the news to Beth right away. As a matter of fact, she'd now told *two* people that she and Drake were engaged. At this point, the entire town probably knew, anyway—thanks to the film and to her visit with Melody.

Luce held her coffee mug between her palms. "Drake's going to hate visiting California, isn't he?"

Blythe leaned back, the slanting sunlight catching the silver in her auburn hair. "He dislikes leaving Wyoming, but for you he'll do it. In my opinion, that's better than an emphatic 'I love you.' The old cliché about actions speaking more loudly than words, you know? He wants you to be happy and you should let him make you happy. And that, in turn, will make him happy. Pretty simple actually. People tend to complicate relationships."

Luce didn't discount that. She'd watched a few of her friends try to change their various boyfriends without success or, perhaps worse, change for them. Compromise was necessary, of course, as her father had once told her, but being true to yourself was the best thing you could do for your marriage. It kept you from resenting your husband or wife. That was why he let her mother give her parties without complaint and she let him play golf as often as he wanted. He couldn't understand her endless need to entertain, and she thought golf was boring, but their marriage worked because they each understood what was important to the other.

The ranch and his family were part of Drake's soul. But he'd have to understand that all the compromise wasn't going to be on Luce's side.

A car coming up the driveway interrupted her reflection.

"It's Lettie." Blythe sounded pleased. "I'll bet she's already heard about Harold somehow. She has a network that's second to none. Mine doesn't even compare, and I've lived here for years. I warn you, she has a tendency to say whatever's on her mind, but she also has the softest heart of anyone I know."

The woman was wearing a tailored suit at— Luce wasn't quite sure of the time, but it couldn't be more than eight. She marched up the steps and walked straight over to where Harold still lay on his blanket, looked him over and nodded. "Jax Locke obviously did his job. Good man."

Harold wagged his tail weakly.

Blythe murmured, "Morning, Lettie. Have you met Luce Hale?"

"The girl Drake's going to marry. Prominent California family. She's here to study wild horses."

Lettie Arbuckle-Calder moved to the table, settled into a chair, then crossed her elegant legs and accepted a cup of coffee. She leveled a stare at Luce, who now felt distinctly grubby even after cleaning up, and asked, "What's your young man going to do about the mountain lion?"

She didn't know what Mrs. Arbuckle-Calder was hoping to hear. "He could've killed it last night, but that isn't Drake. He has a friend who's relocated lions before. He's going to call him and review his options."

Mrs. Arbuckle-Calder relaxed visibly. "I approve of that."

Whew. Right answer.

"What about the wild horses?"

Now, there was a tricky one...

Luce took a gulp of coffee. She hadn't expected an interrogation this morning. "He says they can't stay."

"I have a solution to his problem."

The lady sounded very sure. Luce liked her more by the minute. "I can't wait to hear it."

CHAPTER TWENTY

IF HE KEPT a diary—which he didn't—Drake might've written, *Best day of my life, but not without problems*. First day as an engaged man. That was the happy part. He could also note that Red, although he'd never admit it, seemed to be coming down with something—maybe the flu. Which could be dangerous at Red's age.

Slater was out of town, so he couldn't help, and Mace had gotten in a huge order for Mountain Vineyards wine that had him dancing in the streets but working like a dog.

And speaking of dogs... Harold was doing very well—considering. It still hurt to think they might've lost him. Working with animals his entire life, he tried to not get too attached, but...

Ed Gunnerson answered on the third ring. "Drake. We haven't talked in a while. What's up?"

Drake was multitasking, stacking hay bales and talking on his cell. "I need your help. I've got a problem with a mountain lion, and he needs to go. One way or the other, but I prefer the other. He and my dog got into it, and the dog essentially lost the fight.

Seems like he's going to make it, though. This cat's been raiding my calves since last summer, but he's getting bolder. Thoughts?"

There was a pause. Ed always took his time. "Big cats have big territories."

That wasn't news. "Could you track him?"

"Oh, yeah, if he has a pattern, and they all do. Done it before. Track him and move him."

Maybe he could cross that off his to-worry-about list. "You are officially invited to the Carson ranch."

"I know where he could be content to live to a ripe old age and help keep the deer population under control. I'll try to get the arrangements in place."

"I'd appreciate it."

"I prefer a humane solution myself. That's why we're here."

"Thanks." He ended the call and contemplated what he should do next. There were always chores, needless to say, but he should check on Harold and Violet.

And Luce. When he'd gotten up, she'd still been asleep. Everyone had been asleep.

He rode back to the house and saw a recognizable car in the drive. He liked Lettie Arbuckle-Calder, but the woman was difficult to dissuade when she made a decision. He'd once tried—and failed—to deflect her from purchasing a nearby piece of property. She'd later sold it, and he figured that proved he'd been right, but he was never going to hear that from her. *I was wrong* was not part of her vocabulary.

Why did he have a sinking feeling that this had something to do with him? If Mrs. A-C felt the need to meddle, leave him out of it.

No such luck.

When he walked onto the porch, he saw Harold had gotten up and was eating. An encouraging sign. Violet was keeping him company, munching kibble from her bowl, too. She deserved a double helping.

"Hi," he said lamely to the three women sitting there. "I'm checking on the dogs, but I see they're in good hands. Red isn't feeling well, so I'm feeding the horses." A pause. "Beautiful day, isn't it? See you later."

Just as he spun around, Lettie said in a steely tone, "Not so fast, young man."

At thirty-two, he wouldn't describe himself as young anymore, but with his mother sitting right there, he wasn't going to argue. However, he wasn't going to apologize for his reluctance, either. The fact that he could tell Luce was laughing to herself didn't make the situation any more comfortable. "Yes?"

"I want to talk to you about the horses."

"Which ones?"

What man *wouldn't* be wary with three women looking at him expectantly? He certainly was.

It was Luce, as bewitching in her faded jeans and plain shirt as she was in her stylish dress, who finally said, "The wild ones."

His mother added, "I think it's a brilliant plan."

Oh, a supposedly brilliant plan involving wild

horses and women? Just what every man needed. Both unpredictable. It would be rude to point that out, so he hedged. "I'm listening. I guess."

"The old Winston homestead. The one where you believe the herd winters, correct? I've looked into it. The state owns the property now because it was abandoned and no taxes were being paid. You know how slowly the government works." Mrs. A-C sniffed in disapproval at the slow-moving wheels of bureaucracy. "But I have some influence here and there."

She probably had more influence than the governor, although he refrained from mentioning that. "I'm following you, but only so far. What's your suggestion?"

"I'd like to propose that the state of Wyoming make the property part of their park system on the basis of its being a historical landmark. If you can relocate the horses there, your problem's solved and they won't have to be shipped off anywhere." She seemed very...self-satisfied. Yep, that was the word for it.

He propped one foot on the top step, wishing it was that simple and not knowing how to delicately explain that it wasn't. "Uh, well, it sounds great in theory, but—"

"In *theory*?" Luce interrupted. She plonked down her coffee mug. "It sounds *great*, Drake. In reality. Not just in theory."

He gave her a quelling look. "You've been studying them, right? Doing research? Then you're aware

of how fast the herds grow. By the time this arrangement was set up, my problem would be a lot worse
than it is now. Not to mention that I don't know if the
federal government would even agree to let a state
park keep wild horses when it's allocated land to
manage them. And don't forget that stallion's kicked
through almost every fence *I've* ever put up. Plus,
there's no guarantee the horses would stay put, because he moves them all the time. My bull is easier to contain. Sounds simple, but I promise you, it
won't be."

That reminded him he had to meet Jim Galloway
in a couple of hours to go see a young bull owned
by a friend of his.

Full day. At least Harold seemed to be doing as
well as anyone could hope. Jax had said he'd stop
by later.

Mrs. A-C tapped the table and said thoughtfully,
"Probably valid points. I will ask all the right questions, then. Nothing is insurmountable."

He hoped that was true, but he'd stumbled across
a few situations that were pretty daunting. Yet he
had to admire her confidence. He didn't envy whatever official in the state government got her call.
They'd be scrambling to accommodate her, no doubt
about it.

"I'd better get back to work." He touched his hat.
"Ladies."

Then he beat a hasty retreat—although not as
hasty as he would've liked. Self-preservation was

rarely unwise. He could stand his ground if he had to, but his philosophy was to be polite and get the heck out of there when it was three against one and he was the one. A minority position was always difficult. Besides, he had things to do, plenty of them, and he even took his truck so he wouldn't have to go back to the house.

Of course, when he got to the stable, Red was hard at work. Drake frowned. "I told you to knock off for the day. You really look like you could be running a fever."

"Nonsense." Red continued to brush down a horse. "I don't get sick."

"You don't *admit* you get sick. There's a difference." He plucked the brush from the older man's hand and went to work on the gelding. "I'll finish this. Go take a nap."

"Naps are for old ladies," he said gruffly.

Time to play the trump card. "I told my mother you weren't feeling well. She'll tell Harry. Mrs. Arbuckle-Calder was there, too. Do you want the three of them catching you not resting? If I were you, I'd at least pretend to be asleep. Otherwise, in addition to whatever ails you, there's a lecture in your very near future. Maybe three." He fake-squinted at the door. "I think I see them coming now."

Red was no fool. He beat it. Drake shook his head and laughed sympathetically as he finished grooming the horse. He left a note for Ryder to clean the tack room when he got home from school; it was going to be good when the kid was out of school for the summer, because he did a great job with the smaller chores. Slater was teaching him how to ride, Drake was teaching him how to rope and Mace was teaching him how to shoot. For a city boy, he was catching on, too, and roping a calf when you hadn't been riding long wasn't all that easy. The first few times, the horse went one way and the kid went another and bit the dust, but he was getting the hang of it.

Drake glanced at his phone and saw that it was time to go over to Jim Galloway's. He probably smelled like horse with more than a hint of manure mixed in, but Jim wouldn't mind that one bit.

Jim and Pauline lived in a neat little house in town, perfect for two people, with tidy flower beds out front and a fenced backyard for their dogs. Jim looked younger since he'd married his second wife and won his battle with cancer, and he was grinning when he answered the door. "So you're getting married, eh? That's almost as fast as me when I met Pauline. What are you trying to do, beat my record? Pauline and I got hitched practically the moment we met. Hey, I have a request. Could you play the Texas two-step at the reception? My wife's one hell of a dancer."

How had Jim found out? Was that just a lucky guess?

He hadn't told anyone. That meant Luce had,

which he doubted, or his mother had figured it out. Maybe Mrs. A-C had looked in her crystal ball. Oh, yeah, Red had known Luce was in his bed the night before…

Anyway, he wasn't going to lie to Jim. He admitted, "We've talked about it. I don't think I'll be part of the entertainment committee, but I'll be sure to mention your request. Now, let's go see this bull."

Jim climbed amiably into the truck. "I'm not going to say he's easy to handle. Sherman's moody, too, so you know how to deal with that. Impressive animal. I went and took a look at him before I called you."

"You didn't need to do that."

"I have time on my hands now, so it was a pleasure to pretend I was still running a ranch, even for an afternoon. He's a dandy."

"Bloodlines?" Drake shot off some rapid-fire questions about the bull as he started the truck again, got the answers to his questions, and thirty minutes later, they pulled into the yard.

Jim's friend Mike Gorman was old-school, with overalls and a bald head, and it was clear that he assessed Drake before he nodded and they walked over to the fenced pasture. He liked that. The man wasn't going to give this animal away to just anyone.

"He's a handful," Mike said, keeping it short and sweet. "He'll get the job done and he'll tone down some as he gets a few years on him. No one wants a lazy bull. I named him Tobias, but you can call him whatever you want."

The price was reasonable, and Drake couldn't argue. This was a beautiful creature. He wrote a check then and there, because both he and Red trusted Jim's judgment. They hashed out the details for getting Tobias to his new home, and when they got back into the truck to head for Mustang Creek, Drake was feeling decent about life. The mountain lion was going to be handled, he'd solved the bull problem and Luce had said yes. If Mrs. A-C's ridiculous idea actually worked out, things were looking up.

His phone beeped and he pressed the button that let him talk hands-free. "Yep?"

It was Tripp. "You buy that bull from old Gorman?"

"Sure did."

"My dad's a traitor. I kind of had my eye on it."

"Son, I can hear you." Jim was chortling. "I'm right here. You waited a shade too long, that's all."

Tripp muttered something they couldn't catch, but then he laughed. "So I'm talking to both of you? Since you're there, Dad, I'm supposed to tell you that whatever you're having for dinner tonight, Pauline isn't going to cook it. You choose the place, but you're taking her out. And via Melody to Hadleigh, I'm supposed to tell Drake the ring is ready and he can pick it up whenever. Why *I'm* expected to have time to relay all these messages is a mystery to me, because I'm watching the baby right now and that's no picnic. I'd rather be herding ornery cows."

"Ring? What ring?" The moment the words were out of his mouth, Drake felt he already knew the answer to that question.

"The one your mother ordered for you. Damn, I smell something suspicious. This diaper needs changing… Gotta go. Drake, see you on poker night. Dad, take Pauline someplace nice."

Jim looked as if he was going to burst out laughing as the call ended. "Don't tell me. You didn't know about the ring?"

"No." Drake felt like laughing, too, but his laughter would've had an edge to it.

"You've been corralled. Blythe Carson's always been a woman who gets things done."

He'd be more annoyed, but truthfully, his mother had probably done him a favor. She'd have a much better sense of what Luce might want in a ring than he did.

He wanted a companion on evening rides. He wanted to see her smile, to hear the passion in her voice when she argued with him, to touch her, to taste her kiss, to imagine their children laughing and playing.

So all he said was "You're finding this way too funny. I guess after I drop you off, I need to go pick up a ring."

Jim agreed with a cheerful grin. "I guess you do, son."

LUCE BIT HER lower lip, thought about the sentence she'd just written, then went back and erased it.

She sat with her laptop on the front porch, since Blythe was out running errands. Violet was in the kitchen with Harry, but Harold had hobbled over and was keeping her company, sleeping at her feet. She found it touching that he was guarding her for Drake, even though he could barely get up.

She'd come to Wyoming to gather information, and now she had far more than she needed. The dissertation was getting harder to write as she went; there was a lot of ground to cover.

She was about to give it another try when her phone beeped. A text from Beth. I swear I didn't tell.

What did *that* mean?

She typed back, Clarify?

Operation Wedding has begun.

Luce blew out a breath of frustration. She believed Beth, and she knew Blythe would keep her word and hadn't said anything. So that meant her mother was evidently jumping to conclusions—the correct conclusions.

At that moment, Drake pulled in, parked his truck, and Harold barked in greeting, then settled back down. He rested his head on her foot.

"So *she's* your new best friend?" Drake came up the steps looking accusingly at his dog, but he smiled. "Well, Harold, here's a poorly kept secret. I like her, too."

"It isn't a secret at all," Luce informed him drily,

although she felt the same way about Harold. "I have to tell you something. My mother seems to know about the engagement. She didn't hear it from me, or from my sister *or* your mother. Oh, and Blythe's already booked our flights for the anniversary party."

He was quiet, obviously thinking it through. "Okay," he said finally. "That's not ideal, but we'll work with it." He shoved a hand through his hair. "Harold's choosy about the people he keeps company with. You ought to be flattered."

She definitely was.

"He can sleep on my foot anytime he likes." She studied Drake in silence for a few minutes. "The life of a cowboy," she mused. "Mind if I use that for the title of my dissertation? Part of the title, anyway."

"You creative types," he replied. "You sound like Slate. He'll throw out a title for one of his movies and wait for reactions. Says he prefers first impressions." He sat down across the table, appropriated her glass of lemonade and drained it in a single gulp.

Luce didn't mind at all. They were going to be good together. He'd never pressure her, and she wasn't interested in changing him. Oh, he could use a few nudges here and there—everyone could—but a sexy cowboy had been on her life wish list, and he certainly fit the bill.

"How about 'The Life of a Cowboy: I Can Only Control What I Can Control'?"

One corner of his mouth lifted in a smile. "Shouldn't there be something in there about nosy graduate students? Let me revamp. 'I Can Only Control Certain Things in Nature, and Women Are Not Among Them.'"

Luce was really laughing now. His sardonic sense of humor was one of the things she loved about him, even when he was disheveled and smelled like saddle leather and pine forests. She shook her head. "That's a chapter in *The Cowboy Guide to a Successful Relationship*. Stay focused. We're talking about the most important thing I'll ever write."

"Yeah, guess I forgot for a second there. Let me see if Harry can watch Harold while you and I go for a ride. I've been thinking about Mrs. A-C's suggestion. The valley isn't that far. When we first met, you said you wanted to see it. Besides, I haven't been on a horse all day."

For him, astounding. Horse deficiency.

She wanted to see the place where the horses wintered, no doubt about it. Luce would've jumped up with alacrity, but Harold's head was firmly planted on her shoe. "Your mother's lending me some boots. I'll go put them on."

Drake came over to give Harold a reassuring pat and the animal lifted his head. "We'll be waiting right here."

Luce went to her room, grabbed the boots and tugged them on. They were soft as butter, patterned with horses on the sides and totally comfortable.

Drake nodded in approval when she reappeared. "Nice job, cowgirl."

She didn't qualify for that title yet, but she was trying. "I'm learning, one day at a time, from a very qualified teacher."

He elevated his brows and gave her a devilish male grin. "I think you can hold your own. Oh, wait, we're not talking about riding, are we?"

"Watch it, Carson." She smacked his arm.

He caught her around the waist and pulled her to him. "This being in love business... I'm trying to figure it out and not getting very far."

"You're trying to make sense of something that doesn't actually make sense." Luce kissed him with a lingering pressure of her lips on his. "I'm on the same sinking ship."

"We can drown together."

"We can do a lot of things together, most of them better than drowning! Now, let's go for a horseback ride. I can tell you need an equine fix."

He ran his fingers up her arm. "And I can tell you have more confidence."

"Wait until the first time I fall off!"

"We all take a fall at some point. I've even seen Red bite the dust."

"You have?" That surprised her.

"Hell, yes."

It wasn't funny, and yet, somehow, it was. "That old cowboy fell off his horse?"

"Don't ever bring it up." Drake urged her toward the doorway. "I'd suggest not calling him old, either. He's kind of sensitive on the subject. I've also discovered that it's safer not to tell him he shouldn't do something because then he'll do it just to prove me wrong. So far he's in the winning bracket."

"I didn't mean old in a bad way."

"I know. He's a surprisingly sensitive guy about certain things. Oh, have I mentioned that you have to saddle your horse by yourself?"

He hadn't. Well, that was on her list, too. "I was hoping to bribe Ryder to show me how so I could impress you."

"I'm impressed already. No worries there."

She could live with that.

CHAPTER TWENTY-ONE

SHE WAS AN apt pupil, if a little out of practice. It didn't hurt that Grace's horse, Molly, was tolerant and patient, which, of course, was why Slater had picked her for his wife.

"Tighten the cinch again," Drake advised. "Horses are pretty smart. They'll sometimes take a breath and hold it so the saddle's loose when they let it out. Never underestimate an animal's intelligence. She's very amiable, but not all horses are the same. Always check your saddle twice."

"She's sweet." Luce stroked her silky neck.

"Remember, you're practicing on this horse, but another one might be totally different. Never presume it's going to go well if you don't know each other."

Slater's horse, Heck, wouldn't let her within ten feet of him. He was a beautiful horse but gave *feisty* a new meaning. Drake had helped Red break him, and he'd been hell on wheels. Even now, Drake was cautious around him and had ordered Ryder to leave his stall to more experienced hands. Red could do it, but Ryder couldn't handle that animal and he was a head taller than Luce.

"She likes you," he commented. "Don't get the idea that Smoke would ever allow you to get this close."

"He already has."

Drake thought fainting might severely damage his male image, so he didn't. *"What?"*

Luce acted nonchalant about it, her shoulders lifting in a shrug. "*He* came up to me. I touched him and that was it. He's as curious about me as I am about him and the rest of the horses. And he knows I'm not there to do them any harm. I don't carry a gun or ride a big horse. I just want to watch them. I walk only so close, and then I sit down and leave them alone as I make notes."

He actually took off his hat and threw it on the ground. "You *touched* a wild stallion? Are you loco?"

Luce had the nerve to look offended. "Hey, I was sitting there writing and suddenly realized he was right behind me. He sniffed my hair and I held up my hand. Here it is." She offered Exhibit A, palm up. "He didn't bite it off or anything. He smelled it and went on his way. I'm harmless. Give him credit for knowing that. You've already seen that he's gotten used to me."

Her logic worked, but she also needed to understand that they weren't talking about the placid mare he'd just helped her saddle. "He's a wild animal, and he's a really big one. Sharp teeth and hooves. There are bigger critters than us he wouldn't hesitate to go after, like that cougar."

"I didn't go up to him! I turned around and *he* was right there. Like I said, I was focusing on my notes and I had no idea he was so close."

"You are the greenest greenhorn I've met. That little interaction is exactly why you aren't going anywhere without me." He retrieved his hat and plopped it on his head.

She considered him through slightly narrowed eyes. "I seem to have survived for lo these twenty-six years. I promise you, negotiating multiple lanes of traffic in LA during rush hour is a lot more dangerous than anything you can serve up here, and I've done that many times. Are you always going to be so dictatorial?"

"I'm going to be protective, you can count on that. Now, get your very enticing behind on that horse and let's go for a relaxing ride. I'm not helping you mount this time. You work that out for yourself." He did check the saddle very quickly. She'd have to go solo someday, but if he was there, anyway, he might as well make sure she was as safe as possible.

She glared at him. "No problem."

She did a fair job of it, although part of her success was due to the patient horse. Starburst led the way, Molly followed and Drake was finally able to breathe in a deep lungful of the evening air and relax.

"Next valley over," he said. "It's a beautiful place, but I've never understood why the original homesteaders chose that spot to settle. The cabin's been there a long, long time. Since shortly after the Civil War.

I'm guessing they had sheep, because you can't graze cattle there. I also think that for whatever reason, the guy wanted to be as obscure as he could. Red tells me the legend is that he came to town once a month, bought the essentials—flour, coffee and sugar—but otherwise no one saw him. Everyone thought he had something to hide. Eventually, he stopped showing up and they found the place abandoned, the door still open. No one knows if he went away voluntarily or suffered some severe misfortune. There were no papers besides the deed, but no remains, either."

"Did anyone else ever live there? Lettie mentioned that the property taxes hadn't been paid in years."

"Yeah, there was another recluse there for a while, but I don't know much about him. And he was long gone by the time we came along."

"So the real story is about the original home-steader who mysteriously disappeared..."

"Yeah. Naturally, as kids we rode over, hoping it would be haunted. Unfortunately not. Maybe Slate will get lucky with his cameras. He's putting it in the documentary, and that might help Lettie Arbuckle's plan. If anyone can pull it off, it would be her, but I still think the red tape involved will be prohibitive."

"There's nothing like a good old-fashioned ghost story to charm a girl." Luce was easier with the horse now, her hands more relaxed on the reins. "Scary. In a romantic way, I mean."

"Well, I strive to be ever the romantic. Feel free to fling yourself into my arms anytime." He glanced over at her. "However...all ghost hunting so far has proved fruitless, so maybe neither of us should get our hopes up."

"I've flung myself into your arms already—without a ghost."

"And I loved every minute of it."

Luce had the best laugh. Light and feminine. "You did?"

"Like you didn't know that."

The breeze ruffled her hair, and her smile held a hint of mischief. "I might have noticed it. That aside, you really think Mrs. Arbuckle is being too ambitious? I want to be sure I've got all my facts straight."

Oh, yes, her paper. He rode along, slowly, although he could tell that Starburst would've preferred a faster pace. "Containing the horses isn't going to be simple."

"Very few things in life are simple, cowboy."

"A night like this is." His smile was genuine. "An evening ride with a pretty girl, a fresh breeze, the mountains framing a spectacular sunset... This is a simple joy. Harry said something about steaks for dinner, along with her famous scalloped potatoes. Another simple joy."

"Is there anything Harry makes that isn't famous?" Luce tucked a strand of hair behind her ear. She really was sitting her horse more comfortably, not thinking about it so much.

"No," he admitted. "Some people are born to create wonderful paintings. Some are destined to compose music that's listened to and admired for centuries. She has a talent for making fantastic food and running a household the way a general might direct a battle plan. It doesn't hurt that she and my mother are like sisters. My mother, to her credit, is willing to step back and let Harry run the show. Harry, to *her* credit, has always kept her nose and her opinions out of any parenting decisions unless asked. I see that now as an adult, but I didn't notice it as a kid. Even when you asked her directly, tried to get her involved, she'd say, 'I think that needs to be settled between you and your mother.' She wasn't opposed to letting any of us know if we were out of line, but she didn't meddle."

"And when she was finished telling you to smarten up, she gave you a cookie." Luce smiled.

"Usually," he agreed, since she was right. "Or two. Sometimes a slice of pie if Mace didn't get there first. He's quite the chowhound."

"My impression is that he works as hard as you and Slater do, so that might be the secret to the male Carson persona. Hard work, which equals being perpetually hungry."

"My dad was no slouch, either." He pointed. "The only real entrance to the valley is that narrow corridor up ahead. That's problem one for Lottie's relocation plan."

THE VALLEY WAS as beautiful as Drake had promised.

Steep, green, with a meandering stream running

through, it was sheltered by a towering rock wall to one side. Luce immediately thought that if solitude was what you wanted, this would be the place to go. There wasn't a dramatic mountain view, but there was plenty of privacy.

No wonder Smoke brought his band of horses here for the winter. The storms coming in from the west probably didn't hit this spot as fiercely. She'd run the weather models when she'd embarked on this scientific journey, doing her best to understand how the habitat worked.

She wasn't entirely joking when she said, "I see why people might think this place is haunted. It feels strange, a bit surreal."

The cabin itself was decrepit, a relic of the long-gone past. The ancient logs and a rickety front porch had started to deteriorate, but the chimney looked sound, and there were the ruins of a barn. The last time someone had lived here was more than a few decades ago.

Drake didn't disagree with her. "It's a hidden gem. That makes Mrs. A-C's plan both good and bad. People will love that deserted old cabin and the grazing wild horses, but getting them in here is almost impossible if they aren't riding. There's no road, and I don't want one. It would have to go across Carson property."

"It doesn't have to be a road," Luce reasoned. "Maybe just a trail—a ride to a haunted valley. Toss in a visit to the vineyard, and you'll really have something." She paused, her mind moving at warp speed. "Do you see the state agreeing to open a park? I don't know how these things work."

He'd relaxed visibly, out there in the open spaces. The thought of Drake Carson walking into a corporate office for a meeting was practically incomprehensible; he was meant for *this* life. Glimmering Western sunsets and the soft whisper of the breeze ruffling the aspen leaves—that suited him so much better than skyscrapers and concrete ever could.

Luce was starting to feel that maybe it was the same for her.

He shrugged, his answer carefully considered, as usual. "I suggest we wait to see what Lettie finds out," he began. "That woman knows how to get things done." He smiled, the wind ruffling his hair. "She reminds me of my mother, but with a lot less tact. They're quite a team—one of them will pour you a cup of tea and, while you're distracted, the other will run over you with a bulldozer. In any case, they almost always get whatever they're after."

In Luce's admittedly limited experience, that assessment was dead-on.

"Big, strong men should step back, huh?"

"Big, strong men should run for their lives." Drake grinned. "You do realize you fall into the same category as my mother and Lettie. The Unstoppable Female."

She silenced him by holding up one hand. "Pardon my grammar, but you ain't seen nothin' yet, cowpoke. Wait until you meet my sister and mother. Whoa, you're going to be in for an experience." She pretended to assess his appearance. "You might have to get your hair cut," she speculated.

He looked endearingly perplexed. "My hair? What's wrong with my hair?"

"Nothing, as far as *I'm* concerned, but Mom and Beth are big on making people over. Watch out, that's all I'm saying. If you don't, you might find yourself in a Beverly Hills salon, getting highlights or a spray tan."

"That'll be the day," he drawled.

"Oh, it's very LA," she told him solemnly. "Guys even get facials."

"Not this guy, ma'am."

"I'm joking," she said. "Beth and my mom wouldn't dream of trying to improve you." She erupted into laughter. "Not that I'm saying you're perfect or anything."

Drake gave her a mock glare, then he laughed, too. A moment later, his expression was somber again. "Listen, couldn't we just get married at the ranch? Say, on the ridge where you and I first met? A minister and a few witnesses, and we're in business. Mace and Slater could be there, and Slater's crew could take the pictures. Sound good?" He didn't wait for her answer, which was convenient, because she didn't have one ready. "That way, you'll have a wedding and I'll survive the ceremony and the reception. We can feed each other cake and fly out for our honeymoon."

Actually, Luce rather liked the idea of a simple, rustic wedding. She wasn't really the fuss-and-ruffles type, though she did want the day to be special. Not quite as "special" as their mothers were gearing up for, however. "Do you mean it, Drake? Because if you do, my sister would come out here in a heartbeat to be my maid of honor."

"Oh, believe me, I mean it."

If there was one thing she knew about Drake, it was that he said what he thought and thought about what he said; his opinions were never unconsidered. So she did the same. "I'm in favor of something romantic, memorable and uncomplicated," she said honestly.

He brightened. "You are?"

"Sure." Luce nodded. She was fairly certain her mother would be disappointed; Dorothy Hale was probably planning an event more appropriate to the gardens of Buckingham Palace than the wide-open spaces of Wyoming. Her father wouldn't be a problem, and Beth would be on her side.

Their special day would be lovely.

"I know you wanted to meet Mom and Dad before the news got out," she went on. "We could call them, if you like."

"Or," he countered, "we could see if Tate Calder or Tripp Galloway can find the time to fly us out there to pick up your sister. Think she could talk your folks into taking her to the airfield? That way, at least, I could shake hands with your dad and give your mom a chance to look me over, make sure I don't have three heads or anything."

Meeting her parents in person, prior to the wedding, seemed more important to Drake than it was to her, but she thought she understood his reasons. Like his brothers, he'd been raised rough-and-tumble, but with very good manners.

This, she suspected, was what he thought his father would want him to do. It touched her heart, the realization that he still missed Zeke Carson, after all these years, still cared about doing what would be the right thing in his eyes.

She spoke softly. "Your dad would be wildly proud of you no matter what."

Drake didn't respond to that. "Can Beth manage to get your folks to the airfield or not?" he asked.

That was truly a laughable question. "Beth's been twisting Dad around her little finger, as they say, since the day she was born. It's impressive to watch her in action. My mother and I just look at each other and shake our heads. Dad's no fool. He knows exactly what she's up to, but he can't say no."

"Talk to her. Choose a date for the wedding. I'll see what I can work out on this end."

They'd have a romantic story to tell their children, that was for sure. "I'll call her as soon as we get back."

He squinted at the sky. "Speaking of which, we'd better start back. I'm not Red, but it smells like rain to me and there are clouds rolling in. Looks like a spring storm brewing up there. You think you can handle a slightly faster pace?"

Luce nodded, trying to ignore the small flicker of panic. "I'm going to have to sooner or later, I suppose."

They almost made it before the rain came. When he lifted her from her horse, they were both laughing and soaking wet. Drake didn't let her go but smoothed her damp hair away from her face and kissed her. He said, "You did well, cowgirl. While we wait for the rain to stop, I'll show you how to unsaddle your horse and brush her down."

Facetiously, she answered, "I'm not sure California girls do that."

"If I'm not mistaken, you're about to become a Wyoming girl. Now, pay attention, and if you catch on right quick, I might even help you out of your wet clothes when we get into the house."

Would she ever be able to resist that sexy smile? Somehow she doubted it. "You have a deal, cowboy."

CHAPTER TWENTY-TWO

THEY WERE EXACTLY three minutes behind schedule when the plane touched down and taxied across the tarmac. In Drake's opinion, traveling by private jet beat the commercial airlines anytime—no security hassles, no lost baggage and no layover. The flight had been smooth, due to a high pressure system coming in, and the turnaround would be quick.

It had taken the better part of a week to coordinate everybody's schedules, but he considered it well worth the time and effort.

Luce's sister and father had arrived in a high-end luxury car that had a pedigree that would've impressed the CEO of a Fortune 500 company. His own truck regularly smelled like dried mud and horse, but no one needed to know that, since he had just flown in on a private plane. He'd opted for a regular shirt and slacks, and to his surprise, Luce had told him to go change.

"Be yourself," she'd said before they left the house. "Wear jeans and boots. Drake, you're comfortable with who you are. That's really all that matters. My parents will respect that. It won't be news to them that you live on a ranch."

So he kept the nice shirt and gratefully exchanged the slacks and loafers for jeans and boots.

Takeoff was a little turbulent, but Tripp had mentioned it might be. They flew out of it quickly and the trip was smooth from that point on. Luce didn't talk much, but he sensed that she was nervous.

Once they disembarked, Luce rushed across the tarmac to hug a woman who had to be her mother, given the resemblance. Mrs. Hale was expensively dressed in a long white silk shirt and dark pants, her blond hair cut at chin level. Dangling earrings, high heels and a fancy leather handbag completed the overall image of sophistication. There was a second woman, Luce's sister no doubt, a much younger version of the first.

Both were delighted to see Luce, and there was a lot of happy chatter.

Luce, in comparison to her mother and sister, was different, more the outdoors type.

Perfect in every way, in Drake's opinion.

Mr. Hale waited, benignly patient, for his turn to greet the prodigal daughter. He was distinguished-looking, but clearly good-natured, too. Once he'd greeted Luce, the older man met Drake's eyes. They assessed each other in silence for a moment.

Then Drake stepped forward and put out his hand. "I'm Drake Carson," he said.

"John Hale," Luce's father responded, his voice

reserved but cordial. "This is my wife, Dorothy, and our other daughter, Beth."

Drake smiled, shook each woman's hand.

"We've met before," Dorothy Hale said with a sparkle in her eyes. "You probably don't remember, since you and your brothers were small the last time I visited Blythe—not even in school yet, if I remember correctly."

Drake didn't know what to say to that. The whole situation felt awkward and a little contrived, and he began to wish he'd taken Luce's suggestion and introduced himself by phone or over Skype.

"I've never had the pleasure," Luce's dad said cordially. "Luce speaks very highly of you, though, and God knows we both think the world of your mother."

Luce must have sensed Drake's discomfort, because she hooked her arm through his and leaned against him. "Dad, Mom—this is all about telling you, live and in person, even though you already know that Drake's asked me to marry him and I've said yes."

Drake wasn't the nervous sort, but for some reason, everything he'd planned to say had gone right out of his head. He did some mental scrambling and then said, "I love your daughter very much."

"I can see that," Mr. Hale said with a glint of amusement in his eyes. "I take it you flew all the way here to talk to us about this?" He smiled warmly. "We appreciate that, son." He paused to look around the airfield for a few minutes. "Your method seems a little unorthodox, which makes me think this was Luce's idea. And Beth's." His gaze swept from one daughter to the other, full of affection, and Mrs. Hale gave a soft laugh. "I don't know why women can't do things in a straightforward way, just call up and break the news, or come to the house. They like drama, I guess."

Drake relaxed a little, but not completely. He didn't give a damn what people thought of him, but he wanted the Hales to understand that he would be good to Luce, always. "I realize you don't know much about me, but—"

"I know your family," John broke in, "and your mother and Dorothy are close. Your grandfather's a longtime friend of ours, as well—how is George, anyway? It must have been a blow when your grandmother died."

Drake felt a pang of sorrow, thinking of his grandmother, dead some ten years now. He knew his grandfather missed his wife every moment of every day, but the old man was determined to carry on and ran his California vineyard with the energy and ambition of a much younger man. "He keeps busy and visits the ranch when he can," he said, and his voice came out sounding hoarse.

Mrs. Hale hadn't said much before then, but now she spoke up. Cut right to the chase. "We know our daughters are both smart, sensible young women, Drake. If Luce wants to marry you, and if you're anything like your mother and grandfather, you're a fine human being. You certainly have our blessing."

"Do I get to say anything?" Beth demanded good-naturedly.

Everyone smiled.

"Be our guest," John Hale said with a gesture of one hand.

"My sister is a catch," Beth said pleasantly, but in a direct way, "and if you treat her well, I'll be the best sister-in-law ever. If you don't, I'll be your worst nightmare."

Drake laughed, liking Beth, as he liked Mr. and Mrs. Hale. "Duly noted," he said.

John Hale slapped Drake on the shoulder. "Good luck, young man," he said. Then, kissing Luce, he added, "To you, too, sweetheart."

Mrs. Hale was smiling and crying a little at the same time. "I wish you could stay with us awhile, both of you," she said. "We have a lot of planning to do, Luce. It's not every day a person's daughter gets married."

Behind them, Tripp fired up the airplane's engine, and the props began to turn.

"We've got lots of things to do back at Mustang Creek," Luce said, not quite meeting her mother's eyes. "Drake runs the ranch, you know, and I'm still working on my research project."

"Lucinda can be a bit of a handful," Mr. Hale said with another fatherly smile at Luce. "It's only fair to warn you."

Drake smiled. "She'll keep my life interesting, anyway."

"I can hear what you're saying, both of you," Luce said in lilting tones. Her beautiful eyes sparkled with exaggerated affront. She rose up on tiptoe and kissed her mother, then her father, on the cheek. "Thanks for that, Dad," she teased.

"I hate goodbyes," Dorothy said, blotting her eyes with a tissue. "I'll just wait in the car."

"Women," said John, but tenderly.

"We really have to get back," Luce said.

Beth hugged her. "Come back when you can stay longer, sis," she said. Then she smiled, stood on tiptoe and kissed Drake's cheek. "Take care of my sister, cowboy," she told him in parting, "and nobody will get hurt." With that, she followed her mother.

Drake put his arm around Luce's shoulders, gave her a gentle squeeze and extended a hand to his future father-in-law. "I don't have a lot of experience with father-daughter moments," he said, "but this sure looks like one to me, so I'll leave you to it."

John Hale's grip was firm and friendly. "We'll see you again soon," he said.

Drake nodded, caught and held Luce's eyes for a moment. She nodded back, and he turned and walked back toward the plane, where Tripp was overseeing the refueling process.

"Dad?" Luce said, full of love and benevolent desperation in her voice. "Will you do something for me? Will you please remind Mom that we really and truly want the wedding to be ultrasimple, so she shouldn't go too crazy planning the reception?"

She knew Beth had filled their parents in on the dates and the general plan and would help in Luce's campaign to keep the festivities out of overdrive, but getting her dad on board was important, too.

"Will I at least get to walk you down the aisle?" He asked the question lightly, with a smile in his eyes. Luce knew her answer mattered to this man who had always been a good father to her and to Beth, and a devoted husband to their mother.

She hugged him again, hard. Let her head rest against his strong shoulder for a moment, remembering. Appreciating. And, most of all, loving. "Of course you will, Dad," she assured him, looking up into his kind, strong face. "Although it might be more of a path than an aisle." They both smiled at that. "It's just that, well, for Drake and me, this wedding isn't about one day, it's about setting the tone for our whole future, our marriage." She paused. "And you know me, Dad, I've never been the lace-and-flounces type, have I? That was Beth's department, and when she got married, as you recall, Mom planned, organized and fussed to her heart's content."

Her dad smiled again, a bit wistfully, and shook his head. "I understand, sweetheart. And your mother will, too, with a little convincing. Don't waste a moment worrying about us, because we're on your side. This is your day, and Drake's, and we'll respect that."

"Thank you," Luce said.

He kissed her forehead. "Just be happy," he told her gruffly. "And remember, we love you."

Luce's eyes stung with sudden tears. "And I love you, Dad. You and Mom and Beth."

Holding her shoulders in a gentle grip, her dad looked past her, to Drake and the waiting airplane and probably the years ahead. "Let us know when you get back to Mustang Creek," he said. "Your mother will be anxious until she's sure you're back on solid ground."

"I'll send a text," Luce promised. Then, with a wave toward the car, where her mother and sister waited, and a soft goodbye for her dad, she turned, seeking and finding Drake, walking toward him.

Toward all they would do and be and have together.

CHAPTER TWENTY-THREE

As LUCE WAS to discover over the dizzying course of the next ten days, there was her definition of *simple*—and then there was the Blythe Carson–Dorothy Hale version.

Dorothy and Beth, baby in tow, arrived in Mustang Creek barely a week after the hasty airfield conference, full of happy plans.

Luce, though slightly wary, was thrilled to see her mother, sister and infant nephew.

Dorothy and Blythe hugged and cried and laughed, and they were still chattering long after everyone else had retired that first night.

Luce tried to sleep—upcoming wedding notwithstanding, she was still searching for the herd of wild horses every day, albeit without success, and she'd been spending hours on her research notes, as well. She needed her rest.

Still, knowing her sister and tiny nephew were just down the hall, Luce couldn't lie still long enough to close her eyes, let alone drop off into sweet slumber.

So, barefoot and wearing pajamas, she tiptoed

toward that particular guest room, blushing a little as she passed Drake's closed door.

Alas, there would be no private slumber party tonight, not with Luce's mother in the house, huge as it was. She consoled herself with the reminder that soon enough Drake's room would be her room, too.

Reaching Beth's door, Luce rapped lightly, hoping her sister hadn't already gone to sleep. Motherhood, according to Beth, was strenuous business, and the day had been a busy one.

"In," Beth called quietly. For a moment, it seemed to Luce, time shifted, and she and her sister were girls again, meeting in one of their bedrooms to whisper and giggle and, sometimes, commiserate over a boy or a bad grade or being grounded.

Luce stepped willingly into the time warp.

Beth had just gotten the baby to sleep in the antique cradle hauled over from Slater and Grace's part of the house for his use.

She smiled at Luce and held an index finger to her lips.

Luce smiled and nodded and crept over to admire the sleeping infant. His name was Ben, and he looked downright cherubic lying there, his downy hair fluffing out, his lashes resting lush on his plump little cheeks.

Luce's heart swelled with love for this child and, naturally, she thought of the babies she and Drake would have.

Was it even possible to sustain the kind of happiness she was feeling now?

Probably not, she supposed. Like everyone else, she and Drake would have their ups and downs, but the core of their relationship was solid and lasting, and that was what counted.

She and Beth moved to sit, side by side, on the edge of the bed, speaking in near whispers.

"Okay," Luce began, "let's have it. Is Mom here to see her best friend and help with the preparations, or is she planning a full-scale assault on my wedding plans?"

Beth smiled, took Luce's hand and squeezed it gently. "We're here because you're getting married, and we want to be with you. I think Dad and I have been fairly successful in persuading Mom not to go all Martha Stewart, though I can't guarantee she and Mrs. Carson aren't plotting a takeover even as we speak."

Luce shook her head, but she was smiling as she returned Beth's hand-squeeze. "Whatever happens, I'm so glad you're here. Mom, too, of course."

"Dad and Liam will be here the day of," Beth said. Liam was her husband. "In the meantime, Mom and I just want to be part of the process." She made a cross-my-heart motion with one hand. "We'll behave, I promise."

Luce laughed, very softly. "Who are you," she joked, "and what have you done with my sister?"

Beth stifled a giggle, à la the old days, when they

were teenagers with silly secrets. And her eyes shone as she gazed at Luce. "I'm so happy for you, sis."

Luce teared up briefly and gave Beth a one-armed hug. "Thanks, Bethie. That means a lot to me."

They sat in silence for a little while, just being sisters, side by side, shoulders touching.

Then, with a faux wince, Beth ventured, "You do know about the wedding shower, right? I hope I'm not blowing a big surprise."

"I suspected something was up," Luce admitted, pleased in spite of her no-fuss policy. "I've caught Grace and Harry and Blythe whispering a few times, among other hints."

"So you've made friends here?"

"I haven't had much spare time," Luce answered, "but, yes, I've been meeting new people right and left. Hadleigh, Melody and Bex—they're married to Drake's closest friends—have been great to me. Being neighborly is very big in Mustang Creek."

"Good," Beth said. "I love my husband, but the older I get, the more I cherish my girlfriend time."

Another silence followed, contented and reflective. Again, and typically, Beth was the one to break it.

"Okay, so I do have one question," she said.

"Shoot," Luce responded.

"What about your PhD, and your plans to teach? It's none of my business, I know, and yet—"

"And yet it is," Luce said. "You're my big sister, after all. The answer is, I may modify my plans a little, at least at first, but I'm definitely going forward with the original idea."

"Where would you teach? Is there a college in Mustang Creek?"

"A community college," Luce replied, "with a very good chance of upgrading to a four-year institution in the next few years. They've already approached me about establishing an ecology program this fall, in cooperation with the high school, and that means I can teach while I finish my graduate work."

"And what does Drake think?"

Luce smiled and patted her sister's hand. "He's all for it. Drake is as committed to the environment as I am, if not more so, and I'm counting on his input when I start my syllabus."

Beth fairly beamed. "Wow," she said. "The man is not only hot, he's progressive."

Luce laughed. "I wouldn't go that far. Drake's hot, all right, but progressive?" She shook her head, still amused. "When he decides to dig in his heels, he can be incredibly stubborn, and some of his ideas are distinctly old-fashioned."

"Examples, please, little sister."

"Well, he can be overprotective. He opens doors and tips his hat and says 'Ma'am' when he speaks to a woman over fifty. He stands when any female enters a room and won't hear of going Dutch."

Beth made a mock-sympathetic face. "Poor you," she said.

"Yeah," Luce agreed happily. "Poor me."

Beth yawned then and, since yawns are catchy, Luce did, too. The sisters exchanged good-nights, and Luce went back to her room.

This time, she had no trouble falling asleep.

THE NEXT FEW days were busy ones. Luce saw little of Drake, but this only ratcheted up the anticipation, and when they were together, invisible fireflies lit the atmosphere between them.

As it turned out, literally every woman in Mustang Creek had been invited to the wedding shower, held in the community center, and there was a capacity crowd. By Blythe's decree, and much to Luce's agreement, nobody brought gifts; the gathering was meant to be a getting-acquainted celebration, and it was certainly that and more.

Although the no-gifts rule was observed, it apparently didn't apply to food. Luce had never seen so many cakes, pies, cookies and casseroles supplementing the catered spread. There was plenty of wine—Mace's label, of course—as well as lemonade and punch and that small-town specialty, two large urns of coffee, regular and decaffeinated.

Luce was absolutely dazzled; Melody, Hadleigh and Bex had hung streamers, and there were flowers everywhere.

Luce had a wonderful time, as did her mother and sister, though with all those new faces, she began to wish someone had passed out name tags.

The event lasted some three hours, and Luce was

dizzy by the end, feeling fully welcome in her new community. There was still a great deal of food, but the women of Mustang Creek were prepared; they'd brought plastic containers of all sorts along, and they filled every one to the brim.

Much of it would be eaten later that same day, since, once a week, the community center offered free meals to anyone who showed up. By design, tonight was the night. The remainder of the largesse, mostly desserts, would be taken to the town's two nursing homes as a treat for the residents.

Luce treasured the prospect of friendship with these women, and their generosity, to the less fortunate members of the community as well as to her, was a memory she would hold in her heart forever.

WHEN THEIR WEDDING DAY finally arrived, Luce was in a strange, blissful state, and for the first time, she understood what the old cliché about walking on air really meant.

Blythe and Dorothy had done their best to restrain themselves, but only so much could be expected of the mothers of the bride and groom.

The spacious yard behind the ranch house glittered in the twilight when everyone gathered for the ceremony. Colorful Chinese lanterns glowed in the branches of the maple and oak trees, the rented folding chairs had bows affixed to their backs and a three-piece mini orchestra had set up in the gazebo.

There was an abundance of food, as there had

been at the shower a few days before, but Luce knew not a scrap would be wasted. Once again the leftovers would be shared; this time two local churches had agreed to package what remained and deliver meals to every shut-in in town.

When all was ready, the ceremony began.

Luce wore a simple, ankle-length dress of white eyelet over a silky fabric; Drake, a dark suit that flattered his cowboy frame in a whole new way. The small orchestra played quietly.

Luce's father, recently arrived, proudly escorted the bride to the rose arbor serving as an altar, where Beth waited, beaming, bouquet in hand.

Drake, with his brothers at his side, stood tall and proud and impossibly handsome, facing the Carson family's longtime minister.

"Who gives this woman in marriage?" the pastor asked.

"Her mother and I," answered the father of the bride in a clear voice. Before returning to his seat in the front row, next to Dorothy, Blythe and a happily weepy Harry, he bent his head and kissed Luce gently on the cheek.

The vows were made, the rings were exchanged and Drake and Luce were pronounced husband and wife.

Drake's kiss was long and deep, and when it ended, the guests applauded and cheered, and he whispered mischievously, "There's something to be said for starting off on the right foot, so to speak."

And Luce laughed for joy.

As MUCH AS DRAKE loved his family and friends, there were times, during the picture-taking and the cake-eating and the exuberant congratulations, that he wished they'd all vanish, temporarily of course, into some parallel universe, so that he could be alone with his wife.

It seemed to him that the fussing and the eating and the making of toasts would never end. Drake choked up as he watched his bride and her father share the first waltz.

God, Luce was so beautiful.

And she was his wife.

When it was his turn to dance with the bride, Drake forgot everything but the way it felt to hold this woman in his arms, to see her smiling up at him, her eyes alight.

Eventually, the long-awaited cue came. Slater gave the prearranged signal to take Luce and slip away—a raised fist.

Finally, finally, the honeymoon could begin.

Drake grabbed Luce and led her to the refurbished buckboard awaiting them. Red was at the reins, all spiffed up in his best suit, reserved for weddings and funerals, and grinning from one ear to the other. He jumped down, nimble for a man of his age, and watched proudly as Drake lifted Luce up into the seat, then followed, taking the place Red had occupied.

There were more cheers and good wishes, and then Mr. and Mrs. Drake Carson were on their way.

The honeymoon would be an unconventional one,

Drake supposed, at least in terms of location, but it was exactly what both he and Luce wanted.

Earlier in the day, with the help of his brothers, Drake had set up a tent in the private spot where he and Luce had made love the first time. A campfire was laid, and there were fancy provisions, but just then, Drake didn't care if he ever ate again.

Luce sat close, leaning against him, her arm hooked through his.

"I can still arrange for a hotel, if you've changed your mind," he told her, raising his voice a little to be heard over the two-horse team and the creaking harnesses.

"Not a chance," Luce said. "This is perfect."

The words proved prophetic.

When they reached the campsite, the tent, just big enough for an air mattress equipped with a double sleeping bag, glowed like a palace in the star-spangled moonlight.

For a touch of elegance, there was a small portable picnic table, so they wouldn't have to eat breakfast sitting on the ground. If they ever got around to breakfast, that is.

Luce drew in an audible breath. "Oh, Drake," she whispered. "This is lovely!"

Her pleasure was his pleasure, and not just in bed.

Drake secured the wagon's brake lever, wrapped the reins loosely around it and climbed down. When he reached for Luce, she wrapped her arms around him and slid her body along the length of his as she descended.

He kissed her, long and hard and deep.

"Happy?" he asked when he caught his breath.

She smiled. "Yes," she replied, "and about to be a whole lot happier still."

Drake laughed and swatted her lightly on that delectable backside of hers.

"Like any good frontier husband," he said, "I've got to look after the horses before I can do anything else."

"Then I guess you'd better hurry, cowboy," Luce purred, her eyes dancing.

With that, she headed for the tent, disappeared inside.

If there was a God in heaven, Drake thought, with a silent apology for irreverence, she'd be out of that dress by the time he joined her.

IT WAS DELICIOUSLY DARK inside that small tent, and Luce wasted no time wriggling out of her wedding dress and panty hose and bra. Since there was no place to put the discarded garments, she tossed them through the narrow opening and stretched out to wait for her husband.

He was in the process of stripping when he entered their honeymoon hideaway.

Luce was more than ready for him, and there was no question that he was ready for her.

They'd made love before, of course, but somehow that night was even better. In fact, it was transcendent.

They touched each other everywhere.

They kissed and withdrew, not to tease, but because they needed to catch their breath.

They drew out the foreplay until neither of them could bear the wait any longer, and when they came together, they felt their souls mate along with their bodies.

Intermittently, they slept, satiated, and then woke to love again.

For a solid forty-eight hours, they were alone in their singular world of grass and trees and snow-capped mountains.

Then, inevitably, it was time to go back.

"Could we do this again?" Luce asked. This morning, she was wearing shorts, hiking boots and a tank top from the suitcase they'd brought along in the back of the wagon.

Drake, busy hitching the horses to the wagon, paused long enough to kiss her thoroughly. "I was thinking," he said, working again, "that we ought to build a house here. What do you think, Mrs. Carson?"

She turned him around, flung herself at him, arms around his neck, legs around his hips. "I think you're a genius, Mr. Carson," she cried, and then she kissed him just as deeply as he'd kissed her before.

NO HONEYMOON LASTS FOREVER, Drake reminded himself when they drove up to the ranch half an hour later and found Red waiting for them with a solemn expression on his grizzled old face.

"He doesn't look happy," Luce observed, perched beside Drake on the wagon seat and sounding worried.

"He never looks happy," Drake said.

Luce didn't wait for him to help her down from the wagon this time. She marched over to Red and asked, "What's wrong?"

Red chuckled. "See you're takin' to bein' a ranch wife right off the bat," he remarked, not unkindly.

"You looked so serious," Luce persisted.

"I ain't what you'd call expressive," Red told her. By then, Drake was out of the wagon, coming toward them.

"Stop stalling and spill it," he said.

"Look, I didn't mean to get you all riled up. I just wanted to welcome the bride and groom home proper like, that's all. Let me deal with this wagon and these horses and we'll talk business."

Knowing Luce wanted to take a shower and then drink coffee that hadn't been boiled over a campfire, Drake said, "Go on inside, Luce. Mom and Harry are probably waiting to make sure you're still in one piece after a wilderness honeymoon."

Luce smiled, but she didn't budge. "In a minute," she said. "If this is about the mountain lion, or the wild horses, I want to hear it."

Red looked a little surprised, but he didn't offer an opinion. In his era, women didn't talk back to their husbands.

Drake felt a little sorry for Red's generation, because this particular woman was worth listening to.

"The BLM and the Fish and Wildlife people are all over this," Red said as stolidly cheerful as ever. "They plan to tranquilize the cat and relocate it farther north. If they can find it, anyhow."

Drake was relieved. Relocation was ideal in a case like this, but it wasn't always possible for a variety of reasons, including budgets and manpower.

"Just goes to show change isn't always bad," Red agreed. "Back in my day, they solved problems like this one with a bullet."

"Change isn't good or bad," Drake said. "It just is. And this is *still* your day, Red."

"As long as my eyes open every morning, I reckon that's true." Red scratched his chin, his tone jocular.

"What about the wild horses?" Luce asked.

"No sign of them," Red replied with regret.

"In that case, I'm going inside." Luce stood on her toes and kissed Drake's cheek. "See you around, cowboy," she said, and then she was moving away, headed for the house.

A glint appeared in Red's eyes the moment Luce was gone.

"You've got more to say," Drake prodded. "So say it."

"All the weddin' visitors are gone," Red replied, "but you have some company coming your way."

Given the topic of conversation, the incoming person had to be none other than Lettie Arbuckle-Calder. "Does she have a hyphenated last name by any chance?"

"You got it." Red practically chortled. "She ain't

alone, either. Two lawyers and some other fella's comin' with her. They ought to be here any minute now. Your mother told me to send you in to talk to her soon as you and Luce got back."

Luce was on her way to the shower. If Drake went inside now, he ran a definite risk of following her upstairs. And if that happened, he'd be late for Lettie's meeting.

If he got there at all.

"Damn," Drake muttered. "I hope this doesn't mean Lettie and her bunch have filed some sort of injunction to keep me from capturing that stallion and moving him off this ranch. If that happens, I'll never get my mares back."

"Seems to me you ain't made much headway in that direction anyways," Red said wryly.

"Thanks for pointing that out," Drake retorted. "For a minute there, I'd forgotten."

Red busted loose with one of his gap-toothed grins. "Look on the bright side, son. In a round-about way, that stallion landed you a beautiful wife." He hoisted his rickety old carcass up into the wagon seat and took the reins. Looking down at Drake, he went solemn again. "Just simmer down and listen to what these folks have to say. Like as not, they want the same thing you do, just for different reasons. And Lettie Arbuckle might be a lot of things, but stupid ain't one of 'em."

Drake didn't answer. He just went around to the

back of the wagon, lowered the tailgate and pulled out Luce's suitcase and his leather overnight case.

Soon as he raised the tailgate again, Red drove off.

DRAKE HEADED FOR the house. No sign of anybody.

Not daring to join his wife upstairs, Drake found clean jeans and a shirt in the laundry room, then used the adjoining shower, reserved for men who might dirty up Harry's clean floors or get dust on the furniture.

While he lathered up, he thought about Lettie. She could be pushy as hell, but he'd served on the board of the county humane society with her, and he knew her concern for the welfare of animals was genuine. If she was on the annoying side, well, her heart was in the right place.

Fifteen minutes after he'd gotten dressed and poured himself a cup of coffee, the Lettie Arbuckle-Calder contingent showed up in a caravan of luxury vehicles.

Harry and Blythe instantly reappeared, greeted him cordially and proceeded to welcome their guests.

Everyone gravitated to the dining room and seated themselves around the big table, conference style.

Luce joined them while they were still getting settled, and another round of good wishes ensued.

While Harry bustled off to the kitchen to brew a gallon or two of coffee and arrange the inevitable baked goods on platters, Lettie stated her business.

"We've come to outline our plan concerning that

stallion and his band," she said, and her tone was decisive. "Those beautiful, majestic creatures must be protected at any cost."

Harold, who was now recovered to the point that he could get around, ambled in and settled himself as close to Drake as he could manage, and Violet soon arrived, too.

All eyes swung to Drake, as surely as if he'd bolted to his feet and roared an objection.

Before he could lodge an opinion, before he really *had* an opinion, however, Harry rushed in from the kitchen, clearly panicked. "I just heard from Grace over the intercom," she blurted. "It's time!"

Luce went pale and rushed toward the wide doorway. She turned back to him. "Come on, Drake," she said urgently. "Slater's off on location somewhere, and we've got to get Grace to the hospital!"

Call him slow, but Drake hadn't made the leap from Harry's "It's time!" to the fact that Grace was about to give birth.

Blythe, too, was on her feet, apologizing to the group assembled around the table.

Luce waited impatiently. "You get your truck," she told Drake, "and I'll get Grace. Hurry!"

"I'll call Grace's doctor and let Slater know," Blythe said.

"Oh, dear Lord," Harry said, looking faint.

Somebody led her to a chair and sat her down, made her put her head down low.

Drake ran to the kitchen, grabbed his keys from

the hook next to the back door and hurried outside to fire up the rig.

When Luce appeared, Lettie was with her, and they were supporting Grace between them.

"Get her in the truck," Lettie ordered.

Drake obeyed, hefting a bulky Grace into the backseat.

Harry, apparently recovered, ran outside with a stack of clean towels. "You might need these!"

"I hope to God you're wrong about that," Drake muttered.

Luce bounded into the passenger seat and buckled her seat belt. "Go!" she told Drake.

Grace moaned softly.

Drake laid rubber.

"Why didn't you tell someone you've been having contractions all day?" Luce asked her sister-in-law, sounding surprisingly calm.

Drake was anything but.

"They *were* far apart," Grace protested. "And I get them all the time!"

Another moan, this one deeper and slow to end.

"Well, they sure aren't far apart now," Luce said.

"I'm not sure we're going to make it to the hospital," Grace groaned.

"Don't worry," Luce told her. Easy for her to say, since she wasn't the one fixing to have a baby in the backseat of a pickup.

Drake said nothing. He just drove.

And he prayed.

"If necessary, Drake can fill in for the doctor," Luce went on merrily. "It can't be that different from delivering a calf."

Drake swore under his breath and kept the pedal to the metal. Checking the rearview mirror, he was relieved to see Harry and his mother barreling along behind them in Harry's old station wagon.

Lettie and her bunch followed, on their way back to wherever they'd been before they showed up at the ranch en masse.

It was quite a procession. Grace gave an apologetic little scream.

Holy shit, Drake thought.

"Hold on, Grace," Luce said, rifling through her purse. How was it that, no matter what the emergency, women always managed to have their handbags with them? Triumphantly, she held up a small bottle of hand sanitizer. "Voilà!"

"I can do this," Grace said, panting the words. "I can do this."

That was Grace for you.

"How far to the hospital?" Luce asked, digging in her purse again.

"A lot farther than I'd like," Drake said tightly.

"Everything's going to be all right," Luce said in a singsong voice. She'd extracted a pair of nail scissors and a package of dental floss by then.

Grace wasn't fooled by Luce's eager reassurance.

She was, after all, in pain and possibly on the verge of giving birth to her first child in a truck. "An epidural would be good right about now," she answered, shutting her eyes.

The next thing she said was "Oh, my God, the baby's coming—now!"

Drake was about to whip over to the side of the road, shut off the truck and take care of business, but before he could, Grace spoke again.

"Or not," she said happily. "Whew. That was a bad one."

THEY MADE IT, after all.

Just barely.

In the end, an emergency-room doctor delivered the baby in the backseat of the truck, right there in the hospital parking lot.

At least Drake had dodged *that* bullet.

Luce loved the fact that he would've done whatever he had to, though. It gave her a greater sense of his brother's vision of life in a place like this. His documentary about this area showed how people used to rely on one another. In the old days, with no hospitals handy, midwives, the occasional doctor or sometimes stalwart husbands had to make do. "You almost had to deliver the baby," she said.

Hours had passed, and they were back home in their room.

"*Almost* is good." Drake sank down on the bed and

fell back, crossing his arms behind his head. He was wearing jeans, but no shirt and no boots. "I can deal with that. And, by the way, there is a major difference between delivering a calf and delivering a baby."

Luce smiled winningly, stretching out beside him, running a hand lightly over his chest. "You can do anything," she said.

"Thanks," Drake replied wryly, "but there may be a few flaws in that theory."

"The important thing is Grace and the baby are both doing well."

"You're right. That *is* what's important. Of course, Slater may need treatment for heart failure, now that he's heard the story."

"Poor Slater," Luce agreed, still stroking Drake's chest. "All the way up in northern Alberta. He must be beside himself."

"By now, he's on his way home," Drake said.

"If you're away from home when I have our first baby," Luce said, "I might have you horsewhipped when you get back."

Drake laughed. "I'll keep that in mind."

"Good."

"And if you don't stop doing what you're doing, that baby might come sooner than expected."

Luce kissed him. "Promises, promises," she murmured. "Are you just talking, or do you plan to put your money where your mouth is?"

"I definitely plan to put my mouth in a few places," he answered. "Forget money."

IT HAD TAKEN eight of them that morning, and a care-fully orchestrated dance of experienced horsemen, not to mention a whole lot of luck, but they'd accom-plished their mission.

They'd tracked down the stallion, finally, and cor-nered him, along with his band, in a canyon.

Cutting out Drake's mares wasn't easy, but with some fancy riding and even fancier roping, they'd gotten the job done.

The stallion was outraged, naturally, and he'd get the mares back if he got the chance.

It was Drake's job to make damn sure that didn't happen.

Two riders had kept the stallion and his follow-ing boxed in until the mares, some with foals, were well away.

Back home, he and the others put them in stalls, fed and watered them.

When Luce appeared, Drake pointed at one of the stalls. "Take a look," he said.

Luce gave him an uncertain glance but went to peer over the top of the stall door. The look on her face made it all worthwhile. "Oh, Drake! He's beautiful!"

The colt was truly a fine-looking little horse. The spitting image of his sire, right down to the way he left his mother to come and stare up at Luce, nick-ering quietly.

"You said you wanted a horse of your own," Drake told her. "You'll have to sweet-talk Red into starting him when that high-spirited colt gets old enough.

The old man has a soft spot for you, so that should work out."

"He's gorgeous." She whispered the words, marveling.

So was she.

There was nothing ordinary about her, including the fact that she'd decided to study wild horses even though she'd been skittish about riding at first.

She was made for ranch life.

God, how he loved her. She'd spent her honeymoon in a tent and delighted in every minute of it. She'd jumped into a truck and driven country roads with a pregnant woman about to deliver in the backseat.

Oh, yes. She was his kind of woman.

"This horse is going to be magnificent when he grows up."

"He'll have to be gelded," Drake reminded her.

"You really surprised me this time," she said, and her eyes were alight.

He was fairly sure he'd fallen for those eyes first. The minute she'd stormed at him through that meadow. He couldn't forget her tempting body, either...

But it wasn't only physical. Her adventurous spirit had moved him from the beginning and so had her innate kindness. He searched for the right answer and found honesty the only option. "It might have been," he admitted. "Did it work?"

She smiled and rose on tiptoe to kiss him. "You'll find out tonight."

* * * * *

Keep reading to enjoy an insightful—and delightful—personal essay from Linda Lael Miller, the queen of Western romance!

Growing Up Western

IF I'VE BEEN asked once how I came to understand the West, both old and new, so well, I've been asked a million times. It's a question I never tire of, unlike "Where do you get your ideas?" (my standard and admittedly snarky reply is usually "I go to ideas.com. I'm a subscriber.") and the ever popular "How much money do you make?" (Answer: "How much do *you* make?") Since Skip and Hazel's baby girl was raised up right, as we say out here, I am much more polite to the elderly and the obviously well-intentioned but naive. With them, I simply counter sweetly, "Now, why would you ask a question like that?"

The most accurate answer, as far as I know, is this. I grew up in the old West, as well as the new. I lived it, sometimes vicariously, often straight up, like a shot of whiskey.

For instance, one of my earliest memories is of our first home, affectionately referred to in Lael lore as the Van Horn. (Probably the surname of the good folks who owned the property before my grandfather Jacob Daniel Lael bought a big chunk of land and gave some of it to my father, Grady "Skip" Lael, and some to my uncle, Jack Lael.)

Our "house" would have made the cabin in *Little House on the Prairie* look like the Biltmore Estate. In actuality, it was, I'm told, a converted chicken coop, with no insulation and certainly no indoor facilities. Since I was only about two when my memory kicked in and commenced taking notes, I didn't feel at all deprived. After all, the only other houses I frequented did not seem significantly different.

There was no running water; a daily supply had to be scooped from the nearby creek in buckets and carried back to the house, where, if it was meant for anything besides drinking from the trusty dipper, it would be heated on the potbellied stove. Amazingly, Mom did all the cooking on that little stove, with its crooked chimney poking out of the wall.

Dad, recently discharged from the United States Marine Corps, where he served bravely on Iwo Jima, among other terrifying places, was a resourceful man. He knew we would need insulation, come those cold eastern Washington winters, but he probably didn't have the proverbial two nickels to rub together. He paid a visit to the funeral home in Colville, some forty miles away, and talked the proprietors out of a stack of large cardboard cartons, which had originally housed spanking-new coffins.

He brought the flattened boxes home, trimmed them to fit his purposes and nailed them to the thin board walls of the chicken coop, with all their cracks and knotholes, and lined the inside of the roof, too, since there was no ceiling. He was very careful, he always said, with a twinkle in his blue eyes, to keep the printed side to the wall. That first night, he lay down in bed, pleased with his industry, and there right above his head in bold print were the legendary words *Sunshine Coffin Company*.

Dad owned (and deeply loved) a bay gelding called Peanuts. He used the horse to herd our very few cattle, among other tasks. Mainly, I suspect, he just liked riding, being a cowboy at heart with a history of rodeos behind him. He was, back in the day, a bull rider and traveled widely with his older brother, Jack, who was a serious contender in every rodeo he entered. Known from Northport, Washington, to Madison Square Garden in New York City (we would have pronounced NYC the way that guy in the salsa commercials did) as "Jiggs" Lael, my uncle was the classic bronc-buster. Elvis-handsome, he won numerous buckles and got to kiss Miss America twice—two different Miss Americas on two different occasions—for placing first in the bareback ridin', as we termed it.

In their travels, Dad and Uncle Jack had plenty of adventures, and I've woven several of them into my books over the course of my career. A particular favorite is the tale of a bar fight in a run-down Montana establishment, involving a couple of cowboy brothers sent by their mother to fetch Pa home for supper. Pa was roundly drunk and scrawny as a baby bird, while his sons were big as upended boxcars. One of the cowboys whispered mildly to Dad and Uncle Jack, "Now, friends, you need to stay out of this. It's a family matter."

They stepped up to Pa's bar stool and each gripped one of his arms, hoping for a peaceable departure.

Well, Pa might have been little, but he was mighty, and he wasn't through with the day's drinking, either. He put up one hell of a fight and did some damage to his tough sons before they managed to haul him out of the saloon and home to Ma. A version of that story turned up in my novel *The Bridegroom* years later.

I often went riding with Dad on Peanuts, from the age of two. He called our forays "cuttin' brush," which meant we were chasing stray cattle hither and yon, and he said I sat that saddle like a pro, even then. Today, thanks to a great deal of effort on my brother's part, I own that very saddle, battered and worn, the canticle inscribed with the name "Skip Lael," and it is my most prized possession.

Still more immersion in the Western culture came through our neighbors and dear friends, the Wileys—we're at four generations and counting—where my brother and I spent a lot of time growing up. The Wileys were not blood relations, but Guy Wiley, the mischievous patriarch of the clan, was "Grampa" to us, and his wife, Florence, was "Gramma."

Compared to the Van Horn, the Wiley ranch was J. R. Ewing's Southfork, although in actuality, it was and is a very small, never-painted house, downright tiny by anybody's standards. It never felt cramped because there always seemed to be room for one more, and the place was often filled to the rafters with cousins, neighbors and stray kids in need of a place to be. Guy and Florence raised five children in that two-bedroom house, and several generations have grown up there since. I'm only one of many, many people with fond memories of that house and the kindness of the Wileys.

My favorite part of the ranch house was the kitchen, not just because of the delicious pies, fried chicken, creek trout, venison roasts, garden vegetables and fresh and preserved fruit that were served at the venerable old table over by the windows. I liked the kitchen because Gramma Wiley was always there, doing something at her big old wood-burning cookstove and, better yet, telling stories.

Gramma had so many stories. Her mother, who lived with the family until her death at a very great age, was the widow of an honest-to-God Civil War soldier. As the tale was told, the older of the two Gramma Wileys had been married to a young man serving on the Union side. He'd marched off to war with his best friend, from whom he extracted a solemn vow that if he fell in battle, the best friend would take care of his wife and small children when the fighting was over. The husband did perish, like so many others, and the best friend was as good as his word. He went back home when the war ended, married the widow and fathered several more children, including Florence. This man, whose last name was

Heritage, a fact that seems strangely fitting, was definitely ahead of his time—but I'll get to that.

Eventually, the couple bought a farm outside of Coffeyville, Kansas. In those days following the Civil War, Kansas was still the Wild West, and it wasn't called "bloody Kansas" for nothing. Before, during and after the great conflict, there were plenty of differing opinions, and a lot of them ended in violence. Bands of outlaws—most of them displaced veterans from both the Union and the Confederacy—roamed the countryside, robbing banks, rustling livestock and shooting up saloons. It was a very dangerous time.

Mr. Heritage, however, was a man of peace. He didn't even believe in spanking his children, and I'd be willing to bet that he'd seen all the killing he cared to look upon during the war. Still, a farmer with a family to protect, and to feed, he would have owned a gun or two, for hunting and personal defense.

One day, when Gramma Florence was a very small child, gunshots sounded in town, and repeatedly, audible even from the farm, which was some six miles from Coffeyville. Of all the stories she told me, in the heart of the Wiley ranch house outside Northport, clattering the lids of her cast-iron, chrome-trimmed Kitchen Queen all the while, this one is my second favorite.

Her father did not go to town to participate in the melee. As I said, he was a man of peace.

Word soon reached them, probably via a well-informed neighbor passing by on the road, that the

Dalton brothers, a famous outlaw band of the day, had intended to hold up the bank in Coffeyville. Banks weren't federally insured in those days, so if the money was stolen, it was just plain gone, for good. Folks would be ruined, perhaps see their children go hungry, if the thieves succeeded.

The men of the town, along with ranchers and farmers from the surrounding area, had gotten wind of the plan ahead of time, and they were ready and waiting, sprawled on rooftops, hidden in the narrow spaces between storefronts, crouched behind horse troughs, with their rifles and pistols cocked, when the Daltons rode up and reined in right in front of the bank.

The locals opened fire, releasing a literal hail of bullets.

The Dalton brothers were dead before they could dismount, probably before they realized what was happening.

The townsfolk decided to bring home a salient point: the wages of sin is death, as the Bible rather ungrammatically puts it. They strapped those dead outlaws to boards and doors ripped from their hinges and set them upright along the street, right there on the wooden sidewalk. People came from far and wide to look at them, bloody and fly-specked, and they brought their children, too. The message was abundantly clear: this is what comes of the criminal life. Aspiring outlaws, beware.

There were so many visitors trooping past the bodies, I was told, that guards had to be posted to

keep folks from stealing buttons off the dead outlaws' coats or snipping off a lock of hair for a souve-
nir. Photographs were taken, and can still be seen in
books and online, and the images are grim indeed.

Mr. Heritage was having none of the spectacle,
morally instructive or not. He was not about to march
his children past a bunch of bullet-riddled outlaws,
and that was that. They didn't go into town that day
or any other day, until the Daltons had been taken
off display and decently buried.

I've always admired Mr. Heritage for his sensitivity, among other qualities. As I said before, he was
an unusual man, especially in that time and place.

Still, Gramma Florence remembered that day as
vividly, all those years later, in her plain kitchen,
with me listening raptly, as if it had happened the
previous week.

That being my second favorite story, I will now
tell my first.

One day, on that same farm, at about sundown,
supper was cooking and Mr. Heritage was outside,
probably chopping wood or pumping water, when
a rider approached his gate. The stranger wore a
long, dusty overcoat and his hat was pulled down
low over his eyes.

Mr. Heritage went to the gate to speak to him, that
being the neighborly thing to do. He spoke quietly
with the man for a while, then, as later reported, invited him to come on in and join the family for the
evening meal.

The stranger thanked Mr. Heritage, kindly and quietly, but declined. Mr. Heritage directed him to the barn, where he and his tired horse could pass the night with a roof over their heads. It's pertinent to mention here that, although hospitality was a way of life in those days, especially on lonely farms and ranches, where any visitor was an event, no unknown caller would have been asked to spend the night in the house, because of the women and children.

Presently, Mr. Heritage came inside, where the family was fairly bursting with curiosity. Why hadn't the man seen to his horse and come in to join them at the supper table? He surely looked like someone in need of a hot meal and some pleasant conversation.

Mr. Heritage, probably washing up at the basin prior to sitting down to the meal, was thoughtful. He'd offered, he told his wife and children, but the man had refused, saying he didn't want to endanger them by getting too close.

He was, he had admitted, a fugitive from the law, wanted dead or alive.

And his name was Jesse James.

The notable outlaw was a kind of Robin Hood figure to ordinary folks. He never stole from them, or shot at them. Indeed, he'd been known to meet their mortgage payments, supply food when they might have gone hungry otherwise and protect them from other outlaws.

A little research into Jesse James's life will show that he was, for all practical intents and purposes, a cold-blooded killer and a clever thief, an outlaw in every sense of the word. Growing up on a hard-scrabble farm himself, he and his family had suffered greatly at the hands of renegade Yankees, had their crops trampled and were terrorized to the extent of a mock hanging that left Jesse's beloved stepfather a broken man. From that day until he was shot in the back while hanging a picture in his own living room, James hated the United States government and, by extension, all officialdom, as did his brothers.

The law was probably relieved when the infamous Mr. Howard gunned Jesse down, since it saved them the trouble of hanging him. To the common folks, however, Jesse James died a hero, and he was widely mourned, the subject of song and story.

And he'd spent a night in the Heritage barn, this very man, feeding and watering his horse, grateful to bed down in the hay and straw, probably full of the generous supper Mr. Heritage almost certainly brought out to him on one of his wife's own Blue Willow dinner plates. The next morning, most likely before sunrise, the visitor saddled up and rode on.

I like to think he tipped his hat in farewell as he went.

As an avid student of American history, I'm familiar with the life of Jesse James, and I still marvel at the mysterious complexity of human nature. Truly, with a few notable exceptions, everybody is some combination of very good and very bad, with a great deal of both blending in the middle.

These two stories were integral to my formation as a writer, and I'm sure there were many more, lost to present recollection.

Ranch life was still rustic, even in the 1950s and early '60s, so my immersion continued. Cattle had to be rounded up, fed, watered or milked. There was no branding on the Wiley ranch; they used ear tags to mark their livestock. Kindness was the Wiley way, and animals benefited as well as humans. Gramma, like her own father, would not countenance spanking, and fistfights, a sport on other farms and ranches, were strictly forbidden.

The chores were endless. Water had to be pumped and carried in, eggs gathered, cows milked, cream and milk separated, cream churned into good country butter, with no additives except for a tiny pinch of salt. (Too much salt was considered a dirty trick, since it made the butter set up considerably faster.) The women made quilts—by the light of kerosene lanterns when I was very young, and later by the unreliable light of a single bulb dangling over the kitchen table—and sewed shirts for their men, complicated Western styles with fancy yokes and snap buttons, stitching the seams either by hand or on Gramma's ancient treadle sewing machine. They didn't go to town for fancy store-bought patterns, these necessarily resourceful women; they took measurements and cut the pieces from old newspapers, pinned those to the cloth and snipped out shapes that went together perfectly.

They conjured up hot biscuits, fried chicken (or

grouse or rabbit or venison or, very rarely, beef from the family's own herd), and coffee that would, as the men liked to say, put hair on your chest. They grew vast gardens, baked loaf after loaf of delicious bread and put up preserves for the long, hungry winters, all without running water or electricity. We kids had chores to do—carrying wood for the stoves, weeding and watering the garden, digging potatoes, shelling peas and stringing beans. The cousins milked cows—I never got the knack—and we also gathered eggs and fed the chickens. The coward in the lot, I was scared of roosters, not to mention bulls, and I couldn't "buck" bales (of hay) to save my life.

Still, we lived in a magical world, those days on the ranch, wading in the ice-cold creek, trying to catch fish, riding far and wide on horseback. If the chores were done and there was no hay to cut, load and haul, we were free to mount up and take off. In those days, nobody worried about us unless a horse came back riderless or we were, God forbid, late for supper.

The girls did the dishes after a meal, in basins, the water heated on the Kitchen Queen. The boys lugged buckets up from the creek and split firewood to kindling, because the cookstove was always hungry, even in the heat of summer.

In the evening, Gramma liked to sit in her rocking chair, reading by the light of a kerosene lamp, sewing or darning socks, or playing solitaire with cards bent and nearly colorless with age. At the time, it all seemed normal. In retrospect, I wonder how on earth the woman did so much work, so cheerfully.

We were poor, by most people's standards, but none of us had a clue. Life was real and rich and full of stories.

About the time I was ready for kindergarten, the bottom fell out of the beef market, and we moved into Northport, population five hundred, give or take, but along with my brother and numerous cousins, we still spent lots of time on the Wiley ranch, especially during the summers.

Dad's faithful old horse, Peanuts, had died by then. He'd gotten into some squirrel poison, and I remember Dad spending at least one entire night out in the barn looking after his range buddy. Until he passed away, at eighty-one, my father would still choke up whenever Peanuts was mentioned.

Dad became the town marshal, and I think he took his cues from Matt Dillon on *Gunsmoke*, because he always hurried home to catch the new episode, even when he was on patrol. Besides serving as marshal, he was also the street commissioner (which meant he plowed snow and graded the roads constantly) *and* the water commissioner, a job that entailed digging through frozen ground to repair Northport's century-old wooden water pipes when they were clogged, iced over, or had simply crumbled. All this for the princely sum of five hundred dollars a month, without benefits. In addition, Dad grew a garden and, later on, he and Mom ran Lael's Motel. Admittedly, most of the motel work fell to Mom; we had a total of four rooms, and we practically sang "Happy Days Are Here Again" whenever they were all rented.

By this time, the Western mind-set was firmly implanted in me, and in my brother, too.

Oddly, since I believe I was born to be a writer, I was a slow reader, early on. In retrospect, I realize that the main problem was undiagnosed ADD. The condition was unknown in those days, so my report cards said things like, *Linda daydreams a lot*, and alas, *Linda talks too much*. I didn't much care for books, since concentration was and still is difficult for me, but I loved wandering in my imagination, and I could spend days doing just that.

It was my voracious reader of a mother who turned the tide where reading was concerned, God bless her forever. I was home sick, and it was her day to work at the town's tiny library, which offered only donated books and was open on Tuesday afternoons, period. When she came home, I was whining on the couch, tired of daytime TV.

Mom handed me a stack of Nancy Drew books, suggested I give them a try and heated up a medicinal can of Campbell's chicken noodle soup.

I must have been bored out of my skull, because I leafed through those thin volumes, worn and dog-eared by previous readers, settled on one that didn't seem too terrible and read a page or two.

It was a eureka moment, for sure.

Here was Nancy Drew—a *girl*, no less—who

drove a snazzy "roadster," a convertible to boot, and solved genuine mysteries without adult interference. She and her two girlfriends, George and Bess, investigated crimes *and* saw that the perpetrators were brought to justice. Nancy had a good-looking boyfriend, Ned, but she and George and Bess didn't need him to rescue them; he was window dressing, not muscle.

I was enthralled. Hooked. In for the duration.

After those Nancy Drew books, I read Cherry Ames, Student Nurse, the Hardy Boys, everything the Tuesday-afternoon library had to offer. Then I began to borrow books from the loaner shelves at the grade school. (Only the high school had a library then.) I devoured biographies—Annie Oakley, Abe Lincoln, George and Martha Washington. I gobbled up the Little House stories. I read about astronauts and planned on becoming one, until I found out that astronauts had to be wizards at math and science.

Drat. So much for space travel.

For a while, I wanted to be Annie Oakley, as seen on TV. She wore a great fringed cowgirl outfit with a vest, was a sharpshooter and a trick rider. Furthermore, she rounded up outlaws right and left, just like Nancy Drew, only with more action.

Alas, it finally occurred to me that the job of being Annie Oakley, either the real one, long dead, or the one on TV, with the blond pigtails and the great horse, was filled.

I was stuck with being plain old me, and I wasn't very happy about it, either.

Then, one Saturday night when I was nine, I got my first look at Little Joe Cartwright, of *Bonanza* fame, in glorious black-and-white. The crooked grin, the curly hair, the pinto horse—I was in love. (And, all these many years later, I am *still* in love with Little Joe. A portrait of him, done by my friend, actor/artist Buck Taylor, hangs above my living room fireplace.)

My imagination went into overdrive. I began to daydream in earnest, creating scenarios in my busy little brain for hours, even days, at a time. Usually, I was a long-lost Cartwright sister, riding the range with my handsome brothers and Pa. As puberty commenced, I changed roles and became Little Joe's girlfriend, or his bride. Anyone who remembers *Bonanza* will tell you, marrying Little Joe was a dangerous business. The poor woman was doomed, destined to die tragically, not to mention dramatically, in her heartbroken lover's arms. Never, ever did she survive longer than two episodes. Today, ironically, one of those ill-fated brides, the actress Jess Walton, who still plays Jill Abbott on *The Young and the Restless*, is a good friend.

I began to set some of my stories down on paper. They were fevered and brimming with purple prose and lines like, "Breathe, damn you!" and I absolutely loved writing them.

One day, in fifth grade, the teacher, a man named Bob Hyatt who had the distinction of having served in the army with Elvis Presley, handed back papers we'd written as part of an English lesson. I, the day-dreamer, was astonished to see that I'd not only received an A, but Mr. Hyatt had graciously written something underneath the grade, along the lines of *You have real talent. You could be a writer.*

I had never been good at much of anything, except getting out of doing farm chores so I could stay inside and listen to Gramma Wiley's wonderful stories.

I could be a writer.

Seriously? Writing was an actual *job*? It paid real money?

And I was good at it?

I was blown away. Ten years old, and I was off and running. I wrote and wrote and wrote, frenzied with the pure joy of it. I turned out plays, which I also directed and starred in. I scribbled stories, usually *Bonanza*-themed, and passed them in class the way most kids passed notes.

I remain the only person I know who was sent to the principal's office repeatedly for passing around— or writing—stories when I was supposed to be studying. Or listening. Or reading something educational.

From that long-ago day in fifth grade, I can honestly say I never looked back. I was a writer. In real life, I couldn't be Annie Oakley or an astronaut, but in stories—joy of joys, thrill of thrills—I could be *anyone I wanted.*

In high school, I wrote an entire novel, by hand and in pencil, filling some twenty-six spiral notebooks with what I thought was deathless prose. From my present vantage point, I know I should probably have driven a stake through those notebooks and exposed them to unrelenting sunlight. The title of this tome was *Sea of Faces*, and it was a coming-of-age story—sappy, improbable and surely as bad as anything Jo March wrote in the early chapters of *Little Women*.

Most likely, it was worse.

Now I wish I'd saved that manuscript, along with a few others that were only marginally better. I could have read a few pages aloud at writers' conferences, to show just how bad a writer can be and still find herself making a respectable living at the trade years later. Or it might have come in handy as a replacement for the Sears catalog in the outhouse at the ranch.

Looking back, I can certainly see the wisdom of the old adage about being willing to write a whole heap of lousy stuff before it's even remotely possible to write well. I certainly did my homework on that score.

I was still a Western girl, riding horses when I had the opportunity, attending the Colville rodeo and the now-defunct Diamond Spur event in Spokane, then regarded as the big city with the bright lights. I was the original *Bonanza* freak, but as the years passed, I added *The Big Valley*, *The Virginian*, *The High Chaparral* and several other TV Westerns to my watch-list. I also shamelessly stole the characters and settings for stories of my own, and when the

Beatles came along, I added them, too, even though they weren't cowboys.

I'd taught myself to use punctuation long before we covered it in elementary school, since I read so much, and I learned the concept of scenes from watching my beloved TV Westerns. I clued in that something had better happen at the end of a scene to make the reader/viewer want to come back and find out what happens next.

I married at nineteen, and I continued to write, brave enough now to make up characters of my own. I wrote another bad novel, about a family called Corbin, though by then I owned a portable Smith-Corona—electric, no less. I worked at office jobs, and in my spare time, if I wasn't writing, I was reading.

I had zero money and probably owned a total of four books, one of which was a Bible, but I was living in the big city of Spokane, and the libraries were not only well stocked, they were open five and a half days a week. I consumed books by the stack, especially historical novels by Taylor Caldwell, Lloyd C. Douglas and Janice Holt Giles, and checked out as many back issues of *The Writer* and *Writer's Digest* as the rules allowed. I read every article, took notes, tried to apply what I'd read to whatever project I was banging out on my Smith-Corona at the time. Eventually, I wore that little machine out.

I had—and still have—an insatiable appetite for words, words and more words. These days, I tend to favor audiobooks, if only because my eyes are tired

by the end of a writing day, and listening is easier.
Also, since I still have ADD, I like to be mobile.

Somehow, my now-ex-husband and I managed to
scrounge up the funds for more typewriters—and I
wore those out in turn. I wasn't making a dime, or
publishing anything, but I was undeterred. Now, looking back, I marvel at my own bullheaded persistence.

I don't think I ever doubted that, one fine day, I
would earn a living doing what I loved most—writing.

It's a good thing I was raised by people who could
get an old truck running on a freezing day, work
eighteen-hour days for practically no money and haul
cows out of chest-deep mud, because I still had a
long road ahead of me.

I just never learned to quit, a trait that hasn't always worked in my favor, but certainly served me
well in this case.

In the early 1980s, I managed to place thirty-
seventh in a short story contest run by *Writer's Digest*, and damn, I was proud of that. Soon after, I
placed another short piece in a literary magazine.
I didn't get paid, but there was my story in print,
with my name under the title.

I needed no more encouragement than that.

I wrote another novel and actually submitted it. It
was rejected everywhere, but one kindly editor enclosed a letter, expressing regret at having to turn
the story down. She said I had talent and went to the
trouble, bless her diligent heart, of describing all the
things that were wrong with the book.

I put both the manuscript and the letter away and turned to other things. I took the *Writer's Digest* short story course by correspondence, and that was a turning point. My instructor was a woman named Nan Schram Williams, and she was a ghostwriter, composing autobiographies for famous people, but she also wrote "confession" stories for magazines like *True Romance*, *True Story*, *True Confessions*, etc. She made either five or three cents a word doing that and advised me to give it a shot.

Even now, I chuckle when I remember this, because my mother wouldn't allow me to read "those magazines" as a girl. The titles were wild and, as Mom put it, "suggestive." Hesitant but determined, I skulked into the grocery store and bought a few copies, soon discovering that while the titles were attention-grabbers, the actual stories were sweet little pieces, almost always about love. Although they were written by freelancers, there were no bylines, as the stories were supposed to be "true," set down on paper and submitted by the people who had experienced them. As such, they were always told in first-person.

I decided to try my hand at one. I wrote a gentle story about a young widow falling in love again, mailed it off to *True Romance* and forgot about it. Imagine my delight when, weeks and weeks later, I received a letter offering to buy the story for a future issue. By the time the check arrived, more weeks and weeks later—a whopping one hundred and thirty-five dollars—I'd written and submitted several more heartfelt confessions. We used the money to replace the windshield in our car.

I sold over thirty of these torridly titled tales and even placed a story with *Women's World*, which paid a mind-blowing twelve hundred dollars, a fortune to a young wife and mother.

Encouraged, I got out my rejected novel, reread the editor's thoughtful letter and applied her suggestions to the manuscript. I sent it off and received another round of rejections for my trouble, but one fine day, I spotted a blurb in the marketing section of *The Writer*. Pocket Books was starting a new line of historical romances, called Tapestry, and they were looking for stories.

I figured I didn't have much to lose besides the postage and sent three chapters and an outline off to Linda Marrow, then an assistant editor at Pocket. She called a week later—be still my beating heart—and asked for the rest of the book. As this had happened once before, and the resulting rejection had devastated me, I tried not to get too excited. I sent the book.

On Valentine's Day, 1983, Linda's boss, Kate Duffy, called and made me an offer. The book came out in August of that same year, and I've been gainfully employed ever since, with my total number of published novels somewhere in the range of one hundred and fifty.

What does all this prove?

Never underestimate a cowgirl from Northport, Washington. They just don't know how to quit.

Turn the page for an excerpt from
FOREVER A HERO, the third book in
the *CARSONS OF MUSTANG CREEK trilogy,*
coming to HQN Books March 2017.

CHAPTER ONE

MACE CARSON BRAKED, nice and easy, when he saw the car up ahead fishtail on the rain-slicked pavement and then go into a slow-motion spin. After a full three-sixty, the vehicle came to rest at a precarious slant, with the passenger's side tilted downhill, ready to slip in the mud and roll over the steep slope beyond.

The car's engine was still running as he steered his truck to the roadside, flung open the door and jumped to the ground. He hurried forward but could barely make out the driver through the steady drizzle; he saw only a form sitting rigidly upright behind the steering wheel, probably gripping it for dear life.

Up close, he saw her, and something flickered in the back of his brain, something to do with ghosts, popping out of the past and smack into the present, but he didn't pursue the thought. Priority one—get the woman out of the car.

He reached for the handle and, at the same moment, she came out of freeze-frame long enough to unsnap her seat belt and try to push the door open from her side.

Neither of them was getting anywhere with the effort, since the car was still in Drive.

"Put it in Park," he mouthed.

She stared at him for a few seconds, her face a pale oval behind the rain-specked glass of her window, while he registered that the air bag hadn't deployed.

That was good, anyway, Mace thought, continuing to pull at the door even though he knew the locks were engaged. She probably wasn't hurt, and she didn't look as though she'd been drinking. Still, she might be in shock.

The car lurched a foot or two sideways, farther into the ditch. The woman's eyes rounded, and he saw her gasp.

"Park!" he repeated, only this time he yelled the word.

She finally got the memo and shifted gears. The locks popped.

Mace yanked open the door, gravity working against him, while she pushed desperately from inside. As soon as he could, he took her by the arm and hauled her out. She slammed against him as the sodden earth on the other side gave way again, and the back of the car slid down the slope to stand on end.

Trembling, the woman clung to him, murmuring into his shoulder.

"You all right?" he asked, in no hurry to turn her loose even though the danger was past.

He felt her head bob in an apparent "yes."

Conscious of the rain again, Mace hustled her to

the passenger's side of his truck and hoisted her un-ceremoniously onto the seat. Obviously disoriented, she looked at him blankly at first, then with a start of what seemed to be recognition.

"I—I'm okay," she managed, after a few stam-mered attempts to get the words out.

"You're sure you don't need a doctor?"

She shook her head, smiled tentatively. "No," she said. "I'm not hurt. Really." She swallowed visibly. "Just shaken up, that's all."

Mace nodded, let out a long breath as the rush of adrenaline started to subside. The rainstorm had been a sudden drenching torrent, but it was hardly more than a sprinkle now. All the same, rivulets cas-caded off both sides of the road.

He stood there for a while, staring at her like a damn fool, oddly stricken and more than a little off his game. He had the distinct feeling that he knew this woman from somewhere, but he couldn't place her.

"Thanks," she said, and something in her expres-sion—curious, grateful, mildly amused—reminded him that he was standing in the rain.

Mace walked around the truck, climbed behind the wheel and reached for his cell phone resting be-side the gearshift. "What happened?" he asked.

"One of the front tires must have gone flat," she replied, still smiling slightly. "There was this awful shimmying, and then I lost control of the car. Next thing I knew, I was facing the wrong direction and halfway down the embankment."

He frowned, reviewing the events of the last few minutes. Driving behind her, he hadn't seen the tire blow, or noticed the shimmying. She'd been rolling along at a good clip, a few miles over the speed limit, maybe, but she hadn't been driving recklessly. So why did he feel like reading her the riot act, lecturing her about unfamiliar roads and slick surfaces?

He shoved his fingers through his hair and took another deep breath.

Then, with his free hand, he offered her the cell phone. Her purse, if she had one, was still in the car.

She blinked once, then accepted the phone. He wondered if she was in shock, since she didn't seem to know what to do with the thing.

Mace finally got a grip. Sort of. "You're *sure* you're all right?"

She nodded, glancing from the device in her palm to his face.

He worked the gearshift, then decided he wasn't ready to drive quite yet. Maybe *he* was the one who ought to make a pit stop at the ER.

Mace wasn't much of a talker under any circumstances, but now he thought a bit of idle chitchat might be called for, if only to let his blood pressure trip down a few notches. He'd driven these roads so often, in every conceivable kind of weather, that he could navigate them on autopilot, but the lady, vaguely familiar or not, was new to Bliss County. If he'd met her before, and he was sure he had, the encounter had taken place somewhere else. "That's a bad curve for a flat," he said.

She flicked him that cautious smile again and raised her eyebrows, as if to say, "Duh."

Mace was still spinning his mental wheels; he couldn't seem to get any traction. "You'll need a wrecker," he said, the soul of wit and wisdom, and pointed at the phone.

"It's a rental car," she said, trembling again. "And I'm not from around here, so I don't know who to call."

He reached out, pushed a button on the dashboard to ratchet up the heat, wishing he had a blanket or at least a jacket to offer her. Shock victims had to be kept warm, didn't they?

She looked down at the phone, her lower lip wobbling.

Don't cry, Mace pleaded silently.

He moved to take back the phone, make the necessary call himself, then changed his mind. Along with his two older brothers, Slater and Drake, he'd been raised to get back on the horse when thrown, on the premise that action was always better than hesitation. "Dial 911," he said, surprised that he sounded so calm. "You'll get Junie at the sheriff's office. Tell her what happened and ask her to send out a tow truck." He gave a brief twitch of a grin. "While you're at it, you can ask if it's safe to get into a car with me. My name is Mace Carson." He saw that her color was coming back, and her eyes were brighter. "I'll drive you into Mustang Creek."

She recovered some of her composure, straightening her shoulders, lifting her chin. "I just came through Mustang Creek," she informed him. "I'm headed somewhere else actually." She paused, and mischief danced in her aqua-blue eyes. "And I knew who you were as soon as I saw you, although I appreciate the introduction."

He was taken aback, but not really surprised. After all, there was that déjà vu thing going on.

The rain was still coming down; he hadn't switched on the interior light, and it was getting dark out. He realized his impressions of the damsel in distress had been visceral, intuitive ones, more about essence than physical details. Now he looked more closely, took in her blond hair and compact, womanly shape, noticed that she was wearing a midlength skirt and a filmy loose blouse over a camisole.

Finally he asked, "Have we met?" The question came out sounding raspy, made him want to clear his throat.

"We sure have," she replied cheerfully. "Ten years ago, in California."

The experience eluded him. He had a decent memory, or so he'd thought until now. The recollection stayed just out of reach, and that was frustrating. He'd gone to UCLA and later served an apprenticeship of sorts at his grandfather's winery in the Napa Valley. "In college?" he guessed. "Did we have a class together?"

"No."

He studied her for a moment. "Wait a minute. You're Kelly—the girl that night on campus..."

She seemed pleased, but mildly discomfited, too. And little wonder—the memory was probably still traumatic. "Yes," she answered, so softly that he almost didn't hear her. "I'm Kelly Wright."

It all fell into place then. He was thirty-one now, and a decade had gone by, so he supposed he could be forgiven for not remembering right away; a lot had happened since that night, and he hadn't seen her since.

It had been dark then, too, but warm and sultry, and she'd been in real trouble, scared and upset. Spinning off the road in a rainstorm must seem tame, by comparison.

And now she was here, of all places.

What a weird coincidence. If it *was* a coincidence.

Another tremulous smile surfaced, and she'd stopped shivering. "You do remember me, then," she said. She waggled the cell at him. "No need to ask this Junie person, whoever she is, if it's safe to get into a car with you. I'll call to have the car towed, though. She'll take care of everything? Don't I need to file an accident report or something?"

"She will." Mace peered through the windshield, but the vehicle wasn't visible in the gathering gloom. She wasn't going to be able to drive it out of that ditch, but he needed something to look at, besides Kelly, while he regained his balance. "The accident report will keep till morning." He managed to meet her eyes again. "Where were you headed?"

"There's a resort nearby, on the Bliss River. I have a reservation."

Since his sister-in-law, Slater's wife, Grace ran the resort, he knew where to take her, knew she'd be comfortable there. By morning, she'd be good as new. "I'll take you there," he said. He thought he could drive now, so he pulled onto the road to test the theory and gave the rig some gas. "What brings you to Wyoming?" he asked, once they got rolling, figuring that long-ago night in California wouldn't be the best topic of conversation to start with, since she'd already been shaken up enough, going off the road like that. "A vacation?"

He sounded like a half-wit—resort, vacation, no big leap of logic there—but he couldn't seem to help it. It was a jolt, running into Kelly after all this time, and in about the last place he would have expected.

"I have a business meeting tomorrow afternoon." She swept back her hair, and the jerky motion of her hand betrayed the fact that she was still unsteady but trying hard to pull herself together. Then, in the space of a heartbeat, she seemed to gather all her resources, aim them at casual good cheer. "Would you like to have dinner with me tonight? The on-line reviews of the restaurant at the resort are stellar, as you probably know, and I promise we won't talk business."

Talk business?

Then the light dawned. Oh, yeah. Business meeting. Tomorrow afternoon.

He had a meeting scheduled for the next day himself.

Duh.

"I'd like that. Dinner, I mean. Stefano is the best chef in three states." He hurried through that part of the discussion, hell-bent for the next one. "You're the representative from the California distributor and your meeting tomorrow is with me. I guess the name didn't click before. Kelly Wright. When we met, you were Kelly Arden."

"Yes. I'm divorced. It seemed easier to keep my married name after my ex and I called it quits." She sounded tired, sad. He wondered how long the marriage had lasted, and if the split had been relatively amicable.

Probably, he decided. Otherwise, she wouldn't be using the guy's name anymore.

Anyway, her marital status was none of his business.

"What are the chances?" he asked, thinking aloud. "Of our running into each other as business associates? It's a big world out there."

There was a smile in her voice. "Chance had nothing to do with it, Mace. My coming here, that is. When I saw your name in a trade magazine a few months ago, touting you as an innovator, an award-winning winemaker, it seemed like synchronicity. It wasn't hard to track you down." Another pause, sort of fragile. Mace kept his eyes on the road as she went on. "I'm sure you can understand why I remember *you* so well."

"Yes," he said, sounding grim. He rarely thought of that night on the UCLA campus, but he'd never really forgotten it, either. And he'd never expected to see her again. He felt a strange combination of reluctance and relief, as if he'd misplaced something valuable and then found it when he was no longer even searching for it.

Silence fell while she examined his phone, punched in three numbers and spoke to Junie, identifying herself, describing the accident and asking for a tow truck. She said she'd be at the resort until further notice, then "Thank you" and "Goodbye."

She dropped the phone into the little well by the gearshift.

And then she just sat there, not saying anything at all.

Mace—who loved silence, thrived on it, in fact—suddenly wanted to hear her voice again. Failing that, he'd settle for his own. He turned his head in her direction for a moment, raised both eyebrows. "Dinner sounds like a good idea," he said. Then, "We have some catching up to do, Kelly."

MACE CARSON HADN'T changed all that much. He was older, of course, and more solid, but he was still the same quiet, down-to-earth man Kelly had encountered that night in Los Angeles, the kind who showed up at just the right moment, fought off the fire-breathing dragon and didn't expect credit for his actions. For her, the incident on campus, all those years ago, occasionally curdled ordinary dreams into nightmares, even now. Every aspect of it was etched into her psyche, waking or sleeping, but in the daytime, at least, she could keep all the terrible might-have-beens at an acceptable distance.

Bottom line—if Mace hadn't come along when he had, hauled her attacker off her and basically kicked the crap out of the scumbag, she would've been raped and possibly murdered.

Telling herself that Mace *had* come along at just the right moment, and that it was foolish to dwell on things that could've happened but hadn't, made sense when she was feeling rested, confident, in control. And with all those years of practice, that was most of the time.

Tonight, though, tired and still shaken from the near-miss on the highway, she was particularly vulnerable.

Her very cells remembered the throat-closing sensation when she'd realized she was being followed that moonless night as she walked back from a friend's apartment, taking a shortcut through an alley. And the way her breath had caught when she'd turned around to see that she *wasn't* imagining things, that someone was there. She'd picked up her pace, breaking into a run.

She hadn't been fast enough.

Suddenly, she'd felt the impact of another body slamming into her from behind, sending her hurtling, crashing to the ground. Then came the hard weight of a stranger's hands on her, the explosion of pure, primal fear, the scream that knotted in her throat and throbbed there, painful and without sound. She'd struggled wildly, desperately and completely in vain.

She wasn't going to get away.

But she'd fought, just the same. If there was one thing she knew, it was that she *had* to fight if she wanted to survive. Dear God, she wanted to survive.

Abruptly, remarkably, the tide turned. There was a grunt, and the crushing weight of her attacker shifted, then fell away.

Kelly had sat up, scooted backward, every instinct screaming at her to *run*.

She hadn't run, though, because she'd known her legs wouldn't support her. Instead, she'd watched, half-hysterical, sobbing, as a man in jeans, Western boots and a T-shirt dropped her assailant to the sidewalk with one well-aimed punch.

A cowboy, she'd thought stupidly. *I've been saved by a cowboy.*

The would-be rapist was unconscious when the cowboy got out his phone and called the police, and when they arrived, minutes later, the would-be rapist was still down, bleeding copiously from the nose and mouth, although he'd come around enough to whimper and whine.

Mace Carson had kept an eye on the attacker as he

extended a hand to Kelly. "You okay?" he'd asked, just like he had a few minutes ago, after he'd pulled her from a car about to slide—or roll—into a deep ditch at the side of the highway.

He'd gone with her to the police station after the attack and gotten her back to the dorm when all the questions had been asked and answered. The man who'd come after Kelly like a runaway train had a rap sheet, it turned out, and he was a person of interest in several similar assaults, including at least one brutal rape. He was arrested that night, held without bail and eventually tried and convicted.

Kelly's horrified parents had insisted she leave school temporarily and come home to Bakersfield, where they could look after her. By the time she'd returned to UCLA, the "temporary" break having stretched to cover two full semesters, Mace had graduated and gotten on with his life elsewhere.

She hadn't known about the big ranch in Wyoming back then, although it wouldn't have surprised her, given the jeans and boots and whole-body dexterity.

Kelly hadn't expected that they'd become lifelong friends or anything like that. She'd simply wanted to thank Mace for helping her, both the night of the attack and afterward, when he'd returned at the request of the Los Angeles county prosecutor's office to testify.

Yes, she'd blubbered some incoherent version of "thank you" at the police station immediately after the incident, but in retrospect, that had never seemed like enough. She could've tracked him down during the decade since, of course, and expressed her gratitude in an adult, rational way. But another part of her had flatly refused to make contact, wanting to put the whole thing behind her for good, to move on, to forget.

And that part had won out.

Kelly *had* moved on. She'd gotten a degree in business, made new friends, dated a variety of guys, worked hard, continued to learn and built a career she loved. She'd been through the appropriate therapy and attended support groups for PTSD, and she'd had a white-lace-and-promises wedding, too. The marriage hadn't lasted, it was true, but she'd honestly tried to make it work.

She had her problems—didn't everyone?—and yet she'd made a good life for herself, a life she was proud of, even if it wasn't perfect. Even if she hadn't forgotten, not entirely.

It had been naive, she supposed, to believe that was possible. Traumatic experiences, especially life-threatening ones, didn't just vanish from a person's memory, but they could be managed, coped with, put in perspective. And maybe that was all anybody ought to expect, since living was a complicated and sometimes messy business.

Now, as she and Mace traveled over country roads in the warm semidarkness of his truck, Kelly had a chance to refresh her memory, at least where his appearance was concerned, without openly staring at the man. His thick, longish hair, like before, wasn't exactly brown or exactly red, either, but a mixture of the two, a rich auburn or chestnut, probably lighter in summer. His shoulders were broader, but he was still lean, and he still wore jeans, boots and a T-shirt, faded with wear.

The confident, no-nonsense attitude was in evidence, as well. Mace was clearly the take-charge type, just as he'd been in college.

Beyond these observations, though, and the things she'd read about him in the article and on a few websites, he was still a mystery.

He'd come to her rescue twice, like some cowboy-knight, and it did seem serendipitous that he'd been right behind her on the road when she lost control of her car. On the other hand, this was his home turf, his territory.

"I'm glad I took the extra insurance option when I rented the car," she heard herself say.

Mace grinned, looked her way for a moment, then turned his attention back to the road. "Yeah," he agreed. "There's bound to be some damage."

"The keys are in the ignition," Kelly recalled, fretful now. "You don't suppose somebody would—"

"Steal your car?" He sounded quietly amused. "That would take some doing, I think."

She blushed, feeling foolish. "Right," she said, glad he couldn't see her face. Now that she'd calmed down a bit, potential problems kept coming to mind. "My suitcase is in the back, along with my laptop and my purse."

"Your stuff will be safe until tomorrow," he said.

In her mind, Kelly went on cataloging what she'd need tonight, not tomorrow. Such as her nightgown, her toothbrush, her makeup case, her cell phone. She didn't have to call anyone in particular, but she was addicted to a certain game app, and she doubted she could sleep without listening to part of an audiobook.

And what about clean clothes to put on in the morning?

Mace seemed to know what she was thinking, because he chuckled and said, "The spa has everything you could possibly need for the night. Junie will make sure you get your luggage bright and early. The woman is an organizational genius."

Kelly allowed herself to be reassured. She'd made the reservation at the resort well in advance, using the corporate card, so her payment information would be on file. As for her favorite presleep distractions... surely she could get through a single night without them. If necessary, she'd buy a paperback in the gift shop, provided it was open, and charge the purchase to her room. Or catch a movie on TV.

"Good," she said in belated answer. "Everything's good, then."

She must have sounded hesitant, though, because Mace said, "You'll feel a lot better after a hot meal and a night's sleep. In the meantime, don't worry about your car or your things. Around here, most folks are not only honest, they'll go out of their way to lend a hand."

Kelly was from the big city, and his remark made her feel somewhat wistful. "Must be nice, knowing almost everybody in town."

Mace laughed quietly. "No 'almost' about it. I also know the names of their cats, dogs and horses. Of course, that kind of familiarity works both ways. By tomorrow morning it'll be common knowledge, from one end of Bliss County to the other, that I had dinner at the resort with a lovely young woman from California after she had an accident involving a blown tire. That pretty much sums the place up."

Kelly hadn't missed the compliment tucked away in the middle of that statement, and it warmed her. "So you never thought about living anywhere else?"

His shoulders lifted in a shrug. "Not really. Mustang Creek is home, and it isn't as if I haven't been to plenty of other places. Most people who grow up here either stay put or come back after college or a hitch in the service. You can't beat the scenery, and there's a lot to be said for small-town life." He looked her way again, signaled for a right turn when they came to a crossroads. "Like most roads in this part of Wyoming, the one where you ditched your car is quiet, but I'd bet next year's profits that nobody would have driven by without stopping to help. That's just how it is around here."

Kelly wasn't inclined to refute that, although she hadn't seen another car, except for the truck she was riding in now, which she'd glimpsed in her rearview mirror, since she'd driven out of Mustang Creek.

She might have had a long wait if Mace hadn't been around. For one thing, she wouldn't have had the strength to shove open the driver's-side door, because of how the vehicle was tilted—and, for another, she might've been hurt when the ground gave way.

There it was again, that habit of focusing on what *might* have happened. Annoyed with herself, she shook off the thought. "You do seem to show up just when I need help," she said too brightly.

"Ah, shucks, ma'am," he teased. "T'weren't nothin'."

She laughed at the late-show cowboy line, and he grinned.

They made the turn, and Kelly spotted the lights of the resort up ahead. "Almost there," Mace said. "We'll get you checked in, then you can have a nice glass of wine while you look over the dinner menu." A few seconds passed and, once again, she sensed that he knew what had been going through her mind. "Everything's okay, Kelly Wright. Time to kick back and relax."

Easy for him to say, she thought without rancor. He was probably right, though.

He'd certainly been dead-on when it came to the beauty of their surroundings. She'd been awestruck on the drive, before the wreck, before nightfall, drinking in the Grand Tetons, the rushing Bliss River, the open spaces interspersed with groves of aspen trees. Even the rain hadn't marred the view. "Are you always so philosophical?"

He grinned again. "No," he said, straight out.

"What's your family like?" She didn't know why

she'd asked that question. They'd almost reached the resort, so the curious intimacy of riding together was about to end.

He answered easily. "I have two brothers," he said. "Drake is the practical one. He raises cattle, with the help of a dozen or so ranch hands. Slater is the firstborn, which means he's bossy as hell. He makes documentary films about the West, new and old. Me, I'm the kid brother, so I have to work twice as hard for half the glory. Slater and Drake, well, they can't figure me out, most of the time. I do get some pretty wild ideas."

"For instance?" Kelly prompted, maybe a touch more interested than she should've been.

Mace glanced at her, as if the question left him slightly bemused, then replied, "Last year I decided to try making corn wine. They all thought I was crazy, gave me a lot of guff about turning into a moonshiner. Red—he's the oldest living ranch hand on the planet—said they must've brought Prohibition back and he'd missed it, and wanted to know where I'd hidden the still." He shook his head, smiling. "He loves a bad joke, that old man, and he had a fine time with the white-lightning routine."

They'd reached the big circular driveway in front of the resort by then, but Kelly wished they could stay in Mace's truck awhile longer.

"But your experiment worked," she said as they drew up at the end of a line of cars, waiting for valet service. She'd tasted his blends, as had everyone she worked with, wine snobs all of them. The cautious consensus had been that Mountain Vineyards had potential, and she agreed, although her own assessment had been considerably more enthusiastic. She wouldn't have been in Wyoming otherwise, despite the debt of gratitude she'd owed him for so long.

"It worked," he confirmed, referring, as she had, to the corn wine. "It has to age awhile before I'd feel right about putting it on the market, but just about everybody who's tried it says it's damn decent."

A young man in slacks, a crisp white shirt and a vest rapped at the driver's-side window, his smile eager and toothy.

Mace sighed good-naturedly and lowered the window.

"What are you doing in the valet line, Mace?" the boy asked, apparently delighted. "You usually park in the main lot."

"Tonight, Phil," Mace answered cheerfully, "I feel like living high on the hog, availing myself of your expert services. Besides, the lady here has had a hard day, and I doubt she's up for a hike through the rain."

Phil peered around Mace, clearly trying to get a look at the lady in question, reacting with wry resignation when his view was blocked by a pair of wide shoulders.

"Just park the truck, Phil," Mace said. "And God help you if I find any new scratches or dents when the sun comes up tomorrow morning."

CHAPTER TWO

THE LOBBY OF the resort was as magnificent as the outside. Kelly was used to good hotels, even excellent ones, since her high-profile job required a lot of travel, but in this place, grand as it was, the warmth was almost like an embrace. And here she was, with no luggage and no credit cards, probably looking like the proverbial drowned rat, escorted by one of the hottest men she'd ever seen.

Thank God Mace was a local, and willing to do all the explaining, because Kelly felt off-kilter, damp from head to foot, her skirt and blouse clinging, her expensive shoes caked with mud, the light makeup she'd applied that morning in the bathroom of her LA condo long gone. She wished she'd looked into the side mirror of Mace's truck, made sure her mascara hadn't migrated from her eyelashes to lie in smudged streaks on either side of her face.

And then there was her hair.

Silently, she commanded herself to stop being so silly.

To distract herself, she watched Mace charming the clerk at the fancy reception desk, gesturing once or twice in Kelly's direction, explaining the situation. The pretty young woman basked in his smile the whole time, fingers busy on the keyboard, well-coiffed head nodding at intervals. When she got the chance, the clerk homed in on Kelly, and the pleasant upward curve of her mouth faltered briefly.

So much for distracting herself.

If Mace hadn't been handling the check-in process, Kelly thought with an uncharacteristic lapse of self-confidence, the woman might have called security to have the homeless person discreetly removed.

Soon enough, though, Mace was turning, walking over to Kelly. Even here, in this upscale resort, among guests clad in designer clothes, he seemed completely at ease in his jeans and T-shirt.

He was smiling, and as he came toward her, Kelly could have sworn that time froze for an instant. Sound, too, was suspended; the soft music, the voices of the other people, the chime of elevator bells, all faded into a strange, pulsing silence.

Kelly simply looked at Mace Carson, marveling. Rugged as he was, his features were classic, almost aristocratic. Slap that face onto a Renaissance painting—she'd minored in art—and it would fit right in, five-o'clock shadow and all. His eyes were a remarkable shade of blue, and so expressive that he probably could've gotten any point across without opening his mouth.

There were men, she thought, and there were *men*. Some were just plain handsome, and Mace certainly qualified, but he was attractive for deeper, less definable reasons. Intelligence, sure. Sense of humor? Absolutely. And yet there was more to him, and still more beyond that, an infinity of qualities and secrets to explore.

By degrees, the strange spell began to subside. Kelly was both relieved and saddened by the shift.

Mace reached her. He was smiling, but concern flickered in his eyes. "All set," he said, and Kelly noticed that he wasn't holding a key card. Reading her curious glance correctly, he added, "Your room will be ready by the time we've finished dinner. A tour group checked out late, and the housekeeping people are hustling to catch up."

Kelly's knees wobbled, and she ordered them to hold her upright. "But…they have my reservation, right?" It wasn't like her to be so uncertain, she fretted to herself, not even after a stressful day. What the heck was going on?

"Yep," Mace said, taking a firm but gentle hold on her elbow. "Come on. You need food and at least one glass of wine—the sooner, the better."

He led her toward the restaurant entrance on the other side of the lobby. She recalled from her research that there were several eating establishments in the resort; however, this one was the main attraction.

Kelly might have balked, bedraggled as she was, but Mace was on a direct trajectory, and besides, she was hungry. Starved, in fact. She would have opted for room service, given the choice, but she didn't actually *have* a room yet, so that was out.

They were greeted warmly at the door and seated right away at a quiet table in a cozy corner of the large room. Along the way, Kelly saw that the other tables were all occupied by well-dressed, smiling people, and Mace paused a few times for a friendly word and a handshake when one of the diners called his name or waved him over. Each time, the hostess, sleek in a feminine version of a tuxedo, waited patiently, her smile wide and genuine.

Aware of tailored suits, glamorous evening gowns and jewelry usually stored in safes or bank vaults, Kelly wished she could teleport herself—and Mace—to a fast-food place. Or an ordinary diner with a counter and stools, tables with mismatched chairs and vinyl booths.

Evidently, she reflected ruefully, the dress code, ranging from smart casual to out-and-out formal, judging by the fashions on display tonight, didn't apply to Mace Carson.

Kelly was relieved when they finally reached their table. Mace pulled back her chair, and she practically collapsed onto the seat.

The hostess handed them each a heavy, leatherbound menu, announced that their server this evening would be Danielle and cheerfully instructed them to enjoy their meal.

Kelly studied the impressive offerings for that evening, handwritten in lovely copperplate, and discovered, to her embarrassment, that she was incapable of making a decision, famished though she was.

Once again, Mace stepped up. "Mind if I order for both of us?" he asked.

"Please," Kelly replied with a nod and a wavering smile.

The server, Danielle, materialized beside the table. "Hey, Mace," she said, neatly including Kelly with a nod. Danielle was attractive, but there was an air of anxiety about her, which she was obviously trying to hide.

"Hey, back at you." Mace introduced Kelly as a business associate and Danielle as an old friend.

Kelly *was* a business associate, of course, but she felt a pang of disappointment at those words, just the same. She even went so far as to wonder what *kind* of friend Danielle was, which was none of her damn beeswax, any way you looked at it, and was instantly annoyed with herself.

Mace ordered prime rib for both of them, along with a rich merlot, and Danielle collected the menus and walked away, returning shortly with a bread basket and a bottle bearing the Mountain Vineyards label. Danielle uncorked the wine expertly, filled their glasses and asked if they wanted ice water.

Mace nodded, and they were alone again, unless you counted the hundred or so other diners in the place. For Kelly, those people were drifting into a haze, just as their counterparts in the lobby had minutes before.

Mace lifted his glass, and Kelly raised her own. The rims clinked.

Kelly took a thoughtful sip, savored it for a moment, then widened her eyes at Mace. "Impressive," she said.

He smiled, clearly pleased. "Thanks," he responded, "but we're dangerously close to talking business, and I think we agreed not to do that tonight."

"So we did," Kelly said. "This is a really nice place, isn't it?"

"Yes," Mace answered. "And you're so worn-out you might fall asleep in your salad plate."

"I'm not usually so—"

"Tired?" he finished for her.

The haze dissolved. "Self-conscious," she confessed.

"Self-conscious?" He looked baffled, then apparently something dawned on him. "You do realize you're the most beautiful woman in this restaurant?"

"If that's a line," Kelly replied, smiling over the rim of her wineglass, "it's a darned clever one."

Mace's eyes danced, and he ducked his head, as though taking a bow. "Better yet," he said, "it's true."

Kelly was unsettled, in ways that had nothing to do with their very brief but memorable history. "I think I'd be more comfortable talking about wine," she said.

Danielle brought their salads, lovely crisp Caesars with croutons, and vanished again.

Kelly, who had restrained herself when the bread

basket arrived, fairly dived into her salad, which was delicious. And it took the edge off her hunger—a good thing, since she might have consumed her prime rib, when it was served, with the manners of a peasant feasting at a medieval banquet.

Plus, eating salad kept her too busy to blurt out something stupid like, "So. Tell me all about Danielle. Just how well do you two know each other?"

Between the removal of the salad plates and the delivery of the entrée, she finished her first glass of wine and started on the second as soon as Mace finished pouring it.

"My expertise on corn varieties is nonexistent," she said, returning to their earlier conversation. "I thought there was field corn and sweet corn. Period."

Mace's brow furrowed in confusion, but he was quick on the uptake, this ridiculously attractive cowboy vintner, and picked up the conversational ball right away, as smoothly as if there hadn't been a half-hour gap between their corn-into-wine discussion in his truck and the remark she'd just made. "I have a friend who's a fourth-generation farmer, out in Indiana. I called him and he said the Silver Queen variety was the best option for what I had in mind. Sweet corn is his favorite, and he knows what he's talking about."

"Maybe if you didn't label it corn wine," Kelly mused, in her element again and very glad to be there. "What if you called it Midwestern Blend? Or Heartland Varietal?"

He looked amused. "What about Hayseed Special Vintage? I kind of had that in mind."

Kelly laughed, for real this time, without awkwardness or restraint. "Colorful, but I don't think it'll fly in today's sophisticated marketplace." She felt so much better now that they were back on common ground.

"Spoken like a true sales guru. And forgive the reminder, but I thought we weren't going to talk business."

"I can't help it," she admitted airily. "I find the whole process fascinating, from growing the grapes right on through to store displays and shelving for ideal impact on the consumer."

"Seriously, the corn thing is still in the experimental stage. Truth is, I'm so busy with production now I can barely keep up."

Kelly might have said he'd be even busier if tomorrow's meeting went the way she hoped, but she kept that to herself. The notes for her presentation were on her iPad, anyway, and that was in the rental car, along with everything else she'd brought, besides the clothes on her back and the shoes on her feet. She'd spent days preparing the charts and spreadsheets she intended to show him, and she wanted to be in fine form when she made her pitch.

"I think the rain stopped," she observed, squinting through the window next to their table.

Their dinners arrived, and Kelly managed to eat sedately, enjoying every bite.

"According to the weather reports," Mace said presently, "the storm is headed east. We should see blue skies and sunshine tomorrow."

"Dawn will probably be spectacular," Kelly said. As if she had any intention of being awake in time to see it. "See, I'm taking your advice and looking on the bright side, so to speak."

"Good to know," Mace said, suppressing a grin.

"I'm doing my best." She sighed and looped a lock of hair behind her ear; it was a habit she'd been trying to break, but she was starting to feel nervous again. Why was that? "I was hoping we'd meet again one day, so I could thank you for what you did for me, but I didn't figure blowing a tire and winding up in a ditch into the equation."

Too soon, warned a voice in Kelly's head. *Too soon. First and foremost, you're here on business, not a personal mission. Stay on track.*

"Well," he said easily, "we've met again, haven't we?"

"Guess so," Kelly said and felt utterly inane.

"You thanked me before," Mace reminded her. "That was good enough. I only did what any red-blooded cowboy, or any guy with a shred of decency, would've done. That particular creep is still in prison, you and a lot of other women are safe, from him, anyhow, and that's all that matters, in the end."

"You really are noble," Kelly told him solemnly.

He held up both hands, palms out. "No," he said.

"I'm just a man who happened to be around when somebody needed help."

"You're way too modest, Mr. Carson."

"And you're giving me way too much credit."

"My prerogative," Kelly said.

"Finish your dinner."

"I'm full."

He sighed, leaning back in his chair. He might've been sitting at the table in a ranch-house kitchen instead of a five-star restaurant, he seemed so relaxed. "Me, too."

Danielle stopped by, asked if they were ready for dessert and coffee and carried away the debris when they both said, "No, thanks." Mace watched the other woman leave, his expression serious, and Kelly refused to let that bother her.

Danielle returned with the check, setting the small leather folder in front of Mace, and looked mildly surprised when Kelly reached across the table and picked it up.

For a couple of minutes, Kelly and Mace engaged in a friendly stare-down.

With a nearly imperceptible shrug, Danielle walked away.

Kelly didn't give an inch; this was a business dinner, and besides, Mace had helped her out of the rental car, where she might've been trapped for hours, brought her here and taken over the registration process. "Did you get my room number when you spoke to the receptionist?" she asked, almost primly.

He shook his head, smiling again. "Room 422," he said as though she'd dragged it out of him. "Has it occurred to you that you're ruining my reputation here? By morning, everybody in the county will know I let a woman pay for my dinner, like some yahoo who can't hold down a job. They might have me thrown out of the cowboys' union."

"Tough luck," she said lightly, picking up the accompanying pen, adding a tip and a total and scrawling her signature on the dotted line.

"You're one stubborn woman," Mace told her.

She smiled sweetly. "Keep that in mind," she answered.

Just then, Mace's cell phone rang. He glanced at the number and his mouth tightened. "Do me a favor?" he asked.

"What?"

"Answer this call."

Kelly frowned, confused, but she took the phone when he offered it, still ringing insistently, pressed the button and said, "Hello?"

There was a silence on the other end, followed by a female voice demanding, "Who the *hell* is this?"

Kelly looked at Mace. "Kelly Wright," she said. "Who's this?"

The only response was a muttered curse and the sound of a flip-phone snapping shut.

Slowly, Kelly handed Mace's phone back to him. "What was that all about?"

"Thanks," Mace said grimly, accepting the phone. He'd just screwed up, big-time, and all because he didn't want to deal with Felicity Donovan, then or ever. Considering that he'd drawn Kelly into the drama by asking her to take the call, he owed her an explanation.

Kelly merely raised an eyebrow and waited.

Mace sighed. He'd met Felicity at a conference several months before and they'd gotten a little carried away, after a full day of wine-tasting, followed by a rubber-chicken dinner with more wine, and ended up in Felicity's room, sharing a bed.

With the morning came stone-cold sobriety, the hangover to end all hangovers and a whole lot of regret. Politely, because he knew he was responsible for his part of what had been a truly lousy decision, he'd tried to play down his hasty departure even as he scrambled back into his clothes and practically bolted for the door.

Felicity's fury had surprised him. She'd yelled, and yelled plenty, and Mace had stopped and listened, shocked to discover that what he saw as the end of something that shouldn't have happened in the first place, Felicity had interpreted as a *beginning*.

He'd said he was sorry she'd misunderstood, and fled.

For the rest of the conference, Felicity had turned up everywhere he went, alternately sniffling into a cocktail napkin and scorching his hide with the stink-eye. He'd tried to be diplomatic; that hadn't worked, either. He supposed he should've left the conference early, but there were still meetings he wanted to attend, people he wanted to talk with, and besides, it just wasn't in him to run. So he'd stuck it out to the end. Surely, he'd thought, an intelligent, successful woman like Felicity would see reason once she got home, if not before.

Except she hadn't.

She'd sent emails until he finally blocked her.

She'd raged at him on every available social media site.

And she'd called and called, and called again, relentlessly. Mace had considered changing his number, which would be a huge hassle and, ultimately, a temporary fix. They were in the same industry, with a lot of the same contacts, and she'd manage to charm the new information out of one of them.

He couldn't bring himself to say all that to Kelly. They hardly knew each other.

So he said some of it. "There's a woman," he told her.

"So I gathered," Kelly said flippantly.

"She wanted a relationship, and I didn't. Still don't." God, this was hard. He should've ignored the call when he recognized Felicity's number, let it go to voice mail to delete later, the way he usually did. What had given him the harebrained idea to involve Kelly?

"And you thought if she called, and a woman answered, she'd leave you alone?" Kelly's tone told him nothing, but there might have been a spark of something in her eyes; he couldn't really tell.

Mace nodded. "I'm sorry."

She absorbed the inadequate apology. Nodded.

Silence.

"Say something," he said when he couldn't stand it anymore.

"Fine," Kelly responded coolly. "You don't know much about women if you thought a lame trick like that was going to work."

Mace felt heat rise up his neck and pulse under his jawline. "Not that one, anyhow," he said. Here he was, sitting across a restaurant table from the first woman who'd interested him in a couple of years, and he'd already blown his chances.

Nice work.

Kelly pushed back her chair and stood, leaving Mace with no choice but to do the same.

"Well," she said very quietly, "I guess maybe we're even."

Great. She was going to get a good night's sleep, collect her belongings from the rental car right after breakfast and hightail it back to the airport. He'd never see her again, and worst of all, it served him right.

He stood there, swamped by an emotion so unfamiliar that he couldn't quite put a name to it, taking in Kelly's honey-colored hair, elegantly cut, her delicate features and those incredible aquamarine eyes. He'd wanted to get to know her better, in so far as he could, considering the context. Besides being uncommonly beautiful, Kelly Wright was a representative of one of the largest wine and spirits distributors in the country, with the ability to put his winery in the black for years to come.

She was also the polar opposite of Felicity and women like her.

For the first time in his life, Mace wanted to say, "Don't go."

But he didn't. His tongue was stuck to the roof of his mouth.

Mercifully, she broke the silence. "This," she said, "has been a very, *very* long day. I think I'll turn in, provided my room is ready."

"Right," he said, still not moving.

Kelly walked out of the restaurant and into the lobby, going straight to the reception desk.

Mace followed. If he had half a brain, he'd cut his losses and run. The winery was doing well financially, he reminded himself, and there were other distributors in the world. The problem was, they didn't have Kelly Wright on their payrolls.

She waited at the desk, arms folded, then approached one of the clerks, not once looking back.

When she'd collected her key card, she finally made eye contact. He was only about six feet away, and he probably came off as some kind of weirdo, a stalker even, but it was too late to step back and give her more space. She was holding a small plastic bag filled with travel-size grooming supplies, and it rattled as she shook it at him and smiled.

She actually *smiled*.

"See you at tomorrow's meeting," she said, as if the whole Felicity fiasco hadn't happened at all.

A moment later, she was in one of the elevators, the doors closing in front of her.

SHE'D BEEN UPGRADED from a regular room to a suite, Kelly soon discovered. There was a living room, a spacious bedroom and an en suite bath with a jetted garden tub and one of those fancy shower stalls with strategically placed sprayers.

The space was furnished Western-style, expensively rustic, with a hand-hewn headboard on a king-size bed graced by an exquisite quilt in rich brown, crimson and gold, coordinating nicely with the drapes and the wall decor, which consisted of a few landscape prints and a collection of framed photographs of racing mustangs and snow-covered ski slopes. The desk, where she hoped she'd be drafting a hefty contract with Mountain Vineyards—if she ever got her laptop back—faced a window, promising a glorious view.

For tonight, she wasn't going to think. She'd give herself a break, enjoy the novelty of being unplugged, however temporarily.

She found a fluffy robe in the bedroom closet and hung it on the back of the bathroom door.

After tearing open the plastic package she'd been

given at the desk, she brushed her teeth at one of the two sinks, and immediately felt a little less grubby than before.

Normally, Kelly liked to soak in a bath at night— she got some of her best ideas relaxing in the tub— but for now, she didn't want to linger in the waking world. She was not only exhausted, she was on physical and mental overload.

She kicked off her ruined shoes, stripped off her clothes and took a quick shower, using only one sprayer. Afterward, she dried off and bundled up in the hotel bathrobe, tightening the belt until she felt almost swaddled. Her favorite nightgown would have been less bulky and therefore a lot more comfortable, but the robe would do in a pinch, and this was definitely a pinch.

With luck, she'd have her suitcase and other things by morning.

Keeping her mind closed to thoughts of Mace Carson, the woman who'd called his cell phone at dinner and the disturbing parts of her past, Kelly switched off the lights. She threw back the quilt and top sheet, fluffed her pillow and sank gratefully into bed.

She didn't miss the games on her smartphone or the audiobook she'd nearly finished the night before.

A few seconds after she closed her eyes, she slid into a deep, dreamless sleep.

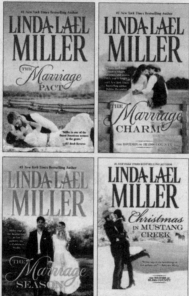

HARLEQUIN®

SPECIAL EDITION

Life, Love and Family

Save $1.00

on the purchase of
ANY Harlequin® Special Edition
book.

Available wherever books are sold, including
most bookstores, supermarkets, drugstores
and discount stores.

Save $1.00

on the purchase of any Harlequin® Special Edition book.

Coupon valid until November 30, 2016. Redeemable at participating
outlets in the U.S. and Canada only. Not redeemable at Barnes and Noble stores.
Limit one coupon per customer.

52614082

5 65373 00076 2   (8100)0 12199

Canadian Retailers: Harlequin Enterprises Limited will pay the face value of
this coupon plus 10.25¢ if submitted by customer for this product only. Any
other use constitutes fraud. Coupon is nonassignable. Void if taxed, prohibited
or restricted by law. Consumer must pay any government taxes. Void if copied.
Inmar Promotional Services ("IPS") customers submit coupons and proof of
sales to Harlequin Enterprises Limited, P.O. Box 3000, Saint John, NB E2L 4L3,
Canada. Non-IPS retailer—for reimbursement submit coupons and proof of
sales directly to Harlequin Enterprises Limited, Retail Marketing Department, 225
Duncan Mill Rd., Don Mills, ON M3B 3K9, Canada.

U.S. Retailers: Harlequin Enterprises
Limited will pay the face value of
this coupon plus 8¢ if submitted by
customer for this product only. Any
other use constitutes fraud. Coupon is
nonassignable. Void if taxed, prohibited
or restricted by law. Consumer must pay
any government taxes. Void if copied.
For reimbursement submit coupons
and proof of sales directly to Harlequin
Enterprises Limited, P.O. Box 880478,
El Paso, TX 88588-0478, U.S.A. Cash
value 1/100 cents.

® and TM are trademarks owned and used by the trademark owner and/or its licensee.

© 2016 Harlequin Enterprises Limited

SECOUP0916

REQUEST YOUR FREE BOOKS!

2 FREE NOVELS
FROM THE ROMANCE COLLECTION,
PLUS 2 FREE GIFTS!

YES! Please send me 2 FREE novels from the Romance Collection and my 2 FREE gifts (gifts are worth about $10). After receiving them, if I don't wish to receive any more books, I can return the shipping statement marked "cancel." If I don't cancel, I will receive 4 brand-new novels every month and be billed just $6.49 per book in the U.S. or $6.99 per book in Canada. That's a savings of at least 18% off the cover price. It's quite a bargain! Shipping and handling is just 50¢ per book in the U.S. and 75¢ per book in Canada.* I understand that accepting the 2 free books and gifts places me under no obligation to buy anything. I can always return a shipment and cancel at any time. Even if I never buy another book, the two free books and gifts are mine to keep forever.

194/394 MDN GH4D

Name	(PLEASE PRINT)
Address	Apt. #
City	State/Prov.	Zip/Postal Code

Signature (if under 18, a parent or guardian must sign)

Mail to the **Reader Service:**
IN U.S.A.: P.O. Box 1867, Buffalo, NY 14240-1867
IN CANADA: P.O. Box 609, Fort Erie, Ontario L2A 5X3

Want to try 2 free books from another line?
Call 1-800-873-8635 or visit www.ReaderService.com.

*Terms and prices subject to change without notice. Prices do not include applicable taxes. Sales tax applicable in N.Y. Canadian residents will be charged applicable taxes. Offer not valid in Quebec. This offer is limited to one order per household. Not valid for current subscribers to the Romance Collection or the Romance/Suspense Collection. All orders subject to credit approval. Credit or debit balances in a customer's account(s) may be offset by any other outstanding balance owed by or to the customer. Please allow 4 to 6 weeks for delivery. Offer available while quantities last.

Your Privacy—The Reader Service is committed to protecting your privacy. Our Privacy Policy is available online at www.ReaderService.com or upon request from the Reader Service.

We make a portion of our mailing list available to reputable third parties that offer products we believe may interest you. If you prefer that we not exchange your name with third parties, or if you wish to clarify or modify your communication preferences, please visit us at www.ReaderService.com/consumerchoice or write to us at Reader Service Preference Service, P.O. Box 9062, Buffalo, NY 14240-9062. Include your complete name and address.

LINDA LAEL MILLER

79999	ARIZONA WILD	___$7.99 U.S.	___$9.99 CAN.
78988	THE COWBOY WAY	___$7.99 U.S.	___$9.99 CAN.
78969	ALWAYS A COWBOY	___$7.99 U.S.	___$9.99 CAN.
78906	BIG SKY COUNTRY	___$7.99 U.S.	___$8.99 CAN.
78895	MONTANA CREEDS: DYLAN	___$7.99 U.S.	___$9.99 CAN.
78845	MONTANA CREEDS: LOGAN	___$7.99 U.S.	___$8.99 CAN.
77996	McKETTRICKS OF TEXAS: AUSTIN	___$7.99 U.S.	___$8.99 CAN.
77968	ONCE A RANCHER	___$7.99 U.S.	___$9.99 CAN.
77953	McKETTRICKS OF TEXAS: GARRETT	___$7.99 U.S.	___$8.99 CAN.
77870	THE MARRIAGE PACT	___$7.99 U.S.	___$8.99 CAN.
77866	THE BRIDEGROOM	___$7.99 U.S.	___$8.99 CAN.
77681	McKETTRICK'S HEART	___$7.99 U.S.	___$9.99 CAN.
77677	McKETTRICK'S PRIDE	___$7.99 U.S.	___$9.99 CAN.

(limited quantities available)

TOTAL AMOUNT	$_____
POSTAGE & HANDLING	$_____
($1.00 FOR 1 BOOK, 50¢ for each additional)	
APPLICABLE TAXES*	$_____
TOTAL PAYABLE	$_____

(check or money order—please do not send cash)

To order, complete this form and send it, along with a check or money order for the total above, payable to HQN Books, to: **In the U.S.:** 3010 Walden Avenue, P.O. Box 9077, Buffalo, NY 14269-9077; **In Canada:** P.O. Box 636, Fort Erie, Ontario, L2A 5X3.

Name: _____
Address: _____ City: _____
State/Prov.: _____ Zip/Postal Code: _____
Account Number (if applicable): _____ .
075 CSAS

*New York residents remit applicable sales taxes.
*Canadian residents remit applicable GST and provincial taxes.

HQN™

www.HQNBooks.com

PHLLM0916BL